PENGUIN CLASSICS

HUMBOLDT'S GIFT

SAUL BELLOW (1915–2005) is the only novelist to receive three National Book awards, for *The Adventures of Augie March, Herzog,* and *Mr. Sammler's Planet.* In 1975, he won the Pulitzer Prize for his novel *Humboldt's Gift.* The Nobel Prize in Literature was awarded to him in 1976 "for the human understanding and subtle analysis of contemporary culture that are combined in his work." In 1990, Mr. Bellow was presented the National Book Award Foundation Medal for distinguished contribution to American letters. He has also received the National Medal of Arts. His books include *Dangling Man* (1944), *The Victim* (1947), *The Adventures of Augie March* (1953), *Seize the Day* (1956), *Henderson the Rain King* (1959), *Herzog* (1964), *Mosby's Memoirs* (1969), *Mr. Sammler's Planet* (1970), *Humboldt's Gift* (1975), *To Jerusalem and Back* (1976), *The Dean's December* (1982), *Him with His Foot in His Mouth and Other Stories* (1984), *More Die of Heartbreak* (1987), *A Theft* (1989), *The Bellarosa Connection* (1989), *Something to Remember Me By* (1991), *It All Adds Up* (1994), *The Actual* (1997), *Ravelstein* (2000) and *Collected Stories* (2001).

JEFFREY EUGENIDES is the author of two novels, *The Virgin Suicides* (Farrar, Straus and Giroux, 1993) and *Middlesex* (Farrar, Straus and Giroux, 2002), which was awarded the 2003 Pulitzer Prize for Fiction. In addition to the Pulitzer, *Middlesex* won the WELT-Literatur Preis in Germany, the Ambassador Book Award, and Spain's Santiago de Compostela Literary Prize, as well as being short-listed for the National Book Critics Circle Award, the Prix Medicis of France, and the IMPAC-Dublin International Literature Award. In 2008, Mr. Eugenides edited the anthology *My Mistress's Sparrow Is Dead: Great Love Stories from Chekhov to Munro.* His fiction has been translated into thirty-six languages. He is professor of creative writing in the Lewis Center for the Performing and Creative Arts at Princeton University.

Contents

Contents

Introduction

Not "The Light" but Light:
Raids on Beauty in Bellow's Humboldt's Gift

In his solemn treatise, *On Moral Fiction*, John Gardner complained about Saul Bellow's habit of "leaning his characters against the wall" while he "lectures to a favorite graduate student." As with his views on the novel in general, Gardner was wrong about this in particular. Bellow didn't lean his heroes against a wall. As a rule, he stretched them out flat.

From *Herzog*: "In his posture of collapse on the sofa, arms abandoned over his head and legs stretched away, lying with no more style than a chimpanzee, his eyes with greater than normal radiance watched his own work in the garden with detachment, as if he were looking through the front end of a telescope at a tiny clear image."

From "A Silver Dish": "Woody, now sixty, fleshy and big, like a figure for the victory of American materialism, sunk in his lounge chair, the leather of its armrests softer to his fingertips than a woman's skin, was puzzled and, in his depths, disturbed by certain blots within him, blots of light in the brain, a blot combining pain and amusement in his breast (how *did* that get there?)."

Humboldt's Gift, the funny, bubbly, unflinchingly esoteric book that Bellow published on the eve of his sixtieth birthday, contains perhaps the most exciting instance of a narrator lying down in American literature. It's on page 111 that Charlie Citrine, the "higher-thought clown" who tells the story, reclines on a green sofa in his Chicago apartment. "Under the circumstances . . . ," Citrine explains, "Renata, Denise, children, courts, lawyers, Wall Street, sleep, death, metaphysics, karma, the presence of the universe in us, our being present in the universe itself) I had not paused to think about Humboldt, a precious friend hid in death's dateless night, a camerade from a former existence (almost), well-beloved but dead." Putting the external world on hold, Citrine commences to do just that—for the next fifty-seven pages. "Cheerful, I dug out my Humboldt papers. I piled notebooks, letters, diaries, and manuscripts on the coffee table and on the covered radiator behind the sofa. Then I lay down, sighing, pulling off my shoes. . . . I took Von Humboldt Fleisher as the subject of my meditation that morning."

Unlike Herzog, who goes belly-up after a failed marriage, or Woody Selbst, who veges out in a nostalgic mood, Citrine's immobility is veritably athletic. He's doing work on that couch. "Of all the meditative methods recommended in the literature I liked this new one best. Often I sat at the end of the day remembering everything that had happened, in minute detail, all that had been seen and done and said. I was able to go backward through the day, viewing myself from the back or the side, physically no different from anyone else."

How a person feels about *Humboldt's Gift* and about Saul Bellow's work in general depends on one's tolerance for the characteristic way Bellow heroes have of checking out of the action. For this reason, it's important to understand what's going on in these hovering moments, to detect the action in the inaction, the passion in the sequestration, the mental exertion in the apparent abdication of will. No other Bellow book brings a character to such a state of strenuous motionlessness as *Humboldt's Gift*. In comparison with Citrine, the other sacked-out heroes of Bellow's fiction are lightweights, mere pretenders to the sofa. Citrine was born to it, and what he does on the couch while doing nothing lies at the philosophical center of this, Bellow's most misunderstood novel.

Humboldt's Gift was first published in 1975, a year before Bellow was awarded the Nobel Prize. It was one of Bellow's popular successes, staying on the *New York Times* best-seller list for nine months. The reviews, however, weren't all that hot. As James Atlas sums up in his biography of Bellow: "Richard Gilman [writing in the *New York Times Book Review*] was equivocal, applauding the portrait of Delmore Schwartz while objecting to the novel's rabbinical didacticism. . . . Most of the other important reviews were equally tough. Jack Richardson, writing in *Commentary*—his review was ominously titled "A Burnt-Out Case"—deplored Bellow's efforts 'to bully and bustle the reader into a point of view about the artist and society that is a mixture of antic exaggeration and simplistic *parti pris*.'" The rap on *Humboldt's Gift* that has solidified over the years is that it is one of Bellow's comedic books, fun but flawed. People maintain a holiday mood about it. Coming after *Mr. Sammler's Planet*, which dealt with the Holocaust and American cultural decadence, *Humboldt's Gift* was a walk at the beach, sunny, vibrant, lined with Coney Island sideshows and attractions. Even Philip Roth, in praising the book, described it as "far and away the screwiest of the euphoric going-every-which-way out-and-out comic novels, the books that materialize at the very tip-top of the Bellovian mood swing. . . ." *Humboldt's Gift* does go every which way. More often than not, this surface untidiness, the shuttling between New York and New Jersey of the forties and Chicago of the seventies, encourages people to conclude that the novel is a big, joyous mess, a high-spirited romp that's wonderful to read (because it is Saul Bellow doing the writing) but which suffers from a lack of focus or intrinsic harmony, becoming not so much a tour de force as a *detour* de force.

Certainly, there's a lot going on. The book opens with brio: "The book of ballads published by Von Humboldt Fleisher in the Thirties was an immediate hit. Humboldt was just what everyone had been waiting for. Out in the Midwest I had certainly been waiting eagerly, I can tell you that. An avant-garde writer, the first of a new generation, he was handsome, fair, large, serious, witty, he was learned. The guy had it all." Here on display are all the typical Bellovian charms: the energy and congeniality of the narrative voice, what Martin Amis has referred to as Bellow's "beguiling shifts of register," along with a nice summary of what the book will be about: a famous poet, the narrator's friendship with that poet, and what America did to both of them, and to their friendship, but especially what it did to the poet, to poor Humboldt, and what this has to say about the artist in America. Before the heyday of the memoir, when people began informing on themselves, the job used to be done by novelists. In *Humboldt's Gift*, Bellow appears to be both telling tales on his old friend, Delmore Schwartz, and eulogizing him.

The other half of the novel involves Charlie Citrine—not the meditative Citrine lying on the sofa but the carnal Citrine lying in bed. This is the Citrine who says of himself: "I could find no shadow of wistful yearning, no remorse, no anxiety. I was with a beautiful bim. She was as full of schemes and secrets as the Court of Byzantium. Was that so bad? I was a goofy old chaser. But what of it?" Charles Citrine is an historian; the millionaire author of a Broadway play; a double Pulitzer winner, a chevalier of the French Legion of Honor; a divorced father of two, currently in a bitter alimony dispute; and an old Chicago hand. To keep up his Chicago credentials, Citrine attends a poker game at which a minor underworld figure, Rinaldo Cantabile, cheats. Citrine cancels his personal check to Cantabile, embroiling himself with the mobster in a series of crazy events. This Citrine, the Chicago Citrine, is responsible for the "screwiness" of the novel.

Humboldt and Cantabile don't seem to belong to the same book—they shouldn't belong—and this is the reason you get the qualified praise. Atlas, for instance, describes *Humboldt's Gift* as "two separate novels that were never reconciled." What all this leaves out, of course, is the *other* Citrine, the one lying on the green sofa. What's he doing there?

Early on, Citrine qualifies his narration with a startling aside:

> I want it to be clear, however, that I speak as a person who had lately received or experienced light. I don't mean "The light." I mean a kind of light-in-the-being. . . . And this light, however it is to be described, was now a real element in me, like the breath of life itself. I had experienced it briefly, but it had lasted long enough to be convincing and also to cause an altogether unreasonable kind of joy. Furthermore, the hysterical, the grotesque

about me, the abusive, the unjust, that madness in which I had often been a willing and active participant, the grieving, now had found a contrast. I say "now" but I knew long ago what this light was. Only I seemed to have forgotten that in the first decade of life I knew this light and even knew how to breathe it in. But this early talent or gift or inspiration, given up for the sake of maturity or realism (practically, self-preservation, the fight for survival), was now edging back.

A susceptibility to loopy doctrines is a feature of many a Bellow protagonist. Kenneth Trachtenberg, the narrator of *More Die of Heartbreak*, goes in for angelology, sitting at the knee of a Russian initiate. The soon-to-be-extradited former professor of "Him with His Foot in His Mouth" dabbles in Swedenborgianism. Certainly, Bellow was aware of the comic potential of crackpot ideas. But the frequent explorations of esoterica in his writing, as well as in his own life, point to a genuine interest in mystical thought. Yeats had his whirl with Madame Blavatsky, leaving behind his very strange book *A Vision*. James Merrill drew the raw material for his epic *The Changing Light at Sandover* from monkeying around with a Ouija board. For Saul Bellow it was a lot of things, but while writing *Humboldt's Gift* it was anthroposophy.

"Toward the end of his labor on the novel," Atlas tell us, "Bellow had discovered the work of Rudolf Steiner, the Austrianborn philosopher. . . . At the heart of Steiner's doctrine—as expounded by Bellow in a foreword to *The Boundaries of Natural Science,* a collection of Steiner's lectures—was the belief that a gulf existed between the private, inward-dwelling experience of human consciousness and the primacy of science in the modern world. It was Steiner's ambition to bridge this gulf, to transcend the limits of empirical human knowledge and attain another, higher form of consciousness, a higher 'spiritual reality.'" Steiner's distrust of science, his claim that the technological mind-set of modern society made phenomena inaccessible, depriving human beings of the imaginative connection with the unseen they'd previously enjoyed and thereby enervating their spiritual lives, was something Bellow had long felt to be the case. Bellow believed in, and insisted on talking about, that very old-fashioned thing: the soul. Like many of his heroes, Herzog in particular, Bellow maintained communications with "his dead." It's tempting to attribute Bellow's lifelong interest in the afterlife to the death of his mother when he was only sixteen. Or it might have been the result of his being hospitalized as a child with peritonitis and pneumonia. "Anyone who's faced death at that age," Bellow said, "is likely to remember something of what I felt. That it was a triumph . . . That I'd better make it worth the while of whoever it was that authorized all this. I've always had some such feeling. Overjoyed. Full of welling vitality . . ."

In his refreshing critical study "Saul Bellow and the Decline of Humanism," Michael Glenday argues that not only *Humboldt's Gift* but all of Bellow's books mount a steady assault on the secular pieties of the age. "*Humboldt's Gift* was clearly to be taken as a part of this new programme, as a novel which demolishes the line which suggests that the reality beyond appearances is unknowable. Under the aegis of this new aesthetic, the task of the writer was to provide man with the images and the vocabulary of this spiritual rebirth. . . . 'Humboldt's Gift' is a work which endeavors to replenish the flow of writing which could help to claw back the territory lost to 'gigantesque outer life.' *The recovery of such territory requires the elevation of language, for this has atrophied in common with the life of the spirit.*" [Italics mine.]

If castigating American culture for its Babbittry was Bellow's only motive in writing *Humboldt's Gift*, then why all the stuff about Citrine? If he wanted to imaginatively slum with Chicago mobsters, then why the anthroposophy, the discussion of the "Consciousness soul"? Why a narrator who makes clear from the outset that he is someone who has experienced light?

Clearly, the mysticism is important here. But is it important as mysticism? In other words, what form does Citrine's mysticism take? Most critics don't pay much attention to it. Despite the prominence of anthroposophy in the novel's architecture and in Citrine's mental life, the general inclination is to treat it as something extraneous to the novel's meaning. To admit that Bellow takes Steiner seriously would be to take Bellow less seriously, and nobody wants to do that. It's easier to lump the anthroposophy with the abundant comic material in the book and, in that way, to think about it no further.

But let's take Citrine at his word as he reposes on his sofa: "I took Von Humboldt Fleisher as the subject of my meditation that morning." A Steinerian meditation of the kind Citrine practices in *Humboldt's Gift* consists of concentrating on an object and, by holding the object in the mind's eye with the utmost intensity, of gradually eliminating the distinction between subject and object. Citrine, picturing a lamppost enshrouded with roses, tries to become the lamppost. Concentrating on Humboldt, he tries to become one with him also. This includes remembering everything he can about his dead friend, summoning him in every loquacious, pill-popping detail, reconstructing his marvelous, alcohol-fueled conversation, the vehicular manslaughter of his driving technique, the dreary New Jersey farm Humboldt bought where "even the bushes were on welfare." Lying on the sofa, Citrine remembers, and grieves, and spins out scene after scene about Humboldt's great, sad life. Citrine is tender, merciless, despairing, fond, he's Mnemosyne herself, inspiring this heroic feat of recollection and reclamation. Humboldt, Citrine says, "made raids behind the lines to bring back beauty." This is the central fact about his life. "[O]ne of Humboldt's themes was the perennial human feeling that there was an original world, a home-world, which was lost. Sometimes he spoke of Poetry as the merciful Ellis Island where a host of aliens began their naturalization and of this planet as a thrilling but insufficiently humanized imitation of that home-world." This is not so different from Steiner's notion that the distinction between self and the world, between subject and object, is illusory, and that by means of the imagination and thinking you can pierce the veil to reach the ultimate spiritual reality. This is what Citrine is doing on the sofa. He's trying to get back to his home-world. *Humboldt's Gift* isn't about Humboldt. It's about Citrine *thinking* about Humboldt. The anthroposophy that confuses critics is exactly the thing that illuminates what the book's about. The Steinerian mumbo jumbo people think extraneous to the plot is actually the key to deciphering the plot's significance. What the two-unreconciled-novels school of criticism fails to reckon with is nothing less than the center of the action. Humboldt's fate has been sealed long before the book begins. Citrine's problems with Cantabile and Renata are just comic relief. The rendering of these things, the relishing of all this life, is what's really at stake here, in an internal, dead-serious reverie by a man, until recently, terrified of death himself. A man who has turned to anthroposophy for some solace against death but who has found something else entirely: not an intimation of the afterlife but a revelation in the form of words. Not The Light. But light.

Bellow was interested in anthroposophy, as he'd been in Reichianism before and Swedenborgianism afterward, not because he believed in these systems entirely, but because they allowed him to imaginatively unshackle himself from a purely rational, mechanistic, college-educated worldview. As a disciple of Steiner, Bellow was a washout. Yet he was able to import anthroposophy into his book and, by hitching a ride on its wild surmises, slingshot himself to an orbit where art and mysticism touch. Citrine's anthroposophical meditations assume a literary form. They are equivalent with the sentences of the novel.

Recall how Citrine, in describing what it means to have experienced light, says: "This early talent or gift or inspiration, given up for the sake of maturity or realism . . . was now edging back." Notice the use of the word "gift." Notice, too, Citrine's diction at the outset of the book: "But I didn't expect him to come at me as in life, driving ninety miles an hour in his Buick fourholer. First I laughed. Then I shrieked. I was transfixed. He bore down on me. He struck me with blessings. Humboldt's gift wiped out many immediate problems." This is some three hundred and fifty pages before Humboldt's actual gift (in the form of a screenplay) turns up in the novel.

Humboldt's Gift ends with the reburial of Humboldt, a scene offering not the slightest spiritual consolation. "So the coffin was enclosed and the soil did not come directly on it. But then, how did one get out? One didn't, didn't, didn't! You stayed, you stayed!" Despite all the talk of spirit and the afterlife, the Humboldt Citrine knew and loved is gone.

And yet Humboldt, sane at the end, sends his old friend a final message: "Remember, we are not natural creatures but supernatural." How so? Immortal spirits? Maybe. But a surer bet is this: immortal on the page. Humboldt's gift is not the screenplay for *Caldofreddo* but this book itself, Citrine's reverie on the sofa and what comes from it, the manifestation of higher consciousness not in a trance or moment of gnosis but in language. Again, Michael Glenday: "*The recovery of such territory requires the elevation of language, for this has atrophied in common with the life of the spirit.*"

A phrase that might also describe Bellow's chief and lasting achievement: he elevated language and, by doing so, reversed the spirit's atrophy. That's what reading Bellow feels like. What makes Bellow's prose better than just about anyone else's is that it is touched, in every clause, by enlightenment. Every clause glows with its own aura. Even the verbs are doing holy work. To think of Citrine's anthroposophy as pointing to an ethereal realm is to miss the point of Bellow's art, which was to bring what he could of the angelic into the human frame of his paragraphs. Bellow, like Humboldt, made raids behind the lines. The sentences of *Humboldt's Gift* are what he brought back from the other side.

Almost alone in his generation, Saul Bellow maintained a connection to the vatic role poets had in earlier ages. He did this in a modern, twentieth-century way, tentatively, probingly, with self-humor and a large measure of dubiety, but not outright rejection. He kept the lines open. It was similar to the way he talked about prayer as "checking in with universal headquarters." Which sounds a lot like "whoever it was that authorized this." Bellow didn't know who it was; he didn't insist on who, or what. But he remained faithful to intuitions of something beyond this life, this world or reality, and he found a way to lightly and comically allow these rays of optimism to pierce the dome of his narratives otherwise so full of the smoke, noise, and human foolishness of Chicago, Illinois.

You can put a darker spin on Citrine's mysticism. You can agree with Philip Roth that it all derives from Citrine's fear of mortality, and be, as Roth is, absolutely right in terms of the psychology of the character. You can decide that Bellow's relish of the physical world constitutes a renunciation of eternal longings, a reiteration of realism. But you can also wonder if it wasn't those hope beams of Bellow's that lit up the world for him, allowing him to see it with a matchless clarity, and to render it in words sanctified by an ancient gift, Humboldt's gift, the one they used to call poetry, back when that counted for something.

JEFFREY EUGENIDES

The book of ballads published by Von Humboldt Fleisher in the Thirties was an immediate hit. Humboldt was just what everyone had been waiting for. Out in the Midwest I had certainly been waiting eagerly, I can tell you that. An avant-garde writer, the first of a new generation, he was handsome, fair, large, serious, witty, he was learned. The guy had it all. All the papers reviewed his book. His picture appeared in *Time* without insult and in *Newsweek* with praise. I read *Harlequin Ballads* enthusiastically. I was a student at the University of Wisconsin and thought about nothing but literature day and night. Humboldt revealed to me new ways of doing things. I was ecstatic. I envied his luck, his talent, and his fame, and I went east in May to have a look at him—perhaps to get next to him. The Greyhound bus, taking the Scranton route, made the trip in about fifty hours. That didn't matter. The bus windows were open. I had never seen real mountains before. Trees were budding. It was like Beethoven's *Pastorale*. I felt showered by the green, within. Manhattan was fine, too. I took a room for three bucks a week and found a job selling Fuller Brushes door to door. And I was wildly excited about everything. Having written Humboldt a long fan letter, I was invited to Greenwich Village to discuss literature and ideas. He lived on Bedford Street, near Chumley's. First he gave me black coffee, and then poured gin in the same cup. "Well, you're a nice-looking enough fellow, Charlie," he said to me. "Aren't you a bit sly, maybe? I think you're headed for early baldness. And such large emotional handsome eyes. But you certainly do love literature and that's the main thing. You have sensibility," he said. He was a pioneer in the use of this word. Sensibility later made it big. Humboldt was very kind. He introduced me to people in the Village and got me books to review. I always loved him.

Humboldt's success lasted about ten years. In the late Forties he started to sink. In the early Fifties I myself became famous. I even made a pile of money. Ah, money, the money! Humboldt held the money against me. In the last years of his life when he wasn't too depressed to talk, wasn't locked up in a loony bin, he went about New York saying bitter things about me and my "million dollars." "Take the case of Charlie Citrine. He arrived from Madison, Wisconsin, and knocked on my door. Now he's got a million bucks. What kind of writer or intellectual makes that kind of dough—a Keynes? Okay. Keynes, a world figure. A genius in economics, a prince in Bloomsbury," said Humboldt. "Married to a Russian ballerina. The money follows. But who the hell is Citrine to become so rich? We used to be close friends," Humboldt accurately said. "But there's something perverse with that guy. After making this dough why does he bury himself in the sticks? What's he in Chicago for? He's afraid to be found out."

Whenever his mind was sufficiently clear he used his gifts to knock me. He did a great job.

And money wasn't what I had in mind. Oh God, no, what I wanted was to do good. I was dying to do something good. And this feeling for good went back to my early and peculiar sense of existence—sunk in the glassy depths of life and groping, thrillingly and desperately, for sense, a person keenly aware of painted veils, of Maya, of domes of many-colored glass staining the white radiance of eternity, quivering in the intense inane and so on. I was quite a nut about such things. Humboldt knew this, really, but toward the end he could not afford to give me any sympathy. Sick and sore, he wouldn't let up on me. He only stressed the contradiction between the painted veils and the big money. But such sums as I made, made themselves. Capitalism made them for dark comical reasons of its own. The world did it. Yesterday I read in *The Wall Street*

Journal about the melancholy of affluence, "Not in all the five millennia of man's recorded history have so many been so affluent." Minds formed by five millennia of scarcity are distorted. The heart can't take this sort of change. Sometimes it just refuses to accept it.

In the Twenties kids in Chicago hunted for treasure in the March thaw. Dirty snow hillocks formed along the curbs and when they melted, water ran braided and brilliant in the gutters and you could find marvelous loot—bottle tops, machine gears, Indian-head pennies. And last spring, almost an elderly fellow now, I found that I had left the sidewalk and that I was following the curb and looking. For what? What was I doing? Suppose I found a dime? Suppose I found a fifty-cent piece? What then? I don't know how the child's soul had gotten back, but it was back. Everything was melting. Ice, discretion, maturity. What would Humboldt have said to this?

When reports were brought of the damaging remarks he made I often found that I agreed with him. "They gave Citrine a Pulitzer prize for his book on Wilson and Tumulty. The Pulitzer is for the birds—for the pullets. It's just a dummy newspaper publicity award given by crooks and illiterates. You become a walking Pulitzer ad, so even when you croak the first words of the obituary are 'Pulitzer prizewinner passes.'" He had a point, I thought. "And Charlie is a double Pulitzer. First came that schmaltzy play. Which made him a fortune on Broadway. Plus movie rights. He got a percentage of the gross! And I don't say he actually plagiarized, but he did steal something from me—my personality. He built my personality into his hero."

Even here, sounding wild, he had grounds, perhaps.

He was a wonderful talker, a hectic nonstop monologuist and improvisator, a champion detractor. To be loused up by Humboldt was really a kind of privilege. It was like being the subject of a two-nosed portrait by Picasso, or an eviscerated chicken by Soutine. Money always inspired him. He adored talking about the rich. Brought up on New York tabloids, he often mentioned the golden scandals of yesteryear, Peaches and Daddy Browning, Harry Thaw and Evelyn Nesbitt, plus the Jazz Age, Scott Fitzgerald, and the Super-Rich. The heiresses of

Henry James he knew cold. There were times when he himself
schemed comically to make a fortune. But his real wealth was
literary. He had read many thousands of books. He said that
history was a nightmare during which he was trying to get a
good night's rest. Insomnia made him more learned. In the small
hours he read thick books—Marx and Sombart, Toynbee, Ros-
tovtzeff, Freud. When he spoke of wealth he was in a position
to compare Roman *luxus* with American Protestant riches. He
generally got around to the Jews—Joyce's silk-hatted Jews outside the Bourse. And he wound up with the gold-plated skull or
death mask of Agamemnon, dug up by Schliemann. Humboldt
could really talk.

His father, a Jewish Hungarian immigrant, had ridden with
Pershing's cavalry in Chihuahua, chasing Pancho Villa in a Mexico of whores and horses (very different from my own father,
a small gallant person who shunned such things). His old man
had plunged into America. Humboldt spoke of boots, bugles,
and bivouacs. Later came limousines, luxury hotels, palaces in
Florida. His father had lived in Chicago during the boom. He
was in the real-estate business and kept a suite at the Edge-
water Beach Hotel. Summers, his son was sent for. Humboldt
knew Chicago, too. In the days of Hack Wilson and Woody
English the Fleishers had a box at Wrigley Field. They drove to
the game in a Pierce-Arrow or a Hispano-Suiza (Humboldt was
car-crazy). And there were lovely John Held, Jr., girls, beautiful, who wore step-ins. And whisky and gangsters and the
pillared doom-dark La Salle Street banks with railroad money
and pork and reaper money locked in steel vaults. Of this Chicago I was completely ignorant when I arrived from Appleton.
I played Piggie-move-up with Polish kids under the El tracks.
Humboldt ate devil's-food coconut-marshmallow layer cake at
Henrici's. I never saw the inside of Henrici's.

I did, once, see Humboldt's mother in her dark apartment on
West End Avenue. Her face was like her son's. She was mute,
fat, broad-lipped, tied up in a bathrobe. Her hair was white,
bushy, Fijian. The melanin was on the back of her hands and
on her dark face still darker spots as large as her eyes. Humboldt bent over to speak to her, and she answered nothing

but stared out with some powerful female grievance. He was gloomy when we left the building and he said, "She used to let me go to Chicago but I was supposed to spy on the old man and copy out bank statements and account numbers and write down the names of his hookers. She was going to sue him. She's mad, you see. But then he lost everything in the crash. Died of a heart attack down in Florida."

This was the background of those witty cheerful ballads. He was a manic depressive (his own diagnosis). He owned a set of Freud's works and read psychiatric journals. Once you had read the *Psychopathology of Everyday Life* you knew that everyday life *was* psychopathology. That was all right with Humboldt. He often quoted me *King Lear:* "In cities, mutinies; in countries, discord; in palaces, treason; and the bond cracked 'twixt son and father. . . ." He stressed "son and father." "Ruinous disorders follow us disquietly to our graves."

Well, that's where ruinous disorders followed him seven years ago. And now as new anthologies came out I went down to Brentano's basement and checked them. Humboldt's poems were omitted. The bastards, the literary funeral directors and politicians who put together these collections, had no use for old-hat Humboldt. So all his thinking, writing, feeling counted for nothing, all the raids behind the lines to bring back beauty had no effect except to wear him out. He dropped dead in a dismal hotel off Times Square. I, a different sort of writer, remained to mourn him in prosperity out in Chicago.

The noble idea of being an American poet certainly made Humboldt feel at times like a card, a boy, a comic, a fool. We lived like bohemians and graduate students in a mood of fun and games. Maybe America didn't need art and inner miracles. It had so many outer ones. The USA was a big operation, very big. The more *it,* the less *we.* So Humboldt behaved like an eccentric and a comic subject. But occasionally there was a break in his eccentricity when he stopped and thought. He tried to think himself clear away from this American world (I did that, too). I could see that Humboldt was pondering what to do between *then* and *now,* between birth and death, to satisfy certain great questions. Such brooding didn't make him any saner. He tried drugs and drink. Finally, many courses of shock treatment had to be administered. It was, as he saw it, Humboldt versus madness. Madness was a whole lot stronger.

I wasn't doing so well myself recently when Humboldt acted from the grave, so to speak, and made a basic change in my life. In spite of our big fight and fifteen years of estrangement he left me something in his will. I came into a legacy.

• • •

He was a great entertainer but going insane. The pathologic element could be missed only by those who were laughing too hard to look. Humboldt, that grand erratic handsome person with his wide blond face, that charming fluent deeply worried man to whom I was so attached, passionately lived out the theme of Success. Naturally he died a Failure. What else can result from the capitalization of such nouns? Myself, I've always held the number of sacred words down. In my opinion Humboldt had too long a list of them—Poetry, Beauty, Love, Waste Land, Alienation, Politics, History, the Unconscious. And, of course, Manic and Depressive, always capitalized. According to him, America's great Manic Depressive was Lincoln. And Churchill with what he called his Black Dog moods was a classic case of Manic Depression. "Like me, Charlie," said Humboldt. "But think—if Energy is Delight and if Exuberance is Beauty, the Manic Depressive knows more about Delight and Beauty than anyone else. Who else has so much Energy and Exuberance? Maybe it's the strategy of the Psyche to increase Depression. Didn't Freud say that Happiness was nothing but the remission of Pain? So the more Pain the intenser the Happiness. But there is a prior origin to this, and the Psyche makes Pain on purpose. Anyway, Mankind is stunned by the Exuberance and Beauty of certain individuals. When a Manic Depressive escapes from his Furies he's irresistible. He captures History. I think that aggravation is a secret technique of the Unconscious. As for great men and kings being History's slaves, I think Tolstoi was off the track. Don't kid yourself, kings are the most sublime sick.

Manic Depressive heroes pull Mankind into their cycles and carry everybody away."

Poor Humboldt didn't impose his cycles for very long. He never became the radiant center of his age. Depression fastened on him for good. The periods of mania and poetry ended. Three decades after *Harlequin Ballads* made him famous he died of a heart attack in a flophouse in the West Forties, one of those midtown branches of the Bowery. On that night I happened to be in New York. I was there on Business—i.e., up to no good. None of my Business was any good. Estranged from everybody, he was living in a place called the Ilscombe. I went later to have a look at it. Welfare lodged old people there. He died on a rotten hot night. Even at the Plaza I was uncomfortable. Carbon monoxide was thick. Throbbing air conditioners dripped on you in the street. A bad night. And on the 727 jet, as I was flying back to Chicago next morning, I opened the *Times* and found Humboldt's obituary.

I knew that Humboldt would soon die because I had seen him on the street two months before and he had death all over him. He didn't see me. He was gray stout sick dusty, he had bought a pretzel stick and was eating it. His lunch. Concealed by a parked car, I watched. I didn't approach him, I felt it was impossible. For once my Business in the East was legitimate and I was not chasing some broad but preparing a magazine article. And just that morning I had been flying over New York in a procession of Coast Guard helicopters with Senators Javits and Robert Kennedy. Then I had attended a political luncheon in Central Park at the Tavern on the Green, where all the celebrities became ecstatic at the sight of one another. I was, as they say, "in great shape" myself. If I don't look well, I look busted. But I knew that I looked well. Besides, there was money in my pockets and I had been window-shopping on Madison Avenue. If any Cardin or Hermès necktie pleased me I could buy it without asking the price. My belly was flat, I wore boxer shorts of combed Sea Island cotton at eight bucks a pair. I had joined an athletic club in Chicago and with elderly effort kept myself in shape. I played a swift hard game of paddle ball, a form of squash. So how could I talk to Humboldt? It was too much.

While I was in the helicopter whopping over Manhattan, viewing New York as if I were passing in a glass-bottomed boat over a tropical reef, Humboldt was probably groping among his bottles for a drop of juice to mix with his morning gin.

I became, after Humboldt's death, an even more intense physical culturist. Last Thanksgiving Day I ran away from a mugger in Chicago. He jumped from a dark alley and I beat it. It was pure reflex. I leaped away and sprinted down the middle of the street. As a boy I was not a remarkable runner. How was it that in my middle fifties I became inspired with flight and capable of great bursts of speed? Later that same night I boasted, "I can still beat a junkie in the hundred-yard dash." And to whom did I brag of this power of my legs? To a young woman named Renata. We were lying in bed. I told her how I took off—I ran like hell, I flew. And she said to me, as if on cue (ah, the courtesy, the gentility of these beautiful girls), "You're in terrific shape, Charlie. You're not a big fellow but you're sturdy, solid, and you're elegant also." She stroked my naked sides. So my pal Humboldt was gone. Probably his very bones had crumbled in potter's field. Perhaps there was nothing in his grave but a few lumps of soot. But Charlie Citrine was still outspeeding passionate criminals in the streets of Chicago, and Charlie Citrine was in terrific shape and lay beside a voluptuous friend. This Citrine could now perform a certain Yoga exercise and had learned to stand on his head to relieve his arthritic neck. About my low cholesterol Renata was well informed. Also I repeated to her the doctor's comments about my amazingly youthful prostate and my supernormal EKG. Strengthened in illusion and idiocy by these proud medical reports, I embraced a busty Renata on this Posturepedic mattress. She gazed at me with love-pious eyes. I inhaled her delicious damp, personally participating in the triumph of American civilization (now tinged with the Oriental colors of Empire). But in some phantom Atlantic City boardwalk of the mind I saw a different Citrine, this one on the border of senility, his back hooked, and feeble. Oh very, very feeble, pushed in a wheelchair past the little salt ripples, ripples which, like myself, were puny. And who was pushing my chair? Was it Renata—the Renata I had taken in the wars of Happiness by a quick Patton-thrust of armor? No, Renata was a grand girl, but I couldn't see her behind my wheelchair. Renata? Not Renata. Certainly not.

Out in Chicago Humboldt became one of my significant dead. I spent far too much time mooning about and communing with the dead. Besides, my name was linked with Humboldt's, for, as the past receded, the Forties began to be valuable to people fabricating cultural rainbow textiles, and the word went out that in Chicago there was a fellow still alive who used to be Von Humboldt Fleisher's friend, a man named Charles Citrine. People doing articles, academic theses, and books wrote to me or flew in to discuss Humboldt with me. And I must say that in Chicago Humboldt was a natural subject for reflection. Lying at the southern end of the Great Lakes—twenty percent of the world's supply of fresh water—Chicago with its gigantesque outer life contained the whole problem of poetry and the inner life in America. Here you could look into such things through a sort of fresh-water transparency.

"How do you account, Mr. Citrine, for the rise and fall of Von Humboldt Fleisher?"

"Young people, what do you aim to do with the facts about Humboldt, publish articles and further your careers? This is pure capitalism."

I thought about Humboldt with more seriousness and sorrow than may be apparent in this account. I didn't love so many people. I couldn't afford to lose anyone. One infallible sign of love was that I dreamed of Humboldt so often. Every time I saw him I was terribly moved, and cried in my sleep. Once I dreamed that we met at Whelan's Drugstore on the corner of Sixth and Eighth in Greenwich Village. He was not the stricken leaden swollen man I had seen on Forty-sixth Street, but still the stout normal Humboldt of middle life. He was sitting beside me at the soda fountain with a Coke. I burst into tears. I said, "Where have you been? I thought you were dead."

He was very mild, quiet, and he seemed extremely well pleased, and he said, "Now I understand everything."

"Everything? What's everything?"

But he only said, "Everything." I couldn't get more out of

him, and I wept with happiness. Of course it was only a dream
such as you dream if your soul is not well. My waking character is far from sound. I'll never get any medals for character.
And all such things must be utterly clear to the dead. They have
finally left the problematical cloudy earthly and human sphere.
I have a hunch that in life you look outward from the ego, your
center. In death you are at the periphery looking inward. You
see your old pals at Whelan's still struggling with the heavy
weight of selfhood, and you hearten them by intimating that
when their turn comes to enter eternity they too will begin to
comprehend and at last get an idea of what has happened. As
none of this is Scientific, we are afraid to think it.

All right, then, I will try to summarize: at the age of twenty-
two Von Humboldt Fleisher published his first book of ballads.
You would have thought that the son of neurotic immigrants
from Eighty-ninth and West End—his extravagant papa hunting Pancho Villa and, in the photo Humboldt showed me, with
a head so curly that his garrison cap was falling off; his mama,
from one of those Potash and Perlmutter yapping fertile baseball-
and-business families, darkly pretty at first, then gloomy mad
and silent—that such a young man would be clumsy, that
his syntax would be unacceptable to fastidious goy critics on
guard for the Protestant Establishment and the Genteel Tradition. Not at all. The ballads were pure, musical, witty, radiant,
humane. I think they were Platonic. By Platonic I refer to an
original perfection to which all human beings long to return.
Yes, Humboldt's words were impeccable. Genteel America had
nothing to worry about. It was in a tizzy—it expected Anti-
Christ to burst out of the slums. Instead this Humboldt Fleisher
turned up with a love-offering. He behaved like a gentleman.
He was charming. So he was warmly welcomed. Conrad Aiken
praised him, T. S. Eliot took favorable notice of his poems,
and even Yvor Winters had a good word to say for him. As
for me, I borrowed thirty bucks and enthusiastically went to
New York to talk things over with him on Bedford Street. This
was in 1938. We crossed the Hudson on the Christopher Street
ferry to eat clams in Hoboken and talked about the problems
of modern poetry. I mean that Humboldt lectured me about

them. Was Santayana right? Was modern poetry barbarous?
Modern poets had more wonderful material than Homer or
Dante. What they didn't have was a sane and steady idealiza-
tion. To be Christian was impossible, to be pagan also. That
left you-know-what.

I had come to hear that great things might be true. This I was
told on the Christopher Street ferry. Marvelous gestures had
to be made and Humboldt made them. He told me that poets
ought to figure out how to get around pragmatic America. He
poured it on for me that day. And there I was, having raptures,
gotten up as a Fuller Brush salesman in a smothering wool suit,
a hand-me-down from Julius. The pants were big in the waist
and the shirt ballooned out, for my brother Julius had a fat
chest. I wiped my sweat with a handkerchief stitched with a J.

Humboldt himself was just beginning to put on weight. He
was thick through the shoulders but still narrow at the hips.
Later he got a prominent belly, like Babe Ruth. His legs were
restless and his feet made nervous movements. Below, shuffling comedy; above, princeliness and dignity, a certain nutty
charm. A surfaced whale beside your boat might look at you
as he looked with his wide-set gray eyes. He was fine as well as
thick, heavy but also light, and his face was both pale and dark.
Golden-brownish hair flowed upward—two light crests and a
dark trough. His forehead was scarred. As a kid he had fallen
on a skate blade, the bone itself was dented. His pale lips were
prominent and his mouth was full of immature-looking teeth,
like milk teeth. He consumed his cigarettes to the last spark
and freckled his tie and his jacket with burns.

The subject that afternoon was Success. I was from the sticks
and he was giving me the low-down. Could I imagine, he said,
what it meant to knock the Village flat with your poems and
then follow up with critical essays in the *Partisan* and the *Southern Review*? He had much to tell me about Modernism, Symbolism, Yeats, Rilke, Eliot. Also, he was a pretty good drinker.
And of course there were lots of girls. Besides, New York was
then a very Russian city, so we had Russia all over the place.
It was a case, as Lionel Abel said, of a metropolis that yearned
to belong to another country. New York dreamed of leaving

North America and merging with Soviet Russia. Humboldt
easily went in his conversation from Babe Ruth to Rosa Lux-
emburg and Béla Kun and Lenin. Then and there I realized that
if I didn't read Trotsky at once I wouldn't be worth conversing
with. Humboldt talked to me about Zinoviev, Kamenev, Bukha-
rin, the Smolny Institute, the Shakhty engineers, the Moscow
trials, Sidney Hook's *From Hegel to Marx*, Lenin's *State and
Revolution*. In fact, he compared himself to Lenin. "I know,"
he said, "how Lenin felt in October when he exclaimed, '*Es
schwindelt!*' He didn't mean that he was *schwindling* everyone
but that he felt giddy. Lenin, tough as he was, was like a young
girl waltzing. Me too. I have vertigo from success, Charlie. My
ideas won't let me sleep. I go to bed without a drink and the
room is whirling. It'll happen to you, too. I tell you this to
prepare you," Humboldt said. In flattery he had a marvelous
touch.

Madly excited, I looked diffident. Of course I was in a state of
intense preparation and hoped to knock everybody dead. Each
morning at the Fuller Brush sales-team pep meeting we said
in unison, "I'm fine and dandy, how are you?" But I actually
was fine and dandy. I didn't have to put it on. I couldn't have
been more eager—eager to greet housewives, eager to come in
and see their kitchens, eager to hear their tales and their complaints. The passionate hypochondria of Jewish women was
new to me then, I was keen to hear about their tumors and
their swollen legs. I wanted them to tell me about marriage,
childbirth, money, sickness, and death. Yes, I tried to put them
into categories as I sat there drinking coffee. They were petty
bourgeois, husband-killers, social climbers, hysterics, etcetera.
But it was no use, this analytical skepticism. I was too enthusiastic. So I eagerly peddled my brushes, and just as eagerly I
went to the Village at night and listened to the finest talkers in
New York—Schapiro, Hook, Rahv, Huggins, and Gumbein.
Under their eloquence I sat like a cat in a recital hall. But Humboldt was the best of them all. He was simply the Mozart of
conversation.

On the ferryboat Humboldt said, "I made it too young, I'm
in trouble." He was off then. His spiel took in Freud, Heine,

Wagner, Goethe in Italy, Lenin's dead brother, Wild Bill Hickok's costumes, the New York Giants, Ring Lardner on grand opera, Swinburne on flagellation, and John D. Rockefeller on religion. In the midst of these variations the theme was always ingeniously and excitingly retrieved. That afternoon the streets looked ashen but the deck of the ferry was bright gray. Humboldt was slovenly and grand, his mind undulating like the water and the waves of blond hair rising on his head, his face with widely separated gray eyes white and tense, his hands deep in his pockets, and his feet in polo boots set close together.

If Scott Fitzgerald had been a Protestant, said Humboldt, Success wouldn't have damaged him so much. Look at Rockefeller Senior, he knew how to handle Success, he simply said that God had given him all his dough. Of course that was stewardship. That was Calvinism. Once he had spoken of Calvinism, Humboldt was bound to go on to Grace and Depravity. From Depravity he moved to Henry Adams, who said that in a few decades mechanical progress would break our necks anyway, and from Henry Adams he went into the question of eminence in an age of revolutions, melting pots, and masses, and from this he turned to Tocqueville, Horatio Alger, and Ruggles of Red Gap. Movie-mad Humboldt followed *Screen Gossip* magazine. He personally remembered Mae Murray like a goddess in sequins on the stage of Loew's inviting kids to visit her in California. "She starred in *The Queen of Tasmania* and *Circe the Enchantress,* but she ended as a poorhouse crone. And what about what's-his-name who killed himself in the hospital? He took a fork and hammered it into his heart with the heel of his shoe, poor fellow!"

This was sad. But I didn't really care how many people bit the dust. I was marvelously happy. I had never visited a poet's house, never drunk straight gin, never eaten steamed clams, never smelled the tide. I had never heard such things said about business, its power to petrify the soul. Humboldt spoke wonderfully of the wonderful, abominable rich. You had to view them in the shield of art. His monologue was an oratorio in which he sang and played all parts. Soaring still higher he began to speak about Spinoza and of how the mind was fed with joy by things eternal and infinite. This was Humboldt the student who had gotten A's in philosophy from the great Morris R. Cohen. I doubt that he would have talked like this to anyone but a kid from the sticks. But after Spinoza Humboldt was a bit depressed and said, "Lots of people are waiting for me to fall on my face. I have a million enemies."

"You do? But why?"

"I don't suppose you've read about the Cannibal Society of the Kwakiutl Indians," said learned Humboldt. "The candidate when he performs his initiation dance falls into a frenzy and eats human flesh. But if he makes a ritual mistake the whole crowd tears him to pieces."

"But why should poetry make you a million enemies?"

He said this was a good question but it was obvious that he didn't mean it. He turned gloomy and his voice went flat—plink—as though there were one note of tin in his brilliant keyboard. He struck it now. "I may think I'm bringing an offering to the altar, but that's not how they see it." No, it was not a good question, for the fact that I asked it meant that I didn't know Evil, and if I didn't know Evil my admiration was worthless. He forgave me because I was a boy. But when I heard the tinny plink I realized that I must learn to defend myself. He had tapped my affection and admiration, and it was flowing at a dangerous rate. This hemorrhage of eagerness would weaken me and when I was weak and defenseless I would get it in the neck. And so I figured, ah ha! he wants me to suit him perfectly, down to the ground. He'll bully me. I'd better look out.

On the oppressive night when I achieved *my* success, Humboldt picketed the Belasco Theatre. He had just been let out of Bellevue. A huge sign, *Von Trenck by Charles Citrine*, glittered above the street. There were thousands of electric bulbs. I arrived in black tie, and there was Humboldt with a gang of pals and rooters. I swept out of the taxi with my lady friend and was caught on the sidewalk in the commotion. Police were controlling the crowd. His cronies were shouting and rioting and Humboldt carried his picket sign as though it were a cross. In streaming characters, mercurochrome on cotton, was written, "The Author of this Play is a Traitor." The demonstrators were pushed back by the police, and Humboldt and I did not meet face to face. Did I want him run in? the producer's assistant asked me.

"No," I said, wounded, trembling. "I used to be his protégé. We were pals, the crazy son of a bitch. Let him alone."

Demmie Vonghel, the lady who was with me, said, "Good man! That's right, Charlie, you're a good man!"

Von Trenck ran for eight months on Broadway. I had the attention of the public for nearly a year, and I taught it nothing.

• • •

Now as to Humboldt's actual death: he died at the Ilscombe around the corner from the Belasco. On his last night, as I have reconstructed it, he was sitting on his bed in this decayed place, probably reading. The books in his room were the poems of Yeats and Hegel's *Phenomenology*. In addition to these visionary authors he read the *Daily News* and the *Post*. He kept up with sports and with night life, with the jet set and the activities of the Kennedy family, with used-car prices and want ads. Ravaged as he was he maintained his normal American interests. Then at about 3 a.m.—he wasn't sleeping much toward the end—he decided to take his garbage down and suffered a heart attack in the elevator. When the pain struck he seems to have fallen against the panel and pressed all the buttons, including the alarm button. Bells rang, the door opened, he stumbled into a corridor and fell, spilling cans, coffee grounds, and bottles from his pail. Fighting for breath, he tore off his shirt. When the cops came to take the dead man to the hospital his chest was naked. The hospital didn't want him now, so they carried him on to the morgue. At the morgue there were no readers of modern poetry. The name Von Humboldt Fleisher meant nothing. So he lay there, another derelict.

I visited his uncle Waldemar not long ago in Coney Island. The old horse-player was in a nursing home. He said to me, "The cops rolled Humboldt. They took away his watch and his dough, even his fountain pen. He always used a real pen. He didn't write poetry with a ball-point."

"Are you sure he had money?"

"He never went out without a hundred dollars minimum in his pocket. You ought to know how he was about money. I miss the kid. How I miss him!"

I felt exactly as Waldemar did. I was more moved by Humboldt's death than by the thought of my own. He had built himself up to be mourned and missed. Humboldt put that sort of weight into himself and developed in his face all the graver, all the more important human feelings. You'd never forget a face like his. But to what end had it been created?

Quite recently, last spring, I found myself thinking about this in an odd connection. I was in a French train with Renata, taking a trip which, like most trips, I neither needed nor desired. Renata pointed to the landscape and said, "Isn't that beautiful out there!" I looked out, and she was right. Beautiful was indeed there. But I had seen Beautiful many times, and so I closed my eyes. I rejected the plastered idols of the Appearances. These idols I had been trained, along with everybody else, to see, and I was tired of their tyranny. I even thought, The painted veil isn't what it used to be. The damn thing is wearing out. Like a roller-towel in a Mexican men's room. I was thinking of the power of collective abstractions, and so forth. We crave more than ever the radiant vividness of boundless love, and more and more the barren idols thwart this. A world of categories devoid of spirit waits for life to return. Humboldt was supposed to be an instrument of this revival. This mission or vocation was reflected in his face. The hope of new beauty. The promise, the secret of beauty.

In the USA, incidentally, this sort of thing gives people a very foreign look.

It was consistent that Renata should direct my attention to the Beautiful. She had a personal stake in it, she was linked with Beauty.

Still, Humboldt's face clearly showed that he understood what was to be done. It showed, too, that he had not gotten around to doing it. And he, too, directed my attention to landscapes. Late in the Forties, he and Kathleen, newlyweds, moved from Greenwich Village to rural New Jersey, and when I visited them he was all earth, trees, flowers, oranges, the sun, Paradise, Atlantis, Rhadamanthus. He talked about William Blake at Felpham and Milton's Eden, and he ran down the city. The city was lousy. To follow his intricate conversation you had to know his basic texts. I knew what they were: Plato's *Timaeus,* Proust on Combray, Virgil on farming, Marvell on gardens, Wallace Stevens's Caribbean poetry, and so on. One reason why Humboldt and I were so close was that I was willing to take the complete course.

So Humboldt and Kathleen lived in a country cottage. Humboldt several times a week came to town on business—poet's business. He was at the height of his reputation though not of his powers. He had lined up four sinecures that I knew of. There may have been more. Considering it normal to live on fifteen bucks a week I had no way of estimating his needs and his income. He was secretive but hinted at large sums. And now he got himself appointed to replace Professor Martin Sewell at Princeton for a year. Sewell was off to give Fulbright lectures on Henry James in Damascus. His friend Humboldt was his substitute. An instructor was needed in the program and Humboldt recommended me. Making good use of my opportunities in the postwar cultural boom I had reviewed bushels of books for *The New Republic* and the *Times*. Humboldt said, "Sewell has read your pieces. Thinks you're pretty good. You *seem* pleasant and harmless with your dark ingenu eyes and your nice Midwestern manners. The old guy wants to look you over."

"Look me over? He's too drunk to find his way out of a sentence."

"As I said, you *seem* to be a pleasant ingenu, till your touchiness is touched. Don't be so haughty. It's just a formality. The fix is already in."

"Ingenu" was one of Humboldt's bad words. Steeped in psychological literature, he looked quite through my deeds. My mooning and unworldliness didn't fool him for a minute. He knew sharpness and ambition, he knew aggression and death. The scale of his conversation was as big as he could make it, and as we drove to the country in his secondhand Buick Humboldt poured it on as the fields swept by—the Napoleonic disease, Julien Sorel, Balzac's *jeune ambitieux,* Marx's portrait of Louis Bonaparte, Hegel's World Historical Individual. Humboldt was especially attached to the World Historical Individual, the interpreter of the Spirit, the mysterious leader who imposed on Mankind the task of understanding him, etcetera. Such topics were common enough in the Village, but Humboldt brought a peculiar inventiveness and a manic energy to such discussions, a passion for intricacy and for Finneganesque double meanings and hints. "And in America," he said, "this Hegelian individual would probably come from left field. Born in Appleton, Wisconsin, maybe, like Harry Houdini or Charlie Citrine."

"Why start on me? With me you're way off."

I was annoyed with Humboldt just then. In the country, one night, he had warned my friend Demmie Vonghel against me, blurting out at dinner, "You've got to watch it with Charlie. I know girls like you. They put too much into a man. Charlie is a real devil." Horrified at what he had blurted out, he then heaved himself up from the table and ran out of the house. We heard him pounding heavily on the pebbles of the dark country road. Demmie and I sat awhile with Kathleen. Kathleen finally said, "He dotes on you, Charlie. But there's something in his head. That you have a mission—some kind of secret thing—and that people like that are not exactly trustworthy. And he likes Demmie. He thinks he's protecting her. But it isn't even personal. You aren't sore, are you?"

"Sore at Humboldt? He's too fantastic to be sore at. And especially as a protector of maidens."

Demmie appeared amused. And any young woman would find value in such solicitude. She asked me later in her abrupt way, "What's this mission stuff about?"

"Nonsense."

"But you once said something to me, Charlie. Or is Humboldt only talking through his hat?"

"I said I had a funny feeling sometimes, as if I had been stamped and posted and they were waiting for me to be delivered at an important address. I may contain unusual information. But that's just ordinary silliness."

Demmie—her full name was Anna Dempster Vonghel—taught Latin at the Washington Irving School, just east of Union Square, and lived on Barrow Street. "There's a Dutch corner in Delaware," said Demmie. "And that's where the Vonghels came from." She had been sent to finishing school, studied classics at Bryn Mawr, but she had also been a juvenile delinquent and at fifteen she belonged to a gang of car thieves. "Since we love each other, you have a right to know," she said. "I have a record—hubcap-stealing, marijuana, sex offenses, hot cars, chased by cops, crashing, hospital, probation officers, the whole works. But I also know about three thousand Bible verses. Brought up on hellfire and damnation." Her Daddy, a backwoods millionaire, raced around in his Cadillac spitting from the window. "Brushes his teeth with kitchen cleanser. Tithes to his church. Drives the Sunday-school bus. The last of the old-time Fundamentalists. Except that there are scads of them down there," she said.

Demmie had blue eyes with clean whites and an upturned nose that confronted you almost as expressively and urgently as the eyes. The length of her front teeth kept her mouth slightly open. Her long elegant head grew golden hair and she parted it evenly, like the curtains of a neat house. Hers was the sort of face you might have seen in a Conestoga wagon a century ago, a pioneer face, a very white sort of face. But I fell first for her legs. They were extraordinary. And these beautiful legs had an exciting defect—her knees touched and her feet were turned outward so that when she walked fast the taut silk of her stockings made a slight sound of friction. In a cocktail crowd, where I met her, I could scarcely understand what she was saying, for she muttered in the incomprehensible fashionable Eastern lockjaw manner. But in her nightgown she was the perfect country girl, the farmer's daughter, and pronounced her words plainly and clearly. Regularly, at about 2 a.m., her nightmares woke her. Her Christianity was the delirious kind. She had unclean spirits to cast out. She feared hell. She moaned in her sleep. Then she sat up sobbing. More than half asleep myself, I tried to calm and reassure her. "There is no hell, Demmie."

"I know there is hell. There *is* a hell—there *is*!"

"Just put your head on my arm. Go back to sleep."

On a Sunday in September 1952 Humboldt picked me up in front of Demmie's apartment building on Barrow Street near the Cherry Lane Theatre. Very different from the young poet with whom I went to Hoboken to eat clams, he now was thick and stout. Cheerful Demmie called down from the third-floor fire escape where she kept begonias—in the morning there was not a trace of nightmare. "Charlie, here comes Humboldt driving the four-holer." He charged down Barrow Street, the first poet in America with power brakes, he said. He was full of car mystique, but he didn't know to park. I watched him trying to back into an adequate space. My own theory was that the way people parked had much to do with their intimate self-image and revealed how they felt about their own backsides. Humboldt twice got a rear wheel up on the curb and finally gave up, turning off the ignition. Then in a checked sport jacket and strap-fastened polo boots he came out, swinging shut a door that seemed two yards long. His greeting was silent, the large lips were closed. His gray eyes seemed more widely separated than ever—the surfaced whale beside the dory. His handsome face had thickened and deteriorated. It was sumptuous, it was Buddhistic, but it was not tranquil. I myself was dressed for the formal professorial interview, all too belted furled and buttoned. I felt like an umbrella. Demmie had taken charge of my appearance. She ironed my shirt, chose my necktie, and brushed flat the dark hair I still had then. I went downstairs. And there we were, with the rough bricks, the garbage cans, the sloping sidewalks, the fire escapes, Demmie waving from above and her white terrier barking at the window sill.

"Have a nice day."

"Why isn't Demmie coming? Kathleen expects her."

"She has to grade her Latin papers. Make lesson plans," I said.

"If she's so conscientious she can do it in the country. I'd take her to the early train."

"She won't do it. Besides, your cats wouldn't like her dog."

Humboldt did not insist. He was devoted to the cats.

So from the present I see two odd dolls in the front seat of the roaring, grinding four-holer. This Buick was all over mud and looked like a staff car from Flanders Field. The wheels were out of line, the big tires pounded eccentrically. Through the thin sunlight of early autumn Humboldt drove fast, taking advantage of the Sunday emptiness of the streets. He was a terrible driver, making left turns from the right side, spurting, then dragging, tailgating. I disapproved. Of course I was much better with a car but comparisons were absurd, because this was Humboldt, not a driver. Steering, he was humped huge over the wheel, he had small-boy tremors of the hands and feet, and he kept the cigarette holder between his teeth. He was agitated, talking away, entertaining, provoking, informing, and snowing me. He hadn't slept last night. He seemed in poor health. Of course he drank, and he dosed himself with pills, lots of pills. In his briefcase he carried the *Merck Manual*. It was bound in black like the Bible, he consulted it often, and there were druggists who would give him what he wanted. This was something he had in common with Demmie. She too was an unauthorized pill-taker.

The car walloped the pavement, charging toward the Holland Tunnel. Close to the large form of Humboldt, this motoring giant, in the awful upholstered luxury of the front seat, I felt the ideas and illusions that went with him. He was always accompanied by a swarm, a huge volume of notions. He said how changed the Jersey swamps were, even in his lifetime, with roads, dumps, and factories, and what would a Buick like this with power brakes and power steering have meant even fifty years ago. Imagine Henry James as a driver, or Walt Whitman, or Mallarmé. We were off: he discussed machinery, luxury, command, capitalism, technology, Mammon, Orpheus and poetry, the riches of the human heart, America, world civilization. His task was to put all of this, and more, together. The car went snoring and squealing through the tunnel and came out in bright sunlight. Tall stacks, a filth artillery, fired silently into the Sunday sky with beautiful bursts of smoke. The acid smell of gas refineries went into your lungs like a spur. The rushes were as brown as onion soup. There were seagoing tankers stuck in the channels, the wind boomed, the great clouds were white. Far out, the massed bungalows had the look of a necropolis-to-be. Through the pale sun of the streets the living went to church. Under Humboldt's polo boot the carburetor gasped, the eccentric tires thumped fast on the slabs of the highway. The gusts were so strong that even the heavy Buick fluttered. We plunged over the Pulaski Skyway while the stripes of girder shadows came at us through the shuddering windshield. In the back seat were books, bottles, beer cans, and paper bags—Tristan Corbière, I remember, *Les Amours Jaunes* in a yellow jacket, *The Police Gazette,* pink, with pictures of vulgar cops and sinful kitty cats.

Humboldt's house was in the Jersey back country, near the Pennsylvania line. This marginal land was good for nothing but chicken farms. The approaches were unpaved and we drove in dust. Briars lashed the Roadmaster as we swayed on huge springs through rubbishy fields where white boulders sat. The busted muffler was so loud that though the car filled the lane there was no need to honk. You could hear us coming. Humboldt yelled, "Here's our place!" and swerved. We rolled over a hummock or earth-wave. The front of the Buick rose and then dived into the weeds. He squeezed the horn, fearing for his cats, but the cats lit out and found safety on the roof of the woodshed which had collapsed under the snow last winter.

Kathleen was waiting in the yard, large, fair-skinned, and beautiful. Her face, in the feminine vocabulary of praise, had "wonderful bones." But she was pale, and she had no country color at all. Humboldt said she seldom went outside. She sat in the house reading books. It was exactly like Bedford Street, here, except that the surrounding slum was rural. Kathleen was glad to see me, and gave my hand a kind touch. She said, "Welcome, Charlie." She said, "Thank you for coming. But where's Demmie, couldn't she come? I'm very sorry."

Then in my head a white flare went off. There was an illumination of curious clarity. I saw the position into which Humboldt had placed Kathleen and I put it into words: Lie there. Hold still. Don't wiggle. My happiness may be peculiar, but once happy I will make you happy, happier than you ever dreamed. When I am satisfied the blessings of fulfillment will

flow to all mankind. Wasn't this, I thought, the message of
modern power? This was the voice of the crazy tyrant speaking, with peculiar lusts to consummate, for which everyone
must hold still. I grasped it at once. Then I thought that Kathleen must have secret feminine reasons for going along. I too
was supposed to go along, and in another fashion I too was
to hold still. Humboldt had plans also for me, beyond Princeton. When he wasn't a poet he was a fanatical schemer. And I
was peculiarly susceptible to his influence. Why that was I have
only recently begun to understand. But he thrilled me continually. Whatever he did was delicious. Kathleen seemed aware of
this and smiled to herself as I came out of the car. I stood on
the down-beaten grass.

"Breathe the air," Humboldt said. "Different from Bedford
Street, hey?" He then quoted, "This castle hath a pleasant seat.
Also, The heaven's breath smells wooingly here."

We then started to play football. He and Kathleen played all
the time. This was why the grass was trampled. Kathleen spent
most of the day reading. To understand what her husband was
talking about she had to catch up, she said, on James, Proust,
Edith Wharton, Karl Marx, Freud, and so on. "I have to make
a scene to get her out of the house for a little football," said
Humboldt. She threw a very good pass—a hard, accurate spiral. Her voice trailed as she ran bare-legged and made the catch
on her breast. The ball in flight wagged like a duck's tail. It flew
under the maples, over the clothesline. After confinement in the
car, and in my interview clothes, I was glad to play. Humboldt
was a heavy choppy runner. In their sweaters he and Kathleen
looked like two rookies, big, fair, padded out. Humboldt said,
"Look at Charlie, jumping like Nijinsky."

I was as much Nijinsky as his house was Macbeth's castle.
The crossroads had eaten into the small bluff the cottage sat
on, and it was beginning to tip. By and by they'd have to prop
it up. Or sue the county, said Humboldt. He'd sue anyone.
The neighbors raised poultry on this slummy land. Burdocks,
thistles, dwarf oaks, cottonweed, chalky holes, and whitish
puddles everywhere. It was all pauperized. The very bushes
might have been on welfare. Across the way, the chickens were

throaty—they sounded like immigrant women—and the small trees, oaks sumacs ailanthus, were underprivileged, dusty, orphaned-looking. The autumn leaves were pulverized and the fragrance of leaf-decay was pleasant. The air was empty but good. As the sun went down the landscape was like the still frame of an old movie on sepia film. Sunset. A red wash spreading from remote Pennsylvania, sheep bells clunking, dogs in the brown barnyards. I was trained in Chicago to make something of such a scant setting. In Chicago you became a connoisseur of the near-nothing. With a clear eye I looked at a clear scene, I appreciated the red sumac, the white rocks, the rust of the weeds, the wig of green on the bluff over the crossroads.

It was more than appreciation. It was already an attachment. It was even love. The influence of a poet probably contributed to the feeling for this place that developed so quickly. I'm not referring to the privilege of being admitted to the literary life, though there may have been a touch of that. No, the influence was this: one of Humboldt's themes was the perennial human feeling that there was an original world, a home-world, which was lost. Sometimes he spoke of Poetry as the merciful Ellis Island where a host of aliens began their naturalization and of this planet as a thrilling but insufficiently humanized imitation of that home-world. He spoke of our species as castaways. But good old peculiar Humboldt, I thought (and I was peculiar enough in my own right), now has taken on the challenge of challenges. You needed the confidence of genius to commute between this patch, Nowhere, New Jersey, and the home-world of our glorious origin. Why did the crazy son of a bitch make things so hard for himself? He must have bought this joint in a blaze of mania. But now, running far into the weeds to catch the waggle-tailed ball as it flew over the clotheslines in the dusk, I was really very happy. I thought, Maybe he can swing it. Perhaps, being lost, one should get loster; being very late for an appointment, it might be best to walk slower, as one of my beloved Russian writers advised.

I was dead wrong. It wasn't a challenge, and he wasn't even trying to swing it.

When it grew too dark to play we went inside. The house

was Greenwich Village in the fields. It was furnished from thrift shops, rummage sales, and church bazaars, and seemed to rest on a foundation of books and papers. We sat in the parlor drinking from peanut-butter glasses. Big fair wan lovely pale-freckled Kathleen with that buoyant bust gave kindly smiles but mostly she was silent. Wonderful things are done by women for their husbands. She loved a poet-king and allowed him to hold her captive in the country. She sipped beer from a Pabst can. The room was low pitched. Husband and wife were large. They sat together on the Castro sofa. There wasn't enough room on the wall for their shadows. They overflowed onto the ceiling. The wallpaper was pink—the pink of ladies' underclothing or chocolate creams—in a rose-and-lattice pattern. Where a stovepipe had once entered the wall there was a gilt-edged asbestos plug. The cats came and glared through the window, humorless. Humboldt and Kathleen took turns letting them in. There were old-fashioned window pins to pull. Kathleen laid her chest to the panes, lifting the frame with the heel of her hand and boosting also with her bosom. The cats entered bristling with night static.

Poet, thinker, problem drinker, pill-taker, man of genius, manic depressive, intricate schemer, success story, he once wrote poems of great wit and beauty, but what had he done lately? Had he uttered the great words and songs he had in him? He had not. Unwritten poems were killing him. He had retreated to this place which sometimes looked like Arcadia to him and sometimes looked like hell. Here he heard the bad things being said of him by his detractors—other writers and intellectuals. He grew malicious himself but seemed not to hear what he said of others, how he slandered them. He brooded and intrigued fantastically. He was becoming one of the big-time solitaries. And he wasn't meant to be a solitary. He was meant to be in active life, a social creature. His schemes and projects revealed this.

At this time he was sold on Adlai Stevenson. He thought that if Adlai could beat Ike in the November election, Culture would come into its own in Washington. "Now that America is a world power, philistinism is finished. Finished and politically dangerous," he said. "If Stevenson is in, literature is in—we're in, Charlie. Stevenson reads my poems."

"How do you know that?"

"I'm not free to tell you how, but I'm in touch. Stevenson carries my ballads with him on the campaign trail. Intellectuals are coming up in this country. Democracy is finally about to begin creating a civilization in the USA. That's why Kathleen and I left the Village."

He had become a man of property by now. Moving into the barren backlands, among the hillbillies, he felt that he was entering the American mainstream. That at any rate was his cover. Because there were other reasons for the move—jealousy, sexual delusions. He told me once a long and tangled story. Kathleen's father had tried to get her away from him, Humboldt. Before they were married the old man had taken her and sold her to one of the Rockefellers. "She disappeared one day," said Humboldt. "Said she was going to the French bakery, and was gone for almost a year. I hired a private detective but you can guess what kind of security arrangements the Rockefellers with their billions would have. There are tunnels under Park Avenue."

"Which of the Rockefellers bought her?"

"Bought is the word," said Humboldt. "She was sold by her father. Never again smile when you read about White Slavery in the Sunday supplements."

"I suppose it was all against her will."

"She's very pliant. You see what a dove she is. One-hundred-percent obedient to that vile old man. He said 'Go,' and she went. Maybe that was her real pleasure, which her pimp father only authorized. . . ."

Masochism, of course. This was part of the Psyche Game which Humboldt had studied under its modern masters, a game far more subtle and rich than any patented parlor entertainment. Out in the country Humboldt lay on his sofa reading Proust, pondering the motives of Albertine. He seldom allowed Kathleen to drive to the supermarket without him. He hid the ignition key from her and kept her in purdah.

He was a handsome man still, Kathleen adored him. He,

however, suffered keen Jewish terrors in the country. He was an Oriental, she a Christian maiden, and he was afraid. He expected the KKK to burn a cross in his yard or shoot at him through the window as he lay on the Castro sofa reading Proust or inventing scandal. Kathleen told me that he looked under the hood of the Buick for booby traps. More than once Humboldt tried to get me to confess that I had similar terrors about Demmie Vonghel.

A neighboring farmer had sold him green logs. These smoked in the small fireplace as we sat after dinner. On the table was the stripped skeleton of a turkey. The wine and beer were going fast. There was an Ann Page coffee cake and melting maple-walnut ice cream. A slight cesspool smell rose to the window, and the Skellgas cylinders resembled silver artillery shells. Humboldt was saying that Stevenson was a man of real culture, the first really since Woodrow Wilson. But Wilson was inferior in this respect to Stevenson and Abraham Lincoln. Lincoln knew Shakespeare well and quoted him at the crises of his life. "There's nothing serious in mortality, All is but toys. . . . Duncan is in his grave; After life's fitful fever he sleeps well . . ." These were Lincoln's premonitions just as Lee was about to surrender. Frontiersmen were never afraid of poetry. It was Big Business with its fear of femininity, it was the eunuchoid clergy capitulating to vulgar masculinity that made religion and art sissy things. Stevenson understood that. If you could believe Humboldt (and I couldn't) Stevenson was Aristotle's great-souled man. In his administration cabinet members would quote Yeats and Joyce. The new Joint Chiefs would know Thucydides. Humboldt would be consulted about each State of the Union message. He was going to be the Goethe of the new government and build Weimar in Washington. "You be thinking what you might like to do, Charlie. Something in the Library of Congress, for a start."

Kathleen said, "There's a good program, on the *Late Late Show.* An old Bela Lugosi movie."

She saw that Humboldt was overexcited. He would not sleep tonight.

Very good. We tuned in the horror picture. Bela Lugosi was

a mad scientist who invented synthetic flesh. He daubed it on himself, making a fearful mask, and he broke into the rooms of beautiful maidens who screamed and fell unconscious. Kathleen, more fabulous than scientists, more beautiful than any of the ladies, sat with a hazy absent freckled half-smile. Kathleen was a somnambulist. Humboldt had surrounded her with the whole crisis of Western Culture. She went to sleep. What else could she do? I understand these decades of sleep. This is a subject I know well. Meantime Humboldt kept us from going to bed. He took Amytal to overcome the Benzedrine, on top of which he drank gin.

I went out and walked in the cold. Light poured from the cottage into ruts and gullies, over the tangled road-crown of wild carrot and ragweed. Yapping dogs, foxes maybe, piercing stars. The late-late spooks jittered through the windows, the mad scientist shot it out with the police, his lab exploded, and he died in flames, the synthetic flesh melting from his face.

Demmie on Barrow Street would be watching this same picture. She didn't have insomnia. She dreaded sleep and preferred horror movies to bad dreams. Toward bedtime Demmie always grew restless. We would take in the 10 o'clock news and walk the dog and play backgammon and double solitaire. Then we would sit on the bed and watch Lon Chaney throwing knives with his feet.

I hadn't forgotten that Humboldt tried to make himself into Demmie's protector, but I no longer had it in for him. As soon as they met, Demmie and Humboldt would begin at once to talk about old movies and new pills. When they discussed Dexamil so passionately and learnedly they lost me. But it pleased me that they had so much in common. "He's a grand man," said Demmie.

And Humboldt said of Demmie, "This girl really knows her pharmaceuticals. This is an exceptional girl." But not to tamper was more than he could bear, so he added, "She's got a few things to get out of her system."

"Bunk. What things? She's already been a juvenile delinquent."

"That's not enough," said Humboldt. "If life is not intoxicating, it's nothing. Here it's burn or rot. The USA is a romantic country. If you want to be sober, Charlie, it's only because you're a maverick and you'll try anything." Then he lowered his voice and spoke looking at the floor. "What about Kathleen, does she look wild? But she let herself be stolen and sold by her father to Rockefeller. . . ."

"I still don't know which Rockefeller bought her."

"I wouldn't make any plans about Demmie, Charlie. That girl has a lot of agony to get through yet."

He was meddling, just meddling. Still, I took this to heart. For there was a lot of agony in Demmie. Some women wept as softly as a watering can in the garden. Demmie cried passionately, as only a woman who believes in sin can cry. When she cried you not only pitied her, you respected her strength of soul.

Humboldt and I were up talking half the night. Kathleen lent me a sweater; she saw that Humboldt would sleep very little and maybe she took advantage of my visit to get a little rest, foreseeing an entire week of manic nights when there would be no guest to spell her.

As a foreword to this Evening of Conversation with Von Humboldt Fleisher (for it was a sort of recital) I should like to offer a succinct historical statement: There came a time (Early Modern) when, apparently, life lost the ability to arrange itself. It had to *be* arranged. Intellectuals took this as their job. From, say, Machiavelli's time to our own this arranging has been the one great gorgeous tantalizing misleading disastrous project. A man like Humboldt, inspired, shrewd, nutty, was brimming over with the discovery that the human enterprise, so grand and infinitely varied, had now to be managed by exceptional persons. He was an exceptional person, therefore he was an eligible candidate for power. Well, why not? Whispers of sane judgment plainly told him why not and made this comical. As long as we were laughing we were okay. At that time I was more or less a candidate myself. I, too, saw great opportunities, scenes of ideological victory, and personal triumph.

Now a word about Humboldt's conversation. What was the poet's conversation actually like?

He wore the look of a balanced thinker when he began, but

he was not the picture of sanity. I myself loved to talk and kept up with him as long as I could. For a while it was a double concerto, but presently I was fiddled and trumpeted off the stage. Reasoning, formulating, debating, making discoveries Humboldt's voice rose, choked, rose again, his mouth went wide, dark stains formed under his eyes. His eyes seemed blotted. Arms heavy, chest big, pants gathered with much belt to spare under his belly, the loose end of leather hanging down, he passed from statement to recitative, from recitative he soared into aria, and behind him played an orchestra of intimations, virtues, love of his art, veneration of its great men—but also of suspicion and skulduggery. Before your eyes the man recited and sang himself in and out of madness.

He started by talking about the place of art and culture in the first Stevenson administration—his role, *our* role, for we were going to make hay together. He began this with an appreciation of Eisenhower. Eisenhower had no courage in politics. See what he allowed Joe McCarthy and Senator Jenner to say about General Marshall. He had no guts. But he shone in logistics and public relations, and he was no fool. He was the best type of garrison officer, easygoing, a bridge-player, he liked girls and read Zane Grey Westerns. If the public wanted a relaxed government, if it had recovered sufficiently from the Depression and now wanted a holiday from war, and felt strong enough to get along without New Dealers and prosperous enough to be ungrateful, it would vote for Ike, the sort of prince who could be ordered from a Sears Roebuck catalogue. Maybe it had had enough of great personalities like FDR and energetic men like Truman. But he didn't wish to underrate America. Stevenson might make it. Now we would see where art would go in a liberal society, whether it was compatible with social progress. Meantime, having mentioned Roosevelt, Humboldt hinted that FDR might have had something to do with the death of Bronson Cutting. Senator Cutting's plane had crashed while he was flying from his home state after a vote recount. How did that happen? Maybe J. Edgar Hoover was involved. Hoover kept his power by doing the dirty work of presidents. Remember how he tried to damage Burton K. Wheeler of Montana. From this Humboldt turned to Roosevelt's sex life. Then from Roosevelt and J. Edgar Hoover to Lenin and Dzerzhinsky of the GPU. Then back to Sejanus, and the origins of secret police in the Roman Empire. Next he spoke of Trotsky's literary theories and how heavy a load great art made in the baggage train of the Revolution. Then he went back to Ike and the peacetime life of professional soldiers in the Thirties. The drinking habits of the military. Churchill and the bottle. Confidential arrangements to protect the great from scandal. Security measures in the male brothels of New York. Alcoholism and homosexuality. The married and domestic lives of pederasts. Proust and Charlus. Inversion in the German Army before 1914. Late at night Humboldt read military history and war memoirs. He knew Wheeler-Bennett, Chester Wilmot, Liddell Hart, Hitler's generals. He also knew Walter Winchell and Earl Wilson and Leonard Lyons and Red Smith, and he moved easily from the tabloids to General Rommel and from Rommel to John Donne and T. S. Eliot. About Eliot he seemed to know strange facts no one else had ever heard. He was filled with gossip and hallucination as well as literary theory. Distortion was inherent, yes, in all poetry. But which came first? And this rained down on me, part privilege, part pain, with illustrations from the classics and the sayings of Einstein and Zsa Zsa Gabor, with references to Polish socialism and the football tactics of George Halas and the secret motives of Arnold Toynbee, and (somehow) the used-car business. Rich boys, poor boys, jewboys, goyboys, chorus girls, prostitution and religion, old money, new money, gentlemen's clubs, Back Bay, Newport, Washington Square, Henry Adams, Henry James, Henry Ford, Saint John of the Cross, Dante, Ezra Pound, Dostoevski, Marilyn Monroe and Joe DiMaggio, Gertrude Stein and Alice, Freud and Ferenczi. With Ferenczi he always made the same observation: nothing could be further from instinct than rationality and therefore, according to Ferenczi, rationality was also the height of madness. As proof, how crazy Newton became! And at this point Humboldt generally spoke of Antonin Artaud. Artaud, the playwright, invited the most brilliant intellectuals in Paris to a lecture. When they were assembled there was no lecture.

Artaud came on stage and screamed at them like a wild beast. "Opened his mouth and screamed," said Humboldt. "Raging screams. While those Parisian intellectuals sat frightened. For them it was a delicious event. And why? Artaud as the artist was a failed priest. Failed priests specialize in blasphemy. Blasphemy is aimed at a community of believers. In this case, what kind of belief? Belief only in intellect, which a Ferenczi has now charged with madness. But what does it mean in a larger sense? It means that the only art intellectuals can be interested in is an art which celebrates the primacy of ideas. Artists must interest intellectuals, this new class. This is why the state of culture and the history of culture become the subject matter of art. This is why a refined audience of Frenchmen listens respectfully to Artaud screaming. For them the whole purpose of art is to suggest and inspire ideas and discourse. The educated people of modern countries are a thinking rabble at the stage of what Marx called primitive accumulation. Their business is to reduce masterpieces to discourse. Artaud's scream is an intellectual thing. First, an attack on the nineteenth-century 'religion of art,' which the religion of discourse wants to replace. . . .

"And you can see for yourself, Charlie," said Humboldt after more of this, "how important it is for the Stevenson administration to have a cultural adviser like me who understands this worldwide process. Somewhat."

Above us, Kathleen was getting into bed. Our ceiling was her floor. The boards were bare and you heard every movement. I rather envied her. I was now shivering and would have liked to get under the covers myself. But Humboldt was pointing out that we were only fifteen minutes from Trenton and two hours from Washington by train. He could shoot right in. He confided that Stevenson had already been in touch with him and that a meeting was being arranged. Humboldt asked me to help him prepare notes for this conversation, and until three in the morning we discussed this. Then I went to my room and left Humboldt pouring himself a last cup of gin.

Next day he was still going strong. It made me giddy to hear so much subtle analysis and to have so much world history poured over my head at breakfast. He hadn't slept at all.

To calm himself he took a run. With slovenly shoes he pounded the gravel. Waist-high in dust, his arms bunched against his chest, he descended the road. He seemed to sink down into it under the sumacs and small oaks, between banks of brittle crab grass, thistle, milkweed, puffballs. Burrs were sticking to his pants when he returned. For running, too, he had a text. When Jonathan Swift was secretary to Sir Wm. Temple he ran miles every day to blow off steam. Thoughts too rich, emotions too dense, dark expressive needs? You could do some roadwork. That way, you sweated out the gin, too.

He took me for a stroll and the cats accompanied us through the dead leaves and brush. They practiced pouncing. They attacked ground gossamers. With grenadier tails they bounded to sharpen their claws on trees. Humboldt was extremely fond of them. The morning air was infused with something very nice. Humboldt went in and shaved and then we drove in the fateful Buick to Princeton.

My job was in the bag. We met Sewell for lunch—a muttering subtle drunken backward-leaning hollow-faced man. He had little to say to me. At the French restaurant he wanted to gossip with Humboldt about New York and Cambridge. Sewell, a cosmopolitan if there ever was one (in his own mind), had never gone abroad before. Humboldt didn't know Europe either. "If you'd like to go, old friend," said Sewell, "we could arrange that."

"I don't feel quite ready," said Humboldt. He was afraid that he would be kidnaped by former Nazis or by GPU agents.

And as Humboldt walked me to the train, he said, "I told you it was just a formality, this interview. We've known each other for years, and we've written about each other, Sewell and I. But there are no hard feelings at all. Only I wonder why Damascus wants to know about Henry James. Well, Charlie, it should be a cheerful season for us. And if I should have to go to Washington, I know I can count on you to run things here."

"Damascus!" I said. "Among those Arabs he'll be the Sheik of Apathy."

Pale Humboldt opened his mouth. Through small teeth he gave his near-silent laugh.

At that time I was an apprentice and a bit player and Sewell had treated me like one. He had seen, I expect, a soft-fibered young man, handsome enough but slack, with large sleepy-looking eyes, a bit overweight, and with a certain reluctance (it showed in his glance) to become enthusiastic about other people's enterprises. That he failed to appreciate me made me sore. But such vexations always filled me with energy as well. And if I later became such a formidable mass of credentials it was because I put such slights to good use. I avenged myself by making progress. So I owed Sewell quite a lot and it was ungrateful of me, years later when I read in the Chicago paper that he was dead, to say, as I sipped my whisky, what I occasionally did say at such moments—death is good for some people. I remembered then the wisecrack I had made to Humboldt as we walked to the Princeton Dinkey connecting with the Junction. People die and the stinging things I said about them come winging back to attach themselves to me. What *about* this apathy? Paul of Tarsus woke up on the road to Damascus but Sewell of Princeton would sleep even deeper there. Such was my wicked meaning. I confess I am sorry now that I had said such a thing. I should add, about that interview, that it was a mistake to let Demmie Vonghel send me down dressed in charcoal gray, in a button-down collar, a knitted maroon necktie, and maroon cordovan shoes, an instant Princetonian.

Anyway, it was not long after I read Sewell's obituary in the Chicago *Daily News*, leaning on the kitchen counter at 4 p.m. with a glass of whisky and a snack of pickled herring, that Humboldt, who had been dead for five or six years, re-entered my life. He came from left field. I shan't be too exact about the time of this. I was then becoming careless about time, a symptom of my increasing absorption in larger questions.

• • •

And now the present. A different side of life—entirely contemporary.

It was in Chicago, and not very long ago by the calendar, that I left the house one morning in December to see Murra, my accountant, and when I got downstairs I found that my Mercedes-Benz had been attacked in the night. I don't mean that it had been banged and scraped by a reckless or drunken driver who ran away without leaving a note under my wipers. I mean that my car had been pounded all over, I assume with baseball bats. This elite machine, no longer new but worth eighteen thousand dollars three years ago, had been mauled with a ferocity difficult to grasp—to grasp, I mean, even in an esthetic sense, for these Mercedes coupes are beautiful, the silver-gray ones in particular. My dear friend George Swiebel had even said once, with a certain bitter admiration, "Murder Jews and make machines, that's what those Germans really know how to do."

The attack on this car was hard on me also in a sociological sense, for I always said that I knew my Chicago and I was convinced that hoodlums, too, respected lovely automobiles. Recently a car was sunk in the Washington Park lagoon and a man was found in the trunk who had tried to batter his way out with tire-tools. Evidently he was the victim of robbers who decided to drown him—get rid of the witness. But I recall thinking that his car was only a Chevrolet. They would never have done such a thing to a Mercedes 280-SL. I said to my friend Renata that *I* might be knifed or stomped on an Illinois Central platform but that this car of mine would never be hurt.

So on this morning I was wiped out as an urban psychologist. I recognized that it hadn't been psychology but only swagger, or perhaps protective magic. I knew that what you needed in a big American city was a deep no-affect belt, a critical mass of indifference. Theories also were very useful in the building of such a protective mass. The idea, anyway, was to ward off trouble. But now the moronic inferno had caught up with me. My elegant car, my shimmering silver motor tureen which I had had no business to buy—a person like me, hardly stable enough to drive this treasure—was mutilated. Everything! The delicate roof with its sliding panel, the fenders, hood, trunk, doors, locks, lights, the smart radiator emblem had been beaten and clubbed. The shatterproof windows had held up, but they looked spat on all over. The windshield was covered with white fracture-blooms. It had suffered a kind of crystal-line internal hemorrhage. Appalled, I nearly broke down, I felt like swooning.

Someone had done to my car as rats, I had heard, did when they raced through warehouses by the thousands and tore open sacks of flour for the hell of it. I felt a similar rip at my heart. The machine belonged to a time when my income was in excess of a hundred thousand dollars. Such an income had attracted the attention of the IRS, which now examined all my returns, yearly. I had set out this morning to see William Murra, that well-dressed marvelous smooth expert, the CPA who was defending me in two cases against the federal government. Although my income had now dropped to its lowest level in many years they were still after me.

I had really bought this Mercedes 280-SL because of my friend Renata. When she saw the Dodge compact I was driving when we met she said, "What kind of car is this for a famous man? There's some kind of mistake." I tried to explain to her that I was too susceptible to the influence of things and people to drive an eighteen-thousand-dollar automobile. You had to live up to such a grand machine, and consequently you were not yourself at the wheel. But Renata dismissed this. She said that I didn't know how to spend money, that I neglected myself, and that I shirked the potentialities of my success and was afraid of it. She was an interior decorator by trade, and style or panache came natural to her. Suddenly I got the idea. I went into what I called an Antony and Cleopatra mood. Let Rome in Tiber melt. Let the world know that such a mutual pair could wheel through Chicago in a silver Mercedes, the engines ticking like wizard-made toy millipedes and subtler than a Swiss Accutron—no, an Audemars Piguet with jeweled Peruvian butterfly wings! In other words, I had allowed the car to become an extension of my own self (on the folly and vanity side), so that an attack on it was an attack on myself. It was a moment terribly fertile in reactions.

How could such a thing happen on a public street? The noise must have been louder than rivet guns. Of course the lessons of jungle guerrilla tactics were being applied in all the great cities of the world. Bombs were exploding in Milan and London. Still, mine is a relatively quiet Chicago neighborhood. I was parked around the corner from my high-rise, in a narrow side street. But wouldn't the doorman have heard such clattering in the middle of the night? No, people generally hide under the covers when there are disturbances. Hearing pistol shots they say, "Backfire," to one another. As for the night-man he locks up at 1 a.m. and washes the floors. He changes in the cellar into a gray denim suit saturated with sweat. Entering the lobby late you smell the combined odors of soap powder and the musk of his denims (like rotting pears). No, the criminals who battered my car would have had no problems with the doorman. Nor with the police. As soon as the squad car had passed, knowing that it wouldn't return for fifteen minutes, they had jumped out of hiding and fallen on my car with bats, clubs, or hammers.

I knew perfectly well who was responsible for this. I had been warned over and over again. Late at night the phone often rang. Stumbling toward consciousness I picked it up and even before I could bring it to my ear I already heard my caller yelling, "Citrine! You! Citrine!"

"Yes? Yes, this is Citrine. Yes?"

"You son of a bitch. Pay me. Look what you're doing to me."

"Doing to you?"

"To me! Fucking-A-right. The check you stopped was to me. Make good, Citrine. Make that lousy check good. Don't force me to do something."

"I was fast asleep—"

"*I'm* not sleeping, why should you be?"

"I'm trying to wake up, Mr.—"

"No names! All we have to talk about is a stopped check. No names! Four hundred and fifty bucks. That's our only subject."

These gangster threats in the night against me—me! of all people! a peculiar soul and, in my own mind, almost comically innocent—made me laugh. My way of laughing has often been criticized. Well-disposed people are amused by it. Others can be offended.

"Don't laugh," said my night caller. "Knock it off. That's not a normal sound. Anyhow, who the hell do you think you're laughing at? Listen, Citrine, you lost the dough to me in a poker game. You'll say it was just a family evening, or you were drunk, but that's a lot of crap. I took your check, and I won't hold still for a slap in the face."

"You know why I stopped payment. You and your buddy were cheating."

"Did you see us?"

"The host saw. George Swiebel swears you were flashing cards to each other."

"Why didn't he speak up, that dumb prick. He should have thrown us out."

"He may have been afraid to tackle you."

"Who, that health fiend, with all the color in his face? For Christ sake he looks like an apple, with all that jogging five miles a day, and the vitamins I saw in his medicine chest. There were seven, eight people at the game. They could have bounced us. Your friend has no guts."

I said, "Well, it wasn't a good evening. I was high, though you don't believe it. Nobody was rational. Everyone was out of character. Let's be sensible."

"What, I have to hear from my bank about your stop order, which is like a kick in the ass, and then be sensible? You think I'm a punk? It was a mistake to get into all that talk about education and colleges. I saw the look you gave when I told the name of the cow-college I went to."

"What's colleges got to do with it?"

"Don't you understand what you're doing to me? You've written all that stuff. You're in *Who's Who*. But you dumb asshole you don't understand anything."

"At two in the morning it's hard for me to understand. Can't we meet in the daytime when my head is clear?"

"No more talk. Talk is finished."

He said this many times, however. I must have received ten such calls from Rinaldo Cantabile. The late Von Humboldt Fleisher had also used the dramatic properties of night to bully and harass people.

George Swiebel had ordered me to stop the check. My friendship with George goes back to the fifth grade, and to me such pals are a sacred category. I have been warned often against this terrible weakness or dependency on early relationships. Once an actor, George had given up the stage decades ago and become a contractor. He was a wide-built fellow with a ruddy color. There was nothing subdued about his manner, his clothing, his personal style. For years he had been my self-designated expert on the underworld. He kept me informed about criminals, whores, racing, the rackets, narcotics, politics, and Syndicate operations. Having been in radio and television and journalism, his connections were unusually extensive, "from putrid to pure," he would say. And I was well up among the pure. I make no such claims for myself. This is to explain how George saw me.

"You lost that money at my kitchen table, and you'd better listen," he said. "Those punks were cheating."

"Then you should have called them on it. Cantabile has a point."

"He's got nothing, and he's nobody. If he owed you three bucks, you'd have to chase him for it. Also he was spaced out on drugs."

"I didn't notice."

"You didn't notice anything. I gave you the high sign a dozen times."

"I didn't see. I can't remember. . . ."

"Cantabile was working on you every minute. He snowed you. He was smoking pot. He was talking art and culture and psychology and the Book-of-the-Month Club and bragging about his educated wife. You bet every hand you were dealt. And every single subject I ever asked you not to mention you were discussing freely."

"George, these night calls of his are wearing me down. I'll pay him. Why not? I pay everybody. I have to get rid of this creep."

"No pay!" Trained as an actor, George had learned to swell his voice theatrically, to glare, to seem startled and to have a startling effect. He shouted at me, "Charlie, you listen!"

"But I'm dealing with a gangster."

"There are no Cantabiles in the rackets any more. They all got thrown out years ago. I told you. . . ."

"He puts on a damned good imitation then. At two a.m. I'm convinced that he's a real hoodlum."

"He's seen *The Godfather* or something, and he's grown a dago mustache. He's only a confused big-mouth kid and a dropout. I shouldn't have let him and his cousin into the house. Now you forget this. They were playing gangster and they cheated. I tried to stop you giving him the check. Then I made you stop payment. I won't let you give in. Anyhow, the whole thing—take it from me—is over."

So I submitted. I couldn't challenge George's judgment. Now Cantabile had hit my car with everything he had. The blood left my heart when I saw what he had done. I dropped back against the building for support. I had gone out one evening to amuse myself in vulgar company and I had fallen into the moronic inferno.

Vulgar company was not my own expression. What I was in fact hearing was the voice of my ex-wife. It was Denise who used terms like "common clay" and "vulgar company." The fate of my poor Mercedes would have given her very deep satisfaction. This was something like war, and she had an intensely martial personality. Denise hated Renata, my lady friend. She correctly identified Renata with this automobile. And she loathed George Swiebel. George, however, took a complex view of Denise. He said that she was a great beauty but not altogether human. Certainly Denise's huge radial amethyst eyes in combination with a low-lined forehead and sharp sibylline teeth supported this interpretation. She is exquisite, and terribly fierce. Down-to-earth George is not without myths of his own, especially where women are concerned. He has Jungian views, which he expresses coarsely. He has fine feelings which frustrate him because they fiddle his heart, and he overreacts grossly. Anyway, Denise would have laughed with happiness at the sight of this ruined car. And I? You would have thought that being divorced I had escaped the marital "I-told-you-so." But here I was, supplying it myself.

For Denise continually spoke to me about myself. She would say, "I just can't believe the way you are. The man who's had all those wonderful insights, the author of all these books, respected by scholars and intellectuals all over the world. I sometimes have to ask myself, 'Is that *my* husband? The man *I* know?' You've lectured at the great Eastern universities and had grants and fellowships and honors. De Gaulle made you a knight of the Legion of Honor and Kennedy invited us to the White House. You had a successful play on Broadway. *Now* what the hell do you think you're doing? Chicago! You hang around with your old Chicago school chums, with freaks. It's a kind of mental suicide, death wish. You'll have nothing to do with really interesting people, with architects or psychiatrists or university professors. I tried to make a life for you when you insisted on moving back here. I put myself out. You wouldn't have London or Paris or New York, you had to come back to this—this deadly, ugly, vulgar, dangerous place. Because at heart you're a kid from the slums. Your heart belongs to the old West Side gutters. I wore myself out being a hostess. . . ."

There were large grains of truth in all of this. My old mother's words for Denise would have been *"Edel, gebildet, gelassen,"* for Denise was an upper-class person. She grew up in Highland Park. She went to Vassar College. Her father, a federal judge, also came from the West Side Chicago gutters. *His* father had been a precinct captain under Morris Eller in the stormy days of Big Bill Thompson. Denise's mother had taken the judge when he was a mere boy, only the son of a crooked politician, and straightened him out and cured him of his vulgarity. Denise had expected to do as much with me. But oddly enough her paternal inheritance was stronger than the maternal. On days when she was curt and tough, in her high tense voice you heard that old precinct captain and bagman, her grandfather. Because of this background, perhaps, she hated George fiercely. "Don't bring him to the house," she said. "I can't bear to see his ass on my sofa, his feet on my rug." Denise said, "You're like one of those overbred race horses that must have a goat in his stall to calm his nerves. George Swiebel is your billy goat."

"He's a good friend to me, an old friend."

"Your weakness for your school chums isn't to be believed. You have the *nostalgie de la boue*. Does he take you around to the whores?"

I tried to give a dignified answer. But as a matter of fact I wanted the conflict to increase, and I provoked Denise. On the maid's night out I once brought George home to dinner. Maid's night out threw Denise into an anguish of spirit. Housework was insufferable. It killed her to have to cook. She wanted to go to a restaurant, but I said I didn't feel like dining out. So at six o'clock, she hastily mixed ground meat with tomatoes, kidney beans, and chili powder. I said to George, "Share our chili con carne tonight. We can open a few bottles of beer."

Denise signaled me to come into the kitchen. She said, "I won't have this." She was warlike and shrill. Her voice was clear, thrilling, and minutely articulate—the rising arpeggios of hysteria.

"Oh, come on. Denise, he can hear you." I lowered my voice and said, "Let George have some of this chili con carne."

"There's not enough. It's just half a pound of hamburger. But that's not the point. The point is I won't serve him."

I laughed. Partly from embarrassment. I am normally a low baritone, almost basso profundo, but under certain kinds of provocation my voice disappears into the higher registers, perhaps into the bat range.

"Listen to that screeching," said Denise. "You give yourself away when you laugh like this. You were born in a coal scuttle. Brought up in a parrot-house."

Her great violet eyes were unyielding.

"All right," I said. I took George to the Pump Room. We ate shashlik brought in flaming by turbaned Moors.

"I don't want to interfere in your marriage, but I notice you've stopped breathing," said George.

George feels that he can speak for Nature. Nature, instinct, heart guide him. He is biocentric. To see him rub his large muscles, his Roman Ben Hur chest and arms with olive oil is a lesson in piety toward the organism. Concluding, he takes a long swig from the bottle. Olive oil is the sun and the ancient Mediterranean. Nothing is better for the bowels, the hair, the skin.

He holds his own body in numinous esteem. He is a priest to the inside of his nose, his eyeballs, his feet. "You're not getting enough air with that woman. You look as if you're suffocating. Your tissues aren't getting any oxygen. She'll give you cancer."

"Oh," I said. "She may think she's offering me the blessings of an American marriage. Real Americans are supposed to suffer with their wives, and wives with husbands. Like Mr. and Mrs. Abraham Lincoln. It's the classic US grief, and a child of immigrants like me ought to be grateful. For a Jew it's a step up."

Yes, Denise would be overjoyed to hear of this atrocity. She had seen Renata speeding past in the silver Mercedes. "And you, the passenger," said Denise, "getting to be as bald as a barber pole, even if you comb your side-hair over to hide it, and grinning. She'll give you something to grin about, that fat broad." From insult Denise went into prophecy. "Your mental life is going to dry out. You're sacrificing it to your erotic needs (if that's the term for what you have). After sex, what can you two talk about . . . ? Well, you wrote a few books, you wrote a famous play, and even that was half ghosted. You associated with people like Von Humboldt Fleisher. You took it into your head that you were some kind of artist. We know better, don't we. And what you really want is to get rid of everybody, to tune out and be a law unto yourself. Just you and your misunderstood heart, Charlie. You couldn't bear a serious relationship, that's why you got rid of me and the children. Now you've got this tramp with the fat figure who wears no bra and shows her big nipples to the world. You've got ignorant kikes and hoodlums around you. You're crazy with your own brand of pride and snobbery. There's nobody good enough for you. . . . I could have helped you. Now it's too late!"

I would not argue with Denise. I felt a certain sympathy with her. She said I was living badly. I agreed. She thought I wasn't all there, and I would have had to be completely crazy to deny it. She said I was writing stuff that made sense to no one. Maybe so. My last book, Some Americans, subtitled The Sense of Being in the USA, was quickly remaindered. The publishers had begged me not to print it. They offered to forget a debt of twenty thousand dollars if I would shelve it. But now I was perversely writing Part II. My life was in great disorder.

I was, however, loyal to something. I had an idea.

"Why did you ever bring me back to Chicago?" said Denise. "Sometimes I think you did it because your dead are buried here. Is that the reason? Land where my Jewish fathers died? And you dragged me to your graveyard so you could get into the anthem? And what's it about? All because you have delusions about being a marvelous noble person. Which you are—like hell!"

Such abuse does Denise more good than vitamins. As for me, I find that certain kinds of misunderstanding are full of useful hints. But my final though silent answer to Denise was always the same. Despite her intelligence, she *had* been bad for my idea. From that standpoint, Renata was the better woman—better for me.

Renata had forbidden me to drive a Dart. I tried to negotiate with the Mercedes salesman for a secondhand 250-C, but in the showroom Renata—roused, florid, fragrant, large—had put her hand on the silver hood and said, "This one—the coupe." The touch of her palm was sensual. Even what she did to the car I felt in my own person.

•   •   •

But now something had to be done about this wreck. I went to the Receiving Room and fetched Roland the doorman—skinny, black, elderly, never-shaven Roland. Roland Stiles, unless I deceived myself (a strong likelihood), was on my side. In my fantasies of solitary death it was Roland whom I saw in my bedroom filling a flight bag with a few articles before calling the police. He did so with my blessing. He particularly needed my electric razor. His intensely black face was pitted and spiky. Shaving with a blade must have been nearly impossible.

Roland, in the electric-blue uniform, was perturbed. He had seen the ruined car when he came to work in the morning but, he said, "I couldn't be the one to tell you, Mist' Citrine." Tenants on their way to work had seen it, too. They knew of course to whom it belonged. "This is a real bitch," said Roland soberly, his lean old face twisted and his mouth and mustache puckered. Quickwitted, he had always kidded me about the beautiful ladies who called on me. "They come in Volkswagens and Cadillacs, on bikes and motorcycles, in taxis and walkin'. They ask when you went out, and when you comin' back, and they leave notes. They come, they come, they come. You some ladies' man. Plenty of husbands got it in for you, I bet." But the amusement was gone. Roland hadn't been a black man sixty years for nothing. He knew moronic infernos. I had lost the immunity which made my ways so entertaining. "You in trouble," he said. He muttered something about "Miss Universe." He called Renata Miss Universe. Sometimes she paid him to entertain her little boy in the Receiving Room. The child played with parcels while his mother lay in my bed. I didn't like it, but you can't be a ridiculous lover by halves.

"Now what?"

Roland twisted his hands outward. He lifted his shoulders. Shrugging, he said, "Call the cops."

Yes, a report had to be filed, if only because of the insurance. The insurance company would find this a very queer case. "Well, flag the squad car when it passes. Have those useless fellows look at this ruin," I said. "And then send them up."

I gave him a dollar for his trouble. I usually did that. And now the flow of malevolence had to be reversed.

Through my apartment door I heard the telephone. It was Cantabile.

"All right, smart-ass."

"Insane!" I said. "Vandalism! Beating a machine . . . !"

"You've seen your car—you saw what you made me do!" He yelled. He forced his voice. Nevertheless it shook.

"What's that? You're blaming me?"

"You were warned."

"*I* made you hammer that beautiful automobile?"

"You made me. Yes, you. You sure did. You think I don't have feelings? You wouldn't believe how I feel about a car like that. You're stupid. This is nobody's fault but yours." I tried to answer but he shouted me down. "You forced me! You made me! Okay, last night was only step one."

"What does that mean?"

"Don't pay me and you'll see what it means."

"What kind of threat is that? This is getting out of hand. Do you mean my daughters?"

"I'm not going to a collection agency. You don't know what you're into. Or who I am. Wake up!"

I often said "Wake up!" to myself, and many people also have cried, "Wake, wake!" As if I had a dozen eyes, and stubbornly kept them sealed. "Ye have eyes and see not." This, of course, was absolutely true.

Cantabile was still speaking. I heard him say, "So, go and ask George Swiebel what to do. He gave you the advice. *He*, like, smashed your car."

"Let's stop all this. I want to settle."

"No settle. Pay. Make good the check. The full amount. And cash. No money orders, no cashier's check, no more fucking around. Cash. I'll call you later. We'll make a date. I want to see you."

"When?"

"Never mind when. You stick by the telephone till I call."

Next instant I heard the interminable universal electronic miaow of the phone. And I was desperate. I had to tell what had happened. I needed to consult.

A sure sign of distress: telephone numbers stormed through my head—area codes, digits. I must telephone someone. The first person I called was George Swiebel, of course; I had to tell him what had happened. I also had to warn him. Cantabile might attack him, too. But George was out with a crew. They were pouring a concrete footing somewhere, said Sharon, his secretary. George, before he became a businessman, was, as I have said, an actor. He started out in the Federal Theater. Afterward he was a radio announcer. He had tried television and Hollywood as well. Among business people he spoke of his show-business experience. He knew his Ibsen and his Brecht and he often flew to Minneapolis to see plays at the Guthrie Theatre. In South Chicago he was identified with Bohemia and the Arts, with creativity, with imagination. And he was vital, generous, had an open nature. He was a good guy. People formed strong attachments to him. Look at this little Sharon, his secretary. She was a hillbilly, dwarfish and queer-faced, and looked like Mammy Yokum in the funnies. Yet George was her brother, her doctor, her priest, her tribe. She had, as it were, surveyed South Chicago and found only one man there, George Swiebel. When I spoke to her, I had enough presence of mind to dissemble, for if I had told Sharon how shocking things were she would not have given George the message. George's average day, as he and his people saw it, was one crisis after another. Her job was to protect him. "Ask George to call me," I said. I hung up thinking of the crisis-outlook in the USA, a legacy from old frontier times, etcetera. I thought these things from force of habit. Just because your soul is being torn to pieces doesn't mean that you stop analyzing the phenomena.

I restrained my real desire, which was to scream. I recognized that I would have to recompose myself unassisted. I didn't dial Renata. Renata is not especially good at giving consolation over the phone. You have to get it from her in person.

Now I had Cantabile's ring to wait for. And the police as well. I had to explain to Murra the CPA that I wouldn't be coming in. He'd charge me for the hour anyway, after the manner of psychiatrists and other specialists. That afternoon I was to have taken my small daughters Lish and Mary to their piano teacher. For, as the Gulbransen Piano Co. used to say on the brick walls of Chicago, "The richest child is poor without a musical education." And mine were rich man's daughters, and it would be a disaster if they grew up unable to play "Für Elise" and the "Happy Farmer."

I had to recover my calm. Seeking stability, I did the one Yoga exercise I know. I took the small change and the keys out of my pockets, I removed my shoes, took a position on the floor, advancing my toes, and, with a flip, I stood on my head. My loveliest of machines, my silver Mercedes 280, my gem, my love-offering, stood mutilated in the street. Two thousand dollars' worth of bodywork would never restore the original smoothness of the metal skin. The headlights were crushed blind. I hadn't the heart to try the doors, they might be jammed shut. I tried to concentrate on hatred and fury—revenge,

revenge! But I couldn't get anywhere with that. I could only see the German steward at the shop in his long white smock, like a dentist, telling me that parts would have to be imported. And I, clutching my half-bald head in both hands as if in despair, fingers interlocked, had my trembling aching legs in the air, tufts of side-hair sticking out, and the green Persian carpet flowing under me. I was heart-injured. I was desolate. The beauty of the carpet was one of my comforts. I have become deeply attached to carpets, and this one was a work of art. The green was soft and varied with great subtlety. The red was one of those surprises that seem to spring straight from the heart. Stribling, my downtown expert, told me that I could get far more than I had paid for this rug. Everything that wasn't mass-produced was zooming in value. Stribling was an obese excellent man who kept horses but now was too heavy to ride. Few people seemed to be consummating anything good, these days. Look at me. I couldn't be serious, becoming involved in this sort of grotesque comic Mercedes-and-Underworld thing. As I stood on my head, I knew (I *would* know!) that there was a sort of theoretical impulse behind this grotesqueness too, one of the powerful theories of the modern world being that for self-realization it's necessary to embrace the deformity and absurdity of the inmost being (we *know* it's there!). Be healed by the humiliating truth the Unconscious contains. I didn't buy this theory, but that didn't mean that I was free from it. I had a talent for absurdity, and you don't throw away any of your talents.

I was thinking that I'd never get a penny from the insurance company on a queer claim like this. I had bought every kind of protection they offered, but somewhere in the small print they were sure to have the usual foxy clauses. Under Nixon the great corporations became drunk with immunity. The good old bourgeois virtues, even as window dressing, are gone forever.

It was from George that I had learned this upside-down position. George warned that I was neglecting my body. Several years ago he began to point out that my throat was becoming crepy, my color was poor, and I was easily winded. At a certain point in middle age you had to make a stand, he argued, before the abdominal wall gives, the thighs get weak and thin, the breasts female. There was a way to age that was physically honorable. George interpreted this for himself with peculiar zeal. Immediately after his gall-bladder operation he got out of bed and did fifty push-ups—his own naturopath. From this exertion, he got peritonitis and for two days we thought he was dying. But ailments seemed to inspire him, and he had his own cures for everything. Recently he told me, "I woke up day before yesterday and found a lump under my arm."

"Did you go to the doctor?"

"No. I tied it with dental floss. I tied it tight, tight, tight. . . ."

"What happened?"

"Yesterday when I examined it, it had swelled up to the size of an egg. Still I didn't call the doctor. To hell with that! I took more dental floss and tied it tight, tight, even tighter. And now it's cured, it's gone. You want to see?"

It was when I told him of my arthritic neck that he prescribed standing on my head. Though I threw up my palms and shrieked with laughter (looking like one of Goya's frog caricatures in the *Visión Burlesca*—the creature with the locks and bolts) I did as he advised. I practiced and learned the headstand, and I was cured of the neck pains. Next, when I had a stricture, I asked George for a remedy. He said, "It's the prostate gland. You start, then you stop, then you trickle again, it burns a bit, you feel humiliated?"

"All correct."

"Don't worry. Now as you stand on your head, tighten your buttocks. Just suck them in as if you were trying to bring the cheeks together."

"Why must this be done as you stand on your head? I already feel like Old Father William."

But he was adamant and said, "On your head."

Again his method worked. The stricture went away. Others may see in George a solid high-colored good-humored building contractor; I see a hermetical personage; I see a figure from the tarot deck. If I was on my head now I was invoking George. When I'm in despair he's always the first person I telephone.

I've reached an age at which you can see your neurotic impulses advancing on you. There's not much that I can do when the dire need of help comes over me. I stand at the edge of a psychic pond and I know that if crumbs are thrown in, my carp will come swimming up. You have, like the external world, your own phenomena inside. At one time I thought the civilized thing to do was to make a park and a garden for them, to keep these traits, your quirks, like birds, fishes, and flowers.

However, the fact that I had no one but myself to turn to was awful. Waiting for bells to ring is a torment. The suspense claws at my heart. Actually, standing on my head did relieve me. I breathed again. But I saw, when I was upside-down, two large circles in front of me, very bright. These occasionally appear during this exercise. Reversed on your cranium, of course you do think of being caught by a cerebral hemorrhage. A physician advising against the headstand said to me that a chicken held upside-down would die in seven or eight minutes. But that's obviously because of terror. The bird is scared to death. I figure that the bright rings are caused by pressure on the cornea. The weight of the body set upon the skull buckles the cornea and produces an illusion of big diaphanous rings. Like seeing eternity. Which, believe me, I was ready for on this day.

Behind me, I had a view of the bookcase, and when my head was readjusted, with more weight shifted to the forearms, the pellucid rings swam away, the shades of a fatal hemorrhage with them. In reverse, I saw rows and rows of my own books. I had stacked them at the back of my closets, but Renata had brought them out again to make a display. I prefer, when I'm on my head, to have a view of the sky and the clouds. It's good fun to study the clouds upside-down. But now I was looking at the titles which had brought me money, recognition, prizes, my play, *Von Trenck,* in many editions and languages, and a few copies of my favorite, the failure *Some Americans: The Sense of Being in the USA. Von Trenck* while it was running brought in about eight thousand dollars a week. The government, which had taken no previous interest in my soul, immediately claimed seventy percent in the result of its creative efforts. But this was not supposed to affect me. You rendered unto Caesar what was

Caesar's. At least you knew that you should. Money belonged to Caesar. There was also *Radix malorum est cupiditas*. I knew all that, too.

I knew everything I was supposed to know and nothing I really needed to know. I had bungled the whole money thing. It was highly educational, of course, and education has become the great and universal American recompense. It has even replaced punishment in the federal penitentiaries. Every great prison is now a thriving seminar. The tigers of wrath are crossed with the horses of instruction, making a hybrid undreamed of in the Apocalypse. Not to labor the matter too much, I had lost most of the money that Humboldt had accused me of making. The dough came between us immediately. He put through a check for thousands of dollars. I didn't contest this. I didn't want to go to law. Humboldt would have been fiercely delighted with a trial. He was very litigious. But the check he cashed was actually signed by me, and I would have had a hard time explaining this in court. Besides, courts kill me. Judges, lawyers, bailiffs, stenotypists, the benches, the woodwork, the carpets, even the water glasses I hate like death. Moreover, I was actually in South America when he cashed the check. He was then running wild in New York, having been released from Bellevue. There was no one to restrain him. Kathleen had gone into hiding. His nutty old mother was in a nursing home. His uncle Waldemar was one of those eternal kid brothers to whom responsibilities are alien. Humboldt was jumping and prancing about New York being mad. Perhaps he was aware dimly of the satisfaction he was giving to the cultivated public which gossiped about his crack-up. Frantic desperate doomed crazy writers and suicidal painters are dramatically and socially valuable. And at that time he was a fiery Failure and I was a newborn Success. Success baffled me. It filled me with guilt and shame. The play performed nightly at the Belasco was not the play I had written. I had only provided a bolt of material from which the director had cut shaped basted and sewn his own Von Trenck. Brooding, I muttered to myself that after all Broadway adjoins the garment district and blends with it.

Cops have their own way of ringing a doorbell. They ring like brutes. Of course, we are entering an entirely new stage in the history of human consciousness. Policemen take psychology courses and have some feeling for the comedy of urban life. The two heavy men who stood on my Persian carpet carried guns, clubs, cuffs, bullets, walkie-talkies. Such an unusual case—a Mercedes beaten in the street—amused them. This pair of black giants had a squad-car odor, the smell of close quarters. Their hardware clinked, their hips and bellies swelled and bulged.

"I never saw such massacre on an automobile," said one of them. "You in trouble with some real bad actors." He was probing, hinting. He didn't actually want to hear about the Mob, about juice men or gang-entanglements. Not one word. But it was all obvious. I didn't *look* like a fellow in the rackets, but maybe I was one. Even the cops had seen *The Godfather, The French Connection, The Valachi Papers,* and other blast-and-bang thrillers. I was drawn to this gang stuff myself, as a Chicagoan, and I said, "I don't know anything." I dummied up, and I believe the police approved of this.

"You keep your car in the street?" said one of the cops—he had volumes of muscle and a great slack face. "If I didn't have a garage, I wouldn't own but a piece of junk." Then he saw my medal, which Renata had framed in plush on the wall, and he said, "Were you in Korea?"

"No," I said. "The French government gave me that. The Legion of Honor. I'm a knight, a *chevalier.* Their ambassador decorated me."

On that occasion, Humboldt had sent me one of his unsigned postcards. *"Shoveleer! Your name is now lesion!"*

He had been on a *Finnegans Wake* kick for years. I remembered our many discussions of Joyce's view of language, of the poet's passion for charging speech with music and meaning, of the dangers that hover about all the works of the mind, of beauty falling into abysses of oblivion like the snow chasms of the Antarctic, of Blake and Vision versus Locke and the *tabula rasa.* As I saw the cops out I was remembering with sadness of heart the lovely conversations Humboldt and I used to have. Humanity divine incomprehensible!

"You better square this thing," the cop advised me, low and kindly. His great black weight moved toward the elevator. The Shoveleer inclined politely. I felt my eyes ache with a helpless craving for help.

Yes, the medal reminded me of Humboldt. Yes, when Napoleon gave the French intellectuals ribbons stars and baubles, he knew what he was doing. He took a boatload of scholars with him to Egypt. He ditched them. They came up with the Rosetta stone. From the time of Richelieu and earlier, the French had been big in the culture business. You'd never catch De Gaulle wearing one of these ridiculous trinkets. He had too much self-esteem. The fellows who bought Manhattan from the Indians didn't wear beads themselves. I would gladly have given this gold medal to Humboldt. The Germans tried to honor him. He was invited to Berlin in 1952 to lecture at the Free University. He wouldn't go. He was afraid of being abducted by the GPU or the NKVD. He was a longtime contributor to the *Partisan Review* and a prominent anti-Stalinist, so he was afraid that the Russians would try to kidnap and kill him. "Also, if I spent a year in Germany I'd be thinking of one thing only," he stated publicly (I was the only one listening). "For twelve months I'd be a Jew and nothing else. I can't afford to give an entire year to that." But I think a better explanation is that he was having a grand time being mad in New York. He was seeing psychiatrists and making scenes. He invented a lover for Kathleen and then he tried to kill the man. He smashed up the Buick Roadmaster. He accused me of stealing his personality for the character of Von Trenck. He drew a check on my account for six thousand seven hundred and sixty-three dollars and fifty-eight cents and bought an Oldsmobile with it, among other things. Anyway, he didn't want to go to Germany, a country where no one could follow his conversation.

From the papers he later learned that I had become a Shoveleer. I had heard that he was living with a gorgeous black girl who studied the French horn at the Juilliard School. But when I last saw him on Forty-sixth Street I knew that he was too destroyed to be living with anyone. He was destroyed—I can't help repeating this. He wore a large gray suit in which he was floundering. His face was dead gray, East River gray. His head looked as if the gypsy moth had gotten into it and tented in his hair. Nevertheless I should have approached and spoken to him. I should have drawn near, not taken cover behind the parked cars. But how could I? I had had my breakfast in the Edwardian Room of the Plaza, served by rip-off footmen. Then I had flown in a helicopter with Javits and Bobby Kennedy. I was skirring around New York like an ephemerid, my jacket lined with jolly psychedelic green. I was dressed up like Sugar Ray Robinson. Only I didn't have a fighting spirit, and seeing that my old and close friend was a dead man I beat it. I went to La Guardia and took a 727 back to Chicago. I sat afflicted in the plane, drinking whisky on the rocks, overcome with horror, ideas of Fate and other humanistic lah-de-dah—compassion. I had gone around the corner and gotten lost on Sixth Avenue. My legs trembled and my teeth were set hard. I said to myself, Humboldt good-by, I'll see you in the next world. And two months after this in the Ilscombe Hotel, which has since collapsed, he started down at 3 a.m. with his garbage pail and died in the corridor.

At a Village cocktail party in the Forties I heard a beautiful girl tell Humboldt, "Do you know what you're like? You're like a person from a painting." Sure, women dreaming of love might have visions of Humboldt at twenty stepping down from a Renaissance or an Impressionist masterpiece. But the picture on the obituary page of the *Times* was frightful. I opened the paper one morning and there was Humboldt, ruined, black and gray, a disastrous newspaper face staring at me from death's territory. That day, too, I was flying from New York to Chicago—wafting back and forth, not always knowing why. I went to the can and locked myself in. People knocked but I was weeping and wouldn't come out.

• • •

Actually Cantabile didn't make me wait too long. He phoned just before noon. Maybe he was getting hungry. I remembered that someone or other in Paris toward the end of the nineteenth century used to see Verlaine drunken and bloated pounding his cane wildly on the sidewalk as he went to lunch, and shortly afterward the great mathematician Poincaré, respectably dressed and following his huge forehead while describing curves with his fingers, also on his way to lunch. Lunchtime is lunchtime, whether you are a poet or a mathematician or a gangster. Cantabile said, "All right, you dumb prick, we're going to meet right after lunch. Bring cash. And that's all you bring. Don't make any more bad moves."

"I wouldn't know what or how," I said.

"That's true, as long as you don't cook up anything with George Swiebel. You come alone."

"Of course. It never even occurred to me—"

"Well now I've said it, but it better not occur. Alone, and bring new bills. Go to the bank and get clean money. Nine bills of fifty. New. I don't want any grease stains on those dollars. And be glad if I don't make you eat that fucking check."

What a fascist! But maybe he was only priming or haranguing himself to keep up the savagery level. By now, however, my only object was to get rid of him by submission and agreement. "Any way you want it," I said. "Where shall I bring this money?"

"The Russian Bath on Division Street," he said.

"That old joint? For the love of God!"

"You be in front, there, at one-forty-five and wait. And alone!" he said.

I answered, "Right." But he hadn't waited for agreement. Again I heard the dial tone. I identified this interminable squalling with the anxiety level of the disengaged soul.

I had to put myself into motion. And I couldn't expect Renata to do anything for me. Renata, at business today, was attending an auction, and she'd have been miffed if I had called the auction rooms to ask her to take me to the Northwest Side. She's an obliging and beautiful woman, she has marvelous breasts, but she takes offense at certain kinds of slights and quickly flares up. Well, I'd manage it all somehow. Perhaps the Mercedes could be driven to the shop. A tow truck might not be needed. And then I'd have to find a taxi or call the Emery Liv-

ery Service or Rent-a-Car. I wouldn't ride the bus. There are
too many armed drunkards and heroin users on the buses and
trains. But, no, wait! First, I must call Murra and then run to
the bank. Also I had to explain that I couldn't drive Lish and
Mary to their piano lesson. This made my heart particularly
heavy, because I'm somewhat afraid of Denise. She still wields
a certain power. Denise made a great production of these lessons. But with her everything was a production, everything was
momentous, critical. All psychological problems relating to the
children were presented with great intensity. Questions of child
development were desperate, dire, mortal. If these kids were
ruined it would be my fault. I had abandoned them at a most
perilous moment in the history of civilization to take up with
Renata. "That whore with fat tits"—was what Denise regularly called her. She spoke of beautiful Renata always as a gross
tough broad. The trend of her epithets, it seemed, was to make
a man of Renata and a woman of me.

Denise, like my wealth, goes back to the Belasco Theatre.
Trenck was played by Murphy Verviger and the star had a reti-
nue (a dresser, a press agent, an errand boy). Denise, who was
living with Verviger at the St. Moritz, arrived with his other
attendants daily, carrying his script. Dressed in a plum velvet
jump-suit she wore her hair down. Elegant, slender, slightly
flat-chested, high-shouldered, wide across the top like an old-
fashioned kitchen chair, she had large violet eyes, a marvelously rich subtle color in her face and a mysterious, seldom
visible down, even over her nose. Because of the August heat
the great doors offstage were open on the cement alleys and the
daylight stealing in showed the appalling baldness and decay of
the antique luxury. The Belasco was like a gilded cake-platter
with grimed frosting. Verviger, his face deeply grooved at the
mouth, was big and muscular. He resembled a skiing instructor. Some concept of intense refinement was eating at him. His
head was shaped like a busby, a high solid arrogant rock covered with thick moss. Denise kept rehearsal notes for him. She
wrote with terrible concentration, as if she were the smartest
pupil in the class and the rest of the fifth grade were in pursuit.
When she came to ask a question she held the script to her

chest and spoke to me in a condition of operatic crisis. Her voice seemed to make her own hair bristle and to dilate her astonishing eyes. She said, "Verviger wants to know how you'd like him to pronounce this word"—she printed it out for me, FINITE. "He says he can do it *fin*-it, or *fine*-it, or *fine-ite*. He doesn't take my word for it—fine-ite!"

I said, "Why so fancy? . . . I don't care what he does with it." I didn't add that I despaired of Verviger anyway. He had the play wrong from top to bottom. Maybe he was getting things right at the St. Moritz. That didn't concern me then. I went home and told my friend Demmie Vonghel about the glaring bristling beauty at the Belasco, Verviger's girlfriend.

Well, ten years later Denise and I were husband and wife. And we were invited to the White House by the President and Mrs. Kennedy in black tie for a cultural evening. Denise consulted twenty or thirty women about dresses, shoes, gloves. Very intelligent, she always read up on national and world problems at the beauty parlor. Her hair was heavy and worn high. It wasn't easy to be sure when she had had it done, but I could always tell from her dinner conversation whether she'd been to the hairdresser that afternoon, because she was a speed reader and covered every detail of world crisis under the dryer. "Do you realize what Khrushchev did in Vienna?" she said. So at the beauty salon, to prepare for the White House, she mastered *Time* and *Newsweek* and *The U.S. News and World Report*. On the flight to Washington we reviewed the Bay of Pigs and the Missile Crisis and the Diem problem. Her nervous intensity is constitutional. After dinner she got hold of the President and spoke to him privately. I saw her cornering him in the Red Room. I knew that she was driving urgently over the tangle of lines dividing her own terrible problems—and they were all terrible!—from the perplexities and disasters of world politics. It was all one indivisible crisis. I knew that she was saying, "Mr. President, what can be done about this?" Well, we woo one another with everything we've got. I tittered to myself when I saw them together. But JFK could take care of himself, and he liked pretty women. I suspected that he read *The U.S. News and World Report*, too, and that his information might not be much better than her own. She'd have made him an excellent Secretary of State, if some way could be found to wake her before 11 a.m. For she's quite marvelous. And a real beauty. And much more litigious than Humboldt Fleisher. He mainly threatened. But from the time of the divorce I have been entangled in endless ruinous lawsuits. The world has seldom seen a more aggressive subtle resourceful plaintiff than Denise. Of the White House I mainly remembered the impressive hauteur of Charles Lindbergh, the complaint of Edmund Wilson that the government had made a pauper of him, the Catskill resort music played by the Marine Corps orchestra, and Mr. Tate keeping time with his fingers on the knee of a lady.

One of Denise's big grievances was that I wouldn't allow her to lead this kind of life. The great captain Citrine who once had burst the buckles of his armor in heroic scuffles now cooled gypsy Renata's lust and in his dotage had bought a luxury Mercedes-Benz. When I came to call for Lish and Mary, Denise told me to make sure the car was well aired. She didn't want it smelling of Renata. Butts stained with her lipstick had to be emptied from the ashtray. She once marched out of the house and did this herself. She said there must be no Kleenexes smeared with God-knows-what.

Apprehensive, I picked out Denise's number on the telephone. I was in luck, the maid answered, and I told her, "I can't fetch the girls today. I've got car trouble."

Downstairs I found that I could squeeze into the Mercedes and though the windshield was bad, I thought I could manage the driving if the police didn't stop me. I tested this by going to the bank where I drew the new money. It was given to me in a plastic envelope. I didn't fold this packet but laid it next to my wallet. Then from a phone booth I made an appointment at the Mercedes shop. You've got to have an appointment—you don't barge in to the garage as you did in the old mechanic days. Then, still on the pay phone, I tried again to get hold of George Swiebel. Apparently I had said, while sounding off during the card game, that George enjoyed going with his old father to the Baths on Division Street near what used to be Robey Street. Probably Cantabile hoped to catch George there.

As a kid I went to the Russian Bath with my own father. This old establishment has been there forever, hotter than the tropics and rotting sweetly. Down in the cellar men moaned on the steam-softened planks while they were massaged abrasively with oak-leaf besoms lathered in pickle buckets. The wooden posts were slowly consumed by a wonderful decay that made them soft brown. They looked like beaver's fur in the golden vapor. Perhaps Cantabile hoped to trap George here naked. Could there be any other reason why he had named this rendezvous? He might beat him, he might shoot him. Why had I talked so much!

I said to George's secretary, "Sharon? He's not back? Now listen, tell him not to go to the *schwitz* on Division Street today. *Not!* It's serious."

George said of Sharon, "She digs emergencies." This is understandable. Two years ago she had her throat cut by a total stranger. This unknown black man stepped into George's South Chicago office with an open razor. He swept it over Sharon's throat like a virtuoso and disappeared forever. "The blood fell like a curtain," said George. He knotted a towel about Sharon's neck and rushed her to the hospital. George digs emergencies himself. He's always looking for something basic, "honest," "of the earth," primordial. When he saw blood, a vital substance, he knew what to do. But of course George is also theoretical; he is a primitivist. This ruddy, big-muscled, blunt-handed George with his brown, humanly comprehensive eyes is not stupid except when he proclaims his ideas. He does this loudly, fiercely. And then I only grin at him because I know how kindly he is. He takes care of his old parents, of his sisters, of his ex-wife and their grown children. He denounces eggheads, but he really loves culture. He spends whole days trying to read difficult books, knocking himself out. Not with great success. And when I introduce him to intellectuals like my learned friend Durnwald, he shouts and baits them and talks dirty, his face gets red. Well, it's that sort of curious moment in the history of human consciousness when the mind universally awakens and democracy originates, an era of turmoil and ideological confusion, the principal phenomenon of the present age. Humboldt, boyish, loved the life of the mind and I shared his enthusiasm. But the intellectuals one meets are something else again. I didn't behave well with the mental beau monde of Chicago. Denise invited superior persons of all kinds to the house in Kenwood to discuss politics and economics, race, psychology, sex, crime. Though I served the drinks and laughed a great deal I was not exactly cheerful and hospitable. I wasn't even friendly. "You despise these people!" Denise said, angry. "Only Durnwald is an exception, that curmudgeon." This accusation was true. I hoped to lay them all low. In fact it was one of my cherished dreams and dearest hopes. They were against the True, the Good, the Beautiful. They denied the light. "You're a snob," she said. This was not accurate. But I wouldn't have a thing to do with these bastards, the lawyers, Congressmen, psychiatrists, sociology professors, clergy, and art-types (they were mostly gallery-owners) she invited.

"You've got to meet real people," George said to me later. "Denise surrounded you with phonies, and now day in, day out you're alone with tons of books and papers in that apartment and I swear you're going to go nuts."

"Why no," I said, "there's yourself and Alec Szathmar, and my friend Richard Durnwald. And also Renata. And what about the people at the Downtown Club."

"Lots of good this guy Durnwald will do you. He's the professor's professor. And nobody can interest him. He's heard it or read it all. When I try to talk to him I feel that I'm playing the Ping-Pong champion of China. I serve the ball, he smashes it back, and that's the end of that. I have to serve again and pretty soon I'm out of balls."

He always came down heavily on Durnwald. There was a certain rivalry. He knew how attached I was to Dick Durnwald. In crude Chicago Durnwald, whom I admired and even adored, was the only man with whom I exchanged ideas. But for six months Durnwald had been at the University of Edinburgh, lecturing on Comte, Durkheim, Tönnies, Weber, and so on. "This abstract stuff is poison to a guy like you," said George. "I'm going to introduce you to guys from South Chicago." He began to shout. "You're too exclusive, you're going to dry out."

"Okay," I said.

So the fateful poker game was organized around me. But the guests knew that they had been invited as low company. Nowadays the categories are grasped by those who belong to them. It would have been obvious to them that I was some sort of mental fellow even if George hadn't advertised me as such, boasting that my name was in reference books and that I was knighted by the French government. So what? It wasn't as if I had been a Dick Cavett, a true celebrity. I was just another educated nut and George was showing me off to them and exhibiting them to me. It was nice of them to forgive me this great public-relations buildup. I was brought there by George to relish their real American qualities, their peculiarities. But they enriched the evening with their own irony and reversed the situation so that in the end my peculiarities were far more conspicuous. "As the game went on they liked you more and more," said George. "They thought you were pretty human. Besides, there was Rinaldo Cantabile. He and his cousin were flashing cards to each other, and you were getting drunk and didn't know what the hell was happening."

"So I was merely a contrast-gainer," I said.

"I thought contrast-gainer was just your term for married couples. You like a lady because she's got a husband, a real stinker, who makes her look good."

"It's one of those portmanteau expressions."

I am not a great poker-player. Besides, I was interested in the guests. One was a Lithuanian in the tuxedo-rental business, another a young Polish fellow getting computer training. There was a plainclothes detective from the homicide squad. Next to me sat a Sicilian-American undertaker, and last there were Rinaldo Cantabile and his cousin Emil. These two, said George, had crashed the party. Emil was a small-time hoodlum, born to twist arms and throw bricks through show windows. He must have taken part in the attack on my car. Rinaldo was extremely good-looking with a dark furry mustache as fine as mink, and he was elegantly dressed. He bluffed madly, spoke loudly, knocked the table with his knuckles, and pretended to be a cast-iron lowbrow. Still, he kept talking about Robert Ardrey, the territorial imperative, paleontology in the Olduvai Gorge, and the views of Konrad Lorenz. He said loudly and harshly that his educated wife left books around. The Ardrey book he had picked up in the toilet. God knows why we are drawn to others and become attached to them. Proust, an author to whom Humboldt introduced me and in whose work he gave me heavy instruction, said that he often was attracted to people whose faces had something in them of a hawthorn hedge in bloom. Hawthorn was not Rinaldo's flower. White calla lily was more like it. His nose was particularly white and his large nostrils, correspondingly dark, reminded me of an oboe when they dilated. People so distinctly seen have power over me. But I don't know which comes first, the attraction or the close observation. When I feel gross, dull, damaged in sensibility, a refined perception, coming suddenly, has great influence.

We sat at a round pedestal table and as the clean cards flew and flickered George got the players to talk. He was the impresario and they obliged him. The homicide cop talked about killings in the street. "It's all different, now they kill the sonofabitch if he doesn't have a dollar in his pocket and they kill the sonofabitch if he gives them fifty dollars. I tell 'em, 'You bastards kill for money? For money? The cheapest thing in the world. I killed more guys than you but that was in the war.'"

The tuxedo man was in mourning for his lady friend, a telephone ad-taker at the *Sun Times*. He spoke with a baying Lithuanian accent, joking, bragging, but gloomy, too. As he got into his story he blazed with grief, he damn-near cried. On Mondays he collected his rented tuxedoes. After the weekend they were stained, he said, with sauce, with soup, with whisky or semen, "You name it." Tuesdays he drove in his station wagon to a joint near the Loop where the suits were put to soak in vats of cleaning fluid. Then he spent the afternoon with a girlfriend. Ah, they couldn't even make it to the bed, they were so hot for each other. They fell to the floor. "She was a good family type of girl. She was my kind of people. But she'd do anything. I told her how, and she did it, and no questions."

"And you saw her on Tuesdays only, never took her to dinner, never visited her at home?" I said.

"She went home at five o'clock to her old mother and cooked dinner. I swear I didn't even know her last name. For twenty years I never had but her phone number."

"But you loved her. Why didn't you marry her?"

He seemed astonished, looking at the other players as if to say, What's with this guy? Then he answered, "What, marry a hot broad who turns on in hotel rooms?"

While everyone laughed the Sicilian undertaker explained to me in the special tone in which you tell the facts of life to educated dummies, "Look, professor, you don't mix things up. That's not what a wife is about. And if you have a funny foot you have to look for a funny shoe. And if you find the right fit you just let it alone."

"Anyhow, my honey is in her grave."

I am always glad to learn, grateful for instruction, good under correction, if I say so myself. I may avoid opposition, but I know when it's true friendship. We sat with whisky, poker chips, and cigars in this South Chicago kitchen penetrated by the dark breathing of the steel mills and refineries, under webs of power lines. I often note odd natural survivals in this heavy-industry district. Carp and catfish still live in the benzine-smelling ponds. Black women angle for them with dough-bait. Woodchucks and rabbits are seen not far from the dumps. Red-winged blackbirds with their shoulder tabs fly like uniformed ushers over the cattails. Certain flowers persist.

Grateful for this evening of human company I let myself go. I dropped nearly six hundred dollars, counting the check to Cantabile. But I'm so used to having money taken from me that I didn't really mind. I had great pleasure that evening, drinking, laughing a good deal, and talking. I talked and talked. Evidently I discussed my interests and projects in some detail, and later I was told that I alone failed to understand what was going on. The other gamblers dropped out when they saw how the Cantabile cousins were cheating. They were flashing cards, finagling the deck, and pouncing on each pot.

"They don't get away with that on my turf," shouted George in one of his theatrical bursts of irrationality.

"But Rinaldo is dangerous."

"Rinaldo is a punk!" George yelled.

•   •   •

Possibly so, but in the Capone era the Cantabiles had been bad eggs. At that time the entire world identified Chicago with blood—there were the stockyards and there were the gang wars. In the Chicago blood-hierarchy the Cantabiles had stood in about the middle rank. They worked for the Mob, they drove whisky trucks, and they beat and shot people. They were average minor hoodlums and racketeers. But in the Forties a weak-minded Cantabile uncle on the Chicago police force brought disgrace upon the family. He got drunk in a bar and two playful punks took away his guns and had fun with him. They made him crawl on his belly and forced him to gobble filth and sawdust from the floor, they kicked his buttocks. After they had tormented and humiliated him and while he lay crying with rage they ran away, full of glee, throwing down the guns. This was their big mistake. He pursued them and shot them dead in the street. Since then, said George, no one would take the Cantabiles seriously. Old Ralph (Moochy) Cantabile, now a lifer at Joliet, ruined the family with the Mob by murdering two adolescents. This was why Rinaldo could not afford to be brushed off by a person like me, well known in Chicago, who lost to him at poker and then stopped his check. Rinaldo, or Ronald, may have had no standing in the underworld but he had done terrible things to my Mercedes. Whether his rage was a real hoodlum's rage, natural or contrived, who could say? But he was evidently one of those proud sensitive fellows who give so much trouble because they are passionate about internal matters of very slight interest to any sensible person.

I was not so completely unrealistic that I failed to ask myself whether by a sensible person I meant myself. Returning from the bank I shaved, and I noticed how my face, framed to be cheerful, taking a metaphysical premise of universal helpfulness, asserting that the appearance of mankind on this earth was on the whole a good thing—how this face, filled with premises derived from capitalist democracy, was now depressed, retracted in unhappiness, sullen, unpleasant to shave. Was I the aforementioned sensible person?

I performed a few impersonal operations. I did a little ontogeny and phylogeny on myself. Recapitulation: the family was called Tsitrine and came from Kiev. The name was Anglicized at Ellis Island. I was born in Appleton, Wisconsin, the birthplace also of Harry Houdini with whom I think I have some affinities. I grew up in Polish Chicago, I went to the Chopin Grammar School, I spent my eighth year in the public ward of a TB sanatorium. Good people donated piles of colored funny papers to the sanatorium. These were stacked high beside each bed. The children followed the adventures of Slim Jim and Boob McNutt. In addition, day and night, I read the Bible. One visit a week was allowed, my parents taking turns, my mother with her bosom in old green serge, big-eyed, straight-nosed, and white with worry—her deep feelings inhibited her breathing—and my father the immigrant desperate battler coming from the frost, his coat saturated with cigarette smoke. Kids hemorrhaged in the night and choked on blood and were dead. In the morning the white geometry of made-up beds had to be coped with. I became very thoughtful here and I think that my disease of the lungs passed over into an emotional disorder so that I sometimes felt, and still feel, poisoned by eagerness, a congestion of tender impulses together with fever and enthusiastic dizziness. Owing to the TB I connected breathing with joy, and owing to the gloom of the ward I connected joy with light, and owing to my irrationality I related light on the walls to light inside me. I appear to have become a Hallelujah and Glory type. Furthermore (concluding) America is a didactic country whose people always offer their personal experiences as a helpful lesson to the rest, hoping to hearten them and to do them good—an intensive sort of personal public-relations project. There are times when I see this as idealism. There are other times when it looks to me like pure delirium. With everyone sold on the good how does all the evil get done? When Humboldt called me an ingenu, wasn't this what he was getting at? Crystallizing many evils in himself, poor fellow, he died as an example, his legacy a question addressed to the public. The death question itself, which Walt Whitman saw as the question of questions.

At all events I didn't care a bit for the way I looked in the mirror. I saw angelic precipitates condensing into hypocrisy, especially around my mouth. So I finished shaving by touch and only opened my eyes when I started to dress. I chose a quiet suit and necktie. I didn't want to provoke Cantabile by appearing showy.

I didn't have to wait long for the elevator. It was just past dog time in my building. During dog-walking hours it's hopeless, you have to use the stairs. I went out to my dented car which, in maintenance alone, ran me fifteen hundred dollars per annum. In the street the air was bad. It was the pre-Christmas season, dark December, and a brown air, more gas than air, crossed the lake from the great steel-and-oil complex of South Chicago, Hammond, and Gary, Indiana. I got in and started the engine, also turning on the radio. When the music began I wished that there might be more switches to turn on, for it was somehow not enough. The cultural FM stations offered holiday concerts of Corelli, Bach, and Palestrina—Music Antiqua, conducted by the late Greenberg, with Cohen on the viola da gamba and Levi on the harpsichord. They performed pious and beautiful cantatas on ancient instruments while I tried to look through the windshield bashed by Cantabile. I had the fresh fifty-dollar bills in a packet together with my specs, billfold, and handkerchief. I hadn't yet decided in what order to proceed. I never decide such things but wait for them to be revealed and, on the Outer Drive, it occurred to me to stop at the Downtown Club. My mind was in one of its Chicago states. How should I describe this phenomenon? In a Chicago state I infinitely lack something, my heart swells, I feel a tearing eagerness. The sentient part of the soul wants to express itself. There are some of the symptoms of an overdose of caffeine. At the same time I have a sense of being the instrument of external powers. They are using me either as an example of human error or as the mere shadow of desirable things to come. I drove. The huge pale lake washed forward. To the east was a white Siberian sky and McCormick Place, like an aircraft carrier, moored at the shore. Life had withdrawn from the grass. It had its wintry buff color. Motorists swerved up alongside to look at the Mercedes, so incredibly mutilated.

I wanted to speak to Vito Langobardi at the Downtown Club to get his views, if any, on Rinaldo Cantabile. Vito was a big-time hoodlum, a pal of the late Murray the Camel and the Battaglias. We often played racquet ball together, I liked Langobardi. I liked him very much, and I thought him fond of me. He was a most important underworld personality, so high in the organization that he had become rarefied into a gentleman and we discussed only shoes and shirts. Among the members only he and I wore tailored shirts with necktie loops on the underside of the collar. By these loops we were in some sense joined. As in a savage tribe I once read about in which, after childhood, brother and sister do not meet until the threshold of old age because of a terrific incest taboo, when suddenly the prohibition ends . . . no, the simile is no good. But I had known many violent kids at school, terrible kids whose adult life was entirely different from mine, and now we could chat about fishing in Florida and custom-made shirts with loops or the problems of Langobardi's Doberman. After games, in the nude democracy of the locker room, we sociably sipped fruit juice, and chatted about X-rated movies. "I never go to them," he said. "What if the show got raided and they arrested me? How would it look in the papers?" What you need for quality is a few million dollars, and Vito with millions salted away was straight quality. Rough talk he left to the commodity brokers and lawyers. On the court he tottered just a little when he ran, for his calf muscles were not strongly developed, a defect common also in nervous children. But his game was subtle. He outgeneraled me always because he always knew exactly what I was doing behind his back. I was attached to Vito.

Racquet ball or paddle ball to which I was introduced by George Swiebel is an extremely fast and bruising game. You collide with other players or run into the walls. You are hit in the backswing, you often catch yourself in the face with your own racquet. The game has cost me a front tooth. I knocked it out myself and had to have a root-canal and a crown job. First I was a puny child, a TB patient, then I strengthened myself, then I degenerated, then George forced me to recover muscle tone. On some mornings I am lame, hardly able to straighten my back when I get out of bed but by midday I am on the court playing, leaping, flinging myself full length on the floor to scoop dead shots and throwing my legs and spinning entrechats like a Russian dancer. However, I am not a good player. I am too tangled about the heart, overdriven. I fall into a competitive striving frenzy. Then, walloping the ball, I continually say to myself, "Dance, dance, dance, dance!" Convinced that mastery of the game depends upon dancing. But gangsters and business-men, translating their occupational style into these matches, outdance me and win. I tell myself that when I achieve mental and spiritual clarity and translate these into play nobody will be able to touch me. Nobody. I'll beat everyone. Meantime, notwithstanding the clouded spiritual state that prevents me from winning, I play violently because I get desperate without strenuous action. Just desperate. And now and then one of the middle-aged athletes keels over. Rushed to the hospital, some players have never come back. Langobardi and I played Cut-Throat (the three-man game) with a man named Hildenfisch, who succumbed to a heart attack. We had noticed that Hilden-fisch had been panting. Afterward he went to rest in the sauna and someone ran out saying, "Hildenfisch has fainted." When the black attendants laid him on the floor he spurted water. I knew what this loss of sphincter control meant. Mechanical resuscitation equipment was sent for but nobody knew how to operate it.

At times when I pushed too hard at the game, Scottie, the athletic director, told me to quit. "Stop and look at yourself, Charlie. You're purple." In the mirror I was gruesome, gush-ing sweat, dark, black, my heart clubbing away inside. I felt slightly deaf. The eustachian tubes! I made my own diagnosis. Owing to the blood pressure my tubes were crinkling. "Walk it off," said Scottie. I walked back and forth on the patch of carpet forever identified with poor Hildenfisch, surly inferior Hildenfisch. In the sight of death I was no better than Hildenfisch. And once when I had overdone things on the court and lay panting on the red plastic couch, Langobardi came over and gave me a look. When he brooded he squinted. One eye seemed to cross over like a piano-player's hand. "Why do you push it, Charlie?" he said. "At our age one short game is plenty. Do you see me play more? One of these days you could seven out. Remember Hildenfisch."

Yes. Seven out. Right. I could roll bad dice. I must stop this tease-act with death. I was touched by Langobardi's concern. Was it personal solicitude, however? These health-club fatalities were bad, and two coronaries in a row would make this a gloomy place. Still Vito wished to do what he could for me. There was little of substance that we could tell each other. When he was on the telephone I sometimes observed him. In his own way he was an American executive. Handsome Langobardi dressed far better than any board chairman. Even his coat sleeves were ingeniously lined, and the back of his waistcoat was made of beautiful paisley material. Calls came in the name of Finch, the shoeshine man "—Johnny Finch, Johnny Finch, telephone, extension five—" and Langobardi took these Finch calls. He was manly, he had power. In his low voice he gave instructions, made rulings, decisions, set penalties, probably. Now then, could he say anything serious to me? But could I tell him what was on my mind? Could I say that that morning I had been reading Hegel's *Phenomenology,* the pages on freedom and death? Could I say that I had been thinking about the history of human consciousness with special emphasis on the question of boredom? Could I say that for years now I had been preoccupied with this theme and that I had discussed it with the late poet Von Humboldt Fleisher? Never. Even with astrophysicists, with professors of economics or paleontology, it was impossible to discuss such things. There were beautiful and moving things in Chicago, but culture was not one of them. What we had was a cultureless city pervaded nevertheless by Mind. Mind without culture was the name of the game,

wasn't it? How do you like that! It's accurate. I had accepted
this condition long ago.

Langobardi's eyes seemed to have the periscope power of
seeing around corners.

"Get smart, Charlie. Do it the way I do," he said.

I had thanked him sincerely for his kindly interest. "I'm trying," I said.

So I parked today under the chill pillars at the rear of the club.
Then I rose in the elevator and came out at the barbershop.
There, the usual busy sight—the three barbers: the big Swede
with dyed hair, the Sicilian, always himself (not even shaved),
and the Japanese. Each had the same bouffant coiffure, each
wore a yellow vest with golden buttons over a short-sleeved
shirt. All three were using hot-air guns with blue muzzles and
shaping the hair of three customers. I entered the club through
the washroom where bulbs were bleaking over the sinks and
Finch, the real Johnny Finch, was filling the urinals with heaps
of ice cubes. Langobardi was there, an early bird. Lately he had
taken to wearing his hair in a little fringe, like an English country churchwarden. He sat nude, glancing at *The Wall Street
Journal,* and gave me a short smile. Now what? Could I throw
myself into a new relationship with Langobardi, hitch a chair
forward and sit with my elbows on my knees, looking into his
face and opening my own features to the warmth of impulse?
Eyes dilated with doubt, with confidentiality, might I say, "Vito,
I need a little help"? Or, "Vito, how bad is this fellow Rinaldo
Cantabile?" My heart knocked violently—as it had knocked
decades earlier when I was about to proposition a woman.
Langobardi had now and then done me small favors, booking
tables in restaurants where reservations were hard to get. But
to ask him about Cantabile would be a professional consultation. You didn't do that at the club. Vito had once bawled out
Alphonse, one of the masseurs, for asking me a bookish question. "Don't bug the man, Al. Charlie doesn't come here to talk
about his trade. We all come to forget business." When I told
this to Renata she said, "So you two have a relationship." Now
I saw that Langobardi and I had a relationship in the same way
that the Empire State Building had an attic.

"You want to play a short game?" he said.

"No, Vito, I came to get something from my locker."

The usual casting about, I was thinking as I went back to the beat-up Mercedes. How typical of me. The usual craving. I looked for help. I longed for someone to do the stations of the cross with me. Just like Pa. And where was Pa? Pa was in the cemetery.

• • •

At the Mercedes shop the distinguished official and technician in the white smock was naturally curious but I refused to answer questions. "I don't know how this happened, Fritz. I found it this way. Fix it. I don't want to see the bill, either. Just send it to the Continental Illinois. They'll pay it." Fritz charged like a brain surgeon.

I flagged a taxi in the street. The driver was wild-looking with an immense Afro like a shrub from the gardens at Versailles. The back of his cab was dusty with cigarette ashes and had a tavern odor. There was a bulletproof screen between us. He made a fast turn and charged due west on Division Street. I could see little, because of the blurred Plexiglas and the Afro, but I didn't really need to look, I knew it all by heart. Large parts of Chicago decay and fall down. Some are rebuilt, others just lie there. It's like a film montage of rise fall and rise. Division Street where the old Bath stands used to be Polish and now is almost entirely Puerto Rican. In the Polish days, the small brick bungalows were painted fresh red, maroon, and candy green. The grass plots were fenced with iron pipe. I always thought that there must be Baltic towns that looked like this, Gdynia for instance, the difference being that the Illinois prairie erupted in vacant lots and tumbleweed rolled down the streets. Tumbleweed is so melancholy.

In the old days of ice wagons and coal wagons householders used to cut busted boilers in half, set them out on the grass plots, and fill them with flowers. Big Polish women in ribboned caps went out in the spring with cans of Sapolio and painted these boiler-planters so that they shone silver against the blar-

ing red of the brick. The double rows of rivets stood out like
the raised-skin patterns of African tribes. Here the women grew
geraniums, sweet William, and other low-grade dusty flowers.
I showed all of this to Humboldt Fleisher years ago. He came
to Chicago to give a reading for *Poetry* magazine and asked me
for a tour of the city. We were dear friends then. I had come
back to see my father and to put the last touches on my book,
New Deal Personalities, at the Newberry Library. I took Humboldt on the El to the stockyards. He saw the Loop. We went to
the lakeshore and listened to the foghorns. They bawled melancholy over the limp silk fresh lilac drowning water. But Humboldt responded mostly to the old neighborhood. The silvered
boiler rivets and the blazing Polish geraniums got him. He listened pale and moved to the buzzing of roller-skate wheels on
the brittle cement. I too am sentimental about urban ugliness.
In the modern spirit of ransoming the commonplace, all this
junk and wretchedness, through art and poetry, by the superior
power of the soul.

Mary, my eight-year-old daughter, has discovered this about
me. She knows my weakness for ontogeny and phylogeny. She
always asks to hear what life was like way-back-when.

"We had coal stoves," I tell her. "The kitchen range was
black, with a nickel trim—huge. The parlor stove had a dome
like a little church, and you could watch the fire through the
isinglass. I had to carry up the scuttle and take down the
ashes."

"What did you wear?"

"A leatherette war-ace cap with rabbit-fur flaps, high-top
boots with a sheath for a rusty jackknife, long black stockings,
and plus fours. Underneath, woolly combinations which left
lint in my navel and elsewhere."

"What else was it like?" my younger daughter wanted to
know. Lish, who is ten years old, is her mother's child and such
information would not interest her. But Mary is less pretty,
though to my mind she is more attractive (more like her father).
She is secretive and greedy. She lies and steals more than most
small girls, and this is also endearing. She hides chewing gum
and chocolates with stirring ingenuity. I find her candy buried

under the upholstery or in my filing cabinet. She has learned that I don't often look at my research materials. She flatters and squeezes me precociously. And she wants to hear about old times. She has her own purposes in evoking and manipulating my emotions. But Papa is quite willing to manifest the old-time feelings. In fact I must transmit these feelings. For I have plans for Mary. Oh, nothing so definite as plans, perhaps. I have an idea that I may be able to pervade the child's mind with my spirit so that she will later take up the work I am getting too old or too weak or too silly to continue. She alone, or perhaps she and her husband. With any luck. I worry about the girl. In a locked drawer of my desk I keep notes and memos for her, many of them written under the influence of liquor. I promise myself to censor these one day, before death catches me off base on the racquet-ball court or on the Posturepedic mattress of some Renata or other. Mary is sure to be an intelligent woman. She interprets "Für Elise" much better than Lish. She feels the music. My heart is often troubled for Mary, however. She will be a straight-nosed thin broad who feels the music. And personally I prefer plump women with fine breasts. So I felt sorry for her already. As for the project or purpose I want her to carry on, it is a very personal overview of the Intellectual Comedy of the modern mind. No one person could do this comprehensively. By the end of the nineteenth century what had been the ample novels of Balzac's Comedy had already been reduced to stories by Chekhov in his Russian *Comédie Humaine*. Now it's even less possible to be comprehensive. I never had a work of fiction in mind but a different kind of imaginative projection. Different also from Whitehead's *Adventures of Ideas*. . . . This is not the moment to explain it. Whatever it was, I conceived of it while still a youngish man. It was actually Humboldt who lent me the book of Valéry that suggested it. Valéry wrote of Leonardo, *"Cet Apollon me ravissait au plus haut degré de moi-même."* I too was ravished with permanent effect—perhaps carried beyond my mental means. But Valéry had added a note in the margin: *"Trouve avant de chercher."* This finding before seeking was my special gift. If I had any gift.

However, my small daughter would say to me with deadly accuracy of instinct, "Tell me what your mother used to do. Was she pretty?"

"I think she was very pretty. I don't look like her. And she did cooking, baking, laundry and ironing, canning and pickling. She could tell fortunes with cards and sing trembly Russian songs. She and my father took turns visiting me at the sanatorium, every other week. In February the vanilla ice cream they brought was so hard you couldn't cut it with a knife. And what else—ah yes, at home when I lost a tooth she would throw it behind the stove and ask the little mouse to bring a better one. You see what kind of teeth those bloody mice palmed off on me."

"You loved your mother?"

Eager swelling feeling suddenly swept in. I forgot that I was talking to a child and I said, "Oh, I loved them all terribly, abnormally. I was all torn up with love. Deep in the heart. I used to cry in the sanatorium because I might never make it home and see them. I'm sure they never knew how I loved them, Mary. I had a TB fever and also a love fever. A passionate morbid little boy. At school I was always in love. At home if I was first to get up in the morning I suffered because they were still asleep. I wanted them to wake up so that the whole marvelous thing could continue. I also loved Menasha the boarder and Julius, my brother, your Uncle Julius."

I shall have to lay aside these emotional data.

At the moment money, checks, hoodlums, automobiles preoccupied me.

Another check was on my mind. It had been sent by my friend Thaxter, the one whom Huggins accused of being a CIA agent. You see Thaxter and I were preparing to bring out a journal, *The Ark*. We were all ready. Wonderful things were to be printed in it—pages from my imaginative reflections on a world transformed by Mind, for example. But meantime Thaxter had defaulted on a certain loan.

It's a long story and one that I'd rather not go into at this point. For two reasons. One is that I love Thaxter, whatever he does. The other is that I actually do think too much about money. It's no good trying to conceal it. It's there and it's base. Earlier when I described how George saved Sharon's life when her throat was cut, I spoke of blood as a vital substance. Well, money is a vital substance, too. Thaxter was supposed to repay part of the defaulted loan. Broke but grandiose he had ordered a check from his Italian bank for me, the Banco Ambrosiano of Milan. Why the Banco? Why Milan? But all of Thaxter's arrangements were out of the ordinary. He had had a transatlantic upbringing and was equally at home in France and in California. You couldn't mention a region so remote that Thaxter didn't have an uncle there, or an interest in a mine, or an old château or villa. Thaxter with his exotic ways was another of my headaches. But I couldn't resist him. However, that too must wait. Only one last word: Thaxter wanted people to believe that he was once a CIA agent. It was a wonderful rumor and he did everything to encourage it. It greatly added to his mysteriousness, and mystery was one of his little rackets. This was harmless and in fact endearing. It was even philanthropic, as charm always is—up to a point. Charm always is a bit of a racket.

The cab pulled up at the Bath twenty minutes early and I wasn't going to loiter there so I said through the perforations of the bulletproof screen, "Go on, drive west. Take it easy, I just want to look around." The cabbie heard me and nodded his Afro. It was like an enormous black dandelion in seed, blown, all its soft spindles standing out.

In the last six months more old neighborhood landmarks had been torn down. This shouldn't have mattered much. I can't say why it made such a difference. But I was in a state. It almost seemed to me that I could hear myself rustling and fluttering in the back seat like a bird touring the mangroves of its youth, now car dumps. I stared with pulsatory agitation through the soiled windows. A whole block had gone down. Lovi's Hungarian Restaurant had been swept away, plus Ben's Pool Hall and the old brick carbarn and Gratch's Funeral Parlor, out of which both my parents had been buried. Eternity got no picturesque interval here. The ruins of time had been bulldozed, scraped, loaded in trucks, and dumped as fill. New

steel beams were going up. Polish kielbasa no longer hung in
butchers' windows. The sausages in the *carnicería* were Caribbean, purple and wrinkled. The old shop signs were gone. The
new ones said HOY. MUDANZAS. IGLESIA.

"Keep going west," I said to the driver. "Past the park. Turn
right on Kedzie."

The old boulevard now was a sagging ruin, waiting for the
wreckers. Through great holes I could look into apartments
where I had slept, eaten, done my lessons, kissed girls. You'd
have to loathe yourself vividly to be indifferent to such destruction or, worse, rejoice at the crushing of the locus of these
middle-class sentiments, glad that history had made rubble of
them. In fact I know such tough guys. This very neighborhood
produced them. Informers to the metaphysical-historical police
against fellows like me whose hearts ache at the destruction of
the past. But I had *come* here to be melancholy, to be sad about
the wrecked walls and windows, the missing doors, the fixtures
torn out, and the telephone cables ripped away and sold as
junk. More particularly, I had come to see whether the house
in which Naomi Lutz had lived was still standing. It was not.
That made me feel very low.

In my highly emotional adolescence I had loved Naomi Lutz.
I believe she was the most beautiful and perfect young girl I
have ever seen, I adored her, and love brought out my deepest
peculiarities. Her father was a respectable chiropodist. He gave
himself high medical airs, every inch the Doctor. Her mother
was a dear woman, slipshod, harum-scarum, rather chinless,
but with large glowing romantic eyes. Night after night I had
to play rummy with Dr. Lutz, and on Sundays I helped him to
wash and simonize his Auburn. But that was all right. When
I loved Naomi Lutz I was safely *within life*. Its phenomena
added up, they made sense. Death was an after all acceptable
part of the proposition. I had my own little Lake Country,
the park, where I wandered with my Modern Library Plato,
Wordsworth, Swinburne, and *Un Cœur Simple*. Even in winter
Naomi petted behind the rose garden with me. Among the frozen twigs I made myself warm inside her raccoon coat. There
was a delicious mixture of coon skin and maiden fragrance. We

breathed frost and kissed. Until I met Demmie Vonghel many years later, I loved no one so much as Naomi Lutz. But Naomi, while I was away in Madison, Wisconsin, reading poetry and studying rotation pool at the Rathskeller, married a pawnbroker. He dealt also in rebuilt office machinery and had plenty of money. I was too young to give her the charge accounts she had to have at Field's and Saks, and I believe the mental burdens and responsibilities of an intellectual's wife had frightened her besides. I had talked all the time about my Modern Library books, of poetry and history, and she was afraid that she would disappoint me. She told me so. I said to her, if a tear was an intellectual thing how much more intellectual pure love was. It needed no cognitive additives. But she only looked puzzled. It was this sort of talk by which I had lost her. She did not look me up even when her husband lost all his money and deserted her. He was a sporting man, a gambler. He had to go into hiding at last, because the juice men were after him. I believe they had even broken his ankles. Anyway, he changed his name and went or limped to the Southwest. Naomi sold her classy Winnetka house and moved to Marquette Park, where the family owned a bungalow. She took a job in the linen department at Field's.

As the cab went back to Division Street I was making a wry parallel between Naomi's husband's Mafia troubles and my own. He had muffed it, too. I couldn't help thinking what a blessed life I might have led with Naomi Lutz. Fifteen thousand nights embracing Naomi and I would have smiled at the solitude and boredom of the grave. I would have needed no bibliography, no stock portfolios, no medal from the Legion of Honor.

So we drove again through what had become a tropical West Indies slum, resembling the parts of San Juan that stand beside lagoons which bubble and smell like stewing tripe. There was the same crushed plaster, smashed glass, garbage in the streets, the same rude amateur blue chalk lettering on the shops.

But the Russian Bath where I was supposed to meet Rinaldo Cantabile stood more or less unchanged. It was also a proletarian hotel or lodging house. On the second floor there had always lived aged workingstiffs, lone Ukrainian grandfathers, retired car-line employees, a pastry cook famous for his icings who had to quit because his hands became arthritic. I knew the place from boyhood. My father, like old Mr. Swiebel, had believed it was healthful, good for the blood to be scrubbed with oak leaves lathered in old pickle buckets. Such retrograde people still exist, resisting modernity, dragging their feet. As Menasha the boarder, an amateur physicist (but mostly he wanted to be a dramatic tenor and took voice lessons: he had worked at Brunswick Phonograph Co. as a punch-press operator), once explained to me, human beings could affect the rotation of the earth. How? Well, if the whole race at an agreed moment were to scuff its feet the revolution of the planet would actually slow down. This might also have an effect on the moon and on the tides. Of course Menasha's real topic was not physics but concord, or unity. I think that some through stupidity and others through perversity would scuff the wrong way. However, the old guys at the Bath do seem to be unconsciously engaged in a collective attempt to buck history.

These Division Street steam-bathers don't look like the trim proud people downtown. Even old Feldstein pumping his Exercycle in the Downtown Club at the age of eighty would be out of place on Division Street. Forty years ago Feldstein was a swinger, a high roller, a good-time Charlie on Rush Street. In spite of his age he is a man of today, whereas the patrons of the Russian Bath are cast in an antique form. They have swelling buttocks and fatty breasts as yellow as buttermilk. They stand on thick pillar legs affected with a sort of creeping verdigris or blue-cheese mottling of the ankles. After steaming, these old fellows eat enormous snacks of bread and salt herring or large ovals of salami and dripping skirt-steak and they drink schnapps. They could knock down walls with their hard stout old-fashioned bellies. Things are very elementary here. You feel that these people are almost conscious of obsolescence, of a line of evolution abandoned by nature and culture. So down in the super-heated subcellars all these Slavonic cavemen and wood demons with hanging laps of fat and legs of stone and lichen boil themselves and splash ice water on their heads by the bucket. Upstairs, on the television screen in the locker room, little dudes and grinning broads make smart talk or leap up and down. They are unheeded. Mickey who keeps the food concession fries slabs of meat and potato pancakes, and, with enormous knives, he hacks up cabbages for coleslaw and he quarters grapefruits (to be eaten by hand). The stout old men mounting in their bed sheets from the blasting heat have a strong appetite. Below, Franush the attendant makes steam by sloshing water on the white-hot boulders. These lie in a pile like Roman ballistic ammunition. To keep his brains from baking Franush wears a wet felt hat with the brim torn off. Otherwise he is naked. He crawls up like a red salamander with a stick to tip the latch of the furnace, which is too hot to touch, and then on all fours, with testicles swinging on a long sinew and the clean anus staring out, he backs away groping for the bucket. He pitches in the water and the boulders flash and sizzle. There may be no village in the Carpathians where such practices still prevail.

Loyal to this place, Father Myron Swiebel came every day of his life. He brought his own herring, buttered pumpernickel, raw onions, and bourbon whisky. He drove a Plymouth, though he had no driver's license. He could see well enough straight ahead, but because there were cataracts on both eyes he side-swiped many cars and did great damage in the parking lot.

I went in to reconnoiter. I was quite anxious about George. His advice had put me in this fix. But then I knew that it was bad advice. Why did I take it? Because he had raised his voice with such authority? Because he had cast himself as an expert on the underworld and I had let him do his stuff? Well, I hadn't used my best mind. But my best mind was now alert and I believed I could handle Cantabile. I reckoned that Cantabile had already worked off his rage against the car and I thought the debt was largely paid.

I asked the concessionaire, Mickey, who stood in the smoke behind the counter searing fatty steaks and frying onions, "Has George come in? Does his old man expect him?"

I thought that if George were here it was not likely that Cantabile would rush fully dressed into the steam to punch or beat or kick him. Of course Cantabile was an unknown quantity. You couldn't guess what Cantabile might do. Either in rage or from calculation.

"George isn't here. The old man is steaming."

"Good. Is he expecting his son?"

"No. George was here Sunday, so he won't come again. He's only once a week with his father."

"Good. Excellent!"

Built like a bouncer with huge bar arms and an apron tied very high under his oxters, Mickey has a twisted lip. During the Depression he had to sleep in the parks and the cold ground gave him a partial paralysis of the cheek. This makes him seem to scoff or jeer. A misleading impression. He is a gentle earnest and peaceful person. A music-lover, he takes a season ticket at the Lyric Opera.

"I haven't seen you in a long time, Charlie. Go steam with the old man, he'll be glad for the company."

But I hurried out again past the cashier's cage with its little steel boxes where patrons left their valuables. I passed the squirming barber pole, and when I got to the sidewalk, which was as dense as the galaxy with stars of broken glass, a white Thunderbird pulled up in front of the Puerto Rican sausage shop across the street and Ronald Cantabile got out. He sprang out, I should say. I saw that he was in a terrific state. Dressed in a brown raglan coat with a matching hat and wearing tan kid boots, he was tall and good-looking. I had noted his dark dense mustache at the poker game. It resembled fine fur. But through the crackling elegance of dress there was a current, a desperate sweep, so that the man came out, so to speak, raging from the neck up. Though he was on the other side of the street I could see how furiously pale he was. He had worked himself up to intimidate me, I thought. But also he was making unusual steps. His feet behaved strangely. Cars and trucks came between us just then so that he could not cross over. Beneath the cars I could see him trying to dodge through. The boots were exquisite. At the first short break in the traffic Cantabile held open his raglan to me. He was wearing a magnificent broad belt. But surely it wasn't a belt that he wanted to display. Just beside the buckle something was sticking out. He clapped his hand to it. He wanted me to know that he was carrying a gun. More traffic came, and Cantabile was jumping up and down, glaring at me over the tops of automobiles. Under the utmost strain he called out to me when the last truck had passed, "You alone?"

"Alone. I'm alone."

He drew himself up toward the shoulders with peculiar twisting intensity. "You got anybody hiding?"

"No. Just me. Nobody."

He threw open the door and brought up two baseball bats from the floor of the Thunderbird. A bat in each hand, he started toward me. A van came between us. Now I could see nothing but his feet moving rapidly in the fancy boots. I thought, He sees I've come to pay. Why should he clobber me? He's got to know I wouldn't pull anything. He's proved his point on the car. And I've seen the gun. Should I run? Since I had discovered on Thanksgiving Day how fast I could still run, I seemed oddly eager to use this ability. Speed was one of my resources. Some people are too fast for their own good, like Asahel in the Book of Samuel. Still it occurred to me that I might dash up the stairs of the Bath and take shelter in the cashier's office where the little steel boxes were. I could crouch on the floor and ask the cashier to pass the four hundred and fifty dollars through the grille to Cantabile. I knew the cashier quite well. But he'd never let me in. He couldn't. I wasn't bonded. He had once referred to this special circumstance when we were having a chat. But I couldn't believe that Cantabile would batter me down. Not in the street. Not as I waited and bowed my head. And just at that moment I remembered Konrad Lorenz's discussion of wolves. The defeated wolf offered his throat, and the victor snapped but wouldn't bite. So I was bowing my head. Yes, but damn my memory! What did Lorenz say next? Humankind was different, but in what respect? How! I couldn't remember. My brain was disintegrating. The day before, in the bathroom, I hadn't been able to find the word for the isolation of the contagious, and I was in agony. I thought, whom should I telephone about this? My mind is going! And then I stood and clutched the sink until the word "quarantine" mercifully came back to me. Yes, quarantine, but I was losing my grip. I take such things hard. In old age my father's memory also failed. So I was shaken. The difference between man and other species such as the wolves never did come back to me. Perhaps the lapse was excusable at a time like this. But it served to show how carelessly I was reading, these days. This inattentiveness and memory-failure boded no good.

As the last of a string of cars passed, Cantabile took a long stride with both bats as if to rush upon me without a pause. But I yelled, "For Christ's sake, Cantabile!"

He paused. I held up open hands. Then he flung one of the bats into the Thunderbird and started for me with the other.

I called out to him, "I brought the money. You don't have to beat my brains out."

"You got a gun?"

"I've got nothing."

"You come over here," he said.

I started willingly to cross the street. He made me stop in the middle.

"Stay right there," he said. I was in the center of heavy traffic, cars honking and the provoked drivers rolling down their windows, already fighting mad. He tossed the second bat back into the T-bird. Then he strode up and took hold of me roughly. He treated me as if I deserved the extreme penalty. I held out the money, I offered it to him on the spot. But he refused to look at it. Furious he pushed me onto the sidewalk and toward the stairs of the Bath and past the squirming barbershop cylinders of red white and blue. We hurried in, past the cashier's cage and along the dirty corridor.

"Go on, go on," said Cantabile.

"Where do you want to go?"

"To the can. Where is it?"

"Don't you want the dough?"

"I said the can! The can!"

I then understood, his bowels were acting up, he had been caught short, he had to go to the toilet, and I was to go with him. He wouldn't allow me to wait in the street. "Okay," I said, "just take it easy and I'll lead you." He followed me through the locker room. The john entrance was doorless. Only the individual stalls have doors. I motioned him forward and was about to sit down on one of the locker-room benches nearby but he gave me a hard push on the shoulder and drove me forward. These toilets are the Bath at its worst. The radiators put up a stunning dry heat. The tiles are never washed, never disinfected. A hot dry urine smell rushes to your eyes like onion fumes. "Jesus!" said Cantabile. He kicked open a stall, still keeping me in front of him. He said, "You go in first."

"The both of us?" I said.

"Hurry up."

"There's space only for one."

He tugged out his gun and shook the butt at me. "You want this in your teeth?" The black fur of his mustache spread as the lip of his distorted face stretched. His brows were joined above the nose like the hilt of a large dagger. "In the corner, you!" He slammed the door and panting, took off his things. He thrust the raglan and the matching hat into my arms, although there was a hook. There was even a piece of hardware I had never before noticed. Attached to the door was a brass fitting, a groove labeled *Cigar,* a touch of class from the old days. He was seated now with the gun held in both palms, his hands between his knees, his eyes first closing then dilating greatly.

In a situation like this I can always switch out and think about the human condition over-all. Of course he wanted to humiliate me. Because I was a *chevalier* of the *Légion d'honneur?* Not that he actually knew of this. But he was aware that I was as they would say in Chicago a *Brain,* a man of culture or intellectual attainments. Was this why I had to listen to him rumbling and slopping and smell his stink? Perhaps fantasies of savagery and monstrosity, of beating my brains out, had loosened his bowels. Humankind is full of nervous invention of this type, and I started to think (to distract myself) of all the volumes of ape behavior I had read in my time, of Kohler and Yerkes and Zuckerman, of Marais on baboons and Schaller on gorillas, and of the rich repertory of visceral-emotional sensitivities in the anthropoid branch. It was even possible that I was a more limited person than a fellow like Cantabile in spite of my concentration on intellectual achievement. For it would never have occurred to me to inflict anger on anyone by such means. This might have been a sign that his vital endowment or natural imagination was more prodigal and fertile than mine. In this way, thinking improving thoughts, I waited with good poise while he crouched there with his hardened dagger brows. He was a handsome slender man whose hair had a natural curl. It was cropped so close that you could see the roots of his curls and I observed the strong contraction of his scalp in this moment of stress. He wanted to inflict a punishment on me but the result was only to make us more intimate.

As he stood and then wiped, and then pulled his shirttails straight, belting his pants with the large oval buckle and sticking back the gun (I hoped the safety catch was on), as I say, when he pulled his shirttails straight and buckled his stylish belt on the hip-huggers, thrusting the gun in, flushing the toilet with his pointed soft boot, too fastidious to touch the lever with his hand—he said, "Christ, if I catch the crabs here . . . !" As if that would be my fault. He was evidently a violent reckless blamer. He said, "You don't know how I hated to sit here. These old guys must piss on the seats." This too he entered on the debit side against me. Then he said, "Who owns this joint?"

Now this was a fascinating question. It had never occurred to me, you know. The Bath was so ancient, it was like the Pyramids of Egypt, the Gardens of Ashurbanipal. It was like water seeking its level, or like gravitational force. But who in fact was its proprietor? "I've never heard of an owner," I said. "For all I know it's some old party out in British Columbia."

"Don't get smart. You're too fucking smart. I only asked for information. I'll find out."

To turn the faucet he used a piece of toilet paper. He washed his hands without soap, none was provided by the management. At this moment I offered him the nine fifty-dollar bills again. He refused to look at them. He said, "My hands are wet." He wouldn't use the roller towel. It was, I must admit, repulsively caked, filthy, with a certain originality in the way of filth. I held out my pocket handkerchief, but he ignored it. He didn't want his anger to diminish. Spreading his fingers wide he shook them dry. Full of the nastiness of the place he said, "Is this what they call a Bath?"

"Well," I said, "the bathing is all downstairs."

They had two long rows of showers, below, which led to the heavy wooden doors of the steam room. There also was a small cistern, the cold plunge. The water was unchanged from year to year, and it was a crocodile's habitat if I ever saw one.

Cantabile now hurried out to the lunch counter, and I followed him. There he dried his hands with paper napkins which he pulled from the metal dispenser angrily. He crumpled these embossed flimsy papers and threw them on the floor. He said to Mickey, "Why don't you have soap and towels in the can? Why don't you wash the goddamn place out? There's no disinfectant in there."

Mickey was very mild, and he said, "No? Joe is supposed to take care of it. I buy him Top Job, Lysol." He spoke to Joe. "Don't you put in mothballs any more?" Joe was black and old, and he answered nothing. He was leaning on the shoe-shine chair with its brass pedestals, the upside-down legs and rigid feet (reminiscent of my own feet and legs during the Yoga headstand). He was there to remind us all of some remote, grand considerations and he would not answer any temporal questions.

"You guys are gonna buy supplies from me," said Cantabile. "Disinfectant, liquid soap, paper towels, everything. The name is Cantabile. I've got a supply business on Clybourne Avenue." He took out a long pitted ostrich-skin wallet and threw several business cards on the counter.

"I'm not the boss," said Mickey. "All I have is the restaurant concession." But he picked up a card with deference. His big fingers were covered with black knife-marks.

"I better hear from you."

"I'll pass it along to the Management. They're downtown."

"Mickey, who owns the Bath?" I said.

"All I know is the Management, downtown."

It would be curious, I thought, if the Bath should turn out to belong to the Syndicate.

"Is George Swiebel here?" said Cantabile.

"No."

"Well, I want to leave him a message."

"I'll give you something to write on," said Mickey.

"There's nothing to write. Tell him he's a dumb shit. Tell him I said so."

Mickey had put on his specs to look for a piece of paper, and now he turned his spectacled face toward us as if to say that his only business was the coleslaw and skirt-steaks and whitefish. Cantabile did not ask for old Father Myron, who was steaming himself below.

We went out into the street. The weather had suddenly cleared. I couldn't decide whether gloomy weather suited the environment better than bright. The air was cold, the light was neat, and the shadows thrown by blackened buildings divided the sidewalks.

I said, "Well, now let me give you this money. I brought new bills. This ought to wrap the whole thing up, Mr. Cantabile."

"What—just like that? You think it's so easy?" said Rinaldo.

"Well, I'm sorry. It shouldn't have happened. I really regret it."

"You regret it! You regret your hacked-up car. You stopped a check on me, Citrine. Everybody blabbed. Everybody knows. You think I can allow it?"

"Mr. Cantabile, who knows—who is everybody? Was it really so serious? I was wrong—"

"Wrong, you fucking ape . . . !"

"Okay, I was stupid."

"Your pal George tells you to stop a check, so you stop it. Do you take that asshole's word for everything? Why didn't he catch Emil and me in the act? He has you pull this sneaky stunt and then you and he and the undertaker and the tuxedo guy and the other dummies spread around the gossip that Ronald Cantabile is a punk. Man! You could never get away with that. Don't you realize!"

"Yes, now I realize."

"No, I don't know what you realize. I was watching at the

game, and I don't dig you. When are you going to do something *and know what you're doing*?" Those last words he
spaced, he accented vehemently and uttered into my face. Then
he snatched away his coat, which I was still holding for him,
the rich brown raglan with its large buttons. Circe might have
had buttons like those in her sewing box. They were very beautiful, really, rather Oriental-treasure buttons.

The last garment I had seen resembling this one was worn
by the late Colonel McCormick. I was then about twelve years
old. His limousine had stopped in front of the Tribune Tower,
and two short men came out. Each man held two pistols, and
they circled on the pavement, crouching low. Then, in this four-
gun setting, the Colonel stepped out from his car in just such
a tobacco-colored coat as Cantabile's and a pinch hat with
gleaming harsh fuzz. The wind was stiff, the air pellucid, the
hat glistened like a bed of nettles.

"You don't think I know what I'm doing, Mr. Cantabile?"

"No you don't. You couldn't find your ass with both
hands."

Well, he may have been right. But at least I wasn't crucifying anyone. Apparently life had not happened to me as it
had happened to other people. For some indiscernible reason
it happened differently to them, and so I was not a fit judge of
their concerns and desires. Aware of this I acceded to more of
these desires than was practical. I gave in to George's low-life
expertise. Now I bent before Cantabile. My only resource was
to try to remember useful things from my ethological reading
about rats, geese, sticklebacks, and dancing flies. What good is
all this reading if you can't use it in the crunch? All I asked was
a small mental profit.

"Anyway, what about these fifty-dollar bills?" I said.

"I'll let you know when I'm ready to take them," he said.
"You didn't like what happened to your car, did you?"

I said, "It's a beautiful machine. It was really heartless to do
that."

Apparently the bats he had threatened me with were what
he had used on the Mercedes and there were probably more
assault weapons in the back seat of the Thunderbird. He made

me get into this showy auto. It had leather bucket seats red as spilt blood and an immense instrument panel. He took off at top speed from a standstill, like an adolescent drag-racer, the tires wildly squealing.

In the car I got a slightly different impression of him. Seen in profile, his nose ended in a sort of white bulb. It was intensely, abnormally white. It reminded me of gypsum and it was darkly lined. His eyes were bigger than they ought to have been, artificially dilated perhaps. His mouth was wide, with an emotional underlip in which there was the hint of an early struggle to be thought full grown. His large feet and dark eyes also hinted that he aspired to some ideal, and that his partial attainment or nonattainment of the ideal was a violent grief to him. I suspected that the ideal itself might be fitful.

"Was it you or your cousin Emil that fought in Vietnam?"

We were speeding eastward on Division Street. He held the wheel in both hands as though it were a pneumatic drill to chop up the macadam. "What! Emil in the Army? Not that kid. He was 4-F, practically psycho. No, the most action Emil ever saw was during the 1968 riots in front of the Hilton. He was twigged out and didn't even know which side he was on. No, I was in Vietnam. The folks sent me to that smelly Catholic college near St. Louis that I mentioned at the game, but I dropped out and enlisted. That was some time back."

"Did you fight?"

"I'll tell you what you want to hear. I stole a tank of gasoline—the truck, trailer, and all. I sold it to some black-market guys. I got caught but my folks made a deal. Senator Dirksen helped. I was only eight months in jail."

He had a record of his own. He wished me to know that he was a true Cantabile, a throwback to the Twenties and no mere Uncle Moochy. A military prison—he had a criminal pedigree and he could produce fear on his own credentials. Also the Cantabiles were evidently in small rackets of the lesser hoodlum sort, as witness the toilet-disinfectant business on Clybourne Avenue. Perhaps also a currency exchange or two—currency exchanges were often owned by former small-time racketeers. Or in the extermination business, another common favorite.

But he was obviously in the minor leagues. Perhaps he was in no league at all. As a Chicagoan I had some sense of this. A real big shot used hired muscle. No Vito Langobardi would carry baseball bats in the back seat of his car. A Langobardi went to Switzerland for winter sports. Even his dog traveled in class. Not in decades had a Langobardi personally taken part in violence. No, this restless striving smoky-souled Cantabile was on the outside trying to get in. He was the sort of unacceptable entrepreneur that the sanitation department still fished out of the sewers after three months of decomposition. Certain persons of this type were occasionally found in the trunks of automobiles parked at O'Hare. The weight of the corpse at the back was balanced by a cinderblock laid on the motor.

Deliberately, at the next corner, Rinaldo ran a red light. He rode the bumper of the car ahead and he made other motorists chicken out. He was elegant, flashy. The seats of the T-bird were specially upholstered in soft leather—so soft, so crimson! He wore the sort of gloves sold to horsemen at Abercrombie & Fitch. At the expressway he swept right and gunned up the slope, running into merging traffic. Cars braked behind us. His radio played rock music. And I recognized Cantabile's scent. It was Canoe. I had once gotten a bottle of it for Christmas from a blind woman named Muriel.

In the squalid closet at the Bath when his pants were down and I was thinking about Zuckerman's apes at the London Zoo it had been clear that what was involved here were the plastic and histrionic talents of the human creature. In other words I was involved in a dramatization. It wouldn't have done much for the image of the Cantabiles, however, if he had actually shot off the gun that he held between his knees. It would make him too much like the crazy uncle who disgraced the family. That, I thought, was the whole point.

• •

Was I afraid of Cantabile? Not really. I don't know what he thought, but what I thought was perfectly clear to me. Absorbed in determining what a human being is, I went along with him. Cantabile may have believed that he was abusing a passive man. Not at all. I was a man active elsewhere. At the poker game, I received a visionary glimpse of this Cantabile. Of course, I was very high that night, if not downright drunk, but I saw the edge of his spirit rising from him, behind him. So when Cantabile yelled and threatened I didn't make a stand on grounds of proper pride—"Nobody treats Charlie Citrine like this, I'm going to the police," and so forth. No, the police had no such things to show me. Cantabile had made a very peculiar and strong impression on me.

What a human being is—I always had my own odd sense of this. For I did not have to live in the land of the horses, like Dr. Gulliver, my sense of mankind was strange enough without travel. In fact I traveled not to seek foreign oddities but to get away from them. I was drawn also to philosophical idealists because I was perfectly sure that *this* could not be *it*. Plato in the Myth of Er confirmed my sense that this was not my first time around. We had all been here before and would presently be here again. There was another place. Maybe a man like me was imperfectly reborn. The soul is supposed to be sealed by oblivion before its return to earthly life. Was it possible that my oblivion might be slightly defective? I never was a thorough Platonist. I never could believe that you could be reincarnated a bird or a fish. No soul once human was locked into a spider. In my case (which I suspect is not so rare as all that) there may have been an incomplete forgetting of the pure soul-life, so that the mineral condition of re-embodiment seemed abnormal, so that from an early age I was taken aback to see eyes move in faces, noses breathe, skins sweat, hairs grow, and the like, finding it comical. This was sometimes offensive to people born with full oblivion of their immortality.

This leads me to recall and reveal a day of marvelous spring and a noontime full of the most heavy silent white clouds, clouds like bulls, behemoths, and dragons. The place is Appleton, Wisconsin, and I am a grown man standing on a crate trying to see into the bedroom where I was born in the year 1918. I was probably conceived there, too, and directed by divine wisdom to appear in life as so-and-so, such-and-such

(C. Citrine, Pulitzer Prize, Legion of Honor, father of Lish and Mary, husband of A, lover of B, a serious person, and a card). And why should this person be perched on a box, partly hidden by the straight twigs and glossy leaves of a flowering lilac? And without asking permission of the lady of the house? I had knocked and rung but she did not answer. And now her husband was standing at my back. He owned a gas station. I told him who I was. At first he was very hard-nosed. But I explained that this was my birthplace and I asked for old neighbors by name. Did he remember the Saunderses? Well, they were his cousins. This saved me a punch in the nose as a Peeping Tom. I could not say, "I am standing on this crate among these lilacs trying to solve the riddle of man, and not to see your stout wife in her panties." Which was indeed what I saw. Birth is sorrow (a sorrow that may be canceled by intercession) but in the room where my birth took place I beheld with sorrow of my own a fat old woman in underpants. With great presence of mind she pretended not to see my face at the screen but slowly left the room and phoned her husband. He ran from the gas pumps and nabbed me, laying oily hands on my exquisite gray suit—I was at the peak of my elegant period. But I was able to explain that I was in Appleton to prepare that article on Harry Houdini, also a native—as I have obsessively mentioned—and I experienced a sudden desire to look into the room where I was born.

"So what you got was an eyeful of my Missus."

He didn't take this hard. I think he understood. These matters of the spirit are widely and instantly grasped. Except of course by people who are in heavily fortified positions, mental opponents trained to resist what everyone is born knowing.

As soon as I saw Rinaldo Cantabile at George Swiebel's kitchen table I was aware that a natural connection existed between us.

• • •

I was now taken to the Playboy Club. Rinaldo was a member. He walked away from his supercar, the Bechstein of automobiles, leaving it to the car jockey. The checkroom Bunny knew him. From his behavior here I began to understand that my task was to make amends publicly. The Cantabiles had been defied. Maybe Rinaldo had been ordered at a family council to go out and repair the damage to their good bad name. And this matter of his reputation would consume a day—an entire day. And there were so many pressing needs, I had so many headaches already that I might justifiably have begged fate to give me a pass. I had a pretty good case.

"Are the people here?"

He threw over his coat. I also dropped mine. We stepped into the opulence, the semidarkness, the thick carpets of the bar where bottles shone, and sensual female forms went back and forth in an amber light. He took me by the arm into an elevator and we rose immediately to the top. Cantabile said, "We're going to see some people. When I give you the high sign, then you pay me the money and apologize."

We were standing before a table.

"Bill, I'd like to introduce Charlie Citrine," said Ronald to Bill.

"Hey, Mike, this is Ronald Cantabile," Bill said, on cue.

The rest was, Hey how are you, sit down, what'll you drink.

Bill was unknown to me, but Mike was Mike Schneiderman the gossip columnist. He was large heavy strong tanned sullen fatigued, his hair was razor styled, his cuff links were as big as his eyes, his necktie was a clumsy flap of silk brocade. He looked haughty, creased and sleepy, like certain oil-rich American Indians from Oklahoma. He drank an old-fashioned and held a cigar. His business was to sit with people in bars and restaurants. I was much too volatile for sedentary work like this, and I couldn't understand how it was done. But then I couldn't understand office jobs, either, or clerking or any of the confining occupations or routines. Many Americans described themselves as artists or intellectuals who should only have said that they were incapable of doing such work. I had many times discussed this with Von Humboldt Fleisher, and now and then with Gumbein the art critic. The work of sitting with people to discover *what was interesting* didn't seem to agree with Schneiderman either. At certain moments he looked blank and almost ill. He knew me, of course, I had once appeared on his television program, and he said, "Hello, Charlie." Then he said to Bill, "Don't you know Charlie? He's a famous person who lives in Chicago incognito."

I began to appreciate what Rinaldo had done. He had gone to great trouble to set up this encounter, pulling many strings. This Bill, a connection of his, perhaps owed the Cantabiles a favor and had agreed to produce Mike Schneiderman the columnist. Obligations were being called in all over the place. The accountancy must be very intricate, and I could see that Bill was not pleased. Bill had a Cosa Nostra look. There was something corrupt about his nose. Curving deeply at the nostrils it was powerful yet vulnerable. He had a foul nose. In a different context I would have guessed him to be a violinist who had become disgusted with music and gone into the liquor business. He had just returned from Acapulco and his skin was dark, but he was not exactly shining with health and well-being. He didn't care for Rinaldo; he appeared contemptuous of him. My sympathy at this moment was with Cantabile. He had attempted to organize what should have been a beautiful spirited encounter, worthy of the Renaissance, and only I appreciated it. Cantabile was trying to crash Mike's column. Mike of course was used to this. The would-be happy few were always after him and I suspected that there was a good deal of trading behind the scenes, *quid pro quo.* You gave Mike an item of gossip and he printed your name in bold type. The Bunny took our drink order. Up to the chin she was ravishing. Above, all was commercial anxiety. My attention was divided between the soft crease of her breasts and the look of business difficulty on her face.

We were on one of the most glamorous corners of Chicago. I dwelt on the setting. The lakeshore view was stupendous. I couldn't see it but I knew it well and felt its effect—the shining road beside the shining gold vacancy of Lake Michigan. Man had overcome the emptiness of this land. But the emptiness had given him a few good licks in return. And here we sat amid the flatteries of wealth and power with pretty maidens and booze and tailored suits, and the men wearing jewels and using scent. Schneiderman was waiting, most skeptically, for an item he could use in his column. In the right context, I was good copy. People in Chicago are impressed with the fact that I am taken seriously elsewhere. I have now and then been asked to cocktail parties by culturally ambitious climbing people and have experienced the fate of a symbol. Certain women have said to me, "You *can't* be Charles Citrine!" Many hosts are pleased by the contrast I offer. Why, I look like a man intensely but incompletely thinking. My face is no match for their shrewd urban faces. And it's especially the ladies who can't mask their disappointment when they see what the well-known Mr. Citrine actually looks like.

Whisky was set before us. I drank down my double Scotch eagerly and, being a quick expander, started to laugh. No one joined me. Ugly Bill said, "What's funny?"

I said, "Well, I just remembered that I learned to swim just down the way at Oak Street before all these skyscrapers went up, the architectural pride of P.R. Chicago. It was the Gold Coast then, and we used to come from the slums on the streetcar. The Division car only went as far as Wells. I'd come with a greasy bag of sandwiches. My mother bought me a girl's bathing suit at a sale. It had a little skirt with a rainbow border. I was mortified and tried to dye it with India ink. The cops used to jab us in the ribs to hurry us across the Drive. Now I'm up here, drinking whisky. . . ."

Cantabile gave me a shove under the table with his whole foot, leaving a dusty print on my trousers. His frown spread upward into his scalp, rippling under the close-cut curls, while his nose became as white as candle wax.

I said, "By the way, Ronald . . ." and I took out the bills. "I owe you money."

"What money?"

"The money I lost to you at that poker game—it was some time back. I guess you forgot about it. Four hundred and fifty bucks."

"I don't know what you're talking about," said Rinaldo Cantabile. "What game?"

"You can't remember? We were playing at George Swiebel's apartment."

"Since when do you book guys play poker?" said Mike Schneiderman.

"Why? We have our human side. Poker has always been played at the White House. Perfectly respectable. President Harding played. Also during the New Deal. Morgenthau, Roosevelt, and so on."

"You sound like a West Side Chicago boy," said Bill.

"Chopin School, Rice and Western," I said.

"Well, put away your dough, Charlie," said Cantabile. "This is drink time. No business. Pay me later."

"Why not now, while I think of it and have the bills out? You know the whole thing slipped my mind, and last night I woke up with a start thinking, 'I forgot to pay Rinaldo his dough.' Christ, I could have blown my brains out."

Cantabile said violently, "Okay, okay, Charlie!" He snatched the money from me and crammed it without counting into his breast pocket. He gave me a look of high irritation, a flaming look. What for? I could not imagine why. What I did know was that Mike Schneiderman had power to put you in the paper and if you were in the paper you hadn't lived in vain. You were not just a two-legged creature, seen for a brief hour on Clark Street, sullying eternity with nasty doings and thoughts. You were—

"What'cha doing these days, Charlie," said Mike Schneiderman. "Another play maybe? A movie? You know," he said to Bill, "Charlie's a real famous guy. They made a terrific flick out of his Broadway hit. He's written a whole lot of stuff."

"I had my moment of glory on Broadway," I said. "I could never repeat it, so why try?"

"Now I remember. Somebody said you were going to publish some kind of highbrow magazine. When is it coming out? I'll give you a plug."

But Cantabile glared and said, "We've got to go."

"I'll be glad to phone when I have an item for you. It would be helpful," I said with a meaning glance toward Cantabile.

But he had already gone. I followed him and in the elevator he said, "What the fuck is the matter with you?"

"I can't think what I did wrong."

"You said you wanted to blow your brains out, and you know damn well, you creep, that Mike Schneiderman's brother-in-law blew *his* brains out two months ago."

"No!"

"You must have read it in the paper—that whole noise about the phony bonds, the counterfeit bonds he gave for collateral."

"Oh, *that* one, you mean Goldhammer, the fellow who printed up his own certificates, the forger!"

"You knew it, don't pretend," said Cantabile. "You did it on purpose, to louse me up, to wreck my plan."

"I didn't, I swear I didn't. Blowing my brains out? That's a commonplace expression."

"Not in a case like this. You knew," he said violently, "you knew. You knew his brother-in-law killed himself."

"I didn't make the connection. It must have been a Freudian slip. Absolutely unintentional."

"You always pretend you never know what you're doing. I suppose you didn't know who that big-nosed fellow was."

"Bill?"

"Yes! Bill! Bill is Bill Lakin, the banker who was indicted with Goldhammer. He took the forged bonds as security."

"Why should he be indicted for that? Goldhammer put them over on him."

"Because, you bird-brain, don't you understand what you read in the news? He bought Lekatride from Goldhammer for a buck a share when it was worth six dollars. Haven't you heard of Kerner either? All these grand juries, all these trials? But you don't care about the things that other people knock themselves out over. You have contempt. You're arrogant, Citrine. You despise us."

"Who's us?"

"Us! People of the world . . ." said Cantabile. He spoke wildly. It was no time for argument. I was to respect and to fear him. It would be provoking if he didn't think I feared him. I didn't think that he would shoot me but a beating was surely possible, perhaps even a broken leg. As we left the Playboy Club he thrust the money again into my hand.

"Do we have to do this over?" I said. He explained nothing. He stood with his head angrily hooked forward until the Thunderbird came around. Once more I had to get in.

Our next stop was in the Hancock Building, somewhere on the sixtieth or seventieth story. It looked like a private apartment, and yet it seemed also to be a place of business. It was furnished in decorator style with plastic, trick art objects hanging on the walls, geometrical forms of the *trompe l'œil* type that intrigue business people. They are peculiarly vulnerable to art racketeers. The gentleman who lived here was elderly, in a brown hopsack sports jacket with gold threads and a striped shirt on his undisciplined belly. White hair was slicked back upon his narrow head. The liver stains on his hands were large. Under the eyes and about the nose he did not look altogether well. As he sat on the low sofa which, judging by the way it gave under him, was stuffed with down, his alligator loafers extended far into the ivory shag carpet. The pressure of his belly brought out the shape of his phallus on his thigh. Long nose, gaping lip, and wattles went with all this velvet, the gold-threaded hopsack, brocade, satin, the alligator skin, and the *trompe l'œil* objects. From the conversation I gathered that his line was jewelry and that he dealt with the underworld. Perhaps he was also a fence—how would I know? Rinaldo Cantabile and his wife had an anniversary coming and he was shopping for a bracelet. A Japanese houseboy served drinks. I am not a great drinker but today I understandably wanted whisky and I took another double shot of Black Label. From the skyscraper I could contemplate the air of Chicago on this short December afternoon. A ragged western sun spread orange light over the dark shapes of the town, over the branches of the river and the black trusses of bridges. The lake, gilt silver and amethyst, was ready for its winter cover of ice. I happened to be thinking that if Socrates was right, that you could learn nothing from trees, that only the men you met in the street could teach you something about yourself, I must be in a bad way, running off into the scenery instead of listening to my human companions. Evidently I did not have a good stomach for human companions. To get relief from uneasiness or heaviness of heart I was musing about the water. Socrates would have given me a low mark. I seemed rather to be on the Wordsworth end of things—trees, flowers, water. But architecture, engineering, electricity, technology had brought me to this sixty-fourth story. Scandinavia had put this glass in my hand, Scotland had filled it with whisky, and I sat there recalling certain marvelous facts about the sun, namely, that the light of other stars, when it entered the sun's gravitational field, had to bend. The sun wore a shawl made of this universal light. So Einstein, sitting thinking of things, had foretold. And observations made by Arthur Eddington during an eclipse proved it. Finding before seeking.

Meantime the phone rang continually and not a single call seemed local. It was all Las Vegas, L.A., Miami, and New York. "Send your boy over to Tiffany and find out what they get for an item like that," our host was saying. I then heard him speak of estate-jewels, and of an Indian prince who was trying to sell a whole lot of stuff in the USA and inviting bids.

At one interval, while Cantabile was fussing over a tray of diamonds (nasty, that white stuff seemed to me), the old gentleman spoke to me. He said, "I know you from somewhere, don't I?"

"Yes," I said. "From the whirlpool at the Downtown Health Club, I think."

"Oh yeah sure, I met you with that lawyer fellow. He's a big talker."

"Szathmar?"

"Alec Szathmar."

Cantabile said, fingering diamonds and not lifting his face from the dazzle of the velvet tray, "I know that son of a bitch Szathmar. He claims to be an old buddy of yours, Charlie."

"True," I said, "we were all boys at school. Including George Swiebel."

"In the old stone age that must have been," said Cantabile.

Yes, I had met this old gentleman in the hot chemical bath at the club, the circular bubbling whirlpool where people sat sweating, gossiping about sports, taxes, television programs, best sellers, or chatting about Acapulco and numbered bank accounts in the Cayman Islands. I didn't know but what this

old fence had one of those infamous *cabañas* near the swimming pool to which young chicks were invited for the siesta.
There had been some scandal and protest over this. What was
done behind drawn drapes in the *cabañas* was no one's business, of course, but some of the old guys, demonstrative and
exhibitionistic, had been seen fondling their little dolls on the
sun-terrace. One had removed his false teeth in public to give
a girl soul kisses. I had read an interesting letter in the *Tribune* about this. A retired history teacher living high up in the
club building had written a letter saying that Tiberius—the old
girl was showing off—Tiberius in the grottoes of Capri had
had nothing on these grotesque lechers. But what did these old
characters, in the rackets or in First Ward politics, care about
indignant school-mams and classical allusions. If they had gone
to see Fellini's *Satyricon* at the Woods Theater it was only to
get more sex ideas not because they were studying Imperial
Rome. I myself had seen some of these spider-bellied old cod-
gers on the sundeck taking the breasts of teen-age hookers into
their hands. It occurred to me that the Japanese houseboy was
also a judo or karate expert as in *007* movies, there were so
many valuables in the apartment. When Rinaldo said he'd like
to see more Accutron watches, the fellow brought out a few
dozen, flat as wafers. These may or may not have been stolen.
My heated imagination couldn't be relied upon for guidance
here. I was excited, I admit, by these currents of criminality.
I could feel the need to laugh rising, mounting, always a sign
that my weakness for the sensational, my American, Chicagoan (as well as personal) craving for high stimuli, for incon-
gruities and extremes, was aroused. I knew that fancy thieving
was a big thing in Chicago. It was said that if you knew one of
these high-rise superrich Fagin-types you could obtain luxury
goods at half the retail price. The actual shoplifting was done
by addicts. They were compensated in heroin. As for the police,
they were said to be paid off. They kept the merchants from
making too much noise. Anyway there was insurance. There
was also the well-known "shrinkage" or annual loss reported
to the Internal Revenue Service. Such information about cor-
ruption, if you had grown up in Chicago, was easy to accept. It

even satisfied a certain need. It harmonized with one's Chicago view of society. Naïveté was something you couldn't afford.

Item by item, I tried to assess what Cantabile wore as I sat there in soft upholstery with my scotch on the rocks, his hat coat suit boots (the boots may have been unborn calf) his equestrian gloves, and I made an effort to imagine how he had obtained these articles through criminal channels, from Field's, from Saks Fifth Avenue, from Abercrombie & Fitch. He was not, so far as I could judge, taken absolutely seriously by the old fence.

Rinaldo was intrigued with one of the watches and slipped it on. His old watch he tossed to the Japanese who caught it. I thought the moment had come to recite my piece and I said, "Oh, by the way, Ronald, I owe you some dough from the other night."

"Where from?" said Cantabile.

"From the poker game at George Swiebel's. I guess it slipped your mind."

"Oh I know that guy Swiebel with all the muscles," said the old gentleman. "He's terrific company. And you know he cooks a great bouillabaisse, I'll give him that."

"I inveigled Ronald and his cousin Emil into this game," I said. "It really was my fault. Anyhow, Ronald cleaned up on us. Ronald is one of the poker greats. I ended up about six hundred dollars in the hole and he had to take my IOU—I've got the dough on me, Ronald, and I better give it to you while we both remember."

"Okay." Again Cantabile, without looking, crumpled the notes into his jacket pocket. His performance was better than mine, though I was doing my very best. But then he had the honor side of the deal, the affront. To be angry was his right and that was no small advantage.

When we were out of the building again I said, "Wasn't that okay?"

"Okay—yes! Okay!" he said loud and bitter. Clearly he wasn't ready to let me off. Not yet.

"I figure that old pelican will pass the word around that I paid you. Wasn't that the object?"

I added, almost to myself, "I wonder who makes pants like the pants the old boy was wearing. The fly alone must have been three feet long."

But Cantabile was still stoking his anger. "Christ!" he said. I didn't like the way he was staring at me under those straight bodkin brows.

"Well, then, that does it," I said. "I can get a cab."

Cantabile caught me by the sleeve. "You wait," he said. I didn't really know what to do. After all, he carried a gun. I had for a long time thought about having a gun too, Chicago being what it is. But they'd never give me a license. Cantabile, without a license, packed a pistol. There was one index of the difference between us. Only God knew what consequences such differences might bring. "Aren't you enjoying our afternoon?" said Cantabile, and grinned.

Attempting to laugh this off I failed. The globus hystericus interfered. My throat felt sticky.

"Get in, Charlie."

Again I sat in the crimson bucket seat (the supple fragrant leather kept reminding me of blood, pulmonary blood) and fumbled for the seat belt—you never can find those cursed buckles.

"Don't fuck with the belt, we're not going that far."

Out of this information I drew what relief I could. We were on Michigan Boulevard, heading south. We drew up beside a skyscraper under construction, a headless trunk swooping up, swarming with lights. Below the early darkness now closing with December speed over the glistening west, the sun like a bristling fox jumped beneath the horizon. Nothing but a scarlet afterglow remained. I saw it between the El pillars. As the tremendous trusses of the unfinished skyscraper turned black, the hollow interior filled with thousands of electric points resembling champagne bubbles. The completed building would never be so beautiful as this. We got out, slamming the car doors, and I followed Cantabile over some plank-bedding laid down for the trucks. He seemed to know his way around. Maybe he had clients among the hard-hats. If he was in the juice racket. Then again if he was a usurer he wouldn't come here after dark and risk getting pushed from a beam by one of these tough guys. They must be reckless. They drink and spend recklessly enough. I like the way these steeplejacks paint the names of their girlfriends on inaccessible girders. From below you often see DONNA or SUE. I suppose they bring the ladies on Sunday to point to their love-offerings eight hundred feet up. They fall to death now and then. Anyway Cantabile had brought his own hard hats. We put them on. Everything was prearranged. He said he was related by blood to some of the supervisory personnel. He also mentioned that he did lots of business hereabouts. He said he had connections with the contractor and the architect. He told me things much faster than I could discount them. However, we rose in one of the big open elevators, up, up.

How should I describe my feelings? Fear, thrill, appreciation, glee—yes I appreciated his ingenuity. It seemed to me, however, that we were rising too high, too far. Where were we? Which button had he pressed? By daylight I had often admired the mantis-like groups of cranes, tipped with orange paint. The tiny bulbs, which seemed so dense from below, were sparsely strung through. I don't know how far we actually went, but it was far enough. We had as much light about us as the time of day had left to give, steely and freezing, keen, with the wind ringing in the empty squares of wound-colored rust and beating against the hanging canvases. On the east, violently rigid was the water, icy, scratched, like a plateau of solid stone, and the other way was a tremendous effusion of low-lying color, the last glow, the contribution of industrial poisons to the beauty of the Chicago evening. We got out. About ten hard-hats who had been waiting pushed into the elevator at once. I wanted to call to them "Wait!" They went down in a group, leaving us nowhere. Cantabile seemed to know where he was going, but I had no faith in him. He was capable of faking anything. "Come on," he said. I followed, but I was going slowly. He waited for me. There were a few windbreaks up here on the fiftieth or sixtieth floor, and those, the wind was storming. My eyes ran. I held on to a pillar and he said, "Come on Granny, come on check-stopper."

I said, "I have leather heels. They skid."

"You better not chicken out."

"No, this is it," I said. I put my arms around the pillar. I wouldn't move.

Actually we had come far enough to suit him. "Now," he said, "I want to show you just how much your dough means to me. You see this?" He held up a fifty-dollar bill. He rested his back on a steel upright and stripping off his fancy equestrian gloves began to fold the money. It was incomprehensible at first. Then I understood. He was making a child's paper glider of it. Hitching back his raglan sleeve, he sent the glider off with two fingers. I watched it speeding through the strung lights with the wind behind it out into the steely atmosphere, darker and darker below. On Michigan Boulevard they had already put up the Christmas ornaments, winding tiny bubbles of glass from tree to tree. They streamed down there like cells under a microscope.

My chief worry now was how to get down. Though the papers underplay it people are always falling off. But however scared and harassed, my sensation-loving soul also was gratified. I knew that it took too much to gratify me. The gratification-threshold of my soul had risen too high. I must bring it down again. It was excessive. I must, I knew, change everything.

He sailed off more of the fifties. Tiny paper planes. Origami (my knowledgeable mind, keeping up its indefatigable pedantry—my lexical busybody mind!), the Japanese paper-folder's art. An international congress of paper-aircraft freaks had been held, I think, last year. It seemed last year. The hobbyists were mathematicians and engineers.

Cantabile's green bills went off like finches, like swallows and butterflies, all bearing the image of Ulysses S. Grant. They brought crepuscular fortune to people down in the streets.

"The last two I'm going to keep," said Cantabile. "To blow them on drinks and dinner for us."

"If I ever get down alive."

"You did fine. Go on, lead the way, start back."

"These leather heels are awfully tricky. I hit an ordinary piece of wax paper in the street the other day and went down. Maybe I should take my shoes off."

"Don't be crazy. Go on your toes."

If you didn't think of falling, the walkways were more than adequate. I crept along, fighting paralysis of the calves and the thighs. My face was sweating faster than the wind could dry it as I took hold of the final pillar. I thought that Cantabile had been treading much too close behind. More hard-hats waiting for the elevator probably took us for union guys or architect's men. It was night now and the hemisphere was frozen all the way to the Gulf. Gladly I fell into the seat of the Thunderbird when we got down. He removed his hard hat and mine. He cocked the wheel and started the motor. He should really let me go now. I had given him enough satisfaction.

But he was off again, driving fast. He sped away toward the next light. My head hung back over the top of the seat in the position you take to stop a nosebleed. I didn't know exactly where we were. "Look, Rinaldo," I said. "You've made your point. You bashed my car, you've run me all day long, and you've just given me the scare of my life. Okay, I see it wasn't the money that upset you. Let's stuff the rest of it down a sewer so I can go home."

"You've had it with me?"

"It's been a whole day of atonement."

"You've seen enough of the whatchamacallems?—I learned some new words at the poker game from you."

"Which words?"

"Proles," he said, "Lumps. Lumpenproletariat. You gave us a little talk about Karl Marx."

"My lord, I did carry on, didn't I. Completely unbuttoned. What got into me!"

"You wanted to mix with riffraff and the criminal element. You went slumming, Charlie, and you had a great time playing cards with us dumbheads and social rejects."

"I see. I was insulting."

"Kind of. But you were interesting, here and there, about the social order and how obsessed the middle class was with the Lumpenproletariat. The other fellows didn't know what in hell you were talking about." For the first time, Cantabile spoke more mildly to me. I sat up and saw the river flashing night-lights on the right, and the Merchandise Mart decorated for Christmas. We were going to Gene and Georgetti's old steak house, just off the spur of the Elevated train. Parking among other sinister luxury cars we went into the drab old building where—hurrah for opulent intimacy!—a crash of jukebox music fell on us like Pacific surf. The high-executive bar was crowded with executive drinkers and lovely companions. The gorgeous mirror was peopled with bottles and resembled a group photograph of celestial graduates.

"Giulio," Rinaldo told the waiter. "A quiet table, and we don't want to sit by the rest rooms."

"Upstairs, Mr. Cantabile?"

"Why not?" I said. I was shaky and didn't want to wait at the bar for seating. It would lengthen the evening, besides.

Cantabile stared as if to say, Who asked you! But he then consented. "Okay, upstairs. And two bottles of Piper Heidsieck."

"Right away, Mr. Cantabile."

In the Capone days hoodlums fought mock battles with champagne at banquets. They jigged the bottles up and down and shot each other with corks and foaming wine, all in black tie, and like a fun-massacre.

"Now I want to tell you something," said Rinaldo Cantabile, "and it's a different subject altogether. I'm married, you know."

"Yes, I remember."

"To a marvelous beautiful intelligent woman."

"You mentioned your wife in South Chicago. That night . . . Do you have children? What does she do?"

"She's no housewife, buddy, and you'd better know it. You think I'd marry some fat-ass broad who sits around the house in curlers and watches TV? This is a real woman, with a mind, with knowledge. She teaches at Mundelein College and she's working on a doctoral thesis. You know where?"

"No."

"At Radcliffe, Harvard."

"That's very good," I said. I emptied the champagne glass and refilled it.

"Don't brush it off. Ask me what her subject is. Of the thesis."

"All right, what is it?"

"She's writing a study of that poet who was your friend."

"You're kidding. Von Humboldt Fleisher? How do you know he was my friend? . . . I see. I was talking about him at George's. Someone should have locked me in a closet that night."

"You didn't have to be cheated, Charlie. You didn't know what you were doing. You were talking away like a nine-year-old kid about lawsuits, lawyers, accountants, bad investments, and the magazine you were going to publish—a real loser, it sounded like. You said you were going to spend your own money on your own ideas."

"I never discuss these things with strangers. Chicago must be giving me arctic madness."

"Now, listen, I'm very proud of my wife. Her people are rich, upper class. . . ." Boasting gives people a wonderful color, I've noticed, and Cantabile's cheeks glowed. He said, "You're asking yourself what is she doing with a husband like me."

I muttered, "No, no," though that certainly was a natural question. However, it was not exactly news that highly educated women were excited by scoundrels criminals and lunatics, and that these scoundrels etcetera were drawn to culture, to thought. Diderot and Dostoevski had made us familiar with this.

"I want her to get her PhD," said Cantabile. "You understand? I want it bad. And you were a pal of this Fleisher guy. You're going to give Lucy the information."

"Now wait a minute—"

"Look this over." He handed me an envelope and I put on my glasses and glanced over the document enclosed. It was signed Lucy Wilkins Cantabile and it was the letter of a model graduate student, polite, detailed, highly organized, with the usual academic circumlocutions—three single-spaced pages, dense with questions, painful questions. Her husband kept me under close observation as I read. "Well, what do you think of her?"

"Terrific," I said. The thing filled me with despair. "What do you two want of me?"

"Answers. Information. We want you to write out the answers. What's your opinion of her project?"

"I think the dead owe us a living."

"Don't horse around with me, Charlie. I didn't like that crack."

"I couldn't care less," I said. "This poor Humboldt, my friend, was a big spirit who was destroyed . . . never mind that. The PhD racket is a very fine racket but I want no part of it. Besides, I never answer questionnaires. Idiots impose on you with their documents. I can't bear that kind of thing."

"Are you calling my wife an idiot?"

"I haven't had the pleasure of meeting her."

"I'll make allowances for you. You got hit in the guts by the Mercedes and then I ran you ragged. But don't be unpleasant about my wife."

"There are things I don't do. This is one of them. I'm not going to write answers. It would take weeks."

"Listen!"

"I draw the line."

"Just a minute!"

"Bump me off. Go to hell."

"All right, easy does it. Some things are sacred. I understand. But we can work everything out. I listened at the poker game and I know that you're in plenty of trouble. You need somebody tough and practical to handle things for you. I've given this a lot of thought, and I have all kinds of ideas for you. We'll trade off."

"No, I don't want to trade anything. I've had it. My heart is breaking and I want to go home."

"Let's have a steak and finish the wine. You need red meat. You're just tired. You'll do it."

"I won't."

"Take the order, Giulio," he said.

• • •

I wish I knew why I feel such loyalty to the deceased. Hearing of their deaths I often said to myself that I must carry on for them and do their job, finish their work. And that of course I couldn't do. Instead I found that certain of their characteristics were beginning to stick to me. As time went on, for instance, I found myself becoming absurd in the manner of Von Humboldt Fleisher. By and by it became apparent that he had acted as my agent. I myself, a nicely composed person, had had Humboldt expressing himself wildly on my behalf, satisfying some of my longings. This explained my liking for certain individuals—Humboldt, or George Swiebel, or even someone like Cantabile. This type of psychological delegation may have its origins in representative government. However, when an expressive friend died the delegated tasks returned to me. And as I was also the expressive delegate of other people, this eventually became pure hell.

Carry on for Humboldt? Humboldt wanted to drape the world in radiance, but he didn't have enough material. His attempt ended at the belly. Below hung the shaggy nudity we know so well. He was a lovely man, and generous, with a heart of gold. Still his goodness was the sort of goodness people now consider out of date. The radiance he dealt in was the old radiance and it was in short supply. What we needed was a new radiance altogether.

And now Cantabile and his PhD wife were after me to recall the dear dead days of the Village, and its intellectuals, poets, crack-ups, its suicides and love affairs. I didn't care much for that. I had no clear view of Mrs. Cantabile as yet, but I saw Rinaldo as one of the new mental rabble of the wised-up world and anyway I didn't feel just now like having my arm twisted. It wasn't that I minded giving information to honest scholars, or even to young people on the make, but I was busy just then, fiercely, painfully busy—personally and impersonally busy: personally, with Renata and Denise, and Murra the accountant, and the lawyers and the judge, and a multitude of emotional vexations; impersonally, participating in the life of my country and of Western Civilization and global society (a mixture of reality and figment). As editor of an important magazine, *The Ark,* which would probably never come out, I was always thinking of statements that must be made and truths of which the world must be reminded. The world, identified by a series of dates (1789–1914–1917–1939) and by key words (Revolution, Technology, Science, and so forth), was another cause of busyness. You owed your duty to these dates and words. The whole thing was so momentous, overmastering, tragic, that in the end what I really wanted was to lie down and go to sleep. I have always had an exceptional gift for passing out. I look at snapshots taken in some of the most evil hours of mankind and I see that I have lots of hair and am appealingly youthful. I am wearing an ill-fitting double-breasted suit of the Thirties or Forties, smoking a pipe, standing under a tree, holding hands with a plump and pretty bimbo—and I am asleep on my feet, out cold. I have snoozed through many a crisis (while millions died).

This is all terrifically relevant. For one thing, I may as well admit that I came back to settle in Chicago with the secret motive of writing a significant work. This lethargy of mine is related to that project—I got the idea of doing something with the chronic war between sleep and consciousness that goes on in human nature. My subject, in the final Eisenhower years, was boredom. Chicago was the ideal place in which to write my master essay—"Boredom." In raw Chicago you could examine the human spirit under industrialism. If someone were to arise with a new vision of Faith, Love, and Hope, he would want to understand to whom he was offering it—he would have to understand the kind of deep suffering we call boredom. I was going to try to do with boredom what Malthus and Adam Smith and John Stuart Mill or Durkheim had done with population, wealth, or the division of labor. History and temperament had put me in a peculiar position, and I was going to turn it to advantage. I hadn't read those great modern boredom experts, Stendhal, Kierkegaard, and Baudelaire, for nothing. Over the years I had worked a lot on this essay. The difficulty was that I kept being overcome by the material, like a miner by gas fumes. I wouldn't stop, though. I'd say to myself that even Rip van Winkle had slept for only twenty years, I had gone him at least two decades better and I was determined to make the lost time yield illumination. So I kept doing advanced mental work in Chicago, and also joined a gymnasium, playing ball with commodity brokers and gentleman-hoodlums in an effort to strengthen the powers of consciousness. Then my respected friend Durnwald mentioned, kiddingly, that the famous but misunderstood Dr. Rudolf Steiner had much to say on the deeper aspects of sleep. Steiner's books, which I began to read lying down, made me want to get up. He argued that between the conception of an act and its execution by the will there fell a gap of sleep. It might be brief but it was deep. For one of man's souls was a sleep-soul. In this, human beings resembled the plants, whose whole existence is sleep. This made a very deep impression on me. The truth about sleep could only be seen from the perspective of an immortal spirit. I had never doubted that I had such a thing. But I had set this fact aside quite early. I kept it under my hat. These beliefs under your hat also press on your brain and sink you down into the vegetable realm. Even now, to a man of culture like Durnwald, I hesitated to mention the spirit. He took no stock in Steiner, of course. Durnwald was reddish, elderly but powerful, thickset and bald, a bachelor of cranky habits but a kind man. He had a peremptory blunt butting even bullying manner, but if he scolded it was because he loved me—he wouldn't have bothered otherwise. A great scholar, one of the most learned people on earth, he was a rationalist. Not narrowly rationalistic, by any means. Nevertheless, I couldn't talk to him about the powers of a spirit separated from a body. He wouldn't hear of it. He had simply been joking about Steiner. I was not joking, but I didn't want to be thought a crank.

I had begun to think a lot about the immortal spirit. Still, night after night, I kept dreaming that I had become the best player in the club, a racquet demon, that my backhand shot skimmed the left wall of the court and fell dead in the corner, it had so much English on it. I dreamed that I was beating all the best players—all those skinny, hairy, speedy fellows who in reality avoided playing with me because I was a dud. I was badly disappointed by the shallow interests such dreams betrayed. Even my dreams were asleep. And what about money? Money is necessary for the protection of the sleeping. Spending drives you into wakefulness. As you purge the inner film from the eye and rise into higher consciousness, less money should be required.

Under the circumstances (and it should now be clearer what I mean by circumstances: Renata, Denise, children, courts, lawyers, Wall Street, sleep, death, metaphysics, karma, the presence of the universe in us, our being present in the universe itself) I had not paused to think about Humboldt, a precious friend hid in death's dateless night, a camerade from a former existence (almost), well-beloved but dead. I imagined at times that I might see him in the life to come, together with my mother and my father. Demmie Vonghel, too. Demmie was one of the most significant dead, remembered every day. But I didn't expect him to come at me as in life, driving ninety miles an hour in his Buick four-holer. First I laughed. Then I shrieked. I was transfixed. He bore down on me. He struck me with blessings. Humboldt's gift wiped out many immediate problems.

The role played by Ronald and Lucy Cantabile in this is something else again.

Dear friends, though I was about to leave town and had much business to attend to, I decided to suspend all practical activities for one morning. I did this to keep from cracking under strain. I had been practicing some of the meditative exercises recommended by Rudolf Steiner in *Knowledge of the Higher Worlds and Its Attainment*. As yet I hadn't attained much, but then my soul was well along in years and very much stained and banged up, and I had to be patient. Characteristically, I had been trying too hard, and I remembered again that wonderful piece of advice given by a French thinker: *Trouve avant de chercher*—Valéry, it was. Or maybe Picasso. There are times when the most practical thing is to lie down.

And so the morning after my day with Cantabile I took a holiday. The weather was fine and clear. I drew the openwork drapes which shut out the details of Chicago and let in the bright sun and the high blue (which in their charity shone and towered even over a city like this). Cheerful, I dug out my Humboldt papers. I piled notebooks, letters, diaries, and manuscripts on the coffee table and on the covered radiator behind the sofa. Then I lay down, sighing, pulling off my shoes. Under my head I put a needlepoint cushion embroidered by a young lady (what a woman-filled life I always led. Ah, this sexually-disturbed century!), a Miss Doris Scheldt, the daughter of the anthroposophist I consulted now and then. She had given me this handmade Christmas gift the year before. Small and lovely, intelligent, strikingly strong in profile for such a pretty young woman, she liked to wear old-fashioned dresses that made her look like Lillian Gish or Mary Pickford. Her footwear, how-ever, was provocative, quite far out. In my private vocabulary she was a little *noli me tangerine*. She did and did not wish to be touched. She herself knew a great deal about anthroposophy and we spent a lot of time together last year, when Renata and I had a falling-out. I sat in her bentwood rocking chair while she put her tiny patent-leather boots up on a hassock, embroi-dering this red-and-green, fresh-grass-and-hot-embers cushion. We chatted, etcetera. It was an agreeable relationship, but it was over. Renata and I were back together.

This is by way of explaining that I took Von Humboldt Fleisher as the subject of my meditation that morning. Such meditation supposedly strengthened the will. Then, gradually strengthened by such exercises, the will might become an organ of perception.

A wrinkled postcard fell to the floor, one of the last Hum-boldt had sent me. I read the phantom strokes, like a fuzzy graph of the northern lights:

> Mice hide when hawks are high;
> Hawks shy from airplanes;
> Planes dread the ack-ack-ack;
> Each one fears somebody.
> Only the heedless lions
> Under the Booloo tree
> Snooze in each other's arms
> After their lunch of blood—
> I call that living good!

Eight or nine years ago, reading this poem, I thought, Poor Humboldt, those shock-treatment doctors have lobotomized him, they've ruined the guy. But now I saw this as a communication, not as a poem. The imagination must not pine away—that was Humboldt's message. It must assert again that art manifests the inner powers of nature. To the savior-faculty of the imagination sleep was sleep, and waking was true waking. This was what Humboldt now appeared to me to be saying. If that was so, Humboldt was never more sane and brave than at the end of his life. And I had run away from him on Forty-sixth Street just when he had most to tell me. I had spent that morning, as I have mentioned, grandly dressed up and revolving elliptically over the city of New York in that Coast Guard helicopter, with the two US Senators and the Mayor and officials from Washington and Albany and crack journalists, all belted up in puffy life jackets, each jacket with its sheath knife. (I've never gotten over those knives.) And then, after the luncheon in Central Park (I am compelled to repeat), I walked out and saw Humboldt, a dying man eating a pretzel stick at the curb, the dirt of the grave already sprinkled on his face. Then I rushed away. It was one of those ecstatically painful moments when I couldn't hold still. I had to run. I said, "Oh, kid, good-by. I'll see you in the next world!"

There was nothing more to be done for him in this world, I had decided. But was that true? The wrinkled postcard now made me reconsider. It struck me that I had sinned against Humboldt. Lying down on the goose-down sofa in order to meditate, I found myself getting hot with self-criticism and shame, flushing and sweating. I pulled Doris Scheldt's pillow from behind my head and wiped my face with it. Again I saw myself taking cover behind the parked cars on Forty-sixth Street. And Humboldt like a bush tented all over by the bagworm and withering away. I was stunned to see my old pal dying and I fled, I went back to the Plaza and phoned Senator Kennedy's office to say that I had been called to Chicago suddenly. I'd return to Washington next week. Then I took a cab to La Guardia and caught the first plane to O'Hare. I return again and again to that day because it was so dreadful. Two drinks, the limit in flight, did nothing for me—nothing! When I landed I drank several double shots of Jack Daniel's in the O'Hare bar, for strength. It was a very hot evening. I telephoned Denise and said, "I'm back."

"You're days and days early. What's up, Charles?"

I said, "I've had a bad experience."

"Where's the Senator?"

"Still in New York. I'll go back to Washington in a day or two."

"Well, come on home, then."

Life had commissioned an article on Robert Kennedy. I had now spent five days with the Senator, or rather near him, sitting on a sofa in the Senate Office Building, observing him. It was, from every point of view, a singular inspiration, but the Senator had allowed me to attach myself to him and even seemed to like me. I say "seemed" because it was his business to leave such an impression with a journalist who proposed to write about him. I liked him, too, perhaps against my better judgment. His way of looking at you was odd. His eyes were as blue as the void, and there was a slight lowering in the skin of the lids, an extra fold. After the helicopter trip we drove from La Guardia to the Bronx in a limousine, and I was in there with him. The heat was dismal in the Bronx but we were in a sort of crystal cabinet. His desire was to be continually briefed. He asked questions of everyone in the party. From me he wanted historical information—"What should I know about William Jennings Bryan?" or, "Tell me about H. L. Mencken"—receiving what I said with a kind of inner glitter that did not tell me what he thought or whether he could use such facts. We pulled up at a Harlem playground. There were Cadillacs, motorcycle cops, bodyguards, television crews. A vacant lot between two tenements had been fenced in, paved, furnished with slides and sandboxes. The playground director in his Afro and dashiki and beads received the two Senators. Cameras stood above us on trestles. The black director, radiant, ceremonious, held a basketball between the two Senators. A space was cleared. Twice the slender Kennedy, carelessly elegant, tossed the ball. He nodded his ruddy, foxy head high with hair and smiled when he missed. Senator Javits could not afford to miss. Compact and bald he too was smiling but squared off at the basket drawing the ball to his breast and binding himself by strength of will to the objective. He made two smart shots. The ball did not arch. It flew straight at the loop and went in. There was applause. What vexation, what labor to keep up with Bobby. But the Republican Senator managed very well.

And this was what Denise wanted me to occupy myself with. Denise had arranged all this for me, phoning the people at *Life*, supervising the whole deal. "Come on home," she said. But she was displeased. She didn't want me in Chicago now.

Home was a grand house in Kenwood on the South Side. Rich German Jews had built Victorian–Edwardian mansions here early in the century. When the mail-order tycoons and other nobs departed, university professors, psychiatrists, lawyers, and Black Muslims moved in. Since I had insisted on returning to become the Malthus of boredom, Denise bought the Kahnheim house. She had done this under protest, saying, "Why Chicago! We can live wherever we like, can't we? Christ!" She had in mind a house in Georgetown, or in Rome, or in London SW3. But I was obstinate, and Denise said she hoped it wasn't a sign that I was headed for a nervous breakdown. Her father the federal judge was a keen lawyer. I know she often consulted him downtown about property, joint-tenancy, widows' rights in the State of Illinois. He advised us to buy Colonel Kahnheim's mansion. Daily at breakfast Denise asked when I was going to make my will.

Now it was night and she was waiting for me in the master bedroom. I hate air conditioning. I kept Denise from installing it. The temperature was in the nineties, and on hot nights Chicagoans feel the city body and soul. The stockyards are gone, Chicago is no longer slaughter-city, but the old smells revive in the night heat. Miles of railroad siding along the streets once were filled with red cattle cars, the animals waiting to enter the yards lowing and reeking. The old stink still haunts the place. It returns at times, suspiring from the vacated soil, to remind us all that Chicago had once led the world in butcher-technology and that billions of animals had died here. And that night the windows were open wide and the familiar depressing multilayered stink of meat, tallow, blood-meal, pulverized bones, hides, soap, smoked slabs, and burnt hair came back. Old Chicago breathed again through leaves and screens. I heard fire trucks and the gulp and whoop of ambulances, bowel-deep and hysterical. In the surrounding black slums incendiarism shoots up in summer, an index, some say, of psychopathology. Although the love of flames is also religious. However, Denise was sitting nude on the bed rapidly and strongly brushing her hair. Over the lake, steel mills twinkled. Lamplight showed the soot already fallen on the leaves of the wall ivy. We had an early drought that year. Chicago, this night, was panting, the big urban engines going, tenements blazing in Oakwood with great shawls of flame, the sirens weirdly yelping, the fire engines, ambulances, and police cars—mad-dog, gashing-knife weather, a rape and murder night, thousands of hydrants open, spraying water from both breasts. Engineers were staggered to see the level of Lake Michigan fall as these tons of water poured. Bands of kids prowled with handguns and knives. And—dear-dear—this tender-minded mourning Mr. Charlie Citrine had seen his old buddy, a dead man eating a pretzel in New York, so he abandoned *Life* and the Coast Guard and helicopters and two Senators and rushed home to be comforted. For this purpose his wife had taken off everything and was brushing her exceedingly dense hair. Her enormous violet and gray eyes were impatient, her tenderness was mixed with glowering. She was asking tacitly how long I was going to sit on the chaise longue in my socks, heart-wounded and full of obsolete sensibility. A nervous and critical person, she thought I suffered from morbid aberrations about grief, that I was premodern or baroque about death. She often declared that I had come back to Chicago because my parents were buried here. Sometimes she said with sudden alertness, "Ah, here comes the cemetery bit!" What's more she was often right. Soon I myself could hear the chain-dragging monotony of my low voice. Love was the remedy for these death moods. And here was Denise, impatient but dutiful, sitting stripped on the bed, and I didn't even take off my necktie. I know this sorrow can be maddening. And it tired Denise to support me emotionally. She didn't take much stock in these emotions of mine. "Oh, you're on *that* kick

again. You must quit all this operatic bullshit. Talk to a psychiatrist. Why are you hung up on the past and always lamenting
some dead party or other?" Denise pointed out with a bright
flash of the face, a sign that she had had an insight, that while
I shed tears for my dead I was also patting down their graves
with my shovel. For I did write biographies, and the deceased
were my bread and butter. The deceased had earned my French
decoration and got me into the White House. (The loss of
our White House connections after the death of JFK was one
of Denise's bitterest vexations.) Don't get me wrong, I know
that love and scolding often go together. Durnwald did this
to me, too. Whom the Lord loveth He chasteneth. The whole
thing was mixed with affection. When I came home in a state
over Humboldt, she was ready to comfort me. But she had a
sharp tongue, Denise did. (I sometimes called her Rebukah.) Of
course my lying there so sad, so heart-injured, was provoking.
Besides, she suspected that I would never finish the *Life* article.
There she was right again.

If I was going to feel so much about death, why didn't I *do*
something about it. This endless sensibility was awful. Such
was Denise's opinion. I agreed with that, too.

"So you feel bad about your pal Humboldt!" she said. "But
how come you haven't looked him up? You had years to do it
in. And why didn't you speak to him today?"

These were hard questions, very intelligent. She didn't let me
get away with a thing.

"I suppose I could have said, 'Humboldt, it's me, Charlie.
What about some real lunch? The Blue Ribbon is just around
the corner.' But I think he might have thrown a fit. A couple of
years ago he tried to hit some dean's secretary with a hammer.
He accused her of covering his bed with girlie magazines. Some
kind of erotic plot against him. They had to put him away
again. The poor man is crazy. And it's no use going back to
Saint Julien or hugging lepers."

"Who said anything about lepers? You're always thinking
what nobody else has remotely in mind."

"Well okay, then, but he looked gruesome and I was all
dressed up. And I'll tell you a curious coincidence. In the heli-

copter this morning I was sitting next to Dr. Longstaff. So naturally I thought of Humboldt. It was Longstaff who promised Humboldt a huge grant from the Belisha Foundation. This was when we were still at Princeton. Haven't I ever told you about that disaster?"

"I don't think so."

"The whole thing came back to me."

"Is Longstaff still so handsome and distinguished? He must be an old man. And I'll bet you pestered him about those old times."

"Yes, I reminded him."

"You would. And I suppose it was disagreeable."

"The past isn't disagreeable to the fully justified."

"I wonder what Longstaff was doing in that Washington crowd."

"Raising money for his philanthropies, I expect."

• • •

Thus went my meditation on the green sofa. Of all the meditative methods recommended in the literature I liked this new one best. Often I sat at the end of the day remembering everything that had happened, in minute detail, all that had been seen and done and said. I was able to go backward through the day, viewing myself from the back or side, physically no different from anyone else. If I had bought Renata a gardenia at an open-air stand, I could recall that I had paid seventy-five cents for it. I saw the brass milling of the three silver-plated quarters. I saw the lapel of Renata's coat, the white head of the long pin. I remembered even the two turns the pin took in the cloth, and Renata's full woman's face and her pleased gaze at the flower, and the odor of the gardenia. If this was what transcendence took, it was a cinch, I could do it forever, back to the beginning of time. So, lying on the sofa, I now brought back to mind the obituary page of the *Times*.

The *Times* was much stirred by Humboldt's death and gave him a double-column spread. The photograph was large. For after all Humboldt did what poets in crass America are supposed to do. He chased ruin and death even harder than he had chased women. He blew his talent and his health and reached home, the grave, in a dusty slide. He plowed himself under. Okay. So did Edgar Allan Poe, picked out of the Baltimore gutter. And Hart Crane over the side of a ship. And Jarrell falling in front of a car. And poor John Berryman jumping from a bridge. For some reason this awfulness is peculiarly appreciated by business and technological America. The country is proud of its dead poets. It takes terrific satisfaction in the poets' testimony that the USA is too tough, too big, too much, too rugged, that American reality is overpowering. And to be a poet is a school thing, a skirt thing, a church thing. The weakness of the spiritual powers is proved in the childishness, madness, drunkenness, and despair of these martyrs. Orpheus moved stones and trees. But a poet can't perform a hysterectomy or send a vehicle out of the solar system. Miracle and power no longer belong to him. So poets are loved, but loved because they just can't make it here. They exist to light up the enormity of the awful tangle and justify the cynicism of those who say, "If *I* were not such a corrupt, unfeeling bastard, creep, thief, and vulture, I couldn't get through this either. Look at these good and tender and soft men, the *best* of us. They succumbed, poor loonies." So this, I was meditating, is how successful bitter hard-faced and cannibalistic people exult. Such was the attitude reflected in the picture of Humboldt the *Times* chose to use. It was one of those mad-rotten-majesty pictures—spooky, humorless, glaring furiously with tight lips, mumpish or scrofulous cheeks, a scarred forehead, and a look of enraged, ravaged childishness. This was the Humboldt of conspiracies, putsches, accusations, tantrums, the Bellevue Hospital Humboldt, the Humboldt of litigations. For Humboldt was litigious. The word was made for him. He threatened many times to sue me.

Yes, the obituary was awful. The clipping was somewhere amongst these papers that surrounded me, but I didn't want to look at it. I could remember verbatim what the *Times* said. It said, in its tinkertoy style of knobs and sticks, that Von Humboldt Fleisher had made a brilliant start. Born on New York's Upper West Side. At twenty-two set a new style in American poetry. Appreciated by Conrad Aiken (who once had to call the cops to get him out of the house). Approved by T. S. Eliot (about whom, when he was off his nut, he would spread the most lurid improbable sexual scandal). Mr. Fleisher was also a critic, essayist, writer of fiction, teacher, prominent literary intellectual, a salon personality. Intimates praised his conversation. He was a great talker and wit.

Here, no longer meditative, I took over myself. The sun still shone beautifully enough, the blue was wintry, of Emersonian haughtiness, but I felt wicked. I was as filled with harsh things to say as the sky was full of freezing blue. Very good, Humboldt, you made it in American Culture as Hart Schaffner & Marx made it in cloaks and suits, as General Sarnoff made it in communications, as Bernard Baruch made it on a park bench. As, according to Dr. Johnson, dogs made it on their hind legs and ladies in the pulpit—exceeding their natural limits curiously. Orpheus, the Son of Greenhorn, turned up in Greenwich Village with his ballads. He loved literature and intellectual conversation and argument, loved the history of thought. A big gentle handsome boy he put together his own combination of symbolism and street language. Into this mixture went Yeats, Apollinaire, Lenin, Freud, Morris R. Cohen, Gertrude Stein, baseball statistics, and Hollywood gossip. He brought Coney Island into the Aegean and united Buffalo Bill with Rasputin. He was going to join together the Art Sacrament and the Industrial USA as equal powers. Born (as he insisted) on a subway platform at Columbus Circle, his mother going into labor on the IRT, he intended to be a divine artist, a man of visionary states and enchantments, Platonic possession. He got a Rationalistic, Naturalistic education at CCNY. This was not easily reconciled with the Orphic. But all his desires were contradictory. He wanted to be magically and cosmically expressive and articulate, able to say *anything*; he wanted also to be wise, philosophical, to find the common ground of poetry and science, to prove that the imagination was just as potent as machinery, to free and to bless humankind. But he was out also to be rich and famous. And of course there were the girls. Freud himself believed that fame was pursued for the sake of the girls. But then the girls were pursuing something themselves. Humboldt said, "They're always looking for the real thing. They've been had and had by phonies, so they pray for the real thing and they rejoice when the real thing appears. That's why they love poets. This is the truth about girls." Humboldt was the real thing, certainly. But by and by he stopped being a beautiful young man and the prince of conversationalists. He grew a belly, he became thick in the face. A look of disappointment and doubt appeared under his eyes.

Brown circles began to deepen there, and he had a bruised sort of pallor in the cheeks. That was what his "frantic profession" did to him. For he always had said that poetry was one of the frantic professions in which success depends on the opinion you hold of yourself. Think well of yourself, and you win. Lose self-esteem, and you're finished. For this reason a persecution complex develops, because people who don't speak well of you are killing you. Knowing this, or sensing it, critics and intellectuals *had* you. Like it or not you were dragged into a power struggle. Then Humboldt's art dwindled while his frenzy increased. The girls were dear to him. They took him for the real thing long after he had realized that nothing real was left and that he was imposing on them. He swallowed more pills, he drank more gin. Mania and depression drove him to the loony bin. He was in and out. He became a professor of English in the boondocks. There he was a grand literary figure. Elsewhere, in one of his own words, he was zilch. But then he died and got good notices. He had always valued prominence, and the *Times* was tops. Having lost his talent, his mind, fallen apart, died in ruin, he rose again on the cultural Dow Jones and enjoyed briefly the prestige of significant failure.

• • •

To Humboldt the Eisenhower landslide of 1952 was a personal disaster. He met me, the morning after, with heavy depression. His big blond face was madly gloomy. He led me into his office, Sewell's office, which was stuffed with books—I had the adjoining room. Leaning on the small desk, the *Times* with the election results spread over it, he held a cigarette but his hands were also clasped in despair. His ashtray, a Savarin coffee can, was already full. It wasn't simply that his hopes were disappointed or that the cultural evolution of America was stopped cold. Humboldt was afraid. "What are we going to do?" he said.

"We'll have to mark time," I said. "Maybe the next administration will let us into the White House."

Humboldt would allow no light conversation this morning.

"But look," I said. "You're poetry editor of *Arcturus,* you're on the staff of Hildebrand & Co. and a paid adviser to the Belisha Foundation, and teaching at Princeton. You have a contract to do a textbook in modern poetry. Kathleen told me that if you lived to be a hundred and fifty you'd never be able to make good on all the advances you've drawn from publishers."

"You wouldn't be jealous, Charlie, if you knew how hard my position is. I seem to have a lot going for me, but it's all a bubble. I'm in danger. You, without any prospects at all, are in a much stronger position. And now there's this political disaster." I sensed that he was afraid of his back-country neighbors. In his nightmares they burned his house, he shot it out with them, they lynched him and carried off his wife. Humboldt said, "What do we do now? What's our next move?"

These questions were asked only to introduce the scheme he had in mind.

"Our move?"

"Either we leave the US during this administration, or we dig in."

"We could ask Harry Truman for asylum in Missouri."

"Don't joke with me, Charlie. I have an invitation from the Free University of Berlin to teach American literature."

"That sounds grand."

He quickly said, "No, no! Germany is dangerous. I wouldn't take a chance on Germany."

"That leaves digging in. Where are you going to dig?"

"I said 'we.' The situation is very unsafe. If you had any sense you'd feel the same. You think because you're such a pretty-boy, and so bright and big-eyed, that nobody would hurt you."

Humboldt now began to attack Sewell. "Sewell really is a rat," he said.

"I thought you were old friends."

"Long acquaintance isn't friendship. Did *you* like him? He *received* you. He condescended, he was snotty, you were treated like dirt. He didn't even talk to you, only to me. I resented it."

"You didn't say so."

"I didn't want to rouse you right away and make you angry, start you under a cloud. Do you think he's a good critic?"

"Can the deaf tune pianos?"

"He's subtle, though. He's a subtle man, in a dirty way. Don't underrate him. And he's a rough infighter. But to become a professor without even a BA . . . it speaks for itself. His father was just a lobsterman. His mother took in washing. She did Kittredge's collars in Cambridge and she wangled library privileges for her son. He went down into the Harvard stacks a weakling and he came up a regular titan. Now he's a Wasp gentleman and lords it over us. You and I have raised his status. He comes on with two Jews like a mogul and a prince."

"Why do you want to make me sore at Sewell?"

"You're too lordly yourself to take offense. You're an even bigger snob than Sewell. I think you may be psychologically one of those Axel types that only cares about inner inspiration, no connection with the actual world. The actual world can kiss your ass," said Humboldt wildly. "You leave it to poor bastards like me to think about matters like money and status and success and failure and social problems and politics. You don't give a damn for such things."

"If true, why is that so bad?"

"Because you stick *me* with all these unpoetic responsibilities. You lean back like a king, relaxed, and let all these human problems happen. There ain't no flies on Jesus. Charlie, you're not place bound, time bound, goy bound, Jew bound. What *are* you bound? Others abide our question. Thou art free! Sewell was stinking to you. He snubbed you and you're sore at him, too, don't deny it. But you can't pay attention. You're always mooning in your private mind about some kind of cosmic destiny. Tell me, what is this great thing you're always working on?"

I was now still lying on my broccoli plush sofa engaged in a meditation on this haughty freezing blue December morning. The heating engines of the great Chicago building made a strong hum. I could have done without this. Though I was beholden to modern engineering, too. Humboldt in the Princeton office stood before my mind, and my concentration was intense.

"Come to the point," I said to him.

His mouth seemed dry but there was nothing to drink. Pills make you thirsty. He smoked some more instead, and said, "You and I are friends. Sewell brought me here. And I brought you."

"I'm grateful to you. But you aren't grateful to him."

"Because he's a son of a bitch."

"Perhaps." I didn't mind hearing Sewell called that. He had snubbed me. But with his depleted hair, his dry-cereal mustache, the drinker's face, the Prufrock subtleties, the would-be elegance of his clasped hands and crossed legs, with his involved literary mutterings he was no wicked enemy. Although I seemed to be restraining Humboldt I loved the way he loused up Sewell. Humboldt's wayward nutty fertility when he let himself go gratified one of my shameful appetites, no doubt about it.

"Sewell is taking advantage of us," Humboldt said.

"How do you figure that?"

"When he comes back we'll be turned out."

"But I always knew it was a one-year job."

"Oh, you don't mind being like a rented article from Hertz's, like a trundle bed or a baby's potty?" said Humboldt.

Under the shepherd's plaid of the blanket-wide jacket his back began to look humped (a familiar sign). That massing of bison power in his back meant that he was up to no good. The look of peril grew about his mouth and eyes and the two crests of hair stood higher than usual. Pale hot radiant waves appeared in his face. Pigeons, gray-and-cream-feathered, walked with crimson feet on the sandstone window sills. Humboldt didn't like them. He saw them as Princeton pigeons, Sewell's pigeons. They cooed for Sewell. At times Humboldt seemed to view them as his agents and spies. After all this was Sewell's office and Humboldt sat at Sewell's desk. The books on the walls were Sewell's. Lately Humboldt had been throwing them into boxes. He pushed off a set of Toynbee and put up his own Rilke and Kafka. Down with Toynbee; down with Sewell, too. "You and I are expendable here, Charlie," Humboldt said. "Why? I'll tell you. We're Jews, shonickers, kikes. Here in Princeton, we're no threat to Sewell."

I remembered thinking hard about this, knitting my forehead. "I'm afraid I still haven't grasped your point," I said.

"Try thinking of yourself as Sheeny Solomon Levi, then. It's safe to install Sheeny Solomon and go to Damascus for a year to discuss *The Spoils of Poynton*. When you come back, your classy professorship is waiting for you. You and I are no threat."

"But I don't want to be a threat to him. And why should Sewell worry about threats?"

"Because he's at war with these old guys, all the billy whiskers, the Hamilton Wright Mabie genteel crappers who never accepted him. He doesn't know Greek or Anglo-Saxon. To them he's a lousy upstart."

"So? He's a self-made man. Now I'm for him."

"He's corrupt, he's a bastard, he's covered you and me with contempt. I feel ridiculous when I walk down the street. In Princeton you and I are Moe and Joe, a Yid vaudeville act. We're a joke—Abie Kabibble and Company. Unthinkable as members of the Princeton community."

"Who needs their community?"

"Nobody trusts that little crook. There's something human he just hasn't got. The person who knew him best, his wife—when she left him she took her birds. You saw all those cages. She didn't even want an empty cage to remind her of him."

"Did she go away with birds sitting on her head and arms? Come on, Humboldt, what do you want?"

"I want you to feel as insulted as I feel, not stick me with the whole thing. Why don't you have any indignation, Charlie— Ah! You're not a real American. You're grateful. You're a foreigner. You have that Jewish immigrant kiss-the-ground-at-Ellis-Island gratitude. You're also a child of the Depression.

You never thought you'd have a job, with an office, and a desk, and private drawers all for yourself. It's still so hilarious to you that you can't stop laughing. You're a Yiddisher mouse in these great Christian houses. At the same time, you're too snooty to look at anyone."

"These social wars are nothing to me, Humboldt. And let's not forget all the hard things you've said about Ivy League kikes. And only last week you were on the side of Tolstoi—it's time we simply refused to be inside history and playing the comedy of history, the bad social game."

It was no use arguing. Tolstoi? Tolstoi was last week's conversation. Humboldt's big intelligent disordered face was white and hot with turbulent occult emotions and brainstorms. I felt sorry for us, for both, for all of us, such odd organisms under the sun. Large minds abutting too close on swelling souls. And banished souls at that, longing for their home-world. Everyone alive mourned the loss of his home-world.

Sunk into the pillow of my green sofa it was all clear to me. Ah, what this existence was! What being human was!

Pity for Humboldt's absurdities made me cooperative. "You've been up all night thinking," I said.

Humboldt said with an unusual emphasis, "Charlie, you trust me, don't you?"

"Christ, Humboldt! Do I trust the Gulf Stream? What am I supposed to trust you in?"

"You know how close I feel to you. Interknitted. Brother and brother."

"You don't have to soften me up. Spill it, Humboldt, for Christ's sake."

He made the desk seem small. It was manufactured for lesser figures. His upper body rose above it. He looked like a three-hundred-pound pro linebacker beside a kiddie car. His nail-bitten fingers held the ember of a cigarette. "First we're going to get me an appointment here," he said.

"You want to be a Princeton prof?"

"A chair in modern literature, that's what I want. And you're going to help. So that when Sewell comes back he finds me installed. With tenure. The US Gov has sent him to dazzle and oppress those poor Syrian wogs with *The Spoils of Poynton*. Well, when he's wound up a year of boozing and mumbling long sentences under his breath he'll come back and find that the old twerps who wouldn't give him the time of day have made me full professor. How do you like it?"

"Not much. Is that what kept you up last night?"

"Call on your imagination, Charlie. You're overrelaxed. Grasp the insult. Get sore. He hired you like a spittoon-shiner. You've got to cut the last of the old slave-morality virtues that still bind you to the middle class. I'm going to put some hardness in you, some iron."

"Iron? This will be your fifth job—the fifth that *I* know of. Suppose I were hard—I'd ask you what's in it for me. Where do I come in?"

"Charlie!" He intended to smile; it was not a smile. "I've got a blueprint."

"I know you have. You're like what's-his-name, who couldn't drink a cup of tea without a stratagem—like Alexander Pope."

Humboldt seemed to take this as a compliment, and laughed between his teeth, silently. Then he said, "Here's what you do. Go to Ricketts and say: 'Humboldt is a very distinguished person—poet, scholar, critic, teacher, editor. He has an international reputation and he'll have a place in the literary history of the United States'—all of which is true, by the way. 'And here's your chance, Professor Ricketts, I happen to know that Humboldt's tired of living like a hand-to-mouth bohemian. The literary world is going fast. The avant-garde is a memory. It's time Humboldt led a more dignified settled life. He's married now. I know he admires Princeton, he loves it here, and if you made him an offer he'd certainly consider it. I might talk him into it. I'd hate for you to miss this opportunity, Professor Ricketts. Princeton has got Einstein and Panofsky. But you're weak on the literary creative side. The coming trend is to have artists on the campus. Amherst has Robert Frost. Don't fall behind. Grab Fleisher. Don't let him get away, or you'll end up with some third-rater.'"

"I won't mention Einstein and Panofsky. I'll start right out with Moses and the prophets. What a cast-iron plot! Ike has inspired you. This is what I call high-minded low cunning."

However, he didn't laugh. His eyes were red. He'd been up all night. First he watched the election returns. Then he wandered about the house and yard gripped by despair, thinking what to do. Then he planned out this putsch. Then filled with inspiration he drove in his Buick, the busted muffler blasting in the country lanes and the great long car skedaddling dangerously on the curves. Lucky for the woodchucks they were already hibernating. I know what figures crowded his thoughts—Walpole, Count Mosca, Disraeli, Lenin. While he thought also, with uncontemporary sublimity, about eternal life. Ezekiel and Plato were not absent. The man was noble. But he was all asmolder, and craziness also made him vile and funny. Heavy-handed, thick-faced with fatigue, he took a medicine bottle from his briefcase and fed himself a few little pills out of the palm of his hand. Tranquilizers, perhaps. Or maybe amphetamines for speed. He swallowed them dry. He doctored himself. Like Demmie Vonghel. She locked herself in the bathroom and took many pills.

"So you'll go to Ricketts," Humboldt told me.

"I thought he was only a front man."

"That's right. He's a stooge. But the old guard can't disown him. If we outsmart him, they'll have to back him up."

"But why should Ricketts pay attention to what I say?"

"Because, friend, I passed the word around that your play is going to be produced."

"You did?"

"Next year, on Broadway. They look on you as a successful playwright."

"Now why the hell did you do that? I'm going to look like a phony."

"No, you won't. We'll make it true. You can leave that to me. I gave Ricketts your last essay in the *Kenyon* to read, and he thinks you're a comer. And don't pretend with me. I know you. You love intrigue and mischief. Right now your teeth are on edge with delight. Besides, it's not just intrigue. . . ."

"What? Sorcery! *Fucking sortilegio!*"

"It's not *sortilegio*. It's mutual aid."

"Don't give me that stuff."

"First me, then you," he said.

I distinctly remember that my voice jumped up. I shouted, "What!" Then I laughed and said, "You'll make me a Princeton professor, too? Do you think I could stand a whole lifetime of this drinking, boredom, small talk, and ass-kissing? Now that you've lost Washington by a landslide, you've settled pretty fast for this academic music box. Thank you, I'll find misery in my own way. I give you two years of this goyish privilege."

Humboldt waved his hands at me. "Don't poison my mind. What a tongue you have, Charlie. Don't say those things. I'll expect them to happen. They'll infect my future."

I paused and considered his peculiar proposition. Then I looked at Humboldt himself. His mind was executing some earnest queer labor. It was swelling and pulsating oddly, painfully. He tried to laugh it all off with his nearly silent panting laugh. I could hardly hear the breath of it.

"You wouldn't be lying to Ricketts," he said. "Where would they get somebody like me?"

"Okay, Humboldt. That is a hard question."

"Well, I am one of the leading literary men of this country."

"Sure you are, at your best."

"Something should be done for me. Especially in this Ike moment, as darkness falls on the land."

"But why this?"

"Well, frankly, Charlie, I'm out of kilter, temporarily. I have to get back to a state in which I can write poetry again. But where's my equilibrium? There are too many anxieties. They dry me out. The world keeps interfering. I have to get the enchantment back. I feel as if I've been living in a suburb of reality, and commuting back and forth. That's got to stop. I have to locate myself. I'm here" (here on earth, he meant) "to do something, something good."

"I know, Humboldt. Here isn't Princeton, either, and everyone is waiting for the good thing."

Eyes reddening still more, Humboldt said, "I know you love me, Charlie."

"It's true. But let's only say it once."

"You're right. I'm a brother to you, too, though. Kathleen also knows it. It's obvious how we feel about one another, Demmie Vonghel included. Humor me, Charlie. Never mind how ridiculous this seems. Humor me, it's important. Call up Ricketts and say you have to talk to him."

"Okay. I will."

Humboldt put his hands on Sewell's small yellow desk and thrust himself back in the chair so that the steel casters gave a wicked squeak. The ends of his hair were confused with cigarette smoke. His head was lowered. He was examining me as if he had just surfaced from many fathoms.

"Have you got a checking account, Charlie? Where do you keep your money?"

"What money?"

"Haven't you got a checking account?"

"At Chase Manhattan. I've got about twelve bucks."

"My bank is the Corn Exchange," he said. "Now, where's your checkbook?"

"In my trench coat."

"Let's see."

I brought out the flapping green blanks, curling at the edges. "I see my balance is only eight," I said.

Then Humboldt reaching into his plaid jacket brought out his own checkbook and unclipped one of his many pens. He was bandoliered with fountain pens and ball-points.

"What are you doing, Humboldt?"

"I'm giving you *carte blanche* power to draw on my account. I'm signing a blank check in your name. And you make one out to me. No date, no amount, just 'Pay to Von Humboldt Fleisher.' Sit down, Charlie, and fill it out."

"But what's it about? I don't like this. I have to understand what's going on."

"With eight bucks in the bank, what do you care?"

"It's not the money. . . ."

He was very moved, and he said, "Exactly. It isn't. That's the whole point. If you're ever up against it, fill in any amount you need and cash it. The same applies to me. We'll take an oath as friends and brothers never to abuse this. To hold it for the worst emergency. When I said mutual aid you didn't take me seriously. Well, now you see." Then he leaned on the desk in all his heaviness and in a tiny script he filled in my name with trembling force.

My control wasn't much better than his. My own arm seemed full of nerves and it jerked as I was signing. Then Humboldt, big delicate and stained, heaved himself up from his revolving chair and gave me the Corn Exchange check. "No, don't just stick it in your pocket," he said. "I want to see you put it away. It's dangerous. I mean it's valuable."

We now shook hands—all four hands. Humboldt said, "This makes us blood-brothers. We've entered into a covenant. This is a covenant."

A year later I had a Broadway hit and he filled in my blank check and cashed it. He said that I had betrayed him, that I, his blood-brother, had broken a sacred covenant, that I was conspiring with Kathleen, that I had set the cops on him, and that I had cheated him. They had lashed him in a strait jacket and locked him in Bellevue, and that was my doing, too. For this I had to be punished. He imposed a fine. He drew six thousand seven hundred and sixty-three dollars and fifty-eight cents from my account at Chase Manhattan.

As for the check he had given me, I put it in a drawer under some shirts. In a few weeks it disappeared and was never seen again.

• • •

Here meditation began to get really tough. Why? Because of Humboldt's invectives and denunciations which now came back to me, together with fierce distractions and pelting anxieties, as dense as flak. Why was I lying here? I had to get ready to fly to Milan. I was supposed to go with Renata to Italy. Christmas in Milan! And I had to attend a hearing in Judge Urbanovich's chambers, conferring first with Forrest Tomchek, the lawyer who represented me in the action brought by Denise for every penny I owned. I needed also to discuss with Murra the CPA the government's tax case against me. Also Pierre Thaxter was due from California to talk to me about *The Ark*—really, to show why he had been right to default on that loan for which I had put up collateral—and to bare his soul and in so doing bare my soul, too, for who was I to have a covered soul? There was even a question about the Mercedes, whether to sell it or pay for repairs. I was almost ready to abandon it for junk. As for Ronald Cantabile, claiming to represent the new spirit, I knew that I could expect to hear from him any minute.

Still, I was able to hold out against this nagging rush of distractions. I fought off the impulse to rise as if it were a wicked temptation. I stayed where I was on the sofa sinking into the down for which geese had been ravished, and held on to Humboldt. The will-strengthening exercises I had been doing were no waste of time. As a rule I took plants as my theme: either a particular rosebush summoned from the past, or plant anatomy. I obtained a large botany book by a woman named Esau and sank myself into morphology, into protoplasts and ergastic substances, so that my exercises might have real content. I didn't want to be one of your idle hit-or-miss visionaries.

Sewell an anti-Semite? Nonsense. It suited Humboldt to hoke that up. As for blood-brotherhood and covenants, they were somewhat more genuine. Blood-brotherhood dramatized a real desire. But not genuine enough. And now I tried to remember our endless consultations and briefings before I called on Ricketts. I said, at last, to Humboldt, "Enough. I know how to do this. Not another word." Demmie Vonghel coached me too. She thought Humboldt very funny. On the morning of the interview she made sure that I was correctly dressed and took me to Penn Station in a cab.

This morning in Chicago I found that I could recall Ricketts without the slightest difficulty. He was youthful but white-haired. His crew cut sat low on his forehead. He was thick, strong, and red-necked, a handsome furniture-mover sort of man. Years after the war, he still clung to GI slang, this burly winsome person. A bit heavy for frolic, in his charcoal-gray flannels, he tried to take a light manner with me. "I hear you guys are going great in Sewell's program, that's the scuttlebutt."

"Ah, you should have heard Humboldt speak on *Sailing to Byzantium*."

"People have said that. I couldn't make it. Administration. Tough titty for me. Now what about you, Charlie?"

"Enjoying every minute here."

"Terrific. Keeping up your own work, I hope? Humboldt tells me you're going to have a Broadway production next year."

"He's a little ahead of himself."

"Ah, he's a great guy. Wonderful thing for us all. Wonderful for me, my first year as chairman."

"Is it, now?"

"Why yes, it's my shakedown cruise, too. Glad to have both of you. You look very cheerful, by the way."

"I feel cheerful, generally. People find fault with it. A drunken lady last week asked me what the hell my problem was. She said I was a compulsive-*heimischer* type."

"Really? I don't think I ever heard that expression."

"It was new to me too. Then she told me I was existentially out of step. And the last thing she said was, 'You're apparently having a hell of a good time, but life will crush you like an empty beer can.'"

Under the crew-cut crown Rickett's eyes were shame-troubled. Perhaps he too was oppressed by my good spirits. In reality I was only trying to make the interview easier. But I began to realize that Ricketts was suffering. He sensed that I had come to do mischief. For why was I here, what sort of call was this? That I was Humboldt's emissary was obvious. I brought a message, and a message from Humboldt meant nothing but trouble.

Sorry for Ricketts, I made my pitch as quickly as possible. Humboldt and I were pals, great privilege for me to be able to spend so much time with him down here. Oh, Humboldt! Wise warm gifted Humboldt! Poet, critic, scholar, teacher, editor, original. . . .

Eager to help me through this, Ricketts said, "He's just a man of genius."

"Thanks. That's what it amounts to. Well, this is what I want to say to you. Humboldt wouldn't say it himself. It's my idea

entirely. I'm only passing through, but it would be a mistake
not to keep Humboldt here. You shouldn't let him get away."

"That's a thought."

"There are things that only poets can tell you about
poetry."

"Yes, Dryden, Coleridge, Poe. But why should Humboldt tie
himself down to an academic position?"

"That's not the way Humboldt sees things. I think he needs
an intellectual community. You can imagine how overpowering
the great social structure of the country would be to inspired
men of his type. Where to turn, is the question. Now the trend
in the universities is to appoint poets, and you'll do it, too,
sooner or later. Here's your chance to get the best."

Making my meditation as detailed as possible, no fact too
small to be remembered, I could see how Humboldt had looked
when he coached me on the way to handle Ricketts. Humboldt's
face, with a persuasive pumpkin smile, came so close to mine
that I felt the warmth or fever of his cheeks. Humboldt said,
"You have a talent for this kind of errand. I know it." Did he
mean I was a born meddler? He said, "A man like Ricketts
didn't make it big in the Protestant establishment. Not fit for
the important roles—corporation president, board chairman,
big banks, Republican National Committee, Joint Chiefs, Budget Bureau, Federal Reserve. To be a prof of his kind means to
be the weak kid brother. Or maybe even sister. They get taken
care of. He's probably a member of the Century Club. Okay
to teach *The Ancient Mariner* to young Firestones or Fords.
Humanist, scholar, scoutmaster, nice but a numbskull."

Maybe Humboldt was right. I could see that Ricketts was
unable to cope with me. His sincere brown eyes seemed to ache.
He waited for me to get on with this, to finish the interview.
I didn't like backing him into a corner, but behind me I had
Humboldt. Because Humboldt didn't sleep on the night Ike was
elected, because he was drugged with pills and booze or toxic
with metabolic wastes, because his psyche didn't refresh itself
by dreaming, because he renounced his gifts, because he lacked
spiritual strength, or was too frail to stand up to the unpoetic
power of the USA, I had to come here and torment Ricketts.

I felt pity for Ricketts. And I couldn't see that Princeton was such a big deal as Humboldt made out. Between noisy Newark and squalid Trenton it was a sanctuary, a zoo, a spa, with its own choochoo and elms and lovely green cages. It resembled another place I was later to visit as a tourist—a Serbian watering place called Vrnatchka Banja. But maybe what Princeton was not counted for more. It was not the factory or department store, not the great corporation office or bureaucratic civil service, it was not the routine job-world. If you could arrange to avoid that routine job-world, you were an intellectual or an artist. Too restless, tremorous, agitated, too mad to sit at a desk eight hours a day, you needed an institution—a higher institution.

"A chair in poetry for Humboldt," I said.

"A chair in poetry! A chair! Oh!—What a grand idea!" said Ricketts. "We'd love it. I speak for everyone. We'd all vote for it. The only thing is the dough! If only we had enough dough! Charlie, we're real poor. Besides, this outfit, like any outfit, has its table of organization."

"Table of organization? Translate, please."

"A chair like that would have to be created. It's a big deal."

"How would a chair be set up?"

"Special endowment, as a rule. Fifteen or twenty grand a year, for about twenty years. Half a million bucks, with the retirement fund. We just ain't got it, Charlie. Christ, how we'd love to get Humboldt. It breaks my heart, you know that." Ricketts was now wonderfully cheerful. Minutely observant, my memory brought back, without my especially asking for it, the white frieze of his vigorous short hair, his brownish oxheart cherry eyes, the freshness of his face, his happy full cheeks.

I figured that was that, when we shook hands. Ricketts, having gotten rid of us, was rapturously friendly. "If only we had the money!" he kept saying.

And though Humboldt was waiting for me in a fever, I claimed a moment for myself in the fresh air. I stood under a brownstone arch, on foot-hollowed stone, while panhandling squirrels came at me from all directions across the smooth quadrangles, the lovely walks. It was chilly and misty, the blond dim November sun binding the twigs in circles of light. Demmie Vonghel's face had such a blond pallor. In her cloth coat with the marten collar, with her sublime sexual knees that touched, and the pointed feet of a princess, and her dilated nostrils presented almost as emotionally as her eyes, and breathing with a certain hunger, she had kissed me with her warm face, and pressed me with her tight-gloved hand, saying, "You'll do great, Charlie. Just great." We had parted at Penn Station that morning. Her cab had waited.

I didn't think that Humboldt would agree.

But I was astonishingly wrong. When I showed up in the doorway he sent away his students. He had them all in a state of exaltation about literature. They were always hanging around, waiting in the corridor with their manuscripts. "Gentlemen," he announced, "something has come up. Appointments are canceled—moved up one hour. Eleven is now twelve. Two-thirty is three-thirty." I came in. He locked the door of the hot book-crammed smoky office. "Well?" he said.

"He hasn't got the money."

"He didn't say no?"

"You're famous, he loves you, admires you, desires you, but he can't create a chair without the dough."

"And that's what he said?"

"Exactly what he said."

"Then I think I've got him! Charlie, I've got him! We've done it!"

"How have you got him? How have we done it?"

"Because—ho, ho! He hid behind the budget. He didn't say, 'no dice.' Or 'under no circumstances.' Or 'get the hell out of here.'" Humboldt was laughing that nearly silent, panting laugh of his, through tiny teeth, while a scarf of smoke flowed about him. He looked Mother-Goosey when he did this. The cow jumped over the moon. The little dog laughed to see such fun. Humboldt said, "Monopoly capitalism has treated creative men like rats. Well, that phase of history is ending. . . ." I didn't quite see how that was relevant, even if true. "We're going places."

"Tell me, then."

"I'll tell you later. But you did great." Humboldt had started to pack, to stuff his briefcase, as he did at all decisive moments. Unbuckling, he threw back the slack flap and began to pull out certain books and manuscripts and pill bottles. He made odd foot movements, as though his cats were clawing at his trouser cuffs. He restuffed the scraped leather case with other books and papers. He lifted his broad-brimmed hat from the coat tree. Like a silent-movie hero taking his invention to the big city, he was off for New York. "Put a note up for the kids. I'll be back tomorrow," he said.

I walked him to the train but he told me nothing more. He sprang into the antique Dinkey car. He wagged his fingers at me through the dirty window. And he left.

I might have gone back to New York with him, because I had come down only for the interview with Ricketts. But he was Manic and it was best to let him be.

• • •

So I, Citrine, comfortable, in the midst of life, extended on a sofa, in cashmere socks (considering how the feet of those interred shredded away like leaf tobacco—Humboldt's feet), reconstructed the way in which my stout inspired pal declined and fell. His talent had gone bad. And now I had to think what to do about talent in this day, in this age. How to prevent the leprosy of souls. Somehow it appeared to be up to me.

I meditated like anything. I followed Humboldt in my mind. He was smoking on the train. I saw him passing quick and manic through the colossal hall of Penn Station with its dusty dome of single-colored glass. And then I saw him get into a cab—the subway was good enough, as a rule. But today each move was unusual, without precedent. This was because he couldn't count on reason. Reason was coming and going in shorter cycles, and one of these days it might go for good. And then what would he do? Should he lose it once and for all, he and Kathleen would need lots of money. Also, as he had said to me, you could be gaga in a tenured chair at Princeton, and would anybody notice? Ah, poor Humboldt! He might have been—no, he *was* so fine!

He was soaring now. His present idea was to go straight to the top. When he got there, this blemished spirit, the top saw the point. Humboldt met with interest and consideration.

Wilmoore Longstaff, the famous Longstaff, archduke of the higher learning in America, was the man Humboldt went to see. Longstaff had been appointed the first head of the new Belisha Foundation. The Belisha was richer than Carnegie and Rockefeller, and Longstaff had hundreds of millions to spend on science and scholarship, on the arts, and on social improvement. Humboldt already had a sinecure with the Foundation. His good friend Hildebrand had gotten it for him. Hildebrand the playboy publisher of avant-garde poets, himself a poet, was Humboldt's patron. He had discovered Humboldt at CCNY, he admired his work, adored his conversation, protected him, kept him on the payroll at Hildebrand & Co. as an editor. This caused Humboldt to lower his voice when he slandered him. "He steals from the blind, Charlie. When the Blind Association mails in pencils, Hildebrand keeps those charity pencils. He never donates a penny."

I remembered saying, "Stingy-rich is just ordinary camp."

"Yes, but he overdoes it. Try eating dinner at his house. He starves you. And why did Longstaff hire Hildebrand for thirty thousand to plan a program for writers? He hired him because of me. If you're a Foundation you don't deal with poets, you go to the man who owns a stable of poets. So I do all the work and get only eight thousand."

"Eight for a part-time job isn't bad, is it?"

"Charlie, it's cheap of you to pull this fair-mindedness on me. I say I'm an underdog and then you slip it in that I'm so privileged, meaning that you're an under-underdog. Hildebrand gets full value from me. He never reads a manuscript. He's always on a cruise or skiing in Sun Valley. Without my advice he'd publish toilet paper. I save him from being a millionaire Philistine. He got to Gertrude Stein because of me. Also to Eliot. Because of me he has something to offer Longstaff. But I'm forbidden absolutely to talk to Longstaff."

"No."

"Yes! I tell you," said Humboldt. "Longstaff has a private

elevator. No one gets to his penthouse from the lower ranks. I see him from a distance as he comes and goes but my instructions are to stay away from him."

Years afterward, I, Citrine, sat next to Wilmoore Longstaff on that Coast Guard helicopter. He was quite old then, finished, fallen from glory. I had seen him when the going was good, and he had looked like a movie star, like a five-star general, like Machiavelli's Prince, like Aristotle's great-souled man. Longstaff had fought technocracy and plutocracy with the classics. He forced some of the most powerful people in the country to discuss Plato and Hobbes. He made airline presidents, chairmen, governors of the Stock Exchange perform *Antigone* in board rooms. Truth, however, is truth and Longstaff was in many respects first rate. He was a distinguished educator, he was even noble. His life would perhaps have been easier if his looks had been less striking.

At any rate, Humboldt did the bold thing, just as we had all seen it done in the old go-getter movies. Unauthorized, he entered Longstaff's private elevator and pushed the button. Materializing huge and delicate in the penthouse, he gave his name to the receptionist. No, he had no appointment (I saw the sun on his cheeks, on his soiled clothes—it was shining as it shines through the purer air in skyscrapers), but he *was* Von Humboldt Fleisher. The name was enough. Longstaff had him shown in. He was very glad to see Humboldt. This he told me during the flight, and I believed him. We sat in the helicopter belted up in orange puffy life jackets, and we were armed with those long knives. Why the knives? Perhaps to fight sharks if one fell into the harbor. "I had read his ballads," Longstaff told me. "I considered him to have great talent." I knew of course that for Longstaff *Paradise Lost* was the last real poem in English. Longstaff was a greatness-freak. What he meant was that Humboldt was undoubtedly a poet and a charming man. That he was. In Longstaff's office Humboldt must have been swooning with wickedness and ingenuity, swollen with manic energy, with spots before his eyes and maculations of the heart. He was going to persuade Longstaff, do in Sewell, outfox Ricketts, screw Hildebrand, and bugger fate. At the moment he looked like the Roto Rooter man come to snake out the drains. Yet he was bound for a chair at Princeton. Ike had conquered, Stevenson had gone down, but Humboldt was vaulting into penthouses and beyond.

Longstaff too was riding high. He bullied his trustees with Plato and Aristotle and Aquinas, he had the whammy on them. And probably Longstaff had old scores to settle with Princeton, a pillbox of the educational establishment at which he aimed his radical flame thrower. I knew from Ickes' *Diaries* that Longstaff had made up to FDR. He wanted Wallace's place on the ticket, and Truman's, later. He dreamed of being Vice President and President. But Roosevelt had strung him along, had kept him waiting on tiptoes but never kissed him. That was Roosevelt all over. In this I sympathized with Longstaff (an ambitious man, a despot, a czar in my secret heart).

So as the helicopter tilted back and forth over New York I studied this handsome aged Dr. Longstaff trying to understand how Humboldt must have looked to him. In Humboldt he perhaps had seen Caliban America, heaving and yapping, writing odes on greasy paper from the fish shop. For Longstaff had no feeling for literature. But he had been delighted when Humboldt explained that he wanted the Belisha Foundation to endow a chair for him at Princeton. "Exactly right!" said Longstaff. "Just the thing!" He buzzed his secretary and dictated a letter. Then and there Wilmoore Longstaff committed the Foundation to an extended grant. Soon Humboldt, palpitating, held a signed copy of the letter in his hand, and he and Longstaff drank martinis, gazing at Manhattan from the sixtieth floor, and talked about Dante's bird imagery.

As soon as he left Longstaff, Humboldt rushed downtown by cab to visit a certain Ginnie in the Village, a Bennington girl to whom Demmie Vonghel and I had introduced him. He pounded on her door and said, "It's Von Humboldt Fleisher. I have to see you." Stepping into the vestibule, he propositioned her immediately. Ginnie said, "He chased me around the apartment, and it was a scream. But I was worried about the puppies underfoot." Her dachshund had just had a litter. Ginnie locked herself in the bathroom. Humboldt shouted, "You don't know what you're missing. I'm a poet. I have a big cock." And Ginnie told Demmie, "I was laughing so hard I couldn't have done it anyway."

When I asked Humboldt about this incident he said, "I felt I had to celebrate, and I understood these Bennington girls went for poets. Too bad about this Ginnie. She's very pretty but she's honey from the icebox, if you know what I mean. Cold sweets won't spread."

"Did you go elsewhere?"

"I gave up on erotic relief. I went around and visited lots of people."

"And showed them Longstaff's letter."

"Of course."

In any case, the scheme worked. Princeton couldn't refuse the Belisha gift. Ricketts was outgeneraled. Humboldt was appointed. The *Times* and the *Herald Tribune* both carried the story. For two or three months things were smoother than velvet and cashmere. Humboldt's new colleagues gave cocktail and dinner parties for him. Nor did Humboldt in his happiness forget that we were blood-brothers. Almost daily he would say, "Charlie, today I had a terrific idea for you. For the title role in your play . . . Victor McLaglen is a fascist of course. Can't have him. But . . . I'm going to get in touch with Orson Welles for you. . . ."

But then, in February, Longstaff's trustees rebelled. They had had enough, I guess, and rallied for the honor of American monopoly-capital. Longstaff's proposed budget was rejected, and he was forced to resign. He was not sent away quite empty-handed. He got some money, about twenty million, to start a little foundation of his own. But in effect they gave him the ax. The appropriation for Humboldt's chair was a tiny item in that rejected budget. When Longstaff fell, Humboldt fell with him. "Charlie," Humboldt said when he was at last able to talk about it, "it was just like my father's experience when he was wiped out in the Florida boom. One year more and we would have made it. I've even asked myself, I've wondered, whether Longstaff knew when he sent the letter that he was on his way out . . . ?"

"I can't believe that," I said. "Longstaff is certainly mischievous, but he isn't mean."

The Princeton people behaved well and offered to do the gentlemanly thing. Ricketts said, "You're one of us now, Hum, you know? Don't worry, we'll find the dough for your chair somehow." But Humboldt sent in his resignation. Then in March, on a back road in New Jersey, he tried to run Kathleen down in the Buick. She jumped into a ditch to save herself.

•   •   •

At this moment I must say, almost in the form of deposition, without argument, that I do not believe my birth began my first existence. Nor Humboldt's. Nor anyone's. On esthetic grounds, if on no others, I cannot accept the view of death taken by most of us, and taken by me during most of my life—on esthetic grounds therefore I am obliged to deny that so extraordinary a thing as a human soul can be wiped out forever. No, the dead are about us, shut out by our metaphysical denial of them. As we lie nightly in our hemispheres asleep by the billions, our dead approach us. Our ideas should be their nourishment. We are their grainfields. But we are barren and we starve them. Don't kid yourself, though, we are watched by the dead, watched on this earth, which is our school of freedom. In the next realm, where things are clearer, clarity eats into freedom. We are free on earth because of cloudiness, because of error, because of marvelous limitation, and as much because of beauty as of blindness and evil. These always go with the blessing of freedom. But this is all I have to say about the matter now, because I'm in a hurry, under pressure—all this unfinished business!

As I was meditating on Humboldt, the hall-buzzer went off. I have a dark little hall where I press the button and get muffled shouts on the intercom from below. It was Roland Stiles, the doorman. My ways, the arrangements of my life, diverted Stiles a lot. He was a skinny witty old Negro. He was, so to speak, in the semifinals of life. In his opinion, so was I. But I didn't seem to see it that way, for some strange white man's reason, and I continued to carry on as if it weren't yet time to think of death. "Plug in your telephone, Mr. Citrine. Do you read me? Your number-one lady friend is trying to reach you." Yesterday my car was bashed. Today my beautiful mistress couldn't get in touch. To him I was as good as a circus. At night Stiles's missus liked stories about me better than television. He told me so himself.

I dialed Renata and said, "What is it?"

"What is it! For Christ's sake! I've called ten times. You have to see Judge Urbanovich at half past one. Your lawyer's been trying to get you, too. And he finally phoned Szathmar, and Szathmar phoned me."

"Half past one! They changed the time on me! For months they ignore me, then they give me two hours' notice, curse them." My spirit began to jump up and down. "Oh hell, I hate them, those crap artists."

"Maybe you can wind the whole thing up now. Today."

"How? I've surrendered five times. Each time I surrender Denise and her guy up their demands."

"In just a few days thank God I'm getting you out of here. You've been dragging your feet, because you don't want to go, but believe me, Charlie, you'll bless me for it when we're in Europe again."

"Forrest Tomchek doesn't even have time to discuss the case with me. Some lawyer Szathmar recommended."

"Now Charlie, how will you get downtown without your car? I'm surprised that Denise hasn't tried to hitch a ride to court with you."

"I'll get a cab."

"I have to take Fannie Sunderland to the Mart, anyway, for her tenth look at upholstery material for one fucking sofa." Renata laughed, but she was unusually patient with her clients. "I must take care of this before we pull out for Europe. We'll pick you up at one o'clock sharp. Be ready, Charlie."

Long ago I read a book called *Ils Ne M'auront Pas (They Aren't Going to Get Me)* and at certain moments I whisper, *"Ils ne m'auront pas."* I did that now, determined to finish my exercise in contemplation or Spirit-recollection (the purpose of which was to penetrate into the depths of the soul and to rec-

ognize the connection between the self and the divine powers).
I lay down again on the sofa. To lie down was no small gesture
of freedom. I am only being factual about this. It was a quarter of eleven, and if I left myself five minutes for a container
of plain yoghurt and five minutes to shave I could continue
for two hours to think about Humboldt. This was the right
moment for it.

Well, Humboldt tried to run down Kathleen in his car. They
were driving home from a party in Princeton, and he was
punching her, steering with the left hand. At a blinking light,
near a package store, she opened the door and made a run for
it in her stocking feet—she had lost her shoes in Princeton. He
chased her in the Buick. She jumped into a ditch and he ran
into a tree. The state troopers had to come and release him
because the doors were jammed by the collision.

Anyhow, the trustees had risen up against Longstaff, and
the Poetry chair had disintegrated. Kathleen later told me that
Humboldt had kept this from her all that day. He put down
the phone and with his shuffling feet and sumo-wrestler's belly
came into the kitchen and poured himself a large jam-jar full of
gin. Standing beside the dirty sink in his sneakers he drank this
as if it had been milk.

"What was that call?" said Kathleen.

"Ricketts called."

"What did he want?"

"Nothing. Just routine," said Humboldt.

"He turned a funny color under the eyes when he drank all
that gin," Kathleen told me. "A kind of light greeny purple.
You sometimes see that shade of purple in artichoke hearts."

A little later on the same morning he seems to have had
another talk with Ricketts. This was when Ricketts told him
that Princeton would not renege. Money would be found. But
this put Ricketts in the morally superior position. A poet could
not allow a bureaucrat to surpass him. Humboldt locked himself in his office with the gin bottle and all day long wrote drafts
of a letter of resignation.

But that evening, on the road as they were driving in to

attend a party at the Littlewoods' he went to work on Kathleen. Why did she let her father sell her to Rockefeller? Yes the old guy was supposed to be just a pleasant character, a bohemian antique from Paris, one of the gang from the Closerie des Lilas, but he was an international criminal, a Dr. Moriarty, a Lucifer, a pimp and didn't he try to have sexual relations with his own daughter? Well, how was it with Rockefeller? Did Rockefeller's penis thrill her more? Did the billions enter in? Did Rockefeller have to take a woman away from a poet in order to get it up? So they drove in the Buick skidding on the gravel and booming through clouds of dust. He began to shout that her great calm-and-lovely act didn't take him in at all. He knew all about these things. From a bookish viewpoint he actually did know a lot. He knew the jealousy of King Leontes in *The Winter's Tale*. Mario Praz he knew. And Proust—caged rats tortured to death, Charlus flogged by some killer-concierge, some slaughterhouse brute with a scourge of nails. "I know all that lust garbage," he said. "And I know the game has to be played with a calm face like yours. I know all about this female masochistic business. I understand your thrills, and you're just using me!"

So they got to the Littlewoods' and Demmie and I were there. Kathleen was white. Her face looked heavily powdered. Humboldt walked in silent. He wasn't talking. This was in fact his last night as the Belisha Professor of Poetry at Princeton. Tomorrow the news would be out. Maybe it was out already. Ricketts behaved honorably but he might not have been able to resist telling everyone. But Littlewood seemed not to know anything. He was trying hard to make his party a success. His cheeks were red and jolly. He looked like Mr. Tomato with a top hat in the juice ad. He had wavy hair and a fine worldly manner. When he took a lady's hand you wondered just what he was going to do with it. Littlewood was an upper-class bad boy, a minister's randy son. He knew London and Rome. He especially knew Shepheard's famous bar in Cairo, and had acquired his British Army slang there. He had friendly endearing spaces between his teeth. He loved to grin, and at every party he did imitations of Rudy Vallee. To cheer up Humboldt and Kathleen I got him to sing "I'm Just a Vagabond Lover." It did not go over well.

I was present in the kitchen when Kathleen made a serious mistake. Holding her drink and an unlit cigarette she reached into a man's pocket for a match. He was not a stranger, we knew him well, his name was Eubanks, and he was a Negro composer. His wife was standing near him. Kathleen was beginning to recover her spirits and was slightly drunk herself. But just as she was getting the matches out of Eubanks's pocket Humboldt came in. I saw him coming. First he stopped breathing. Then he clutched Kathleen with sensational violence. He twisted her arm behind her back and ran her out of the kitchen into the yard. A thing of this sort was not unusual at a Littlewood party, and others decided not to notice, but Demmie and I hurried to the window. Humboldt punched Kathleen in the belly, doubling her up. Then he pulled her by the hair into the Buick. As there was a car behind him he couldn't back out. He wheeled over the lawn and off the sidewalk, hacking off the muffler on the curb. I saw it there next morning like the case of a superinsect, flaky with rust, and a pipe coming out of it. Also I found Kathleen's shoes stuck by the heels in the snow. There was fog, ice, dirty cold, the bushes glassy, the elm twigs livid, the March snow brocaded with soot.

And now I recalled that the rest of the night had been a headache because Demmie and I were overnight guests, and when the party broke up Littlewood took me aside and proposed man to man that we do a swap. "An Eskimo wife deal. What say we have a romp," he said. "A wingding."

"Thanks, no, it isn't cold enough for this Eskimo stuff."

"You're refusing on your own? Aren't you even going to ask Demmie?"

"She'd haul off and hit me. Perhaps you'd like to try her. You wouldn't believe how hard she can punch. She looks like a fashionable broad, and elegant, but she's really a big honest hick."

I had my own reasons for giving him a soft answer. We were overnight guests here. I didn't want to go at 2 a.m. to sit in the Pennsylvania waiting room. Entitled to my eight hours of oblivion and determined to have them, I got into bed in the smoky study through which the party had swirled. But now Demmie had put on her nightgown and was a changed person. An hour ago in a black chiffon dress and the hair brushed gold and long on her head and fastened with an ornament she was a young lady of breeding. Humboldt, when he was in a balanced state, loved to cite the important American social categories, and Demmie belonged to them all. "She's pure Main Line. Quaker schools, Bryn Mawr. Real class," Humboldt said. She had chatted with Littlewood, whose subject was Plautus, about Latin translation and New Testament Greek. I didn't love the farmer's daughter in Demmie less than the society girl. She now sat on the bed. Her toes were deformed by cheap shoes. Her large collarbones formed hollows. When they were children, she and her sister, similarly built, filled up these collarbone hollows with water and ran races.

Anything to stave off sleep. Demmie took pills but she deeply feared to sleep. She said she had a hangnail and sat on the bed filing away, the long flexible file going zigzag. Suddenly lively, she faced me cross-legged with round knees and a show of thigh. In this position she released the salt female odor, the bacterial background of deep love. She said, "Kathleen shouldn't have reached for Eubanks's matches. I hope Humboldt didn't hurt her, but she shouldn't have done it."

"But Eubanks is an old friend."

"Humboldt's old friend? He's known him a long time—there's a difference. It means something if a woman goes into a man's pocket. And we saw her do it. . . . I don't completely blame Humboldt."

Demmie was often like this. Just as I was ready to close my eyes for the night, having had enough of my conscious and operating self, Demmie wanted to talk. At this hour she preferred exciting topics—sickness, murder, suicide, eternal punishment, and hellfire. She got into a state. Her hair bristled and her eyes deepened with panic and her deformed toes twisted in all directions. She then closed her long hands upon her smallish breasts. With baby tremors of the lip she sank at times into a preverbal baby stammer. It was now three o'clock in the morning and I thought I heard the depraved Littlewoods carrying on above us in the master bedroom, perhaps to give us an idea of what we were missing. This was probably imaginary.

I rose, anyway, and took away Demmie's nail file. I tucked her in. Her mouth was naïvely open as she gave up the file. I got her to lie down but she was disturbed. I could see that. As she laid her head on the pillow, in profile, one large lovely eye stared out childishly. "Off you go," I said. She shut the staring eye. Her sleep was instantaneous and seemed deep.

But in a few minutes I heard what I expected to hear—her night voice. It was low hoarse and deep almost mannish. She moaned. She spoke broken words. She did this almost every night. The voice expressed her terror of this strange place, the earth, and of this strange state, being. Laboring and groaning she tried to get out of it. This was the primordial Demmie beneath the farmer's daughter beneath the teacher beneath the elegant Main Line horsewoman, Latinist, accomplished cocktail-sipper in black chiffon, with the upturned nose, this fashionable conversationalist. Thoughtful, I listened to this. I let her go on awhile, trying to comprehend. I pitied her and loved her. But then I put an end to it. I kissed her. She knew who it was. She pressed her toes to my shins and held me with powerful female arms. She cried "I love you" in the same deep voice, but her eyes were still shut blind. I think she never actually woke up.

● ● ●

In May, when the Princeton term was ended, Humboldt and I met, as blood-brothers, for the last time.

As deep as the huge cap of December blue behind me entering the window with thermal distortions from the sun, I lay on my Chicago sofa and saw again everything that had happened. One's heart hurt from this sort of thing. One thought, How sad, about all this human nonsense which keeps us from the large truth. But perhaps I can get through it once and for all by doing what I am doing now.

Very good, Broadway was the word then. I had a producer,

a director, and an agent. I was part of the theater world, in Humboldt's eyes. There were actresses who said "dahling" and kissed you when you met. There was a Hirschfeld caricature of me in the *Times*. Humboldt took much credit for this. By bringing me to Princeton he had put me in the majors. Through him I met useful people in the Ivy League. Besides, he felt I had modeled Von Trenck, my Prussian hero, on him. "But look out, Charlie," he said. "Don't be taken in by the Broadway glamour and the commercial stuff."

Humboldt and Kathleen descended on me in the repaired Buick. I was in a cottage on the Connecticut shore, down the road from Lampton, the director, making revisions under his guidance—writing the play he wanted, for that was what it amounted to. Demmie was with me every weekend, but the Fleishers arrived on a Wednesday, when I was alone. Humboldt had just given a reading at Yale and they were going home. We sat in the small stone kitchen drinking coffee and gin, having a reunion. Humboldt was being "good," serious, high-minded. He had been reading *De Anima* and was full of ideas about the origins of thought. I noticed, however, that he didn't let Kathleen out of his sight. She had to tell him where she was going. "I'm just getting my cardigan." Even to go to the bathroom, she needed permission. Also he seemed to have punched her in the eye. She sat quietly and low in her chair, arms folded and long legs crossed, but she had a shiner. Humboldt finally spoke of it himself. "It wasn't me this time," he said. "You won't believe it, Charlie, but she fell against the dashboard when I made a fast stop. Some clunk in a truck came barreling out of a side road and I had to jump the brakes."

Perhaps he hadn't hit her, but he did watch her; he watched like a bailiff escorting a prisoner from one jail to another. He moved his chair all the while he was lecturing about *De Anima*, to make sure we didn't exchange eye-signals. He laid it on so thick that we were bound to try to outwit him. And we did. We managed at last to have a few words at the clothesline in the garden. She had rinsed her stockings and came out into the sunshine to hang them. Humboldt was probably satisfying a natural need.

"Did he sock you or not?"

"No, I fell on the dashboard. But it's hell, Charlie. Worse than ever."

The clothesline was old and dark gray. It had burst open and was giving up its white pith.

"He says I'm carrying on with a critic, a young, unimportant, completely innocent fellow named Magnasco. Very nice, but my God! And I'm tired of being treated like a nymphomaniac and told how I'm doing it on fire escapes or standing up, in clothes closets, every chance I get. And at Yale he made me sit on the platform during his reading. Then he blamed me for showing my legs. At every service station he forces his way into the ladies' room with me. I can't go back to New Jersey with him."

"What will you do?" said eager, heart-melting, concerned Citrine.

"Tomorrow when we get back to New York I'm going to get lost. I love him but I can't take any more. I'm telling you to prepare you, because you guys love each other, and you'll have to help him. He has some money. Hildebrand fired him. But he did get a Guggenheim, you know."

"I didn't even know he applied."

"Oh he puts in for everything. . . . Now he's watching us from the kitchen."

And there indeed was Humboldt bulging out the coppery webbing of the screen door like a fisherman's strange catch.

"Good luck."

As she went back to the house her legs were eagerly beaten by the grass of May. Through stripes of shrub shadow and country sunshine, the cat was strolling. The clothesline surrendered the pith of its soul, and Kathleen's stockings, hung at the wide end, now suggested lust. Such was Humboldt's effect. He came straight to me at the clothesline and ordered me to tell him what we had been talking about.

"Oh lay off, will you Humboldt? Don't force me into this neurotic superdrama." I was appalled by what I foresaw. I wished they would go—pile into their Buick (more than ever the muddy Flanders Field staff car) and pull out, leaving me with my Trenck troubles, the tyranny of Lampton, and the clean Atlantic shore.

But they stayed over. Humboldt didn't sleep. The wooden treads of the backstairs creaked all night under his weight. The tap ran and the refrigerator door slammed. When I came into the kitchen in the morning I found that the quart of Beefeater's gin, the house present they had brought, was empty on the table. The cotton wads of his pill bottles were all over the place, like rabbit droppings.

So Kathleen disappeared from Rocco's Restaurant on Thompson Street and Humboldt went wild. He said she was with Magnasco, that Magnasco kept her hidden in his room at the Hotel Earle. Somewhere Humboldt obtained a pistol and he hammered on Magnasco's door with the butt until he shredded the wood. Magnasco called the desk, and the desk sent for the cops, and Humboldt took off. But next day he jumped Magnasco on Sixth Avenue in front of Howard Johnson's. A group of lesbians gotten up as longshoremen rescued the young man. They had been having ice-cream sodas, and they came out and broke up the fight, pinning Humboldt's arms behind him. It was a blazing afternoon and the women prisoners at the detention center on Greenwich Avenue were shrieking from the open windows and unrolling toilet-paper streamers.

Humboldt phoned me in the country and said, "Charlie, where is Kathleen?"

"I don't know."

"Charlie, I think you do know. I saw her talking to you."

"But she didn't tell me."

He hung up. Then Magnasco called. He said, "Mr. Citrine? Your friend is going to hurt me. I'll have to swear out a warrant."

"Is it really that bad?"

"You know how it is, people go further than they mean to, and then where are you? I mean, where am I? I'm calling because he threatens me in your name. He says you'll get me if he doesn't—his blood-brother."

"I won't lay a hand on you," I said. "Why don't you leave town for a while?"

"Leave?" said Magnasco. "I only just got here. Down from Yale."

I understood. He was on the make, had long prepared for his career.

"The *Trib* is trying me out as a book reviewer."

"I know how it is. I have a show opening on Broadway. My first."

When I met Magnasco, he proved to be overweight, round-faced, young in calendar years only, steady, unflappable, born to make progress in cultural New York. "I won't be driven out," he said. "I'll put him on a peace bond."

"Well, do you need my permission?" I said.

"It won't exactly make me popular in New York to do this to a poet."

I then said to Demmie, "Magnasco is afraid of getting in bad with the New York culture crowd by calling the cops."

Night-moaning, hell-fearing, pill-addicted Demmie was also a most practical person, a supervisor and programmer of genius. When she was in her busy mood, domineering and protecting me, I used to think what a dolls' generalissimo she must have been in childhood. "And where you're concerned," she would say, "I'm a tiger-mother and a regular Fury. Isn't it about a month since you saw Humboldt? He's staying away. That means he's beginning to blame you. Poor Humboldt, he's flipped out, hasn't he! We have to help him. If he keeps attacking this Magnasco character they're going to lock him up. If the police put him in Bellevue, what you have to do is get ready to bail him out. He'll have to be sobered up, calmed down, and cooled off. The best place for that is Payne Whitney. Listen, Charlie, Ginnie's cousin Albert is the admitting physician at Payne Whitney. Bellevue is hell. We should raise some money and transfer him to Payne Whitney. Maybe we could get him a sort of scholarship."

She went into this with Ginnie's cousin Albert, and, in my name, she telephoned people and collected money for Humboldt, taking over because I was busy with *Von Trenck*. We had come back from Connecticut and were going into rehearsal at the Belasco. Efficient Demmie soon raised about three thousand dollars. Hildebrand alone contributed two thousand but he was still sore at Humboldt. He stipulated that the money was for psychiatric treatment and for bare necessities only. A Fifth Avenue lawyer, Simkin, held this fund in escrow. Hildebrand knew, by now we all knew, that Humboldt had hired a private detective, a man named Scaccia, and that this Scaccia had already gotten most of Humboldt's Guggenheim grant. Kathleen herself had done an uncharacteristic thing. Leaving New York at once she headed for Nevada to file for divorce. But Scaccia kept telling Humboldt that she was still in New York and doing lascivious things. Humboldt elaborated a new Proustian sensational scandal involving, this time, a vice ring of Wall Street brokers. If he could catch her in adultery, he would get the "property," the shack in New Jersey, worth about eight thousand dollars, with a mortgage of five, as Orlando Huggins told me—Orlando was one of those radical bohemians who knew money. In avant-garde New York everybody knew money.

The summer went quickly. In August rehearsals began. The nights were hot, tense, and tiring. Each morning I rose already worn out and Demmie gave me several cups of coffee and at the breakfast table also a good deal of counsel about the theater and Humboldt and the conduct of life. The little white terrier, Cato, begged for crusts and snapped his teeth while dancing backward on his hind legs. I thought that I too would prefer sleeping all day on his cushion by the window, near Demmie's begonias, than sit in the antique filth of the Belasco and listen to dreary actors. I began to hate the theater, the feelings wickedly distended by histrionics, all the old gestures, clutchings, tears, and supplications. Besides, *Von Trenck* was no longer my play. It belonged to goggled Harold Lampton for whom I obligingly wrote new dialogue in the dressing rooms. His actors were a bunch of sticks. All the talent in New York seemed to be in the melodrama enacted by feverish, delirious Humboldt. Pals and admirers were his audience at the White Horse on Hudson Street. There he lectured and hollered. He also consulted lawyers and was seeing a psychiatrist or two.

Demmie, I felt, could understand Humboldt better than I

because she too swallowed mysterious pills. (There were other affinities as well.) An obese child, she had weighed two hundred and eighty pounds at the age of fourteen. She showed me pictures I could hardly believe. She was given hormone injections and pills and she grew slender. Judging by the exophthalmic bulge, it must have been thyroxine that they put her on. She thought her pretty breasts disfigured by the rapid weight loss. The insignificant wrinkles in them were a grief to her. She sometimes cried, "They hurt my titties with their goddamn medicine." Brown-paper packets were still arriving from the Mount Coptic Drugstore. "But I am attractive, though." Indeed she was. Her Dutch hair positively gave light. She wore it sometimes combed to the side, sometimes with bangs, depending on what she had done to herself at the hairline with her nails. She often scratched herself. Her face was either childishly circular or like a frontierwoman's, gaunt. She was sometimes a van der Weyden beauty, sometimes Mortimer Snerd, sometimes a Ziegfeld girl. The slight silken scrape of her knock-knees when she walked quickly was, I repeat, highly prized by me. I thought that if I were a locust such a sound would send me soaring over mountain ranges. When Demmie's face with the fine upturned nose was covered with pancake make-up her big eyes, all the more mobile and clear because she had laid on so much dust, revealed two things: one was that she had a true heart and the other that she was a dynamic sufferer. More than once I rushed into Barrow Street to flag down a cab and take Demmie to the emergency room at St. Vincent's. She sun-bathed on the roof and was burned so badly that she became delirious. Then, slicing veal, she cut her thumb to the bone. She went to throw garbage down the incinerator and a gush of flame from the open chute singed her. As a good girl, she did her Latin lesson-plans for an entire term, she laid away scarves and gloves in labeled boxes, she scrubbed the house. As a bad girl she drank whisky, she had hysterics, or took up with thieves and desperadoes. She stroked me like a fairy princess or punched me in the ribs like a cowhand. In hot weather she stripped herself naked to wax the floors on her knees. Then there appeared big tendons, lanky arms, laboring feet. And when it was seen from behind the organ I adored in a different context as small, fine, intricate, rich in delightful difficulties of access, stood out like a primitive limb. But after the waxing, a seizure of sweating labor, she sat with lovely legs in a blue frock having a martini. Fundamentalist Father Vonghel owned Mount Coptic. He was a violent man. There was a scar on Demmie's head where he had banged the child's head on a radiator, there was another on her face where he had jammed a wastepaper basket over it—the tinsmith had to cut her free. With all this she knew the gospels by heart, she had been a field-hockey star, she could break Western horses, and she wrote charming bread-and-butter notes on Tiffany paper. Still, when she took a spoonful of her favorite vanilla custard, she was again the fat child. She savored the dessert at the tip of her tongue, open-mouthed, and the great blue mid-summer ocean-haze eyes in a trance, so that she started when I said, "Swallow your pudding." Evenings we played backgammon, we translated Lucretius, she expounded Plato to me. "People take credit for their virtues. But *he* sees—what else *can* you be but virtuous? There *is* nothing else."

Just before Labor Day Humboldt threatened Magnasco again, and Magnasco went to the police and persuaded a plainclothesman to come back to the hotel with him. They waited in the lobby. Then Humboldt roared in and went for Magnasco. The dick got between them, and Humboldt said, "Officer, he has my wife in his room." The reasonable thing was to make a search. They went upstairs, all three. Humboldt looked in all the closets, he searched under the pillows for her nightgown, he ran his hand under the lining papers of the drawers. There were no underthings. Nothing.

The plainclothesman said, "So, where is she? Was it you who banged hell out of this door with the butt of your gun?"

Humboldt said, "I have no gun. You want to frisk me?" He lifted his arms. Then he said, "Come to my room and look, if you like. See for yourself."

But when they got to Greenwich Street, Humboldt put the key in the lock and said, "You can't come in." He shouted, "Have you got a search warrant?" Then he whirled in and slammed and bolted his door.

This was when Magnasco filed the complaint or took a peace bond—I don't know which—and on a smoggy and stifling night the police came for Humboldt. He fought like an ox. He struggled also in the police station. An anointed head rolled on the filthy floor. Was there a strait jacket? Magnasco swore there wasn't. But there were handcuffs, and Humboldt wept. On the way to Bellevue he had diarrhea, and they locked him away for the night in a state of filth.

Magnasco let it transpire that he and I together had decided to do this, to prevent Humboldt from committing a crime. Everyone then said that the man responsible was Charles Citrine, Humboldt's blood-brother and protégé. I suddenly had many detractors and enemies, unknown to me.

And I'll tell you how I saw it from the plush decay and heated darkness of the Belasco Theatre. I saw Humboldt whipping his team of mules and standing up in his crazy wagon like an Oklahoma land-grabber. He rushed into the territory of excess to stake himself a claim. This claim was a swollen and quaking heart-mirage.

I didn't mean, The poet is off his nut. . . . Call the cops and damn the clichés. No, I suffered when the police laid hands on him, it threw me into despair. What then *did* I mean? Something perhaps like this: suppose the poet had been wrestled to the ground by the police, strapped into a strait jacket or handcuffed, and rushed off dingdong in a paddy wagon like a mad dog, arriving foul, and locked up raging! Was this art versus America? To me Bellevue was like the Bowery: it gave negative testimony. Brutal Wall Street stood for power, and the Bowery, so near it, was the accusing symbol of weakness. And so with Bellevue, where the poor and busted went. And so even with Payne Whitney where the monied derelicts lay. And poets like drunkards and misfits or psychopaths, like the wretched, poor or rich, sank into weakness—was that it? Having no machines, no transforming knowledge comparable to the knowledge of Boeing or Sperry Rand or IBM or RCA? For could a poem pick you up in Chicago and land you in New York two hours later? Or could it compute a space shot? It had no such powers. And interest was where power was. In ancient times poetry was a force, the poet had real strength in the material world. Of course, the material world was different then. But what interest could a Humboldt raise? He threw himself into weakness and became a hero of wretchedness. He consented to the monopoly of power and interest held by money, politics, law, rationality, technology because he couldn't find the next thing, the new thing, the necessary thing for poets to do. Instead he did a former thing. He got himself a pistol, like Verlaine, and chased Magnasco.

From Bellevue he phoned me at the Belasco Theatre. I heard his voice shaking, raging but rapid. He yelled, "Charlie, you know where I am, don't you? All right, Charlie, this isn't literature. This is life."

In the theater I was in the world of illusion while he, Humboldt, had broken out—was that it?

But no, instead of being a poet he was merely the figure of a poet. He was enacting "The Agony of the American Artist." And it was not Humboldt, it was the USA that was making its point: "Fellow Americans, listen. If you abandon materialism and the normal pursuits of life you wind up at Bellevue like this poor kook."

He now held court and made mad-scenes at Bellevue. He openly blamed me. Scandal-lovers were tisking when my name was mentioned.

Then Scaccia the private eye came to the Belasco with a note from Humboldt. He wanted the money I had raised and wanted it right now. So Mr. Scaccia and I faced each other in the gloomy musty cement exit alley outside the stage door. Mr. Scaccia wore open sandals and white silk socks, very soiled. At the corners of his mouth was a grimy deposit.

"The fund is held in escrow by a lawyer, Mr. Simkin, on Fifth Avenue. It's for medical expenses only," I said.

"You mean psychiatric. You think Mr. Fleisher is off his nut?"

"I don't make diagnoses. Just tell Humboldt to talk to Simkin."

"We're speaking of a man of genius. Who says a genius needs treatment?"

"You've read his poems?" I said.

"Fucking right. I won't take a put-down from you. You're supposed to be his friend? The man loves you. He loves you still. Do you love him?"

"And where do you come in?"

"I'm retained by him. And for a client I go all out."

If I didn't give the private eye the money he would go to Bellevue and tell Humboldt that I thought he was insane. My impulse was to kill Scaccia in this back alley. Natural justice was on my side. I could grab this blackmailer by the throat and strangle him. O, that would be delicious! And who could blame me! A gust of murderous feeling made me look modestly at the ground. "Mr. Fleisher will have to explain to Simkin what he wants the money for," I said. "It wasn't raised for you."

After this there came a series of calls from Humboldt. "The cops put me in a strait jacket. Did you have anything to do with that? My blood-brother? They manhandled me, too, you fucking Thomas Hobbes!"

I understand the reference. He meant that I cared only for power.

"I'm trying to help," I said. He hung up. Immediately the phone rang again.

"Where's Kathleen?" he said.

"I don't know."

"She talked to you out by the clothesline. You know where she is all right. Listen to me, handsome, you're sitting on this money. It's mine. You want to put me away with the little guys in the white coats?"

"You need calming down, that's all."

He called later in the day when the afternoon was gray and hot. I was having a tinny-tasting sandwich of crumbling wet tuna fish at the Greek's across the street when they summoned me to the telephone. I took the call in the star's dressing room.

"I've talked to a lawyer," shouted Humboldt. "I'm prepared to sue you for that money. You're a crook. You're a traitor, a liar, a phony, and a Judas. You had me locked up while that whore Kathleen was going to orgies. I'm charging you with embezzlement."

"Humboldt, I only helped to raise that money. I haven't got it. It's not in my hands."

"Tell me where Kathleen is and I'll call off my suit."

"She didn't tell me where she was going."

"You've broken your oath to me, Citrine. And now you want to put me away. You envy me. You always envied me. I'll put you in jail if I can. I want you to know what it's like when the police come for you, and what a strait jacket is like." Then, bam! he hung up, and I sat sweating in the star's grimy dressing room, the rotten tuna salad coming up on me, and a green ptomaine sensation, a cramp, a very sore spot in my side. Actors were trying on costumes that day and passed the door in their knickers, dresses, and cocked hats. I desired help but I felt like an arctic survivor in a small boat, an Amundsen hailing ships on the horizon which turned out to be icebergs. Trenck and Lieutenant Schell passed with their rapiers and wigs. They couldn't tell me that I was *not* an obvious phony, a crook, and a Judas. I couldn't tell them what I thought was really wrong with me: namely that I suffered from an illusion, perhaps a marvelous illusion, or perhaps only a lazy one, that by a kind of inspired levitation I could rise and dart straight to the truth. Straight to the truth. For I was too haughty to bother with Marxism, Freudianism, Modernism, the avant-garde, or any of these things that Humboldt, as a culture-Jew, took so much stock in.

"I'm going to the hospital to see him," I told Demmie.

"You are not. That's the worst thing you can do."

"But look at the state he's in. I've got to go there, Demmie."

"I won't allow it. He'll attack you. I couldn't bear for you to fight, Charlie. He'll hit you, and he's twice your size and crazy and strong. Besides, I won't have you disturbed when you're doing the play. Listen," she deepened her voice, "I'll take care of it. I'll go there myself. And I forbid you."

She never actually got to see him. Dozens of people were in the act by now. The drama at Bellevue drew crowds from Greenwich Village and Morningside Heights. I compared them to the residents of Washington who drove out in carriages to watch the Battle of Bull Run and then got in the way of the Union troops. Since I was no longer his blood-brother, bearded stammering Orlando Huggins became Humboldt's chief friend. Huggins obtained Humboldt's release. Then Humboldt went to Mount Sinai Hospital and signed himself in. Acting on my instructions, lawyer Simkin paid a week in advance for his private care. However, Humboldt checked out again on the very next day and collected from the hospital an unused balance of about eight hundred dollars. Out of this he paid Scaccia's latest bill. Then he started legal actions against Kathleen, against Magnasco, against the Police Department, and against Bellevue. He continued to threaten me but didn't actually file suit. He was waiting to see whether *Von Trenck* would make money.

I was still at the primer level in my understanding of money. I didn't know that there were many people, persistent ingenious passionate people, to whom it was perfectly obvious that *they* should have all your money. Humboldt had the conviction that there was wealth in the world—not his—to which he had a sovereign claim and that he was bound to get it. He had told me once that he was fated to win a big lawsuit, a million-dollar suit. "With a million bucks," he said, "I'll be free to think of nothing but poetry."

"How will this happen?"

"Somebody will wrong me."

"Wrong you a million dollars' worth?"

"If I'm obsessed by money, as a poet shouldn't be, there's a reason for it," was what Humboldt had told me. "The reason is that we're Americans after all. What kind of American would I be if I were innocent about money, I ask you? Things have to be combined as Wallace Stevens combined them. Who says 'Money is the root of evils'? Isn't it the Pardoner? Well the Pardoner is the most evil man in Chaucer. No, I go along with Horace Walpole. Walpole said it was natural for free men to think about money. Why? Because money *is* freedom, that's why."

In the enchanting days we had had such marvelous talks, only touched a little by manic depression and paranoia. But now the light became dark and the dark turned darker.

Still reclining, holding tight on my padded sofa, I saw those gaudy weeks in review.

Humboldt riotously picketed *Von Trenck* but the play was a hit. To be closer to the Belasco and my celebrity, I took a suite at the St. Regis. The *art nouveau* elevators had gilded gates. Demmie taught Virgil. Kathleen played blackjack in Nevada. Humboldt had returned to his command post at the White Horse Tavern. There he held literary, artistic, erotic, and philosophic exercises till far into the night. He coined a new epigram which was reported to me uptown: "I never yet touched a fig leaf that didn't turn into a price tag." This gave me hope. He could still get off a good wisecrack. It sounded as if normalcy might be returning.

But no. Each day Humboldt gave himself a perfunctory shave, drank coffee, took pills, studied his notes, and went to midtown to see his lawyers. He had lots of lawyers—he collected lawyers and psychoanalysts. Treatment was not the object of his visits with the analysts. He wanted to talk, to express himself. The theoretical climate of their offices stimulated him. As to lawyers, he had them all preparing papers and discussing strategies. Lawyers didn't often meet writers. How was any lawyer to know what was going on? A famous poet calls for an appointment. Referred by so-and-so. The entire office is excited, the typists put on make-up. Then the poet arrives, stout and ill but still handsome pale hurt-looking terrifically agitated, timid in a way, and with strikingly small gestures or tremors for such a large man. Even seated he has leg tremors, his body is vibrating. At first the voice is from another world. Trying to smile, the man can only wince. Odd small stained teeth control a trembling lip. Although thickset, really a big bruiser, he is also a delicate plant, an Ariel, and so on. Can't make a fist. Never heard of aggression. And he unfolds a tale—you'd think it was Hamlet's father: fraud, deceit, betrayal of pledges; finally, as he slept in his garden, someone crept up with a vial and tried to pour stuff into his ear. At first he refuses to name his false friends and would-be murderers. They are only X and Y. Then he refers to "This Person." "I went along with this X-Person," he says. In his innocence he entered into agreements, exchanged promises with X, this Claudius Person. He said yes to everything. He signed a paper without reading it, about joint tenancy of the New Jersey house. He was also disappointed in a blood-brother who turned fink. Shakespeare was right, There's no art to find the mind's construction in the face: he was a gentleman on whom I built an absolute trust. But now recovering from shock he's building a case against the said gentleman. Building cases is one of the master preoccupations of human beings. He has Citrine dead to rights—Citrine grabbed his money. But restitution is all he asks. And he fights, or seems to fight, the rising fury. This Citrine is a deceptively handsome fellow. But Jakob Boehme was wrong, the outer is not the inner visible. Humboldt says he is struggling for decency. His father had no friends, he has no friends—so much for the human material. Fidelity is for phonographs. But let's be restrained. Not all turn into poisoned rats biting one another. "I don't want to hurt the son of a bitch. All I want is justice." Justice! He wanted the fellow's guts in a shopping bag.

Yes, he spent much time with lawyers and doctors. Lawyers and doctors would best appreciate the drama of wrongs and the drama of sickness. He didn't want to be a poet now. Symbolism, his school, was used up. No, at this time he was a performing artist who was being *real*. Back to direct experience. Into the wide world. No more art-substitute for real life. Lawsuits and psychoanalysis were real.

As for the lawyers and the shrinkers, they were delighted with him not because he represented the real world but because he was a poet. He didn't pay—he threw the bills out. But these people, curious about genius (which they had learned from Freud and from movies like *Moulin Rouge* or *The Moon and Sixpence* to esteem), were hungry for culture. They listened with joy as he told his tale of unhappiness and persecution. He spilled dirt, spread scandal, and uttered powerful metaphors. What a combination! Fame gossip delusion filth and poetic invention.

Even then shrewd Humboldt knew what he was worth in professional New York. Endless conveyor belts of sickness or litigation poured clients and patients into these midtown offices

like dreary Long Island potatoes. These dull spuds crushed psychoanalysts' hearts with boring character problems. Then suddenly Humboldt arrived. Oh, Humboldt! He was no potato.
He was a papaya a citron a passion fruit. He was beautiful
deep eloquent fragrant original—even when he looked bruised
in the face, hacked under the eyes, half-destroyed. And what
a repertory he had, what changes of style and tempo. He was
meek at first—shy. Then he became childlike, trusting, then
he confided. He knew, he said, what husbands and wives said
when they quarreled, bickerings so important to them and so
tiresome to everyone else. People said ho-hum and looked at
the ceiling when you started this. Americans! with their stupid
ideas about love, and their domestic tragedies. How could you
bear to listen to them after the worst of wars and the most
sweeping of revolutions, the destruction, the death camps, the
earth soaked in blood and fumes of cremation still in the air of
Europe. What did the personal troubles of Americans amount
to? Did they really suffer? The world looked into American
faces and said, "Don't tell me these cheerful well-to-do people
are suffering!" Still, democratic abundance had its own peculiar difficulties. America was God's experiment. Many of the
old pains of mankind were removed, which made the new
pains all the more peculiar and mysterious. America didn't like
special values. It detested people who represented these special
values. And yet, *without* these special values—you see what I
mean, said Humboldt. Mankind's old greatness was created in
scarcity. But what may we expect from plenitude? In Wagner
the giant Fafnir—or is it a dragon?—sleeps on a magical ring.
Is America sleeping, then, and dreaming of equal justice and
of love? Anyway, I'm not here to discuss adolescent American love-myths—this was how Humboldt talked. Still, he said,
I'd like you to listen to this. Then he began to narrate in his
original style. He described and intricately embroidered. He
worked in Milton on divorce and John Stuart Mill on women.
After this came disclosure, confession. Then he accused, fulmi-
nated, stammered, blazed, cried out. He crossed the universe
like light. He struck off X-ray films of the true facts. Weakness,
lies, treason, shameful perversion, crazy lust, the viciousness of

certain billionaires (names were named). The truth! And all of
this melodrama of impurity, all these erect and crimson nipples,
bared teeth, howls, ejaculations! The lawyers had heard this
thousands of times but they wanted to hear it again, from a
man of genius. Had he become their pornographer?

Ah Humboldt had been great—handsome, high-spirited,
buoyant, ingenious, electrical, noble. To be with him made
you feel the sweetness of life. We used to discuss the loftiest
things—what Diotima said to Socrates about love, what Spinoza meant by the *amor dei intellectualis*. To talk to him was
sustaining, nourishing. But I used to think, when he mentioned
people who had been his friends, that it could be only a question of time before I too was dropped. He had no old friends,
only ex-friends. He could become terrible, going into reverse
without warning. When this happened, it was like being caught
in a tunnel by the Express. You could only cling to the walls, or
lie between the rails, praying.

To meditate, and work your way behind the appearances,
you have to be calm. I didn't feel calm after this summary
of Humboldt, but thought of something he himself liked to
mention when he was in a good humor and we were finishing
dinner, a scramble of dishes and bottles between us. The late
philosopher Morris R. Cohen of CCNY was asked by a student
in the metaphysics course, "Professor Cohen, how do I know
that I exist?" The keen old prof replied, "And *who* is asking?"

I directed this against myself. After entering so deeply into
Humboldt's character and career it was only right that I should
take a deeper look also at myself, not judge a dead man who
could alter nothing but keep step with him, mortal by mortal,
if you know what I mean. I mean that I loved him. Very well,
then, *Von Trenck* was a triumph (I shrank from the shame of
it) and I was a celebrity. Humboldt now was only a crazy sans-
culotte picketing drunkenly with a mercurochrome sign while
malicious pals cheered. At the White Horse on Hudson Street,
Humboldt won hands down. But the name in the papers, the
name that Humboldt stifling with envy saw in Leonard Lyons's
column, was Citrine. It was my turn to be famous and to make
money, to get heavy mail, to be recognized by influential people,

to be dined at Sardi's and propositioned in padded booths by
women who sprayed themselves with musk, to buy Sea Island
cotton underpants and leather luggage, to live through the
intolerable excitement of vindication. (I was right all along!) I
experienced the high voltage of publicity. It was like picking up
a dangerous wire fatal to ordinary folk. It was like the rattle-
snakes handled by hillbillies in a state of religious exaltation.

Demmie Vonghel who had coached me all along steered me
now, acting as my trainer, my manager, my cook, my lover,
and my straw boss. She had her work cut out for her and was
terribly busy. She wouldn't let me see Humboldt at Bellevue.
We quarreled over it. She needed a little help with all this and
felt it would be a good idea for me to consult a psychiatrist
also. She said, "To look as collected as you look when I know
you're falling apart and dying of excitement just isn't good."
She sent me to a man named Ellenbogen, a celebrity himself,
appearing on many talk shows, the author of liberating books
on sex. Ellenbogen's dry lean long face had big grinning sin-
ews, redskin cheekbones, teeth like the screaming horse in
Picasso's *Guernica*. He hit a patient hard in order to free him.
The rationality of pleasure was his ideological hammer. He was
tough, New York tough, but he smiled, and how it all added
up he told you with New York emphasis. Our span is short
and we must make up for the shortness of the human day in
frequent, intense sexual gratification. He was never sore, never
offended, he repudiated rage and aggression, the bondage of
conscience, etcetera. All such things were bad for copulation.
Bronze figurines of amatory couples were his bookends. The
air in his office was close. Dark paneling, the comfort of deep
leather. During sessions he lay fully extended, shoeless feet on
a hassock, his long hand under his waistband. Was he fondling
his own parts? Utterly relaxed he released a lot of gas which
dissolved and impregnated the confined air. His plants anyway
thrived on it.

He lectured me as follows: "You are a guilty anxious man.
Depressive. An ant longing to be a grasshopper. Can't bear success. Melancholia, I'd say, interrupted by fits of humor. Women
must be chasing you. Wish I had your opportunities. Actresses.

Well, give the women a chance to give you pleasure, that's really what they want. To them the act itself is far less important than the occasion of tenderness." Perhaps to increase my self-confidence he told me of his own wonderful experiences. A woman in the Deep South had seen him on television and came straight north to be laid by him, and when she got what she came for said with a sigh of luxury, "When I saw you on the box I knew you'd be good. And you *are* good." Ellenbogen was no friend of Demmie Vonghel when he heard of her ways. He sucked sharply and said, "Bad, a bad case. Poor kid. Pushing to get married, I bet. Development immature. A pretty baby. And weighed three hundred pounds when she was thirteen. One of those greedy parties. Domineering. She'll swallow you."

Demmie was unaware that she had sent me to the enemy. She said daily, "We must get married, Charlie," and she planned a big church wedding. Fundamentalist Demmie became an Episcopalian in New York. She talked to me about a wedding dress and veil, calla lilies, ushers, photographs, engraved announcements, morning coats. As best man and maid of honor she wanted the Littlewoods. I never had told her of the wingding Eskimo-style private party Littlewood had proposed to me in Princeton saying, "We can have a good show, Charlie." Demmie, if I had told her, would have been vexed with Littlewood rather than shocked. By now she had fitted herself into New York. The miraculous survival of goodness was the theme of her life. Dangerous navigation, monsters attracted by her boundless female magnetism—spells charms prayers divine protection secured by inner strength and purity of heart—this was how she saw things. Hell breathed from doorways over her feet as she passed, but she did pass safely. Boxes of pills still came in the mail from the home-town pharmacy. The delivery kid from Seventh Avenue came more and more and more often with bottles of Johnnie Walker Black Label. She drank the best. After all, she was an heiress. Mount Coptic belonged to her Daddy. She was a Fundamentalist princess who liked to drink. After a few highballs Demmie was grander, statelier, her eyes great circles of blue, her love stronger. She growled in Louis Armstrong style, "You are mah man." Then she said in earnest,

"I love you with my heart. No other man better try and touch me." When she made a fist it was surprisingly big.

Attempts to touch were often made. Her dentist as he worked on her fillings took her hand and placed it on what she assumed to be the armrest of the chair. It was no such thing. It was his excited member. Her physician concluded an examination by kissing her violently wherever he could reach. "I can't say that I blame the man for being carried away, Demmie. You have a bottom like a white valentine greeting."

"I punched him right in the neck," she said.

On a warm day when the air conditioning had broken down, her psychiatrist said to her, "Why don't you take off your dress, Miss Vonghel." A millionaire host on Long Island spoke through the ventilator of his bathroom into hers. "I need you. Give me your bod . . ." He said in a choking perishing voice, "Give me! I am dying. Save, save . . . save me!" And this was a burly strong jolly man who piloted his own airplane.

Sexual ideas had distorted the minds of people who were under oath, who were virtually priests. Were you inclined to believe that mania and crime and catastrophe were the destiny of mankind in this vile century? Demmie by her innocence, by beauty and virtue, drew masses of evidence from the environment to support this. A strange demonism revealed itself to her. But she was not intimidated. She told me that she was sexually fearless. "And they've tried to pull everything on me," she said. I believed her.

Dr. Ellenbogen said that she was a bad marriage-risk. He was not amused by the anecdotes I related about Mother and Daddy Vonghel. The Vonghels had made a bus tour of the Holy Land, obese Mother Vonghel bringing her own peanut-butter jars and Daddy his cans of Elberta cling peaches. Mother squeezed into the tomb of Lazarus but could not get out again. Arabs had to be sent for to free her. But I was delighted, despite Ellenbogen's warnings, with the oddities of Demmie and her family. When she lay suffering, her deep eye sockets filled with tears and she gripped the middle finger of her left hand convulsively with the other fingers. She was strongly drawn to sickbeds, hospitals, terminal cancers, and funerals. But her goodness was genuine and deep. She bought me postage stamps and commuter tickets, she cooked briskets of beef and pots of *paella* for me, lined my dresser drawers with tissue paper, put away my scarf in moth-flakes. She couldn't do elementary arithmetic but she could repair complicated machines. Guided by instinct she went into the colored wires and tubes of the radio and made it play. It seldom stopped broadcasting hillbilly music and religious services from everywhere. She received from home *The Upper Room, A Devotional Guide for Family and Individual Use,* with its Thought of the Month: "Christ's Renewing Power." Or "Read and consider: Habakkuk 2:2–4." I read this publication myself. The Song of Solomon 8:7: "Many waters cannot quench love, neither can the floods drown it." I loved her clumsy knuckles, her long head growing gold hair. We sat on Barrow Street playing gin rummy. She gripped and shuffled the deck, growling, "I'm going to clean you out, sucker." She snapped down the cards and shouted, "Gin! Count 'em up!" Her knees were apart.

"It's the open view of Shangri-La that takes my mind off these cards, Demmie," I said.

We also played double solitaire hearts and Chinese checkers. She led me to antique-jewelry shops. She loved old brooches and rings all the more because dead ladies once had worn them, but what she mostly wanted of course was an engagement ring. She made no secret of that. "Buy me this ring, Charlie. Then I can show my family that it's on the up-and-up."

"They won't like me no matter how big an opal you get," I said.

"No, that's true. They'll hit the roof. There's all kinds of sin in you. They wouldn't be impressed by Broadway. You write things that aren't so. Only the Bible is true. But Daddy is flying down to South America to spend Christmas at his Mission. The one he's such a big giver to, down in Colombia, near Venezuela. I'm going with him and tell him that we're getting married."

"Ah, don't go, Demmie," I said.

"Down in that jungle with savages all around you'll seem a lot more normal to him," she said.

"Tell him what I'm making. The money should help do it

all," I said. "But I don't want you to go. Is your mother coming too?"

"Not here. I couldn't take that. No, she's staying back in Mount Coptic, giving a Christmas party for the kids in the hospital. *They'll* be sorry."

These meditations were supposed to make you tranquil. To look behind the appearances you had to cultivate an absolute calm. And I didn't feel very calm now. The heavy shadow of a jet from Midway airport crossed the room, reminding me of the death of Demmie Vonghel. Just before Christmas in the year of my success she and Daddy Vonghel died in a plane crash in South America. Demmie was carrying my Broadway scrapbook. Perhaps she had just begun to show it to him when the crash occurred. No one ever knew quite where this was— somewhere in the vicinity of the Orinoco River. I spent several months in the jungle looking for her.

It was at this time that Humboldt put through the blood-brother check I had given him. Six thousand seven hundred and sixty-three dollars and fifty-eight cents was a smashing sum. But it wasn't the money that mattered much. What I felt was that Humboldt should have respected my grief. I thought, What a time he chose to make his move! How could he do that! To hell with the money. But he reads the papers. He knows she's gone!

• • •

I now lay there grieving. Again! This wasn't what I was looking for when I lay down. And I was actually grateful when a brassy hammering at the door made me get up. It was Cantabile on the knocker, forcing his way into my sanctuary. I was annoyed with old Roland Stiles. I paid Stiles to keep intruders and pests away while I was meditating but he wasn't at his post in the receiving room today. Just before Christmas tenants wanted help with trees and such. He was much in demand, I suppose.

Cantabile had brought a young woman with him.

"Your wife, I presume?"

"Don't presume. She's not my wife. This is Polly Palomino.

She's a friend. Of the family, she's a friend. She was Lucy's roommate at the Woman's College in Greensboro. Before Radcliffe."

White-skinned, wearing no brassiere, Polly entered the light and began strolling about my parlor. The red of her hair was entirely natural. Stockingless (in December, in Chicago), minimally dressed, she walked on platform shoes of maximum thickness. Men of my generation never have gotten used to the strength, size, and beauty of women's legs, formerly covered up.

Cantabile and Polly examined my flat. He touched the furniture, she stooped to feel the carpet, turning over a corner to read the label. Yes, it was a genuine Kirman. She studied the pictures. Cantabile then sat down on the silky plush bolstered sofa, saying, "*This* is whorehouse luxury."

"Don't make yourself too comfortable. I have to go to court."

Cantabile said to Polly, "Charlie's ex-wife goes on suing and suing him."

"For what?"

"For everything. You've given her a lot already, Charlie?"

"A lot."

"He's shy. He's ashamed to say how much," Cantabile told Polly.

I said to Polly, "Apparently I told Rinaldo the whole story of my life at a poker game."

"Polly knows it. I told her about yesterday. You did most of the talking after the poker game." He turned toward Polly. "Charlie was too smashed to drive his 280-SL so I took him home and Emil brought the T-bird. You told me plenty, Charlie. Where do you get these fancy goose-quill toothpicks? They're scattered all over. You seem very neurotic about having crumbs between your teeth."

"They're sent from London."

"Like your cashmere socks, and your face soap from Floris?"

Yes, I must have been eager to talk. I had given Cantabile plenty of information and he had made extensive inquiries

besides, obviously intending to develop a relationship with me.
"Why do you let your Ex bug you like this? And you have
a lousy big-shot lawyer. Forrest Tomchek. You see I asked
around. Tomchek is top-drawer in the divorce-establishment.
He divorces corporation biggies. But you're nothing to him. It
was your pal Szathmar who put you on to this prick, isn't that
right? Now, who is your wife's lawyer?"

"A fellow named Maxie Pinsker."

"Yiy! Pinsker, that man-eating kike! She's picked the worst
there is. He'll chop up your liver with egg and onion. Yuch,
Charlie! this side of your life is disgusting. You refuse to be
alert about your interests. You let people dump on you. It starts
with your pals. I know something about your friend Szathmar.
Nobody asks you to dinner, they invite him and he puts on
his louse-up Charlie routine. He feeds confidential information
about you to gossip columnists. Always kissing Schneiderman's
ass, which is so low to the ground you have to stand in a foxhole
to reach it. He'll get a kickback from Tomchek. Tomchek will
sell you to that cannibal Pinsker. Pinsker will throw you to the
judge. The judge will give your wife . . . what's her name?"

"Denise," I said, habitually helpful.

"He'll give Denise your skin and she'll hang it in the den.—
Well, Polly, does Charles look like Charles is supposed to
look?"

Of course Cantabile couldn't bear his elation. Last night he
naturally had to tell someone what he had done. As Humboldt
after his triumph with Longstaff ran straight to the Village to
get on top of Ginnie so Cantabile had roared off in his Thunderbird to spend the night with Polly, to celebrate his triumph
and my abasement. It made me think what a tremendous force
the desire to be interesting has in the democratic USA. This is
why Americans can't keep secrets. In WWII we were the despair
of the British because we couldn't shut our mouths. Luckily the
Germans couldn't believe we were so gabby. They figured we
were deliberately leaking false information. And it's all done to
prove that we're not so tedious as we seem but are running over
with charm and inside information. So I said to myself, Okay,
be elated, you mink-mustached bastard. Brag about what you

did to me and the 280-SL. I'll catch up with you. At the same time I was glad that Renata was taking me away, forcing me to go abroad again. Renata had the right idea. For Cantabile obviously was making plans for our future. I wasn't at all sure that I could defend myself from his singular attack.

Polly was considering how to answer Cantabile's question and he himself, pale and handsome, was studying me almost with affection. Still buttoned in the raglan coat and wearing the pinch hat, his beautiful boots on my Chinese lacquer coffee table, he was dark-bristled and wore a look of fatigue and satisfaction. He was not fresh now, he was smelly, but he was flying high.

"I think Mr. Citrine is still a good-looking man," Polly said.

"Thank you, dear girl."

"He must have been. Slim but solid, with big Oriental eyes and probably a thick dick. Now he's a faded beauty," said Cantabile. "I know it's killing him. He's losing the clean jawline. Notice the dewlaps and the neck wrinkles. His nostrils are getting big and hungry-like, and they have white hair. It's a sign with beagles and horses too, turning white around the muzzle. Oh, he's unusual all right. A rare animal. Like the last of the orange flamingos. He should be protected as a national resource. And a sexy little bastard. He's slept with everything under the sun. Awfully vain, too. Charlie and his pal George jog and train like a couple of adolescent jocks. They stand on their heads, take vitamin E, and play racquet ball. Though they tell me you're a dog on the courts, Charlie."

"It's a bit late for the Olympics."

"He has a sedentary trade and needs the exercise," said Polly. She had a slightly bent nose as well as the fresh, shining red hair. I was growing fond of her—disinterestedly, for her human qualities.

"The main reason for all the fitness is that he has a young broad, and young broads, unless they have a terrific sense of humor, don't like being squeezed by a potbelly."

I explained to Polly, "I exercise because I suffer from an arthritic neck. Or did. As I grew older my head seemed to become heavier, my neck weaker."

The strain was largely at the top. In the crow's-nest from which the modern autonomous person keeps watch. But of course Cantabile was right. I was vain, and I hadn't reached the age of renunciation. Whatever that is. It wasn't entirely vanity, though. Lack of exercise made me feel ill. I used to hope that there would be less energy available to my neuroses as I grew older. Tolstoi thought that people got into trouble because they ate steak and drank vodka and coffee and smoked cigars. Overcharged with calories and stimulants and doing no useful labor they fell into carnality and other sins. At this point I always remembered that Hitler had been a vegetarian, so it wasn't necessarily the meat that was to blame. Heart-energy, more likely, or a wicked soul, maybe even karma—paying for the evil of a past life in this one. According to Steiner, whom I was now reading heavily, the spirit learns from resistance—the material body resists and opposes it. In the process the body wears out. But I had not gotten good value for my deterioration. Seeing me with my young daughters, silly people sometimes asked if these were my grandchildren. Me! Was it possible! And I saw that I was getting that look of a badly stuffed trophy or mounted specimen that I always associated with age, and was horrified. Also I recognized from photographs that I wasn't the man I had been. I should have been able to say, "Yes, maybe I do seem about to cave in but you should see my spiritual balance sheet." But as yet I was in no position to say that, either. I look better than the dead, of course, but at times only just.

I said, "Well, thanks for dropping in, Mrs. Palomino. You'll have to excuse me, though. I'm being called for and I haven't shaved or eaten lunch."

"How do you shave, electric or steel?"

"Remington."

"The electric Abercrombie & Fitch is the only machine. I think I'll shave, too. And what's for lunch?"

"I'm having yoghurt. But I can't offer you any."

"We've just eaten. Plain yoghurt? Do you put anything in it? What about a hard-boiled egg? Polly will boil you an egg. Polly, go in the kitchen and boil Charlie an egg. How did you say you were getting downtown?"

"I'm being called for."

"Don't be upset about the Mercedes. I'll get you three 280-SLs. You're too big a man to hold a mere car against me. Things are going to be different. Look, why don't we meet after court and have a drink? You'll need it. Besides, you should talk more. You listen too much. It's not good for you."

He relaxed even more conspicuously, supporting both arms on the round back of the sofa as if to show that he was not a man I could shoo out. He wished also to transmit a sense of luxurious intimacy with pretty and fully gratified Polly. I had my doubts about that. "This kind of life is very bad for you," he said. "I've seen guys come out of solitary confinement and I know the signs. Why do you live South, surrounded by the slums? Is it because you have egghead friends on the Midway? You spoke about this Professor Richard What's-His-Face."

"Durnwald."

"That's the man. But you also told how some pork-chop chased you down the middle of the street. You should rent near-North in a high-security building with an underground garage. Or are you here because of these professors' wives? The Hyde Park ladies are easy to knock over." Then he said, "Do you own a gun at least?"

"No I don't."

"Christ, here's another example of what I mean. All you people are soft about the realities. This is a Fort Dearborn situation, don't you know that? And only the redskins have the guns and tomahawks. Did you read about the cabbie's face last week, blown off with a shotgun? It'll take a year for plastic surgery to rebuild. Don't you want revenge when you hear about that? Or have you really become so flattened out? If you have, then I don't see how your sex life can be any good either! Don't tell me you wouldn't be thrilled to waste the buffalo that chased you—just turning around and shooting him through the fucking head. If I give you a gun, will you carry it? No? You liberal Jesuses are disgusting. You'll go downtown today and it'll be more of the same with this Forrest Tomchek and this Cannibal Pinsker. They'll eat your ass. But you tell yourself they're gross, while you have class. You want a gun?" He thrust his quick hand under the raglan. "Here's a gun."

I had a weakness for characters like Cantabile. It was no accident that the Baron Von Trenck of my Broadway hit, the source of the movie-sale money—the blood-scent that attracted the sharks of Chicago who were now waiting for me downtown—had also been demonstrative exuberant impulsive destructive and wrong-headed. This type, the impulsive–wrong-headed, was now making it with the middle class. Rinaldo was ticking me off for my decadence. Damaged instincts. I wouldn't defend myself. His ideas probably went back to Sorel (acts of exalted violence by dedicated ideologists to shock the bourgeoisie and regenerate its dying nerve). Although he didn't know who Sorel was, these theories do get around and find people to exemplify them—highjackers, kidnapers, political terrorists who murder hostages or fire into crowds, the Arafats one reads of in the papers and sees on television. Cantabile was manifesting these tendencies in Chicago, wildly exalting some human principle—he knew not what. In my own fashion I myself knew not what. Why was it that I enjoyed no relations with anyone of my own mental level? I was attracted instead by these noisy bumptious types. They did something for me. Maybe this was in part a phenomenon of modern capitalist society with its commitment to personal freedom for all, ready to sympathize with and even to subsidize the mortal enemies of the leading class, as Schumpeter says, actively sympathetic with real or faked suffering, ready to accept peculiar character-distortions and burdens. It was true that people felt it gave them moral distinction to be patient with criminals and psychopaths. To understand! We love to understand, to have compassion! And there I was. As for the broad masses, millions of people born poor now had houses and power tools and other appliances and conveniences and they endured the social turbulence, lying low, hanging on to their worldly goods. Their hearts were angry but they put up with the disorders and formed no mobs in the streets. They took all the abuse, doggedly waiting it out. No rocking the boat. Apparently I shared in their condition. But I couldn't see what good it would do me to fire a gun. As if I could shoot my way out of my perplexities—the chief perplexity being my character!

Cantabile had invested much boldness and ingenuity in me and now he seemed to feel that we must never part. Also he wanted me to draw him upward, to lead him to higher things. He had reached the stage reached by bums, con men, freeloaders, and criminals in France in the eighteenth century, the stage of the intellectual creative man and theorist. Maybe he thought he was Rameau's nephew or even Jean Genet. I didn't see this as the wave of the future. I wanted no part of it. In creating Von Trenck of course I had contributed my share to this. On the *Late Late Show* Von Trenck was still often seen fighting duels, escaping from prison, seducing women, lying and bragging, trying to set fire to his brother-in-law's villa. Yes, I had done my bit. Possibly, too, I continually gave hints of a new interest in higher things, of a desire to advance in the spirit, so that it was only fair that Cantabile should ask me to tell him something of this, to share with him, to give him a hint at least. He was here to do me good, he told me. He was eager to help me. "I can put you into a good thing," he said. He began to describe some of his enterprises to me. He had money in this and money in that. He was president of a charter-flight company, perhaps one of those that had stranded thousands of people in Europe last summer. He had also a little abortion-referral racket and advertised in college newspapers all over the country as a disinterested friend. *"Call us if this misfortune occurs. We will advise and help free of charge."* This was quite accurate, said Cantabile. There was no charge but the doctors kicked back a percentage of the fee. It was normal business.

Polly did not seem bothered by this. I thought her far too good for Cantabile. But then in every couple there is a contrast-gainer. I could see that he amused Polly, with her white skin, red hair, fine legs. That was why she was with him. He really amused her. For his part he pushed me to admire her. He also boasted about his wife's education—what an achiever she was—and he showed me off to Polly. He was proud of us all. "Watch Charlie's mouth," he told Polly. "You'll notice that it

moves even when he isn't talking. That's because he's thinking. He thinks all the time. Here, I'll show you what I mean."
He grabbed up a book, the biggest on the table. "Take this
monster—*The Hastings Encyclopedia of Religion and Ethics*—
Jesus Christ, what the hell is that! Now Charlie tell us, what
were you reading here?"

"I was checking something about Origen of Alexandria.
Origen's opinion was that the Bible could not be a collection of
mere stories. Did Adam and Eve really hide under a tree while
God walked in the Garden in the cool of the day? Did angels
really climb up and down ladders? Did Satan bring Jesus to
the top of a high mountain and tempt him? Obviously these
tales must have a deeper meaning. What does it mean to say
'God walked'? Does God have feet? This was where the thinkers began to take over, and—"

"Enough, that's enough. Now what's this book say, *The Triumph of the Therapeutic*?"

For reasons of my own I wasn't unwilling to be tested in this
way. I actually did read a great deal. Did I know what I was
reading? We would see. I shut my eyes, reciting, "It says that psy-
chotherapists may become the new spiritual leaders of mankind.
A disaster. Goethe was afraid the modern world might turn into
a hospital. Every citizen unwell. The same point in *Knock* by
Jules Romains. Is hypochondria a creation of the medical profession? According to this author, when culture fails to deal with
the feeling of emptiness and the panic to which man is disposed
(and he does say 'disposed') other agents come forward to put
us together with therapy, with glue, or slogans, or spit, or as that
fellow Gumbein the art critic says, poor wretches are recycled on
the couch. This view is even more pessimistic than the one held
by Dostoevski's Grand Inquisitor who said: mankind is frail,
needs bread, cannot bear freedom but requires miracle, mystery,
and authority. A natural disposition to feelings of emptiness and
panic is worse than that. Much worse. What it really means is
that we human beings are insane. The last institution which con-
trolled such insanity (on this view) was the Church—"

He stopped me again. "Polly, you see what I mean. Now
what's this, *Between Death and Rebirth*?"

"Steiner? A fascinating book about the soul's journey past the gates of death. Different from Plato's myth—"

"Whoa, hold it," said Cantabile, and he pointed out to Polly: "All you have to do is ask him a question and he turns on. Can you see this as an act in a night club? We could book him into Mr. Kelly's."

Polly glanced past him at me with full and reddish-brown eyes and said, "He wouldn't go for that."

"It depends how they sock it to him downtown today. Charlie, I had another idea on the way out here. We could tape you reading some of your essays and articles and rent the tapes to colleges and universities. You'd get a pretty nice little income out of that. Like that piece on Bobby Kennedy which I read at Leavenworth, in *Esquire*. And the thing called 'Homage to Harry Houdini.' But not 'Great Bores of the Modern World.' I couldn't read that at all."

"Well, don't get ahead of yourself, Cantabile," I said.

I was perfectly aware that in business Chicago it was a true sign of love when people wanted to take you into money-making schemes. But I couldn't lay hold of Cantabile in this present mood or get a navigational fix or reading of his spirit, which was streaming all over the place. He was a highly excited and, in that Goethean hospital, a sick citizen. I wasn't perhaps in such great shape myself. It occurred to me that yesterday Cantabile had taken me up to a high place, not exactly to tempt me, but to sail away my fifty-dollar bills. Wasn't he facing a challenge of the imagination now—I mean, how was he going to follow such an act? However, he seemed to feel that yesterday's events had united us in a near-mystical bond. There were Greek words for this—*philia, agape,* and so on (I had heard a famous theologian, Tillich the Toiler, expound their various meanings, so that now I was permanently confused about them). What I mean was that the *philia,* at this particular moment in the career of mankind, expressed itself in American promotional ideas and commercial deals. To this, along the edges, I added my own peculiar embroidery. I elaborated people's motives all too profusely.

I looked at the clock. Renata wouldn't be here for forty

minutes yet. She would arrive fragrant painted fresh and even majestic in one of her large soft hats. I didn't want Cantabile to meet her. For that matter I didn't know that it was such a good idea for her to meet Cantabile. When she looked at a man who interested her she had a slow way of detaching her gaze from him. It didn't mean much. It was only her upbringing. She was schooled in charm by her mama, the Señora. Though I suppose that if you are born with such handsome eyes you work out your own methods. In Renata's method of womanly communication piety and fervor were important. The main point, however, was that Cantabile would see an old guy with a young chick and that he might try, as they say, to get leverage out of this.

I want it to be clear, however, that I speak as a person who had lately received or experienced light. I don't mean "The light." I mean a kind of light-in-the-being, a thing difficult to be precise about, especially in an account like this, where so many cantankerous erroneous silly and delusive objects actions and phenomena are in the foreground. And this light, however it is to be described, was now a real element in me, like the breath of life itself. I had experienced it briefly, but it had lasted long enough to be convincing and also to cause an altogether unreasonable kind of joy. Furthermore, the hysterical, the grotesque about me, the abusive, the unjust, that madness in which I had often been a willing and active participant, the grieving, now had found a contrast. I say "now" but I knew long ago what this light was. Only I seemed to have forgotten that in the first decade of life I knew this light and even knew how to breathe it in. But this early talent or gift or inspiration, given up for the sake of maturity or realism (practicality, self-preservation, the fight for survival), was now edging back. Perhaps the vain nature of ordinary self-preservation had finally become too plain for denial. Preservation for what?

For the moment Cantabile and Polly were not paying a great deal of attention to me. He was explaining to her how a convenient little corporation might be set up to protect my income. He spoke of "estate-planning," with a one-sided grimace. In Spain working-class women give themselves a three-fingered prod in the cheek and twist their faces to denote the highest irony. Cantabile grimaced in the same way. It was a question of keeping assets from the enemy, Denise, and her lawyer, Cannibal Pinsker, and maybe even Judge Urbanovich himself.

"My sources tell me the judge is in the lady's corner. How do we know he isn't on the take? There's plenty of funny business at the crossroads. In Cook County is there anything else? Charlie, have you thought of making a move to the Cayman Islands? That's the new Switzerland, you know. I wouldn't put my dough in Swiss banks. After the Russians have gotten what they want out of us in this détente, they'll make their move into Europe. And you know what'll happen to the dough stashed in Switzerland—all that Vietnam dough and Iranian dough and Greek colonels' and Arab oil dough. No, get yourself an air-conditioned condominium in the Caymans. Lay in a supply of underarm antiperspirant and live happy."

"And where's the dough for this?" said Polly. "Has he got it?"

"That I don't know. But if he has no money why are they peeling his toes downtown? Without an anesthetic? I can put you onto a good thing, Charlie. Buy some contracts in commodity futures. I've cleaned up."

"On paper you have. If this fellow Stronson is straight," Polly said.

"What are you talking about—Stronson? A multimillionaire. Didn't you see his big house in Kenilworth? The marketing degree from the Harvard Business School on his wall? Besides, he's been trading for the Mafia and you know how those fellows resent being took. They alone would keep him in line. But he's completely kosher. He has a seat on the Mid America Commodity Exchange. The twenty Gs I gave him five months ago he doubled for me. I'll bring you his company's literature. Anyway, Charlie only has to lift his hand to make a pile. Don't forget he had a Broadway hit and a big box-office movie, once. Why not again? Look at all this paper lying around. These scripts and shit could be worth plenty. There's probably a gold mine right here, you want to bet? For instance, I know that you and your pal Von Humboldt Fleisher once wrote a movie scenario together."

"Who told you that?"

"My researcher wife."

I laughed at this, quite loudly. A movie scenario!

"You remember it?" said Cantabile.

"Yes, I remember. How did your wife hear of it? From Kathleen ... ?"

"Mrs. Tigler in Nevada. Lucy is in Nevada now interviewing her. Has been for about a week, staying at this Mrs. Tigler's dude ranch. She's running it alone."

"Why, where's Tigler, did he take off?"

"For good, he took off. The guy is dead."

"Dead, is he? She's a widow. Poor Kathleen. She's got no luck, poor woman. I'm sorry about Kathleen."

"She's sentimental about you, too. Lucy told her that I knew you, and she sent you regards. You got any message for her? Lucy and I talk on the telephone every day."

"How did Tigler die?"

"Shot in a hunting accident."

"That figures. He was a sporting man. Used to be a cowboy."

"And a pain in the ass?" said Cantabile.

"Could be."

"You knew him personally, then. Not much regret, hey? All you say is poor Kathleen. Now what about this movie that you and Fleisher wrote?"

"Oh yes, tell us," said Polly. "What was all that about? Two minds like yours, collaborating—wow!"

"It was piffle. Nothing to it. At Princeton we diverted ourselves that way. Simply horseplay."

"Haven't you got a copy of it? You might be the last to know, commercially, what there was in it," said Cantabile.

"Commercially? The Hollywood big-money days are over. No more of those fancy prices."

"That side of it you can leave to me," said Cantabile. "If we have a real property, I'll know how to promote it— director, star, financing, the whole ball of wax. You have a track record, don't forget, and Fleisher's name hasn't been completely forgotten yet. We'll get Lucy's thesis published, and that'll revive it."

"But what was the story?" said Polly, bent-nosed, fragrant, idling her legs.

"I have to shave. I need my lunch. I have to go to court. I'm expecting a friend from California."

"Who's that?" said Cantabile.

"His name is Pierre Thaxter, and we edit a journal together called *The Ark*. It's really none of your business anyway. . . ."

But of course it was his business, because he was a demon, an agent of distraction. His job was to make noise and to deflect and misdirect and send me foundering into bogs.

"Well, tell us a little about the movie," said Cantabile.

"I'll try. Just to see how good my memory is," I said. "The thing started with Amundsen the polar explorer and Umberto Nobile. In Mussolini's time Nobile was an Air Force officer, an engineer, a dirigible commander, a brave man. In the Twenties he and Amundsen headed an expedition over the North Pole, and flew from Norway to Seattle. But they were rivals and came to hate each other. On the next expedition, with Mussolini's backing, Nobile went it alone. Only his lighter-than-air ship crashed in the Arctic and his crew were scattered over the ice floes. When Amundsen heard of this, he said, 'My comrade Umberto Nobile'—whom he detested, mind you—'is down at sea. I shall rescue him.' So he chartered a French plane and filled it with equipment. The pilot warned him it was over-loaded and wouldn't fly. Like Sir Patrick Spens, I remember saying to Humboldt."

"What Spens?"

"Just a poem," Polly told Cantabile. "And Amundsen was the fellow who beat the Scott expedition to the South Pole."

Pleased to have an educated dolly to brief him, Cantabile took the patrician attitude that drudges and bookworms would give him what trifling historical information he needed.

"The French pilot warned him, but Amundsen said, 'Don't teach me how to run a rescue expedition.' So the plane rose from the runway but it fell into the sea. Everyone was killed."

"Is that the picture? But what about the guys on the ice?"

"The men on the ice sent out radio messages and these were picked up by the Russians. An icebreaker named the *Krassin* was sent to find them. It cruised among the floes and rescued two men, an Italian and a Swede. There had been a third survivor— where was he? The explanations given were fishy and the Italian was suspected of cannibalism. The Russian doctor aboard the *Krassin* pumped his stomach and under the microscope he identified human tissue. Well, there was a frightful scandal. A jar containing the contents of this fellow's stomach was put on display in Red Square with a huge sign: "This is how fascist imperialist capitalist dogs devour each other. Only the proletariat knows morality brotherhood and self-sacrifice!"

"What the hell kind of movie would this make," said Cantabile. "So far it's a real dumdum idea."

"I told you."

"Yes, but now you're sore at me, and you're glaring. You think I'm a moron, in your department. I'm not artistic and I'm unfit to have an opinion."

"This is only background," I said. "The picture, as Humboldt and I worked it out, opened in a Sicilian village. The cannibal, whom Humboldt and I called Signor Caldofreddo, is now a kindly old man and sells ice cream, the kids love him, he has an only daughter who's a beauty and a darling. Here nobody remembers the Nobile expedition. But a Danish journalist turns up to interview the old guy. He's writing a book about the *Krassin* rescue. The old man meets him in secret and says, 'Leave me alone. I've been a vegetarian for fifty years. I churn ice cream. I am an old man. Don't disgrace me now. Find a different subject. Life is full of hysterical situations. You don't need mine. Lord, let now thy servant depart in peace.'"

"So the Amundsen and Nobile part of it is worked around this?" said Polly.

"Humboldt admired Preston Sturges. He loved *The Miracle of Morgan's Creek* and also *The Great McGinty*, with Brian Donlevy and Akim Tamiroff, and Humboldt's idea was to work in Mussolini, Stalin, Hitler, and even the Pope."

"How the Pope?" said Cantabile.

"The Pope gave Nobile a large cross to drop on the North Pole. And we saw the movie as a vaudeville and farce but with elements of *Oedipus at Colonus* in it. Violent spectacular sinners in old age acquire magical properties, and when they come to die they have the power to curse and to bless."

"If it's supposed to be funny, leave the Pope out of it," said Cantabile.

"Backed into a corner, the old Caldofreddo flares up. He makes an attempt on the journalist's life. He pries loose a boulder on a mountainside. But then he has a change of heart and throws himself on the rock and fights it till the man's car passes in the road below. After this Caldofreddo blows his ice-cream vendor's bugle in the village square, he summons everyone and makes a public confession to the townspeople. Weeping, he tells them that he's a cannibal. . . ."

"Which punctures his daughter's romance, I suppose," said Polly.

"Just the reverse," I said. "The villagers hold a public hearing. The daughter's young man says, 'Think of what our ancestors ate. As apes, as lower animals, as fishes. Think what animals have eaten since the beginning of time. And we owe our existence to them.'"

"No, it doesn't sound like a winner to me," said Cantabile.

I said it was time to shave, and they both accompanied me to the bathroom.

"No," Cantabile said again. "I don't think it's any good. But have you got a copy of this thing?"

I had started the electric shaver but Cantabile took it from me. He said to Polly, "Don't sit down. Go fix that egg for Charlie's lunch. Go on, now, go to the kitchen." Then he said, "I'll shave first. I don't like to use the machine when it's heated up. The temperature of the other guy upsets me." He ran the buzzing shining machine up and down, pulling at his skin and twisting his face. "She'll fix your lunch. Pretty, isn't she! What do you make of her, Charlie?"

"A stunning girl. Signs of intelligence, too. I see by the left hand that she's married."

"Yes, to a drip who makes TV commercials. He's a hard worker. Never at home. I see a lot of Polly. Every morning when Lucy leaves for her job at Mundelein, Polly arrives and gets in bed with me. I see this makes a bad impression on you. But don't put on with me, you lit up when you saw her, and you've been trying to make a hit with her, showing off. That extra little try. You don't have it when you're among men."

"I admit I like to shine when there are ladies."

He lifted his chin to get at his neck with the razor. The bulb of his pale nose was darkly lined. "Would you like to make it with Polly?" he said.

"I? Is that an abstract question?"

"Nothing abstract. You do things for me, I do things for you. Yesterday I bashed your car, I ran you around town. Now we're on a different basis. I know you're supposed to have a pretty lady friend. But I don't care who she is and what she knows, compared to Polly she's a bush leaguer. Polly makes other girls look sick."

"In that case, I ought to thank you."

"That means you don't want to. You're refusing. Take your razor, I'm finished." He put the warm small machine into my hand with a slap. Then he stood away from the basin and leaned against the bathroom wall with his arms crossed and one foot posed on its toe. He said, "You'd better not reject me."

"Why not?"

His face, the colorless-intense type, filled with pale heat. But he said, "There's a thing the three of us can do together. You lie on your back. She gets on top of you and at the same time goes down on me."

"Let's not have any more filth. Stop it. I can't even visualize this."

"Don't put on with me. Don't be superior." He explained again. "I'm at the head of the bed, standing. You lie down. Polly straddles you, leaning forward to me."

"Stop these disgusting propositions. I want no part of your sexual circuses."

He gave me a bloody-murder look but I couldn't have cared less. There were lots of people ahead of him in the bloody-murder line—Denise and Pinsker, Tomchek and the court, the Internal Revenue Service. "You're no puritan," said Cantabile, sullen. But sensing my mood he changed the subject. "Your friend George Swiebel was talking at the game about a beryllium mine in East Africa—what is this beryllium stuff?"

"It's needed for hard alloys used in space ships. George claims he has friends in Kenya. . . ."

"Oh, he has an inside track with some jungle-bunnies. I bet they all love him. He's so natural healthy and humane. I bet he's a lousy businessman. You'd be better off with Stronson and the commodity futures. There's a real smart guy. I know you can't believe it but I'm trying to help you. They're going to mangle you in court. Haven't you stashed something away? You can't be as dumb as all that. Haven't you got a bagman somewhere?"

"I never thought of one."

"You want me to believe you have nothing in your thoughts except angels on ladders and immortal spirits but I can see from the way you live that it can't be true. First of all you're a dude. I know your tailor. Secondly you're an old sex-pot. . . ."

"Did I talk to you that night about the immortal spirit?"

"You sure as hell did. You said that after it gets through the gates of death—this is a quote—your soul spreads out and looks back at the world. Charlie, I had a thought this morning about you—shut the door. Go on, shut it. Now, listen, we could pretend to kidnap one of your kids. You pay the ransom, and I put the dough away in the Cayman Islands for you."

"Let me see that gun of yours now," I said.

He handed it to me and I pointed it at him. I said, "I'll certainly use this on you if you try any such thing."

"Put that Magnum down. It's only an idea. Don't get all shook up."

I removed the bullets and threw them in the wastepaper basket, handing back the pistol. That he made such suggestions to me was, I recognized, my own fault. The arbitrary can become the pets of the rational. Cantabile seemed to recognize that he was my pet arbitrary. In some sense he played up to this. Maybe it was better to be a pet arbitrary than a mere nut. But *was* I so rational?

"The kidnap idea is too gaudy. You're right," he said. "Well, how about getting to the judge? After all, a county judge has to be put on the ballot for re-election. Judges are in politics, too, and you'd better know it. There are little characters in the Organization who put 'em on and take 'em off the ballot. For thirty or forty Gs, the right guy will call on Judge Urbanovich."

I puffed, and blew the tiny clippings out of the shaver.

"You don't go for that either?"

"No."

"Maybe the other side has already gotten to him. Why be such a gentleman? It's like a kind of paralysis. Absolutely unreal. Behind the glass in the Field Museum, that's where you belong. I believe you got stuck in your childhood. If I said to you, 'Liquidate and go abroad,' what would you answer?"

"I'd say that I wouldn't leave the USA just because of money."

"That's right. You're no Vesco. You love your country. Well, you're not fit to have this money. Maybe the other guys should get it from you. People like the President pretended to be fine clean Americans from *The Saturday Evening Post*. They were boy scouts, they delivered the newspaper at dawn. But they were fakes. The real American is a freak like you, a highbrow Jew from the West Side of Chicago. *You* ought to be in the White House."

"I'm inclined to agree."

"You'd love the Secret Service protection." Cantabile opened the bathroom door to check on Polly. She was not eavesdropping. He shut it again and said, low-voiced, "We could put a contract on your wife. Does she wanna fight? Let her have it. There could be a car accident. She could die in the street. She could be pushed in front of a train, dragged into an alley and stabbed. Crazy buffaloes are doing women in left and right, so who's to know. She's bugging *you* to death—well, how would it be if *she* died? I know you'll say no, and treat it as a joke— Wildass Cantabile, a joker."

"You'd better be joking."

"I'm only reminding you this is Chicago, after all."

"Ninety-eight-percent nightmare, so you think I should total it? I'll just assume that you're kidding. I'm sorry Polly wasn't listening to this. Okay, I appreciate your great interest in my welfare. Don't offer any more suggestions. And don't make me a horrible Christmas present, Cantabile. You're casting about to make a dynamic impression. Don't make any more criminal offers, you understand? If I hear another whisper of this I'll tell the homicide squad."

"Relax. I wouldn't lift a finger. I just thought I'd point out the whole range of options. It helps to see them from end to end. It clears your head. You know she'll be damn glad when you're dead, you rascal you."

"I don't know any such thing," I said.

I was lying. She had told me exactly that herself. Really, to be having a conversation like this served me right. I had brought it on myself. I had rooted and sorted my way through mankind experiencing disappointment upon disappointment. What was my disappointment? I had, or assumed that I had, needs and perceptions of a Shakespearian order. But they were only too sporadically of that high order. And so I found myself now looking into the moony eyes of a Cantabile. Ah my higher life! When I was young I believed that being an intellectual assured me of a higher life. In this Humboldt and I were exactly alike. He too would have respected and adored the learning, the rationality, the analytical power of a man like Richard Durnwald. For Durnwald the only brave, the only passionate, the only manly life was a life of thought. I had agreed, but I no longer thought in the same way. I had decided to listen to the voice of my own mind speaking from within, from my own depths, and this voice said that there was my body, in nature, and that there was also me. I was related to nature through my body, but all of me was not contained in it.

Because of this kind of idea I now found myself under Cantabile's gaze. He examined me. He also looked tender concerned threatening punitive and even lethal.

I said to him, "Years ago there was a little kid in the funnies called Desperate Ambrose. Before your time. Now don't you play Desperate Ambrose with me. Let me out of here."

"Just a minute. What about Lucy's thesis?"

"Curse her thesis."

"She's coming back from Nevada in a few days."

I made no answer. In a few days' time I'd be safely abroad—away from this lunatic, though probably mixed up with others.

"One more thing," he said. "You can make it with Polly through me. Only. Don't try on your own."

"Rest easy," I said.

He remained in the bathroom. I suppose he was getting his bullets out of the wastepaper basket.

Polly had the yoghurt and the egg ready for me.

"I'll tell you," she said, "don't get mixed up in the commodity market. He's losing his shirt."

"Does he know that?"

"What do you think," she said.

"Then he's bringing in new investors perhaps to make a deal to recover some of his losses?"

"I couldn't say. That's beyond me," said Polly. "He's a very intricate person. What is that beautiful medal on the wall?"

"It's my French decoration, framed by my lady friend. She's an interior decorator. Actually, the medal is a kind of phony. Major decorations are red, not green. They gave me the sort of thing they give to pig-breeders and to people who improve the garbage cans. A Frenchman told me last year that my green ribbon must be the lowest rank of the Legion of Honor. In fact he had never actually seen a green ribbon before. He thought it might be the Mérite Agricole."

"I don't think it was very nice of him to tell you that," said Polly.

• • •

Renata was punctual, and she had the engine of the old yellow Pontiac idling, waiting to be off. I shook hands with Polly and told Cantabile, "I'll be seeing you." I didn't introduce them to Renata. They tried hard to get a look at her but I got in, slammed the door, and said, "Go!" She went. The crown of Renata's large hat touched the roof of the car. It was amethyst felt and of the seventeenth-century cut you see in portraits by

Frans Hals. She was wearing her long hair down. I preferred it in a bun, showing the shape of her neck.

"Who are your pals, and what's the big hurry?"

"That was Cantabile, who did in my car."

"Him? I wish I'd known. Was that his wife?"

"No, his wife is out of town."

"I watched you coming through the lobby. She's quite a number. And he's a good-looking man."

"He was dying to meet you—trying to get a load of you through the window."

"Why should you be so flustered by that?"

"Just now he offered to have Denise rubbed out for me."

Renata, laughing, shouted, "What?"

"A hit man, a mechanic, he suggested a contract. Everybody knows the lingo now."

"It must have been a put-on."

"I'm sure it was. On the other hand there's my 280-SL in the shop."

"It's not as though Denise didn't deserve it," said Renata.

"She is a maddening pest, that's true enough, and I always laughed when I read how old Mr. Karamazov rushed into the street when he heard that his wife was gone shouting, 'The bitch is dead!'—But Denise," said Citrine the lecturer, "is a comical, not a tragic personality. Besides, she shouldn't die to gratify *me*. Most important are the girls, they need a mother. Anyhow it's idiotic to hear people say kill, murder, die, death—they haven't the faintest idea what they're talking about. There isn't one person in ten thousand that understands the first thing about death."

"What do you suppose will happen downtown today?"

"Oh, the usual thing. They'll mobbalize me, as we used to say in grammar school. I'll represent human dignity, and they'll give me hell."

"Well, must you do the dignity bit? You're stuck with it, while they have all the fun. If you could find some way to crush 'em, it would be so nice. . . . Well, here's my client on the corner. Isn't she built like a bouncer in a clip joint! You don't have to take part in the conversation, it's enough that she bores and badgers me. You just tune out and meditate. If she doesn't choose her upholstery material today I'll cut her throat."

Immense and fragrant in black and white silk, large polka dots covering her bosom (which I could, and did, visualize), Fannie Sunderland got in. I withdrew to the back seat, warning her about the hole in the floor, covered by a square of tin. The heavy samples carried by her salesman ex-husband had actually worn out the metal of Renata's Pontiac. "Unfortunately," said Renata, "our Mercedes is in the shop for repairs."

In the mental discipline I had recently begun, and of which I already felt the good effects, stability equipoise and tranquillity were the prerequisites. I said to myself, "Tranquillity, tranquillity." As on the racquet-ball court I said, "Dance, dance, dance!" And it always had some result. The will is a link which connects the soul to the world as-it-is. Through the will the soul frees itself from distraction and mere dreams. But when Renata told me to tune out and meditate she struck a note of malice. She was needling me about Doris, the daughter of Dr. Scheldt, the anthroposophist from whom I had been getting instruction. Renata was terribly jealous of Doris. "That baby bitch!" Renata cried. "I know she couldn't wait to jump into your bed." But this was Renata's own fault, her very own doing. She and her mother, the Señora, had decided that I needed a lesson. They shut the door in my face. By invitation, I came to Renata's apartment for dinner one night and found myself locked out. Someone else was with her. For several months I was too depressed to be alone. I moved in with George Swiebel and slept on his sofa. I would sit up suddenly in the night with a crying fit, sometimes waking George who came out and turned on a lamp, his wrinkled pajamas baring powerful legs. He made this measured statement: "A man in his fifties who can break up and cry over a girl is a man I respect."

I said, "Oh hell! What are you talking about! I'm a moron. It's disgraceful to carry on like this."

Renata had taken up with a man named Flonzaley. . . .

But I'm getting ahead of myself. I sat behind the two fragrant chatting ladies. We turned into Forty-seventh Street, the boundary between rich man's Kenwood and poor man's Oakwood, passing the locked tavern which lost its license because a fellow had gotten twenty stab wounds there over a matter of eight dollars. This was what Cantabile meant by "crazy buffaloes." Where was the victim? He was buried. Who was he? Nobody could tell you. And now others, casually regardant, passed the place in automobiles still thinking of an "I," and of the past and the prospects of this "I." If there was nothing in this but some funny egoism, some illusion that fate was being outwitted, avoidance of the reality of the grave, perhaps it was scarcely worth the trouble. But that remained to be seen.

George Swiebel, that vitality-worshiper, thought it was a wonderful thing that an elderly man should still keep up an active erotic and vivid fluent emotional life. I did not agree. But when Renata called me up, weeping on the phone, and said she had never cared for this Flonzaley, she wanted me back, I said, "Oh, thank God, thank God!" and hurried straight over. That was the end of Miss Doris Scheldt, of whom I had been very fond. But fond was not enough. I was a nymph-troubled man and a person of frenzied longings. Perhaps the longings were not even specifically for nymphs. But whatever they were, a woman like Renata drew them out. Other ladies were critical of her. Some said she was gross. Maybe so, but she was also gorgeous. And one must bear in mind the odd angle or slant that the rays of love have to take in order to reach a heart like mine. From George Swiebel's poker game, at which I drank so much and became so garrulous, I carried away one useful idea—for an atypical foot you need an atypical shoe. If in addition to being atypical you are fastidious—well, you have your work cut out for you. And is there still any typical foot? I mean by this that such emphasis has fallen on the erotic that all the eccentricity of the soul pours into the foot. The effects are so distorting, the flesh takes such florid turns that nothing will fit. So deformity has overtaken love and love is a power that can't let us alone. It can't because we owe our existence to acts of love performed before us, because love is a standing debt of the soul. This is the position as I saw it. The interpretation given by Renata, something of an astrologer, was that my sign was to blame for my troubles. She had never come across a more divided screwed-up suffering Gemini, so incapable of pulling himself together. "Don't smile when I talk about the stars. I know that to you I'm a beautiful palooka, a dumb broad. You'd like me to be your *Kama Sutra* dream-girl."

But I hadn't been smiling at her. I smiled only because I had yet to read any account of the Gemini type in Renata's astrological literature which was not entirely correct. One book in particular impressed me; it spoke of Gemini as a mental feeling-mill, where the soul is sheared and shredded. As to her being my *Kama Sutra* girl, she was a very fine woman, I still say that, but she was by no means fully at ease in sex. There were times when she was sad and quiet and spoke of her "hang-ups." Now we were going to Europe on Friday, our second trip this year. There were serious personal reasons for these European flights. And if I couldn't offer mature sympathy to a young woman, what did I have to offer? As it happened I took a genuine interest in her problems, I sympathized fully with her.

Still, I owed it to common realism to see the thing as others might see it—an old troubled lecher was taking a gold-digging floozy to Europe to show her a big time. Behind this, to complete the classic picture, was the scheming old mother, the Señora, who taught commercial Spanish in a secretarial college on State Street. The Señora was a person of some charm, one of those people who thrive in the Midwest because they are foreign and dotty. Renata's beauty was not inherited from her. And on the biological or evolutionary side Renata was perfect. Like a leopard or a race horse, she was a "noble animal" (see Santayana, *The Sense of Beauty*). Her mysterious father (and our trips to Europe were made to discover just who this was) must have been one of those old-time strongmen who bent iron bars, pulled locomotives with his teeth, or supported twenty people on a plank across his back, a grand figure of a man, a model for Rodin. The Señora I believe was really a Hungarian. When she told family anecdotes I could see her transposing from the Balkans to Spain. I was convinced that I understood her, and for this claim I gave myself a strange reason; this was that I understood my mother's Singer sewing machine. At the age of ten I had dismantled the machine and put it together again. You pushed the wrought-iron treadle. This moved the smooth pulley, the needle went up and down. You pried up a smooth steel plate and there found small and intricate parts that gave off an odor of machine oil. To me the Señora was a person of intricate parts and smelled slightly of oil. It was on the whole a positive association. But certain bits were missing from her mind. The needle went up and down, there was thread on the bobbin, but the stitching failed to occur.

The Señora's chief claim to sanity was founded upon motherhood. She had many plans for Renata. These were extravagant in the distant reaches, but near at hand they were quite practical. She had invested a lot in Renata's upbringing. She must have spent a fortune on orthodontia. The results were of a very high order. It was a privilege to see Renata open her mouth, and when she kidded me and laughed brilliantly I was struck with admiration. All my mother could do for my teeth in the ignorant old days was to wrap a lid from the coal stove in flannel, or to put hot dry buckwheat in a Bull Durham tobacco sack to apply to my face when I had toothaches. Hence my respect for those beautiful teeth. Also, for a big girl, Renata had a light voice. When she laughed she ventilated her entire being—down to the uterus, I thought. She put up her hair with silk scarves, showing the line of a wonderfully graceful feminine neck, and she walked about—how she walked about! No wonder her mother didn't want to waste her on me with my dewlaps and my French medal. But since Renata did have a weakness for me, why not set up housekeeping? The Señora was for this. Renata was going on thirty, divorced, with a nice little boy named Roger, of whom I was very fond. The old woman (like Cantabile, come to think of it) urged me to buy a condominium on the near-North Side. She omitted herself from these suggested arrangements. "I need privacy. I have my *affaires de cœur*." "But," said the Señora, "Roger should be in a household that has a male figure in it."

Renata and the Señora collected news items about May–December marriages. They sent me clippings about old husbands and interviews with their brides. In one year they lost Steichen, Picasso, and Casals. But they still had Chaplin and

Senator Thurmond and Justice Douglas. From the sex columns of the *News* the Señora even culled scientific statements about sex for the aging. And even George Swiebel said, "Maybe this would be a good deal for you. Renata wants to settle down. She's been around and seen a lot. She's had it. She's ready."

"Well, she's certainly not one of those little *noli me tangerines*," I said.

"She's a good cook. She's lively. She has plants and knick-knacks and the lights are on and the kitchen is steaming and goy music plays. Does she flow for you? Does she get wet when you lay a hand on her? Stay away from those dry mental broads. I have to be basic with you otherwise you'll shilly-shally. You'll be trapped again by a woman who says she shares your mental interests or understands your higher aims. That type already has shortened your life. One more will kill you! Anyhow, I know you want to make it with Renata."

I most certainly did! It's hard for me to stop praising her. In her hat and fur coat she drove the Pontiac, her outthrust leg in spangled textured panty hose bought in a theatrical-specialty house. Her personal emanations affected even the skins of the animals which composed her coat. They not only covered her body but were still in there trying. There was a certain similarity here. I too was trying. Yes, I longed to make it with Renata. She was helping me to consummate my earthly cycle. She had her irrational moments but she was also kindly. True, as a carnal artist she was disheartening as well as thrilling, because, thinking of her as wife-material, I had to ask myself where she had learned all this and whether she had taken the PhD once and for all. Furthermore our relationship made me entertain vain and undignified ideas. An ophthalmologist told me in the Downtown Club that a simple incision would remove the bags under my eyes. "It's just a hernia of one of the tiny muscles," Dr. Klosterman said, and described the plastic surgery and how the skin would be sliced and tucked back. He added that I had plenty of backhair left which could be transplanted to the top. Senator Proxmire had it done and for a time wore a turban on the Senate floor. He had claimed a deduction, disallowed by the IRS—but one could try again. I considered these suggestions but realized presently that I must stop this foolishness! I must fix my whole attention on the great and terrible matters that had put me to sleep for decades. Besides, something might be done at the front of a person but what about the rear? Even if the baggy eyes were fixed and the hair was fixed, wasn't there still the back of my neck? I was trying on a fancy check overcoat at Saks not long ago and in the triple mirror I saw how fissured, how deeply hacked I was between the ears.

I bought the coat anyway, Renata urged me to, and I was wearing it today. When I got out at the county building, giant Mrs. Sunderland said, "Golly, what a jazzy coat!"

• • •

Renata and I had met in this same skyscraper, the new county building, while doing jury duty.

There was, however, an earlier, indirect connection between us. George Swiebel's father, old Myron, knew Gaylord Koffritz, Renata's ex-husband. These two had had an unusual encounter in the Russian Bath on Division Street. George had told me about it.

He was a simple modest person, George's father. All he wanted was to live forever. George came by his vitalism directly. He got it from Myron who had it in a more primitive form. Myron declared that he owed his longevity to heat and vapor, to black bread raw onion bourbon whisky herring sausage cards billiards race horses and women.

Now in the steam room with its wooden bleachers and its sizzling boulders and buckets of ice water the visual distortion was considerable. From the rear if you saw a slight figure with small buttocks you thought it to be a child, but there were no children here and from the front you discovered a rosy and shrunken old man. Father Swiebel, clean-shaven and seen from the back just like a little boy, met a bearded man in the steam and because of the glittering beard took *him* to be much older. He was however only in his thirties, and very well built. They sat down together on the wooden trestles, two bodies covered with drops of moisture, and Father Swiebel said, "What do you do?"

The bearded man was unwilling to say what he did. Father Swiebel urged him to talk. This was wrong. It was, in the demented jargon of the educated, against the "ethos" of the place. Here, as at the Downtown Club, business was not discussed. George liked to say that the steam bath was like the last refuge in the burning forest where hostile animals observed a truce and the law of fang and claw was suspended. I'm afraid he got this from Walt Disney. The point he wanted to remind me of was that it was wrong to ply your trade or make a pitch while steaming. Father Swiebel was to blame and admitted it. "This fellow with the hair didn't want to talk. I egged him on. So then he let me have it."

Where men are as nude as the troglodytes of Stone Age Adriatic caverns and sit together dripping and red, like sunset in a mist, and, as in this case, one has a full brown sparkling beard, and eyes are meeting eyes through streaming sweat and vapor, strange things are apt to be spoken. It turned out that the stranger was a salesman whose line was crypts tombs and mausoleums. When Father Swiebel heard this he wanted to back off. But now it was too late. With arched brows, with white teeth and living lips within the dense fell of the beard, the man spoke:

Has your last rest been arranged? Is there a family plot? Are you provided? No? But why not? Can you afford such neglect? Do you know how they will bury you? Amazing! Has anybody talked to you about conditions in the new cemeteries? Why, they're nothing but slums. Death deserves dignity. Out there the exploitation is terrible. It's one of the biggest real-estate swindles going. They cheat you. They don't give the statutory number of feet. You have to lie cramped forever. The disrespect is ferocious. But you know what politics and rackets are. High and low, everybody is on the take. One of these days there'll be a grand-jury investigation and a scandal. Guys will go to jail. But it'll be too late for the dead. They aren't going to open your grave and rebury you. So you'll lie there short-sheeted. Frogged. As kids do to each other in summer camp. And there you are with hundreds of thousands of bodies in a flattened-out death-tenement, with your knees up. Aren't you entitled to a full stretch? And in these cemeteries they don't allow you a headstone. You have to settle for a brass plate with your name and your dates. Then machines come to cut the grass. They use a gang-mower. You might as well be buried in a public golf course. The blades nick away the brass letters. Pretty soon they're obliterated. Then you can't even be located. Your kids can't find the place. You're lost forever—"

"Stop!" Myron said. The fellow continued:

Now in a mausoleum it's different. It doesn't cost as much as you think. These new jobs are prefabricated but they're copies from the best models, starting with Etruscan tombs, up through Bernini and finally there's Louis Sullivan, *art nouveau*. People are mad now for *art nouveau*. They'll pay thousands for a Tiffany lamp or ceiling fixture. By comparison, an *art nouveau* prefab tomb is cheap. And then you're out of the crowd. You're on your own property. You don't want to get caught for eternity in a kind of expressway traffic jam or subway rush.

Father Swiebel said that Koffritz looked very sincere and that he saw in the steam only a respectful sympathetic troubled bearded face—an expert, a specialist, fair-minded, sensible. But the by-intimations were devastating. The vision got me, too—death seething under the treeless fairway, and the glitterless brass of nameless name plates. This Koffritz with his devilish sales-poetry clutched the heart of Father Swiebel. He grabbed mine as well. For at the time this was reported to me I was suffering intense death-anxieties. I wouldn't even attend funerals. I couldn't bear to see the coffin shut and the thought of being screwed into a box made me frantic. This was aggravated when I read a newspaper account of some Chicago children who found a heap of empty caskets near the crematory of a cemetery. They dragged them down to a pond and boated in them. Because they were reading *Ivanhoe* at school they tilted like knights, with poles. One kid was capsized and caught in the silk lining. They saved him. But there gaped in my mind a display of coffins lined with puffy rose taffeta and pale green satin, all open like crocodiles' jaws. I saw myself put down to suffocate and rot under the weight of clay and stones—no, under sand; Chicago is built on Ice Age beaches and marshes (Late Pleistocene).

For relief, I tried to convert this into serious intellectual subject matter. I believe I did this kind of thing rather well—thinking how the death problem is *the* bourgeois problem, relating to material prosperity and the conception of life as pleasant and comfortable, and what Max Weber had written about the modern conception of life as an infinite series of segments, gainful advantageous and "pleasant," failing to provide the feeling of a life cycle, so that one couldn't die "full of years." But these learned high-class exercises didn't take the death-curse off for me. I could only conclude how bourgeois it was that I should be so neurotic about stifling in the grave. And I was furious with Edgar Allan Poe for writing so accurately about this. His tales of catalepsy and live burial poisoned my childhood, and still killed me. I couldn't even bear to have the sheet over my face at night or my feet tucked in. I spent a lot of time figuring out how to be dead. Burial at sea might be the answer.

The samples that had worn a hole in Renata's Pontiac were, then, models of crypts and tombs. When I met her I not only had been brooding over death (would it help to have a wooden partition in the grave, a floor just above the coffin to keep off the direct smothering weight?) but I had also developed a new oddity. On business errands on La Salle Street, zooming or plunging in swift elevators, every time I felt a check in the electrical speed and the door was about to open, my heart spoke up. Entirely on its own. It exclaimed, "My Fate!" It seems I expected some woman to be standing there. "At last! You!" Becoming conscious of this hungry demeaning elevator phenomenon I tried to do the right thing and get back on a mature standard. I even attempted to be scientific. But all science can do for you is to affirm again that when something like this happens there must be a natural necessity for it. This being sensible got me nowhere. What was there to be so sensible about if, as I felt, I had waited many thousands of years for God to send my soul to this earth? Here I was supposed to capture a true and clear word before I returned, as my human day ended. I was afraid to go back empty-handed. Being sensible could do absolutely nothing to mitigate this fear of missing the boat. Anyone can see that.

Called to jury duty I grumbled at first that it was a waste of time. But then I became a happy eager juror. To leave the house in the morning like everybody else was bliss. Wearing a numbered steel badge I sat joyfully with hundreds of others in the jury pool, high up in the new county skyscraper, a citizen among fellow citizens. The glass walls, the russet and plum steel beams were very fine—the large sky, the ruled space, the far-away spools of storage tanks, the orange delicate distant filthy slums, the green of the river strapped by black bridges. Looking out from the jurors' hall I began to have Ideas. I brought books and papers downtown (so it shouldn't be a total loss). For the first time I read through the letters my colleague Pierre Thaxter had been sending me from California.

I am not a careful letter reader and Thaxter's letters were very long. He composed and dictated them in his orange grove near Palo Alto where he sat thinking in a canvas officer's chair. He wore a black carabiniere cloak, his feet were bare, he drank Pepsi-Cola, he had eight or ten children, he owed money to everyone, and he was a cultural statesman. Adoring women treated him like a man of genius, believed all that he told them, typed his manuscripts, gave birth to his kids, brought him Pepsi-Cola to drink. Reading his voluminous memoranda which dealt with the first number of *The Ark* (in the planning stage for three years, and the costs were staggering), I realized that he had been pressing me to complete a group of studies on "Great Bores of the Modern World." He kept suggesting possible lines of approach. Certain types were obvious, of course—political, philosophical, ideological, educational, therapeutic bores—but there were others frequently overlooked, for instance innovative bores. I however had lost interest in the categories and came presently to care only for the general and theoretical aspect of the project.

I had a lively time in the vast jurors' hall going over my boredom notes. I saw that I had stayed away from problems of definition. Good for me. I didn't want to get mixed up with theological questions about *accidia* and *tedium vitae*. I found it necessary to say only that from the beginning mankind experienced states of boredom but that no one had ever approached the matter front and center as a subject in its own right. In modern times the question had been dealt with under the name of *anomie* or Alienation, as an effect of capitalist conditions of labor, as a result of leveling in Mass Society, as a consequence of the dwindling of religious faith or the gradual using up of charismatic or prophetic elements, or the neglect of Unconscious powers, or the increase of Rationalization in a technological society, or the growth of bureaucracy. It seemed to me, however, that one might begin with this belief of the modern world—either you burn or you rot. This I connected with the finding of old Binet the psychologist that hysterical people had fifty times the energy, the endurance, the power of performance, the keenness of faculties, the creativity in their hysterical fits as they had in their quiet periods. Or as William James put it, human beings really lived when they lived at the top of their energies. Something like the *Wille zur Macht.* Suppose then that you began with the proposition that boredom was a kind of pain caused by unused powers, the pain of wasted possibilities or talents, and was accompanied by expectations of the optimum utilization of capacities. (I try to guard against falling into the social-science style on these mental occasions.) Nothing actual ever suits pure expectation and such purity of expectation is a great source of tedium. People rich in abilities, in sexual feeling, rich in mind and in invention—all the highly gifted see themselves shunted for decades onto dull sidings, banished exiled nailed up in chicken coops. Imagination has even tried to surmount the problems by forcing boredom itself to yield interest. This insight I owe to Von Humboldt Fleisher who showed me how it was done by James Joyce, but anyone who reads books can easily find it out for himself. Modern French literature is especially preoccupied with the theme of boredom. Stendhal mentioned it on every page, Flaubert devoted books to it, and Baudelaire was its chief poet. What is the reason for this peculiar French sensitivity? Can it be because the *ancien régime,* fearing another Fronde, created a court that emptied the provinces of talent? Outside the center, where art philosophy science manners conversation thrived, there was nothing. Under Louis XIV, the upper classes enjoyed a refined society,

and, whatever else, people didn't need to be alone. Cranks like
Rousseau made solitude glamorous, but sensible people agreed
that it was really terrible. Then in the eighteenth century being
in prison began to acquire its modern significance. Think how
often Manon and Des Grieux were in jail. And Mirabeau and
my own buddy Von Trenck and of course the Marquis de Sade.
The intellectual future of Europe was determined by people
impregnated with boredom, by the writings of prisoners. Then,
in 1789, it was young men from the sticks, provincial lawyers
scribblers and orators, who assaulted and captured the center
of interest. Boredom has more to do with modern political revolution than justice has. In 1917, that boring Lenin who wrote
so many boring pamphlets and letters on organizational questions was, briefly, all passion, all radiant interest. The Russian
revolution promised mankind a permanently interesting life.
When Trotsky spoke of permanent revolution he really meant
permanent interest. In the early days the revolution was a work
of inspiration. Workers peasants soldiers were in a state of
excitement and poetry. When this short brilliant phase ended,
what came next? The most boring society in history. Dowdi-
ness shabbiness dullness dull goods boring buildings boring
discomfort boring supervision a dull press dull education boring bureaucracy forced labor perpetual police presence penal
presence, boring party congresses, etcetera. What was permanent was the defeat of interest.

What could be more boring than the long dinners Stalin
gave, as Djilas describes them? Even I, a person seasoned in
boredom by my years in Chicago, marinated, *mithridated* by
the USA, was horrified by Djilas's account of those twelve-
course all-night banquets. The guests drank and ate, and ate
and drank, and then at 2 a.m. they had to sit down to watch an
American Western. Their bottoms ached. There was dread in
their hearts. Stalin, as he chatted and joked, was mentally picking those who were going to get it in the neck and while they
chewed and snorted and guzzled they knew this, they expected
shortly to be shot.

What—in other words—would modern boredom be without
terror? One of the most boring documents of all time is the

thick volume of Hitler's *Table Talk*. He too had people watching movies, eating pastries, and drinking coffee with *Schlag* while he bored them, while he discoursed theorized expounded. Everyone was perishing of staleness and fear, afraid to go to the toilet. This combination of power and boredom has never been properly examined. Boredom is an instrument of social control. Power is the power to impose boredom, to command stasis, to combine this stasis with anguish. The real tedium, deep tedium, is seasoned with terror and with death.

There were even profounder questions. For instance, the history of the universe would be very boring if one tried to think of it in the ordinary way of human experience. All that time without events! Gases over and over again, and heat and particles of matter, the sun tides and winds, again this creeping development, bits added to bits, chemical accidents—whole ages in which almost nothing happens, lifeless seas, only a few crystals, a few protein compounds developing. The tardiness of evolution is so irritating to contemplate. The clumsy mistakes you see in museum fossils. How could such bones crawl, walk, run? It is agony to think of the groping of the species—all this fumbling, swamp-creeping, munching, preying, and reproduction, the boring slowness with which tissues, organs, and members developed. And then the boredom also of the emergence of the higher types and finally of mankind, the dull life of Paleolithic forests, the long long incubation of intelligence, the slowness of invention, the idiocy of peasant ages. These are interesting only in review, in thought. No one could bear to experience this. The present demand is for a quick forward movement, for a summary, for life at the speed of intensest thought. As we approach, through technology, the phase of instantaneous realization, of the realization of eternal human desires or fantasies, of abolishing time and space the problem of boredom can only become more intense. The human being, more and more oppressed by the peculiar terms of his existence—one time around for each, no more than a single life per customer—has to think of the boredom of death. O those eternities of nonexistence! For people who crave continual interest and diversity, O! how boring death will be! To lie in the grave, in one place, how frightful!

Socrates tried to soothe us, true enough. He said there were only two possibilities. Either the soul is immortal or, after death, things would be again as blank as they were before we were born. This is not absolutely comforting either. Anyway it was natural that theology and philosophy should take the deepest interest in this. They owe it to us not to be boring themselves. On this obligation they don't always make good. However, Kierkegaard was not a bore. I planned to examine his contribution in my master essay. In his view the primacy of the ethical over the esthetic mode was necessary to restore the balance. But enough of that. In myself I could observe the following sources of tedium: 1) The lack of a *personal* connection with the external world. Earlier I noted that when I was riding through France in a train last spring I looked out of the window and thought that the veil of Maya was wearing thin. And why was this? I wasn't seeing what was there but only what everyone sees under a common directive. By this is implied that our world-view has used up nature. The rule of this view is that I, a subject, see the phenomena, the world of objects. They, however, are not necessarily in themselves objects as modern rationality defines objects. For in spirit, says Steiner, a man can step out of himself and let things speak to him about themselves, to speak about what has meaning not for him alone but also for them. Thus the sun the moon the stars will speak to nonastronomers in spite of their ignorance of science. In fact it's high time that this happened. Ignorance of science should not keep one imprisoned in the lowest and weariest sector of being, prohibited from entering into independent relations with the creation as a whole. The educated speak of the disenchanted (a boring) world. But it is not the world, it is my own head that is disenchanted. The world *cannot* be disenchanted. 2) For me the self-conscious ego is the seat of boredom. This increasing, swelling, domineering, painful self-consciousness is the only rival of the political and social powers that run my life (business, technological-bureaucratic powers, the state). You have a great organized movement of life, and you have the single self, independently conscious, proud of its detachment and its absolute immunity, its stability and its power to remain unaffected by anything whatsoever—by the sufferings of others or by society or by politics or by external chaos. In a way it doesn't give a damn. It is asked to give a damn, and we often urge it to give a damn but the curse of noncaring lies upon this painfully free consciousness. It is free from attachment to beliefs and to other souls. Cosmologies, ethical systems? It can run through them by the dozens. For to be fully conscious of oneself as an individual is also to be separated from all else. This is Hamlet's kingdom of infinite space in a nutshell, of "words, words, words," of "Denmark's a prison."

These were some of the notes that Thaxter wanted me to expand. I was however in too unstable a condition. Several times a week I went downtown to see my lawyers and discuss my problems. They told me how complex my predicament was. Their news was worse and worse. I soared in elevators looking for salvation in female form whenever a door opened. A person in my condition should lock himself in his room, and if he hasn't the strength of character to take Pascal's advice to stay put he ought to throw the key out of the window. Then the door rolled open in the county building and I saw Renata Koffritz. She too wore a numbered steel badge. We were both taxpayers, voters, citizens. But oh, what citizens! And where was the voice that said, "My Fate!"? It was silent. Was she, then, it? She certainly was all woman, soft and beautifully heavy in a mini-skirt and nursery-school shoes fastened with a single strap. I thought, God help me. I thought, Better think twice about this. I even thought, At your age a Buddhist would already be thinking of disappearing forever into the forest. But it was no use. She may not have been the Fate I was looking for but she was nevertheless a Fate. She even knew my name. "You must be Mr. Citrine," she said.

The year before I had been given an award by the Zig-Zag Club, a Chicago cultural society of bank executives and stockbrokers. I was not invited to become a member. I did however receive a plaque for the book I wrote about Harry Hopkins and my picture was in the *Daily News*. Perhaps the lady had seen it there. But she said, "Your friend Mr. Szathmar is my divorce lawyer and he thought we should get to know each other."

Ah, she had me. How quickly she informed me that she was being divorced. Those love-pious eyes were already sending messages of love and depravity to the Chicago-boy sector of my soul. A gust of the old West Side sex malaria came over me.

"Mr. Szathmar is devoted to you. He adores you. He practically closes his eyes and looks poetic when he discusses you. And he's such a stout man, you don't expect it. He told me about your love who crashed in the jungle. And also about your first romance—with the doctor's daughter."

"Naomi Lutz."

"That's a crazy name."

"Yes, it is, isn't it."

It was true that my boyhood friend Szathmar loved me but he loved matchmaking or procuring also. He had a passion for arranging affairs. This was useful to him professionally, as it tied many clients to him. In special cases he took over all the practical details for them—the rent of a mistress's apartment, her car, and her charge accounts, her dental bills. He even covered suicide attempts. Even funerals. Not the law but fixing people up was his real calling. And we two boyhood pals were going to continue lustful to the end, if he had his way. He made this decorous. He did it all with philosophy, poetry, ideology. He quoted, he played records, and he theorized about women. He tried to keep up with the rapidly changing erotic slang of successive generations. So were we to end our lives as cunt-struck doddering wooers left over from a Goldoni farce? Or like Balzac's Baron Hulot d'Ervy whose wife on her deathbed hears the old man propositioning the maid?

Alec Szathmar a few years ago, while under great stress in the vaults of the First National Bank, suffered a heart attack. I loved foolish Szathmar. I worried terribly about him. As soon as he was out of the intensive care unit, I ran down to see him and found that he was already being sexual. After heart attacks this is common, apparently. Under the powerful crown of white hair, bushy on the cheekbones in the new style of adornment, his gloomy eyes dilated as soon as a nurse entered his room though he still looked purple in the face. My old friend who now was stout, massive, was restless in bed. He threw himself about, kicked away the sheets, and exposed himself as if by fretful accident. If I was making a sympathy call he didn't need my goddamn sympathy. Those eyes of his were grim and alert. At last I said, "Now Alec stop this flashing. You know what I'm talking about—stop uncovering your parts every time some poor old lady comes to mop under the bed."

He glared. "What? You're stupid!" he said.

"That's all right. Quit pulling up your gown."

Bad examples can be elevating—you can win a quick promotion in taste and say, "Poor old Alec, flashing. By the grace of God, there never goes me." Yet here I was in the jury box with an erection for Renata. I was excited, amused, I was slightly mortified. Before us was a personal-injury case. In fairness I should have gone to the judge and asked to be disqualified. "Your honor, I can't keep my mind on the trial because of the glorious lady juror next to me. I'm sorry to be such an adolescent. . . ." (Sorry! I was in seventh heaven.) Besides, the case was only one of those phony whiplash suits against the insurance company filed by the lady passenger in a taxi collision. My personal business was more important. The trial was only background music. I kept the time with metronomic pulsations.

Two floors below, I myself was defendant in a post-decree action to deprive me of all my money. You might have thought that this would sober me. Not in the least!

Excused for lunch I hurried to La Salle Street to get information from Alec Szathmar about this wonderful girl. As I ran into the Chicago crowd I felt my pegs slipping, the strings slacker, my tone going lower. But what was I to do single-handed about a force that had seized the whole world?

There was a genteel and almost Harvard air about Alec's office, though he was a night-school lawyer. The layout was princely, sets of torts and statutes, an atmosphere of high jurisprudence, photographs of Justice Holmes and Learned Hand. Before the Depression Alec had been a rich kid. Not big-rich, only neighborhood-rich. But I knew rich kids. I had studied rich kids at the very top of society—as in the case of Bobby Kennedy. Von Humboldt Fleisher who always claimed that he had been one was not a real rich boy while Alec Szathmar who had been a rich boy told everyone that he was really a poet. In college he proved this by possession. He owned the works of Eliot, Pound, and Yeats. He memorized "Prufrock," which became one of his assets. But the Depression hit the Szathmars hard and he didn't get the silk-stocking education his doting scheming old father hoped to give him. However, just as Alec in boyhood had had bikes and chemistry sets and BB guns and fencing foils and tennis rackets and boxing gloves and skates and ukuleles, he now owned all the latest IBM equipment, conference phones, desk computers, transistor wristwatches, Xerox machines, tape recorders, and hundreds of thick law books.

He had gained weight after his coronary, when he should have thinned down. Always a conservative dresser he tried to cover his broad can with double-vented jackets. So he looked like a giant thrush. The exceedingly human face of this bird was framed with stormy white sideburns. The warm brown eyes full of love and friendship were not especially honest. One of C. G. Jung's observations helped me to make sense of Szathmar. Some minds, said Jung, belong to earlier periods of history. Among our contemporaries there are Babylonians and Carthaginians or types from the Middle Ages. To me Szathmar was an eighteenth-century cavalryman, a follower of Pandour von Trenck, the cousin of my lucky Trenck. His padded swarthy cheeks, his Roman nose, his mutton-chop whiskers, his fat chest wide hips neat feet and virile cleft chin attracted women. Whom women will embrace is one of the unfathomable mysteries. But of course the race has to keep going. Anyway, here was Szathmar waiting to receive me. In his chair his posture suggested clumsy but unshakable sexual horsemanship atop pretty ladies. His arms were crossed, like the arms of Rodin's *Balzac*. Unfortunately he still looked a bit ill. Almost everyone downtown seemed to me a touch sick these days.

"Alec, who is this Renata Koffritz? Brief me." Szathmar took a warm interest in his clients, especially the attractive women.

They got sympathy from him, psychiatric guidance practical advice and even touches of art and philosophy. And he briefed me: only child; kooky mother; no father in sight; ran away to Mexico with her high-school art teacher; fetched back; ran away later to Berkeley; found in one of those California touch-therapy groups; married off to Koffritz, a salesman whose line was crypts and tombs—

"Hold it. Have you seen him? A tall fellow? Brown beard? Why, he's the man who gave old Myron Swiebel a sales pitch in the Russian Bath on Division Street!"

Szathmar was not impressed by the coincidence. He said, "She's just about the finest piece I ever got a divorce for. She's got a little boy who's quite sweet. I thought of you. You can see action with this woman."

"Have you already seen some?"

"What, her lawyer?"

"Don't give me the ethical bit. If you haven't made a pass it's because she hasn't paid the retainer."

"I know your view of my profession. To you all business is fraud."

"Since Denise went on the warpath I've seen plenty of business. You fixed me up with Forrest Tomchek, one of the biggest names in this branch of law. It was like laying a speck of confetti in front of a jumbo vacuum cleaner."

Gigantically glowering, Szathmar said, "Poo!" He spat air to the side, symbolically. "You stupid prick, I had to beg Tomchek to take the case. He did me a favor as a colleague. A man like that! Why he wouldn't put you in his fish tank for an ornament. Board chairmen and bank presidents beg for his time, you twerp. Tomchek! Tomchek belongs to a family of legal statesmen. And an ace fighter-pilot in the Pacific."

"He's a crook all the same and he's incompetent besides. Denise is a thousand times smarter. She studied the documents and caught him in a minute. He didn't even make a routine check of titles to see who legally owned what. Don't give *me* the dignity of the bar, friend! But let's not hassle. Tell me about this girl."

He rose from his office chair. I've been in the White House,

I've sat in the President's chair in the Oval Room, and Szathmar's, I swear, is finer leather. Framed pictures of his father and his grandfather on the wall reminded me of old days on the West Side. My feeling toward Szathmar was after all family feeling.

"I picked her for you as soon as she came through that door. I keep you in mind, Charlie. Your life hasn't been happy."

"Don't exaggerate."

"Unhappy," he insisted. "Wasted talent and advantages, obstinate as hell, perverse proud and pissing everything away. All those connections of yours in New York Washington Paris London and Rome, all your achievements, your knack with words, your luck—because you've been lucky. What I could have done with that! And you had to marry that yenta West Side broad from a family of ward politicians and punchboard gamblers of candy-store kikes and sewer inspectors. That pretentious Vassar girl! Because she talked like a syllabus, and you were dying for understanding and conversation and she had culture. And I who love you, who always loved you, you stupid son of a bitch, I who have had this big glow for you since we were ten years old, and lie awake nights thinking: how do I save Charlie now; how do I protect his dough; find him tax shelters; get him the best legal defense; fix him up with good women. Why you nitwit, you low-grade moron, you don't even know what such love means."

I must tell you that I enjoyed Szathmar in this vein. As he was giving me the works like this his eyes kept turning to the left, where no one stood. If someone were standing there, some objective witness, he would support indignant Szathmar. Szathmar's dear mother had this same trait. She too summoned justice from empty space in this outraged way, laying both hands on her bosom. In Szathmar's breast there was a large true virile heart whereas I had no heart at all, only a sort of chicken giblet—that was how he saw things. He pictured himself as a person of heroic vitality, mature, wise, pagan, Tritonesque. But his real thoughts were all of getting on top, of intromission and all the dirty tricks that he called sexual freedom. But he also had to think how to make his monthly nut. His expenses were high. How to combine these different needs was the question. He told me once, "I was into the sexual revolution before anybody even heard of it."

But I have another thing to tell you. I was ashamed of us both. I had no business to look down on Szathmar. All this reading of mine has taught me a thing or two, after all. I understand a little the middle-class endeavor of two centuries to come out looking well, to preserve a certain darling innocence—the innocence of Clarissa defending herself against the lewdness of Lovelace. Hopeless! Even worse is the discovery that one has been living out certain greeting-card sentiments, with ribbons of middle-class virtue tied in a bow around one's heart. This sort of abominable American innocence is rightly detested by the world, which scented it in Woodrow Wilson in 1919. As schoolchildren we were taught boy-scout honor and goodness and courtesy; strange ghosts of Victorian gentility still haunt the hearts of Chicago's children, now in their fifties and sixties. This appeared in Szathmar's belief in his own generosity and greatness of heart, and also in my thanking God that I would never be as gross as Alec Szathmar. To atone I let him go on denouncing me. But when I thought that he had ranted long enough, I said to him, "How's your health?"

He didn't like this. He acknowledged no infirmities. "I'm fine," he said. "Not that you ran from court to ask me that. I just have to lose some weight."

"Shave your sideburns, too, while you're making improvements. They make you look like the bad guy in an old Western—one of those fellows who sold guns and firewater to the redskins."

"Okay, Charlie, I'm nothing but a would-be swinger. I'm a decaying squaw man, while you think only of higher things. You're noble. I'm a creep. But did you or did you not come to ask about this broad!"

"That's true, I did," I said.

"Don't knock yourself out for that. It's at least a sign of life, and you haven't got all that many. I just about gave up on you when you turned down that Felicia with the beautiful knockers. She's a nice middle-aged woman and would have been grateful

to you. Her husband plays around. She adored you. She would
have blessed you to the end of her days for treating her right.
This is a decent housewife and mother who would have taken
care of you from top to bottom, and washed and cooked and
baked and shopped, and even done your accounts, and nice in
the sack. She would have kept her mouth shut because she's
married. Perfect. But to you it was only another of my vulgar
ideas." He stared angrily. Then he said, "Okay, I'll fix it with
this chick. Take her for a drink at the Palmer House tomorrow.
I'll arrange the details."

If I was susceptible to the West Side sex malaria, Szathmar
could not resist the arranging fever. His one aim now was get
Renata and me into bed, where he would be present in spirit.
Maybe he hoped it would eventually develop into a threesome.
He, like Cantabile, occasionally suggested fantasy combinations. "Now, listen," he said. "During daylight hours you can
get a hotel room at what they call Conference Rates. I'll reserve
one. I'm holding money for you in escrow and they can bill
me."

"If we're only having a drink, how do you know it'll get as
far as the room?"

"That's up to you. The bartender will be holding the room
key. Slip him five bucks and he'll hand over the envelope."

"In what name will the envelope be?"

"Not the stainless name of Citrine, hey?"

"What about Crawley as a name."

"Our old Latin teacher. Old Crawley! *Est avis in dextra
melior quam quattuor extra.*"

So the next day Renata and I went to have a drink in the
dark bar below street level. I promised myself that this would
be absolutely my last idiocy. To myself I put it all as intelligently as possible: that we couldn't evade History, and that
this was what History was doing to everybody. History had
decreed that men and women had to become acquainted in
these embraces. I was going to find out whether or not Renata
was really my Fate, whether the true Jungian anima was in
her. She might turn out to be something far different. But one
sexual touch would teach me that, for women had peculiar

effects on me, and if they didn't make me ecstatic they made me ill. There were no two ways about it.

On this wet gloomy day the Wabash El was dripping but Renata redeemed the weather. She wore a plastic raincoat divided into red, white, and black bands, a Rothko design. In this gleamy hard-surfaced coat she sat fully buttoned in the dark booth. A broad, bent-brim hat was part of the costume. The banana-fragrant lipstick of her beautiful mouth matched the Rothko red. Her remarks made little sense but then she spoke little. She laughed considerably and quickly turned extremely pale. A candle in a round-bottomed glass wrapped in a fish-net kind of thing gave a small quantity of light. Presently her face settled low on the hard buckling glamorous plastic of her coat and became very round. I couldn't believe that the kind of broad described by Szathmar—so ready for action, so experienced, would down four martinis and that her face would grow so white, whiter than the moon when seen at 3 p.m. I wondered at first whether she might not be feigning timidity out of courtesy to a man of an older generation, but a cold gin moisture came out on her beautiful face and she appeared to be appealing to me to do something. In all this so far there was an element of *déjà vu,* for after all I had been through this more than once. What was different now was that I felt sympathetic and even protective toward this young woman in her unexpected weakness. I thought I understood simply enough why I was in the black and subcellar bar. Conditions were very tough. One couldn't make it without love. Why not? I was unable to budge this belief. It had perhaps the great weight of stupidity in it. This need for love (in such a generalized state) was an awful drag. If it should ever become publicly known that I whispered "My Fate!" as elevator doors were opening the Legion of Honor might justifiably ask to have its medal back. And the most constructive interpretation I could find at the time was the Platonic one that Eros was using my desires to lead me from the awful spot I was in toward wisdom. That was nice, it had class, but I don't think it was a bit true (for one thing there was not perhaps all that much Eros left). The big name if I must have one, if any supernatural powers troubled themselves about me, was not Eros, it was probably Ahriman, the principal potentate of darkness. Be that as it might, it was time to get Renata out of this joint.

I went to the bar and leaned over discreetly. I interposed myself among the drinkers. On any ordinary day I would have described these people as barflies and lushes but now their eyes all seemed to me as big as portholes and shed a moral light. The bartender came over. Between the knuckles of my left hand was folded a five-dollar bill. Szathmar had told me exactly how to do this. I asked the bartender whether there was an envelope in the name of Crawley. Immediately he took the five bucks. He had the kind of alertness you find only in a big town. "Now," he said, "what's this envelope?"

"Left for Crawley."

"I got no Crawley."

"Crawley must be there. Look again, if you don't mind."

He rattled through his envelopes again. Each contained a room key.

"What's your first name, buddy? Give me another clue."

Tormented, I said in a low voice, "Charles."

"That's better. Could this be you—C-I-T-R-I-N-E?"

"I know how to spell it, for Christ's sake," I said, faint but furious. I muttered, "Stupid fucking baboon Szathmar. Never did anything right in all his life. And me!—still depending on him to make my arrangements." Then I became aware that someone was trying to get my attention from behind, and I turned. I saw a middle-aged person smiling. She obviously knew me and was bursting with gladness. This lady was stout and gentle, snub-nosed, high in the bust. She appealed for recognition but at the same time tacitly confessed that the years had changed her. But was she as changed as all that? I said, "Yes?"

"You don't know me, I see. But you're still the same old Charlie."

"I can never understand why bars have to be dark as all this," I said.

"But Charlie, it's Naomi—your school-days' sweetheart."

"Naomi Lutz!"

"How wonderful to run into you, Charlie."

"How do you happen to be at the bar of this hotel?"

A woman alone at a bar is, as a rule, a hooker. Naomi was too old for that trade. Besides, it was inconceivable that Naomi who had been my girl at fifteen should have turned into a bar broad.

"Oh, no," she said. "My dad is here. He'll be right back. I bring him downtown from the nursing home at least once a week for a drink. You remember how he always adored to be in the Loop."

"Old Doc Lutz—just think!"

"Yes, alive. Very old. And he and I've been watching you with that lovely thing in the booth. Forgive me Charlie, but how you men keep going is unfair to females. How marvelous for you. Daddy was saying that he shouldn't have interfered with us, child sweethearts."

"I was more than your childhood sweetheart," I said. "I loved you with my soul, Naomi." Saying this I was aware that I had brought one woman to the bar and was making a passionate declaration to another. However, this was the truth, involuntary spontaneous truth. "I've often thought, Naomi, that I lost my character altogether because I couldn't spend my life with you. It distorted me all over, it made me ambitious cunning complex stupid vengeful. If I had been able to hold you in my arms nightly since the age of fifteen I would never have feared the grave."

"Oh Charlie, tell it to the Marines. It always was wonderful the way you talked. But off-putting too. You've had lots and lots of women. I can see by your behavior in that booth."

"Ah, yes—to the Marines!" I was grateful for this antique slang. First of all it checked my effusion, which would have led to nothing. Secondly it relieved me of the weight of another impression that had been gathering in the dark bar. I traced this to the idea that soon after death, when the lifeless body fell into decay and became a lot of minerals again, the soul awoke to its new existence, and an instant after death I expected to find myself in a dark place similar to this bar. Where all who had ever loved each other might meet again, etcetera. And this was my impression here in the bar. With the "Conference Room" key in my hand, the links clinking, I knew I must get back to Renata. If she was still drinking her martini she would be too bombed to rise to her feet and get out of the booth. But I had to wait now for Dr. Lutz. And here he came from the men's room, very weak and bald, and snub-nosed like his daughter. His Twenties Babbittry had faded into old-fashioned courtliness. He had demanded a strange courtesy from us, for though he had never been a real doctor, only a foot doctor (he had kept offices downtown and at home too), he insisted on being called Doctor and flew into a rage if anyone said Mr. Lutz. Fascinated by being a doctor he treated diseases of many kinds, up to the knee. If feet, why not legs? I recalled that he asked me in to assist him when he was laying a purple jelly of his own mixture on horrible sores that punctured the legs of a lady who worked at the National Biscuit factory. I held the jar and the applicators for him and as he filled these holes he made confident quack conversation. I valued this woman for she always brought the doctor a shoe box filled with chocolate-marshmallow puffs and devil's-food bars. As I remembered this, pulsations of chocolate sweetness came into the roof of my mouth. And then I saw myself sitting ecstatic in Dr. Lutz's treatment chair while a snowstorm blackened the tiny offices painted clinical white and I read *Herodias*. Moved by the decapitation of John the Baptist I went into Naomi's room. We were alone during the blizzard. I took off her warm terrycloth blue pajamas and saw her naked. These were the recollections that closed in on my heart. Naomi was no foreign body to me. That was just it. There was nothing alien in Naomi. My feeling for her went into her cells, into the very molecules that, being hers, all had her properties. Because I had conceived of Naomi without otherness, because of this passion, I was trapped by old Doc Lutz in a Jacob-Laban relationship. I had to help him wash his Auburn, a celestial blue car with white-wall tires. I poured from the hose and rubbed with the shammy while the Doctor in white linen golf knickers stood smoking a Cremo cigar.

"Oh Charlie Citrine, you surely have gone places," said the old gentleman. His voice was still lyrical, high, and quite empty. He never had been able to make you feel that he was saying anything at all substantial. "Though I was a Coolidge and Hoover Republican myself, still when the Kennedys had you to the White House I was so proud."

"Is that young woman your speed?" said Naomi.

"I can't honestly say that I know. And what are you doing with yourself, Naomi?"

"My marriage was no good at all and my husband went on the loose. I think you know that. I brought two kids up anyway. You didn't happen to read some articles by my son in the *Southwest Township Herald*?"

"No. I wouldn't have known they were by your son."

"He wrote about kicking the drug habit, based on personal experience. I wish you would give me an opinion on his writing. My daughter is a doll but the boy is a problem."

"And you, Naomi, my dear?"

"I don't do much any more. I have a man friend. Part of the day I'm a crossing guard at the grammar school."

Old Doc Lutz seemed to hear none of this.

"It's a pity," I said.

"About you and me? No it's not. You and your mental life would have been a strain on me. I'm into sports. My bag is football on TV. It's a big outing when we get passes to Soldiers' Field or to the hockey game. Early dinner at the Como Inn, we take the bus to the stadium, and I actually wait for fights on the ice and holler when they knock out their teeth. I'm afraid I'm just a common woman."

When Naomi said "common" and Doc Lutz said "Republican" they meant that they had joined the great American public and thus found contentment and fulfillment. To have been a foot doctor in the Loop during the Thirties gave the old fellow joy. His daughter delivered a similar message about herself. They were pleased with themselves and with each other and happy in their likeness. Only I, mysteriously a misfit, stood between them with my key. Obviously what ailed me was my unlikeness. I was an old friend, only I was not wholly American.

"I've got to go," I said.

"Couldn't we have a beer together sometime? I'd love to see

you," said Naomi. "You could advise me about Louie better than anybody. You haven't got hippie kids yourself have you?" And as I took her number she said, "Oh, look Doc, what a neat little book he writes in. Everything about Charlie is so elegant. What a handsome old guy you're turning into. But you're not the type any woman could ever tie down." As they watched I went back to the booth and raised up Renata. I put on my hat and coat and pretended that we were going outside. I felt the dishonor of everybody.

The conference-rate room was just what lechers and adulterers deserved. Not much bigger than a broom closet it opened on the air shaft. Renata dropped into a chair and ordered two more martinis from room service. I pulled the shade, not for privacy—there were no windows opposite—and not as a seducer, but only because I hate to look into brick air shafts. Against the wall was a sofa bed covered in green chenille. As soon as I saw this object I knew it would defeat me. I was sure I would never be able to get it open. Once anticipated this challenge would not leave my head. I had to meet it at once. The trapezoid foam-rubber bolsters weighed nothing. I pushed them away and pulled off the fitted spread. The sheets under it were perfectly clean. Then I knelt and groped under the sofa frame for a lever. Renata watched silent as my face grew tight and reddened. I crouched and pulled, furious with manufacturers who made such junk, and with the management for taking money from afternoon conferees and crucifying them in spirit.

"This thing is like an IQ test," I said.

"So?"

"I'm flunking. I can't get the thing to open."

"So? Leave it."

There was room for only one on this narrow bed. To tell the truth however I had no desire to lie down.

Renata went into the bathroom. There were two chairs. I sat in the *fauteuil*. It had wings. Between my shoes was a square of colonial American hooked rug. The blood rustled circulating over my eardrums. Surly room service brought the martinis. A dollar tip was taken without thanks. Then Renata came out, the gleamy coat still fully buttoned. She sat on the sofa bed, sipped once or twice at her martini, and passed out. Through the plastic I tried to listen to her heart. She didn't have a cardiac condition, did she? Suppose this were serious. Could one call an ambulance? I felt her pulse, stupidly studying my watch, losing count. For comparison I took my own pulse. I couldn't coordinate the results. Her pulse seemed no worse than mine. Unconscious she had, if anything, the better of it. She was damp and felt cold. I wiped the chill from her with a corner of the sheet and tried to think what George Swiebel, my health counselor, would do in an emergency like this. I knew exactly what he'd do—straighten her legs remove her shoes and unbutton her coat to help the breathing. I did just that.

Under the coat Renata was naked. She had gone into the bathroom and taken off her clothes. After undoing the top button I might have stopped, but I didn't. Of course I had appraised Renata and tried to guess how she might be. My generous guesses had been far behind the facts. I hadn't expected everything to be so large and faultless. I had observed in the jury box that the first joint of her fingers was fleshy and began to swell slightly before it tapered. My conjecture was that her beautiful thighs must also swell toward each other in harmony with this. I found that to be the case, absolutely, and felt more like an art lover than a seducer. My quick impression, for I didn't keep her uncovered very long, was that every tissue was perfect, every fiber of hair was shining. The deep female odor arose from her. When I saw how things were I buttoned her up from sheer respect. I got things back into place as well as I knew how. Next I raised the window. Unfortunately it drove off her wonderful odor but she had to have fresh air. I took her clothing from behind the bathroom door and stuffed it into her large handbag, checking to make sure that we didn't lose her juror's badge. Then in my overcoat, with hat and gloves in hand, I waited for her to come to.

The same things are done by us, over and over, with terrible predictability. One may be forgiven, in view of this, for wishing at least to associate with beauty.

• • •

And now—with her fur coat and her wonderful, soft, versatile, flexible amethyst hat, with belly and thighs under an intermediate sheath of silk—Renata dropped me in front of the county building. And she and her client, the big potent-looking lady in the polka-dot poplin, said, "*Ciao,* so long." And there was the handsome russet and glass skyscraper, and there was the insignificant Picasso sculpture with its struts and its sheet metal, no wings, no victory, only a token, a reminder, only the *idea* of a work of art. Very similar, I thought, to the other ideas or reminders by which we lived—no more apples but the idea, the pomologist's reconstruction of what an apple once was, no more ice cream but the idea, the recollection of something delicious made of substitutes, of starch, glucose, and other chemicals, no more sex but the idea or reminiscence of that, and so with love, belief, thought, and so on. On this theme I rose in an elevator to see what the court, with its specters of equity and justice, wanted of me. When the door of the elevator opened, it merely opened, no voice said, "My Fate!" Either Renata really filled the bill, or the voice had become too discouraged to speak.

I got out and saw my lawyer Forrest Tomchek and his junior associate Billy Srole waiting at the end of the wide open light gray corridor outside Judge Urbanovich's courtroom—two honest-looking deceitful men. According to Szathmar (Szathmar who couldn't even remember a simple name like Crawley), I was represented by Chicago's finest legal talent.

I said, "Then why don't I feel safe with Tomchek?"

"Because you're hypercritical, nervous, and a damn fool," said Szathmar. "In his branch of the law nobody has more respect and clout. Tomchek is one of the most powerful guys in the legal community. In Divorce and Post-Decree these guys form a club. They commute, they play golf, they fly to Acapulco together. Behind the scenes, he tells the other guys how it's all going to be done. Understand? That includes the fees, the tax consequences. Everything."

"You mean," I said, "they'll study my tax returns and so forth and then decide how to cut me up."

"My God!" said Szathmar. "Keep your opinion of lawyers to yourself." He was deeply offended, infuriated really, by my disrespect for his profession. Oh, I agreed with him that I must keep my feelings to myself. I made every effort to be pleasant and deferential to Tomchek, but I wasn't very good at this. The harder I tried, murmuring at Tomchek's pretensions, saying the right thing, the more he mistrusted and disliked me. He kept score. In the end I would pay a heavy price, an enormous fee, I knew that. So here was Tomchek. With him stood Billy Srole, the associate. Associate is a wonderful word, a wonderful category. Srole was chubby, pale, his attitude highly professional. He wore his hair long and kept it flowing by stroking it with a heavy white palm and looping it behind the ears. His fingers bent backward at the tips. He was a bully. These were bully refinements. I know bullies.

"What's up," I said.

Tomchek put his arm about my shoulder and we went into a brief huddle.

"Nothing to worry about," said Tomchek. "Urbanovich was suddenly free to meet with both parties."

"He wants to wrap the thing up. He's proud of his record as a negotiator," Srole told me.

"Look, Charlie," said Tomchek. "Here's the technique Urbanovich uses. He'll throw a scare into you. He'll tell you how much harm he can do and stampede you into an agreement. Don't panic. Legally we've put you in a good position."

I saw the healthy grim folds of Tomchek's close-shaven face. His breath was sourly virile. He gave off an odor which I associated with old-fashioned streetcar brakes, and with metabolism, and with male hormones. "No, I won't give any more ground," I said. "It doesn't work. If I meet her demands she makes brand-new ones. Since the Emancipation Proclamation there's been a secret struggle in this country to restore slavery by other means." This was the sort of statement that caused Tomchek and Srole to be suspicious of me.

"Okay, draw the line and hold it," said Srole. "And leave

the rest to us. Denise makes things tough for her own lawyer. Pinsker doesn't want a hassle. He only wants his dough. He doesn't like this situation. She's getting legal advice on the side from that fellow Schwirner. Completely unethical."

"I hate Schwirner! That son of a bitch," said Tomchek, violent. "If I could prove that he was banging the plaintiff and interfering in my case I'd fix his clock for him. I'd have him before the Ethics Committee."

"Is Gumballs Schwirner still carrying on with Charlie's wife?" said Srole, "I thought he just got married."

"So what if he got married? He still hasn't stopped meeting this crazy broad in motels. She gets strategy ideas from him in the sack, then she bugs Pinsker with them. They're confusing the hell out of Pinsker. How I'd love to get that Schwirner."

I offered no comment and scarcely seemed to hear what they were saying. Tomchek wanted me to suggest that we hire a private investigator to get the goods on Schwirner. I recalled Von Humboldt Fleisher and Scaccia, the private eye. I was having no part of this. "I expect you guys to restrain Pinsker," I said. "Don't let him tear at my guts."

"What, in chambers? He'll behave himself. He rags you on the witness stand but in conference it's different."

"He's an animal," I said.

They answered nothing.

"He's a beast, a cannibal."

This made an unpleasant impression. Tomchek and Srole, like Szathmar, were touchy about the profession. Tomchek remained silent. It was for Srole, the associate and stooge, to deal with captious Citrine. Mild, distant, Srole said, "Pinsker is a very tough man. Tough opponent. A gut fighter."

Okay, they weren't going to let me knock lawyers. Pinsker belonged to the club. Who, after all, was I? A filmy transient figure, eccentric and snooty. They disliked my style entirely. They hated it. But then why should they like it? Suddenly I saw the thing from their viewpoint. And I was extremely pleased. In fact I was illuminated. Maybe these sudden illuminations of mine were an effect of the metaphysical changes I was undergoing. Under the recent influence of Steiner I seldom thought of death in the horrendous old way. I wasn't experiencing the suffocating grave or dreading an eternity of boredom, nowadays. Instead I often felt unusually light and swift-paced, as if I were on a weightless bicycle and sprinting through the star world. Occasionally I saw myself with exhilarating objectivity, literally as an object among objects in the physical universe. One day that object would cease to move and when the body collapsed the soul would simply remove itself. So, to speak again of the lawyers, I stood between them, and there we were, three naked egos, three creatures belonging to the lower grade of modern rationality and calculation. In the past the self had had garments, the garments of station, of nobility or inferiority, and each self had its carriage, its looks, wore the sheath appropriate to it. Now there were no sheaths and it was naked self with naked self burning intolerably and causing terror. I saw this now, in a fit of objectivity. It felt ecstatic.

What was I to these fellows anyway? An oddball and a curiosity. To build himself up Szathmar bragged about me, he oversold me, and people became horribly annoyed because he told them to look me up in reference books and read about my prizes and my medals and Zig-Zag awards. He hammered them with this, he said they should be proud to have a client like me so of course they detested me sight unseen. The quintessence of their prejudice was once expressed by Szathmar himself when he lost his temper and shouted, "You're nothing but a prick with a pen!" He was so sore that he surpassed himself and yelled even louder, "With or without a pen you're a prick!" But I wasn't offended. I thought this was a whopping epithet and I laughed. If you only put it right you could say what you liked to me. However, I knew exactly how I made Tomchek and Srole feel. From their side they inspired me with an unusual thought. This was that History had created something new in the USA, namely crookedness with self-respect or duplicity with honor. America had always been very upright and moral, a model to the entire world, so it had put to death the very idea of hypocrisy and was forcing itself to live with this new imperative of sincerity, and it was doing an impressive job. Just consider Tomchek and Srole: they belonged to a prestigious honorable profession; that profession had its own high standards and everything was hotsy-totsy until some impossible exotic like me who couldn't even keep a wife in line, an idiot with a knack for stringing sentences together, came and disseminated a sense of wrongdoing. I carried an old accusing smell. It was, if you see what I mean, totally unhistorical of me. Owing to this I got a filmy side glance from Billy Srole, as if he were bemused by all the things he could do to me, under law or near the law, if I should ever step out of line. Watch out! He'd hack me up, he'd chop me into bits with his legal cleaver. Tomchek's eyes, unlike Srole's, needed no film, for his deeper opinions never reached his gaze. And I was completely dependent upon this fearful pair. In fact this was part of my ecstasy. It was terrific. Tomchek and Srole were just what I deserved. It was only right that I should pay a price for coming on so innocent and expecting the protection of those less pure, of people completely at home in the fallen world. Where did I get off, laying the fallen world on everyone else! Humboldt had used his credit as a poet when he was a poet no longer, but only crazy with schemes. And I was doing much the same thing, for I was really far too canny to claim such unworldliness. I believe the word is disingenuous. But Tomchek and Srole would set me straight. They had the assistance of Denise, Pinsker, Urbanovich, and a cast of thousands.

"I wish I knew what the hell made you look so pleased," said Srole.

"Only a thought."

"Lucky you, with your nice thoughts."

"But when do we go in?" I said.

"When the other side comes out."

"Oh, are Denise and Pinsker talking to Urbanovich now? Then I think I'll go and relax in the courtroom, my feet are beginning to hurt." A little of Tomchek and Srole went a long way. I wasn't going to stand chatting with them until we were summoned. My consciousness couldn't take much more of them. They quickly tired me.

I refreshed myself by sitting on a wooden bench. I had no book to read, I took this opportunity to meditate briefly. The object I chose for meditation was a bush covered with roses. I often summoned up this bush, but sometimes it made its appearance independently. It was filled, it was dense, it was choked with tiny dark garnet roses and fresh healthy leaves. So for the moment I thought "rose"—"rose" and nothing else. I visualized the twigs, the roots, the harsh fuzz of the new growth hardening into spikes, plus all the botany I could remember: phloem xylem cambium chloroplasts soil sun water chemistry, attempting to project myself into the very plant and to think how its green blood produced a red flower. Ah, but new growth in rosebushes was always red before it turned green. I recalled very accurately the inset spiral order of rose petals, the whitey faint bloom over the red and the slow opening that revealed the germinating center. I concentrated all the faculties of my soul on this vision and immersed it in the flowers. Then I saw, next to these flowers, a human figure standing. The plant, said Rudolf Steiner, expressed the pure passionless laws of growth, but the human being, aiming at higher perfection, assumed a greater burden—instincts, desires, emotions. So a bush was a sleeping life. But mankind took a chance on the passions. The wager was that the higher powers of the soul could cleanse these passions. Cleansed, they could be reborn in a finer form. The red of the blood was a symbol of this cleansing process. But even if all this wasn't so, to consider the roses always put me into a kind of bliss.

After a while I contemplated something else. I visualized an old black iron Chicago lamppost from forty years back, the type with a lid like a bullfighter's hat or a cymbal. Now it was night, there was a blizzard. I was a young boy and I watched from my bedroom window. It was a winter gale, the wind and snow banged the iron lamp, and the roses rotated under the light. Steiner recommended the contemplation of a cross wreathed with roses but for reasons of perhaps Jewish origin I preferred a lamppost. The object didn't matter as long as you went out of the sensible world. When you got out of the sensible world, you might feel parts of the soul awakening that never had been awake before.

I had made quite a lot of progress in this exercise when Denise came out of the chambers and passed through the swinging gate to join me.

This woman, the mother of my children, though she made so much trouble for me, often reminded me of something Samuel Johnson had said about pretty ladies: they might be foolish, they might be wicked, but beauty was of itself very estimable. Denise was in this way estimable. She had big violet eyes and a slender nose. Her skin was slightly downy—you could see this down when the light was right. Her hair was piled on top of her head and gave it too much weight. If she hadn't been beautiful you wouldn't have noticed the disproportion. The very fact that she wasn't aware of the top-heavy effect of her coiffure seemed at times a proof that she was a bit nutty. At court, having dragged me here with her suit, she always wanted to be chummy. And as she was unusually pleasant today I figured she had had a successful session with Urbanovich. The fact that she was going to beat me like a dog released her affections. For she was fond of me. She said, "Ah, you're waiting?" and her voice was high and tremulous, breaking slightly, but also militant. The weak, at war, never know how hard they are hitting you. She wasn't of course so weak. The strength of the social order was on her side. But she always felt weak, she was a burdened woman. Getting out of bed to make breakfast was almost more than she could face. Taking a cab to the hairdresser was also very hard. The beautiful head was a burden to the beautiful neck. So she sat down beside me, sighing. She hadn't been to the beauty salon lately. When her hair was thinned out by the hairdresser she didn't look quite so huge-eyed and goofy. There were holes in her stockings, for she always wore rags to court. "I'm absolutely exhausted," she said. "I never get any sleep before these court days."

I muttered, "Dreadfully sorry."

"You don't seem so well yourself."

"The girls tell me sometimes, 'Daddy, you look like a million dollars—green and wrinkled.' How are they, Denise?"

"As well as they can be. They miss you."

"That's normal, I suppose."

"Nothing is normal for them. They miss you painfully."

"You are to sorrow what Vermont is to syrup."

"What do you want me to say?"

"Only 'okay,' or 'not okay,'" I said.

"Syrup! As soon as something enters your head you blurt it out. That's your big weakness, your worst temptation."

This was my day to see the other fellow's point of view. How does anyone strengthen himself? Denise had it right, you know—by overcoming the persistent temptation. There've been times when just because I kept my mouth shut and didn't say what I thought, I felt my strength increasing. Still, I don't seem to know what I think till I see what I say.

"The girls are making Christmas plans. You're supposed to take them to the pageant at the Goodman Theater."

"No, nothing doing. That's your idea."

"Are you too big a figure to take them to a show like any ordinary father? You told them you would."

"Me? Never. You did that yourself, and now you imagine that I told them."

"You're going to be in town, aren't you?"

I wasn't in fact. I was leaving on Friday. I hadn't gotten around to informing Denise of this, and I said nothing now.

"Or are you planning a trip with Renata Fat-Tits?"

On this level, I was no match for Denise. Again, Renata! She wouldn't even allow the children to play with little Roger Koffritz. She once said, "Later they'll become immune to that kind of whore influence. But they came home once shaking their little behinds and I knew you had broken your promise to keep them away from Renata." Denise's information network was unusually effective. She knew all about Harold Flonzaley, for instance. "How is your rival the undertaker?" she sometimes asked me. For Renata's suitor Flonzaley owned a chain of funeral parlors. One of her ex-husband's business connections, Flonzaley had a ton of money, but his degree from the state university, it couldn't be denied, was in embalming. This gave our romance a gloomy tinge. I quarreled once with Renata because her apartment was filled with flowers and I knew that they were surplus funeral flowers abandoned by heartbroken mourners and delivered in Flonzaley's special flower-Cadillac.

I made her throw them down the rubbish chute. Flonzaley was still wooing her.

"Are you working at all?" said Denise.

"Not too much."

"Just playing paddle ball with Langobardi, relaxing with the Mafia? I know you aren't seeing any of your serious friends on the Midway. Durnwald would give you what-for but he's in Scotland. Too bad. I know he doesn't like Fat-Tits much more than I do. And he told me once how he disapproved of your buddy Thaxter, and your being involved in *The Ark*. You've spent a barrel of money probably on that magazine, and where is the first issue? *Nessuno sa*." Denise was an opera lover and she took a season ticket at the Lyric and quoted often from Mozart or from Verdi. *Nessuno sa* was from *Così Fan Tutte*. Where does one find the fidelity of women, sings Mozart's worldly wise man—*dove sia? dove sia? Nessu-no sa!* Again she was referring to the curious delinquency of Renata, and I knew it perfectly well.

"As a matter of fact, I'm expecting Thaxter. Maybe today."

"Sure, he'll blow into town like the entire cast of *A Midsummer Night's Dream*. You'd rather foot his bills than give the money to your children."

"My children have plenty of money. You have the house and hundreds of thousands. You got all the *Trenck* money, you and the lawyers."

"I can't keep that barn going. The fourteen-foot ceilings. You haven't seen the fuel bills. But then again you could squander your money on worse people than Thaxter, and you do. Thaxter at least has some style. He took us to Wimbledon in plenty of style. Remember? With a hamper. With champagne and smoked salmon from Harrods. From what I understand, it was the CIA that was picking up his tab in those days. Why not get the CIA to pay for *The Ark*?"

"Why the CIA?"

"I read your prospectus. I thought this was just the kind of serious intellectual magazine the CIA could use abroad for propaganda. You imagine you're some kind of cultural statesman."

"All I wanted to say in the prospectus was that America didn't have to fight scarcity and we all felt guilty before people who still had to struggle for bread and freedom in the old way, the old basic questions. We weren't starving, we weren't bugged by the police, locked up in madhouses for our ideas, arrested, deported, slave laborers sent to die in concentration camps. We were spared the holocausts and nights of terror. With our advantages we should be formulating the new basic questions for mankind. But instead we sleep. Just sleep and sleep, and eat and play and fuss and sleep again."

"When you get solemn you're a riot, Charlie. And now you're going in for mysticism, as well as keeping that fat broad, as well as becoming an athlete, as well as dressing like a dude—all symptoms of mental and physical decline. I'm so sorry, really. Not just because I'm the mother of your children, but because you once had brains and talent. You might have stayed productive if the Kennedys had lived. Their kind of action kept you responsible and sane."

"You sound like the late Humboldt. He was going to be Czar of Culture under Stevenson."

"The old Humboldt hang-up, too. You've still got that. He was the last serious friend you had," she said.

In these conversations, always somewhat dreamlike, Denise believed that she was concerned, solicitous, even loving. The fact that she had gone into judge's chambers and dug another legal pit for me was irrelevant. In her view we were like England and France, dear enemies. For her it was a special relationship, permitting intelligent exchanges.

"People tell me about this Dr. Scheldt, your anthroposophist guru. They say he's very kind and nice. But his daughter is a real little popsie. A small opportunist. She wants you to marry her, too. You're a fearful challenge to females who have dreams of glory about you. But you can always hide behind poor Demmie Vonghel."

Denise was pelting me with the ammunition she stored up daily in her mind and heart. Again, however, her information was accurate. Like Renata and the old Señora, Miss Scheldt also spoke of May–December marriages, of the happiness and creativity of Picasso's declining years, of Casals and Charlie Chaplin and Justice Douglas.

"Renata doesn't want you to be a mystic, does she?"

"Renata doesn't meddle that way. I'm not a mystic. Anyway I don't know why mystic should be such a bad word. It doesn't mean much more than the word 'religion,' which some people still speak of with respect. What does religion say? It says that there's something in human beings beyond the body and brain and that we have ways of knowing that go beyond the organism and its senses. I've always believed that. My misery comes, maybe, from ignoring my own metaphysical hunches. I've been to college so I know the educated answers. Test me on the scientific world-view and I'd score high. But it's just head stuff."

"You're a born crank, Charlie. When you said you were going to write that essay on boredom, I thought, There he goes! Now you're degenerating quickly, without me. Sometimes I feel you might be certifiable or committable. Why don't you go back to the Washington-in-the-Sixties book? The stuff you published in magazines was fine. You've told me lots more that never got into print. If you've lost your notes, I could remind you. I can still straighten you out, Charlie."

"You think you can?"

"I understand the mistakes we both made. And the way you live is too grotesque—all these girls, and the athletics and trips, and now the anthroposophy. Your friend Durnwald is upset about you. And I know your brother Julius is worried. Look, Charlie, why don't you marry me again? For starters we could stop the legal fight. We should become reunited."

"Is this a serious proposition?"

"It's what the girls want more than anything. Think it over. You're not exactly leading a life of joy. You're in bad shape. I'd be taking a risk." She stood up and opened her purse. "Here are a few letters that came to the old address."

I looked at the postmarks. "They're months old. You might have turned them over before, Denise."

"What's the difference? You get too much mail as it is. You don't answer most of it, and what good does it do you?"

"You've opened this one and resealed it. It's from Humboldt's widow."

"Kathleen? They were divorced years before he died. Anyway, here comes your legal talent."

Tomchek and Srole entered the courtroom, and from the other side came Cannibal Pinsker in a bright yellow double-knit jazzy suit and a large yellow cravat that lay on his shirt like a cheese omelette, and tan shoes in two tones. His head was brutally hairy. He was grizzled and he carried himself like an old prizefighter. What might he have been in an earlier incarnation, I wondered. I wondered about us all.

• • •

We were not meeting with Denise and Pinsker after all, only with the judge. Tomchek, Srole, and I entered his chambers. Judge Urbanovich, a Croatian, perhaps a Serbian, was plump and bald, a fatty, and somewhat flat-faced. But he was cordial, he was very civilized. He offered us a cup of coffee. I referred his cordiality to the Department of Vigilance. "No, thanks," I said.

"We've now had five sessions in court," Urbanovich began. "This litigation is harmful to the parties—not to their lawyers, of course. Being on the stand is frightful for a sensitive creative person like Mr. Citrine. . . ." The judge meant me to feel the ironic weight of this. Sensitivity in a mature Chicagoan, if genuine, was a treatable form of pathology, but a man whose income passed two hundred thousand dollars in his peak years was putting you on about sensitivity. Sensitive plants didn't make that kind of dough. "It can't be pleasant," Judge Urbanovich now said to me, "to be examined by Mr. Pinsker. He belongs to the hard-edge school. He can't pronounce the titles of your works, or the names of French, Italian, or even English companies you deal with. Besides, you don't like his tailor, his taste in shirts and ties. . . ."

In short it was too bad to turn this ugly violent moron Pinsker loose on me but if I remained uncooperative, the judge would unleash him.

"Three, four, five separate times we've negotiated with Mrs. Citrine," said Tomchek.

"Your offers weren't good enough."

"Your honor, Mrs. Citrine has received large amounts of money," I said. "We offer more and she always increases her demands. If I capitulate, will you guarantee that I won't be back in court next year?"

"No, but I can try. I can make it *res judicata*. Your problem, Mr. Citrine, is your proven ability to earn big sums."

"Not lately."

"Only because you're upset by the litigation. If I end the litigation, I set you free and there's no limit to what you can make. You'll thank me. . . ."

"Judge, I'm old-fashioned and maybe even obsolete. I never learned mass-production methods."

"Don't be so nervous about this, Mr. Citrine. We have confidence in you. We've seen your articles in *Look* and in *Life*."

"But *Life* and *Look* have gone out of business. They're obsolete, too."

"We have your tax returns. They tell a different story."

"Still," said Forrest Tomchek. "In terms of reliable business forecast. How can my client promise to produce?"

Urbanovich said, "It's inconceivable, whatever happens, for Mr. Citrine ever to fall below the fifty-percent tax bracket. So if he pays Mrs. Citrine thirty thousand per annum it only costs him fifteen thousand in real dollars. Until the majority of the littlest daughter."

"So for the next fourteen years, or until I'm about seventy, I must earn one hundred thousand dollars a year. I can't help being a little amused by this, your Honor. Ha ha! I don't think my brain is strong enough, it's my only real asset. Other people have land, rent, inventories, management, capital gains, price supports, depletion allowances, federal subsidies. I have no such advantages."

"Ah but you're a clever person, Mr. Citrine. Even in Chicago that's obvious. So there's no need to put this on a special-case basis. In the property division under the decree Mrs. Citrine got less than half and she alleges that records were falsified.

You are a bit dreamy and probably were not aware of this. Perhaps the records were falsified by others. Nevertheless you are responsible under the law."

Srole said, "We deny any kind of fraud."

"Well, I don't think fraud is a great issue here," said the judge—and made an "out-the-window" gesture with open hands. Pisces was evidently his astrological sign. He wore tiny fish cuff links, tail to head.

"As for Mr. Citrine's lowered productivity of recent years, this may be deliberate to balk the plaintiff. Or it may actually be that he is mentally in transition." The judge was having a good time, I could see that. Evidently he disliked Tomchek the Divorce Statesman, he agreed that Srole was only a stooge, and he was diverting himself with me. "I am sympathetic to the problems of intellectuals and I know you may get into special preoccupations that aren't lucrative. But I understand that this Maharishi fellow by teaching people to turn their tongues backward past the palate so that they can get the tip of the tongue into their own sinuses has become a multimillionaire. Many ideas are marketable and perhaps your special preoccupations are more lucrative than you realize," he said.

Anthroposophy was having definite effects. I couldn't take any of this too hard. Other-worldliness tinged it all and every little while my spirit seemed to disassociate itself. It left me and passed out of the window to float a bit over the civic plaza. Or else the meditative roses would start to glow in my head, set in dewy green. But the judge was giving me a going-over, reinterpreting the twentieth century for me, lest I forget, deciding how the rest of my life was to be spent. I was to quit being an old-time artisan and adopt the methods of soulless manufacture (Ruskin). Tomchek and Srole, at either side of the desk, in their hearts consented and agreed. They said almost nothing. Feeling deserted, vexed, I therefore spoke up for myself.

"So it's about half a million dollars more. And even if she remarries she wants a guaranteed income of ten thousand dollars?"

"True."

"And Mr. Pinsker is asking for a fee of thirty thousand—ten thousand dollars for each month he spent on the case?"

"That's not really so unreasonable," said the judge. "You haven't been hurt hard in the way of fees."

"It doesn't come to more than five hundred dollars an hour. That's what I figure my own time to be worth, especially when I have to do what I dislike," I said.

"Mr. Citrine," the judge said to me, "you've led a more or less bohemian life. Now you've had a taste of marriage, the family, middle-class institutions, and you want to drop out. But we can't allow you to dabble like that."

Suddenly my detachment ended and I found myself in a state. I understood what emotions had torn at Humboldt's heart when they grabbed him and tied him up and raced him to Bellevue. The man of talent struggled with cops and orderlies. And, up against the social order, he had had to fight his Shakespearian longing, too—the longing for passionate speech. This had to be resisted. I could have cried aloud now. I could have been eloquent and moving. But what if I were to burst out like Lear to his daughters, like Shylock telling off the Christians? It would get me nowhere to utter burning words. The daughters and the Christians understood. Tomchek, Srole, and the judge didn't. Suppose I were to exclaim about morality, about flesh and blood and justice and evil and what it felt like to be me, Charlie Citrine? Wasn't this a court of equity, a forum of conscience? And hadn't I tried in my own confused way to bring some good into the world? Yes, and having pursued a higher purpose although without even getting close, now that I was aging, weakening, disheartened, doubting my endurance and even my sanity, they wanted to harness me to an even heavier load for the last decade or so. Denise was not correct in saying that I blurted out whatever entered my head. No sir. I crossed my arms on my chest and kept my mouth shut, taking a chance on heartbreak through tongue-holding. Besides, as suffering went, I was only in the middle rank or even lower. So out of respect for the real thing I clammed up. I shunted my thoughts onto a different track. At least I tried to. I wondered what Kathleen Fleisher Tigler was writing to me about.

These were very tough guys. I had their attention because of my worldly goods. Otherwise I would already have been behind the steel meshes of the county jail. As for Denise, that marvelous lunatic with the great violet eyes, the slender downy nose, the breaking martial voice—suppose I were to offer her all of my money? It would make no difference whatever, she would want to get more. And the judge? The judge was a Chicagoan and a politician, and his racket was equal justice under the law. A government of laws? This was a government of lawyers. But no, no, inflammation of the heart and burning words would only aggravate matters. No, the name of the game was silence, hardness and silence. I wasn't going to talk. A rose, or something that glowed like a rose, intruded itself, it wagged for an instant in my skull, and I felt that my decision was endorsed.

The judge now began to strafe me in earnest. "I understand that Mr. Citrine has been leaving the country often and is planning to go abroad again."

"This is the first I hear of it," said Tomchek. "Are you going anywhere?"

"For the Christmas holidays," I said. "Is there any reason why I shouldn't go?"

"None," said the judge, "if you're not trying to escape jurisdiction. The plaintiff and Mr. Pinsker have suggested that Mr. Citrine is planning to leave the country for good. They say he hasn't renewed his apartment lease and is selling his valuable collection of Oriental rugs. I assume that there are no numbered Swiss accounts. But what's to prevent him taking his head, which is his big asset, to Ireland or to Spain, countries that have no reciprocal agreements with us?"

"Is there any evidence for this, your honor?" I said.

The lawyers began to discuss the matter and I wondered how Denise had come to know that I was going away. Renata of course told the Señora everything and the Señora, singing for her supper all over Chicago, needed bright items to sing about. If she couldn't find something interesting to say at the dinner table, she might as well be dead. However, it was also possible that Denise's spy network had a contact in Poliakoff's Travel Bureau.

"These frequent flights to Europe are thought to have a purpose." Judge Urbanovich had his hand on the valve now and increased the heat still more. His genial glance said brilliantly, "Look out!" And suddenly Chicago was not my town at all. It was totally unrecognizable. I merely imagined that I had grown up here, that I knew the place, that I was known by it. In Chicago my personal aims were bunk, my outlook a foreign ideology, and I made out what the judge was telling me. It was that I had avoided all the Cannibal Pinskers and freed myself from unpleasant realities. He, Urbanovich, as clever a man as myself, with as much sensibility and better looks, bald or not, had paid his social dues in full, had played golf with all the Pinskers, had lunched with them. He had had to put up with this as man and citizen while I was at liberty to sail up and down elevator shafts expecting that a lovely being— "My Fate!"—would be smiling at me the next time the door opened. They'd give me Fate.

"Plaintiff has asked for an order of *ne exeat*. I am considering whether a bond should not be posted," said Urbanovich. "Two hundred thousand, say."

Indignant, Tomchek said, "With no evidence that my client is running out?"

"He's a very absent-minded fellow, your honor," said Srole. "Not signing a lease is a normal oversight, for him."

"If Mr. Citrine owned a little retail business, a little factory, if he had a professional practice or a position in an institution," said Urbanovich, "there would be no question of sudden flight." With round-eyed terrible lightness he was gazing at me, speculative.

Tomchek argued, "Citrine is a lifetime Chicagoan, a figure in this city."

"I understand that a great deal of money has slipped away this year. I hesitate to use the word 'squandered'—it's his money." Urbanovich consulted a memo. "Large losses in a publishing enterprise called *The Ark*. A colleague, Mr. Thaxter . . . bad debts."

"Is it suggested these are not genuine losses and he's been squirreling away money? These are Mrs. Citrine's allegations

Visit the Cafe!

Now through 3/31/2024

Buy 1
Fresh Baked Cookie
Get 50% OFF a
2nd Cookie

Mix or Match any flavor!!!

See Cafe for details.

and suspicions," said Tomchek. "Does the court believe them to be facts?"

The judge said, "This is a private conversation in chambers and only that. I feel, however, in view of the one indisputable fact that so much money is suddenly taking wing, Mr. Citrine should give me a full and current financial statement so that I can determine a bond figure, should that be necessary. You won't refuse me that, will you, Mr. Citrine?"

Oh bad! Very bad! What if Cantabile had the right idea after all—run her down in a truck, kill the bitch.

"I'll have to sit down with my accountant, your honor," I said.

"Mr. Citrine, you have a slightly persecuted look. I hope you understand that I am impartial, that I shall be fair to both parties." When the judge smiled certain muscles which unsubtle people never develop at all became visible. That was interesting. What did nature originally intend such muscles for? "I myself don't think you intend to run away. Mrs. Citrine admits you're a very affectionate father. Still, people do get desperate, and then they can be persuaded to do rash things."

He wanted me to know that my relations with Renata were no secret.

"I hope that you and Mrs. Citrine and Mr. Pinsker will leave me a little something to live on, Judge."

Then we, the defendant's group, were in the light gray speckled heavy polished stone corridor again and Srole said, "Charles, just as we told you, it's the man's technique. Now you're supposed to be terrified and beg us to settle and save you from being butchered and hacked to pieces."

"Well, it's working," I said. I wished that I could spring from this official skyscraper with its multiple squares into another life, never to be seen again. "I am terrified," I said. "And I'm dying to settle."

"Yes, but you can't. She won't accept it," said Tomchek, "she'll only pretend. She won't hear of settle. It's all in the books and at every dinner table every psychoanalyst I ever discussed it with told me the same thing—castration, that's all it is, when a woman is after the money."

"It isn't clear to me why Urbanovich is so keen to assist her."

"With him it seems a terrific fun thing," said Srole. "I often think so."

"And in the end most of the money will go for legal fees," I said. "I have asked myself sometimes why not give up and take a vow of poverty. . . ." But this was idle theorizing. Yes, I might surrender my small fortune and live and die in a hotel room like Humboldt. I was better equipped to lead a mental life as I was not a manic depressive and it might suit me very well. Only it wouldn't suit me well enough. For then there would be no more Renatas, no more erotic life, and no more of the exciting anxieties associated with the erotic life, which were perhaps even more important to me than sex itself. A vow of poverty was not the vow Renata was looking for.

"The bond—the bond is what's bad. That's a low blow," I said. "I really felt that you should have objected more. Put up a fight."

"But what was there to fight?" said Billy Srole. "It's all a bluff. He's got nothing to hang it on. You forgot to sign a lease. You're taking trips to Europe. Those might be professional trips. And listen, how come that woman knows every single move you're going to make?"

I was sure that Mrs. Da Cintra at the travel bureau, the one with the paisley turban, gave Denise information because Renata was impolite to her, even overbearing. As to Denise's knowledge of my actions, I had an analogy for it. Last year I took my little girls to the Far West camping and we visited a beaver lake. Along the shore the Forest Service had posted descriptions of the beaver's life cycle. The beavers were unaware of this and went on gnawing damming feeding and breeding. My own case was quite similar. With Denise it was, in the Mozartian Italian that she liked, *Tutto tutto già si sa.* Everything, everything about me was known.

I now realized that I had offended Tomchek by criticizing his handling of the bond question. No, I had incensed him. However, to protect the client relationship, he took it out on Denise. "How could you marry such a vile bitch!" he said. "Where the hell was your judgment! You're supposed to be a clever man. And if a woman like that decides to bug you to death what do you expect a couple of lawyers to do?" Already out of breath with exasperation he could say no more but snapped his attaché case under his arm and left us. I wished that Srole would go too, but he felt that he must tell me how strong my legal position really was (thanks to him). He stood in my way repeating that Urbanovich couldn't impound my money. He had no grounds for it. "But if it *should* come to the worst and he does lay a bond on you I know a guy who can give you a real buy in tax-exempt municipals so you don't lose the income of the frozen money."

"Good thinking," I said.

To get away I went to the men's room. As he followed me there I entered one of the stalls and was free at last to read Kathleen's letter.

•   •   •

As expected, Kathleen informed me of the death of her second husband, Frank Tigler, in a hunting accident. I knew him well, for while putting in my six weeks in Nevada to qualify for a divorce I had been a paying guest at the Tigler dude ranch. This was a lonely run-down god-forsaken place on Volcano Lake. My relations with Tigler were memorable. I had even the right to claim that I had saved his life, for when he fell out of a boat I jumped into the water to rescue him. Rescue? This event never seemed to deserve such a description. But he was a nonswimming cowboy, a cripple when he was not on horseback. On the ground in boots and Western hat he looked injured in the knees, and when he toppled into the water—the bold bronze face with ginger tufted brows, the bent horse-disfigured legs—I went after him immediately because water was not his element. He was a dry-land man of the extreme type. Then why were we in a boat? Because Tigler was keen to catch fish. He was not so much a fisherman as he was intent always on getting something for nothing. And it was spring and the toobie-fish were running. The toobies, a biological antiquity related to the coelacanth of the Indian Ocean, lived in Volcano Lake, coming up from a great depth to spawn. Crowds of people, Indians mostly, gaffed them in. The fish were awkward, strange to look at, living fossils. They were cured in the sun and stank up the Indian village. Words like "pellucid" and "voltaic" can be applied to the waters of Volcano Lake. When Tigler fell in I was instantly afraid that I might never see him again, the Indians having told me that the lake was miles deep and that bodies seldom were recovered. So I jumped and the cold was electrifying. I boosted Tigler into the boat again. He did not admit that he couldn't swim. He admitted nothing, he said nothing, but caught up the gaff and hooked in his floating hat. His cowboy boots had filled with water. Acknowledgments were neither asked nor given. It was an incident between two men. I mean, I felt it to be the manly silent West. The Indians would surely have let him drown. They didn't want white men coming in their boats, filled with the something-for-nothing fever, and taking their toobies. Besides, they hated Tigler for price-gouging and cheating, and for letting his horses graze everywhere. Furthermore, and Tigler himself had said this to me, the redskins didn't interfere with death but seemed simply to let it happen. Once, he told me, he was present when an Indian named Winnemucca was shot down in front of the post office. No one called a doctor. The man had bled to death in the road while men women and children, sitting on benches and in their old automobiles, watched silently. But at the present moment, high in the county building, I could see the late Tigler's Western figure as if it were cast in bronze, turning over and over in the electrical icy water, and then I saw myself, who had learned swimming in a small chlorinated tank in Chicago, pursuing him like an otter.

From Kathleen's letter I learned that he died in action. "Two fellows from Mill Valley California wanted to hunt deer with crossbows," wrote Kathleen. "Frank was guiding and took them into the hills. There was a run-in with the game warden. I think you met this warden, an Indian named Tony Calico, a Korean War veteran. One of the hunters turned out to have a criminal record. Poor Frank, you know, loved to be a little outside the law. He wasn't, in this case, but still there was a touch of it. There were shotguns in the Land Rover. I won't go into the details, they're too painful. Frank didn't fire but he was the only one shot. He bled to death before Tony could get him to the hospital.

"It hit me very hard, Charlie," she continued. "We were married twelve years, you know. At any rate, not to dwell on this too long, there was a big funeral. Quarter-horse people came from three states. Business associates from Las Vegas and Reno. He was very well liked."

I knew that Tigler had been a rodeo-rider and broncobuster, winner of many prizes, and that he enjoyed some esteem in the horse world, but I doubt that he was dear to anyone except Kathleen and his old mother. The income from the dude ranch, such as it was, he put into his quarter horses. Some of these horses were registered under phony papers, their sires having been ruled off the track as doped or doctored. The hereditary attainder rule was very strict. Tigler was bound to try to get around it with forged documents. So he was on the move from track to track and left Kathleen to manage the business. There wasn't much business to manage. He milked it of income to buy feed and trailers. The guest cabins folded and fell. They reminded me of Humboldt's collapsing chicken farm. Kathleen was in exactly the same fix in Nevada. Fate—fate within—was too strong for her. Tigler put her in charge of the ranch and told her to pay nothing but essential horse-bills, and those only on violent demand.

I had plenty of troubles of my own, but the double solitude of Kathleen's life—first in New Jersey, then in the West—moved me strongly. I leaned against the partition of the biffy in the county building trying to get light from above on her letter, typed with a faded ribbon. "I know you liked Tigler, Charlie. You had such a good time trout fishing with him and playing poker. It took your mind off your troubles."

That was so, although he was furious when I caught the first trout. We were trawling from his boat and I was using his lure, so he said it was his trout. He made a scene and I tossed the fish into his lap. The surroundings were unearthly. It was not a fish setting—only bare rock, no trees, pungent sagebrush, and marl dust floating when a truck passed.

However, it was not to discuss Tigler that Kathleen wrote to me. She wrote because Orlando Huggins was asking for me. Humboldt had left me something. Huggins was his executor. Huggins, that old left-wing playboy, was a decent man, at bottom an honorable person. He too cherished Humboldt. After I was denounced as a false blood-brother Huggins was called in to sort out Humboldt's business affairs. He eagerly rushed into the act. Then Humboldt accused him of cheating and threatened to sue him, too. But Humboldt's mind had evidently cleared toward the last. He had identified his true friends, naming Huggins as administrator of his estate. Kathleen and I were remembered in the will. What she got from him she didn't say, but he couldn't have had much to give. Kathleen mentioned, however, that Huggins had turned over to her a posthumous letter from Humboldt. "He talked about love, and the human opportunities he missed," she wrote. "He mentioned old friends, Demmie and you, and the good old days in the Village and out in the country."

I can't think what made those old days so good. I doubt that Humboldt had had a single good day in all his life. Between fluctuations and the dark qualms of mania and depression, he had had good spells. Perhaps not so many as two consecutive hours of composure. But Humboldt would have appealed to Kathleen in ways in which I was too immature twenty-five years ago to understand. She was a big substantial woman whose deep feelings were invisible because her manner was so quiet. As for Humboldt he had some nobility even when he was crazy. Even then he was constant to some very big things indeed. I remember the shine of his eyes when he dropped his voice to pronounce the word "relume" spoken by a fellow about to commit a murder, or when he spoke Cleopatra's words "I have immortal longings in me." The man loved art deeply. We loved him for it. Even when the decay was raging there were incorruptible places in Humboldt that were not rotted out. But I think he wanted Kathleen to protect him when he entered the states a poet needed to be in. These high dreaming states, always being punctured and torn by American flak, were what he wanted Kathleen to preserve for him. Enchantment. She did her best to help him with the enchantment. But he could never come up with enough enchantment or dream material to sheathe himself in. It would not cover. However, I saw what Kathleen had tried to do and admired her for it.

The letter went on. She reminded me of our long talks under the trees at Rancho Tigler. I suppose I had been telling her about Denise, busy with self-justification. I can recall the trees she referred to, a few box elders and cottonwoods. Tigler advertised the gaiety of his resort, but the bleached boards were sprung and falling from the bunkhouses, the swimming pool was all cracks and covered with leaves and scum. The fences were down and Tigler's mares strolled about freely like beautiful naked matrons. Kathleen wore dungarees and her gingham shirt was laundered to an ectoplasmic degree. I can remember Tigler squatting, repainting his decoy ducks. He wasn't speaking at that time, for his jaw had been broken by someone in anger over a feed bill and was now wired shut. Also that week the utilities were cut off, the guests were freezing, the water was not running. Tigler said that this was the West the dudes really loved. They didn't come out here to be pampered. They wanted it rough and ready. But to me Kathleen said, "I can only handle this a day or two more."

Luckily a movie company turned up to make a picture about the Mongol hordes and Tigler was hired to be the horse expert. He recruited Indians to wear quilted Asiatic costumes and to gallop shrieking and do stunts in the saddle. It was a big thing for Volcano Lake. Credit for this windfall was claimed by Father Edmund, the Episcopal minister who in his youth had been a silent-movie star and very beautiful. In the pulpit he wore marvelous old negligees. The Indians were all film-fans. They whispered that his garments had been donated by Marion Davies or Gloria Swanson. He, said Father Edmund, with his Hollywood connections, had induced the company to come to Volcano Lake. Anyway, Kathleen became acquainted with movie people. I mention this because in her letter she spoke of selling the ranch, putting Mother Tigler out to board with people in Tungsten City while she took a job in the picture industry. People in transition often develop an interest in the movies. Either that or they begin to talk about going back to school for a degree. There must be twenty million Americans who dream of returning to college. Even Renata was forever about to enroll herself at De Paul.

I went back to the courtroom to pick up my primrose path youthful check overcoat deeply considering what to do for money if Urbanovich laid a bond on me. What a bastard he was, this Croatian American bald judge. He knew neither the children nor Denise nor me, and what right had he to take away money earned in thought and fever by such peculiar operations of the brain! Oh yes I knew how to be high-minded about money too. Yea let them take all! And I could fill out a psychological questionnaire with the best of them, certain of being in the top ten percent for magnanimity. But Humboldt—I was full of Humboldt today—used to accuse me of trying to spend my whole life in the upper stories of higher consciousness. Higher consciousness, Humboldt said, lecturing me, was "innocent, aware of no evil in itself." When you tried to live entirely in high consciousness, purely reasonable, you saw evil in other people only, never in yourself. From this Humboldt went on to insist that in the unconscious, in the irrational core of things, money was a vital substance like the blood or fluids that bathed the brain tissues. Since he was always so earnest about the higher significance of money, had he perhaps returned my six thousand seven hundred and sixty-odd bucks in his last will and testament? Of course he hadn't, how could he? He had died broke in a flophouse. But six thousand bucks wouldn't go far now. Szathmar alone owed me more than that. I had lent Szathmar money to buy a condominium. Then there was Thaxter. Thaxter, by defaulting on a loan, had cost me fifty shares of IBM stock posted as collateral. After many letters of warning, the bank, with ethical gestures and regrets, almost weeping to see me so cruelly stung by a conniving friend, took away those shares. Thaxter pointed out that this was a deductible loss. Both he and Szathmar often comforted me in this way. By appealing also to dignity and to absolute value. (Didn't I,

myself, aim at magnanimity, and wasn't friendship a far bigger thing than money?) People kept me broke. And now what
was I to do? I owed publishers about seventy thousand dollars
in advances for books I was too paralyzed to write. I had lost
interest in them utterly. I could sell my Oriental rugs. I had
told Renata that I was tired of them, and she knew an Arme-
nian dealer who was willing to take them on commission. Now
that foreign currencies were booming and the oil-rich Persians
no longer wished to work at the loom. German and Japanese
buyers and even Arabs were raiding the Midwest and carrying
off the carpets. As for the Mercedes, perhaps it would be better to get rid of it. I was always greatly shaken when forced to
fret about money. I felt like a falling rigger or dangling window washer, caught under the arms by his safety harness. I was
strained across the chest and seemed to be deprived of oxygen. I considered sometimes storing a cylinder of oxygen in the
clothes closet for just such spells of worry. I should of course
have opened a numbered Swiss bank account. How was it, that
having lived most of my life in Chicago, I hadn't thought to
provide myself with a bagman? And now what had I to sell?
Thaxter was sitting on two articles of mine, a reminiscence of
Kennedy Washington (now as far behind us as the founding of
the Capuchin Order) and an article from the unfinished series
"Great Bores of the Modern World." There was no money
there. It was excellent, but who would publish a serious study
of bores?

I was even willing now to consider George Swiebel's scheme
for mining beryllium in Africa. I had scoffed at this when
George proposed it but wilder ideas were commercially sound
and no man ever knew what form his Dick Whittington's cat
might take. A man named Ezekiel Kamuttu, George's guide to
the Olduvai Gorge two years ago, claimed to own a mountain
of beryllium and semiprecious stones. A sack of exotic burlap
was at this moment lying under George's bed, filled with peculiar minerals. George had given me a sweat sock filled with
these and asked me to get them assayed at the Field Museum by
Ben Isvolsky, one of our schoolmates, now a geologist. Sober
Ben said they were the real thing. At once he lost his scholar's

air and began to put business questions to me. Could we get these stones in marketable quantities on a regular basis? And with what machinery, and how get into the bush and out? And who was this Kamuttu? Kamuttu, George said, would lay down his life for him. He had invited George to marry into his family. He wanted to sell him his sister. "But," I said to Ben, "you know George's boon-companion complex. He has a few drinks with natives, they see how real he is and that his heart is bigger than the Mississippi. It really is, too. But how can we be sure that this Kamuttu hasn't got some con? Maybe he's stolen these beryllium samples. Or maybe he's bonkers. There's no world shortage of that."

Knowing Isvolsky's domestic troubles, I understood why he dreamed of making a killing in minerals. "Anything," he told me, "to get away from Winnetka for a while." Then he said, "Okay, Charlie, I know what's on your mind. When you come back here to see me you want to be shown those birds." He referred to the museum's great collection of birds, hoarded up over decades and stored in classified drawers. The huge workshops and laboratories behind the scenes, the sheds, storerooms, and caverns were infinitely more fascinating than the museum's public exhibits. The preserved birds were collapsed, their legs tagged. And mainly I liked to see the hummingbirds, thousands upon thousands of little bodies, some no bigger than my fingertip, endless varieties of them, all spattered minutely with a whole Louvre of iridescent colors. So Ben took me to inspect them again. He had full cheeks and woolly hair, bad skin but an agreeable face. The museum treasures now bored him and he said, "If this Kamuttu really has a mountain of beryllium we should go there and grab it."

"I'm leaving soon for Europe," I said.

"Ideal. George and I can pick you up. We can all fly to Nairobi together."

Thoughts of beryllium and Oriental rugs showed how nervous I was, and impractical. When I was in this state only one man in all the world could help me, my practical brother Julius, a real-estate operator in Corpus Christi, Texas. I loved my stout and now elderly brother. Perhaps he loved me too.

In principle he was not in favor of strong family bonds. Possibly he saw brotherly love as an opening for exploitation. My feelings for him were vivid, almost hysterically intense, and I could not blame him for trying to resist them. He wished to be a man entirely of today, and he had forgotten or tried to forget the past. Unassisted he could remember nothing, he said. For my part there was nothing that I could forget. He often said to me, "You inherited the old man's terrific memory. And before him there was that old bastard, his old man. Our grandfather was one of ten guys in the Jewish Pale who knew the Babylonian Talmud by heart. Lots of good that did. I don't even know what it is. But that's where you get your memory." The admiration was not unmixed. I don't think he was always grateful to me for remembering so well. My own belief was that without memory existence was metaphysically injured, damaged. And I couldn't conceive of my own brother, irreplaceable Julius, having metaphysical assumptions different from mine. So I would talk to him about the past, and he would say, "Is that so? Is that a fact? And you know I can't remember a thing, not even the way Mama looked, and I was her favorite, after all."

"You must remember how she looked. How could you forget her? I don't believe that," I said. My family sentiments tormented my stout brother sometimes. He thought me some sort of idiot. He himself, a wizard with money, built shopping centers, condominiums, motels, and contributed greatly to the transformation of his part of Texas. He wouldn't refuse to help me. But this was purely theoretical, for although the idea of help was continually in the air between us, I never actually asked him to give me any. In fact I was extremely reserved about making such a request. I was, if I may say so, merely obsessed, filled by the need to make it.

As I was picking up my coat, Urbanovich's bailiff came up to me and took a piece of paper from the pocket of his cardigan. "Tomchek's office phoned this message in," he said. "There's a fellow with a foreign name—is it Pierre?" said the old man.

"Pierre Thaxter?"

"I wrote down what they gave me. He wants you to meet

him at three at the Art Institute. Also a couple came to ask for
you. Fellow with a mustache. Girl with red hair, mini-skirt."

"Cantabile," I said.

"He didn't leave no name."

It was now half past two. Much had happened in a short
time. I went to Stop and Shop and bought sturgeon and fresh
rolls, also Twining's breakfast tea and Cooper's vintage marmalade. If Thaxter was staying overnight I wanted to give him the
breakfast he was accustomed to. He always fed me extremely
well. He took pride in his table and told me in French what
I was eating. I ate no mere tomatoes but *salade de tomates,*
no bread and butter but *tartines,* and so it went with *bouilli,*
brûlé, farci, fumé, and excellent wines. He dealt with the best
tradespeople and nothing disagreeable to eat or drink was ever
set before me.

As a matter of fact I looked forward to Thaxter's visit. I was
always delighted to see him. Perhaps I even had the illusion that
I could open my oppressed heart to him, although I really knew
better than that. He would blow in from California wearing his
hair long like a Stuart courtier and, under his carabiniere cloak,
dressed in a charming blue velvet lounging suit from the King's
Road. His broad-brimmed hat was bought in a shop for black
swingers. About his neck would be apparently valuable chains,
and also a piece of knotted, soiled, but uniquely tinted silk. His
light-tan boots, which came up to the ankle, were ingeniously
faced with canvas, and on each of the canvas sides there was
an ingenious fleur-de-lis of leather. His nose was strongly distorted, his dark face flaming, and when I saw his leopard eyes
I'd give a secret cheer. There was a reason why, when the bailiff
told me that he was in town, I immediately laid out five dollars
on sturgeon. I was extremely fond of Thaxter. Now, then, the
great question: did he or did he not know what he was doing?
In a word, was he a crook? This was a question a shrewd man
should be able to answer, and I couldn't answer. Renata, when
she did me the honor of treating me as her future husband,
often said, "Don't drop any more money on Thaxter. Charm?
All charm. Talent? Buckets of talent. But a phony."

"He's really not."

"What? Have a little self-respect, Charlie, about what you swallow. All that Social Register stuff of his?"

"Oh that! Yes, but people have to boast. They're dead if they can't say good things about themselves. Good things *have* to be said. Have a heart."

"All right then, his special wardrobe. His special umbrella. The only umbrella with class is a natural-hook umbrella. You don't buy an umbrella with a manufactured steam-bent hook. For Christ's sake it's got to grow that way. Then there's his special wine cellar, and his special attaché case which you can buy only in one shop in London, and his special water bed with special satin sheets, where he was lying in Palo Alto with his special tootsie-roll and they were watching Davis Cup tennis on a special color TV. Not to mention a special putz named Charlie Citrine who pays for everything. Why the guy's delirious."

The above conversation had taken place when Thaxter telephoned to say that he was en route to New York to sail on the *France* and would stop in Chicago to discuss *The Ark*.

"What's he going to Europe for?" said Renata.

"Well, he is a crack journalist, you know."

"Why is a crack journalist sailing First Class on the *France*? That's five days. Has he got all that time to kill?"

"He must have a little, yes."

"And we're flying Economy," said Renata.

"Yes, but he has a cousin who's a director of the French Line. His mother's cousin. They never pay. The old woman knows all the plutocrats in the world. She brings out their debutante daughters."

"I notice he doesn't stick those plutocrats for fifty shares of anything. The rich know their deadbeats. How could you do such a dumb thing?"

"Really, the bank might have waited a few days more. His check was on the way from the Banco Ambrosiano of Milano."

"How did the Italians get in the act? He told you his family funds were in Brussels."

"No, in France. You see his share of his aunt's estate was in the Crédit Lyonnais."

"First he swindles you, then he fills you with garbage explanations which you go around repeating. All those high European connections are straight out of old Hitchcock movies. So now he's coming to Chicago, and what does he do, he has his office girl get you on the phone. It's beneath him to dial a number or answer a ring. But you answer in person and the chick says, 'Hold the line, Mr. Thaxter is coming,' so you stand waiting with the phone to your ear. And the whole thing, mind you, is charged to your bill. Then he tells you he's arriving but later he'll let you know when."

As far as it went this was all true. By no means did I tell Renata everything about Thaxter. There were also blacklists and scandals at country clubs and gossip about larceny charges. My friend's taste in trouble was old-fashioned. There were no more bounders unless, from pure love of antiquity, someone like Thaxter revived the type. But I also felt that something deep was at work and that Thaxter's eccentricities would eventually reveal a special spiritual purpose. I knew it was risky to put up the collateral because I had seen him do other people in the eye. But not me, I thought. There has to be *one* exception. Thus I gambled on immunity and I lost. He was a dear friend. I loved Thaxter. I knew also that I was the last man in the world he would wish to harm. But it came to that, finally. He had run out of harmable men. As there was no one else left, it was friendship versus his life-principle. Besides, I could now call myself a patron of Thaxter's form of art. Such things must be paid for.

He had just lost his house in the Bay Area with the swimming pool and the tennis court, the orange grove he had had put in, the formal garden, the MG, the station wagon, and the wine cellar.

Last September I flew to California to find out why our magazine, *The Ark,* was not appearing. It was a wonderfully pleasant affectionate visit. We walked out to inspect his estate under the California sunshine. At the time I was beginning to develop a new cosmological feeling for the sun. That it was in part our Creator. That there was a sun-band in our spirits. That light rose within us and came forward to meet the sun's light.

That this sun light was not just an external glory revealed to our dark senses and that as light was to the eye, thought was to the mind. So here we were. A happy blessed day. The sky was giving its marvelous temperate pulsating blue heat, while oranges hung about us. Thaxter wore his favorite outdoor garment, the black cloak, and the toes of his bare feet were pressed together like Smyrna figs. He was now having roses put in and asked me not to talk to the Ukrainian gardener. "He was a concentration-camp guard and still insanely anti-Semitic. I don't want him to start raving." So in this beautiful place I felt that demon-selves and silly-selves and loving-selves were intermingling. Some of Thaxter's newest children, fair and innocent, were allowed to play with dangerous knives and poisonous rose-dust containers. Nobody came to harm. Lunch was a big production, served beside the sparkling swimming pool with two wines poured by himself in somber dignity and intense connoisseurship, with cloak and curved pipe and bare toes writhing. His darkly pretty young wife gladly attended to all preparations and presided practically in the background. She was utterly delighted with her life and there was no dough, absolutely none. The gas station at the corner refused to take his check for five dollars. I had to pay with my credit card. And behind the scenes the young woman was holding off the tennis-court and swimming-pool people, the wine people, the car people, the grand-piano people, the bank people.

The Ark was going to be produced on new IBM equipment without expensive compositors. Never has any country given its people so many toys to play with or sent such highly gifted individuals to the remotest corners of idleness, as close as possible to the frontiers of pain. Thaxter was building a wing to house *The Ark*. Our magazine had to have its own premises and not interfere with his private life. He recruited some college students on a Tom Sawyer basis to dig a foundation. He went about in his MG visiting building sites to get construction hints from the hard-hats and scrounge pieces of plywood. This was an expansion I refused to subsidize. "I predict your house will slide into this hole," I said. "Are you sure you're within the building code?" But Thaxter had that willingness to try that makes field marshals and dictators. "We'll throw twenty thousand men into this sector, and if we lose more than half, we'll take a different tack."

In *The Ark* we were going to publish brilliant things. Where were we to find such brilliancy? We knew it must be there. It was an insult to a civilized nation and to humankind to assume that it was not. Everything possible must be done to restore the credit and authority of art, the seriousness of thought, the integrity of culture, the dignity of style. Renata, who must have had an unauthorized look at my bank statements, apparently knew how much I was spending as a patron. "Who needs this *Ark* of yours, Charlie, and who are these animals you're gonna save? You're not really such an idealist—you're full of hostility, dying to attack a lot of people in your very own magazine and insult everyone right and left. Thaxter's arrogance is nothing compared to yours. You let him think he's getting away with murder, but that's really because you can double his arrogance in spades."

"My money is running out anyhow. I'd rather spend it on this—"

"Not spend but squander," she said. "Why do you finance this California setup?"

"Better than giving it to lawyers and to the government."

"When you start to talk about *The Ark* you lose me. For once tell me simply—what, why?"

I was grateful for such a challenge really. As an aid to concentration I shut my eyes to answer. I said, "The ideas of the last few centuries are used up."

"Who says! See what I mean by arrogance," Renata interrupted.

"But so help me, they are used up. Social ideas, political, philosophical theories, literary ideas (poor Humboldt!), sexual ones, and, I suspect, even scientific ones."

"What do you know about all these things, Charlie? You've got brain fever."

"As the world's masses arrive at the point of consciousness, they take these exhausted ideas for new ones. How should they know? And people's parlors are papered with these projections."

"This is too serious for tongue twisters."

"I *am* serious. The greatest things, the things most necessary for life, have recoiled and retreated. People are actually dying of this, losing all personal life, and the inner being of millions, many many millions, is missing. One can understand that in many parts of the world there is no hope for it because of famine or police dictatorships, but here in the free world what excuse have we? Under pressure of public crisis the private sphere is being surrendered. I admit this private sphere has become so repulsive that we are glad to get away from it. But we accept the disgrace ascribed to it and people have filled their lives with so-called 'public questions.' What do we hear when these public questions are discussed? The failed ideas of three centuries. Anyhow the end of the individual, whom everyone seems to scorn and detest, will make our destruction, our superbombs, superfluous. I mean, if there are only foolish minds and mindless bodies there'll be nothing serious to annihilate. In the highest government positions almost no human beings have been seen for decades now, anywhere in the world. Mankind must recover its imaginative powers, recover living thought and real being, no longer accept these insults to the soul, and do it soon. Or else! And this is where a man like Humboldt, faithful to failed ideas, lost his poetry and missed the boat."

"But he went insane. You can't lay all the blame on him. I never knew the guy but sometimes I think you're too hard when you attack him. I know," she said, "you feel that he lived out the poet's awful life in just the way the middle class expected and approved. But nobody makes the grade with you. Thaxter is just your private pet. He certainly doesn't make it."

Of course she was right. Thaxter was always saying, "What we want is a major statement." He suspected that I had a major statement up my sleeve.

I told him, "You mean something like a life reverence, or Yogis and Commissars. You have a weakness for such terrible stuff. You'd give anything to be a Malraux and talk about the West. What is it with you and these seminal ideas? Major statements are hot air. The disorder is here to stay." And so it is—rich, baffling, agonizing, and diverse. As for striving to be exceptional, everything was already strange enough.

Pierre Thaxter was absolutely mad for Culture. He was a classicist, heavily trained by monks in Latin and Greek. He learned French from a governess, and studied it in college as well. He had taught himself Arabic also, and read esoteric books, and hoped to astonish everyone by publishing in learned journals in Finland or Turkey. He spoke with peculiar respect of Panofsky or Momigliano. He saw himself also as Burton of Arabia or T. E. Lawrence. Sometimes he was a purple genius of the Baron Corvo type, sordidly broke in Venice, writing something queer and passionate, rare and distinguished. He could not bear to leave anything out. He played Stravinsky on the piano, knew much about the Ballets Russes. On Matisse and Monet he was something of an authority. He held views on ziggurats and Le Corbusier. He could tell you, and often did, what sort of articles to buy and where to buy them. This was what Renata was talking about. No proper attaché case, for instance, fastened at the top, the clasps had to be on the side. He was bugs about attaché cases and umbrellas. There were plantations in Morocco where proper umbrella handles grew. And on top of it all Thaxter described himself as a Tolstoyan. If you pressed him he would say that he was a Christian pacifist anarchist and confess his faith in simplicity and purity of heart. So of course I loved Thaxter. How could I help it? Besides, the fever that afflicted his poor head made him an ideal editor. The diversity of interests, you see, and his cultural nosiness. He was an excellent journalist. This was widely recognized. He had worked on good magazines. Each and every one of them had fired him. What he needed was an ingenious and patient editor to send him on suitable assignments.

He was waiting between the lions in front of the Institute, exactly as expected in the cloak and blue velvet suit and boots with canvas sides. The only change was in his hair which he was now wearing in the Directoire style, the points coming down over his forehead. Because of the cold his face was deep red. He had a long mulberry-colored mouth, and impressive stature, and warts, and the distorted nose and leopard eyes.

Our meetings were always happy and we hugged each other. "Old boy, how are you? One of your good Chicago days. I've missed the cold air in California. Terrific! Isn't it. Well, we may as well start right with a few of those marvelous Monets." We left attaché case, umbrella, sturgeon, rolls, and marmalade in the checkroom. I paid two dollars for admission and we mounted to the Impressionist collection. There was one Norwegian winter landscape by Monet that we always went to see straightaway: a house, a bridge, and the snow falling. Through the covering snow came the pink of the house, and the frost was delicious. The whole weight of snow, of winter, was lifted effortlessly by the astonishing strength of the light. Looking at this pure rosy snowy dusky light, Thaxter clamped his pince-nez on the powerful twisted bridge of his nose with a gleam of glass and silver and his color deepened. He knew what he was doing. With this painting his visit began on the right tone. Only, familiar with the whole span of his thoughts, I was sure that he was also thinking how a masterpiece like this might be stolen from the museum, and that his mind quickly touched upon twenty daring art thefts from Dublin to Denver, complete with getaway cars and fences. Maybe he even dreamed up some multimillionaire Monet fanatic who had built a secret shrine in a concrete bunker and would be willing to pay a ton of money for this landscape. Scope was what Thaxter longed for (me, too, for that matter). Still he was a puzzle to me. He was either a kindly or a brutal man, and deciding which was a torment. But now he collapsed the trick pince-nez, and turned toward me with the ruddy swarthy face, his big-cat gaze heavier than before, gloomy, and even a touch cross-eyed.

"Before the shops close," he said, "I have an errand in the Loop. Let's go out. I can't take in anything more after this picture." So we retrieved our things and passed through the revolving door. In the Mallers Building there was a dealer named Bartelstein, who sold antique fish knives and forks. Thaxter wanted to obtain a set. "There's a controversy over the silver," he said decisively. "Fish on silver is now supposed to give a bad flavor. But I believe in the silver."

Why fish knives? And with what, and for whom? The bank

was putting him out of his Palo Alto house, still he never ran out of resources. He occasionally spoke of other houses that he owned, one in the Italian Alps, one in Brittany.

"The Mallers Building?" I said.

"This Bartelstein has a world reputation. My mother knows him. She needs the knives for one of her Social Register clients."

At this moment Cantabile and Polly approached us, both breathing December vapor, and I saw the white Thunderbird idling at the curb, its door hanging open, and the blood-red upholstery. Cantabile was smiling and his smile was somewhat unnatural, less an expression of pleasure than something else. Perhaps it was a reaction to Thaxter's cloak and hat and zooty shoes and flaming face. I, too, felt red in the face. Cantabile, on the other hand, was peculiarly white. He breathed the air as if he were stealing it. He had a look of eagerness and of distemper. The Thunderbird, puffing fumes, was beginning to block traffic. Because I had been immersed for much of the day in Humboldt's life and because Humboldt had in turn been immersed in T. S. Eliot, I thought as he might have done of the violet hour when the human engine waits like a taxi throbbing, waiting. But I cut this out. The moment required my full presence. I made quick introductions left and right: "Mrs. Palomino Mr. Thaxter—and Cantabile."

"Hurry, quick, jump in," said Cantabile, a man to be obeyed.

I wasn't having any of this. "No," I said. "We've got lots to discuss and I'd just as soon walk two blocks to the Mallers Building than be stuck in traffic with you."

"For Christ's sake get in the car." He had been stooping over me. But then he cried this out so loud that he jerked himself straight.

Polly lifted her pleasant face. She enjoyed it all. Her straight hair, Japanese in texture but very red and cut like a fall, showed thick and even against her green loden coat. The pleasant cheeks meant that one could be sexually pleasant with Polly. It would gratify, it would be a success. Why was it that some men knew how to find women who naturally pleased and could be pleased? By their cheeks and smiles, even I could identify them—after they had been found. Meantime bits of snow fell from the gray invisibility that lay upon the skyscrapers and something like soft thunder occurred behind us. This might have been sonic boom or jet noise over the lake, for thunder meant warmth and the chill was biting at our reddened faces. In this deepening dusky gray the lake surface would be pearly, and its polar fringe had formed early this winter, white—soiled but white. In the matter of natural beauty Chicago had its piece of the action despite the fact that its over-all historical destiny made it materially coarse, the air coarse, the soil coarse. The trouble was that such pearly water with its arctic edging and the gray air snowing could not be appreciated while these Cantabiles were carrying on, pushing me toward the Thunderbird and gesturing with the finest of fox-hunter's gloves. Nevertheless, one goes to a concert to think one's thoughts against the fine background of chamber music and one may make similar use of a Cantabile. A man who had been for years closely shut up and sifting his inmost self with painful iteration, deciding that the human future depended on his spiritual explorations, frustrated utterly in all his efforts to reach an understanding with those representatives of modern intellect whom he had tried to reach, deciding instead to follow the threads of spirit he had found within himself to see where they might lead, found a peculiar stimulus in a fellow like this Cantabile fellow.

"Let's go!" he bawled at me.

"No. Mr. Thaxter and I have our own business to discuss."

"Oh, there's time for that—plenty of time," said Thaxter.

"And what about the fish knives? Suddenly you're not so keen on the fish knives," I said to Thaxter.

Cantabile's voice was jagged and high with exasperation. "I'm trying to do you some good, Charlie! Fifteen minutes of your time is all, and then I'll whip you back to the Mallers Building for these fucking knives. How'd you do in court, pal? I know how you did! They've got a case full of nice clean bottles waiting for your blood. You already look drained. You've got a damn haggard look. You've aged ten years since lunchtime. But I've got the answer for you and I'll prove it. Charlie, ten grand today will get you fifteen by Thursday—if not, I'll let you beat me on the head with the bat I used on your Mercedes. I've got Stronson waiting. He needs cash badly."

"I want no part of that. I'm not a juice man," I said.

"Don't be stupid. We've got to move fast."

I glanced at Polly. She had warned me against Cantabile and Stronson and I checked silently with her. Her smile confirmed the caution she had given me. But she was highly amused by Cantabile's determination to drive us into the Thunderbird, to cram us into the red leather upholstery of the throbbing open car. He made it seem like a kidnap. We were on the broad sidewalk in front of the Institute, and lovers of criminal legend could tell you that the celebrated Dion O'Banion used to drive his Bugatti at a hundred mph over the very spot where we were standing while pedestrians fled. I had in fact mentioned this to Thaxter. Wherever he went, Thaxter wished to experience the characteristic thing, the essence. Getting the essence of Chicago, he was delighted, he was grinning, and he said, "If we miss Bartelstein now we can stop in the morning en route to the airport."

"Poll," said Cantabile, "get behind the wheel. I see the squad car." Buses were trying to squeeze past the parked Thunderbird. Traffic was tied up. The cops were already spinning their blue lights at Van Buren Street. Thaxter followed Polly to the car and I said to Cantabile, "Ronald, go away. Let me alone."

He gave me a look of open and terrible disclosure. I saw a spirit striving with complications as dense as my own, in another, faraway division. "I didn't want to spring this on you," he said, "but you force me to twist your arm." His fingers in the horseman's gloves, skin-tight, took me by the sleeve. "Your lifelong friend Alec Szathmar is in hot trouble, or could be in hot trouble—that's up to you."

"Why? How come?"

"I'm telling you. There's this pretty young woman—her husband is one of my people—and she's a kleptomaniac. She was caught in Field's pinching a cashmere cardigan. And Szathmar is her lawyer, dig? It was me that recommended Szathmar. He went to court and told the judge not to send her to jail, she needed psychiatric treatment and he'd see that she got it. So the court released her in his custody. Then Szathmar brought this chick straight to a motel and took her clothes off, but before he could screw her she escaped. She didn't have more on than the strip of paper they stretch across the toilet seat when she streaked out. There are plenty of witnesses. Now this girl is straight. She doesn't go for the motel bit. Her only bag is stealing. For your sake, I'm restraining the husband."

"All I hear from you, Cantabile, is nonsense, more and more and more nonsense. Szathmar can act like a jerk, but he's not a monster."

"All right, I'll unleash the husband. You think your buddy wouldn't be disbarred? He would be—fucking-A-right."

"You've hoked up all this for some goofy reason," I said. "If you had anything on Szathmar you'd be blackmailing him right now."

"So have it your way, don't cooperate, I'll slaughter and butcher the son of a bitch."

"I don't care."

"You don't have to tell me that. You know what you are? You're an isolationist, that's what you really are. You don't want to know what other people are into."

Everyone is forever telling me what my faults are, while I stand with great hungry eyes, believing and resenting all. Without metaphysical stability a man like me is the Saint Sebastian of the critical. The odd thing is that I hold still for it. As now, clutched by the sleeve of my checked coat, with Cantabile steaming intrigues and judgments at me from the flues of his white nose. With me it's not how all occasions do inform against me, but how I employ occasions to extract buried information. The latest information seemed to be that I was by inclination the sort of person who needed microcosmic-macrocosmic ideas, or the belief that everything that takes place in man has world significance. Such a belief warmed the environment for me, and brought out the sweet glossy leaves, the hanging oranges of the groves where the unpolluted self was virginal and gratefully communed with its Maker, and so on. It was possible that this was the only way for me to be my own true self. But in the actual moment we were on the wide freezing pavement, on Michigan Boulevard, the Art Institute behind us, and over against us all the colored lights of Christmas traffic and the white façades of Peoples Gas and other companies.

"Whatever I am, Cantabile, my friend and I aren't going with you." I hurried to the Thunderbird to try to stop Thaxter, who was getting in. He was already pulling in his cloak about him, sinking into the supple upholstery. He looked very pleased. I put my head in and said, "Come out of there. You and I are walking."

But Cantabile shoved me into the car beside Thaxter. He put his hands on my rear and thrust me in. Then he jammed the front seat back to keep me there. In the next motion he pulled the door shut with a slam and said, "Take off, Polly." Polly did just that.

"Now what the hell do you think you're doing, pushing and trapping me in here," I said.

"The cops are right on top of us. I didn't have time to argue," Cantabile said.

"Well, this is nothing but a kidnap," I told him. And as soon as I pronounced the word "kidnap" my heart was instantly swollen with a childish sense of terrible injury. But Thaxter was laughing, chuckling through his wide mouth, and his eyes were wrinkling and twinkling. He said, "Hee-hee, don't take it so hard, Charlie. It's a very funny moment. Enjoy it."

Thaxter couldn't have been happier. He was having a real Chicago treat. For his sake, the city was living up to its reputation. Observing this, I cooled off somewhat. I guess I really love to entertain my friends. Hadn't I brought sturgeon and fresh rolls and marmalade when the bailiff said that Thaxter was in town? I was still holding the paper bag from Stop and Shop.

Traffic was thick but Polly's mastery of the car was extraordinary. She worked the white Thunderbird into the left lane without touching the brake, without a jolt, with fearless competency, a marvelous driver.

Restless Cantabile twisted about to the rear to face us and said to me, "Look what I've got here. An early copy of tomorrow morning's paper. I bought it from a guy in the press room.

It cost me plenty. You want to know something? You and I made Mike Schneiderman's column. Listen," he read. " 'Charlie Citrine, the Chevrolet of the French Legion and Chicago scribe, who authored the flick *Von Trenck,* made a card-debt payoff to an underworld figure at the Playboy Club. Better go take a poker seminar at the University, Charles.' What do you say, Charlie. It's a pity Mike didn't know all the facts about your car and the skyscraper and all the rest of it. *Now* what do you think?"

"What do I think? I won't accept 'author' as a verb. I also want to get out at Wabash Avenue."

Chicago was more bearable if you didn't read the papers. We had turned west on Madison Street and passed under the black frames of the El. "Don't pull up, Polly," said Cantabile. We moved on toward the Christmas ornaments of State Street, the Santa Clauses and the reindeer. The only element of stability in this moment lay in Polly's wonderful handling of the machine.

"Tell me about the Mercedes," said Thaxter. "What happened to it? And what was the skyscraper thing, Mr. Cantabile? Is the underworld figure at the Playboy Club you yourself?"

"Those in the know will know," said Cantabile. "Charlie, how much will they charge for the bodywork on your car? Did you take it back to the dealer? I hope you keep away from those rip-off specialists. Four hundred bucks a day for one grease monkey. What crooks! I know a good cheap shop."

"Thank you," I said.

"Don't be ironical with me. But the least I can do is make you back some of the money this will cost."

I made no answer. My heart hammered upon a single theme: I urgently desired to be elsewhere. I simply didn't want to be here. It was utter misery. This was not the moment to remember certain words of John Stuart Mill, but I remembered them anyway. They went something like this: The tasks of noble spirits at a time when the works which most of us are appointed to do are trivial and contemptible—da-da-*da,* da-da-*da,* da-da-*da.* Well the only thing valuable in these contemptible works is the spirit in which they are done. I couldn't see any values in the vicinity at all. But if the tasks of the *durum genus hominum,* said the great Mill, were performed by a supernatural agency and there was no demand for wisdom or virtue O! then there would be little that man could prize in man. This was exactly the problem America had set for itself. The Thunderbird would do as the supernatural agency. And what else was man prizing? Polly was transporting us. Under that mass of red hair lay a brain which certainly knew what to prize, if anyone cared to ask. But no one was asking, and she didn't need much brain to drive this car.

We now passed the towering upswept frames of the First National Bank, containing layer upon layer of golden lights. "What's this beautiful structure?" asked Thaxter. No one answered. We charged up Madison Street. At this rate, and due west, we would have reached the Waldheim Cemetery on the outskirts of the city in about fifteen minutes. There my parents lay under snow-spattered grass and headstones; objects would still be faintly visible in the winter dusk, etcetera. But of course we were not bound for the cemetery. We turned into La Salle Street where we were held up by taxicabs and newspaper trucks and the Jaguars and Lincolns and Rolls-Royces of stockbrokers and corporation lawyers—of the deeper thieves and the loftier politicians and the spiritual elite of American business, the eagles in the heights far above the daily, hourly, and momentary destinies of men.

"Hell, we're going to miss Stronson. That fat little son of a bitch is always tearing off in his Aston-Martin as soon as he can lock his office," said Cantabile.

But Polly sat silent at the steering wheel. Traffic was jammed. Thaxter succeeded at last in getting Cantabile's attention. And I sighed and, left to myself, tuned out. Just as I had done yesterday when forced, practically at gunpoint, into the stinking closet of the Russian Bath. This is what I thought: certainly the three other souls in the warm darkness of this glowing, pulsating and lacquered automobile had thoughts just as peculiar as my own. But they were apparently less aware of them than I. And what was it that I was so aware of? I was aware that I used to think that I knew where I stood (taking the universe as a frame of reference). But I was mistaken. However, I

could at least say that I had been spiritually efficient enough
not to be crushed by ignorance. However, it was now apparent
to me that I was neither of Chicago nor sufficiently beyond it,
and that Chicago's material and daily interests and phenomena
were neither actual and vivid enough nor symbolically clear
enough to me. So that I had neither vivid actuality nor symbolic clarity and for the time being I was utterly nowhere. This
was why I went to have long mysterious conversations with
Professor Scheldt, Doris's father, on esoteric subjects. He had
given me books to read about the etheric and the astral bodies, the Intellectual Soul and the Consciousness Soul, and the
unseen Beings whose fire and wisdom and love created and
guided this universe. I was far more thrilled by Dr. Scheldt's
talks than by my affair with his daughter. She was a good kid
actually. She was attractive and lively, a fair, sharp-profiled,
altogether excellent small young woman. True, she insisted on
serving fancy dishes like Beef Wellington and the pastry crust
was always underdone, and so was the meat, but those were
minor matters. I had taken up with her only because Renata
and her mother had expelled me and put Flonzaley in my place.
Doris couldn't hold a candle to Renata. Renata? Why, Renata
didn't need an ignition key to start a car. One of her kisses on
the hood would turn it on. It would roar for her. Moreover,
Miss Scheldt was ambitious socially. In Chicago, husbands with
higher mental interests aren't easy to find, and it was obvious
that Doris wanted to be Madame Chevalier Citrine. Her father
had been a physicist at the old Armour Institute, an executive of IBM, a NASA consultant who improved the metal used
in space ships. But he was also an anthroposophist. He didn't
wish to call this mysticism. He insisted that Steiner had been a
Scientist of the Invisible. But Doris, with reluctance, spoke of
her father as a crank. She told me many facts about him. He
was a Rosicrucian and a Gnostic, he read aloud to the dead.
Also at a time when girls have to do erotic things whether or
not they have the talent for them, the recent situation being
what it is, Doris behaved quite bravely with me. But it was all
wrong, I was simply not myself with her and at the wrongest
possible time I cried out, "Renata! Oh Renata!" Then I lay

there shocked with myself and mortified. But Doris didn't take my outcry at all hard. She was thoroughly understanding. That was her main strength. And when my talks with the Professor began she was decent about that as well, understanding that I was not going to sleep with the daughter of my guru.

Sitting in the Professor's clean parlor—I have seldom sat in a room so utterly clean, the parquet floors of light wood limpid with wax and the Oriental scatter rugs lint-free, and the park below with the equestrian statue of General Sherman prancing on clean air—I was entirely happy. I respected Dr. Scheldt. The strange things he said were at least deep things. In this day and age people had ceased to say such things. He was from another time, entirely. He even dressed like a country-club member of the Twenties. I had caddied for men of this type. A Mr. Masson, one of my regulars at Sunset Ridge in Winnetka, had been the image of Professor Scheldt. I assumed that Mr. Masson had long ago joined the hosts of the dead and that in all the universe there was only me to remember how he had looked when he was climbing out of a sand trap.

"Dr. Scheldt. . . ." The sun is shining clear, the water beyond is as smooth as the inner peace I have not attained, as wrinkled as perplexity, the lake is strong with innumerable powers, flexuous, hydromuscular. In the parlor is a polished crystal bowl filled with anemones. These flowers are capable of nothing except grace and they are colored with an untranslatable fire derived from infinity. "Now Dr. Scheldt," I say. I'm speaking to his interested and plain face, calm as a bull's face and trying to determine how dependable his intelligence is—i.e., whether we are real here or crazy here. "Let me see if I understand these things at all—thought in my head is also thought in the external world. Consciousness in the self creates a false distinction between object and subject. Am I getting it right?"

"Yes, I think so, sir," the strong old man says.

"The quenching of my thirst is not something that begins in my mouth. It begins with the water, and the water is out there, in the external world. So with truth. Truth is something we all share. Two plus two for me is two plus two for everyone else and has nothing to do with my ego. That I understand. Also the answer to Spinoza's argument that if the dislodged stone had consciousness it could think, 'I am flying through the air,' as if it were freely doing it. But if it were conscious, it would not be a mere stone. It could also originate movement. Thinking, the power to think and to know, is a source of freedom. Thinking will make it obvious that spirit exists. The physical body is an agent of the spirit and its mirror. It is an engine and a reflection of the spirit. It is the spirit's ingenious memorandum to itself and the spirit sees itself in my body, just as I see my own face in a looking glass. My nerves reflect this. The earth is literally a mirror of thoughts. Objects themselves are embodied thoughts. Death is the dark backing that a mirror needs if we are to see anything. Every perception causes a certain amount of death in us, and this darkening is a necessity. The clairvoyant can actually see that when he learns how to obtain the inward view. To do this, he must get out of himself and stand far off."

"All this is in the texts," says Dr. Scheldt, "I can't be sure that you have grasped it all, but you're fairly accurate."

"Well, I understand in part, I think. When our understanding wants it, divine wisdom will flow toward us."

Then Dr. Scheldt begins to speak on the text, *I am the light of the world*. To him that light is understood also as the sun itself. Then he speaks of the gospel of Saint John as drawing upon the wisdom-filled Cherubim, while the gospel of Saint Luke draws upon the fiery love of the Seraphim—Cherubim, Seraphim, and Thrones being the three highest spiritual hierarchy. I am not at all certain that I am following. "I have no experience of any of this advanced stuff, Dr. Scheldt, but I still find it peculiarly good and comforting to hear it all said. I don't at all know where I'm at. One of these days when life is quieter I'm going to buckle down to the training course and do it in earnest."

"When will life be quieter?"

"I don't know. But I suppose people have told you before this how much stronger the soul feels after such a conversation."

"You shouldn't wait for things to become quieter. You must decide to make them quieter."

He saw that I was fairly skeptical still. I couldn't make my peace with things like the Moon Evolution, the fire spirits, the

Sons of Life, with Atlantis, with the lotus-flower organs of spiritual perception or the strange mingling of Abraham with Zarathustra, or the coming together of Jesus and the Buddha. It was all too much for me. Still, whenever the doctrine dealt with what I suspected or hoped or knew of the self, or of sleep, or of death, it always rang true.

Moreover, there were the dead to think of. Unless I had utterly lost interest in them, unless I were satisfied to feel only a secular melancholy about my mother and my father or Demmie Vonghel or Von Humboldt Fleisher, I was obliged to investigate, to satisfy myself that death *was* final, that the dead *were* dead. Either I conceded the finality of death and refused to have any further intimations, condemned my childish sentimentality and hankering, or I conducted a full and proper investigation. Because I simply didn't see how I could refuse to investigate. Yes, I could force myself to think of it all as the irretrievable loss of shipmates to the devouring Cyclops. I could think of the human scene as a battlefield. The fallen are put into holes in the ground or burned to ash. After this, you are not supposed to inquire after the man who gave you life, the woman who bore you, after a Demmie whom you had last seen getting into a plane at Idlewild with her big blond legs and her make-up and her earrings, or after the brilliant golden master of conversation Von Humboldt Fleisher, whom you had last beheld eating a pretzel in the West Forties. You could simply assume that they had been forever wiped out, as you too would one day be. So if the daily papers told of murders committed in the streets before crowds of neutral witnesses, there was nothing illogical about such neutrality. On the metaphysical assumptions about death everyone in the world had apparently reached, everyone would be snatched, ravished by death, throttled, smothered. This terror and this murdering were the most natural things in the world. And these same conclusions were incorporated into the life of society and present in all its institutions, in politics, education, banking, justice. Convinced of this, I saw no reason why I shouldn't go to Dr. Scheldt to talk about Seraphim and Cherubim and Thrones and Dominions and Exousiai and Archai and Angels and Spirits.

I said to Dr. Scheldt at our last meeting, "Sir, I have studied the pamphlet called *The Driving Force of Spiritual Powers in World History,* and it contains a fascinating passage about sleep. It seems to say that mankind doesn't know how to sleep any more. That something should be happening during sleep that simply isn't happening and that this is why we wake up feeling so stale and unrested, sterile, bitter, and all the rest of it. So let me see if I've got it right. The physical body sleeps, and the etheric body sleeps, but the soul goes off."

"Yes," said Professor Scheldt. "The soul, when you sleep, enters the supersensible world, or at least one of its regions. To simplify, it enters its own element."

"I'd like to think that."

"Why shouldn't you?"

"Well, I will, just to see if I understand it. In the supersensible world the soul meets the invisible forces which were known by initiates in the ancient world in their Mysteries. Not all the beings of the hierarchy are accessible to the living, only some of them, but these are indispensable. Now, as we sleep, the pamphlet says, the words that we have spoken all day long are vibrating and echoing about us."

"Not literally, the words," Dr. Scheldt corrected.

"No, but the feeling-tones, the joy or pain, the purpose of the words. Through the vibrations and echoes of what we have thought and felt and said we commune as we sleep with the beings of the hierarchy. But now, our daily monkeyshines are such, our preoccupations are so low, language has become so debased, the words so blunted and damaged, we've said such stupid and dull things, that the higher beings hear only babbling and grunting and TV commercials—the dog-food level of things. This says nothing to them. What pleasure can these higher beings take in this kind of materialism, devoid of higher thought or poetry? As a result, all that we can hear in sleep is matter creaking and hissing and washing, the rustling of plants, and the air conditioning. So we are incomprehensible to the higher beings. They can't influence us and they themselves suffer a corresponding privation. Have I got it right?"

"Yes, by and large."

"It makes me wonder about a late friend of mine who used to complain of insomnia. He was a poet. And I can see now why he may have had such a problem about sleeping. Maybe he was ashamed. Out of a sense that he had no words fit to carry into sleep. He may actually have preferred insomnia to such a nightly shame and disaster."

Now the Thunderbird pulled up beside the Rookery on La Salle Street. Cantabile jumped out. As he was holding the door open for Thaxter I said to Polly, "Now Polly—tell me something helpful, Polly."

"This Stronson fellow is in big trouble," she said, "big, big, big trouble. Look in tomorrow's paper."

We went through the tiled, balustraded Rookery lobby and up in a swift elevator, Cantabile repeating, as though he wanted to hypnotize me, "Ten grand today will get you fifteen by Thursday. That's fifty percent in three days. Fifty percent." We came out into a white corridor and then up against two grand cedar doors lettered *Western Hemisphere Investment Corporation.* On these doors Cantabile gave a coded set of knocks: three times; pause; once; then a final once. It was odd that this should be necessary, but after all a man who could give such a return on money must be fighting off investors. A beautiful receptionist let us in. The anteroom was carpeted heavily. "He's here," said Cantabile. "Just wait a few minutes, you guys."

Thaxter sat down on a low orange loveseat sort of thing. A man was vacuuming loudly around us, wearing a gray porter's jacket. Thaxter removed his wide dude hat and smoothed the Directoire points over his irregularly formed forehead. He took the stem of his curved pipe into his straight lips and said, "Sit down." I gave him the sturgeon and marmalade to hold and overtook Cantabile at the door to Stronson's private office. I pulled tomorrow's paper from under his arm. He grabbed at it and we both tugged. His coat came open and I saw the pistol in his belt but this no longer deterred me. "What do you want?" he said.

"I just want to have a look at Schneiderman's column."

"Here, I'll tear it out for you."

"You do that and I'm leaving."

He pushed the paper at me violently and went into Stronson's office. Rapidly leafing, I found an article in the financial section describing the difficulties of Mr. Stronson and the Western Hemisphere Investment Corporation. A complaint had been filed by the Securities and Exchange Commission against him. He was charged with violation of the federal securities regulations. He had used the mails to defraud and had dealt in unregistered securities. An explanatory affidavit filed by the SEC alleged that Guido Stronson was a complete phony, not a Harvard graduate, but only a New Jersey high-school dropout and gas-station attendant, until recently a minor employee in a bill-collecting agency in Plainfield. He had abandoned a wife and four children. They were now on welfare in the East. Coming to Chicago, Guido Stronson had opened a grand office on La Salle Street and produced glittering credentials, including a degree from the Harvard Business School. He said he had been conspicuously successful in Hartford as an insurance executive. His investment company soon had a very large clientele for hog bellies, cocoa, gold ore. He had bought a mansion on the North Shore and said he wanted to go in for fox hunting. Complaints lodged by clients had led to these federal investigations. The report concluded with the La Salle Street rumor that Stronson had many Mafia clients. He had apparently cost these clients several millions of dollars.

By tonight Greater Chicago would know these facts and tomorrow this office would be mobbed by cheated investors and Stronson would need police protection. But who would protect him the day after tomorrow from the Mafia? I studied the man's photograph. Newspapers distort faces peculiarly—I knew that from personal experience, but this photograph, if it did Stronson justice in any degree, inspired no sympathy. Some faces gain by misrepresentation.

Now why had Cantabile brought me here? He promised me fast profits, but I knew *something* about modern life. I mean, I could read a little in the great mysterious book of urban America. I was too fastidious and skittish to study it closely—I had used the conditions of life to test my powers of immunity; the sovereign consciousness trained itself to avoid the phenomena and to be immune to their effects. Still, I did know, more or less, how swindlers like Stronson operated. They hid away a good share of their stolen dollars, they were sentenced to prison for eight or ten years, and when they got out, they retired quietly to the West Indies or the Azores. Maybe Cantabile was now trying to get his hands on some of the money Stronson had stashed—in Costa Rica, perhaps. Or maybe if he was losing twenty thousand dollars (some of it possibly Cantabile family money) he intended to make a big scene. He would want me to see such a scene. He liked me to be present. Because of me he had gotten into Mike Schneiderman's column. He must have been thinking of something even more brilliant, more sensationally inventive. He needed me. And why was I so often involved in such things? Szathmar too did this to me; George Swiebel had staged a poker party in order to show me a thing or two; this afternoon even Judge Urbanovich had acted up in chambers for my sake. I must have been associated in Chicago with art and meaning, with certain upper values. Wasn't I the author of *Von Trenck* (the movie), honored by the French government and the Zig-Zag Club? I still carried in my wallet a thin wrinkled length of silk ribbon for the buttonhole. And O! we poor souls, all of us so unstable, ignorant, perturbed, so unrested. Couldn't even get a good night's sleep. Failing in the night to make contact with the merciful, regenerative angels and archangels who were there to strengthen us with their warmth and their love and wisdom. Ah, poor hearts that we were, how badly we were all doing and how I longed to make changes or amends or corrections. Something!

Cantabile had shut himself up in conference with Mr. Stronson, and this Stronson, represented in the paper with a brutally thick face and hair done in pageboy style, was probably frantic. Maybe Cantabile was offering him deals—deals upon deals upon deals. Advice on how to come to terms with his furious Mafia customers.

Thaxter was lifting his legs to let the porter vacuum under them.

"I think we'd better go," I said.

"Leave? Now?"

"I think we should get out of here."

"Oh, come on, Charlie, don't make me leave. I want to see what happens. There'll never be another occasion like this. This man Cantabile is absolutely wild. He's fascinating."

"I wish you hadn't rushed into his Thunderbird without asking me. So excited by gangland Chicago you just couldn't wait. I suppose you expect to make use of this experience, send it to the *Reader's Digest* or something nonsensical like that—you and I have all kinds of things to discuss."

"They can wait, Charles. You know I'm sort of impressed by you. You always complain that you're isolated, then I come to Chicago and find you bang in the middle of things." He flattered me. He knew how much I liked to be thought a Chicago expert. "Is Cantabile one of the ballplayers at your club?"

"I don't think Langobardi would let him join. He doesn't suffer minor hoodlums gladly."

"Is that what Cantabile is?"

"I don't know exactly what he is. He carries on like a Mafia Don. He's some sort of silly-billy. He has a wife who's getting a PhD."

"You mean that smashing redhead with the platform shoes?"

"She's not the one."

"Wasn't it grand how he gave that code knock on the door? And the pretty receptionist opened? Notice these glass cases with the pre-Columbian art and the collection of Japanese fans. I tell you, Charles, nobody actually knows this country. This is some country. The leading interpreters of America stink. They do nothing but swap educated formulas about it. *You*, yes *you!* Charles, should write about it, describe your life day by day and apply some of your ideas to it."

"Thaxter, I told you how I took my little girls to see the beavers out in Colorado. All around the lake the Forestry Service posted natural-history placards about the beaver's life cycle. The beavers didn't know a damn thing about this. They just went on chewing and swimming and being beavers. But we human beavers are all shook up by descriptions of ourselves. It affects us to hear what we hear. From Kinsey or Masters or

Eriksen. We read about identity crisis, alienation, etcetera, and it all affects us."

"And you don't want to contribute to the deformation of your fellow man with new inputs?—God, how I loathe the word 'input.' But you yourself continually make high-level analyses. What about the piece for *The Ark* you sent me—I think it's right here in my attaché case—in which you offer an economic interpretation of personal eccentricities. Let's see, I'm sure I've got it here. You argue that there may be a connection at this particular stage of capitalism between the shrinking of investment opportunities and the quest for new roles or personality investments. You even quoted Schumpeter, Charlie. Yes, here it is: 'These dramas may appear purely internal but they are perhaps economically determined . . . when people think they are being so subtly inventive or creative they merely reflect society's general need for economic growth.'"

"Put away that paper," I said. "For God's sake, don't quote my big ideas at me. If there's one thing I can't take today, it's that."

It was really very easy for me to generate great thoughts of this sort. Instead of regretting this glib weakness with me, Thaxter envied it. He longed to be a member of the intelligentsia, to stand in the pantheon and to make a Major Statement like Albert Schweitzer or Arthur Koestler or Sartre or Wittgenstein. He didn't see why I distrusted this. I was too grand; too snobbish, even, he said, sharply resentful. But there it was, I simply did not wish to be a leader of the world intelligentsia. Humboldt had pursued it with all his might. He believed in victorious analysis, he preferred "ideas" to poetry, he was prepared to give up the universe itself for the subworld of higher cultural values.

"Anyway," said Thaxter, "you should go around Chicago like Restif de la Bretonne in the streets of Paris and write a chronicle. It would be sensational."

"Thaxter, I want to talk to you about *The Ark*. You and I were going to give a new impulse to the mental life of the country and outdo the *American Mercury* and *The Dial*, or the *Revista de Occidente*, and so on. We discussed and planned it for years. I've spent a pot of money on it. I've paid all the bills for two and a half years. Now where is *The Ark*? I think you're a great editor, a born editor, and I believe in you. We announced our magazine and people sent in material. We've been sitting on their manuscripts for ages. I've gotten bitter letters and even threats. You've made me the fall guy. They all blame me, and they all quote you. You've set yourself up as a Citrine expert and interpret me all over the place—how I function, how little I understand women, all the weaknesses of my character. I don't take that too hard. I'd be glad though, if you didn't interpret me quite so much. And the words you put into my mouth—that X is a moron, or Y is an imbecile. *I* have no prejudices against X or Y. The one who's out to get 'em is you."

"Frankly, Charles, the reason why our first number isn't out is that you sent me so much anthroposophical material. You're no fool so there must be something to anthroposophy. But for God's sake, we can't come out with all this stuff about the soul."

"Why not? People talk about the psyche, why not the soul?"

"Psyche is scientific," said Thaxter. "You have to accustom people gradually to these terms of yours."

I said, "Why did you buy such a huge supply of paper?"

"I wanted to be ready to publish five issues in succession without worrying about supplies. Besides, we got a good buy."

"Where are all these tons of paper now?"

"In the warehouse. But I don't think that it's *The Ark* that bothers you. It's really Denise that's eating at you, the courts and the dollars and all that grief and harassment."

"No, that's not what it is," I said. "Sometimes I'm grateful to Denise. You think I should be like Restif de la Bretonne, in the streets? Well, if Denise weren't suing me, I'd never get out of the house. Because of her I have to go downtown. It keeps me in touch with the facts of life. It's been positively enlightening."

"How so?"

"Well, I realize how universal the desire to injure your fellow man is. I guess it's the same in the democracies as in dictatorships. Only here the government of laws and lawyers puts a palisade up. They can injure you a lot, make your life hideous, but they can't actually do you in."

"Your love of education really does you credit, Charles. No kidding. I can tell you after a friendship of twenty years," said Thaxter. "Your character is a very peculiar one but there is a certain—I don't know what to call it—dignity that you do have. If you say soul and I say psyche, you have your reason for it, probably. You probably do have a soul, Charles. And it's a pretty startling fact about anyone."

"You have one yourself. Anyway, I think we had better give up our plan to publish *The Ark* and liquidate our assets remaining if any."

"Now, Charles, don't be hasty. We can straighten this business out very easily. We're almost there."

"I can't put any more money into it. I'm not doing well, financially."

"You can't compare your situation to mine," said Thaxter. "I've been wiped out in California."

"How bad is it there?"

"Well, I've kept your obligations down to a minimum. You promised to pay Blossom her salary. Don't you remember Blossom, the secretary? You met her in September?"

"My obligations? In September we agreed to lay Blossom off."

"Ah, but she was the only one who really knew how to operate all the IBM machinery."

"But the machinery was never operated."

"That wasn't her fault. We were prepared. I was ready to go at any time."

"What you mean, really, is that you're too grand a personage to do without a staff."

"Have a heart, Charles. Just after you left, her husband was killed in a car crash. You wouldn't want me to fire her at such a time. I know your heart, whatever else, Charles. So I took it on myself to interpret your attitude. It's only fifteen hundred bucks. There is actually another thing I must mention, the lumber bill for the wing we started."

"I didn't tell you to build the wing. I was dead against it."

"Why, we agreed there was to be a separate office. You didn't expect me to bring all of that editorial confusion into my house."

"I definitely said I'd have no part of it. I warned you even, that if you dug that big hole next to your house you'd undermine the foundations."

"Well, it isn't very serious," said Thaxter. "The lumber company can damn well dismantle it all and take back their wood. Now, as for the slip-up between banks—I'm damn sorry about that, but it was not my fault. The payment from the Banco Ambrosiano di Milano was delayed. It's these damn bureaucracies! Besides, it's just anarchy and chaos now in Italy. Anyway, you have my check. . . ."

"I have not."

"You haven't? It's got to be in the mail. Postal service is outrageous. It was my last installment of twelve hundred dollars to the Palo Alto Trust. They had already closed me out. They owe you twelve hundred."

"Is it possible that they never received it? Maybe it was sent out from Italy by dolphin."

He did not smile. The moment was solemn. We were speaking, after all, of his money. "Those California crumbs were supposed to reissue it and send you their cashier's check."

"Maybe the Banco Ambrosiano's check hasn't cleared yet," I said.

"Now, then," he took a legal pad from his attaché case. "I've worked out a schedule to repay the money you lost. You must have the original cost of the stock. I absolutely insist. I believe you bought it at four hundred. You overpaid, you know, it's way down now. However, that's not your fault. Let's say that when you posted it for me it was worth eighteen thousand. Nor will I forget the dividends."

"You don't have to do dividends, Thaxter."

"No, I insist. It's easy enough to find out what sort of dividend IBM is paying. You send me the figure and I'll send you the check."

"In five years you paid off less than one thousand dollars on this loan. You kept up the interest payments and little else."

"The interest rate was out of sight."

"In five years you reduced the amount of the principal by two hundred dollars a year."

"The exact figures don't come to me now," said Thaxter. "But I know that the bank will owe you something after it sells the stock."

"IBM is now under two hundred a share. The bank gets hurt, too. Not that I care what happens to banks."

But Thaxter was now busy explaining how he would return the money, dividends and all, over a five-year period. The split black pupils of his long grape-green eyes moved over the figures. He was going to do the whole thing handsomely, with dignity, aristocratically, fully sincere, shirking no part of his obligation to a friend. I could see that he entirely meant what he said. But I also knew that this elaborate plan to do right by me would be, in his mind, tantamount to doing right. These long yellow sheets from the legal pad filled with figures, these generous terms of repayment, the care for detail, the expressions of friendship, settled our business fully and forever. This was magically it.

"It's a good idea to be scrupulously precise with you in these petty deals. To you the small sums are more important than big ones. What sometimes surprises me is that you and I should be fooling around with trifles. You could make any amount of money. You don't know your own resources. Odd, isn't it? You could turn a crank and money would fall into your lap."

"What crank?" I said.

"You could go to a publisher with a project and name your own advance."

"I've already taken big advances."

"Peanuts. You could get lots more. I've come up with some ideas myself. For starters you and I could do that cultural Baedeker I'm always after you about, a guide for educated Americans who go to Europe and get tired of shopping for Florentine leather and Irish linen. They're fed up with the thundering herd of common rubbernecks. Are these cultivated Americans in Vienna, for instance? In our guide they can find lists of research institutes to visit, small libraries, private collections, chamber-music groups, the names of cafés and restaurants where one can meet mathematicians or fiddlers, and there would be listings of the addresses of poets, painters, psychologists, and so on. Visit their studios and labs. Have conversations with them."

"You might as well bring over a firing squad and shoot all these poets dead as put such information into the hands of culture-vulture tourists."

"There isn't a ministry of tourism in Europe that wouldn't get excited by this. They'd all cooperate fully. They might even kick in some money. Charlie, we could do this for every country in Europe, for all major cities as well as the capitals. This idea is worth a million dollars to you and me. I would take charge of the organization and research. I'd do most of the work. You'd cover atmospheric stuff and ideas. We'll need a staff for the details. We could start in London and move on to Paris and Vienna and Rome. Say the word and I'll go to one of the big houses. Your name will pull down an advance of two hundred and fifty thousand. We split it two ways and your worries are over."

"Paris and Vienna! Why not Montevideo and Bogotá? There's just as much culture there. Why are you sailing and not flying to Europe?"

"It's my favorite way to travel, deeply restful. One of my old mother's remaining pleasures in life is to arrange these trips for her only child. She's done more, this time. The Brazilian football champions are touring Europe, and she knows I love football. I mean superb football. So she's wangled me tickets for four matches. Besides, I have business reasons for going. And I want to see some of my children."

I refrained from asking how he could travel first class on the *France* when he was dead broke. Asking got me nowhere. I never succeeded in assimilating his explanations. I did remember being told, however, that the velvet suit with a blue silk scarf knotted in the Ronald Colman manner made perfectly acceptable evening wear. In fact the black-tie millionaires looked tacky by comparison. And women adored Thaxter. One evening during his last crossing an old Texas lady, if you could believe him, dropped a chamois sack full of gems into his lap, under the tablecloth. He discreetly passed them back to her. He would not service rich old Texas frumps, he told me. Not even those who were magnanimous in Oriental or Renaissance style. Because after all, he continued, this was a big gesture suitable to a big ocean and a big character. But he was remarkably dignified, virtuous, and faithful to his wife—to all his wives. He was warmly devoted to his extended family, the many children he had had by several women. If he didn't make a Major Statement he would at least leave his genetic stamp upon the world.

"If I had no cash, I'd ask my mother to put me in steerage. How much do you tip when you get off the *France* in Le Havre?" I asked him.

"I give the chief steward five bucks."

"You're lucky to leave the boat alive."

"Perfectly adequate," said Thaxter. "They bully the American rich and despise them for their cowardice and ignorance."

He told me now, "My business abroad is with an international consortium of publishers for whom I'm developing a certain idea. Originally, I got it from you, Charlie, but you won't remember. You said how interesting it would be to go around the world interviewing a lot of second-, third-, and fourth-rank dictators—the General Amins, the Qaddafis, and all that breed."

"They'd have you drowned in their fishpond if they thought you were going to call them third-rate."

"Don't be silly, I'd never do such a thing. They're leaders of the developing world. But it's actually a fascinating subject. These shabby foreign-student-bohemians a few years ago, future petty blackmailers, now they're threatening the great nations, or formerly great nations, with ruin. Dignified world leaders are sucking up to them."

"What makes you think they'll talk to you?" I said.

"They're dying to see somebody like me. They're longing for a touch of the big time, and I have impeccable credentials. They all want to hear about Oxford and Cambridge and New York and the London season, and discuss Karl Marx and Sartre. If they want to play golf or tennis or Ping-Pong, I can do all of that. To prepare myself for writing these articles I've been reading some good things to get the right tone—Marx on Louis Napoleon is wonderful. I've also looked into Suetonius and Saint-Simon and Proust. Incidentally, there's going to be an international poets' congress in Taiwan. I may cover that. You have to keep your ear to the ground."

"Whenever I try that I get nothing but a dirty ear," I said.

"Who knows, I may get to interview Chiang Kai-shek before he kicks off."

"I can't imagine that he has anything to tell you."

"Oh, I can take care of that," said Thaxter.

"How about getting out of this office?" I said.

"Why don't you, for once, go along with me and do the thing my style. Not to overprotect. Let the interesting thing happen. How bad can it be? We can talk just as well here as anywhere. Tell me what's going on personally, what's with you?"

Whenever Thaxter and I met we had at least one intimate conversation. I spoke freely to him and let myself go. In spite of his eccentric nonsense, and my own, there was a bond between us. I was able to talk to Thaxter. At times I told myself that talking to him was as good for me as psychoanalysis. Over the years, the cost had been about the same. Thaxter could elicit what I was really thinking. A more serious learned friend like Richard Durnwald would not listen when I tried to discuss the ideas of Rudolf Steiner. "Nonsense!" he said. "Simply nonsense! I've looked into that." In the learned world anthroposophy was not respectable. Durnwald dismissed the subject sharply because he wished to protect his esteem for me. But Thaxter said, "What is this Consciousness Soul, and how do you explain the theory that our bones are crystallized out of the cosmos itself?"

"I'm glad you asked me that," I said. But before I could begin I saw Cantabile approaching. No, he didn't approach, he descended on us in a peculiar way, as if he weren't using the floor with its carpeting but had found some other material basis.

"Let me borrow this," he said, and took up the black dude hat with the swerving brim. "All right," he said, promotional and tense. "Get up, Charlie. Let's go and visit the man." He gave my body a rough lift. Thaxter also rose from the orange loveseat but Cantabile pushed him down again and said, "Not you. One at a time." He took me with him to the presidential door. There, he paused. "Look," he said, "you let me do the talking. It's a special situation."

"This is one more of your original productions, I see. But no money is going to change hands."

"Oh, I wouldn't really have done that to you. Who else but a guy in bad trouble would give you three for two? You saw the item in the paper, hey?"

"I certainly did," I said. "And what if I hadn't?"

"I wouldn't let you get hurt. You passed my test. We're friends. Come meet the guy anyway, I figure it's like your duty to examine American society from White House to Skid Row. Now all I want you to do is stand still while I say a few words. You were a terrific straight man yesterday. There was no harm in that, was there?" He belted my coat tightly as he spoke and put Thaxter's hat on my head. The door to Stronson's office opened before I could get away.

The financier was standing beside his desk, one of those deep executive desks of the Mussolini type. The picture in the paper was misleading in one respect only—I had expected a bigger man. Stronson was a fat boy, his hair light brown and his face sallow. In build he resembled Billy Srole. Brown curls covered his short neck. The impression he made was not agreeable. There was something buttocky about his cheeks. He wore a turtleneck shirt, and swinging ornaments, chains, charms hung on his chest. The pageboy bob gave him a pig-in-a-wig appearance. Platform shoes increased his height.

Cantabile had brought me here to threaten this man. "Take a good look at my associate, Stronson," he said. "He's the one I told you about. Study him. You'll see him again. He'll catch up with you. In a restaurant, in a garage, in a movie, in an elevator." To me he said, "That's all. Go wait outside." He faced me toward the door.

I had turned to ice. Then I was horrified. Even to be a dummy impersonating a murderer was dreadful. But before I could indignantly deny, remove the hat, stop Cantabile's bluff, the voice of Stronson's receptionist came, enormously amplified and room-filling, from the slotted box on the desk. "Now?" she said.

And he answered, "Now!"

Immediately the porter in the gray jacket entered the office, pushing Thaxter before him. His I.D. card was open in his hand. He said, "Police, Homicide!" and he pushed all three of us against the wall.

"Wait a minute. Let's see that card. What do you mean, homicide?" said Cantabile.

"What do you think, I was just going to let you make threats and hold still? After you said how you'd have me killed I went to the State's Attorney and swore a warrant," said Stronson. "Two warrants. One John Doe for the hit man, your friend."

"Are you supposed to be Murder Incorporated?" said Thaxter to me. Thaxter seldom laughed aloud. His deepest delight was always more than half-silent, and his delight at this moment was wonderfully deep.

"Who's the hit man, me?" I said, trying to smile.

No one replied.

"Who has to threaten you, Stronson?" said Cantabile. His brown eyes, challenging, were filled with moisture, while his face turned achingly dry and pale. "You lost more than a million bucks for the guys in the Troika, and you're finished, kid. You're dead! Why should anybody else get in the act? You've got no more chance than a shit-house rat. Officer, this man is unreal. You want to see the story in tomorrow's paper. Western Hemisphere Investment Corporation is wiped out. Stronson wants to pull a few people down with him. Charlie, go and get the paper. Show it to the man."

"Charlie ain't going anywhere. Everybody just lean on the wall. I hear you carry a gun, and your name is Cantabile. Bend over, sweetheart—that's the way." We all obeyed. His own weapon was under his arm. His harness creaked. He took the pistol from Cantabile's ornate belt. "No ordinary .38, a Saturday-Night Special. It's a Magnum. You could kill an elephant with this."

"There it is, just as I told you. That's the gun he shoved under my nose," said Stronson.

"It must run in the Cantabile family to be silly with guns. That was your Uncle Moochy, wasn't it, who wasted those two kids? No effing class at all. Goofy people. Now we'll see if you've got any grass on you. It would also be nice if there was a little parole violation to go with this too. We'll fix you fine, buddy boy. Goddamn bunch of kid-killers."

Thaxter was now being frisked under the cloak. His mouth was wide and his nose strongly distorted and flaming across the bridge with all the mirth, the joy of this marvelous Chicago experience. I was angry with Cantabile. I was furious. The detective ran his hands over my sides, under the arms, up between my legs and said, "You two gentlemen can turn around. You're quite a pair of dressers. Where did you get those shoes with the canvas sides?" he asked Thaxter. "Italy?"

"The King's Road," said Thaxter pleasantly.

The detective took off the gray porter's jacket—under it he wore a red turtlenecked shirt—and emptied Cantabile's long black ostrich-skin wallet on the desk. "And which one is supposed to be the hit man? Errol Flynn in the cape, or the check coat?"

"The coat," said Stronson.

"I should let you make a fool of yourself and arrest him," said Cantabile, still facing the wall. "Go ahead. On top of the rest."

"Why, is he somebody?" said the policeman. "A big shot?"

"Fucking-A-right," said Cantabile. "He's a well-known distinguished man. Look in tomorrow's paper and you'll see his name in Schneiderman's column—Charles Citrine. He's an important Chicago personality."

"So what, we're sending important personalities to jail by the dozen. Governor Kerner didn't even have the brains to get a smart bagman." The detective was enjoying himself. He had a plain seamed face, now jolly, a thoroughly experienced police face. Under the red shirt his breasts were fat. The dead hair of his wig did not agree with his healthy human color and was lacking in organic symmetry. It took off from his head in the wrong places. You saw such wigs on the playful, gaily-colored seats of the changing booths at the Downtown Club—hair pieces like Skye terriers waited for their masters.

"Cantabile came to see me this morning with wild propositions," said Stronson. "I said, no way. Then he threatened he'd murder me, and he showed me the gun. He's really crazy. Then he said he'd be back with his hit man. He described how the hit would be done. The guy would track me for weeks. Then he'd shoot half my face off like a rotten pineapple. And the smashed bone and the brains and blood running out of my nose. He even told me how the murder weapon, the evidence, would be destroyed, how the killer would saw it up with a power hacksaw and hammer the pieces out and drop them down different manholes in all the suburbs. Every little detail!"

"You're dead anyway, fat-ass," said Cantabile. "They'll find you in a sewer in a few months and they'll have to scrape an inch of shit off your face to see who it was."

"There's no permit for a gun. Beautiful!"

"Now take these guys out of here," said Stronson.

"Are you going to charge everybody? You only got two warrants."

"I'm going to charge everybody."

I said, "Mr. Cantabile himself has just told you that I had nothing to do with this. My friend Thaxter and I were coming out of the Art Institute and Cantabile made us come here to discuss an investment, supposedly. I can sympathize with Mr. Stronson. He's terrified. Cantabile is out of his mind with some kind of vanity, eaten up with conceit, violent egomania—bluff. This is just one of his original hoaxes. Maybe the officer can tell you, Mr. Stronson, that I'm not the Lepke type of hired killer. I'm sure he's seen a few."

"This man never killed anybody," said the cop.

"And I have to leave for Europe and I have lots of things to attend to."

This last point was the main one. The worst of this situation was that it interfered with my anxious preoccupations, my complicated subjectivity. It was my inner civil war versus the open life which is elementary, easy for everyone to read, and characteristic of this place, Chicago, Illinois.

As a fanatical reader, walled in by his many books, accustomed to look down from his high windows on police cars, fire engines, ambulances, an involuted man who worked from thousands of private references and texts, I now found relevance in the explanation T. E. Lawrence had given for enlisting in the RAF—"To plunge crudely among crude men and find myself . . ." How did it go, now? ". . . for these remaining years of prime life." Horseplay, roughhouse, barracks obscenity, garbage detail. Yes, many men, Lawrence said, would take the death-sentence without a whimper to escape the life-sentence which fate carries in her other hand. I saw what he meant. So it was time that someone—and why not someone like me?—did more with this baffling and desperate question than had been done by other admirable men who attempted it. The worst thing about this absurd moment was that my stride was broken. I was expected at seven o'clock for dinner. Renata would be upset. It vexed her to be stood up. She had a temper, her temper always worked in a certain way; and also, if my suspicions were correct, Flonzaley was never far off. Substitutes are forever haunting people's minds. Even the most stable and balanced individuals have a secretly chosen replacement in reserve somewhere, and Renata was not one of the stablest. As she often fell spontaneously into rhymes, she had surprised me once by coming out with this:

> When the dear
> Disappear
> There are others
> Waiting near.

I doubt that anyone appreciated Renata's wit more deeply than I did. It always opened breath-taking perspectives of candor. But Humboldt and I had agreed long ago that I could take anything that was well said. That was true. Renata made me laugh. I was willing to deal later with the terror implicit in her words, the naked perspectives suddenly disclosed. She had for instance also said to me, "Not only are the best things in life free, but you can't be too free with the best things in life."

A lover in the lockup gave Renata a classic floozy opportunity for free behavior. Because of my habit of elevating such mean considerations to the theoretical level it will surprise no one that I started to think about the lawlessness of the unconscious and its independence from the rules of conduct. But it was only antinomian, not free. According to Steiner, true freedom lived in pure consciousness. Each microcosm had been separated from the macrocosm. In the arbitrary division between Subject and Object the world had been lost. The zero self sought diversion. It became an actor. This was the situation of the Consciousness Soul as I interpreted it. But there now passed through me a qualm of dissatisfaction with Rudolf Steiner himself. This went back to an uncomfortable passage in Kafka's *Diaries* pointed out to me by my friend Durnwald, who felt that I was still capable of doing serious intellectual work and wanted to save me from anthroposophy. Kafka too had been attracted by Steiner's visions and found the clairvoyant states he described similar to his own, feeling himself on the outer boundaries of the human. He made an appointment with Steiner at the Victoria Hotel on Jungmannstrasse. It is recorded in the *Diaries* that Steiner was wearing a dusty and spotted Prince Albert and that he had a terrible head cold. His nose ran and he kept working his handkerchief deep into his nostrils with his fingers while Kafka, observing this with disgust, told Steiner that he was an artist stuck in the insurance business. Health and character, he said, prevented him from following a literary career. If he added theosophy to literature and the insurance business, what would become of him? Steiner's answer is not recorded.

Kafka himself of course was crammed to the top with this same despairing fastidious mocking Consciousness Soul. Poor fellow, the way he stated his case didn't do him much credit. The man of genius trapped in the insurance business? A very banal complaint, not really much better than a head cold. Humboldt would have agreed. We used to talk about Kafka and I knew his views. But now Kafka and Steiner and Humboldt were together in death where, presently, all the folk in Stronson's office would join them. Reappearing, perhaps, centuries hence in a more sparkling world. It wouldn't have to sparkle much to sparkle more than this one. Nevertheless, Kafka's description of Steiner upset me.

While I was engaged in these reflections, Thaxter had gotten into the act. He came on with malice toward none. He was going to straighten matters out most amiably, not patronizing people too much. "I really don't think you want to take Mr. Citrine away on this warrant," he said, gravely smiling.

"Why not?" said the cop, with Cantabile's pistol, the fat nickel-plated Magnum, stuck in his belt.

"You agreed that Mr. Citrine doesn't resemble a killer."

"He's tired-out and white. He should go to Acapulco for a week."

"It's preposterous, a hoax like this," said Thaxter. He was showing me the beauty of his common touch, how well he understood and got around his fellow Americans. But it was obvious to me how exotic the cop found Thaxter, his elegance, his Peter Wimsey airs. "Mr. Citrine is internationally known as an historian. He really *was* decorated by the French government."

"Can you prove that?" said the cop. "You wouldn't have your medal on you by any chance, would you?"

"People don't carry medals around," I said.

"Well, what kind of proof have you got?"

"All I have is this bit of ribbon. I have the right to wear it in my buttonhole."

"Let's have a look at that," he said.

I drew out the tangled faded insignificant bit of lime green silk.

"That?" said the cop. "I wouldn't tie it on a chicken leg."

I agreed with the cop completely, and as a Chicagoan I scoffed inwardly with him at these phony foreign honors. I was the Shoveleer, burning with self-ridicule. It served the French right, too. This was not one of their best centuries. They were doing everything badly. What did they mean by handing out these meager bits of kinky green string? Because Renata insisted in Paris that I must wear it in my buttonhole, we had been exposed to the insults of the real *chevalier* whom Renata and I met at dinner, the man with the red rosette, the "hard scientist," to use his own term. He gave me the snubbing of my life. "American slang is deficient, nonexistent," he said. "French has twenty words for 'boot.'" Then he was snooty about the Behavioral Sciences—he took me for a behavioral scientist—and he was very rough on my green ribbon. He said, "I am sure you have written some estimable books but this is the kind of decoration given to people who improve the *poubelles*." Nothing but grief had ever come of my being honored by the French. Well, that would have to pass. The only real distinction at this dangerous moment in human history and cosmic development has nothing to do with medals and ribbons. Not to fall asleep is distinguished. Everything else is mere popcorn.

Cantabile was still facing the wall. The cop, I was glad to note, had it in for him. "You just hold it, there," he said. It seemed to me that we in this office were under something like a huge transparent wave. This enormous transparent thing stood still above us, flashing like crystal. We were all within it. When it broke and detonated we would be scattered for miles and miles along some far white beach. I almost hoped that Cantabile would have his neck broken. But, no, when it happened I saw each of us cast up safe and separate on a bare white pearly shore.

As all parties continued—Stronson, stung by Cantabile's evocation of his corpse fished from the sewer, crying in a kind of pig's soprano voice, "I'll see that *you* get it, anyway!" while Thaxter was coming in underneath, trying to be persuasive—I tuned out and gave my mind to one of my theories. Some people embrace their gifts with gratitude. Others have no use for them and can think only of overcoming their weaknesses. Only their defects interest and challenge them. Thus those who hate people may seek them out. Misanthropes often practice psychiatry. The shy become performers. Natural thieves look for positions of trust. The frightened make bold moves. Take the case of Stronson, a man who entered into desperate schemes to swindle gangsters. Or take myself, a lover of beauty who insisted on living in Chicago. Or Von Humboldt Fleisher, a man of powerful social instincts burying himself in the dreary countryside.

Stronson didn't have the strength to carry through. Seeing how self-deformed he was, fat but elegant; short of leg and ham, on platform shoes; given to squealing, but sending his voice deep, I was sorry, oh! deeply sorry for him. It seemed to me that his true nature was quickly reclaiming him. Had he forgotten to shave that morning or did terror make his beard suddenly rush out? And long awful bristles were coming up from his collar. A woodchuck look was coming over him. The pageboy wave went lank with sweat. "I want all these guys handcuffed," he said to the plainclothesman.

"What, with one pair of cuffs?"

"Well, put 'em on Cantabile. Go, put 'em on."

I completely agreed with him, in silence. Yes, manacle the son of a bitch, twist his arms behind him, and cut into the flesh. But having said these savage things to myself, I didn't necessarily wish to see them happen.

Thaxter drew the cop aside and said a few words in an undertone. I wondered later whether he hadn't passed him a secret CIA code word. You couldn't be sure with Thaxter. To this day I have never been able to decide whether or not he had ever been a secret agent. Years ago he invited me to be his guest in Yucatán. Three times I changed planes to get there, and then I was met at a dirt landing strip by a peon in sandals who drove me in a new Cadillac to Thaxter's villa, fully staffed with Indian servants. There were cars and jeeps, and a wife and little children, and Thaxter had already mastered the local dialect and ordered people around. A linguistic genius, he quickly learned new languages. But he was having trouble with a bank in Mérida, and there was, of all things, a country club in his neighborhood where he had run up a tab. I arrived just as he was completing the invariable pattern. He said on the second day that we were leaving this damn place. We packed his steamer trunks with fur coats and tennis equipment, with temple treasures and electrical appliances. As we drove away I was holding one of his babies on my lap.

The cop took us out of Stronson's office. Stronson called after us, "You bastards are going to get it. I promise you. No matter what happens to me. Especially you, Cantabile."

Tomorrow he himself would get it.

As we waited for the elevator, Thaxter and I had time to confer. "No, I'm not being booked," said Thaxter. "I'm almost sorry about that. I'd love to go along, really."

"I expect you to get busy," I said. "I felt that Cantabile was going to pull something like this. And Renata's going to be very upset, that's the worst of it. Don't go off and forget me now, Thaxter."

"Don't be absurd, Charles. I'll get the lawyers right on this. Give me some names and numbers."

"First thing is to call up Renata. Take Szathmar's number. Also Tomchek and Srole."

Thaxter wrote the information on an American Express receipt form. Could it be that he was still a cardholder?

"You'll lose that flimsy bit of paper," I said.

Thaxter spoke to me rather seriously about this. "Watch it, Charlie," he said. "You're being a nervous Nellie. This is a trying moment, sure. Exactly why you have to watch it all the more. *A plus forte raison.*"

You knew that Thaxter was in earnest when he spoke French. And whereas George Swiebel always shouted at me not to abuse my body, Thaxter forever warned me about my anxiety level. Now there was a man whose nerves were strong enough for his chosen way of life. And notwithstanding his weakness for French expressions, Thaxter was a real American in that, like Walt Whitman, he offered himself as an archetype—"What I assume you will assume." At the moment, that didn't particularly help. I was under arrest. My feelings toward Thaxter were those of a man with many bundles trying to find the door key and hampered by the house cat. But the truth was that the people from whom I looked for help were by no means my favorites. Nothing was to be expected from Thaxter. I even suspected that his efforts to help might be downright dangerous. If I cried out that I was drowning, he would come running and throw me a life preserver of solid cement. If odd feet call for odd shoes, odd souls have odd requirements and affection comes to them in odd modes. A man who longed for help was fond of someone incapable of giving any.

I suppose that it was the receptionist who had sent for the blue-and-white squad car now waiting for us. She was a very pretty young woman. I had looked at her as we were leaving the office and thought, Here's a sentimental girl. Well brought up. Lovely. Distressed to see people arrested. Tears in her eyes.

"In the front seat, you," said the plainclothesman to Cantabile, who, in his pinch hat, white in the face, hair sticking out at the sides, got in. At this moment, disheveled, he seemed for the first time genuinely Italian.

"The main thing is Renata. Get in touch with Renata," I told Thaxter as I got into the back seat. "I'll be in trouble if you don't—trouble!"

"Don't worry. People won't let you disappear from sight forever," said Thaxter.

His words of comfort gave me my first moment of deeper anxiety.

He did indeed try to get in touch with Renata and with Szathmar. But Renata was still at the Merchandise Mart with her client, picking fabrics, and Szathmar had already closed his office. Somehow Thaxter forgot what I had told him about Tomchek and Srole. To kill time, therefore, he went to a Black Kung Fu movie on Randolph Street. When the show let out he reached Renata at home. He said that since she knew Szathmar so well he thought he could leave things to her, entirely. After all, he was a stranger in town. The Boston Celtics were playing the Chicago Bulls and Thaxter bought a ticket to the basketball game from a scalper. En route to the Stadium the cab stopped at Zimmerman's and he bought a bottle of Piesporter. He couldn't get it chilled properly, but it went well with the sturgeon sandwiches.

Cantabile's dark form was riding before me in the front seat of the squad car, I addressed my thoughts to it. A man like Cantabile took advantage of my inadequate theory of evil, wasn't that it? He filled all the gaps in it to the best of his histrionic ability with his plunging and bluffing. Or did I, as an American, *have* a theory of evil? Perhaps not. So he entered the field from that featureless and undemarcated side where I was weak, with his ideas and conceits. This pest delighted the ladies, it

seemed—he pleased Polly and, apparently, his wife the graduate student as well. It was my guess that he was an erotic lightweight. But after all it's the imagination that counts for most
with women. So he made his progress through life with his fine
riding gloves and his calfskin boots, and the keenly gleaming
fuzz of his tweeds, and the Magnum he carried in his waistband, threatening everybody with death. Threats were what he
loved. He had called me in the night to threaten me. Threats
had affected his bowels yesterday on Division Street. This
morning he had gone to threaten Stronson. In the afternoon he
offered, or threatened, to have Denise knocked off. Yes, he was
a queer creature, with his white face, his long ecclesiastical-
wax nose with its dark flues. He was very restless in the front
seat. He seemed to be trying to get a look at me. He was almost
limber enough to twist his head about and preen his own back
feathers. What might it mean that he had tried to pass me off
as a murderer? Did he find the original suggestion for that in
me? Or was he trying in his own way to bring me out, to carry
me into the world, a world from which I had the illusion that
I was withdrawing? On the Chicago level of judgment I dismissed him as ready for the bughouse. Well, he was ready for
the bughouse, certainly. I was sophisticated enough to recognize that in what he proposed that we two should do with Polly
there was a touch of homosexuality, but that wasn't very serious. I hoped that they would send him back to prison. On the
other hand I sensed that he was doing something for me. In his
gleaming tweed fuzz, the harshness of which suggested nettles,
he had materialized in my path. Pale and crazy, with his mink
mustache, he seemed to have a spiritual office to perform. He
had appeared in order to move me from dead center. Because
I came from Chicago no normal and sensible person could do
anything of this sort for me. I couldn't be myself with normal
sensible people. Look at my relations with a man like Richard
Durnwald. Much as I admired him, I couldn't be mentally comfortable with Durnwald. I was slightly more successful with Dr.
Scheldt the anthroposophist, but I had my troubles with him
too, troubles of a Chicago nature. When he spoke to me of
esoteric mysteries I wanted to say to him, "Don't give me that

spiritual hokum, friend!" And after all, my relations with Dr.
Scheldt were tremendously important. The questions I raised
with him couldn't have been more serious.

All this went to my head, or flowed to my head, and I recalled
Humboldt in Princeton quoting to me, *"Es schwindelt!"* The
words of V. I. Lenin at the Smolny Institute. And things were
schwindling now. Now was it because, like Lenin, I was about
to found a police state? It was from a flux or inundation of
sensations, insights, and ideas.

Of course the cop was right. Strictly speaking, I was no killer.
But I did incorporate other people into myself and consume
them. When they died I passionately mourned. I said I would
continue their work and their lives. But wasn't it a fact that I
added their strength to mine? Didn't I have an eye on them in
the days of their vigor and glory? And on their women? I could
already see the outline of my soul's purgatorial tasks, when it
entered the next place.

"Watch it, Charlie," Thaxter had admonished me. He wore
his cape and held the ideal attaché case and the natural hook
umbrella, as well as the sturgeon sandwiches. I watched it. *A
plus forte raison,* I watched it. Watching, I was aware that in
the squad car I was following in Humboldt's footsteps. Twenty
years ago in the hands of the law, he had wrestled with the
cops. They had forced him into a strait jacket. He had had diarrhea in the police wagon as they rushed him to Bellevue. They
were trying to cope, to do something with a poet. What did the
New York police know about poets! They knew drunks and
muggers, they knew rapists, they knew women in labor and
hopheads, but they were at sea with poets. Then he had called
me from a phone booth in the hospital. And I had answered
from that hot grimy flaking dressing room at the Belasco. And
he had yelled, "This is life, Charlie, not literature!" Well, I
don't suppose the Powers, Thrones and Dominions, the Archai,
the Archangels and the Angels read poetry. Why should they?
They are shaping the universe. They're busy. But when Humboldt cried, "Life!" he didn't mean the Thrones, Exousiai, and
Angels. He only meant realistic, naturalistic life. As if art hid

the truth and only the sufferings of the mad revealed it. *This* was impoverished imagination?

We arrived and Cantabile and I were separated. They kept him at the desk, I went inside.

Anticipating the job I had cut out for me in purgatory, I didn't find it necessary to take jail too seriously. What was it, after all? A lot of bustle, and people who specialized in giving you a hard time. They photographed me, front and sides. Good. After these mug shots I was fingerprinted too. Very well. Following this, I expected to go into the lockup. There was a fat domestic-looking policeman waiting to take me to the slammer. Inside duties make these cops obese. There he was, housewifely, in a coat sweater and slippers, with belly and gun, a big pouting lip, and fat furrows at the back of his head. He was steering me in when someone said, "You! Charles Citrine! Outside!" I went back into the main corridor. I wondered how Szathmar had gotten here so fast. But it wasn't Szathmar who was waiting for me, it was Stronson's young receptionist. This beautiful girl said that her employer had decided to drop the case against me. He was going to concentrate on Cantabile.

"And did Stronson send you over?"

She explained, "Well, I really wanted to come. I knew who you were. As soon as I found out your name, I did. So I explained it to my boss. He's been like in shock these days. You can't exactly blame Mr. Stronson, when people come and say he's going to be murdered. But I finally got him to understand that you were a famous person, not a hit man."

"Ah, I see. And you're a dear girl as well as a beautiful one. I can't tell you how grateful I am. Talking to him couldn't have been easy."

"He really was scared. Now he's mostly depressed. Why are your hands so dirty?" she said.

"Fingerprinting. The ink they used."

She was upset. "My God! Imagine fingerprinting a man like you!" She opened her purse and began to moisten paper tissues and to rub my stained fingertips.

"No, thank you. No, no, don't do that," I said. Such attentions always get to me, and it seemed a dreadfully long time since anyone had done me any intimate kindness like this. There are days when one wants to go to the barber, not for a haircut (there's not much hair to cut) but just for the sake of the touch.

"Why not?" said the girl. "I feel that I've always known you."

"From books?"

"Not books. I'm afraid I never read any of your books. I understand they're history books and history has never been my bag. No, Mr. Citrine, through my mother."

"Do I know your mother?"

"Since I was a kid, I've heard you were her school-days sweetheart."

"Your mother isn't Naomi Lutz!"

"Yes, she was. I can't tell you how thrilled she and Doc were when they ran into you at that bar downtown."

"Yes, Doc was with her."

"When Doc passed away, Mother was going to call you. She says now you're the only one she can talk old times with. There are things she wants to remember and can't place. Just the other day she couldn't recall the name of the town where her Uncle Asher lived."

"Her Uncle Asher lived in Paducah, Kentucky. Of course I'll call her. I loved your mother, Miss . . ."

"Maggie," she said.

"Maggie. You've inherited her curves from the waist down. I never saw another back-curve so lovely till this moment, and in jail, of all places. You also have her gums and teeth, a bit short in the teeth, and the same smile. Your mother was beautiful. You'll excuse me for saying this, it's an exciting moment, but I always felt that if I could have embraced your mother every night for forty years, as her husband, of course, my life would have been completely fulfilled, a success—instead of this. How old are you, Maggie?"

"Twenty-five."

"O Lord!" I said as she washed my fingers in the freezing drinking water. My hand is very sensitive to a feminine touch. A kiss in the palm can send me out of my head.

She took me home in her Volkswagen, weeping a little as she drove. She was thinking perhaps of the happiness her mother and I had missed. And when, I wondered, would I rise at last above all this stuff, the accidental, the merely phenomenal, the wastefully and randomly human, and be fit to enter higher worlds?

* * *

So before leaving town I paid a visit to Naomi. Her married name was Wolper.

But I didn't go immediately to see her. I had a hundred chores to do first.

The last days in Chicago were crowded. As if to make up for the hours Cantabile's mischief had cost me, I followed a busy schedule. My accountant, Murra, gave me a whole hour of his time. In his smooth offices, decorated by the famous Richard Himmel and overlooking the lightest green part of the Chicago River, he told me that he had failed to convince the IRS that it had no case against me. His own bill was high. I owed him fifteen hundred dollars for getting nowhere. When I left his building I found myself in the gloom of Michigan Avenue in front of the electric-light shop near Wacker Drive. Always drawn to this place, with its ingenious new devices, the tints and shapes of bulbs and tubes, I bought a 300-watt flood reflector. I had no use for this article. I was going away. What did I need it for? The purchase only expressed my condition. I was still furnishing my retreat, my sanctuary, my Fort Dearborn deep in Indian (Materialistic) Territory. Also I was in the grip of departure anxieties—jet engines would tear me from the ground at two thousand miles per hour but where was I going, and what for? The reasons for this terrific speed remained unclear.

No, buying a bulb didn't help much. What did give me great comfort was to talk with Dr. Scheldt. I questioned him about the Spirits of Form, the Exousiai, known in Jewish antiquity by another name. These shapers of destiny should long ago have surrendered their functions and powers to the Archai, the Spirits of Personality who stand one rank closer to man in the

universal hierarchy. But a number of dissident Exousiai, playing a backward role in world history, had for centuries refused
to let the Archai take over. They obstructed the development of
a modern sort of consciousness. Refractory Exousiai belonging to an earlier phase of human evolution were responsible
for tribalism and the persistence of peasant or folk consciousness, hatred of the West and of the New, they nourished atavis-
tic attitudes. I wondered whether this might not explain how
Russia in 1917 had put on a revolutionary mask to disguise
reaction; and whether the struggle between these same forces
might not lie behind Hitler's rise to power as well. The Nazis
also adopted the modern disguise. But you couldn't entirely
blame these Russians, Germans, Spaniards, and Asiatics. The
terrors of freedom and modernity were fearful. And this was
what made America appear so giddy and monstrous in the eyes
of the world. It also made certain countries seem, to American
eyes, desperately, monumentally dull. Fighting to retain their
inertias the Russians had produced their incomparably boring and terrifying society. And America, under the jurisdiction
of the Archai, or Spirits of Personality, produced autonomous
modern individuals with all the giddiness and despair of the
free, and infected with a hundred diseases unknown during the
long peasant epochs.

    After visiting with Dr. Scheldt I took my small daughters,
Lish and Mary, to the Christmas pageant after all, outmaneu-
vered by Denise, who had put them on the phone in tears.
Unexpectedly, however, the pageant was very stirring. I do love
theatricals, with their breaking voices, missed cues, and silly
costumes. All the fine costumes were in the audience. Hundreds of excited kiddies were brought by their Mamas, many of
these Mamas being tigresses of the subtlest sort. And dressed,
arrayed, perfumed to a degree! *Rip van Winkle* was given as a
curtain raiser. To me it was immensely relevant. It was all very
well to blame the dwarfs for making Rip drunk, but he had
his own good reasons for passing out. The weight of the sense
world is too heavy for some people, and getting heavier all the
time. His twenty years of sleep, let me tell you, went straight
to my heart. My heart was sensitive today—worry, anticipated

problems, and remorse made it tender and vulnerable. An idiotic old lecher was leaving two children to follow an obvious gold digger to corrupt Europe. As one of the few fathers in the audience I felt how wrong this was. I was encompassed by feminine judgment. The views of all these women were unmistakably expressed. I saw for instance that the mothers resented the portrayal of Mrs. van Winkle, clearly the American Bitch in an early version. Myself, I reject all such notions about American Bitches. The mothers, however, were angry, they smiled but were hostile. The kids, though, were innocent, and they clapped and cheered when Rip was told that his wife had died of apoplexy during a fit of rage.

I was thinking of the higher significance of these things—naturally. For me the real question was how Rip would have spent his time if the dwarfs had not put him to sleep. He had an ordinary human American right, of course, to hunt and fish and roam the woods with his dog—much like Huckleberry Finn in the Territory Ahead. The following question was more intimate and difficult: what would I have *done* if I hadn't been asleep in spirit for so long? Amid the fluttering and squealing and clapping and writhing of little children, so pure of face, so fragrant (even the small gases released, inevitably, by a crowd of children were pleasant if you breathed them in a paternal spirit), so *savable,* I forced myself to stop and answer—I was *obliged* to do it. If you believed one of the pamphlets Dr. Scheldt had given me to read, this sleeping was no trifling matter. Our unwillingness to come out of the state of sleep was the result of a desire to evade an impending revelation. Certain spiritual beings must achieve their development through men, and we betray and abandon them by this absenteeism, this will-to-snooze. Our duty, said one bewitching pamphlet, is to collaborate with the Angels. They appear within us (as the Spirit called the *Maggid* manifested himself to the great Rabbi Joseph Karo). Guided by the Spirits of Form, Angels sow seeds of the future in us. They inculcate certain pictures into us of which we are "normally" unaware. Among other things they wish to make us see the concealed divinity of other human beings. They show man how he can cross by means of thought the abyss that separates him from Spirit. To the soul they offer freedom and to the body they offer love. These facts must be grasped by waking consciousness. Because, when he sleeps, the sleeper *sleeps*. Great world events pass him by. Nothing is momentous enough to rouse him. Decades of calendars drop their leaves on him just as the trees dropped leaves and twigs on Rip. Moreover, the Angels themselves are vulnerable. Their aims must be realized in earthly humanity itself. Already the brotherly love they put into us has been corrupted into sexual monstrosity. What are we doing with each other in the sack? Love is being disgracefully perverted. Then, too, the Angels send us radiant freshness and we, by our own sleeping, make it all dull. And in the political sphere we can hear, semi-conscious though we are, the grunting of the great swine empires of the earth. The stink of these swine dominions rises into the upper air and darkens it. Is it any wonder that we invite slumber to come quickly and seal our spirits? And, said the pamphlet, the Angels, thwarted by our sleep during waking hours, have to do what they can with us in the night. But then their work cannot touch our feeling or thinking, for these are absent during sleep. Only the unconscious body and the sustaining vital principle, the ether body, lie there in bed. The great feelings and the thoughts are gone. So also in the day, sleepwalking. And if we will not awaken, if the Spiritual Soul can't be brought to participate in the work of the Angels, we will be sunk. For me the clinching argument was that the impulses of higher love were corrupted into sexual degeneracy. That really went home. Perhaps I had more basic, ultimate reasons for going off with Renata, leaving two little girls in dangerous Chicago, than I was aware enough to produce at a moment's notice. I might, just possibly, justify what I was doing. After all, Christian in *Pilgrim's Progress* had taken off, too, and left his family to pursue salvation. Before I could do the children any real good, I had to wake up. This muddiness, this failure to focus and to concentrate, was very painful. I could see myself as I had been thirty years ago. I didn't need to look in the picture album. That damning photograph was unforgettable. There I was, a pretty young man under a tree, holding hands with an attractive girl. But I might as well have been wearing flannel pajamas as that flapping double-breasted suit—the gift of my brother Julius—for in the flower of my youth and at the height of my powers I was out cold.

As I sat in the theater I allowed myself to imagine that there were spirits near, that they wished to reach us, that their breathing enlivened the red of the little dresses the kids were wearing, just as oxygen brightened fire.

Then the children started to scream. Rip was staggering up from the mass of leaves that had dropped on him. Knowing what he was up against, I groaned. The real question was whether he could stay awake.

During intermission I ran into Dr. Klosterman from the Downtown Club. He was the one who had urged me in the sauna to go to a plastic surgeon and do something about the bags under my eyes—a simple operation to make me look years younger. All I had for him was a cold nod when he came forward with his children. He said, "We haven't seen you around lately."

Well, I hadn't been around lately. But only last night, unconscious in Renata's arms, I had dreamed again that I was playing paddle ball like a champion. My dream-backhand skimmed the left wall of the court and dropped with deadly english into the corner. I beat Scottie the club-player, and also the unbeatable Greek chiropractor, a skinny athlete, very hairy, pigeon-toed but a fiery competitor from whom in real life I could never win a single point. But on the court of my dreams I was a tiger. So in dreams of pure wakefulness and forward intensity I overcame my inertia, my mooning and muddiness. In dreams at any rate I had no intention of quitting.

As I was thinking of all this in the lobby, Lish remembered that she had brought a note for me from her mother. I opened the envelope and read, "Charles: my life has been threatened!"

There was no end to Cantabile. Before kidnaping Thaxter and me on Michigan Boulevard, perhaps at the very moment when we were admiring the beautiful Monet Sandvika winter scene, Cantabile was on the telephone with Denise, doing what he loved best, i.e., making threats.

Once when he was speaking of Denise, George Swiebel had

explained to me (although knowing his Nature System I could have provided this explanation myself), "Denise's struggle with you is her whole sex life. Don't talk to her, don't argue with her, unless you still want to give her kicks." Undoubtedly he would have interpreted Cantabile's threats in the same way. "This is how the son of a bitch gets his nuts off." But it was just possible that Cantabile's death-dealing fantasy, his imaginary role as Death's highest-ranking deputy, was intended also to wake me up—"*Brutus, thou sleep'st,*" etcetera. This had occurred to me in the squad car.

But he had really done it now. "Does your mother expect an answer?" I asked the kid.

Lish looked at me with her mother's eyes, those wide amethyst circles. "She didn't say, Daddy."

Denise had certainly reported to Urbanovich that there was a plot to murder her. This would clinch the matter with the judge. He didn't trust or like me anyway, and he could impound my money. I could forget about those dollars, they were gone. What now? I began again with the usual haste and inaccuracy to tot up my fluid resources, twelve hundred here, eighteen hundred there, the sale of my beautiful carpets, the sale of the Mercedes, very disadvantageous given its damaged condition. So far as I knew, Cantabile was locked up at Twenty-sixth and California. I hoped he would get it in the neck. Lots of people were killed in jail. Perhaps someone would do him in. But I didn't believe that he would spend much time behind bars. Getting out was very easy now and he'd probably draw another suspended sentence. The courts now gave them as freely as the Salvation Army gave out doughnuts. Well, it didn't really matter, I was leaving for Milan.

So, as I said, I paid a sentimental visit to Naomi Lutz, now Wolper. I hired a limousine from the livery service to take me out to Marquette Park—why stint myself now? It was wintry, wet, sleety, a good day for a schoolboy to fight the weather with his satchel and feel dauntless. Naomi was at her post, stopping traffic while kids trotted, straggled, dragged their raincapes and stamped through the puddles. Under the police uniform she wore layers of sweaters. On her head was a garrison cap and a Sam Browne belt crossed her chest—the works: fleece boots, mittens, her neck protected by an orange havelock, her figure obliterated. She waved her coat-hampered wet arms, gathering kids about her, she stopped the traffic and then, heavy in the back, she turned and footed slowly to the curb on her thick soles. And this was the woman for whom I once felt perfect love. She was the person with whom I should have been allowed to sleep for forty years in my favorite position (the woman backed up to me and her breasts in my hands). In a city like brutal Chicago could a man really expect to survive without such intimate, such private comfort? When I came up to her I saw the young woman within the old one. I saw her in the neat short teeth, the winsome gums, the single dimple in the left cheek. I thought I could still breathe in her young woman's odor, damp and rich, and I heard the gliding and drawling of her voice, an affectation she and I had both thought utterly charming once. And even now, I thought, Why not? The rain of the Seventies looked to me like the moisture of the Thirties when our adolescent lovemaking brought out tiny drops in a little band, a Venetian mask across the middle of her face. But I knew better than to try to touch her, to take off the police coat and the sweaters and the dress and the underclothes. Nor would she want me to see what had happened to her thighs and her breasts. That was all right for her friend Hank—Hank and Naomi had grown old together—but not for me, who knew her way-back-when. There was no prospect of this. It was not indicated, not hinted, not possible. It was only one of those things that had to be thought.

We drank coffee in her kitchen. She had invited me to brunch and served fried eggs, smoked salmon, nutbread, and comb honey. I felt completely at home with her old ironware and hand-knitted pot holders. The house was all that Wolper left her, she said. "When I saw how fast he was losing money on the horses I insisted that he should make the title over."

"Smart thinking."

"A little later my husband's nose and ankle were broken, just as a warning, by a juice man. Till then I didn't know Wolper was paying the gangsters juice. He came home from the hospital with his face all purple around the bandages. He said I shouldn't sell the bungalow to save his life. He cried and said he was no damn good and he decided to disappear. I know you're surprised that I live in this Czech neighborhood. But my father-in-law, a smart old Jew, bought investment property in this nice safe Bohunk district. So this was where we wound up. Well, Wolper was a jolly man. He didn't give me trouble the way you would have. For a wedding present he made me a present of my own convertible and a charge account at Field's. That was what I wanted most in life."

"I always felt it would have given me strength to be married to you, Naomi."

"Don't idealize so much. You were a violent kid. You almost choked me to death because I went to a dance with some basketball player. And once, in the garage, you put a rope on your neck and threatened to hang yourself if you didn't get your way. Do you remember?"

"I'm afraid I do, yes. Superkeen needs were swelling up in me."

"Wolper is married again and has a bike shop in New Mexico. He may feel safer near the border. Yes, you were thrilling but I never knew where you were at with your Swinburne and your Baudelaire and Oscar Wilde and Karl Marx. Boy, you certainly did carry on."

"Those were intoxicating books and I was in the thick of beauty and wild about goodness and thought and poetry and love. Wasn't that merely adolescence?"

She smiled at me and said, "I don't really think so. Doc told Mother that your whole family were a bunch of greenhorns and aliens, too damn emotional, the whole bunch of you. Doc died last year."

"Your daughter told me that."

"Yes, he fell apart finally. When old men put two socks on one foot and pee into the bathtub I suppose it's the end."

"I'm afraid so. I myself think that Doc overdid the Yankee Doodle stuff. Being a Babbitt inspired him almost the way

Swinburne did me. He was dying to say good-by to Jewry, or to feudalism. . . ."

"Do me a favor—I still freeze when you use a word like feudalism on me. That was the trouble between us. You came down from Madison raving about that poet named Humboldt Park or something and borrowed my savings to go to New York on a Greyhound bus. I really and truly loved you, Charlie, but when you rolled away to see this god of yours, I went home and painted my nails and turned on the radio. Your father was furious when I told him you were a Fuller Brush salesman in Manhattan. He needed your help in the wood business."

"Nonsense, he had Julius."

"Jesus, your father was handsome. He looked like—what the girls used to say—The Spaniard Who Ruined My Life. And Julius?"

"Julius is disfiguring south Texas with shopping centers and condominiums."

"But you people all loved each other. You were like real primitive that way. Maybe that's why my father called you greenhorns."

"Well, Naomi, my father became an American too and so did Julius. They stopped all that immigrant loving. Only I persisted, in my childish way. My emotional account was always overdrawn. I never have forgotten how my mother cried out when I fell down the stairs or how she pressed the lump on my head with the blade of a knife. And what a knife—it was her Russian silver with a handle like a billy club. So there you are. Whether it was a lump on my head, or Julius's geometry, or how Papa could raise the rent, or poor Mama's toothaches, it was the most momentous thing on earth for us all. I never lost this intense way of caring—no, that isn't so. I'm afraid the truth is that I did lose it. Yes, sure I lost it. But I still required it. That's always been the problem. I required it and apparently I also promised it. To women, I mean. For women I had this utopian emotional love aura and made them feel I was a cherishing man. Sure, I'd cherish them in the way they all dreamed of being cherished."

"But it was a phony," said Naomi. "You yourself lost it. You didn't cherish."

"I lost it. Although anything so passionate probably remains in force somewhere."

"Charlie, you put it over on lots of girls. You must have made them awfully unhappy."

"I wonder whether mine is such an exceptional case of longing-heart-itis. It's unreal, of course, perverse. But it's also American, isn't it? When I say American I mean uncorrected by the main history of human suffering."

Naomi sighed as she listened to me and then said, "Ah, Charlie, I'll never understand how or why you reach your conclusions. When you used to lecture me, I never could follow you at all. But at the time your play opened on Broadway, you were in love with a girl, they tell me. What happened to her?"

"Demmie Vonghel. Yes. She was the real thing, too. She was killed in South America with her father. He was a millionaire from Delaware. They took off from Caracas in a DC-3 and crashed in the jungle."

"Oh how sad and terrible."

"I went down to Venezuela to look for her."

"I'm glad you did that. I was going to ask."

"I took the same flight out of Caracas. They were old planes and patched up. Indians flying around with their chickens and goats. The pilot invited me to sit in the cockpit. There was a big crack in the windshield and the wind rushed in. Flying over the mountains I was afraid we wouldn't make it either, and I thought, O Lord, let it happen to me the way it happened to Demmie. Looking at those mountains I frankly didn't care much for the way the world was made, Naomi."

"What do you mean by that?"

"Oh I don't know, but you get disaffected from nature and all its miracles and stupendous achievements, from subatomic to galactic. Things play too rough with human beings. They chafe too hard. They stick you in the veins. As we came over the mountains and I saw the Pacific throwing a fit of epilepsy against the shore I thought, To hell with *you,* then. You can't always like the way in which the world was molded. Sometimes I think, Who wants to be an eternal spirit and have more existences! Screw all that! But I was telling you about the flight. Up and down about ten times. We landed on bare earth. Strips of red dirt on coffee plantations. Waving at us under the trees were little naked kids with their brown bellies and bent dinguses hanging."

"You never found anything? Didn't you search in the jungle?"

"Sure I searched. We even found a plane, but not the missing DC-3. This was a Cessna that went down with some Japanese mining engineers. Vines and flowers were growing all over their bones, and God knows what spiders and other animals were making themselves at home in their skulls. I didn't want to discover Demmie in that condition."

"You didn't like the jungle much."

"No. I drank lots of gin. I developed a taste for straight gin, like my friend Von Humboldt Fleisher."

"The poet! What happened to him?"

"He's dead, too, Naomi."

"Isn't all this dying something, Charlie!"

"The whole thing is disintegrating and reintegrating all the time, and you have to guess whether it's always the same cast of characters or a lot of different characters."

"I suppose you finally got to the mission," said Naomi.

"Yes, and there were lots of Demmies there, about twenty Vonghels. They were all cousins. All with the same long heads golden hair knock-knees and upturned noses, and the same mumbling style of speech. When I said that I was Demmie's fiancé from New York they thought I was some sort of nut. I had to attend services and sing hymns, because the Indians wouldn't understand a white visitor who was not a Christian."

"So you sang hymns while your heart was breaking."

"I was glad to sing the hymns. And Dr. Tim Vonghel gave me a bucket of gentian violet to sit in. He told me I had a bad case of *tinia crura*. So I stayed among these cannibals, hoping that Demmie would show up."

"Were they cannibals?"

"They had eaten the first group of missionaries that came

there. As you sang in the chapel and saw the filed teeth of somebody who had probably eaten your brother—Dr. Timothy's brother was eaten, and he knew the fellows who had done it—well, Naomi, there's lots of peculiar merit in people. I wouldn't be surprised if my experiences in the jungle put me in a forgiving frame of mind."

"Who was there to forgive?" said Naomi.

"This friend of mine, Von Humboldt Fleisher. He drew a check on my account while I was knocking myself out over Demmie in the jungle."

"Did he forge your signature?"

"I had given him a blank check, and he put it through for more than six thousand dollars."

"No! But you, of course, you didn't expect a poet to act that way about money, did you? Excuse me for laughing. But you always did provoke people into doing the dirty human thing to you by insisting that they should do the Goody Two-Shoes bit. I'm awfully sorry you lost that girl in the jungle. She sounds to me like your type. She was like you, wasn't she? You could both have been out of it together, and perfectly happy."

"I see what you mean, Naomi. I failed to understand the deeper side of human nature. Until recently I couldn't bear to think of it."

"Only you could get mixed up with this goofy fellow that threatened Stronson. This Italian Maggie described to me."

"You may be right," I said. "And I must try to analyze my motives for going along with people of the Cantabile type. But think how I felt to have a child of yours, that beautiful girl, come and get me out of jail—the daughter of the woman I loved."

"Don't get sentimental, Charlie. Please!" she said.

"I have to tell you, Naomi, that I loved you cell by cell. To me you were a completely nonalien person. Your molecules were my molecules. Your smell was my smell. And your daughter reminded me of you—same teeth, same smile, same everything, for all I know."

"Don't get carried away. You'd marry her, wouldn't you, you old sexpot. Are you testing to see if I'd say go ahead? It's a real compliment that you're ready to marry her because she reminds you of me. Well, she's a wonderful kid, but what you need is a woman with a heart as big as a washing machine, and that's not my daughter. Anyway, you're still with that chick I saw in the bar—the gorgeous kind of Oriental one, built like a belly dancer, and big dark eyes. Aren't you?"

"Yes, she is gorgeous, and I'm still the boyfriend."

"A boyfriend! I wonder what it is with you—a big important clever man going around so eager from woman to woman. Haven't you got anything more important to do? Boy, have women ever sold you a bill of goods! Do you think they're really going to give you the kind of help and comfort you're looking for? As advertised?"

"Well, it is advertised, isn't it?"

"It's like an instinct with women," she said. "You communicate to them what you have to have and right away they tell you they've got exactly what you need, although they never even heard of it until just now. They're not even necessarily lying. They just have an instinct that they can supply everything that a man can ask for, and they're ready to take on any size or shape or type of man. That's what they're like. So you go around looking for a woman like yourself. There ain't no such animal. Not even this Demmie could have been. But the girls tell you, 'Your search is ended. Stop here. I'm it.' Then you award the contract. Of course nobody can deliver and everybody gets sore as hell. Well, Maggie isn't your type. Why don't you tell me about your wife?"

"Don't put temptation before me. Just pour me another cup."

"What's the temptation?"

"Oh, the temptation? The temptation is to complain. I could tell you how bad Denise is with the kids, how she dumps them when she can, has the court tie me in knots and the lawyers rip me off, and so on. Now that's a Case, Naomi. A Case can be a work of art, the beautiful version of one's sad life. Humboldt the poet used to perform his Case all over New York. But these Cases are bad art, as a rule. How will all this complaining seem when the soul has flowed out into the universe and looks back on the complete scene of earthly suffering?"

"You've only changed physically," said Naomi. "This is how you used to talk. What do you mean, 'the soul flows out into the universe'? . . . When I was an ignorant girl and loved you, you tried out your ideas on me."

"I found when I made my living by writing people's personal memoirs that no successful American had ever made a real mistake, no one had sinned or ever had a single thing to hide, there have been no liars. The method practiced is concealment through candor to guarantee duplicity with honor. The writer would be drilled by the man who hired him until he believed it all himself. Read the autobiography of any great American—Lyndon Johnson for instance—and you'll see how faithfully his brainwashed writers reproduce his Case. Many Americans—"

"Never mind many Americans," said Naomi. How comfortable she looked in slippers, smiling in the kitchen, her fat arms crossed. I kept repeating that it would have been bliss to sleep with her for forty years, that it would have defeated death, and so on. But could I really have borne it? The fact was that I became more and more fastidious as I grew older. So now I was honor-bound to face the touchy question: could I really have embraced this faded Naomi and loved her to the end? She really didn't look good. She had been beaten about by biological storms (the mineral body is worn out by the developing spirit). But this was a challenge that I could have met. Yes, I could have done it. Yes, it would have worked. Molecule for molecule she was still Naomi. Each cell of those stout arms was still a Naomi cell. The charm of those short teeth still went to my heart. Her drawl was as effective as ever. The Spirits of Personality had done a real job on her. For me the Anima, as C. G. Jung called it, was still there. The counterpart soul, the missing half described by Aristophanes in the *Symposium*.

"So you're going away to Europe with that young broad?" she said.

I was astonished. "Who told you that?"

"I ran into George Swiebel."

"I wish George wouldn't tell my plans to everyone."

"Oh, come, we've all known each other a lifetime."

"These things get back to Denise."

"You think you have secrets from that woman? She could see through a wall of steel, and you're no wall of steel. She doesn't have to figure you, anyway, she only has to figure out what the young lady wants you to do. Why are you going twice a year to Europe with this broad?"

"She's got to find her father. Her mother isn't certain which of two men . . . And last spring I had to be in London on business. So we stopped in Paris, too."

"You must be right at home, over there. The French made you a knight. I kept the clipping."

"I'm the cheapest type of low-grade *chevalier*."

"And did it tickle your vanity to travel with a great big beautiful doll? How did she make out with your high-class European friends?"

"Do you know that Woodrow Wilson sang 'Oh You Beautiful Doll' on the honeymoon train with Edith Bolling? The Pullman porter saw him dancing and singing in the morning when he came out."

"That's just the sort of fact you'd know."

"And he was just about our most dignified President," I added. "No, Renata wasn't a big hit with women abroad. I took her to a fancy dinner in London and the hostess thought her terribly vulgar. It wasn't the beige lace see-through dress. Nor even her wonderful coloring, her measurements, her vital emanations. She was just Sugar Ray Robinson among the paraplegics. She turned on the Chancellor of the Exchequer. He compared her to a woman in the Prado, by one of the Spanish masters. But the ladies were rough on her and she cried afterward and said it was because we weren't married."

"So next day you bought her thousands of dollars' worth of gorgeous clothes instead, I bet. But be you what you may, I get a big kick out of seeing you. You're a sweet fellow. This visit is a wonderful treat for a poor plain old broad. But would you humor me about one thing?"

"Sure, Naomi, if I can."

"I was in love with you, but I married a regular kind of Chicago person because I never really knew what you were talking about. However, I was only eighteen. I've often asked myself, now that I'm fifty-three, whether you'd make more sense today. Would you talk to me the way you talk to one of your intelligent friends—better yet, the way you talk to yourself? Did you have an important thought yesterday, for instance?"

"I thought about sloth, about how slothful I've been."

"Ridiculous. You've worked hard. I know you have, Charlie."

"There's no real contradiction. Slothful people work the hardest."

"Tell me about this. And remember, Charlie, you're not going to tone this down. You're going to say it to me as you would to yourself."

"Some think that sloth, one of the capital sins, means ordinary laziness," I began. "Sticking in the mud. Sleeping at the switch. But sloth has to cover a great deal of despair. Sloth is really a busy condition, hyperactive. This activity drives off the wonderful rest or balance without which there can be no poetry or art or thought—none of the highest human functions. These slothful sinners are not able to acquiesce in their own being, as some philosophers say. They labor because rest terrifies them. The old philosophy distinguished between knowledge achieved by effort *(ratio)* and knowledge received *(intellectus)* by the listening soul that can hear the essence of things and comes to understand the marvelous. But this calls for unusual strength of soul. The more so since society claims more and more and more of your inner self and infects you with its restlessness. It trains you in distraction, colonizes consciousness as fast as consciousness advances. The true poise, that of contemplation or imagination, sits right on the border of sleep and dreaming. Now, Naomi, as I was lying stretched out in America, determined to resist its material interests and hoping for redemption by art, I fell into a deep snooze that lasted for years and decades. Evidently I didn't have what it took. What it took was more strength, more courage, more stature. America is an overwhelming phenomenon, of course. But that's no excuse, really. Luckily, I'm still alive and perhaps there's even some time still left."

"Is this really a sample of your mental processes?" asked Naomi.

"Yes," I said. I didn't dare mention the Exousiai and the Archai and the Angels to her.

"Oh Christ, Charlie," said Naomi, sorry for me. She pitied me, really, and reaching over and breathing kindly into my face she patted my hand. "Of course you've probably become even more peculiar with time. I see now it's lucky for us both that we never got together. We would have had nothing but maladjustment and conflict. You would have had to speak all this highflown stuff to yourself, and everyday gobbledygook to me. In addition, there may be something about me that provokes you to become incomprehensible. Anyway you already took one trip to Europe with your lady and you didn't find Daddy. But when you go away, there are two more little girls with a missing father."

"I've had that very thought."

"George says that the little one is your favorite."

"Yes, Lish is just like Denise. I do love Mary more. I fight my prejudice, however."

"I'd be surprised if you didn't love those children a lot in your dippy way. Like everybody else I have my own child worries."

"Not with Maggie."

"No, I didn't like the job she had with Stronson, but now that he's washed up she'll get another, easy. It's my son that upsets me. Did you ever get around to reading his articles in the neighborhood paper on kicking the drug habit? I sent them to you for your opinion."

"I didn't read them."

"I'll give you another set of clippings. I want you to tell me if he has talent. Will you do that for me?"

"I wouldn't dream of refusing."

"You ought to dream of it oftener. People lay too much on you. I know I shouldn't be doing this. You're leaving town and must have plenty to do. But I want to know."

"Is the young man like his sister?"

"No, he isn't. He's more like his dad. You could do something for him. As a good man who's led a cranky life, you might reach him. He's already begun a cranky career."

"So what's missing is the goodness I'm alleged to have."

"Well, you are a crackpot, but you do have a real soul. The kid grew up without a father," said Naomi, tears coming to her eyes. "You don't have to do much. Just let him get to know you. Take him to Africa with you."

"Ah, did George sound off about the beryllium mine?"

This was all that I needed to add to my other enterprises and commitments, to Denise and Urbanovich, to the quest for Renata's father and the exploratory study of anthroposophy, and to Thaxter and *The Ark*. A hunt for valuable minerals in Kenya or Ethiopia. Just the thing! I said, "There's really nothing in this beryllium stuff, Naomi."

"I didn't actually think there was. But how wonderful it would be for Louie to go with you on safari. It isn't that I buy *King Solomon's Mines* or anything like that. And before you go, let me suggest something, Charlie. Don't wear yourself out proving something with these giant broads. Remember, your great love was for me, just five feet tall."

• • • •

We were accompanied to O'Hare by the gloomy Señora. In the cab she coached Renata in whispers and stayed with us as we checked in, went through skyjacking inspection. At last we took off. Renata told me in the plane not to worry about leaving Chicago. "At last you're doing something for yourself," she said. "It's funny about you. You're self-absorbed but you don't know the ABC of selfishness. Think of it this way, without a me, there's neither thee nor we." Renata was a perfect whiz at rhymed sayings. Her couplet for Chicago was, "Without O'Hare, it's sheer despair." And when I asked her once what she thought of another fascinating woman she said, "Would Paganini pay to hear Paganini play?" I often wished that the London hostess who thought her so gross, such a slob, could have heard her when she got going. When we reached the take-off position and suddenly began to race, tearing from the runway with an adhesive-plaster sound, she said, "So long, Chicago. Charlie, you wanted to do this town some good. Why that bunch of low bastards, they don't deserve a man like you here. They know fuck-all about quality. A lot of ignorant crooks are in the papers. The good guys are ignored. I only hope when you write your essay on boredom that you'll let this city have it right in the teeth."

We tilted backward as the 727 climbed and heard the grinding of the retracted landing gear. The dark wool of clouds and mist came between us and the bungalows, industries, the traffic, and the parks. Lake Michigan gave one glint and became invisible. I said to her, "Renata, it's sweet of you to stand up for me. The truth is that my attitude toward the USA—and Chicago is just the USA—hasn't been one hundred percent either. I've always hunted for some kind of cultural protection. When I married Denise I thought I had an ally."

"Because of her college degrees, I suppose."

"She turned out to be the head of the Fifth Column. But now I can see why this was. Here was this beautiful slender girl."

"Beautiful?" said Renata. "She's witchy-looking."

"This beautiful slender aspiring martial bookish young woman. She told me that her mother once saw her in the bath and gave a cry, 'You are a golden girl.' And then her mother burst into tears."

"I understand the disappointment of such women," Renata said. "That's the upper-middle-class Chicago scene, with the driving mothers. What are those daughters supposed to rise to? They can't all marry Jack Kennedy or Napoleon or Kissinger or write masterpieces or play the harpsichord at Carnegie Hall dressed in gold lamé with a purple backdrop."

"So Denise would start up in the night and sob and say that she was *nothing*."

"Were you supposed to make her something?"

"Well, there was an ingredient missing."

"You never found it," said Renata.

"No, and she went back to the faith of her fathers."

"Who were the fathers?"

"A bunch of ward-heelers and tough guys. But I'm bound to say that I didn't have to be such a sensitive plant. After all, Chicago is my own turf. I should have been able to take it."

"She cried in the night about her wasted life and that was

what did it. You've got to have your sleep. You could never forgive a woman who kept you awake with her conflicts."

"I'm thinking about sensitive plants in Business America because we're headed for New York to find out about Humboldt's will."

"A complete waste of time."

"And I ask myself, Must Philistinism hurt so much?"

"I talk to you, and you lecture me. All our Milan arrangements had to be changed. And for what! He had nothing to leave you. He died in a flophouse, out of his mind."

"He was sane again before he died. I know that from Kathleen. Don't be a bad sport."

"I'm the best sport you'll ever know. You've got me confused with that uptight bitch who drags you to court."

"To get back to the subject, Americans had an empty continent to subdue. You couldn't expect them to concentrate on philosophy and art as well. Old Doc Lutz, because I read poetry to his daughter, called me a damn foreigner. To pare corns in a Loop office was an American calling."

"Please fold my coat and lay it on the rack. I wish the stewardesses would stop gossiping and take our drink orders."

"Certainly, my darling. But let me finish what I was saying about Humboldt. I know you think I'm talking too much, but I am excited, and I feel remorseful about the children besides."

"Just what Denise wants you to be," said Renata. "When you go away and won't leave a forwarding address she tells you, 'Okay, if the kids get killed you can read about it in the paper.' But don't get into a tragic bind about this, Charlie. Those kids will have their Christmas fun, and I'm sure Roger will have a marvelous time with his Milwaukee grandparents. How children love that square family stuff."

"I hope he is all right," I said. "I'm very fond of Roger. He's an engaging kid."

"He loves you too, Charlie."

"To get back to Humboldt then."

Renata's face took on an I'm-going-to-let-you-have-it-straight look and she said, "Charlie, this will is just a gag from the grave. You said yourself, once, that it could be a posthumous prank. The guy died nuts."

"Renata, I've read the textbooks. I know what clinical psychologists say about manic depressives. But they didn't know Humboldt. After all, Humboldt was a poet. Humboldt was noble. What does clinical psychology know about art and truth?"

For some reason this provoked Renata. She became huffy. "You wouldn't think he was so wonderful if he was alive. It's only because he's dead. Koffritz sold mausoleums, so he had business reasons for his death hang-up. But what is it with you?"

I had it in mind to reply, "What about yourself? The men in your life have been, were, or are Mausoleum Koffritz, Flonzaley the Undertaker, and Melancholy Citrine." But I bit my tongue.

"What you do," she said, "is invent relationships with the dead you never had when they were living. You create connections they wouldn't allow, or you weren't capable of. I heard you say once that death was good for some people. You probably meant that you got something out of it."

This made me thoughtful and I said, "That's occurred to me, too. But the dead are alive in us if we choose to keep them alive, and whatever you say I loved Humboldt Fleisher. Those ballads moved me deeply."

"You were just a boy," she said. "It was that glorious time of life. He only wrote ten or fifteen poems."

"It's true he didn't write many. But they were most beautiful. Even one is a lot, for certain things. You should know that. His failure is something to think about. Some say that failure is the only real success in America and that nobody who 'makes it' is ever taken into the hearts of his countrymen. This lays the emphasis on the countrymen. Maybe that's where Humboldt made his big mistake."

"Thinking about his fellow citizens?" said Renata. "When will they bring our drinks?"

"Be patient and I'll entertain you till they come. There are a few things I have to get off my chest about Humboldt. Why should Humboldt have bothered himself so much? A poet is what he is in himself. Gertrude Stein used to distinguish between a person who is an 'entity' and one who has an 'identity.' A significant man is an entity. Identity is what they give you socially. Your little dog recognizes you and therefore you have an identity. An entity, by contrast, an impersonal power, can be a frightening thing. It's as T. S. Eliot said of William Blake. A man like Tennyson was merged into his environment or encrusted with parasitic opinion, but Blake was naked and saw man naked, and from the center of his own crystal. There was nothing of the 'superior person' about him, and this made him terrifying. That is an entity. An identity is easier on itself. An identity pours a drink, lights a cigarette, seeks its human pleasures, and shuns rigorous conditions. The temptation to lie down is very great. Humboldt was a weakening entity. Poets have to dream, and dreaming in America is no cinch. God 'giveth songs in the night,' the Book of Job says. I've devoted lots of thought to all these questions and I've concentrated hard on Humboldt's famous insomnia. But I think that Humboldt's insomnia testified mostly to the strength of the world, the human world and all its wonderful works. The world was interesting, really interesting. The world had money, science, war, politics, anxiety, sickness, perplexity. It had all the voltage. Once you had picked up the high-voltage wire and were *someone,* a known name, you couldn't release yourself from the electrical current. You were transfixed. Okay, Renata, I'm summarizing: the world has power, and interest follows power. Where are the poets' power and interest? They originate in dream states. These come because the poet is what he is in himself, because a voice sounds in his soul which has a power equal to the power of societies, states, and regimes. You don't make yourself interesting through madness, eccentricity, or anything of the sort but because you have the power to cancel the world's distraction, activity, noise, and become fit to hear the essence of things. I can't tell you how terrible he looked last time I saw him."

"You've told me."

"I can't get over it. You know the color of rivers that run through cities—the East River, the Thames, the Seine? He was that shade of gray."

Renata had nothing to say to this. As a rule her own reflections satisfied her perfectly and she used my conversation as a background to think her own thoughts. These thoughts, so far as I could tell, had to do with her desire to become Mrs. Charles Citrine, the wife of a Pulitzer *chevalier*. I therefore turned the tables on her and used her thoughts as a background for my thoughts. The Boeing tore off through shawls of cloud, the hurtling moment of risk and death ended with a musical *Bing!* and we entered the peace and light above. My head lay on the bib and bosom of the seat and when the Jack Daniel's came I strained it through my irregular multicolored teeth, curling my forefinger over the top of the glass to hold back the big perforated ice cubes—they always put in too many. The thread of whisky burned pleasantly in the gullet and then my stomach, like the sun outside, began to glow, and the delight of freedom also began to expand within me. Renata was right, I was away! Once in a while, I get shocked into upper wakefulness, I turn a corner, see the ocean, and my heart tips over with happiness—it feels so free! Then I have the idea that, as well as beholding, I can also be beheld from yonder and am not a discrete object but incorporated with the rest, with universal sapphire, purplish blue. For what is this sea, this atmosphere, doing within the eight-inch diameter of your skull? (I say nothing of the sun and the galaxy which are also there.) At the center of the beholder there must be space for the whole, and this nothing-space is not an empty nothing but a nothing reserved for everything. You can feel this nothing-everything capacity with ecstasy and this was what I actually felt in the jet. Sipping whisky, feeling the radiant heat that rose inside, I experienced a bliss that I knew perfectly well was not mad. They hadn't done me in back there, Tomchek, Pinsker, Denise, Urbanovich. I had gotten away from them. I couldn't say that I knew really what I was doing, but did it matter so much? I felt clear in the head nevertheless. I could find no shadow of wistful yearning, no remorse, no anxiety. I was with a beautiful bim. She was as full of schemes and secrets as the Court of Byzantium. Was that so bad? I was a goofy old chaser. But what of it?

Before leaving Chicago I had had a long talk about Renata with George Swiebel. We were exactly of an age, and approximately in the same physical condition. George was wonderfully kind. He said, "You've got to blow now. Get out of town. I'll take care of the details for you. You just sit on that plane, pull off your shoes, order a drink, and take the fuck off. You'll be okay. Don't worry." He sold the Mercedes for four thousand dollars. He took charge of the Persian carpets and made me an advance of another four. They must have been worth fifteen because they had been appraised by the insurance company at ten. But although George was in the building-repairs racket, he was utterly honorable. You couldn't find a single cheating fiber in his heart.

We drank a bottle of whisky together and he made me a parting speech about Renata. It was full of his own kind of Nature-wisdom. He said, "All right, friend, you're going away with this gorgeous chick. She belongs to the new swinging generation and in spite of the fact that she's so developed she just isn't a grown-up woman. Charlie, she doesn't know a prick from a popsicle. Her mother is a gloomy sinister old character, a real angler. That mother is not my kind of people at all. She figures you for a cunt-crazy old man. You were once a winner with a big reputation. Now you're staggering a bit and here's a chance to marry you, grab off a piece of you before Denise gets it all. Maybe even rebuild you as a name and a money-maker. You're a bit mysterious to those types because there aren't many of you around. Now Renata is her mother's big, big, big prize apple from the Washington State Fair, a perfect Wenatchee, raised under scientific conditions, and she's hell-bent on cashing in while she's in her prime."

Working himself up, George got to his feet, a broad healthy figure of a man, rosy and vigorous, his nose bent like an Indian's, and his thin hair centered like a scalp lock. As always when he expounded his Nature-philosophy he started to shout. "This is no ordinary cunt. She's worth taking a chance on. All right, you might be humiliated, you might have to take a lot of shit, you might be robbed and plundered, you might lie sick with nobody looking after you or have a coronary or lose a leg. Okay, but you're alive, a flesh and blood brave instinct person. You've got guts. And I'll be standing by you. Cable me from anywhere and I'll arrive. I liked you all right when you were younger, but not the way I love you now. When you were younger you were on the make. You may not realize it but you were damn clever and canny about your career. But now, thank God, you're in a real dream and a fever over this young woman. You don't know what you're doing. And that's just what's great about it."

"You make it sound much too romantic, George."

"Never mind," he said. "Now Renata's 'real father' bit is baloney. Let's figure this out together. What does a broad like that need with a real father? She's already got this old pimp mother. Renata wouldn't know what to do with a father. She's got just the daddy she needs, a sex daddy. No, the whole thing was hoked up to get these trips to Europe. But that's just the finest part of it. Go on and blow all your money. Go broke, and the hell with the whole courthouse gang. Now you told me before about April in Paris with Renata but brief me again."

"Here it is," I said. "Until Renata was twelve she thought her father was a certain Signor Biferno, a fancy leather-goods dealer from the Via Monte Napoleone, in Milan. That's the big luxury-goods street. But when she was thirteen or so the old girl told her that Biferno might not be the man. The Señora and Biferno had been skiing in Cortina, she broke her ankle, her foot was in a cast, she quarreled with Biferno and he went home to his wife and kids. She revenged herself on him with a young Frenchman. Now when Renata was ten her mother had taken her to Milan to confront Biferno. They got all dressed up and made a scene on the Via Monte Napoleone."

"That old broad is one of the big-time troublemakers."

"The real Mrs. Biferno called the police. And much later, back in Chicago, her mother told Renata, 'Biferno may not be your father after all.'"

"So you went to Paris to see the young Frenchman, who is

now an old Frenchman? That was a hell of a thing for a mother to tell a girl just as she enters adolescence."

"I had to be in London anyway and we were at the Ritz. Then Renata said she must go to Paris to look over this man who was perhaps her father and she wanted to go alone. She planned to come back three days later. So I took her to Heathrow. She was carrying a large bag, which was open. Right at the top, like a large compact, was her diaphragm case."

"Why was she taking her birth control?"

"You can never tell when the chance of a lifetime may present itself."

"Tactics, Charlie, just stupid tactics. Keep the fellow guessing. She was putting you off balance. I think she's really okay. She just does certain stupid things. One thing I want to say, Charlie. I don't know what your habits are but don't let her blow you. You'll be dead in a year. Now tell me the rest about Paris."

"Well, the man was homosexual, elderly, tedious, and garrulous. When she didn't return to London on the fourth day I went to look for her at the Hotel Meurice. She said she hadn't had the nerve to face him yet and she'd been shopping and going to the Louvre and seeing Swedish films—*I Am Curious Yellow* or something. The old guy remembered her mother and he was pleased to think that he might have a daughter but he was cagey and said that legal recognition was absolutely out of the question. His family would disinherit him. But he wasn't the man anyway. Renata said there was no resemblance. I looked him over myself. She was right. Of course, there's no way of knowing how nature does its stuff. An angry woman with a cast on her ankle gets a gay skier to make an exception for her, and they beget this beautiful daughter with the perfect skin and dark eyes and those eyebrows. Think of an El Greco beauty raising her eyes to heaven. Then substitute sex for heaven. That's Renata's pious look."

"Well, I know you love her," said George. "When she locked you out because she had another guy in there with her and you came to me crying—you remember what I said? A man your age sobbing over a girl is a man I respect. Furthermore, you've still got all your strength."

"I should have, I never used any of it."

"Well, okay, you saved it. Now you're coming down the stretch and it's time to pull ahead. Maybe you should marry Renata. Only don't get faint on your way to the license bureau. Do the whole thing like a man. Otherwise she'll never forgive you. Otherwise she'll turn you into an old errand boy. Poor old Charlie with a watering eye going out to buy cigars for his missus."

• • •

We made our approach over the steely patch of evening water and landed at La Guardia in the tawny sundown. We then rode to the Plaza Hotel imprisoned in the low seats in one of New York's dog-catcher taxis. They make you feel that you have bitten someone and are being rushed to the pound, frothing with rabies, to be put down. I said this to Renata and she appeared to feel that I was using my imagination to spoil her pleasure, already somewhat damaged by the fact that we traveled, unlicensed, as a married pair. The doorman helped her out at the Plaza and, in her high boots, she strode under the heated marquee with its glowing orange rods. Over her miniskirt she wore a long suède Polish coat lined with lambskin. I had bought it for her from Cepelia. Her beautifully pliant velvet hat inspired by seventeenth-century Dutch portrait painters was pushed off from her forehead. Her face, evenly and purely white, broadened toward the base. This gourdlike fullness was her only defect. Her throat was ever so slightly ringed or rippled by some enriching feminine deposit. This slight swell appears also on her hips and on the inside of her thighs. The first joint of her fingers revealed the same signs of sensual superabundance. Following her, admiring, thinking, I walked in the checked coat. Cantabile and Stronson had agreed that it gave me the cut of a killer. But I couldn't have looked less killer-like than I now did. My hair was blown out of position so that I felt the radiant heat of the marquee on my bald spot. The winter air swept into my face and made my nose red. Under my eyes the pouches were heavy. Teatime musicians in the Palm Court played their swooning, ingratiating, kiss-ass music. I registered Mr. and Mrs. Citrine under a false Chicago address, and we went up in the elevator with a crowd of charming college girls down for the holidays. They seemed to give out a wonderful fragrance of unripeness, a sort of green-banana odor.

"You certainly got a load of those darling kids," said Renata, perfectly good-humored again—we were in an endless corridor of golden carpet, endlessly repeating its black scrolls and flourishes, flourishes and scrolls. My manner of observing people entertained her. "You're such an eager looker," she said.

Yes, but for decades I had neglected my innate manner of doing it, my personal way of looking. I saw no reason why I shouldn't resume it now. Who cared?

"But what's this?" said Renata as the bellhop opened the door. "What kind of room did they give us?"

"These are the accommodations with mansard windows. The very top of the Plaza. The best view in the house," I said.

"We had a marvelous suite last time. What the hell are we doing in the attic? Where's our suite?"

"Oh, come, come, my darling. What's the difference? You sound like my brother, Julius. He gets into such a state when hotels don't give him the best—so haughty and furious."

"Charles, are you having one of your stingy fits? Don't forget what you told me once about the observation car."

I was sorry now that I had ever made her familiar with Gene Fowler's saying that money was something to throw off the back end of a train. That was journalistic Hollywood of the golden age, the boozy night-club magnificence of the Twenties, the Big-Spender Syndrome. "But they're right, Renata. This is the best spot in the whole hotel for seeing Fifth Avenue."

Indeed the view, if you cared for views, was remarkable. I was very good myself at putting other people on to views for the purpose of absenting myself. Below, Fifth Avenue glowed with Christmas decorations and the headlights of the jammed traffic, solid between the Seventies and the Thirties, and shop illuminations, multicolored, crystalline, and like the cells in a capillary observed through a microscope, elastically changing shape, bumping and pulsatory. All this I saw in a single

instant. I was like a deft girl, scooping all the jacks before the
ball bounced back. It was as it had been with Renata last spring
when we took the train to Chartres, "Isn't that beautiful out
there!" she had said. I looked and yes, it was indeed beautiful.
No more than a glance was necessary. You saved yourself a lot
of time that way. The question was what you were going to do
with the minutes gained by these economies. This, I may say,
was all due to the operation of what Steiner describes as the
Consciousness Soul.

Renata didn't know that Urbanovich was about to rule on
the impounding of my money. By the movement of her eyes,
however, I saw that money thoughts were on her mind. Her
brows often were tilted heavenward with love but now and
then a strongly practical look swept over her which, however,
I also liked very much. But then she gave her head a quick lift
and said, "As long as you're in New York, you may as well see
a few editors and peddle your essays. Did Thaxter give them
back?"

"Reluctantly. He still expects to bring out *The Ark*."

"Sure. He himself is every kind of animal."

"He called me yesterday and invited us to a Bon Voyage
party on the *France*."

"His aging mother is throwing him a party too? She must be
quite an old dame."

"She understands style. For generations she's arranged the
coming out of debutantes and she's connected with the Rich.
She always knows where there's a chalet vacant for her boy
or a shooting box or a yacht. If he feels run-down she sends
him to the Bahamas or the Aegean. You ought to see her. She's
skinny clever capable and she glowers at me, I'm low company
for Pierre. She stands on guard for monied families defending
their right to drink themselves to death, their ancient privilege
to amount to nothing."

Renata laughed and said, "Spare me his party. Let's get your
Humboldt business over and go on to Milan. I have a deep
anxiety about it."

"Do you think this Biferno really is your father? Better he
than that queer Henri."

"Honestly I wouldn't think about a father if we were married. My insecure position forces me to look for solid ground. You'll say I have been married, but the ground with Koffritz wasn't very solid. And now there's my responsibility for Roger. By the way, we must send out toys to all the kids from F. A. O. Schwarz and I haven't got a cent. Koffritz is six months behind in payments. He says I have a rich man-friend. I will not drag him into court though, or throw him in jail. As for you, you carry so many freeloaders and I don't want to come under that heading. If I may say so, though, I at least care for you and do you some good. If you fell into the hands of that anthroposophist's daughter, that little blonde fox, you'd soon known the difference. She's a toughie."

"What has Doris Scheldt got to do with anything?"

"What? You wrote her a note before we left Chicago. I read the impression on your note pad. Don't look so truthful, Charlie. You're the world's worst liar. I wish I knew how many ladies you had in reserve."

I was not indignant over her spying. I no longer made scenes. Pleasant in themselves, our European trips also took me away from Miss Scheldt. Renata considered her a dangerous person and even the Señora had tried to scold me about her.

"But Señora," I had replied, "Miss Scheldt didn't enter the picture until the Flonzaley incident."

"Now, Charles, the matter of Mr. Flonzaley must be dropped. You are not just a middle-class provincial person but a man of letters," said the old Spanish lady. "Flonzaley belongs to the past. Renata is very sensitive to pain and when the man was in agony what could you expect her to do? She cried the entire night he was there. He is in a vulgar business and there is no comparison between you. She simply felt she owed him the consideration. And as you are an *homme de lettres* and he is an undertaker, the higher person must be more tolerant."

I couldn't argue with the Señora. I had seen her one morning before she was made up, hurrying toward the bathroom, completely featureless, a limp and yellow banana skin, without brows or lashes and virtually without lips. The sorrow of this sight took me by the heart, I never again wanted to win a

point from the Señora. When I played backgammon with her I
cheated against myself.

"The main thing about Miss Scheldt," I told Renata at the
Plaza, "is her father. I couldn't have a love affair with the
daughter of a man who was teaching me so much."

"He fills you with such bunk," she said.

"Renata, let me quote you a text: 'Though you are said to be
alive you are dead. Wake up and put some strength into what
is left, which must otherwise die.' That's from the Revelation of
Saint John, more or less."

Indulgently smiling, Renata rose and straightened her mini-
skirt, saying, "You'll wind up with bare feet in the Loop carrying one of those where-will-you-spend-eternity signs. Get
on the phone, for God's sake, and talk to this man Huggins,
Humboldt's executor. And for dinner don't try to take me to
Rumpelmayer's again."

Huggins was going to an opening at the Kootz Gallery and
invited me to meet him there when I mentioned my business.

"Is there anything to this. What is this legacy stuff?" I said.

"There is something," said Huggins.

In the late Forties when Huggins was a celebrity in Greenwich
Village I was a very minor member of the group that discussed
politics, literature, and philosophy in his apartment. There were
people like Chiaromonte and Rahv and Abel and Paul Goodman and Von Humboldt Fleisher. What Huggins and I had in
common was our love for Humboldt. There wasn't much else.
In many respects we irritated each other. Some years ago at the
Democratic convention in Atlantic City, that old pleasure-slum,
we watched Hubert Humphrey pretending to relax with his
delegation while Johnson dangled him, and something about
the dinky desolation, the torn fibers of holiday gaiety provoked
Huggins against me. We went out on the boardwalk and as we
faced the horrid Atlantic, tamed here to saltwater taffy and
the foam-like popcorn pushed by the sweeper's brush, Huggins became disagreeable to me. Fearing no man and urging
home his arguments with his white billy-goat beard, he made
hostile comments on the book about Harry Hopkins I had
published that spring. Huggins was covering the convention

for the *Women's Wear Daily*. A better journalist than I would
ever be, he was also a famous bohemian dissenter and revolu-
tionist. Why had I been so kind to the New Deal and seen so
much merit in Hopkins? I was forever sneaking praises of the
American system of government into my books. I was an apol-
ogist, a front man and stooge, practically an Andrei Vishinsky.
At Atlantic City as elsewhere, he was informal in chino wash
pants and tennis sneakers, tall, rosy, bearded, stammering, and
argumentative.

I could actually see myself as I studied him on the boardwalk.
In my eyes were specks of green and amber in which he might
have seen whole aeons of sleep and waking. If he thought I
disliked him he was wrong. I liked him better and better all the
time. He was quite old now, and the unkind forces of human
hydrostatics were beginning to make a strained and wrinkled
bag of his face, but his color remained fresh and he was still
the Harvard radical of the John Reed type, one of those ever-
youthful lightweight high-spirited American intellectuals, faithful to his Marx or his Bakunin, to Isadora, Randolph Bourne,
Lenin and Trotsky, Max Eastman, Cocteau, André Gide, the
Ballets Russes, Eisenstein—the beautiful avant-garde pantheon
of the good old days. He could no more give up his delightful
ideological capital than the bonds he had inherited from his
father.

In Kootz's crowded gallery he was talking with several people. He knew how to carry on a conversation at a noisy cocktail party. Din and drink stimulated him. He was not perhaps
too clear in the head, but the actual head I always appreciated.
It was long and high, banked with well-brushed silver hair, the
uneven ends of long strands giving a spiky effect at the back.
Over his tall-man's belly was a shirt of Merrymount stripes,
broad crimson and diabolical purple, like the ribbons of the
revelers' Maypole. It came back to me that more than twenty
years ago I had found myself at a beach party in Montauk, on
Long Island, where Huggins, naked at one end of the log, discussed the Army McCarthy hearings with a lady sitting naked
and astride opposite him. Huggins was speaking with a cigarette holder in his teeth, and his penis which lay before him on

the water-smooth wood expressed all the fluctuations of his interest. And while he was puffing and giving his views in a neighing stammer, his genital went back and forth like the slide of a trombone. You could never feel unfriendly toward a man of whom you kept such a memory.

He was uncomfortable with me at the gallery. He sensed the peculiarities of my perspective. I was not proud of the same. Moreover, I was more warmly friendly than he wanted me to be. If he was not too clear in the head, neither was I. I was full of unmastered intimations and transitional thoughts and I judged no one. As a matter of fact I was fighting the judgments I had made in my days of rashness. I told him I was glad to see him and that he looked well. This was no lie. His color was fresh and despite the increased grossness of his nose, the distortions of age, and the bee-stung swelling of his lips, I still liked his looks. The rube-constable chin beard he could have done without.

"Ah, Citrine, they let you out of Chicago? Going somewhere?"

"Abroad," I said.

"Nice young lady you're with. Terribly att-att-ractive." Huggins's fluency was increased, not impeded, by his stammer. The boulders in a mountain stream show you how fast the water is flying. "So you want to collect your leg-leg . . . ?"

"Yes, but first I want you to tell me why you're so uncordial. We've known each other more than thirty years."

"Well, apart from your political views—"

"Most political views are like old newspapers chewed up by wasps—faded clichés and buzzing."

Huggins said, "Some people care where mankind is going. Besides, you can't expect me to be cor-cor-cor when you make such cracks about me. You said I was the Tommy Manville of the left and that I espoused cau-causes the way he ma-married broads. A couple of years ago-go you insulted me on Madison Avenue because of the protest buttons I was wearing. You said I used to have i-i-ideas and now I had only buttons." Aggrieved, inflamed, facing me with my own effrontery, he waited to hear what I could say for myself.

"I'm sorry to say that you quote me correctly. I admit this

low vice. In the sticks, away from the Eastern scene, I think up wicked things to say. Humboldt brought me around in the Forties, but I never became part of your gang. When everybody was on Burnham or on Koestler I was somewhere else. The same for the *Encyclopedia of Unified Science,* or Trotsky's Law of Combined Development, or Chiaromonte's views on Plato or Lionel Abel on theater or Paul Goodman on Proudhon, or almost everybody on Kafka or Kierkegaard. It was like poor old Humboldt's complaint about girls. He wanted to do them good but they wouldn't hold still for it. I wouldn't hold still either. Instead of being grateful for my opportunity to get into the cultural life of the Village at its best—"

"You were reserved," said Huggins. "But what were you re-re-reserving yourself for? You had the star attitude, but where was the twi-twi-twink. . . ."

"Reserved is the right word," I said. "If other people had a bad content, I had a superior emptiness. My sin was that I thought in secret that I was more intelligent than all you enthusiasts for 1789, 1848, 1870, 1917. But you all had a much nicer and gayer time with your parties and all-night discussions. All I had was the subjective, anxious pleasure of thinking myself so smart."

"Don't you still think so?" said Huggins.

"No, I don't. I've given up on that."

"Well, you're out in Chicago where they think the earth is flat and the moon is made of green cheese. You've returned to your mental home," he said.

"Have it your way. That's not what I came to see you about. We still have one bond, anyway. We both adored Humboldt. Maybe we have something else in common, we're both amorous old dogs. We don't take each other seriously. But women seem to, still. Now what about the legacy?"

"Whatever it is, it's in an envelope labeled 'Citrine,' and I haven't read it because old Wald-Waldemar, Humboldt's uncle, grabbed it off. I don't know how I became exec-executor."

"Humboldt gave you lumps too, didn't he, after you joined the gang at Bellevue and he said I stole his money. You may have been at the Belasco when he picketed me."

"No, but it had a certain ch-cha-charm."

Laughing, Huggins puffed at his holder. Was it the old Russian actress, Ouspenskaya, who had made these holders popular in the Thirties, or FDR, or John Held, Jr.? Like Humboldt, like myself for that matter, Huggins was an old-movie buff. Humboldt's picketing and his own behavior at the White House he might see as moments from René Clair.

"I never thought you stole his money," said Huggins. "I understand he got into you for a few thousand. Did he forge a check?"

"No. We once exchanged blank checks sentimentally. He used his," I said. "And it wasn't a few, it was nearly seven."

"I took care of finances for him. I got Kathleen to way-way-waive rights. But he said I took kickbacks. Sore as a boil. So I didn't see him ever again, poor Humboldt. He accused some switch-switchboard old woman at a hotel of covering his bed with cen-centerfold girls from *Playboy*. Grabbed a hammer and tried to hit the old broad. Took him away. More shock-shock therapy! Enough to make you cry when you think how viv-viv, how fresh, handsome, wonderful, and what masterpieces. Ah! This society has a lot to an-answer for."

"Yes, he was wonderful and generous. I loved him. He was good." Strange words these at a clamorous cocktail party. "He wanted with all his heart to give us something exquisite and delicate. He put a heavy demand on himself. But you say that his horse-playing uncle took most of his papers?"

"And clothes and valuables."

"He must have been hit very hard, losing his nephew, and frightened, probably."

"He came running in from Co-Coney Island. Humboldt kept him in a nursing home. The old bookie must have fi-figured that the pa-papers of a man who rated such a long obituary in the *Times* must be valuable."

"Did Humboldt leave him some money?"

"There was an insurance policy, and if he didn't drop it all on the horses he's okay."

"Was Humboldt in his right mind toward the end or am I mistaken?"

"He wrote me a beauti-beauti-beautiful letter. He copied out some poems for me on good paper. The one about his Hungarian Pa, riding with Pershing's cavalry to capture Pancho."

"The toothy horses, the rattler's castanet, the cactus thorn, and the banging guns . . ."

"You're not quoting quite right," said Huggins.

"And it was you that gave Kathleen Humboldt's bequest?"

"It was, and she's in New York right now."

"Is she? Where is she? I'd love to see her."

"On her way to Europe, like you. I don't know where she's stay-staying."

"I must find out. But first I have to get on to Uncle Waldemar in Coney Island."

"He may not give you anything," said Huggins. "He's can-cantankerous. And I've written him and phoned him. No soap."

"Probably a phone call isn't good enough. He's holding out for a real visit. You can't blame him for that, if nobody comes. Wasn't Humboldt's mother the last of his sisters? He wants somebody to go to Coney Island. He's using Humboldt's papers as a bait. Maybe he'll give them to me."

"I'm sure you'll be irre-ree. You'll be irresistible," said Huggins.

● ● ●

Renata was greatly annoyed when I said that she must come to Coney Island with me.

"What, go to a nursing home? On the subway? Don't drag me into this. Go alone."

"You've got to do it. I need you, Renata."

"You're wrecking my day. I have a professional thing I need to do. It's business. Homes for the aged depress me. Last time I set foot in one I became hysterical. At least spare me the subway."

"There's no other transportation. And give old Waldemar a break. He's never seen a woman like you, and he was a sporting man."

"Save the sweet talk. I didn't hear any when the girl at the switchboard called me Mrs. Citrine. You clammed up."

Later on the boardwalk she was still vexed, and strode ahead of me. The subway had been awful, the filth, the spray-can graffiti were not to be believed. She kicked out the skirts of her maxi-coat as she marched, and the hanging fleeces fluttered at the front. The high-crowned Netherlands hat was pushed back. Henri, the Señora's old friend in Paris, the man who was clearly not Renata's father, had been impressed by her forehead. "Un beau front!" he said, over and over again. "Ah, ce beau front!" A fine brow. But what was behind it? Now I couldn't see it. She was striding away, offended, ruffled. She wished to punish me. But really I couldn't lose on Renata. I was pleased with her even when she was cross. People looked after her as she passed. Walking behind her I admired the action of her hips. I might not have cared to know what went on behind that beau front; and her dreams might have shocked me but her odor alone was a great solace in the night. The pleasure of sleeping with her went far beyond the ordinary pleasure of sharing a bed. Even to lie unconscious beside her was a distinct event. As for insomnia, Humboldt's complaint, she made that agreeable, too. Energizing influences passed into my hands from her breasts during the night. I allowed myself to imagine that these influences entered my finger bones like a sort of white electricity and surged upward to the very roots of my teeth.

A white December sky overlay the Atlantic gloom. The message of Nature seemed to be that conditions were severe, that things were tough, very tough, and that people should console one another. In this Renata thought I was not doing my part, for when the operator at the Plaza had called her Mrs. Citrine, Renata had put down the phone and turned to me, her face lighted, saying, "She called me Mrs. Citrine!" I failed to answer. People are really far more naïve and simple-hearted than we commonly suppose. It doesn't take much to make them glow. I'm that way myself. Why withhold your kindliness from them when you see the glow appearing? To increase Renata's happiness, I might have said, "Why of course, kid. You'd make a wonderful Mrs. Citrine. And why not?" What would that have cost me . . . ? Nothing but my freedom. And I wasn't, after all, doing much with this precious freedom. I was assuming that I had world enough and time to do something with it later. And which was more important, this pool of unused freedom or the happiness of lying beside Renata at night which made even unconsciousness special, like a delectable way to be stricken? When that cursed operator called her "Mrs." my silence seemed to accuse her of being just a whore, no Mrs. at all. This burned her up. The pursuit of her ideal made Renata intensely touchy. But I too pursued ideals—freedom, love. I wanted to be loved for myself alone. Noncapitalistically, as it were. This was one of those American demands or expectations which, as a native of Appleton and a kid from the Chicago streets, I had all too many of. What caused me a certain amount of anguish was that I suspected that the time had passed when I might still have been loved for myself alone. Oh with what speed conditions had worsened!

I had told Renata that marriage would have to wait until my case with Denise was settled.

"Ah, come on, she'll quit suing when you're out in Waldheim beside your Pa and your Ma. She's good for the rest of the century," said Renata. "Are you?"

"Of course solitary old age would be horrible," I said. Then I ventured to add, "But you can see yourself pushing my wheelchair?"

"You don't understand real women," said Renata. "Denise wanted to knock you out of action. Because of me she hasn't succeeded. It wasn't that pale little fox Doris, in the Mary Pickford getup. It's all me—*I've* kept your sex powers alive. I know how. Marry me and you'll still be balling me at eighty. By ninety, when you can't, I'll love you still."

Thus we were walking on the Coney Island boardwalk. And as I, when a boy, had rattled my stick on fence palings, so Renata, when she passed the popcorn men, the caramel-corn and hot-dog men, got a rise out of each one. I followed her, elderly but fit, wrinkled with anxieties yet smiling. In fact I was feeling unusually high. I'm not altogether sure why I was in this glorious condition. It couldn't have been only the result of physical well-being, of sleeping with Renata, of good chemistry. Or of the temporary remission of difficulties which, according to certain grim experts, is all that people need to make them happy and is, in fact, the only source of happiness. No, I was inclined to think as I vigorously walked behind Renata that I owed it to a change in my attitude toward death. I had begun to entertain other alternatives. This in itself was enough to make me soar. But even more joyful was the possibility that there might be something to soar into, a space unused, neglected. All this while the vastest part of the whole had been missing. No wonder human beings went mad. For suppose that we—as we are in this material world—are the highest of all beings. Suppose that the being-series ends with us and there is nothing more beyond us. On such assumptions who can blame us for going into convulsions! Assume a cosmos, however, and it's metaphysically a more spacious situation.

Then Renata turned and said, "Are you sure the old dodo knows you're coming?"

"Sure. We're expected. I phoned him," I said.

We entered one of the alley-like streets, where garment workers used to pass their summer holidays, and found the address. An old brick building. On its wooden stoop were wheelchairs and walking frames for invalids who had had strokes.

At another time I might have been astonished by what happened next. But now that the world was being reconstituted and the old structure, death and all, was no more solid than a Japanese lantern, human matters came over me with the greatest vividness, naturalness, even with gaiety—I mustn't leave out the gaiety. The saddest of sights might have it. Anyway, we were indeed expected. Leaning on a stick someone was watching for us between the door and the storm door of the nursing home and came out shouting, "Charlie, Charlie," as soon as we reached the stairs.

I said to this man, "You're not Waldemar Wald, are you?"

"No, Waldemar is here. But I'm not Waldemar, Charlie. Now look at me. Listen to my voice." He began to sing something in an old raven tenor. He took me by the hand and sang "La donna è mobile" in the style of Caruso, but miserably, poor old boy. I took him in, I studied his hair, once kinky and red, the busted nose and eager nostrils, the dewlaps, the Adam's apple, the skinny stoop of his figure. Then I said, "Ah yes, you're Menasha! Menasha Klinger! Chicago Illinois 1927."

"That's right." For him this was sublime. "It's me. You recognized me!"

"Holy mackerel! What a pleasure! I swear I don't deserve such a surprise." In putting off my search for Humboldt's uncle it seems that I had been avoiding good luck, wonderful things, miracles almost. Immediately I met a person whom I loved way-back-when. "It's dreamlike," I said.

"No," said Menasha. "For an ordinary guy, maybe it would be. But when you turn into a personage, Charlie, it's much less of a coincidence than you think. There must be friends and acquaintances like me all over the place who used to know you but are too shy to approach and remind you. I would have been too shy myself if it wasn't that you were coming to see my buddy Waldemar." Menasha turned to Renata. "And this is Mrs. Citrine," he said.

"Yes," I said, looking her in the face. "This is Mrs. Citrine."

"I knew your husband as a kid. I boarded with his family when I came down from Ypsilanti, Michigan, to work at Western Electric as a punch-press operator. What I really came for was to study singing. Charlie was a wonderful boy. Charlie was the best-hearted little kid on the whole Northwest Side. I could talk to him when he was only nine or ten, and he was my only friend. I'd take him downtown with me Saturdays for my music lesson."

"Your teacher," I said, "was Vsevelod Kolodny, room eight sixteen in the Fine Arts Building. Basso profundo with the Imperial Opera, Petersburg, bald, four-feet-ten, wore a corset and Cuban heels."

"He recognized me, too," said Menasha, infinitely pleased.

"You were a dramatic tenor," I said. I had only to say this to see how he rose on his toes, clasping his punch-press-callused palms and singing "In questa tomba oscura," tears of ardor filling up his eyes, and his voice so roosterish, with so much heart, so much cry and hackle and hope—tuneless. Even as a boy I knew he'd never make stardom. I did believe, however, that he might have become a singer but for the fact that on the Ypsilanti YMCA boxing team someone had hit him in the nose and this had ruined his chances in art. The songs that were sung through this disfigured nose would never be right.

"Tell me, my boy, what else do you remember?"

"I remember Tito Schipa, Titta Ruffo, Werrenrath, McCormack, Schumann-Heink, Amelita Galli-Curci, Verdi, and Boito. And when you heard Caruso sing *Pagliacci*, life was never the same again, right?"

"Oh, yes!"

Love made these things unforgettable. In Chicago fifty years ago, we had been passengers on the double-deck open-topped bus down to the Loop on Jackson Boulevard, Menasha explaining to me what bel canto was, telling me, radiant, about *Aida*, envisioning himself in brocade robes as a priest or warrior. After his singing lesson he took me to Kranz's for a chocolate-fudge sundae. We went to hear Paul Ash's sizzling band, we also heard vaudeville seals who played "Yankee Doodle" by nipping the syringe bulbs of automobile horns. We swam at Clarendon Beach, where everyone peed in the water. At night he taught me astronomy. He explained Darwin to me. He married his high-school sweetheart from Ypsilanti. Her name was Marsha. She was obese. She was homesick and she lay in bed and cried. I once saw her sitting in the bathtub trying to wash her hair. She took water in her hands but her arms were too fat to raise it in her palms as high as the head. This dear girl was dead. Menasha had been an electrician in Brooklyn for most of his life. Of his dramatic tenor nothing was left but the yelping of an old man, greatly moved. Of his stiff red hair there remained only this orange-whitey cirrhus formation. "Very kind people, the Citrines. Maybe not Julius. He was rough. Is Julius still Julius? Your mother was so helpful to Marsha. Your kind poor mother. . . . But let's go and see Waldemar. I'm only the greeting committee and he's waiting. They keep him in a back room by the kitchen."

We found Waldemar sitting on the edge of his bed, a man with wide shoulders, and his hair wet-brushed very like Humboldt's, the same broad face, and the eyes gray and set wide. Within ten miles of Coney Island, perhaps, sucking in and straining tons of water, puffing vapor from his head, there was a whale with eyes similarly positioned.

"So you were my nephew's buddy," said the old gambler.

"This is Charlie Citrine," said Menasha. "You know, Waldemar, he recognized me. The boy recognized me all right. Gosh, Charlie, you should, you know, I paid out a fortune on sodas and treats. There ought to be some justice."

Through Humboldt I knew Uncle Waldemar, of course. He was an only son, with four older sisters and a doting mother, much pampered, idle, a poolroom bum, a dropout, mooching from his sisters and stealing from their purses. Eventually he placed Humboldt in the senior position as well. Becoming rather a brother than an uncle. The kid role was the only role he understood.

I was thinking that life was a hell of a lot more bounteous than I had ever realized. It rushed over us with more than our senses and our judgment could take in. One life with its love affairs, its operatic ambitions, its dollars and horse races and marriage-designs and old people's homes is, after all, only a tin dipperful of this superabundance. It rushes up also from within. Take a room like Uncle Waldemar's, smelling of wieners boiling for lunch, with Waldemar squatting on the edge of the bed, all dressed up for a visit, his face, his head blearily similar to Humboldt's, but with the effect of a blown dandelion, all the yellow gone gray; take the old gentleman's green shirt, buttoned to the collar; take his good suit on the wire hanger in the corner (he would have a dressy funeral); take the satchels under his bed and the pin-ups of horses and prizefighters and the book-jacket photograph of Humboldt in the days when Humboldt was impossibly beautiful. If this is literally all what life is, then Renata's little rhyme about Chicago is right on the head: "Without O'Hare, it's sheer despair." And all O'Hare can do is change the scene for you and take you from dismal to dismal, from boredom to boredom. But why did a kind of faintness come over me at the start of this interview with Uncle

Waldemar in the presence of Menasha and Renata? Because there is far more to any experience, connection, or relationship than ordinary consciousness, the daily life of the ego, can grasp. Yes. You see, the soul belongs to a greater, an all-embracing life outside. It's got to. Learning to think of this existence of mine as merely the present existence, one in a series, I was not really surprised to meet Menasha Klinger. He and I obviously held permanent membership in some larger, more extended human outfit, and his desire to stand in brocade and sing Rhadames in *Aida* was like my eagerness to go far, far beyond fellow intellectuals of my generation who had lost the imaginative soul. Oh, I admired some of these intellectuals without limits. Especially the princes of science, astrophysicists, pure mathematicians, and the like. But nothing had been done about the main question. The main question, as Walt Whitman had pointed out, was the death question. And music drew me toward Menasha. By means of music a man affirmed that the logically unanswerable was, in a different form, answerable. Sounds without determinate meaning became more and more pertinent, the greater the music. This was such a man's assignment. I, too, in spite of lethargy and weakness, was here for a big reason. Just what this was I would consider later, when I looked back on my life in the twentieth century. Calendars would disintegrate under the gaze of the spirit. But there would be a December spot for a subway ride in cars disfigured by youth gangs, and a beautiful woman whom I followed on the boardwalk while hearing the peppery pang of shooting galleries and smelling popcorn and hot dogs, thinking of the sex of her figure, the consumerism of her garments, and of my friendship with Von Humboldt Fleisher which had brought me to Coney Island. In my reflective purgatory I would see it all from a different perspective and know, perhaps, how all these peculiarities added up—know why an emotional estuary should have opened up in me when I laid eyes on Waldemar Wald.

Waldemar was now saying, "What a dog's age since anybody visited. I've been forgot. Humboldt would never have stuck me in a dump like this. It was temporary. The chow is awful, and the help is rough. They say, 'Shut up, you're gaga.' They're all from the Caribbean. Everybody else is a kraut. Menasha and me are practically the only Americans. Humboldt once made a joke, 'Two is company, three is a kraut!' "

"But he did put you here," said Renata.

"Just till he could iron out some problems. The whole week before he died he was looking for an apartment for us both. Once we lived together for three months and that was heaven. Up in the morning like a real family, bacon and eggs, and then we'd talk baseball. I made a real fan of him, you know that? Fifty years ago I bought him a first-baseman's mitt. I taught him to field a grounder and throw a guy out. Football, too. I showed him how to toss a forward pass. My mother's railroad apartment had a long, long corridor where we played. When his dad took off it was a houseful of women and it was up to me to make an American boy out of him. Those women did plenty of damage. Look at the names they gave us—Waldemar! The kids called me Walla-Walla. And he had it rough, too. Humboldt! My goofy sister named him after a statue in Central Park."

All this was familiar to me from Humboldt's charming poem "Uncle Harlequin." Waldemar Harlequin, in the old days on West End Avenue, after his wage-earning sisters went to business, rose at eleven, bathed for an hour, shaved with a new Gillette blade, and then lunched. His mother sat beside him to butter his rolls, to skin his whitefish and bone it, to pour his coffee while he read the papers. Then he took a few bucks from her and went out. He talked at the dinner table about Jimmy Walker and Al Smith. He, in Humboldt's opinion, was his family's American. This was his function among the ladies and with his nephew. When the national conventions were broadcast on the radio he could call the roll of the states together with the announcer—"Idaho, Illinois, Indiana, Iowa"—and patriotic tears filled his eyes.

"Mr. Wald, I've come to see you about the papers Humboldt left. I told you on the phone. I have a note from Orlando Huggins."

"Yes, I know Huggins, that long drink of water. Now I want to ask you about the papers. Is this stuff valuable or ain't it?"

"Sometimes we see in the *Times*," said Menasha, "a letter by

Robert Frost fetches eight hundred bucks. As for Edgar Allan Poe, don't ask."

"What's actually in those papers, Mr. Wald?" asked Renata.

"Well, I have to tell you," said Waldemar. "*I* never understood any of his stuff. I'm not a big reader. What he wrote was way over my head. Humboldt could hit like a sonofabitch on the sandlot. With his shoulders, just imagine how much beef there went into his swing. If I had my way he would have ended up in the majors. But he started in to hanging around the Forty-second Street library and bull-shitting with those bums on the front steps. First thing I knew he was printing highbrow poems in the magazines. I mean, the kind of magazines without pictures."

"Come on, Waldemar," said Menasha. His chest was high with feeling and his voice rose and rose. "I've known Charlie from a kid. I want to tell you you can trust Charlie. Long ago, soon as I laid eyes on him, I said to myself, This kid's heart is right up there in his face. He's getting along in years himself. Although compared to us he's a strong fellow still. Now Waldemar, whyn't you come clean and tell him what's on your mind?"

"In Humboldt's papers, as papers, there probably isn't much money," I said. "One might try to sell them to a collector. But perhaps there is something in what he left that could be published."

"It's mostly the sentiment," said Renata. "Like a message from an old friend in the next world."

Waldemar looked at her, obstinate. "But suppose it *is* valuable, why should I get screwed? Am I entitled to get something out of it or not? I mean, why should I stick in this lousy home here? As soon as they showed me Humboldt's obituary in the *Times*—Christ! Imagine what that did to me! Like my own kid, the last of the family, my own flesh and blood! I got on the BMT as fast as I could and went up to his room. His stuff was half gone already. The cops and the hotel management were grabbing it off. The cash and the watch and his fountain pen and the typewriter disappeared."

"What's the use of sitting on this stuff and dreaming you'll make a killing?" said Menasha. "Hand it over to somebody who knows."

"Don't fink on me," said Waldemar to Menasha. "We're in here together. This much I'm willing—I'll level with you, Mr. Citrine. I could have peddled this stuff long ago. If you ask me there is a real property in this."

"You have read it then," I said.

"Hell, sure I've read it. What the hell else have I got to do? I couldn't make heads or tails out of it."

"I wouldn't dream of doing you out of anything," I said. "If it has got value I'll tell you honestly."

"Why don't we get a lawyer to draw up a legal document?" said Waldemar.

He was Humboldt's uncle all right. I became very persuasive. I am never so reasonable as when I badly want something. I can make it seem natural justice itself that I should have it. "We can make things as legal as you like," I said. "But shouldn't I read it all? How can I tell without examining it?"

"Then read it here," said Waldemar.

Menasha said, "You've always been a sport, Charlie. Take a gamble."

"Along that line my record isn't so hot," said Waldemar. I thought he would cry, he sounded so shaky. So little stood between him and death, you see. On the bald harsh crimson of the threadbare carpet, a pale patch of weak December warmth said, "Don't cry, old boy." Inaudible storms of light, ninety-three million miles away, used a threadbare Axminster, a scrap of human manufacture, to deliver a message through the soiled window of a nursing home. My own heart became emotional. I wished to convey something important. We have to go through the bitter gates of death, I wanted to say to him, and give back these loaned minerals that comprise us, but I want to tell you, brother Waldemar, that I deeply suspect things do not end there. The thought of the life we are now leading may pain us as greatly later on as the thought of death pains us now.

Well, finally I got around him with my good sense and honesty and we all went down on our knees and began to pull all

sorts of stuff from under his bed—bedroom slippers, an old
bowling ball, a toy baseball game, playing cards, odd dice,
cardboard boxes, and valises, and, finally, a relic that I could
identify—Humboldt's briefcase. It was Humboldt's old bag
with the frayed straps, the one that was always riding, crammed
with books and pill bottles, in the back seat of his Buick.

"Wait, I've got my files in there," Waldemar said, fussing.
"You'll screw it all up. I'll do this."

Renata, on the floor with the rest of us, wiped the dust with
paper tissues. She was always saying, "Here's a Kleenex," and
producing paper tissues. Waldemar removed several insurance
policies and a bundle of computer-perforated Social Security
cards. There were several horse photographs, which he identified as an almost complete set of Kentucky Derby winners.
Then like a blindish postman, he went through numerous envelopes. "Quicker!" I wanted to say.

"This is the one," he said.

There was my name written in Humboldt's tight, scratchy
hand.

"What's in it? Let me see," said Renata.

I took it from him, an outsized heavy manila envelope.

"You'll have to give me a receipt," said Waldemar.

"Certainly I will. Renata, would you mind making out a
form? Like, received from Mr. Waldemar Wald, papers willed
to me by Von Humboldt Fleisher. I'll sign it."

"Papers of what kind? What's actually here?"

"What's in them?" said Waldemar. "One thing is a long personal letter to Mr. Citrine. Then a couple of sealed envelopes
which I never broke open at all because there are instructions
that say if you open them something goes wrong with the copyright. Anyhow, they're duplicates, or duplicates of duplicates.
I can't tell you. Most of it doesn't add up, to me. Maybe for
you it will. Anyhow, if I, the last member of my family, can tell
you what's on my mind, my dead are all over the place, one
grave here, and the other to hell and gone, my sister in that
joint they call Valhalla for the German Jews and my nephew
buried in potter's field. What I really want is to reunite the family again."

Menasha said, "It bugs Waldemar that Humboldt is buried in a bad place. Way out in no man's land."

"If there's any value in this legacy, the first money should be spent to dig the kid up and move him. It doesn't have to be the Valhalla. That was my sister keeping up with the Joneses. She had a thing about them German Jews. But I want to bring us all together. Gather up my dead," the old horse-player said.

This solemnity was unexpected. Renata and I looked at each other.

"Count on Charlie to do right by you," said Menasha.

"I'll write and tell you what I find in these papers," I said. "And just as soon as we get back from Europe, I promise you we'll attend to everything. You can start lining up a cemetery. Even if these papers have no commercial value I'd be perfectly willing to pick up the burial tab."

"Just what I told you," said Menasha to Waldemar. "A kid like this kid was bound to grow up into a gentleman."

We now went out. I held each of the old boys by a wasted arm, by the big double knobs of the elbow where radius and ulna meet, promising to stay in touch. Sauntering behind us, Renata with her white face and great hat was incomparably more substantial in person than any of us. She said unexpectedly, "If Charles says it, Charles'll do it. We'll go away and he'll be thinking of you."

In a corner of the cold porch stood the wheelchairs, glittering, lightweight, tubular, stainless metal, with batlike folds. "I wonder if anyone would object if I sat in one of these wheelchairs," I said.

I got into one of them and said to Renata, "Give us a ride."

The old men didn't quite know what to make of my being trundled back and forth on the stoop by this large, laughing, brilliant woman with the wonderful teeth. "Don't carry on like a fool. You'll offend them, Renata," I said. "Just push."

"These damn handles are damn cold," she said.

She drew on the long gloves with charming swagger, I must say.

• ● • ● •

In the racketing speed of the howling, weeping subway I began to read the long letter, the preface to Humboldt's gift, handing on the onionskin pages to Renata. Incurious after she had glanced at a few of these, she said, "When you get to the story, let me know. I'm not big on philosophy." I can't say that I blame her. He was not *her* precious friend hid in death's dateless night. There was no reason why she should be moved, as I was. She made no effort to enter into my feelings, nor did I want her to try.

"Deer Shoveleer," wrote Humboldt. "I am in a bad position, getting more sane as I become weaker. By a damn peculiar arrangement, lunatics always have energy to burn. And if old William James was right, and happiness is living at the energetic top and we are here to pursue happiness, then madness is pure bliss and also has supreme political sanction." This was the sort of thing that Renata objected to. I agree that it was not a restful habit of mind. "I am living in a bad place," he went on. "And eating bad meals. I've now eaten sixty or seventy delicatessen dinners in a row. You can't get sublime art on a diet like this. On the other hand pastrami and peppery potato salad seem to nourish calm judgment. I don't go out to dinner. I stay in my room. There is a colossal interval between supper and bedtime and I sit beside a drawn window shade (who can look out eighteen hours a day?) correcting certain old mistakes. It occurs to me sometimes that I may be petitioning death to lay off because I am deep in good works. Would I be trying, also, to keep the upper hand in dying as in the sexual act?—Do this, do that, hold still, wriggle now, kiss my ear, graze my back with your nails, but don't touch my testicles. However, death is the passionate party in this case."

"Poor fellow, I can see him now. I understand his type," said Renata.

"So, Charlie, as these weaker saner days come and go I think often about you, and think with end-of-the-line lucidity. That

I wronged you is very true. I knew even when I loused you up so elaborately and fiercely that you were in Chicago trying to do me good, consulting people behind my back to get me jobs. I called you a sell-out, Judas, fink, suck-ass, climber, hypocrite. I had first a deep black rage against you, and then a red hot rage. Both were very luxurious. The fact is that I was remorseful about the blood-brother check. I knew you were mourning the death of Demmie Vonghel. I was panting with cunning and I put one over on you. You were a Success. And if that weren't enough and you wanted to be a big moral figure as well, then the hell with you, it was going to cost you a few thousand bucks. It was entrapment. I was going to give you a chance to forgive me. In forgiving you would be lying your head off. This fool kindliness would damage your sense of reality, and with your sense of reality damaged you'd be suffering what I suffered. All this crazy intricacy was unnecessary, of course. You were going to suffer anyway because you were stricken with the glory and the gold. Your giddy flight through the florid heavens of success, and so on! Your innate sense of truth, if nothing else, would make you sick. But my 'reasoning,' in endless formulae like chemistry formulae on a college blackboard, put me into swoons of rapture. I was manic. I was chattering from the dusty top of my crazy head. Afterward I was depressed and silent for long, long days. I lay in the cage. Grim gorilla days.

"I ask myself why you figured so prominently in my obsessions and fixations. You may be one of those people who arouse family emotions, you're a son-and-brother type. Mind, you want to arouse feeling but not necessarily to return it. The idea is that the current should flow your way. You stimulated the blood-brother oath. I was certainly wild, but I acted on a suggestion emanating from you. Nevertheless, in the words of the crooner, 'With all your faults, I love you still.' You are a promissory nut, that's all.

"Let me say a word about money. When I used your blood-brother check, I didn't expect it to clear the bank. I put it through, outraged because you didn't come to see me at Bellevue. I was suffering; you didn't draw near, as a loving friend should. I decided to punish hurt and fine you. You accepted the penalty, and therefore the sin, too. You borrowed my spirit to put into Trenck. My ghost was a Broadway star. All this daylight delusion, cracked, spoiled, and dirty! I don't know how else to put it. Your girl died in the jungle. She wouldn't let you come to Bellevue—I found that out. Oh! the might of money and the entanglement of art with it—the dollar as the soul's husband: a marriage nobody has had the curiosity to study.

"And do you know what I did with the six thousand bucks? I bought an Oldsmobile with part of it. What I thought I was going to do with this big powerful car on Greenwich Street, I can't tell you. It cost me lots of dough to keep it in a garage, more than the rent in my fifth-floor walk-up. And what happened to this automobile? I had to be hospitalized and when I got out, after a course of shock treatments, I couldn't remember where I left it. I couldn't find the claim check, or the registration either. I had to forget about it. But for a while I drove a hell of a car. I became capable of observing some of my own symptoms. My eyelids became deep violet with manic insomnia. Late at night I drove past the Belasco Theatre with some buddies and I said, 'There's the hit that paid for this powerful machine.' I declare I had it in for you because you thought I was going to be the great American poet of the century. You came down from Madison, Wisconsin, and told me so. But I wasn't! And how many people were waiting for that poet! How many souls hoped for the strength and sweetness of visionary words to purge consciousness of its stale dirt, to learn from a poet what had happened to the three-fourths of life that are obviously missing! But during these last years I haven't been able to even read poetry, much less write it. Opening the *Phaedrus* a few months ago, I just couldn't do it. I broke down. My gears are stripped. My lining is shot. It is all shattered. I didn't have the strength to bear Plato's beautiful words, and started to cry. The original, fresh self isn't there any more. But then I think, Maybe I can recover. If I play it smart. Playing it smart means simpler kinds of enjoyment. Blake had it right with Enjoyment the food of Intellect. And if the intellect can't digest meat (the *Phaedrus*) you coddle it with zwieback and warm milk."

When I read his words about the original fresh self, I began
to cry myself, and big benign Renata shook her head when she
observed this as if to say, "Men!" As if to say, "These poor
mysterious monsters. You work your way down into the laby-
rinth and there you find the minotaur breaking his heart over
a letter." But I saw Humboldt in the days of his youth, covered
in rainbows, uttering inspired words, affectionate, intelligent.
In those days his evil was only an infinitesimal black point, an
amoeba. The mention of zwieback brought back to me, also,
the pretzel he was chewing on the curb on that hot day. On that
day I made a poor showing. I behaved very badly. I should have
gone up to him. I should have taken his hand. I should have
kissed his face. But is it true that such actions are effective?
And he was dreadful. His head was all gray webbing, like an
infested bush. His eyes were red and his big body was floundering in the gray suit. He looked like an old bull bison on his
last legs, and I beat it. Maybe that was the very day on which
he wrote this beautiful letter to me. "Now come on, kid," said
Renata, kindly. "Dry your eyes." She gave me a fragrant hankie, oddly redolent, as if she kept it not in her pocketbook but
between her legs. I put it to my face and curiously enough it did
something, it gave me some comfort. That young woman had
a good understanding of certain fundamentals.

"This morning," Humboldt went on, "the sun was bright.
For certain of the living it was a very fine day. Though without sleep for several nights I remembered how it used to be to
bathe and shave and breakfast and go into the world. A mild
lemon light rinsed the streets. (Hope for this wild combined
human operation called America?) I thought I would stroll to
Brentano's and look into a copy of Keats's *Letters*. During the
night I had thought of something Keats had said about Robert
Burns. How a luxurious imagination deadens its delicacy in
vulgarity and in things attainable. For the first Americans were
surrounded by thick forests, and then they were surrounded
by things attainable, and these were just as thick. The problem
became one of faith—a faith in the equal sovereignty of the
imagination. Standing at Brentano's I started to copy out this
sentence but a clerk came up to me and took the Keats *Letters*

away. He thought I was from the Bowery. So I went out, and that was the end of the fine day. I felt like Emil Jannings in one of his pictures. The former tycoon ruined by drink and whores comes home an old bummer and tries to peep into the window of his own house where his daughter's wedding is being celebrated. The cop makes him move on, and so he shuffles away and a cello plays Massenet's 'Elégie.'

"Now, Charles, I come to the zwieback and warm milk. Big enterprises are beyond me, obviously, but my wit oddly enough is intact. This wit, developed to cope with the disgraces of life, real or imaginary, is like a companion to me these days. It stands by me and we are on good terms. In short, my sense of humor has not disappeared and now that bigger ambitious passions have worn themselves out it has been coming before me with an old-fashioned bow out of Molière. A relationship has developed.

"You remember how we amused ourselves in Princeton with a movie scenario about Amundsen and Nobile and Caldofreddo the Cannibal? I always thought it would make a classic. I handed it to a fellow named Otto Klinsky in the RCA Building. He promised to get it to Sir Laurence Olivier's hairdresser's cousin who was the sister of a scrubwoman at Time and Life who was the mother of the beautician who did Mrs. Klinsky's hair. Somewhere in these channels our script got lost. I still have a copy of this. You will find it among these papers." Indeed I did. I was curious to read it again. "But that is not my gift to you. After all, we collaborated, and it would be chintzy of me to call it a gift. No, I have dreamed up another story and I believe it is worth a fortune. This small work has been important to me. Among other things it has given me hours of sane enjoyment on certain nights and brought relief from thoughts of doom. The fitting together of the parts gave me the pleasure of a good intricacy. The therapy of delight. I tell you as a writer—we have had some queer American bodies to fit into art's garments. Enchantment didn't have enough veiling material for this monstrous mammoth flesh, for such crude arms and legs. But this preface is getting too long. On the next page begins my Treatment. I've tried to sell it. I've offered it to some people but they weren't interested. I haven't got the strength to follow through. People don't want to see me. You remember how I went to see Longstaff? No more. Receptionists turn me away. I guess I look like the sheeted dead who squeaked and gibbered in the streets of Rome. Now, Charlie, you are still in the midst of life and are rich in contacts. People will pay attention to the Shoveleer, the author of *Trenck,* the chronicler of Woodrow Wilson and Harry Hopkins. This will not reach you unless I kick the bucket. But then it will be a fabulous legacy and I want you to have it. For you are, at one and the same time, no good at all and also a darling man.

"Good old Henry James, of whom Mrs. Henry Adams said that he chewed more than he bit off, tells us that the creative mind is better off with hints than with extensive knowledge. I have never suffered from a knowledge handicap. The *donnée* for this treatment comes from the gossip columns, which I have always read faithfully. *Verbum sapientiae*—I think that's the dative. The original is apparently true.

TREATMENT

I.

A fellow named Corcoran, a successful author, has been barren for many years. He has tried skin diving and parachute jumping as subjects but nothing has resulted. Corcoran is married to a strong-minded woman. A woman of her sort might have made Beethoven a powerful wife, but Beethoven wasn't having any of that. To play the part of Corcoran I have in mind someone like Mastroianni.

II.

Corcoran meets a beautiful young woman with whom he has an affair. Had she lived, poor Marilyn Monroe would have been ideal for this role. For the first time in many years Corcoran tastes happiness. Then in a fit of enterprise, ingenuity, daring, he escapes with her to a faraway place. His disagreeable wife is nursing a sick father. Taking advantage of this, he and his girl go off. I don't know where. To Polynesia, to New Guinea, to Abyssinia, with dulcimers, wonderful and far off. The place is still quite pure in its beauty and enchanting weeks follow. Chieftains receive Corcoran and his girl. Hunts occur, and dances and banquets are laid on. The girl is an angel. They bathe in pools together, they float among gardenias and hibiscus. At night the spots of heaven draw near. The sensors open. Life is renewed. Dross and impurities evaporate.

III.

Returning, Corcoran writes a marvelous book—a book of such potency and beauty that it must not be kept from the world. But

IV.

He cannot publish. It would hurt his wife and destroy his marriage. He himself had a mother and few people have character enough to cast off their new superstitions about mothers and sons. He would have no identity, he would not even be an American without this bitch-affliction. If Corcoran hadn't been a writer he would not have sullied the heart of this angelic girl by writing a book about their adventure. Unfortunately, he is one of those writing fellows. He is a mere writer. Not to publish would kill him. And he is comically afraid of his wife. This wife should be matronly, jolly, frank, a bit tough but not altogether forbidding. In her own way rather attractive. A good broad, a bossy all-American girl. I think she should be a food faddist who drinks Tiger's Milk and eats Queen-Bee Jelly. You may be able to do something with that.

V.

Corcoran takes the book to his agent, a Greek American named Zane Bigoulis. This is a most important role. It should be played by Zero Mostel. He is a comedian of genius. But if he isn't restrained, he runs away with everything. At all events, I have him in mind for this part. Zane reads the book and cries "Magnificent." "But I can't publish it, it would finish my marriage." Now Charlie, *My Marriage*! Marriage having become one of the idols-of-the-tribe (Francis Bacon), the source of this comedy is the low seriousness which has succeeded the high seriousness of the Victorians. Corcoran has enough imagination to write a wonderful book, but he is enslaved by middle-class attitudes. As the wicked flee when none pursueth, so does the middle-class wrestle when none contendeth. They cried out for freedom, it came down on them in a flood. Nothing remains but a few floating timbers of psychotherapy. "What shall I do?" Corcoran cries. They deliberate. Then Bigoulis says, "All you can do is take the same trip with Hepzibah that you took with Laverne. Exactly the same trip, following the book faithfully, at the same season. Having reproduced the trip, you can publish the book."

VI.

"I won't let a word be changed," says Corcoran. "No impurity, no betrayal of the Experience." "Leave it to me," says Bigoulis. "I will precede you everywhere with transistors, panty hose, pocket computers, and so on, and bribe the chieftains. I'll get them to put on the same hunts and banquets and duplicate the dances. When your publisher sees this manuscript he'll be glad to pick up the tab." "It's really a frightful idea to do all this with Hepzibah. And I'll have to lie to Laverne. She feels as I do about our miraculous month on the Island. There's something sacred about it." But, Charlie, as *The Scarlet Letter* shows, love and lying have always gone together in this country. Truth is actually fatal. Dimmesdale tells it and dies. But Bigoulis argues, "You want the book published? You don't want Hepzibah to leave you, and you want to hang on to Laverne as well? From a male viewpoint the whole thing makes complete sense. So . . . we go to the Island. I can swing it for you. If you bury this book I lose a hundred grand in commissions, with picture-rights maybe more."

I see, Charlie, that I have now made the place an Island. Thinking of *The Tempest*. Prospero is a Hamlet who gets his revenge through art.

VII.

Thus Corcoran repeats with Hepzibah the journey he made with Laverne. Oh what a difference! All now is parody, desecration, wicked laughter. Which must be suffered. To the high types of Martyrdom the twentieth century has added the farcical martyr. This, you see, is the artist. By wishing to play a great role in the fate of mankind he becomes a bum and a joke. A double punishment is inflicted on him as the would-be representative of meaning and beauty. When the artist-agonist has learned to be sunk and shipwrecked, to embrace defeat and assert nothing, to subdue his will and accept his assignment to the hell of modern truth, perhaps his Orphic powers will be restored, the stones will dance again when he plays. Then heaven and earth will be reunited. After long divorce. With what joy on both sides, Charlie! What joy!

But this has no place in our picture. In the picture, Corcoran and his wife are bathing in a pool covered with hibiscus. She adores it. He fights his depression and prays for strength to play his role. Meantime, Bigoulis goes ahead staging each event, bribing chieftains, and hiring musicians and dancers. In this Island he sees also, on his own score, the investment opportunity of a lifetime. He is already planning to build the world's greatest resort here. At night he sits in his tent with a map, laying out a pleasure dome. The natives will become waiters, cooks, porters, and caddies on his golf course.

VIII.

The terrible trip over, Corcoran comes back to New York and publishes his book. It is a great success. His wife leaves him and sues for divorce. She knows she is not the heroine of those tender scenes. Laverne is outraged when she discovers that he repeated the same trip, sacred to her, with Hepzibah. She can never, she says, love a man capable of such a betrayal. To make love with another woman among those flowers, by moonlight! She knew he was a married man. That, she was willing to tolerate. But not this, not the breaking of the faith. She never wants to see him again.

He is therefore alone with his success, and his success is enormous. You know what that means. . . .

"Charles, here is my gift to you. It is worth a hundred times more than the check I put through. A picture like this should gross millions and fill Third Avenue with queues for a year. Insist on a box-office percentage.

"You will make a good script of this outline if you will remember me as I kept remembering you in plotting this out. You took my personality and exploited it in writing your *Trenck*. I have borrowed from you to create this Corcoran. Don't allow the caricatures to get out of hand. Let me call your attention to the opinion of Blake on this subject. 'Fun I love,' he says, 'but too much Fun is of all things the most loathsome. Mirth is better than Fun, & Happiness is better than Mirth. I feel that a Man may be happy in This World. And I know that This World Is a World of Imagination & Vision. . . . The tree which moves some to tears of joy is in the Eyes of others only a Green thing which stands in the way. Some see Nature all Ridicule & Deformity, & by these I shall not regulate my proportions.' "

Humboldt added a few sentences more. "I have explained why I wrote such a Treatment. I wasn't really strong enough to bear the great burdens. I haven't made it here, Charlie. Not to be guilty of a final failure of taste, I will avoid the heavy declaration. Let's say I have a leg already over the last stile and I look back and see you far back laboring still in fields of ridicule.

"Help my Uncle Waldemar all you can. Be sure that if there is a hereafter I will be pulling for you. Before you sit down to work at this scenario play a few sides of *The Magic Flute* on the phonograph, or read *The Tempest*. Or E. T. A. Hoffmann. You are lazy, disgraceful, tougher than you think but not yet a dead loss. In part you are humanly okay. We are supposed to do something for our kind. Don't get frenzied about money. Overcome your greed. Better luck with women. Last of all— remember: we are not natural beings but supernatural beings.

Lovingly, Humboldt"

• • • •

"So now I know why we missed the Scala," said Renata. "We had tickets for tonight. All that glow—that gorgeous performance of *The Barber of Seville*—a chance to be part of the greatest musical audience in Europe! And we sacrificed it. And for what? To go to Coney Island. Coming back with what? A goofy outline. I could laugh about it," she said. In fact she was laughing. She was in a good humor and had seldom been more beautiful, the dark hair drawn back and secured at the top, giving a sense—well, a sense of rescue, silken and miraculous. The dark hues with the red suited Renata best. "*You* don't mind missing out on the Scala. In spite of all your credentials you don't really care much for culture. Deep down, you're from Chicago after all."

"Let me make it up to you. What's at the Met tonight?"

"No, it's Wagner, and that "Liebestod" drags me. Actually, as everybody is talking about it, let's see if we can get in to see *Deep Throat*. All right, I can see you getting ready to make a remark about sex films. Don't do it. I'll tell you what your attitude is—When it's done it's fun, but when it's seen it's unclean. And remember that your wisecracks show no respect for me. First I do things for you, and then I become a woman of a certain class."

Still, she was in good heart, chatty and highly affectionate. We were lunching at the Oak Room, far from the beans and wieners of the nursing home. We should have given those two old geezers a treat and taken them out. At lunch Menasha might have told me much about my mother. She died when I was an adolescent and I longed to hear her described by a mature man, if such Menasha was. She had come to be a sacred person. Julius always insisted that he couldn't remember her at all. He had his doubts about my memory altogether. Why such keenness (approaching hysteria) for the past? Clinically speaking, I guess the problem was hysteria. Philosophically, I came out better. Plato links recollection with love. But I couldn't ask Renata to creep along with two old boys to some seafood joint on the boardwalk and spend a whole afternoon helping them to read the menu and to deal with clams, wiping butter from their pants, looking away when they popped out their detachable bridges, just so I could discuss my mother. To her it was odd that an elderly fellow like me should be so eager to hear reminiscences of his mother. Contrast with these very old guys might make me look a bit younger, still it was also possible that she would lump us all together in her irritation. Thus Menasha and Waldemar were deprived of a treat.

In the Oak Room she ordered Beluga caviar. She said it was her reward for taking the subway. "And after that," she told the waiter, "lobster salad. For dessert, the *profiterole*. Mr.

Citrine will have the *omelette fines-herbes*. I'll let him order the wine." And so I did, having been told what she wanted. I commanded a bottle of Pouilly-Fuissé. When the waiter left, Renata said, "I notice that your eye goes from right to left as you read the menu. There is no reason for the poor-boy bit. You can always make money, piles of it. Especially if you team up with me, I promise we'll be Lord and Lady Citrine. I know the visit to Coney Island has made you downhearted. So I'll give you a blessing to count. Look around this dining room and look at the women—see what kind of dogs important brokers, corporation executives, and big-time lawyers get stuck with. Then compare."

"You are certainly right. My heart bleeds for all parties."

The wine waiter came and made the usual phony passes, showed the label, and ducked down with his corkscrew. He then poured some wine for me to taste, and harassed me with perfunctory courtesies that had to be acknowledged.

"Still, coming to New York was right, I now agree," she said. "Your mission here is accomplished, and that's all to the good because it's about time your life was set on a real basis and you cleared away a few tons of rubbish. Your sentiments and deep feelings may do you credit, but you're like a mandolin-player. You tickle every note ten times. It's cute, but a little goes a long way. Were you about to say something?"

"Yes, the strangeness of life on this earth is very oppressive."

"You're always saying 'on this earth.' It gives me a creepy feeling. This old Professor Scheldt, the father of your pussycat Doris, has filled you up with his esoteric higher worlds and when you talk to me about this I feel we're both going bonkers: knowledge that doesn't need a brain, hearing without real ears, sight without eyes, the dead are with us, the soul leaves the body when we sleep. Do you believe all this stuff?"

"I take it seriously enough to examine it. As to the soul leaving the body when we sleep, my mother absolutely believed that. She told me so when I was a kid. I find nothing strange in that. Only my head-culture opposes it. My hunch is that Mother was right. This can't lead me into oddity, I already am in oddity. People as ingenious, as fertile in wishes as I am, and also my wonderful betters, have gone to their death. And what is this death? Again, *nessuno sa.* But ignorance of death is destroying us. And this is the field of ridicule in which Humboldt sees me still laboring. No honorable person can refuse to lend his mind, to give his time, to devote his soul to this problem of problems. Death now has no serious challenge from science or from philosophy or religion or art. . . ."

"So you think crank theories are the best bet?"

I muttered something to myself, for she had heard this quotation from Samuel Daniel before, and her mandolin-playing figure prevented me from repeating it aloud. It was, "While timorous knowledge stands considering, audacious ignorance hath done the deed." My thought was that life on this earth was actually everything else as well, provided that we learned how to apprehend it. But, not knowing, we were oppressed to the point of heartbreak. *My* heart was breaking all the time, and I was sick and tired of it.

Renata said, "Really, what do I care—worship as you please is American and fundamental. It's just that when you open your eyes there's a sort of gloony gleam in them. That's a made-up word, gloony. I loved it, by the way, when Humboldt said you were a promissory nut. I just loved that."

For my part, I loved Renata's cheerfulness. Her roughness and frankness were infinitely better than her loving-pious bit. I had never bought that—never. But her cheerfulness as she laid caviar, chopped egg, and onion on Melba toast for me gave me wonderful extravagant comfort. "Only," she went on, "you've got to stop twittering like a ten-year-old girl. And now let's take this Humboldt thing straight on. He thought he was leaving you a valuable property. Poor character. What a gas! Who'd buy such a story? What's it got? You'd have to do everything twice, first with the girl and then with the wife. It would drive an audience nuts. Producers are looking to go beyond *Bonnie and Clyde, The French Connection, The Godfather.* Murder on an El train. Naked lovers who bounce up and down when machine-gun slugs tear into their bodies. Dudes on massage tables who get bullets straight through their eyeglasses." Ruthless, perfectly good-natured Renata laughed, sipping Pouilly-

Fuissé, aware of how I admired her throat and the feminine subtlety of its white rings (here the veil of Maya was as vivid as ever). "Well, isn't that it, Charles? And how does Humboldt compete? He dreamed about having magic with his public. But you didn't have it either. Without your director, *Trenck* could never have made a big box office. You told me so yourself. What did you get for those *Trenck* movie rights?"

"The price was three hundred thousand. The producer took half, the agent took ten percent, the government took sixty percent of the rest, I put fifty into the house in Kenwood which now belongs to Denise...." Renata's face, when I recited figures and percentages, was wonderfully at peace. "That's how my commercial success breaks down," I said. "And I would never have been capable of doing it on my own, I agree. It was all Harold Lampton and Kermit Bloomgarden. As for Humboldt he was not the first man to go down trying to combine worldly success with poetic integrity, blasted with poetic fire, as Swift says, and consequently unfit for Church or Law or State. But he thought of me, Renata. His scenario gives his opinion of me—foolishness, intricacy, wasted subtlety, a loving heart, some kind of disorganized genius, a certain elegance of construction. His legacy is also his affectionate opinion of me. And he did his very best. It was an act of love—"

"Charlie, look, they're bringing you the telephone," said Renata. "It's terrific!"

"You're Mr. Citrine?" said the waiter.

"Yes."

He plugged in the instrument and I spoke to Chicago. The call was from Alec Szathmar. "Charlie, you're in the Oak Room?" he said.

"I am."

He laughed with excitement. We two who had sparred in the alley with boxing gloves as children hitting each other in the face until we were winded and dazed were now men, and had risen in the world. I was lunching elegantly in New York; he was phoning me from a paneled office on La Salle Street. Unfortunately, the messages he gave me did not suit the plush occasion. Or did it? "Urbanovich is going along with Denise and Pinsker. The court says you must post a bond. The figure is two hundred thousand dollars. This is what happens when you ignore my advice. I told you to hide some money in Switzerland. No, you had to be aboveboard. You weren't going to do anything gross. That's the kind of snobbery that does you in. You want austerity? Well, you're two hundred grand closer to it than you were yesterday."

A slight echo told me that he was using an amplifier. My replies were heard on the squawk box in his office. This meant that his secretary, Tulip, was listening. Because of the affectionate interest this woman took in my doings, Szathmar, always the showman, sometimes invited her to listen in on our conversations. She was a fine woman, somewhat pale and heavy, and carried herself in the sad high-hearted style of the old West Side. She was devoted to Szathmar, whose weaknesses she knew and forgave. Only Szathmar himself was conscious of no weaknesses. "What will you do for dough, Charlie?" he said.

The first thing to do was to conceal the facts from Renata.

"There's no immediate problem. I've got a small balance with you, still, haven't I?"

"We agreed that I would repay the condominium loan in five annual installments, and you've already gotten this year's payment. I suppose the decades of free legal advice I gave you don't count for a thing."

"You also put me on to Tomchek and Srole."

"The finest domestic-relations people in Chicago. They couldn't work with you. No one could."

Renata passed me another bit of Melba toast with caviar, grated egg, onion, and sour cream.

"Now I've given you message number one," said Szathmar. "Message number two is to call your brother in Texas. His wife has been trying to reach you. Nothing has happened. Don't lose your head. Julius is going to have open-heart surgery. Your sister-in-law says they're going to transplant a few arteries for the angina. She thought his only brother should know. They're going up to Houston for the operation."

"Your face is completely changed, what is it?" said Renata as I put down the telephone.

"My brother is going to have open-heart surgery."

"Oh-oh!" she said.

"Quite right. I must go there."

"You're not asking me to postpone this trip again?"

"We can easily fly from Texas."

"You've got to go?"

"Of course, I must."

"I've never met your brother, but I know he's a rough man. He wouldn't cancel his plans for you."

"Now Renata he's my only brother, and these are frightful operations. As I understand it, they break into your chest, remove the heart, lay it on a towel or something, while they circulate the blood by machine. It's one of those demonic modern technological things. Poor humankind, we're all hurled down into the object world now. . . ."

"Ugh," said Renata, "I hope they never make such a jigsaw puzzle of me."

"Darling Renata, in your case the very thought is blasphemous." Renata's breasts, when the support of clothing was removed, fell slightly to the right and to the left, owing to a certain enchanting fullness at the base of each and perhaps because of their connection with the magnetic poles of the earth. You did not think of Renata as having a chest in the usual human way—certainly not my brother's human way, gray-haired and stout.

"You want me to go to Texas with you, don't you," she said.

"It would mean a great deal to me."

"And to me, too, if we were husband and wife. I'd go there twice a week if you needed support. But don't expect to take me in tow and show me off to a dirty old man as your floozy. Don't go by my behavior as a single woman."

This last was a reference to the night she locked me out and lay beside Flonzaley the mortuary king. She had been weeping, to hear her tell it, while I telephoned frantically. "Marry me," she said to me now. "Change my status. That's what I need. I'll make you a wonderful wife."

"I should do it. You're a glorious woman. Why should I bandy arguments with you?"

"There's nothing to argue about. I'm going to Italy tomorrow, and you can meet me in Milan. But I'll be walking into the Biferno leather shop in a weak position. As a divorced woman who floats around with a lover I can't expect my father to be enthusiastic, and, practically speaking it'll be harder for him to have an emotional catharsis over me than if I were an innocent girl. As for me, I still remember how Mother and I were put out on the street—right on the Via Monte Napoleone, and how I stood in front of his show window with all the beautiful leather and cried. To this day when I go into Gucci and see the luxury luggage and handbags I feel almost like fainting from rejection and heartbreak."

Some statements are meant to pass, some to echo. The words "my behavior as a single woman" continued to reverberate, as it was her tactical intention that they should. But it was impossible to marry her just to keep her honest for a few days in Milan.

I went up to the mansard room and got the operator to connect me with my brother in Corpus Christi.

"Ulick?" I said, using his family name.

"Yes, Chuckie."

"I'm coming down to Texas tomorrow."

"Ah, they've told you," he said. "They're going to hack me open on Wednesday. Well, come along if you haven't got anything else to do. I thought I heard that you were going to Europe."

"I can leave the country from Houston."

He was of course pleased that I wanted to come but he was distrustful, and he wondered whether I might not be angling for some advantage. Julius in fact loved me but affirmed and even believed that he didn't. My brotherly intensity flattered him. But he was too clear-headed to deceive himself. He was not a lovable man and if he held an important place in my feelings, and those feelings were intricate and keen, the reason was either that I was queerly undeveloped, immature, or that possibly without knowing what I was doing I was involved in a con. Ulick saw rackets everywhere. A stout character, sharp-faced, handsome, his eyes were big alert and shrewd. A mustache in

the style of the late Secretary Acheson mitigated the greedi-
ness of his mouth. He was a strutting heavy graceful rapa-
cious man who wore checks, stripes, gaudy but elegantly fitted.
Somewhere between business and politics he had once made a
fortune in Chicago, connected with the underworld although
without being a part of it. But he fell in love and left his wife
for the other woman. In the divorce he was wiped out, losing
his Chicago possessions. However, he made a second fortune
in Texas and raised a second family. It was impossible to think
of him without his wealth. It was necessary for him to be in the
money, to have dozens of suits and hundreds of pairs of shoes,
shirts beyond inventory, cuff links, pinkie rings, large houses,
luxury automobiles, a grand-ducal establishment over which
he ruled like a demon. Such was Julius, my big brother Ulick,
whom I loved.

"For the life of me," said Renata, "I can't figure why you're
so crazy about this brother of yours. The more he puts you
down, the more you worship the ground. Let me recall a few of
the things you told me about him. When you were a kid playing with toys on the floor he would step on your fingers. He
rubbed your eyes with pepper. He hit you on the head with a
bat. When you were an adolescent he burned your collection of
Marx and Lenin pamphlets. He had fist fights with everyone,
even a colored maid."

"Yes, that was Bama, she was six feet tall and she gave him
a hard punch on the ear, which he had coming."

"He's been in a hundred scandals and lawsuits. He fired shots
ten years ago at a car that used his driveway to turn around."

"He only meant to shoot out a tire."

"Yes, but he hit the windows, and he was being sued for
assault with a deadly weapon—didn't you tell me? He sounds
like one of those crazy brutes who get entangled in your life. Or
was it the other way around?"

"The odd thing is that he isn't a brute, he's charming, a gentleman. But mainly he's my brother Ulick. Some people are so
actual that they beat down my critical powers. Once they're
there—inarguable, incontestable—nothing can be done about
them. Their reality matters more than my practical interests.

Beyond a certain point of vividness I become passionately attached."

Obviously Renata herself belonged to this category. I was passionately attached to her because she was Renata. She had an additional value, too—she knew a lot about me. I had a vested interest in her because I had told her so much about myself. She was educated in the life and outlook of Citrine. You needed no such education in the life of Renata. All you had to do was look at her. And conditions were such that I had to purchase her consideration. The more facts I put into her the more I needed her, and the more I needed her the more her price increased. In the life to come there will be no such personal or erotic bondage. You won't have to bribe another soul to listen while you explain what you're about, and what you had meant to do, and what you had done, and what others had done, et cetera. (Although the question naturally arises, why should anyone listen gratis to such stuff?) Spiritual science says that in the life to come the moral laws have the priority, and they are as powerful there as the laws of nature are in the physical world. Of course I was just a beginner, in theosophical kindergarten.

But I was serious about it. I meant to make a strange jump and plunge into the truth. I had had it with most contemporary ways of philosophizing. Once and for all I was going to find out whether there was anything behind the incessant hints of immortality that kept dropping on me. Besides, this was the biggest and most revolutionary thing one could undertake to do, and of the greatest value. Socially, psychologically, politically, the very essence of human institutions was an extract of what we assumed about death. Renata said I was furious and arrogant and vengeful toward intellectuals. I always said that they were wasting their time and ours, and that I wanted to trample and clobber them. Possibly so, though she exaggerated my violence. I had the strange hunch that nature itself was not *out there*, an object world eternally separated from subjects, but that everything external corresponded vividly with something internal, that the two realms were identical and interchangeable, and that nature was my own unconscious being. Which I could come to know through intellectual work, scientific study, and intimate contemplation. Each thing in nature was an emblem for something in my own soul. At this moment in the Plaza, I took a rapid reading on my position. I had a slightly outer-space feeling. The frame of reference was tenuous and shuddering all around me. So it was necessary to be firm and to put metaphysics and the conduct of life together in some practical way.

Suppose, then, that after the greatest, most passionate vividness and tender glory, oblivion is all we have to expect, the big blank of death. What options present themselves? One option is to train yourself gradually into oblivion so that no great change has taken place when you have died. Another option is to increase the bitterness of life so that death is a desirable release. (In this the rest of mankind will fully collaborate.) There is a further option seldom chosen. That option is to let the deepest elements in you disclose their deepest information. If there is nothing but nonbeing and oblivion waiting for us, the prevailing beliefs have not misled us, and that's that. This would astonish me, for the prevailing beliefs seldom satisfy my need for truth. Still the possibility must be allowed. Suppose, however, that oblivion is *not* the case? What, then, have I been doing for about six decades? I think that I never believed that oblivion *was* the case and by five and a half decades of distortion and absurdity I have challenged and disputed the alleged rationality and finality of the oblivion view.

These were the thoughts whirling through my head in the top story of the Plaza Hotel. Renata was still criticizing the mansard room. I always gave her a grand time in New York, spent magnificently, blew my money like a Klondike miner. Urbanovich had grounds for his opinion that I was a wild old guy, that I was jettisoning the capital to keep it out of enemy hands, and he was restraining me. But it wasn't his money, was it? However, the matter was very odd, for all kinds of people with whom I was scarcely acquainted had claims on it. There was, for instance, Pinsker, Denise's lawyer, the hairy man with the cheese-omelette cravat. I didn't even know the man, we had never exchanged a single personal word. How did he get his hand into my pocket?

"What arrangements are we going to make?" said Renata.

"For you, in Italy? Will a thousand dollars hold you for a week?"

"The most awful things are said about you back in Chicago, Charlie. You should hear what a reputation you have. Of course Denise sees to that. She even works on the kids and they spread her view, too. You're supposed to be unbearable. Mother hears that everywhere. But when a person gets to know you, you turn out to be sweet—as sweet a guy as I ever knew. What do you say we make love? We don't have to take off all our clothes. I know you sometimes like it half-and-half." She removed her bottom garments, unhooking her bra for easy access, and settled herself on a corner of the bed in all the fullness, smoothness, and beauty of her nether half, her face white and her brows going up with piety. I faced her in my shirttails. She said, "Let's store up a little comfort for our separation."

Then, behind us on the night table, the small light of the telephone began to beat silently, to pulsate. Someone was trying to reach me. Whose pulsations came first, was the question.

Renata began to laugh. "You know the most talented nuisances," she said. "They always know when to bother you. Well? Answer it. The occasion is ruined anyway. You look anxious. You probably are thinking about the kids."

The caller was Thaxter. He said, "I'm downstairs. Are you busy? Can you come to the Palm Court? I have important news."

"To be continued," said Renata, cheerful enough. We put our clothing on and went downstairs to find Thaxter. I didn't recognize him at first, for he was wearing a new outfit, a Western hat and his velvet trousers were tucked into cowboy boots.

"What's this?" I said.

"The good news is that I've just signed a contract for that book on the temperamental dictators," he said. "Qaddafi, Amin, and those other types. What's more, Charlie, we can get another contract. Today. Tonight, if you like. And I think we should. It would be a really good deal for you. And oh, by the way, on the house phone next to me there was a lady also asking for you. She's the widow of the poet Fleisher, I believe, or his divorced wife."

"Kathleen? Where has she gone? Where is she?" I said.

"I told her we had urgent business and she said she had some shopping to do anyway. She said you could meet in the Palm Court in about an hour."

"You sent her away?"

"Before you get sore, remember that I'm giving a cocktail party on the *France*. I'm a little pressed for time."

"What's the Western getup about?" said Renata.

"Well, I thought it would be a good idea to look more American, like a guy from the heartland. I felt I should show that I had nothing to do with the liberal media and the Eastern Establishment."

"You'll pretend to take those fellows from the Third World seriously," I said, "and then you'll write them up as vulgarians, imbeciles, blackmailers, and killers."

"No, there's a serious side to it," said Thaxter. "I plan to avoid out-and-out satire. This question has its serious side. I want to examine them not just as soldier-demagogues and bad-boy buffoons but also as leaders defying the West. I want to say something about their resentment over the failure of civilization to lead the world beyond technology and banking. I intend to analyze the crisis of values—"

"Don't tamper with that stuff. Stay away from the values, Thaxter. I'd better give you a few words of advice. First of all, don't push forward, don't intrude yourself into these interviews, and don't ask long questions. Secondly, don't fool around with these dictators and stay away from competitive games. If you play backgammon or Ping-Pong or bridge with them you'll get carried away—you'll be sunk. You don't know Thaxter," I said to Renata, "until you've seen him with a cue in his hand or a paddle or a racquet or golf club. He's vicious, he leaps, he cheats, he gets fiery in the face, and he'll trounce everybody without pity, man woman or child—are you getting a big advance?"

He was prepared, of course, for such a question.

"Not bad, considering. But there are so many liens against me in California that my lawyers have advised me to take monthly installments, not a lump sum, so I'm drawing five hundred a month."

The Palm Court was silent, the musicians were taking their break. Renata, reaching under the table, began to rub my leg. She took my foot into her lap and slipped off the loafer, stroking my sole and caressing the instep. Presently she applied the foot to herself, unremittingly sensual, secretly making love to me—or to herself with me. This had happened before, at dinner parties where the company annoyed or bored her. She was wearing the beautiful velour hat copied from the *Syndics of Amsterdam*, under it the dreaming white face, full toward the bottom, expressed its amusement, it affection, its comment upon my relations with Thaxter, its enjoyment of secrecy. How easy and natural she made everything seem—goodness, badness, lustfulness. I envied her this. At the same time I didn't really believe that it was all so very natural or easy. I suspected—no, I actually *knew* better.

"So if you're thinking about payment, I haven't got anything to give you on account," said Thaxter. "Instead I'm going to do better by you. I'm here to make a practical proposal. You and I should do that cultural Baedeker of Europe. There's an idea that really turns my editor on. Stewart really went for it. Frankly, your name is important in a deal like this. But I'd organize the whole project. You know I have a talent for that. And you wouldn't have a thing to worry about. I'd definitely be the junior partner and you'd get fifty thousand bucks on signing. All you have to do is put down your name."

Renata didn't seem to hear our conversation. She entirely missed the mention of the fifty thousand dollars. She had now left us, as it were, and was pressing me closer and closer. Her need was strong. She was gross, brilliant, endearing, and if she had to suffer fools she knew what measures to take to compensate herself. I loved her for this. The conversation meantime continued. I was glad to hear that I could still command big advances.

Thaxter was not an especially observant man. He entirely missed what Renata was doing, the dilation of her eyes and the biological seriousness in which her fine joke ended. She went from fun to mirth to happiness and finally to a climax, her body straightening in the French provincial Palm Court chair. She nearly passed out with a fine long quiver. This was almost fish-like in its delicacy. Then her eyes shone at me as she smoothed my foot, gentle and calm.

Thaxter meantime was saying, "Of course you worry about working with me. Of course you're afraid I'll run off with my end of the advance, and you'll either have to refund your end or do the book alone. That would be a nightmare to a man with an anxious character like yours."

"I could use the money," I said, "but don't ask me to commit suicide. If I got stuck with a responsibility like that, if you were to beat it and I had to do work alone, my head would go off like a bomb."

"Well, you'd be fully covered. You could protect yourself con-tractually. It would be stipulated that your only obligation by contract would be to do the major essay on each of the coun-tries. There'll be six countries—England, France, Spain, Italy, Germany, and Austria. The serial rights to those would be yours, completely. Those alone, if you handle them right, might be worth fifty thousand dollars. So my proposal is this, Charlie, we start with Spain, the simplest country, and see how it goes. Now listen to this, Stewart says he'll stake you to a month at the Ritz in Madrid. On approval. You couldn't ask anything fairer. You'd both love it. The Prado is right around the corner. The Michelin Guide lists quite a few first-class restaurants now, like the Escuadrón. I'll set up all the interviews. There'll be a stream of painters, poets, critics, historians, sociologists, architects, musicians, and underground leaders coming to you at the Ritz. You could sit there all day conversing with excellent people and eating and drinking fantastically and making a fortune besides. In three weeks' time you could write a piece called 'Contempo-rary Spain, a Cultural Overview' or something like that."

Renata, returning to consciousness, was now listening with interest to what Thaxter was saying. "Would this publisher really pick up the tab? Madrid sounds like a wonderful deal," she said.

"You know what these giant conglomerates are," said Thaxter. "What would a few thousand bucks mean to Stewart?"

"I'll think about it."

"It generally means 'No' when Charlie says he'll think about it."

Thaxter bent toward me in his Stetson hat. "I can follow your train of thought," he said. "You're thinking that I better do my book on the dictators first. Thaxter, *avec tout ce qu'il a sur son assiette*? Too many irons in the fire. But that's just it. Other people would burn themselves but with me, the more irons the better I function. I can wrap up five dictators in three months," Thaxter asserted.

"Madrid sounds enchanting," said Renata.

"The old country for your mother, isn't it?" I said.

"Let me give you the rundown on the international Ritz Hotel situation," said Thaxter. "The London Ritz is played out—soiled, run-down. The Paris Ritz belongs to the Arab oil billionaires, the Onassis types, and the Texas barons. No waiter will pay attention to you there. Right now, with those Portuguese upheavals, the Lisbon Ritz isn't a restful place. But Spain is still stable and feudal enough to give the real old-fashioned Ritz treatment."

Thaxter and Renata had this in common: they fancied themselves to be Europeans, Renata because of the Señora, Thaxter because of his French governess, his international family connections, his BA in French at Olivet College, Michigan.

Money apart, Renata saw in me the hope of an interesting life, Thaxter saw the hope of a higher one leading perhaps to a Major Statement. We were sipping tea and sherry and eating pastries iced in beautiful colors while I waited for Kathleen to arrive.

"Trying to keep up with your interests," said Thaxter, "I've been reading your man Rudolf Steiner, and he's fascinating. I expected something like Madame Blavatsky, but he turns out to be a very rational kind of mystic. What's his angle on Goethe?"

"Don't start that, Thaxter," said Renata.

But I needed a serious conversation. I longed for it. "It isn't mysticism," I said. "Goethe simply wouldn't stop at the boundaries drawn by the inductive method. He let his imagination pass over into objects. An artist sometimes tries to see how close he can come to being a river or a star, playing at becoming one or the other—entering into the forms of the phenomena painted or described. Someone has even written of an astronomer keeping droves of stars, the cattle of his mind, in the meadows of space. The imaginative soul works in that way, and why should poetry refuse to be knowledge? For Shelley, Adonais in death became part of the loveliness he had made more lovely. So according to Goethe the blue of the sky *was* the theory. There was a thought in blue. The blue became blue when human vision received it. A wonderful man like my late friend Humboldt was overawed by rational orthodoxy, and because he was a poet this probably cost him his life. Isn't it enough to be a poor naked forked creature without also being a poor naked forked spirit? Must the imagination be asked to give up its own full and free connection with the universe—the universe as Goethe spoke of it? As the living garment of God? And today I found out that Humboldt really believed that human beings were supernatural beings. He too!"

"There he goes," said Renata. "What did you want to start him spouting for?"

"Thought is a real constituent of being," I tried to continue.

"Charlie! Not now," said Renata.

Thaxter who was normally polite to Renata spoke stiffly to her when she barged into these higher conversations. He said, "I take a real interest in the way Charles's mind works." He was smoking his pipe, his mouth drawn wide and dark, under the big Western brim.

"Try living with it," said Renata. "Charlie's kinky theorizing puts together combinations nobody else could imagine, like the way the US Congress does its business, with Immanuel Kant, Russian Gulag camps, stamp collecting, famine in India, love and sleep and death and poetry. The less said about the way his mind works, the better. But if you do have to be a guru, Charlie, go the whole distance—wear a silk gown, get a turban, grow a beard. You'd make a hell of a good-looking spiritual

leader with a beard and those paisley nostrils of yours. I'd dress
up with you, and we'd be a smash. The way you carry on and
for free! I sometimes have to pinch myself. I think I've taken
fifty Valiums and am hearing things."

"People of powerful intellect never are quite sure whether or
not it's all a dream."

"Well, people who don't know whether they're awake or
dreaming don't necessarily have that powerful intellect,"
Renata answered. "My theory is that you're punishing me with
this anthroposophy. You know what I mean. That blonde runt
introduced you to her dad, and since then it's all been really
spooky."

"I wish you'd finish what you started to say," Thaxter turned
again to me.

"It comes to this, that the individual has no way to prove
out what's in his heart—I mean the love, the hungering for the
external world, the swelling excitement over beauty for which
there are no acceptable terms of knowledge. True knowledge
is supposed to be a monopoly of the scientific world-view. But
human beings have all sorts of knowledge. They don't have to
apply for the right to love the world. But to see what goes on
in this respect, take the career of someone like Von Humboldt
Fleisher. . . ."

"Ah, that guy again," said Renata.

"Is it true that as big-time knowledge advances poetry must
drop behind, that the imaginative mode of thought belongs to
the childhood of the race? A boy like Humboldt, full of heart
and imagination, going to the public library and finding books,
leading a charmed life bounded by lovely horizons, reading old
masterpieces in which human life has its full value, filling himself with Shakespeare, where there is plenty of significant space
around each human being, where words mean what they say,
and looks and gestures also are entirely meaningful. Ah, that
harmony and sweetness, that art! But there it ends. The significant space dwindles and disappears. The boy enters the world
and learns its filthy cutthroat tricks, the enchantment stops.
But is it the world that is disenchanted?"

"No," said Renata. "I know the answer to that one."

"It's rather our minds that have allowed themselves to be convinced that there is no imaginative power to connect every individual to the creation independently."

It occurred to me suddenly that Thaxter in his home-on-the-range outfit might as well have been in church and that I was behaving like his minister. This was not a Sunday, but I was in my Palm Court pulpit. As for Renata, smiling—her dark eyes, red mouth, white teeth, smooth throat—though she interrupted and heckled during these sermons she got a kick out of the way I delivered them. I knew her theory well. Whatever was said, whatever was done, either increased or diminished erotic satisfaction, and this was her practical test for any idea. Did it produce a bigger bang? "We could have been at the Scala tonight," she said, "and part of a brilliant audience hearing Rossini. Instead, do you know what we were doing today, Thaxter? We went out to Coney Island so Charlie could collect his inheritance from his dear dead old pal Humboldt Fleisher. It's been Humboldt, Humboldt, Humboldt, like 'Figaro, Figaro.' Humboldt's eighty-year-old uncle gave Charlie a bunch of papers, and Charlie read 'em and wept. Well, for a month now I've heard nothing but Humboldt and death and sleep and metaphysics and how the poet is the arbiter of the diverse and Walt Whitman and Emerson and Plato and the World Historical Individual. Charlie is like Lydia the Tattooed Lady, covered with information. You remember that song, 'You Can Learn a Lot from Lydia'?"

"Could I see those papers?" said Thaxter.

"Come with me to Italy tomorrow," said Renata to me.

"Darling, I'll join you there in a few days."

The Palm Court Trio, returning, began to play Sigmund Romberg, and Renata said, "Why, it's four o'clock. I don't want to miss *Deep Throat*. It starts at four-twenty."

"Yes, and I've got to go to the dock," said Thaxter. "You are coming, aren't you, Charlie?"

"I hope to. I've got to wait here for Kathleen."

"I've written out my itinerary for the dictators," said Thaxter, "so you can get in touch if you have a mind to go to Madrid and start our project. Say the word, and I'll begin organizing.

I know people are giving you the business in Chicago. I'm sure
you'll be needing lots of money. . . ." He glanced at Renata,
who was organizing herself to leave. "And there's real dough
in my proposal."

"I've got to run," said Renata. "I'll see you back here later."
She slung the bag over her shoulder and preceded Thaxter
across the vast luxurious carpet, part of the Christmas display, a blast of gold within the bristling green, and through the
swinging doors.

• •   •   ••

In her large bag Renata carried off my shoe. I realized this
when I looked under the table for it. Gone! She had taken it. By
means of this prank she told me how she felt about going to the
movies alone while I visited sentimentally with an old friend,
recently widowed and possibly available. I couldn't go upstairs
now, Kathleen would arrive any minute, so I sat waiting, feeling the chill in one foot while the music played. Renata in high
spirits had symbolic reasons for pinching my loafer; I was hers.
Was she correspondingly mine? When she was proprietary I
became uneasy. I felt that as soon as she was sure of one man
she became free to contemplate her future with another. And
I? Evidently I longed most to possess most the woman that
threatened me most.

"Ah, Kathleen, I'm glad to see you," I said as Kathleen came
up. I rose, my peculiar foot missing its peculiar shoe. She kissed
me—an old friend's warm kiss on the cheek. The Nevada sun
hadn't given her an outdoor color. Her fair hair was lighter
from the admixture of gray. She hadn't grown stout but she
was fleshier, a big woman. This was only the normal effect of
the decades, a slackening and softening and a saddening of the
cheeks, an attractive melancholy or hollowing. She had once
had pale freckles. Now her face had larger spots. Her upper
arms were heavier, her legs were thicker, her back wider, her
hair paler. Her dress was black chiffon, thinly trimmed with
gold at the neck.

"Lovely to see you," I said, for so it was.

"And to see you, Charlie."

She sat down but I remained standing. I said, "I took off a shoe to be more comfortable and now the thing is gone."

"How odd. Maybe the busboy took it. Why don't you try Lost and Found?" So for form's sake I beckoned to the waiter. I made a distinguished inquiry but then I said, "I'll have to go up and get another pair."

Kathleen offered to come with me but as Renata's under-clothes were all over the floor and the bed was unmade at one corner in a way that I thought baldly telling, I said, "No, no, why don't you wait for me. This lousy high-toned pimble-pamble music is driving me nuts. I'll come right down and we'll go out for a drink. I want to get my coat, anyway."

So I went up again in the luxurious cage of the elevator think-ing what a bold original Renata was and what a struggle she made continually against the threat of passivity, the universal threat. If I thought it, it had to be universal. I wasn't fooling around these days. This universalizing was becoming a craze with me, I suspected, as I put on my other pair of shoes. These were light, weightless red shoes from Harrods, a little short in the toe, but admired by the black shoeshine man at the Down-town Club for their weightlessness and style. In these, a little cramped but fine, I went down again.

This day belonged to Humboldt, it was charged with his spirit. I realized how emotional I was becoming under this influ-ence when, trying to adjust my hat, I felt uncontrollable trem-ors in my arms. As I approached Kathleen, one side of my face also twitched. I thought, Old Dr. Galvani has got me. I saw two men, husbands, in their graves, decomposing. This beautiful lady's affections had not saved them from death. Next a vision of Humboldt's shade went through my head in the form of a dark gray cloud. His cheeks were fat and the abundant hair was piled on his head. I walked toward Kathleen as the three-piece group played what Renata called "frill-paper cup-cake music." They had dipped into *Carmen* now and I said, "Let's go to a dark, quiet bar. Above all, quiet." I signed the waiter's stagger-ing check and Kathleen and I walked up and down in the cold streets until we found an agreeable place on West Fifty-sixth, dark enough for any taste and not too Christmasy.

We had a lot of catching up to do. First of all we had to speak of poor Tigler. I couldn't bring myself to say what a nice man he had been, for he hadn't been nice at all. The old wrangler could stamp his foot like Rumpelstiltskin and flew into tantrums when he was crossed. It gave him keen satisfaction to stick and screw people. He despised them all the more if they were too timid to complain. His dudes, and I had been one of them, got no hot water. The lights went out and they sat in the dark. If they went to Kathleen to beef they came away pitying and forgiving, hating him and loving her. She was not, however, one of my contrast-gainers. Her own merits were clear, this large-limbed pale freckled quiet woman. Her quietness was most important. While Humboldt played the Furious Turk she was his Christian Captive, reading in the book-stuffed cottage parlor set in the barren chicken country while the ruddy sun persisted in trying to force color through the soiled small-framed windows. Then Humboldt ordered her to put on a sweater and come outside. They chased a football like two fair-haired rookies. Staggering backward on clumsy heels he threw passes over the clothesline and through the autumn maples. My recollection of this was complete—how as Kathleen ran to make the catch her voice trailed and she reached out her arms and brought the wagging ball to her bosom, and how she and Humboldt had sat together on the Castro sofa drinking beer. I recalled this so fully that I saw the cats, one with a Hitler mustache, at the window. I heard my own voice. Twice now she had been a sleeping maiden under the spell of demon lovers. "You know what my hillbilly neighbors say," Humboldt told me, "they say, keep 'em in their stocking feet. Sometimes," he said, "I think of Eros and Psyche." He flattered himself. Eros was beautiful and he came and went in dignity. Where was Humboldt's dignity? He confiscated Kathleen's driver's license. He hid the car keys. He wouldn't allow her to keep a garden because, he said, gardening expressed the Philistine-improving impulse of city people when they bought a dream house in the country. A few tomatoes grew at the kitchen door but these had reseeded themselves when raccoons overturned the garbage cans. He said seriously, "Kathleen and I have mental work to do. Besides, if we had fruits and flowers it would make us conspicuous out here." He was afraid of sheeted night-riders and of burning crosses in his yard.

I sympathized greatly with Kathleen because she was a sleeper. I wondered about her dreaminess. Was she born to be kept in the dark? Not to reach consciousness was a condition of Psyche's bliss. But perhaps there was a more economical explanation. Tigler's tight denims had revealed an enormous sexual lump in front, and Humboldt, when he pursued Demmie's friend to her apartment, among the dachshund puppies, had shouted, "I'm a poet, I have a big cock!" But my guess was that Humboldt had the character of a tyrant who wanted a woman to hold still and that his lovemaking was frenzied dictatorship. Even his last letter to me confirmed this interpretation. Still, how was one to know? And a woman without secrets was no woman at all. And probably Kathleen had decided to marry Tigler only because life in Nevada was so lonely. Enough of this ingenious analysis.

Giving in to my weakness for telling people what they wish to hear, I said to Kathleen, "The West has agreed with you." It was, however, more or less true.

"You look well but a little drawn, Charlie."

"Life is too vexatious. Maybe I should try the West myself. When the weather was nice I did like lying under the elder trees at your ranch watching the mountains all day long. Anyway, Huggins says you've got some sort of job in the picture business and you're on your way to Europe."

"Yes. You were there when that company came out to Volcano Lake to make a movie about Outer Mongolia and all the Indians were hired to ride their ponies."

"And Tigler was technical consultant."

"And Father Edmund—you remember him, the silent-film-star Episcopal minister—was so excited. Poor Father Edmund never got ordained. He hired somebody to take his written exam in theology and they were caught. It's too bad because

the Indians loved him and they were so proud that his robes
were those stars' negligees. But yes, I'm going to Yugoslavia
and then to Spain. Those are big for film-making these days.
You can hire Spanish soldiers by the regiment, and Andalusia
is perfect for Westerns."

"It's odd that you should mention Spain. I've thought of
going there myself."

"Have you? Well, from March first I'm going to be in the
Grand Hotel of Almería. Wouldn't it be wonderful to see you
there."

"It's a good change for you," I said.

"You always wished me well, Charlie. I know that," said
Kathleen.

"This has been a big Humboldt day, a major day, an accel-
erating spiral since this morning and I'm in a very emotional
state. At Uncle Waldemar's nursing home, to add to the excitement, I met a man I've known since I was a kid. Now you're
here. I'm all worked up."

"I heard from Huggins that you were going to Coney Island.
You know, Charlie, there were times in Nevada when I thought
you were overdoing your attachment to Humboldt."

"That's possible, and I've tried to check it. I ask myself, why
so much enthusiasm? As a poet or thinker his record wasn't
all that impressive. And I'm not longing for the good old days.
Is it that the number of people who got serious about Art and
Thought in the USA is so small that even those who flunked
out are unforgettable?" Here we were closer to the real topic. I
meant to interpret the good and evil of Humboldt, understand
his ruin, translate the sadness of his life, find out why such gifts
produced negligible results, and so forth. But these were aims
difficult to discuss even when I was flying high, full of affection
for Kathleen and of wonderful pangs. "For me he had charm,
he had the old magic," I said.

"I guess you loved him," she said. "Of course I was crazy
about him. We went to New Jersey—that would have been hell
even if he had had no crazy spells. The little cottage seems now
like part of a terrible frame-up. But I would have gone to the
Arctic with him. And the college girl's thrill at getting into the

literary life was only a small part of it. I didn't care for most of
his literary friends. They came to watch the show Humboldt
put on, his routines. When they left, and he was still inspired,
he'd go after me. He was a sociable person. He used to say how
much he would like to move in brilliant circles, be a part of the
literary world."

"That's just it. There never was such a literary world," I said.
"In the nineteenth century there were several solitaries of the
highest genius—a Melville or a Poe had no literary life. It was
the customhouse and the barroom for them. In Russia, Lenin
and Stalin destroyed the literary world. Russia's situation now
resembles ours—poets, in spite of everything against them,
emerge from nowhere. Where did Whitman come from, and
where did he get what he had? It was W. Whitman, an irre-
pressible individual, that had it and that did it."

"Well, if there had been a rich literary life, and if he had been
able to drink tea with Edith Wharton and see Robert Frost and
T. S. Eliot twice a week, poor Humboldt would have felt supported and appreciated and rewarded for his talent. He just
didn't feel able to fill up all the vacancy he felt around him,"
said Kathleen. "Of course he was a wizard. He made me feel
so slow, slow slow! He invented the most ingenious things
to accuse me of. All that invention should have gone into his
poetry. Humboldt had too many personal arrangements. Too
much genius went into the arrangements. As his wife I had to
suffer the consequences. But let's not go on talking about it. Let
me ask . . . you two wrote a scenario once . . . ?"

"Just some nonsense to pass the time in Princeton. You said
something about it to that young woman, Mrs. Cantabile.
What is Mrs. Cantabile like?"

"She's pretty. She's polite in an old-fashioned Emily Post way,
and sends proper notes to thank you for a delicious lunch. At
the same time she paints her nails in gaudy colors, wears flashy
clothes, and has a harsh voice. When she chats with you she's
screaming. She sounds like a gun-moll but asks graduate-student
questions. Anyway I'm getting into the film business now, and I'm
curious about something that you and Humboldt did together.
After all a successful movie was made of your play."

"Oh, our scenario could never have made a picture. Our cast included Mussolini, the Pope, Stalin, Calvin Coolidge, Amundsen, and Nobile. Our hero was a cannibal. We had a dirigible and a Sicilian village. W. C. Fields might have loved it, but only a mad producer would ever have put a penny into it. Of course no one ever does know about these things. In 1913, who would have looked twice at an advance-scenario of World War One? Or if, before I was born, you had submitted the tale of my own life to me and invited me to live with it, wouldn't I have turned you down flat?"

"But what about your hit play?"

"Kathleen, believe me. I was just the worm that spit out the silk thread. Other people created the Broadway garment. Now tell me, what did Humboldt leave you?"

"Well, first of all, he wrote me an extraordinary letter."

"Me too. And a perfectly sane one."

"Mine is more mixed. It's too personal to show, even now. He spelled out all the crimes I was supposed to have committed. His purpose was to forgive me, whatever I had done, but he forgave in full detail and he was still talking about the Rockefellers. But there were patches of perfect sanity. Really moving, true things."

"Was that all you got from him?"

"Well, no, Charlie, there was something else he gave me. A document. Another idea for a movie. This is why I was asking you about the thing you two invented in Princeton. Tell me, what did he leave you, apart from this letter?"

"Astonishing!" I said.

"What's astonishing?"

"What Humboldt did. Sick as he was, dying, decaying, but still so ingenious."

"I don't understand you."

"Tell me, Kathleen, is this document, this film idea, about a writer? And does the writer have a domineering wife? And does he also have a beautiful young mistress? And do they take a journey? And does he then write a book he can't publish?"

"Ah, yes. I see. Of course. That's it, Charlie."

"What a son of a bitch. How marvelous! He duplicated

everything. The same journey with the wife. And the same document for us both."

Silent, she studied me. Her mouth moved. She smiled. "Why do you suppose he gave the same gift to each of us?"

"Are you perfectly sure that we're his only heirs? Ha-ha, well, let's drink to his crazy memory. He was a dear man."

"Yes, he was a dear man. And how I wish—you think it was all done according to plan?" said Kathleen.

"Who was it, Alexander Pope, who couldn't drink a cup of tea without a stratagem? That was Humboldt, too. And he kept dreaming about miraculous money until the end. He was dying and still he wanted to make us both rich. Anyway, if he kept his sense of humor, or traces of it, to the last, that was astonishing. And crazy as he was he wrote two sane letters at least. I'm going to make an odd comparison—Humboldt had to break out of his case of hardened madness to do that. You might say that he had emigrated into this madness long ago. Became a settler there. For us, maybe, he managed a visit to the Old Country. To see his friends once more? And it may have been as hard for him to do it as it might be for someone—myself, for instance—to go from this world to the spirit world. Or, another odd comparison—he made a Houdini escape from the hardened projections of paranoia, or manic depression, or whatever it was. Sleepers do awaken. Exiles and emigrants do make it back, and dying genius can revive. 'End-of-the-line lucidity,' he wrote in my letter."

"I don't think at the end he had the strength for two separate gifts, one for each of us," she said.

"Or look at it this way," I said. "He showed us what he had most of—scheming, plotting, and paranoia. He did as much with it as any man could. Don't you remember the famous Longstaff scheme?"

"Do you think he might have had anything else in mind?" said Kathleen.

"One single thing?" I said.

"A kind of posthumous character test," she said.

"He was absolutely sure that my character was hopeless. Yours, too, maybe. Well, he's given us a very lively moment.

Here we are laughing and admiring, and how sad it is. I'm very touched. We both are."

Quiet and large, Kathleen was mildly smiling, but the color of her large eyes suddenly changed. Tears came into them. Still she sat passive. That was Kathleen. It was not appropriate to mention this, but possibly Humboldt's idea was to bring us together. Not to become man and wife necessarily, but perhaps to combine our feelings for him and create a sort of joint memorial. For after he died, we would continue (for a time) to be active in life in this deluded human scene, and perhaps it would be a satisfaction to him and ease the boredom of the grave to think that we were busy with his enterprises. For when a Plato or a Dante or Dostoevski argued for immortality, Humboldt, a deep admirer of these men couldn't say, "They were geniuses, but we don't have to take their ideas seriously." But did he himself take immortality seriously? He didn't say. What he said was that we were supernatural, not natural. I would have given anything to find out what he meant.

"These scenarios or treatments are very hard to copyright," Kathleen explained. "And Humboldt must have gotten professional advice about legal protection. . . . He sealed a copy of his script in an envelope and went to the post office and registered it and had it delivered to himself by registered mail. So that it's never been opened. We've read the duplicates."

"That's right. I have two such sealed envelopes."

"Two?"

"Yes," I said. "The other is the one we'd dreamed up at Princeton. Now I know how Humboldt was amusing himself in that rotten hotel. He spent his time working all this out in meticulous detail and with ceremonious formalities. That was right up his alley."

"Listen, Charles, we must go fifty-fifty," Kathleen said.

"Bless you, commercially it's zero," I told her.

"On the contrary," Kathleen said firmly. I looked again at her, hearing this. It was out of character for Kathleen, normally diffident, to be so positively contradictory. "I submitted this to people in the business and I actually signed a contract and took an option payment of three thousand dollars. Half of that is yours."

"You mean that someone has actually paid out money for this?"

"I had two offers to choose from. I accepted the one from Steinhals Productions. Where shall I send your check?"

"At the moment I have no address. I'm in transit. But no, Kathleen, I won't take any of this money." I was thinking how I would give this news to Renata. She had ridiculed Humboldt's gift so brilliantly, and on behalf of our vanishing generation, Humboldt's and mine, I had felt hurt. "And is a script being written?"

"It's receiving serious consideration," said Kathleen. Occasionally her voice soared into a girlish treble. It broke.

"How interesting. How goofy. A solid mass of improbabilities," I said. "Although I've always been a little proud of my personal oddities, I've begun to suspect that they may be only faint images of a thousand real and much more powerful oddities out there, somewhere—that they may not be so personal after all and that maybe this is a general condition. That's why Humboldt's burlesque of love and ambition and all the rest of those monkeyshines can sound plausible to business people."

"I had good legal advice and my contract with Steinhals is for a minimum of thirty thousand dollars if the option is picked up. We could go over seventy thousand, depending on the budget. We should know in about two months. End of February. And what I feel now, Charlie, is that as joint owners you and I should draw a separate contract."

"Now, Kathleen, let's not add to the unreality of things. No contracts. And I don't need this money."

"I would have thought so too, before today, with everybody talking about your million-dollar fortune. But before you signed the check at the Palm Court you added it twice from top to bottom and again from the bottom. You lost your color. And then I saw you struggling to decide on a tip. Now don't be embarrassed, Charles."

"No, no, Kathleen. I've got plenty. It's only one of my Depression hang-ups. Besides, what a rip-off! It makes old-timers indignant."

"But I know you're being sued. I know what happens when the judges and lawyers get after a man. I haven't run a Nevada dude ranch for nothing."

"Hanging on to money is hard, of course. It's like clutching an ice cube. And you can't just make it and then live easy. There's no such thing. That's what Humboldt probably didn't understand. I wonder, did he think money made the difference between success and failure? Then he didn't understand. When you get money you go through a metamorphosis. And you have to contend with terrific powers inside and out. There's almost nothing personal in success. Success is always money's own success."

"You're merely trying to change the subject. You've always been a great observer. For years I've watched you looking at people cannily. As if you saw them but they didn't see you. But come now, Charlie, you aren't the only observer."

"Would I be staying at the Plaza if I were going broke?"

"With a young lady you might, yes."

This large, altered but still handsome woman with the occasionally breaking piercing voice, her cheeks looped inward with attractive melancholy, had been studying me. Her glance, though still a bit averted and oblique from the long habit of passivity, was warm and kindly. I am quickly and deeply touched when people take the trouble to note my situation.

"I understand you're on your way to Europe with this lady. So Huggins told me."

"True," I said, "that's right."

"To . . . ?"

"To what?" I said, "God knows." I might have told her more. I might have confessed that I no longer took seriously questions taken seriously by many serious people, questions of metaphysics or of politics, wrongly formulated. Was there then any reason why I should have a precise or practical motive for flying to Italy with a beautiful creature? I was pursuing a special tenderness, I was pursuing love and gratification from motives that would have been appropriate thirty years ago. What would it be like to overtake in my sixties what I had longed for in my twenties? What would I do with it when I got it? I had half a mind to open my heart to this fine woman. I believed that I saw signs that she too was coming out of a state of spiritual sleep. We might have discussed lots of fascinating subjects—for instance, why slumber sealed people's spirits, why waking was so convulsive, and whether she thought that the spirit could move independently of the body and if she felt that there might not be a kind of consciousness that needed no biological footing. I was tempted to tell her that I, personally, had some notion of doing something about the problem of death. I considered whether to discuss with her seriously the assignment set for writers by Walt Whitman, who was convinced that democracy would fail unless its poets gave it great poems of death. I felt that Kathleen was a woman to whom I could talk. But the position was an embarrassing one. An old chaser who had lost his head over a beautiful gold-digging palooka, a romancer who was going to fulfill the dreams of his youth, suddenly wanting to discuss supersensible consciousness and democracy's great poem of death! Come, Charlie, let's not make the world queerer than it already is. It was precisely because Kathleen *was* a woman to whom I could talk that I kept silent. Out of respect. I thought I would wait until I had considered all these questions more ripely, until I knew more.

She said, "I'll be at the Metropol in Belgrade next week. Let's stay in touch. I'm going to have a contract drawn, and I'll sign it and send it to you."

"No, no, let's not bother."

"Why, because I'm a widow you won't accept your own money from me? But *I* don't want *your* share. Think of it that way."

She was a kind woman. And she recognized the truth—I was spending big money on Renata and I was quickly going broke.

• • •

"My dear, why did you steal my shoe?"

"I couldn't resist," said great Renata. "How did you hobble upstairs on one shoe? What did your friend think? I bet it was a riot. Charlie, humor is a bond we have. That I know for a fact."

Humor had an edge over love in this relationship. My character and my ways entertained Renata. This entertainment was so extensive that I thought it might merge by degrees with love. For I didn't under any circumstances propose to do without love.

"You also took off my boot under the table in Paris."

"Yes, that was the night that horrible fellow told you how worthless your Legion ribbon was and put you in a class with garbage collectors and pig breeders. It was like revenge, consolation, kicks, all at the same time," said Renata. "Do you remember what I said afterward, that I thought was so funny?"

"Yes, I remember."

"What did I say, Charlie?"

"You said, to air it is human."

"To air it is human, to bare it divine." All made up, dark-haired and dressed in a crimson traveling costume, she laughed. "Oh, Charlie, give up this dumb trip to Texas. I need you in Milan. It isn't going to be easy for me with Biferno. Your brother doesn't want your visit and you don't owe him anything. You love him but he bullies you, and you have no defenses against bullies. You go to them with an aching heart and they always kick you in the ass. You know and I know what he's going to think. He's going to think that you're flying down at a tender moment to con him into putting you in one of his profitable deals. Let me ask you something, Charlie, will he be partly right? I don't want to pry into your present situation, but I suspect you may need a break financially right now. There's one thing more: it'll be nip and tuck between you and his wife as to who has the right to be chief mourner if something happens, and why should he want to face both of his chief mourners just as he goes under the knife? In short, you're wasting your time. Come with me. I dream of marrying you in Milan under my true maiden name, Biferno, with my real father giving me away."

I wanted to humor Renata. She deserved to have things her way. We were at Kennedy now and, in her incomparable hat and the suède maxi-coat, her Hermès scarves, her elegant boots, she was no more to be privately possessed than the Tower of Pisa. And yet she claimed her private rights, the right to an identity-problem, the right to a father, a husband. How silly, what a comedown! However, from the next hierarchical level, and to an invisible observer, I might appear to be making similar claims to order, rationality, prudence, and other middle-class things.

"Let's have a drink in the VIP Lounge. I don't want to drink where it's so noisy and the glasses are sticky."

"But I don't belong any more."

"Charles," she said, "there is that guy Zitterbloom—the one who lost you twenty thousand dollars in oil wells a year ago when he was supposed to be buying you tax shelter. Get him on the phone and have him fix it. He suggested it himself last year. 'Anytime at all, Charlie.'"

"You make me feel like the fisherman in *Grimm's Fairy Tales,* the one whose wife sent him to the seashore to ask the magic fish for a palace."

"Watch how you talk. I'm no nag," she said. "We have a right to our last drink with a little class, not pushed around by a lousy crowd."

So I telephoned Zitterbloom, whose secretary easily arranged the matter. It made me think how much a man might salvage from his defeats and losses if he wanted to put his mind to it. In a gloomy farewell spirit, I sipped my bloody mary, thinking what a risk I was running for my brother's sake and how little he would appreciate it. Still, I *must* have confidence in Renata. Ideal manhood demanded it and practical judgment would have to live with the demand of ideal manhood. I did not, however, wish to be asked on the spot to predict how it would all come out, for if I had to predict, everything would disappear in a whirlwind. "What about a bottle of 'Ma Griffe,' duty-free?" she said. I bought her a large-sized bottle, saying, "They'll deliver it on the plane and I won't be there to smell it."

"Don't you worry, we're going to save everything for the reunion. Don't let your brother fix you up with women in Texas."

"That would be about the last thing on his mind. But what about you, Renata, when was the last time you spoke with Flonzaley?"

"You can forget Flonzaley. We've made a clean break. He's a nice man, but I can't go along with the undertaking business."

"He's very rich," I said.

"He's worth his wreaths in wraiths," she said, in the style I loved her for. "As president he doesn't have to handle corpses any more but I can never help remembering his embalming background. Of course I don't hold with this guy Fromm, when he says how necrophilia has crept up on civilization. To be perfectly serious, Charlie, with a build like mine if I don't stay strictly normal where am I at?"

I was quite sad, nevertheless, wondering what part of the truth she was telling me and even whether we would see each other again. But despite the many pressures I was under I felt that I was making progress spiritually. At the best of times, separations and departures unnerve me and I experienced great anxiety now but felt I had something reliable within.

"So good-by, darling. I'll phone you from Milan tomorrow in Texas," said Renata, and we kissed many times. She seemed on the point of crying, but there were no tears.

I walked through the TWA tunnel, like an endless arched gullet or a corridor in an expressionistic film, and then I was searched for weapons and got on a plane to Houston. All the way to Texas I read occult books. There were many stirring passages in them, to which I shall come back in a while. I reached Corpus Christi in the afternoon and checked into a motel. Then I went over to Julius's house, which was large and new and surrounded by palms and jacarandas and loquats and lemon trees. The lawns looked artificial, like green excelsior or packing material. Expensive automobiles were parked in the driveway, and when I rang the bell there was a great gonging and tolling and dogs began to bark inside. The security arrangements were elaborate. Heavy locks were undone and then my sister-in-law, Hortense, opened the wide door covered with Polynesian carvings. She hollered at the dogs but with underlying affection. Then she turned to me. She was a blunt, decent person with blue eyes and chub lips. A bit blinded by the smoke of her own cigarette, which she did not remove from her mouth, she said, "Charles! How did you get here?"

"Hired a car from Avis. How are you, Hortense?"

"Julius is expecting you. He's dressing. Go on in."

The dogs were not much smaller than horses. She restrained them and I went toward the master bedroom, greeting the children, my nephews, who answered nothing. I wasn't altogether sure that for them I was a full member of the family. Entering, I found Ulick, my brother, in candy-striped boxer shorts reaching to his knees. "I thought that must be you, Chuckie," he said.

"Well, Ulick, here we are," I said. He did not look well. His belly was large and his titties were pointed. Between them grew profuse gray silk. He was, however, in full control, as usual. His long head was masterful with its straight nose and well-barbered smooth white hair, the commanding mustache and witty, hard-glinting pouchy eyes. He had always worn roomy shorts, he liked them better. Mine were as a rule shorter and snugger. He gave me one of his undershot glances. A whole lifetime was between us. With me it was continuous, but Ulick was the sort of man who wanted to renegotiate the terms again and again. Nothing was to be assumed permanently. The brotherly emotions I brought with me mystified and embarrassed him, flattered him, and filled him with suspicion. Was I a nice fellow? Was I really innocent? And was I really any good? Ulick had, with me, the difficulties of a final determination which I myself had with Thaxter.

"If you had to come, you could have gone direct to Houston," he said. "That's where we go tomorrow." I could see that he was fighting his brotherly feelings. They were heavily present still. Ulick had by no means gotten rid of them all.

"Oh, I didn't mind the extra trip. And I had nothing special to do in New York."

"Well, I have to go and look at some property this afternoon. You want to come with me or do you want to swim in the pool? It's heated." Last time I slid into his pool one of his great dogs had bitten me in the ankle and drawn quite a lot of blood. And I hadn't come for the bathing, he knew that. He said, "Well, I'm pleased you're here." He turned away his powerful face and stared elsewhere while his brain, intensely trained in calculation, calculated his chances. "This operation is fucking up the kids' Christmas," he said, "and you're not even going to be with yours."

"I sent them a load of toys from F. A. O. Schwarz. I'm sorry to say I didn't think of bringing presents for your boys."

"What would you give them? They've got everything. It's a goddamn guessing game to buy them a toy. I'm set for the operation. They kept me in bed for all the tests, up in Houston. I made a twenty-thousand-dollar donation to that joint in memory of Papa and Mama. And I'm ready for the operation except that I'm a few pounds overweight. Chuck, they saw you open and I even think the bastards lift the heart right out of your chest. Their team does these heart jobs by the thousands. I expect to be back in my office by the first of February. Are you fluid? Have you got about fifty thousand? I may be able to put you into something."

From time to time Ulick telephoned me from Texas and said, "Send me a check for thirty, no, make it forty-five." I simply wrote the check and mailed it. There were no receipts. Occasionally a contract arrived six months later. Invariably my money was doubled. It pleased him to do this for me, although it also irritated him that I failed to understand the details of these deals and that I didn't appreciate his business subtlety. As for my profits, they had been entrusted to Zitterbloom, they paid Denise, they subsidized Thaxter, they were taken by the IRS, they kept Renata in the Lake Point Tower, they went to Tomchek and Srole.

"What have you got in mind?" I said.

"A few things," he said. "You know what bank rates are. I'd be surprised if they didn't hit eighteen percent before long." Three different television sets were turned on, adding to the streaming colors of the room. The wallpaper was gold-embossed. The carpet seemed a continuation of the dazzling lawn. Indoors and outdoors fell into each other through a picture window, garden and bedroom mingling. There was a blue

Exercycle, and there were trophies on the shelves, for Hortense was a famous golfer. Enormous closets, specially built, were thick with suits and with dozens of pairs of shoes arranged on long racks and with hundreds of neckties and stacks of hatboxes. Showy, proud of his possessions, in matters of taste he was a fastidious critic and he reviewed my appearance as if he were the Douglas MacArthur of dress. "You were always a slob, Chuckie, and now you spend money on clothes and go to a tailor, but you're still a slob. Who sold you those goddamn shoes? And that horse-blanket overcoat? Hustlers used to sell shoes like that to the greenhorns fifty years ago with a buttonhook for a bonus. Now take this coat." He threw into my arms a black vicuña with a Chesterfield collar. "Down here it's too warm to get much use out of it. It's yours. The boys will take your coat to the stable, where it belongs. Take it off, put this on." I did as I was ordered. This was the form his affection took. When it was necessary to resist Ulick, I did it silently. He put on a pair of double-knit slacks, beautifully cut, with flaring cuffs, but he couldn't fasten them over his belly. He shouted to Hortense in the next room that the cleaner had shrunk them.

"Yah, they shrank," she answered.

This was the style of the house. None of your Ivy League muttering and subdued statement.

I was given a pair of his shoes, too. Our feet were exactly the same. So were the big extruded eyes and the straight noses. I don't clearly know what these features did for me. His gave him an autocratic look. And now that I was beginning to think of every earthly life as one of a series, I puzzled over Ulick's spiritual career. What had he been before? Biological evolution and Western History could never create a person like Ulick in sixty-five lousy years. He had brought his deeper qualities here with him. Whatever his earlier form, I was inclined to believe that in this life, as a rich rough American, he had lost some ground. America was a harsh trial to the human spirit. I shouldn't be surprised if it set everyone back. Certain higher powers seemed to be in abeyance, and the sentient part of the soul had everything its own way, with its material conveniences.

Oh the creature comforts, the animal seductions. Now which journalist was it that had written that there were countries in which our garbage would have been delicatessen?

"So you're going to Europe. Any special reason? Are you on a job? Or just running, as usual? You never go alone, always with some bim. What kind of cunt is taking you this time? . . . I can force myself into these slacks, but we're going to do a lot of driving and I won't be comfortable." He pulled them off angrily and threw them on the bed. "I'll tell you where we're going. There's a gorgeous piece of property, forty or fifty acres of a peninsula into the Gulf, and it belongs to some Cubans. Some general who was dictator before Batista ripped it off years ago. I'll tell you what his racket was. When currency wore out, the old bills were picked up at the Havana banks and trucked away to be destroyed. But this currency was never burned. No sir, it was shipped out of the country and deposited to the old general's account. With this he bought US property. Now the descendants are sitting on it. They're no damn good, a bunch of playboys. The daughters and daughters-in-law are after these playboy heirs to act like men. All they do is sail and drink and sleep and whore and play polo. Drugs, fast cars, planes—you know the scene. The women want a developer to size this property up. Bid on it. It'll take millions, Charlie, it's a whole damn peninsula. I've got some Cubans of my own, exiles who knew these heirs in the old country. I believe we have the inside track. By the way, I got a letter about you from Denise's lawyer. You owned one point in my Peony Condominiums and they wanted to know what it was worth. Did you have to tell them everything? Who is this fellow Pinsker?"

"I had no choice. They subpoenaed my tax returns."

"Ah, you poor nut, you overeducated boob. You come from good stock, and you weren't born dumb, you thrust it on yourself. And if you had to be an intellectual, why couldn't you be the tough type, a Herman Kahn or a Milton Friedman, one of those aggressive guys you read in *The Wall Street Journal*! You with your Woodrow Wilson and other dead numbers. I can't read the crap you write. Two sentences and I'm yawning. Pa should have slapped you around the way he did me. It would

have woken you up. Being his favorite did you no good. Then
you up and marry this fierce broad. She'd fit in with the Symbionese or the Palestine Liberation terrorists. When I saw her
sharp teeth and the way her hair grew twisty at the temples I
knew you were bound for outer space. You were born trying to
prove that life on this earth was not feasible. Okay, your case
is practically complete. Christ I wish I had your physical condition. You still play ball with Langobardi? Christ they say he's a
gentleman now. Tell me, how is your lawsuit?"

"Pretty bad. The court ordered me to post a bond. Two hundred thousand."

The figure made him pale. "They tied up your money? You'll
never see it again. Who's your lawyer, still your boyhood chum,
that fat-ass Szathmar?"

"No, it's Forrest Tomchek."

"I knew Tomchek at law school. The legal-statesman type of
crook. He's smoother than a suppository, only his supposito-
ries contain dynamite. And the judge is who?"

"A man named Urbanovich."

"Him I don't know. But he's been ruling against you and it's
all clear to me. They've gotten to him. Dirty work at the crossroads. He's using you to make some payoff. He owes somebody something and he's settling the score with your dough. I'll
check it out for you right now. You know a guy named Flanko,
in Chicago?"

"Solomon Flanko? He's a Syndicate lawyer."

"He'll know." Ulick rapidly punched out the numbers on
the telephone. "Flanko," he said when he got through, "this
is Julius Citrine down in Texas. There's a guy in domestic-
relations court named Urbanovich. Is he on the take?" He listened keenly. He said, "Thanks, Flanko, I'll get back to you
later." After hanging up, he chose a sport shirt. He said, "No,
Urbanovich doesn't seem to be on the take. He wants to make
a record on the bench. He's very slick. He's callous. If he is after
you, you and that money are going to be separated like yolks
and whites. Okay, write it off. We'll make you some more. Did
you put anything aside?"

"No."

"Nothing in a box? No numbered account anywhere? No bagman?"

"No."

He stared at me sternly. And then his face, grooved with age with worry and with indurated attitudes, relented somewhat and he smiled under the Acheson mustache. "To think that we should be brothers," he said. "It's positively a subject for a poem. You ought to suggest it to your pal Von Humboldt Fleisher. What ever happened, by the way, to your sidekick the poet? I came in a cab and took you night-clubbing in New York once in the Fifties. We had fun at the Copacabana, you remember?"

"That night on the town was great. Humboldt loved it. He's dead," I said.

Ulick put on a shirt of flame-blue Italian silk, a beautiful garment. It seemed to hunger for an ideal body. He drew it over his chest. On my last visit Ulick was slender and wore magnificent hip-huggers, melon-striped and ornamented on the seams with Mexican silver pesos. He had achieved this new figure in a crash diet. But even then the floor of his Cadillac was covered with peanut shells, and now he was fat again. I saw the fat old body which I had always known and which was completely familiar to me—the belly, the freckles on his undisciplined upper arms, and his elegant hands. I still saw in him the obese, choked-looking boy, the lustful conniving kid whose eyes continually pleaded not guilty. I knew him inside-out, even physically, remembering how he gashed open his thigh on a broken bottle in a Wisconsin creek fifty years ago and that I stared at the yellow fat, layers and layers of fat through which the blood had to well. I knew the mole on the back of his wrist, his nose broken and reset, his fierce false look of innocence, his snorts, and his smells. Wearing an orange football jersey, breathing through the mouth (before we could afford the nose-job), he held me on his shoulders so that I could watch the GAR parade on Michigan Boulevard. The year must have been 1923. He held me by the legs. His own legs were bulky in ribbed black stockings and he wore billowing, bloomerlike golf knickers. Afterward he stood behind me in the men's room of the Public

Library, the high yellow urinals like open sarcophagi, helping
me to fish my child's thing out from the complicated under-
clothes. In 1928 he became a baggage-smasher at American
Express. Then he worked at the bus terminal changing the
huge tires. He slugged it out with bullies in the street, and was
a bully himself. He put himself through the Lewis Institute,
nights, and through law school. He made and lost fortunes.
He took his own Packard to Europe in the early Fifties and
had it airlifted from Paris to Rome because driving over mountains bored him. He spent sixty or seventy thousand dollars
a year on himself alone. I never forgot any fact about him.
This flattered him. It also made him sore. And if I put so much
heart into remembering, what did it prove? That I loved Ulick?
There are clinical experts who think that such completeness of
memory is a hysterical symptom. Ulick himself said he had no
memory except for business transactions.

"So that screwball friend of yours Von Humboldt is dead.
He talked complicated gobbledygook and was worse dressed
than you, but I liked him. He sure could drink. What did he
die of?"

"Brain hemorrhage." I had to tell this virtuous lie. Heart
disease was taboo today. "He left me a legacy."

"What, he had dough?"

"No. Just papers. But when I went to the nursing home to
get them from his old uncle, whom should I run into but Menasha Klinger."

"Don't tell me—Menasha! The dramatic tenor, the redhead!
The fellow from Ypsilanti who boarded with us in Chicago?
I never saw such a damn deluded crazy bastard. He couldn't
carry a tune in a bucket. Spent his factory wages on lessons and
concert tickets. The one time he tried to do himself some good
he caught a dose, and then the clap-doctor shared his wages
with the music teacher. Is he old enough to be in a nursing
home? Well, I'm in my middle sixties and he was about eight
years ahead of me. You know what I found the other day? The
deed to the family burial plots in Waldheim. There are two
graves left. You wouldn't want to buy mine, would you? I'm
not going to lie around. I'm having myself cremated. I need

action. I'd rather go into the atmosphere. Look for me in the weather reports."

He too had a thing about the grave. He said to me on the day of Papa's funeral, "The weather is too damn warm and nice. It's awful. Did you ever see such a perfect afternoon?" The artificial grass carpet was rolled back by the diggers and under it in the tan sandy ground was a lovely cool hole. Aloft, far behind the pleasant May weather stood something like a cliff of coal. Aware of this coal cliff bearing down on the flowery cemetery—lilac time!—I broke out into a sweat. A small engine began to lower the coffin on smooth-running canvas bands. There never was a man so unwilling to go down, to pass through the bitter gates as Father Citrine—never a man so unfit to lie still. Papa, that great sprinter, that broken-field runner, and now brought down by the tackle of heavy death.

Ulick wanted to show me how Hortense had redecorated the children's rooms, he said. I knew that he was looking for candy bars. In the kitchen the cupboards were padlocked, and the refrigerator was out of bounds. "She's absolutely right," he said, "I must stop eating. I know you always said it was all false appetite. You advised me to put my finger down my throat and gag when I thought I was hungry. What's that supposed to do, reverse the diaphragm muscle or something? You were always a strong-willed fellow and a jock, chinning yourself and swinging dubs and dumbbells and punching the bag in the closet and running around the block and hanging from the trees like Tarzan of the Apes. You must have had a bad conscience about what you did when you locked yourself in the toilet. You're a sexy little bastard, never mind your big-time mental life. All this fucking art! I never understood the play you wrote. I went away in the second act. The movie was better, but even that had dreary parts. My old friend Ev Dirksen had a literary period, too. Did you know the Senator wrote poems for greeting cards? But he was a deep old phony—he was a real guy, as cynical as they come. He at least kidded his own hokum. Say, listen, I knew the country was headed for trouble as soon as there began to be big money in art."

"I don't know about that," I said. "To make capitalists out

of artists was a humorous idea of some depth. America decided to test the pretensions of the esthetic by applying the dollar measure. Maybe you read the transcript of Nixon's tape where he said he'd have no part of this literature and art shit. That was because he was out of step. He lost touch with the spirit of Capitalism. Misunderstood it completely."

"Here, here, don't start one of your lectures on me. You were always spouting some theory to us at the table—Marx, or Darwin, or Schopenhauer, or Oscar Wilde. If it wasn't one damn thing it was another. You had the biggest collection of Modern Library books on the block. And I'd bet you fifty to one you're ass-deep in a crank theory this minute. You couldn't live without it. Let's get going. We have to pick up the two Cubans and that Boston Irishman who's coming along. I never went for this art stuff, did I?"

"You tried becoming a photographer," I said.

"Me? When was that?"

"When they had funerals in the Russian Orthodox church—you remember, the stucco one with the onion dome on Leavitt, corner of Haddon?—they opened the coffins on the front steps and took pictures of the family with the corpse. You tried to make a deal with the priest and be appointed official photographer."

"Did I? Good for me!" It pleased Ulick to hear this. But somehow he smiled quietly, with mild fixity, musing at himself. He felt his hanging cheeks and said that he had shaved too close today, his skin was tender. It must have been a rising soreness from the breast that made him touchy about the face. This visit of mine, with its intimations of final parting, bothered him. He acknowledged that I had done right to come but he loathed me for it, too. I could see it his way. Why did I come flapping around him with my love, like a death-pest? There was no way for me to win, because if I hadn't come here he'd have held it against me. He needed to be wronged. He luxuriated in anger, and he kept accounts.

For fifty years, ritualistically, he had been repeating the same jokes, laughing at them because they were so infantile and stupid. "You know who's in the hospital? Sick people"; and, "I took first prize in history once, but they seen me taking it and made me put it back." And in the days when I still argued with him I would say, "You're a real populist and know-nothing, you've given your Russian Jewish brains away out of patriotism. You're a self-made ignoramus and a true American." But I had long ago stopped saying such things. I knew that he shut himself up in his office with a box of white raisins and read Arnold Toynbee and R. H. Tawney, or Cecil Roth and Salo Baron on Jewish history. When any of this reading cropped up in conversation he made sure to mispronounce the key words.

He drove his Cadillac under the glittering sun. Shadows that might have been cast by all the peoples of the earth flickered over it. He was an American builder and millionaire. The souls of billions fluttered like spooks over the polish of the great black hood. In distant Ethiopia people with dysentery as they squatted over ditches, faint and perishing, opened copies of *Business Week*, abandoned by tourists, and saw his face or faces like his. But it seemed to me that there were few faces like his, with the ferocious profile that brought to mind the Latin word *rapax* or one of Rouault's crazed death-dealing arbitrary kings. We passed his enterprises, the Peony Condominiums, the Trumbull Arms. We reviewed his many building projects. "Peony almost did me in. The architect talked me into putting the swimming pool on the roof. The concrete estimate was short by tons and tons, to say nothing of the fact that we overran the lot by a whole foot. Nobody ever found out, and I got rid of the damn thing. I had to take lots of paper." He meant a large second mortgage. "Now listen, Chuck, I know you need income. That crazy broad won't be satisfied until she's got your liver in her deepfreeze. I'm astonished, really astonished, that you didn't put away some dough. You must be bananas. People must be into you for some pretty good sums. You've invested plenty with this fellow Zitterbloom in New York who promised to shelter you, protect your income from Uncle Sam. He screwed you good. You'll never get a penny out of him. But others must owe you thousands. Make them offers. Take half, but in cash. I'll show you how to launder your money and we'll make it disappear. Then you go to Europe and stay there. What the hell do you want to be in Chicago for? Haven't you had enough of that boring place? For me it wasn't boring, because I went out and saw action. But you? You get up, look out, it's gray, you pull the curtain, and pick up a book. The town is roaring, but you don't hear it. If it hasn't killed your fucking heart you must be a man of iron, living like that. Listen, I have an idea. We'll buy a house on the Mediterranean together. My kids ought to learn a foreign language, have a little culture. You can tutor them. Listen, Chuck, if you can scrape together fifty thousand bucks I'll guarantee you a twenty-five-percent return, and you can live abroad on that."

So he talked to me, and I kept thinking about his fate. His fate! And I couldn't tell him my thoughts. They were not transmissible. Then what good were they? Their oddity and idiosyncrasy was a betrayal. Thoughts should be real. Words should have a definite meaning, and a man should believe what he said. This was Hamlet's complaint to Polonius when he said, "Words, words, words." The words are not *my* words, the thoughts not *my* thoughts. It's wonderful to have thoughts. They can be about the starry heavens and the moral law, the majesty of the one, the grandeur of the other. Ulick was not the only one that took lots of paper. We were all taking paper, plenty of it. And I wasn't about to pass any paper off on Ulick at a time like this. My new ideas, yes. They were more to the point. But I wasn't ready to mention them to him. I should have been ready. In the past, thoughts were too real to be kept like a cultural portfolio of stocks and bonds. But now we have mental assets. As many world-views as you like. Five different epistemologies in an evening. Take your choice. They're all agreeable, and not one is binding or necessary or has true strength or speaks straight to the soul. It was this paper-taking, this passing of highbrow currency that had finally put my back up. But my back had gone up slowly, reluctantly. So now I wasn't ready to tell Ulick anything of genuine interest. I had nothing to offer my brother, bracing himself for death. He didn't know what to think about it and was furious and frightened. It was my business as the thoughtful brother to tell him something. And actually I had important intimations to communicate as he faced the end. But intimations weren't much use. I hadn't done my homework. He'd say, "What do you mean, Spirit! Immortality? You mean that?" And I wasn't yet prepared to explain. I was just about to go into it seriously myself. Maybe Renata and I would take a train to Taormina and there I could sit in a garden and concentrate on this, giving it my whole mind.

Our serious Old World parents certainly had produced a pair of American clowns—one demonic millionaire clown, and one higher-thought clown. Ulick had been a fat boy I adored, he was a man precious to me, and now the fatal coastline was in view before him and I wanted to say, as he sat looking sick behind the wheel, that this brilliant, this dazing shattering delicious painful thing (I was referring to life) when it concluded, concluded only what we knew. It did not conclude the unknown, and I suspected that something further would ensue. But I couldn't prove a thing to this hardheaded brother of mine. He was terrified by the approaching blank, the flowering pleasant-day-in-May conclusion with the cliff of coal behind it, the nice cool hole in the ground. So all I could really say to him if I spoke would go as follows: "Listen here, do you remember when we moved down to Chicago from Appleton and lived in those dark rooms on Rice Street? And you were an obese boy and I a thin boy? And Mama doted on you with black eyes, and Papa flew into a fit because you dunked your bread in the cocoa? And before he escaped into the wood business he slaved in the bakery, the only work he could find, a gentleman but laboring at night? And came home and hung his white overalls behind the bathroom door so that the can always smelled like a bakeshop and the stiff flour fell off in scales? And he slept handsome and angry, on his side all day, with one hand under his face and the other between his drawn-up knees? While Mama boiled the wash on the coal stove, and you and I disappeared to school? Do you remember all that? Well, I'll tell you why I bring it up— there are good esthetic reasons why this should not be wiped from the record eternally. No one would put so much heart into things doomed to be forgotten and wasted. Or so much love. Love is gratitude for being. This love would be hate, Ulick, if the whole thing was nothing but a gyp." But a speech like this was certainly not acceptable to one of the biggest builders of southeast Texas. Such communications were prohibited under the going mental rules of a civilization that proved its right to impose such rules by the many practical miracles it performed, such as bringing me to Texas from New York in four hours, or sawing open his sternum and grafting new veins into his heart. To accept the finality of death was part of his package, however. There was to be no sign of us left. Only a few holes in the ground. Only the dirt of certain mole-runs cast up by extinct creatures that once burrowed here.

Meantime Ulick was saying that he was going to help me. For fifty thousand dollars he would sell me two points in an already completed project. "That ought to throw off between twenty-five and thirty percent. So if you got an income of fifteen thousand, plus what you picked up by your scribbles, you could be comfortable in one of the cheap countries like Yugoslavia or Turkey, and tell the Chicago gang to fuck itself."

"Lend me the fifty grand, then," I said. "I can raise that much in a year's time and repay you."

"I'd have to go to the bank for it myself," he said. But I was a Citrine, the same blood ran in our veins, and he couldn't expect me to accept so obvious a lie. He then said, "Charlie, don't ask me to do such an unbusinesslike thing."

"You mean that if you advanced me the dough, and if you didn't make a little something on me, your self-respect would suffer."

"With your gift for putting things succinctly, what things I could write," he said, "seeing that I know a thousand times as much as you. Of course I have to take a little advantage. After all, I'm the guy who puts the thing together—the whole ball of wax. But it would be the minimum basic. On the other hand, if you're tired of your way of life, and you sure ought to be, you could settle here in Texas and become filthy rich yourself. This place has big dimensions, Charlie, it's got scale."

But this reference to scale, to large dimensions, didn't fill me with business ambitions, it only reminded me of a stirring lecture by a clairvoyant that I had read on the plane. Now that did impress me deeply and I tried to comprehend it. After the two

Cubans and the man from Boston got into the Cadillac with us and began to smoke cigars, so that I became carsick, to think about clairvoyance was as good a thing to do as any other. The car tore out of town, following the coastline. "There's a great fish place along here," said Ulick. "I want to stop and buy Hortense some smoked shrimp and smoked marlin." We pulled in and got some. Starving, Ulick ate pieces of marlin before the fish was removed from the scale. Before it could be wrapped he had already pulled off the tail-end.

"Don't gorge," I said.

He paid no attention to this, and he was quite right. He gorged. Gaspar, his Cuban crony, took the wheel and Ulick sat in the back with his fish. He kept it under the seat. "I want to save this for Hortense, she dotes on it," he said. But at this rate nothing would be left for Hortense. It wasn't for me to conjure away a whole lifetime of such extraordinary greed, and I should have let him be. But I had to put in my brotherly two cents, giving him just the touch of remorse you wanted from your family on the eve of open-heart surgery as you crammed yourself with smoked fish.

At the same time I was concentrating on the vision the clairvoyant had described in such extraordinary detail. Just as soul and spirit left the body in sleep, they could also be withdrawn from it in full consciousness with the purpose of observing the inner life of man. The first result of this conscious withdrawal is that everything is reversed. Instead of seeing the external world as we normally do with senses and intellect, initiates can see the circumscribed self from without. Soul and spirit are poured out upon the world which normally we perceive from within—mountains clouds forests seas. This external world we no longer see, for we are *it*. The outer world is now the inner. Clairvoyant, you are in the space you formerly beheld. From this new circumference you look back to the center, and at the center is your own self. That self, your self, is now the external world. Dearest God, there you see the human form, your own form. You see your own skin and the blood inside, and you see this as you see an external object. But what an object! Your eyes are now two radiant suns, filled with light. Your eyes are

identified by this radiance. Your ears are identified by sound.
From the skin comes a glow. From the human form emanate
light, sound, and sparkling electrical forces. This is the physical
being when the Spirit looks at it. And even the life of thought is
visible within this radiance. Your thoughts can be seen as dark
waves passing through the body of light, says this clairvoyant.
And with this glory comes also a knowledge of stars which exist
in the space where we formerly felt ourselves to stand inert. We
are not inert but in motion together with these stars. There is
a star world within us that can be seen when the Spirit takes a
new vantage point outside its body. As for the musculature it is
a precipitate of Spirit and the signature of the cosmos is in it. In
life and in death the signature of the cosmos is within us.

We were now driving through swampy, reefy places. There
were mangroves. Here was the Gulf sparkling alongside. There
was also a great deal of clutter, for the peninsula was a dumping
ground and an old-car cemetery. The afternoon was hot. The
great black Cadillac opened and we got out. The men, excited,
striding off in all directions, studying the ground, trying to get
the lay of the land and already struggling with future building problems. Gorgeous palaces, stunning towers, and thrilling
gardens of crystal dew arose from their flaming minds.

"Solid rock," said the Boston Irishman, scraping the ground
with his white calfskin shoe.

He had confided to me that he wasn't an Irishman at all,
he was a Pole. His name, Casey, was shortened from Casi-
mirz. Because I was Ulick's brother, he took me for a businessman. With a name like Citrine what else would I be?
"This guy is a real creative entrepreneur. Your brother Julius
is imaginative—a genius builder," said Casey. As he spoke, his
flat freckled face gave me the false smile that swept the country
about fifteen years ago. To achieve it, you drew your upper lip
away from the teeth, while looking at your interlocutor with
charm. Alec Szathmar did it better than anyone. Casey was
a large, almost monumental and hollow-looking person who
resembled a plainclothes dick from Chicago—same type. His
ears were amazingly crinkled, like Chinese cabbage. He spoke
with pedantic courtliness, as if he had taken a correspondence

course originating in Bombay. I rather liked that. I saw that he wanted me to put in a good word for him with Ulick, and I understood his need. Casey was retired, a partial invalid, and he was seeking ways to protect his fortune from inflationary shrinkage. Also he was looking for action. Action or death. Money can't mark time. Now that I was committed to spiritual investigation, many matters presented themselves to me in a clearer light. I saw, for instance, what volcanic emotions Ulick was dissembling. He stood on a rubble elevation, eating smoked shrimps from the paper bag, and pretended to take a cool view of this peninsula as a development site. "It's promising," he said. "It's got possibilities. But there'd be some terrible headaches here. You'd have to start by blasting. There'll be a hell of a water problem. Sewage, too. And I don't even know how this is zoned."

"Why, what you could do with this is a first-class hotel," said Casey. "Apartment houses on each side, with ocean frontage, beaches, a yacht basin, tennis courts."

"It sounds easy," said Ulick. Oh cunning Ulick, my darling brother! I could see that he was in an ecstasy of craftiness. This was a place that might be worth hundreds of millions, and he came upon it just as the surgeons were honing up for him. A fat cumbered clogged ailing heart threatened to lay him in the grave just as his soul came into its most brilliant opportunity. You could be sure that when you were dreaming your best somebody would start banging at the door—the famous Butcher Boy from Porlock. In this case, the kid's name was Death. I understood Ulick and his passions. Why not? I was a lifetime Ulick subscriber. So I knew what a paradise he saw in this dumping ground—the towers in a sea-haze, the imported grass gemmy with moisture, the pools surrounded by gardenias where broads sunned their beautiful bodies, and all the dark Mexican servitors in embroidered shirts murmuring *"Sí, señor"*—there were plenty of wetbacks crossing the border.

I also knew how Ulick's balance sheets would look. They'd read like Chapman's *Homer,* illuminated pages, realms of gold. If zoning ordinances interfered with this opportunity he was prepared to lay out a million bucks in bribes. I saw that in his face. He was the positive, I the negative sinner. He might have been wearing sultry imperial colors. I might have been buttoned into a suit of Dr. Denton's Sleepers. Of course I had a big thing to wake up to, a very big challenge. Now I was only simmering, still, and it would be necessary at last to come to a full boil. I had business on behalf of the entire human race—a responsibility not only to fulfill my own destiny but to carry on for certain failed friends like Von Humboldt Fleisher who had never been able to struggle through into higher wakefulness. My very fingertips rehearsed how they would work the keys of the trumpet, imagination's trumpet, when I got ready to blow it at last. The peals of that brass would be heard beyond the earth, out in space itself. When that Messiah, that savior faculty the imagination was roused, finally we could look again with open eyes upon the whole shining earth.

The reason why the Ulicks of this world (and also the Cantabiles) had such sway over me was that they knew their desires clearly. These desires might be low but they were pursued in full wakefulness. Thoreau saw a woodchuck at Walden, its eyes more fully awake than the eyes of any farmer. Of course that woodchuck was on his way to wipe out some hard-working farmer's crop. It was all very well for Thoreau to build up woodchucks and fume at farmers. But if society is a massive moral failure farmers have something to sleep about. Or look at the present moment. Ulick was awake to money; I, with a craving to do right swelling in my heart, was aware that the good liberal sleep of American boyhood had lasted half a century. And even now I had come to get something from Ulick—I was revisiting the conditions of childhood under which my heart had been inspired. Traces of the perfume of that sustaining time, that early and sweet dream-time of goodness still clung to him. Just as his face was turning toward (perhaps) his final sun, I still wanted something from him.

Ulick treated his two Cubans as deferentially as the Polish Casey treated him. These were his indispensable negotiators. They had gone to school with the proprietors. At times they hinted that they were all cousins. To me they looked like Caribbean playboys, a recognizable type—strong fatty men with fresh round faces and blue, not especially kindly, eyes. They were golfers, water-skiers, horsemen, polo-players, racing-car drivers, twin-engine pilots. They knew the Riviera, the Alps, Paris, and New York as well as the night clubs and gambling joints of the West Indies. I said to Ulick, "These are sharp guys. Exile hasn't dulled them any."

"I know they're sharp," said Ulick. "I'll have to find a way to put them into the deal. This is no time to be petty—my God, Chuckie, there's plenty here for everybody this time," he whispered.

Before this conversation occurred we had made two stops. As we were returning from the peninsula, Ulick said he wanted to stop at a tropical fruit farm he knew. He had promised Hortense to bring home persimmons. The fish had been eaten. We sat with him under a tree sucking at the breast-sized, flame-colored fruit. The juice spurted over his sport shirt, and seeing that it now had to go to the cleaner anyway he wiped his fingers on it as well. His eyes had shrunk, and moved back and forth rapidly in his head. He was not, just then, with us. The Cubans took Hortense's golf bag from the trunk of the car and began to amuse themselves by driving balls across the fields. They were superb powerful golfers, despite their heavy bottoms and the folds of flesh that formed under their chins as they addressed the ball. They took turns, and with elastic strength whacked the elastic balls—crack!—into the unknown. It was pleasing to watch this. But when we were ready to leave it turned out that the ignition keys had gotten locked up in the trunk. Tools were borrowed from the persimmon farmer, and in half an hour the Cubans had punched out the lock. Of course they damaged the paint of the new Cadillac. But that was nothing. "Nothing, nothing!" said Ulick. He was burned up, too, naturally, but these Gonzalez cousins could not be freely hated now. Ulick said, "What is it—some hardware, a touch of paint?" He rose, heavy, and said, "Let's stop now and get a drink and something to eat."

We went to a Mexican restaurant where he devoured an order

of chicken breasts with *molé* sauce—a bitter spicy chocolate gravy. I could not finish mine. He took my plate. He ordered pecan pie à la mode, and then a cup of Mexican chocolate.

When we got home I said I would go to my motel and lie down; I was very tired. We stood together in his garden for a while.

"Do you even begin to get the picture of this peninsula?" he said. "With this land I could do the most brilliant piece of business in my life. These smart-ass Cubans will have to go along. I'll sweep those bastards with me. I'll develop a plan—while I'm convalescing I'll get a survey done, and a map, and when I make my pitch to those lazy Spanish jet-set bastards, I'll be prepared with architect's models and all my financing ready. I mean *if,* you know. Do you want to try some of these loquats?" He reached gloomily into one of his trees and picked handfuls of fruit.

"I'm bilious now," I said, "from all I've eaten."

He stood plucking and eating, spitting out stones and skins, his gaze fixed beyond me. He wiped at his Acheson mustache from time to time. Arrogant, haggard, he was filled with incommunicable thoughts. These were written dense and small on every inch of his inner surface. "I won't see you in Houston before the operation, Charlie," he said. "Hortense is against it. She says you'll make me too emotional, and she's a woman who knows what she's talking about. Now this is what I want to say to you, Charlie. If I die, you marry Hortense. She's a better woman than you'll ever find by yourself. She's straight as they come. I trust her one hundred percent, and you know what that means. She acts a little rough but she's made me a wonderful life. You'll never have another financial problem, I can tell you that."

"Have you discussed this with Hortense?"

"No, I've written it in a letter. She probably guesses that I want her to marry a Citrine, if I die on the table." He stared hard at me and said, "She'll do what I tell her. So will you."

Late noon stood like a wall of gold. And a mass of love was between us, and neither Ulick nor I knew what to do with it. "Well, all right, good-by." He turned his back on me. I got into the rented car and took off.

Hortense, on the telephone, said, "Well, he made it. They took veins from his leg and attached them to his heart. He's going to be stronger than ever now."

"Thank God for that. He's out of danger?"

"Oh, sure, and you can see him tomorrow."

During the operation Hortense hadn't wanted my company. I attributed this to wife/brother rivalry, but later I changed my mind. I recognized a kind of boundlessness or hysteria in my affection which, in her place, I would have avoided, too. But on the phone there was a tone in her voice I had never heard before. Hortense raised exotic flowers and hollered at dogs and men—that was her style. This time, however, I felt that I shared what as a rule she reserved for the flowers and my attitude toward her changed entirely. Humboldt used to tell me, and he was a harsh judge of character himself, that far from being mild I was actually too tough. My reform (if it was one) would have pleased him. In this critical age, following science (fantasy-science is really what it is) people think they are being "illusionless" about one another. The law of parsimony makes detraction more realistic. Therefore I had had my reservations about Hortense. Now I thought she was a good broad. I had been lying on the king-sized motel bed reading some of Humboldt's papers and books by Rudolf Steiner and his disciples, and I was in a state.

I don't know what I expected to see when I entered Ulick's room—bloodstains, perhaps, or bone-dust from the power saw; they had pried open the man's rib cage and taken out his heart; they had shut it off like a small motor and laid it aside and started it up again when they were ready. I couldn't get over this. But I came into a room filled with flowers and sunlight. Over Ulick's head was a small brass plate engraved with the names of Papa and Mama. His color was green and yellow, the bone of his nose stuck out, his white mustache grew harshly under it. His look, however, was happy. And his fierceness was still there, I was glad to see. He was weak, of course,

but he was all business again. If I had told him that I thought
he looked a shade other-worldly he would have listened with
contempt. Here was the polished window, here were the grand
roses and dahlias, and here was Mrs. Julius Citrine in a knitted
trouser-suit, her legs plump, low to the ground, an attractive
short strong woman. Life went on. What life? This life. And
what was this life? But now was not a time to be metaphysical.
I was very eager, very happy. I kept things under my peculiar
hat, however.

"Well, kid," he said, his voice still thin. "You're glad, aren't
you?"

"That's right, Ulick."

"A heart can be fixed like a shoe. Resoled. Even new uppers.
Like Novinson on Augusta Street . . ."

I suppose that I was Ulick's nostalgia-man. What he couldn't
himself remember, he loved to hear from me. Tribal chieftains
in Africa had had official remembrancers about them; I was
Ulick's remembrancer. "Novinson in his window had trench
souvenirs from 1917," I said. "He had brass shell casings and
a helmet with holes in it. Over his bench was a colored cartoon
made by his son Izzie of a customer squirted in the face and
leaping into the air yelling, 'Hilp!' The message was, Don't Get
Soaked for Shoe Repairs."

Ulick said to Hortense, "All you have to do is turn him on."

She smiled from her upholstered chair, her legs crossed. The
color of her knitted suit was old rose, or young brick. She was
as white-faced as a powdered Kabuki dancer, for despite her
light eyes her face was Japanese—the cheekbones and the chub
lips, painted crimson, did that.

"Well, Ulick, I'll be going, now that you're out of the
woods."

"Listen, Chuck, there's something I've always wanted that
you can buy for me in Europe. A beautiful seascape. I've
always loved paintings of the sea. Nothing but the sea. I don't
want to see a rock, or a boat, or any human beings. Only mid-
ocean on a terrific day. Water water everywhere: Get me that,
Chuckie, and I'll pay five grand, eight grand. Phone me if you
come across the right thing and I'll wire the money."

It was implied that I was entitled to a commission—unofficial, of course. It would be unnatural for me not to chisel a little. This was the form his generosity sometimes took. I was touched.

"I'll go to the galleries," I said.

"Good. Now what about the fifty thousand—have you thought about my offer?"

"Oh, I'd certainly like to take you up on that. I need the income badly. I've already cabled a friend of mine—Thaxter. He's on his way to Europe on the *France*. I told him that I was willing to go to Madrid to try my hand at a project he dreamed up. A cultural Baedeker . . . So I'm going to Madrid now."

"Fine. You need projects. Get back to work. I know you. When you stop work you're in trouble. That broad in Chicago has brought your work to a standstill, with her lawyers. She knows what the stoppage does to you—Hortense, we have to look after Charlie a little, now."

"I agree we should," said Hortense. From moment to moment I more and more admired and loved Hortense. What a wonderful and sensitive woman she was, really, and what emotional versatility the Kabuki mask concealed. Her gruffness had put me off. But behind the gruffness, what goodness, what a rose garden. "Why not make more of an effort to settle with Denise?" she said.

"She doesn't want to settle," said Ulick. "She wants his gizzard in a glass on her mantelpiece. When he offers her more dough she raises the ante again. It's no use. The guy is pissing against the wind in Chicago. He needs broads, but he picks women who cripple him. So get back to business, Chuck, and start turning the stuff out. If you don't keep your name before the public people will assume you're gone and they missed your obituary. How much can you get out of this culture-guide deal? Fifty? Hold out for a hundred. Don't forget the taxes. Did you get caught in the stock market too? Of course you did. You're an America expert. You have to experience what the whole country experiences. You know what I'd do? I'd buy old railroad bonds. Some of them are selling for forty cents on the dollar. Only railroads can move the coal, and the energy crisis is bringing coal back strongly. We ought to acquire some coal-lands, too. Under Indiana and Illinois, the whole Midwest is a solid mass of coal. It can be crushed, mixed with water, and pumped through pipelines, but that's not economical. Even water is getting to be a scarce commodity," said Ulick, off on one of his capitalistic fugues. On this subject of coal he was a romantic poet, a Novalis speaking of earth-mysteries. "You get together some dough. Send it and I'll invest for you."

"Thank you, Ulick," I said.

"Right. Bug off. Stay in Europe, what the hell do you want to come back for? Get me a seascape."

He and Hortense went back to their development plans for the Cubans' peninsula. He fiercely applied his genius to maps and blueprints while Hortense dialed bankers for him on the telephone. I kissed my brother and his wife and drove my Avis to the airport.

• • •

Although I was full of joy, I knew that things were not going well in Milan. Renata troubled my mind. I didn't know what she was up to. From the motel last night I had talked with her on the telephone. I asked her what was happening. She said, "I'm not going into this on a transatlantic call, Charlie, it's too expensive." But then she wept for two solid minutes. Even Renata's intercontinental sobs were fresher than other women's close at hand. After this, still tearful, she laughed at herself and said, "Well, that was two-bits a tear, at least. Yes, I'll meet you in Madrid, you bet I will."

"*Is* Signor Biferno your father?" I said.

"You sound as if the suspense is killing you. Imagine what it's doing to me. Yes, I think Biferno is my dad. I *feel* he is."

"What does he feel? He must be a glorious-looking man. No punk could beget a woman like you, Renata."

"He's old and caved in. He looks like somebody they forgot to take off from Alcatraz. And he hasn't talked to me. He won't do it."

"Why?"

"Before I left, Mother didn't tell me that she was all set to sue him. Her papers were served on him the day before I arrived. It's a paternity suit. Child support. Damages."

"Child support? You're almost thirty. And the Señora didn't tell you that she was plotting this?" I said.

"When you sound incredulous, when you take that I-can't-believe-it tone I know you're really in a furious rage. You're sore about the money this trip is costing."

"Renata, why did the Señora have to sock Biferno with summonses just as you're about to solve the riddle of your birth?—to which she should have the answer, by the way. You go on this errand for the sake of your heart, or your identity—you've spent weeks fretting about your identity crisis—and then your own mother pulls this. You can't blame me for being baffled. It's wild. What a plan for conquest the old girl has hatched. All this—fire-bombing, victory, unconditional surrender."

"You can't bear to hear of women suing men. You don't know what I owe my mother. Bringing up a girl like me was a pretty rough project. As for what she pulled on me, remember what people pull on you. This Cantabile, may he rot in hell, or Szathmar or Thaxter. Watch out for Thaxter. Take the month at the Ritz but don't sign any contract or anything. Thaxter will take his money and stick you with all the work."

"No, Renata, he's peculiar, but he is basically trustworthy."

"Good-by, darling," she said. "I've missed you like mad. Remember what you once said to me about the British lion standing up with his paw on the globe? You said that when you set your paw on my globe it was better than an empire. The sun never sets on Renata! I'll be waiting in Madrid."

"You seem to be washed up in Milan," I said.

She answered by telling me, like Ulick, that I must begin to work again. "Only for God's sake don't write that pedantic stuff you're unloading on me lately," she said.

But now the whole Atlantic must have surged between us; or perhaps the communications satellite was peppered with glittering particles in the upper air. Anyway, the conversation crumpled and ended.

But when the plane took off I felt unusually free and light—trundled out on the bowed eagle legs of the 747, lifted into flight on the great wings, the machine passing from level to level into brighter and brighter atmospheres while I gripped my briefcase between my feet like a rider and my head lay on the bosom of the seat. On balance I believed that the Señora's wicked and goofy lawsuit improved my position. She discredited herself. My kindliness, my patience, my sanity, my superiority would gain on Renata. All I had to do was to keep my mouth shut and to sit tight. Thoughts about her came thick and fast—all kinds of things connecting what-beautiful-girls-contributed-to-the-unfolding-destiny-of-capitalist-Democracy to, far beyond this, deeper questions. Let me see if I can clarify any of it. Renata was very nearly aware, as many people now are, of "leading a life in history." Now Renata was, as a biologically noble beauty, in a false category—Goya's *Maja* smoking a cigar, or Wallace Stevens's Fretful Concubine who whispered "Pfui!" That is she wished to defy and outsmart the category to which she was assigned by common opinion. But with this she also collaborated. And if there is one historical assignment for us it is to break with false categories. Vacate the personae. I once suggested to her, "A woman like you can be called a dumb broad only if Being and Knowledge are entirely separate. But if Being is also a form of Knowledge, one's own Being is one's own accomplishment in some degree. . . ."

"Then I'm not a dumb broad after all. I can't be, if I'm so beautiful. That's super! You've always been kind to me, Charlie."

"Because I really love you, kid."

Then she wept a little because, sexually, she was not all that she was cracked up to be. She had her hang-ups. Sometimes she accused herself wildly, crying, "The truth! I'm a phony! I like it better under the table." I told her not to exaggerate. I explained to her that the Ego had emancipated itself from the Sun and it must undergo the pain of this emancipation (Steiner). The modern sexual ideology could never counteract this. Programs of uninhibited natural joy could never free us from the universal tyranny of selfhood. Flesh and blood never could live up to such billing. And so on.

Anyway, we were lofted to an altitude of six miles in a great

747, an illuminated cavern, a theater, a cafeteria, the Atlantic in pale daylight raging below. According to the pilot, ships were taking hard punishment in the storm. But from this altitude the corrugations of the seas looked no higher to the eye than the ridges of your palate feel to the tongue. The stewardess served whisky and Hawaiian macadamia nuts. We plunged across the longitudinal lines of the planet, this deep place that I was learning to think of as the great school of souls, the material seat of the spirit. More than ever I believed that the soul with its occasional glimmers of the Good couldn't expect to get anywhere in a single lifetime. Plato's theory of immortality was not, as some scholars tried to make it, a metaphor. He literally meant it. A single span could only make virtue desperate. Only a fool would try to reconcile the Good with one-shot mortality. Or as Renata, that dear girl, might put it, "Better none than only one."

In a word, I allowed myself to think what I pleased and let my mind go in every direction. But I felt that the plane and I were headed the right way. Madrid was a smart choice. In Spain I could begin to set myself straight. Renata and I would enjoy a quiet month. I put it to myself—thinking of the carpenter's level—that maybe our respective bubbles could be coaxed back to the center. Then the things that really satisfied, naturally satisfied, all hearts and minds might be attempted. If people felt like fakers when they spoke of the True and the Good this was because their bubble was astray, because they believed they were following the rules of scientific thought, which they didn't understand one single bit. But I had no business to be toying with fire either, or playing footsie with the only revolutionary ideas left. Actuarially speaking, I had only a decade left to make up for a life-span largely misspent. There was no time to waste even on remorse and penitence. I felt also that Humboldt, out there in death, stood in need of my help. The dead and the living still formed one community. This planet was still the base of operations. There was Humboldt's bungled life, and my bungled life, and it was up to me to do something, to give a last favorable turn to the wheel, to transmit moral understanding from the earth where you can get it to the next existence where you needed it. Of course I had my other dead. It wasn't Humboldt alone. I also had a substantial suspicion of lunacy. But why should my receptivity fall under such suspicion? On the contrary, etcetera. I concluded, We'll see what we shall see. We flew through unshadowed heights, and in the pure upper light I saw that the beautiful brown booze in my glass contained many crystalline corpuscles and thermal lines of heat-generating cold fluid. This was how I entertained myself and passed the time. We were held up in Lisbon for quite a while and reached Madrid hours off schedule.

The 747, with its whale's anterior hump, opened, and passengers poured out, eager Charlie Citrine among them. Tourists in this year, I had read in the airline magazine, outnumbered the Spanish population by about ten million. Still, what American could believe that his arrival in the Old World was not a special event? Behavior under these skies meant more than in Chicago. It had to. There was significant space here. I couldn't help feeling this. And Renata, also surrounded by significant space, was waiting at the Ritz. Meantime, my charter-flight countrymen, a party of old folks from Wichita Falls, shuffled fatigued down the long corridors and resembled ambulatory patients in a hospital. I passed them like a streak. I was first at the passport window, first at the baggage conveyor. And then—my bag was the last bag of all. The Wichita Falls party was gone and I was beginning to think my bag with its elegant wardrobe, its Hermès neckties, its old chaser's monkey-jackets, and so forth was lost when I saw it wobbling, solitary, on the long, long trail of rollers. It came toward me like an uncorseted woman sauntering over cobblestones.

Then in the cab to the hotel I was pleased with myself again and thought I had done well to arrive late at night when the roads were empty. There was no delay; the taxi drove furiously fast, I could go to Renata's room at once and get out of my clothes and into bed with her. Not from lust but from eagerness. I was full of a boundless need to give and take comfort. I can't tell you how much I agreed with Meister Eckhart about the eternal youth of the soul. From first to last, he says, it remains the same, it has only one age. The rest of us, however, is not so stable. So overlooking this discrepancy, denying decay, and always starting life over and over doesn't make much sense. Here, with Renata, I wanted to have another go at it, swearing up and down that I would be more tender and she would be more faithful and humane. It didn't make sense, of course. But it mustn't be forgotten that I had been a complete idiot until I was forty and a partial idiot after that. I would always be something of an idiot. Still, I felt that there was hope and raced in the cab toward Renata. I was entering the final zones of mortality, expecting that here in Spain of all places, here in a bedroom, all the right human things would—at last!—happen.

Dignified flunkies in the circular reception hall of the Ritz took my bag and briefcase and I came through the revolving door looking for Renata. Certainly she would not be waiting for me in one of those stately chairs. A queenly woman couldn't sit in the lobby with the night staff at 3 a.m. No, she must be lying awake, beautiful, humid, breathing quietly, and waiting for her extraordinary, her one-and-only Citrine. There were other suitable men, handsomer, younger, energetic, but of me Charlie there was only one, and Renata I believed was aware of this.

For reasons of self-respect she had objected on the telephone to sharing a suite with me. "It doesn't matter in New York but in Madrid, with different names on our passports, it's just too whorey. I know it's going to cost double but that's the way it's got to be."

I asked the man at the switchboard to ring Mrs. Koffritz.

"We have no Mrs. Koffritz," was his answer.

"A Mrs. Citrine, then?" I said.

There was no Mrs. Citrine either. That was a wicked disappointment. I walked across the circular carpet under the dome to the concierge. He handed me a wire from Milan. SLIGHT DELAY. BIFERNO DEVELOPING. PHONING TOMORROW. I ADORE YOU.

I was then shown to my room, but I was in no condition to admire its effects: richly Spanish, with carved chests and thick drapes, with Turkish carpets and *fauteuils*, a marble bathroom and old-fashioned electrical fixtures in the grand old *Wagon-*

Lit style. The bed stood in a curtained alcove and was covered in watered silk. My heart was behaving badly as I crept in naked and laid my head on the bolster. There was no word from Thaxter, either, and he should have reached Paris by now. I had to communicate with him. Thaxter would have to inform Stewart in New York that I was accepting his invitation to stay in Madrid for a month as his guest. This was a fairly important matter. I was down to four thousand dollars and couldn't afford two suites at the Ritz. The dollar was taking a beating, the peseta was unrealistically high, and I didn't believe that Biferno was developing into anything.

My heart was dumbly aching. I refused to give it the words it would have uttered. I condemned the state I was in. It was idle, idle, idle. Many thousands of miles from my last bed in Texas I lay stiff and infinitely sad, my body temperature at least three degrees below normal. I had been brought up to detest self-pity. It was part of my American training to be energetic, and positive, and a thriving energy system, and an achiever, and having achieved two Pulitzer prizes and the Zig-Zag medal and a good deal of money (of which I was robbed by a Court of Equity), I had set myself a final and ever higher achievement, namely, an indispensable metaphysical revision, a more correct way of thinking about the question of death! And now I remembered a quotation from Coleridge, cited by Von Humboldt Fleisher in the papers he had left me, about quaint metaphysical opinions. How did it go? Quaint metaphysical opinions, in an hour of anguish, were playthings by the bedside of a child deadly sick. I got up then to rummage in the briefcase for the exact quotation. But then I stopped. I recognized that to be afraid that Renata was ditching me was far different from being deadly sick. Besides, damn her, why should she give me an hour of anguish and make me stoop and rummage naked, pulling out a dead man's papers by the light of this *Wagon-Lit* lamp. I decided that I was only overtired and suffering from jet lag.

I turned from Humboldt and Coleridge to the theories of George Swiebel. I did what George would have done. I ran myself a hot bath and stood on my head while the tub was filling. I went on to do a wrestler's bridge, resting all my weight on my heels and on the back of my head. After this I performed some of the exercises recommended by the famous Dr. Jacobsen, the relaxation and sleep expert. I had studied his manual. You were supposed to cast out tension toe by toe and finger by finger. This was not a good idea, for it brought back to me what Renata did with toes and fingers in moments of erotic ingenuity. (I never knew about the toes until Renata taught me.) After all this I simply went back to bed and prayed my upset soul to go out for a while, please, and let the poor body have some rest. I picked up her telegram, fixing my eyes on I ADORE YOU. Studying this hard, I decided to believe that she was telling the truth. As soon as I performed this act of faith I slept. For many hours I was out cold in the curtained alcove.

Then my telephone rang. In the shuttered curtained blackness I felt for the switch. It was not to be found. I picked up the phone and asked the operator, "What time is it?"

It was twenty minutes after eleven. "A lady is on her way up to your room," the switchboard told me.

A lady! Renata was here. I dragged the drapes aside from the windows and ran to brush my teeth and wash my face. I pulled on a bathrobe, gave a swipe at my hair to cover the bald spot, and was drying myself with one of the heavy luxurious towels when the knocker ticked many times, like a telegraph key, only more delicately, suggestively. I shouted, "Darling!" I swept the door open and found Renata's old mother before me. She was wearing her dark travel costume, with many of her own arrangements, including the hat and the veil. "Señora!" I said.

She entered in her medieval garments. Just over the threshold she reached a gloved hand behind her and brought in Renata's little boy, Roger. "Roger!" I said. "Why is Roger in Madrid? What are you doing here, Señora?"

"Poor baby. He was sleeping on the plane. I had them carry him off."

"But Christmas with the grandparents in Milwaukee—what about that?"

"His grandfather had a stroke. May die. As for his father, we can't locate the man. I couldn't keep Roger with me, my apartment is small."

"What about Renata's apartment?"

No, the Señora, with her *affaires de cœur*, couldn't take care of a small child. I had met some of her gentlemen friends. It was wise not to expose the child to them. As a rule I avoided thinking about her romances.

"Does Renata know?"

"Of course she knows we're coming. We discussed it on the telephone. Please order breakfast for us, Charles. Will you eat some nice Frosted Flakes, Roger darling? For me, hot chocolate and also some *croissants* and a glass of brandy."

The child sat bowed over the arm of the tall Spanish chair.

"Come on, kid," I said, "lie on my bed." I pulled off his small shoes and led him into the alcove. The Señora watched as I covered him and drew the curtains. "So Renata told you to bring him here."

"Of course. You may be here for months. It was the only thing to do."

"When is Renata arriving?"

"Tomorrow is Christmas," said the Señora.

"Terrific. What does your statement mean? Will she be here for Christmas or is she having Christmas with her father in Milan? Is she getting anywhere? How can she, if you're suing Mr. Biferno?"

"We've been in the air for ten hours, Charles. I'm not strong enough to answer questions. Please order breakfast. I wish you would shave also. I really can't bear a man's unshaven face across the table."

This made me consider the Señora's own face. She had wonderful dignity. She sat in her wimple like Edith Sitwell. Her power with her daughter, whom I so badly needed, was very great. There was a serpentine dryness about her eyes. Yes, the Señora was bananas. However, her composure, with its large content of furious irrationality, was unassailable.

"I'll shave while you're waiting for your cocoa, Señora. Why, I wonder, did you choose such a time to sue Signor Biferno?"

"Isn't that my own business?"

"Isn't it Renata's business also?"

"You speak like Renata's husband," she said. "Renata went

to Milan to give that man a chance to acknowledge his daughter. But there is a mother in the case too. Who brought the girl up and made such an extraordinary woman of her? Who taught her class and all the important lessons of a woman? The whole injustice should be dealt with. The man has three plain ugly daughters. If he wants this marvelous child he had by me, let him settle his bill. Don't try to teach a Latin woman about such things, Charles."

I sat in my not entirely clean beige silk robe. The sash was too long and the tassels had dragged on the floor for many years. The waiter came, the tray was uncovered with a flourish, and we breakfasted. As the Señora snuffed up her cognac I observed the grain of her skin, the touch of whisker on her lip, the arched nose with its operatic nostrils and the peculiar chicken luster of her eyeballs. "I got the TWA tickets from your travel agent, that Portuguese lady who wears a paisley turban, Mrs. Da Cintra. Renata told me to charge them. I didn't have a cent." The Señora was like Thaxter in this regard—people who could tell you with pride, even with delight, how broke they were. "And I've taken a room here for Roger and me. My institute is closed this week. I will have a holiday."

At the mention of institute, I thought of a loony bin, but no, she was speaking of the secretarial school where she taught commercial Spanish. I had always suspected that she was actually a Magyar. Be that as it might, the students appreciated her. No school without spectacular eccentrics and crazy hearts is worth attending. But she would have to retire soon, and who would push the Señora's wheelchair? Was it possible that she now saw me in that capacity? But perhaps the old woman, like Humboldt, dreamed that she could make her fortune in a lawsuit. And why not? Perhaps there was a judge in Milan like my Urbanovich.

"So we will have Christmas together," said the Señora.

"The kid is very pale. Is he sick?"

"It's only fatigue," said the Señora.

Roger, however, came down with the flu. The hotel sent an excellent Spanish doctor, a graduate of Northwestern who reminisced with me about Chicago and soaked me. I paid him an American fee. I gave the Señora money for Christmas presents and she bought all kinds of objects. On Christmas Day, thinking of my own girls, I felt quite low. I was glad to have Roger there and kept him company, reading him fairy tales and cutting and pasting long chains from the Spanish newspapers. There was a humidifier in the room which heightened the odors of paste and paper. Renata did not telephone.

I recalled that I had spent the Christmas of 1924 in the TB sanatorium. The nurses gave me a thick-striped peppermint candy cane and a red openwork Christmas stocking filled with chocolate coins wrapped in gilt, but it was depressing joy and I longed for Papa and Mama and for my wicked stout brother, Julius, even. Now I had survived this quaking and heartsickness and was an elderly fugitive, the prey of Equity, sitting in Madrid, cutting and pasting with sighs. The kid was pale with fever, his breath flavored with the chocolate and paste, and he was absorbed in a paper chain that went twice about the room and had to be strung over the chandelier. I tried to be nice and calm but now and then my feelings gave a wash (oh those lousy feelings) like the water in a ferry slip when the broad-beamed boat pushes in and the backing engines churn up the litter and drowned orange rinds. This happened when my controls failed and I imagined what Renata might be doing in Milan, the room she was in, the man who was with her, the positions they took, the other fellow's toes. I was determined that no, I wouldn't tolerate being wrung abandoned sea-sick ship-wrecked castaway. I tried quoting Shakespeare to myself—words to the effect that Caesar and Danger were two lions whelped on the same day, and Caesar the elder and more terrible. But that was aiming too high and it didn't work. In addition the twentieth century is not easily impressed by pains of this nature. It has seen everything. After the holocausts, you can't blame it for lacking interest in private difficulties of this sort. I myself recited a brief list of the real questions before the world—the oil embargo, the collapse of Britain, famines in India and Ethiopia, the future of democracy, the fate of humankind. This did no more good than Julius Caesar. I remained personally downhearted.

It wasn't until I was sitting in a French brocade armchair of the Ritz's private eighteenth-century barber's cubicle—I was here not because I needed a haircut but, as so often, only because I longed for a human touch—that I began to have clearer ideas about Renata and the Señora. How was it, for instance, that as soon as grandfather Koffritz had suffered his stroke and became paralyzed on one side Roger was ready to go? How did that old broad get him a passport so quickly? The answer was that the passport, when I went up and examined it on the quiet, proved to have been issued back in October. The ladies were very thorough planners. Only I failed to think ahead. So now it occurred to me to take the initiative.

It would be a clever move to marry Renata before she could learn that I was broke. This should not be done merely to hit back. No, in spite of her shenanigans I was mad about her. Loving her, I was willing to overlook certain trifles. She had provoked me by locking me out one night and by the conspicuous display of her birth-control device at the top of her open bag in Heathrow last April when we were parting for three days. But was that, after all, very significant? Did it mean more than that one never knew when one was going to meet an interesting man? The serious question was whether I, with all my thoughts, or because of them, would ever be able to understand what sort of girl Renata was. I wasn't like Humboldt, given to jealous seizures. I recalled how he had looked in Connecticut, when he quoted me King Leontes in my yard by the sea. "I have tremor cordis on me: my heart dances; but not for joy, not joy." That heart-dancing was classic jealousy. I didn't suffer from classic jealousy. Renata did gross things, to be sure. But perhaps these were war measures. She was campaigning to get me and would be different when we were settled down as husband and wife. No doubt she was a dangerous person but I would never be greatly interested in any woman incapable of harm, in any woman who didn't threaten me with loss. Mine was the sort of heart that had to overcome melancholy and free itself from many depressing weights. The Spanish setting was right for this. Renata was acting like Carmen, and Flonzaley,

for it probably was Flonzaley, was being Escamillo the Tore-
ador, while I, at two and a half times the age for the role, was
cast as Don José.

Quickly I sketched the immediate future. Civil marriages
probably didn't exist in this Catholic country. The knot could
be tied at the American Embassy by the military attaché, perhaps, or even a notary public for all I knew. I would go to the
antique shops (I loved the Madrid antique shops) to look for
two wedding bands and I could throw a champagne supper at
the Ritz, no questions asked about Milan. After we had sent the
Señora back to Chicago, the three of us might move to Segovia,
a town I knew. After Demmie's death I traveled widely, so I had
been to Segovia before. I was beguiled by the Roman aqueduct,
I recalled that I had really gone for those tall knobby stone
arches—stones whose nature was to fall or sink were sitting
there lightly in the air. That was an achievement that had gone
home—an example to me. For purposes of meditation Segovia
couldn't be beat. We could live there *en famille* in one of the
old back streets, and while I tried to see if I could really move
from mental consciousness to the purer consciousness of spirit,
it might amuse Renata to comb the town for antiques she could
sell to decorators in Chicago. Perhaps she would even make a
buck. Roger could attend nursery school and eventually my
little girls might join us, because when Denise won her case and
collected her money she'd want to get rid of them immediately.
I had just enough cash left to settle in Segovia and give Renata a
commercial start. Perhaps I would even write the essay on contemporary Spanish culture suggested by Thaxter, if that could
be done without too much faking. And how would Renata take
my deception? She would take it as good comedy, which she
valued more highly than anything in the world. And when I
told her after the marriage that we were down to our last few
thousand dollars she would laugh brilliantly, larger than life,
and say, "Well, *there's* a twist." I evoked Renata laughing brilliantly because I was in reality undergoing a major attack of
my lifelong trouble—the longing, the swelling heart, the tearing eagerness of the deserted, the painful keenness or infinitiz-
ing of an unidentified need. This condition was apparently

stretching from earliest childhood to the border of senescence. I thought, Hell, let's settle this once and for all. Then, not wanting the nosy Ritz staff to talk, I went to the central post office of Madrid, with its sonorous halls and batty-looking steeples (Spanish bureaucratic Gothic) and sent a cable to Milan. MARVELOUS IDEA, RENATA DARLING. MARRY ME TOMORROW. YOUR TRULY LOVING FAITHFUL CHARLIE.

After this I lay awake all night because I had used the word "faithful." This might queer the whole deal, with its implied accusation and the hint or shadow of forgiveness. But I had really meant no harm. I was betwixt and between. I mean, if I were a true hypocrite I wouldn't forever be putting my foot in my mouth. On the other hand, if I were a real innocent, pure in heart, I wouldn't have to fret the night out over Renata's conduct in Milan or her misinterpretation of my wire. But I lost a night's sleep for nothing. The wording of the message didn't matter. She didn't reply at all.

So that night, in the romantic dining room of the Ritz where every bite cost a fortune, I said to the Señora, "You'll never guess who's been on my mind today." Without waiting for an answer I then uttered the name "Flonzaley!" as a surprise assault on her defenses. But the Señora was made of terribly hard material. She seemed hardly to notice. I repeated the name. "Flonzaley! Flonzaley! Flonzaley!"

"What is this loudness, what is the matter, Charles?"

"Maybe you'd better tell me what's the matter. Where is Mr. Flonzaley?"

"Why should his whereabouts be my problem? Would you mind asking the *camarero* to pour the wine?" It was not only because she was the lady and I the gentleman that the Señora wished me to speak to waiters. She was fluent in Spanish all right, but her accent was pure Hungarian. Of this there was no doubt now. I learned a thing or two from the Señora. For instance, did I think that people concluding their lives would all be in a fever to come to terms with their souls? I went through agonies of preparation before I blurted out Flonzaley's name and then she asked for more wine. And yet it must have been she that masterminded the plan to bring Roger to Madrid. It was she who made certain that I was pinned down here and prevented me from rushing to Milan to burst in on Renata. For Flonzaley was there with her, all right. He was mad for her and I didn't blame him. A man who met more people on the mortuary slab than he met socially could not be blamed for losing his head that way. A body like Renata's was not often seen in the living flesh. As for Renata, she complained of the morbid element in his adoration, but could I be altogether sure that it was not one of his attractions? I was certain of nothing. I sat trying to make myself drunk on a bottle of acid wine, but I made no headway against my bitter sobriety. No I didn't understand.

The activities of higher consciousness didn't inevitably improve the understanding. The hope of such understanding was raised by my manual—*Knowledge of the Higher Worlds and Its Attainment*. This gave specific instructions. One suggested exercise was to try to enter into the intense desire of another person on a given occasion. To do this one had to remove all personal opinions, all interfering judgments; one should be neither for nor against this desire. In this way one might come gradually to feel what another soul was feeling. I had made this experiment with my own child Mary. For her last birthday she desired a bicycle, the ten-speed type. I wasn't convinced that she was old enough to have one. When we went to the shop it was by no means certain that I would buy it. Now what was her desire, and what did she experience? I wanted to know this, and tried to desire in the way that she desired. This was my kid, whom I loved, and it should have been elementary to find out what a soul in its fresh state craved with such intensity. But I couldn't do this. I tried until I broke into a sweat, humiliated, disgraced by my failure. If I couldn't know this kid's desire could I know any human being? I tried it on a large number of people. And then, defeated, I asked where was I anyway? And what did I really know of anyone? The only desires I knew were my own and those of nonexistent people like Macbeth or Prospero. These I knew because the insight and language of genius made them clear. I bought Mary the bike and then shouted at her, "For Christ's sake, don't ride over the curbs, you'll bust hell out of the wheel." But this was an explosion of despair over my failure to know the kid's heart. And yet I was prepared to know. I was all set up to know in the richest colors, with the deepest feelings, and in the purest light. I was a brute, packed with exquisite capacities which I was unable to use. There's no need to go into this yet once again and tickle each mandolin note ten times as that dear friend of mine accused me of doing. The job, once and for all, was to burst from the fatal self-sufficiency of consciousness and put my remaining strength over into the Imaginative Soul. As Humboldt too should have done.

I don't know who the other gentlemen in the Ritz may have been dining with, the human scene was too pregnant and dense in complications for me at this moment, and all I can say was that I was glad the aims of the pimping old bitch across the table were merely conventional aims. If she had gone after my soul, what was left of it, I would have been sunk. But all she wanted was to market her daughter at her finest hour. And was I through? And was it over? For a few years I had had it good with Renata—the champagne cocktails, the table set with orchids, and this warm beauty serving dinner in feathers and G string while I ate and drank and laughed till I coughed at her erotic teasing, the burlesque of the amorous greatness of heroes and kings. Good-by, good-by to those wonderful sensations. Mine at least had been the real thing. And if hers were not, she had at least been a true and understanding pal. In her percale bed. In her heaven of piled pillows. All that was probably over.

And what could you be at the Ritz but a well-conducted diner? You were attended by servitors and chefs and *maîtres* and grooms, waiters, and the little *botónes* who was dressed like an American bellhop and was filling the glasses with crystalline ice water and scraping crumbs from the linen with a broad silver blade. Him I liked best of all. There was nothing I could do under the circumstances about my desire to give a sob. It was my heartbreak hour. For I didn't have the dough and the old woman knew it. This tunicate withered bag the Señora had my financial number. Flonzaley with his corpses would never run out of money. The course of nature itself was behind him.

Cancers and aneurysms, coronaries and hemorrhages stood behind his wealth and guaranteed him bliss. All these dead, like the glorious court of Jerusalem, chanting, "Live forever, Solomon Flonzaley!" And so Flonzaley was getting Renata while I yielded a moment to bitter self-pity and saw myself very old and standing dazed in the toilet of some tenement. Perhaps like old Doc Lutz I would put two socks on one foot and pee in the bathtub. That, as Naomi said, was the end. It was just as well that the title to those graves in Waldheim had turned up in Julius's desk. I might just need them, untimely. Tomorrow, heavy of heart, I was going to the Prado to look for the Velásquez, or was it the Murillo that resembled Renata—the one mentioned by the Chancellor of the Exchequer in Downing Street. So I sat in this scene of silver service and brandy flames and the superb flash of chafing dishes.

"I wired Renata yesterday and asked her to marry me," I said.

"Did you? How nice. That should have been done long ago," said the relentless Señora. "You can't treat proud women like this. But I would be happy to have such a distinguished son-in-law and Roger loves you like his own daddy."

"But she hasn't answered me."

"The postal system isn't working. Haven't you heard, Italy is breaking down?" she said. "Did you telephone too?"

"I tried, Señora. I hesitate to call in the middle of the night. Anyway there's never an answer."

"She may have gone with her father for the holiday. Maybe Biferno still owns his house in the Dolomites."

"Why don't you use your influence for me, Señora," I said. This capitulation was a mistake. To appeal to certain peculiar powers is the worst thing you can do. These vulcanized hearts, they only become more resistant when you ask for mercy. "You know I'm in Spain to work on a new type of Baedeker. After Madrid Renata and I, if we got married, would be going on to Vienna, Rome, and Paris. I'm going to buy a new Mercedes-Benz. We could hire a governess for the boy. There's a great deal of money in this." I now dropped names, I bragged of my connections in European capitals, I babbled. She was less and less impressed. Maybe she had had a talk with Szathmar. I don't know why, but Szathmar loved to give my secrets away. Then I said, "Señora, why don't we go to the Flamenco Cabaret—the whatchamacallit that advertises all over the place? I really love strong voices and people hammering with their heels. We can get a sitter for Roger."

"Oh, very good," she said.

So we spent the evening with gypsies, and I splurged and behaved like a man with plenty of money. I discussed rings and wedding gifts with the crazy old woman at every interval in the guitar music and hand-clapping.

"What have you seen, going back and forth in Madrid, that might appeal to Renata?" I asked her.

"Oh, the most elegant leather and suède. Coats and gloves and bags and shoes," she said. "But I found a street where they sell exquisite cloaks and I talked with the president of the International Cloak Society, Los Amigos de la Capa, and he showed me, with hoods and without hoods, the most stunning velvet dark-green items."

"I'll buy one for her first thing tomorrow," I said.

If the Señora had given even the slightest hint of discouragement I might have known where I stood. But she gave me only a dry look. A blink crossed the table. It even seemed to come from the bottom of her eye upward, like a nictitating membrane. My impression was of a forest, and of a clearing from which a serpent departed just as I got to it on a dry and golden autumn afternoon fragrant with leaf mold. I mention this for what it may be worth. Nothing, probably. But I had been going around to the Prado, around the corner from the Ritz, looking at some strange pictures every free moment and especially the burlesque visions of Goya and the paintings of Hieronymus Bosch. My mind was prepared therefore for visiting images and even hallucinations.

"I congratulate you on finally making sense," said the old woman. She didn't say, mind you, that I had done this in time. She said, "I brought Renata up to make a perfect wife to a serious man."

A born patsy, I concluded from this that I was the serious

man she meant and that these women had not yet reached an irrevocable decision. I celebrated this possibility by drinking a large amount of Lepanto brandy. As a result I slept soundly and woke rested. In the morning I opened the high windows and enjoyed the traffic wheeling in the sun, the dignified plaza with the white Palace Hotel on the far side. Delicious rolls and coffee were brought with sculptured butter and Hero jam. For ten years I had lived in style, well tailored, with custom-made shirts and cashmere stockings and silk neckties, esthetically satisfying. Now this silly splendor was ending but I, with my experience of the great Depression, knew austerity perfectly well. I had spent most of my life in it. The hardship was not living in a rooming house but becoming just another old guy, no longer capable of inspiring the minds of pretty ladies with May–December calculations or visions of being mistress of a castle like Mrs. Charlie Chaplin, having ten children by an autumnal-to-wintry husband of great stature. Could I bear to live without having this effect on women? And then possibly, just possibly, Renata loved me well enough to accept conditions of austerity. On an income of fifteen thousand dollars, promised by Julius if I were to invest fifty thousand with him, something very nice could be arranged in Segovia. I could even put up with the Señora for the rest of her life. Which I hoped would not be long. No hard feelings, you understand, but it would be nice to lose her soon.

I tried to reach Thaxter in Paris—the Hotel Pont-Royal was his address there. I also put in a call for Carl Stewart in New York. I wanted to discuss the cultural Baedeker with Thaxter's publisher myself. I also wanted to make certain that he would pay my bill at the Ritz. Thaxter was not registered at the Pont-Royal. Maybe he was staying with his mother's friend, the Princesse de Bourbon-Sixte. I was not disturbed. Having discussed the details of my New York call with the switchboard I gave myself ten minutes of tranquillity by the window. I enjoyed the winter freshness and the sun. I tried to experience the sun not as a raging thermonuclear pile of gases and fissions but as a being, an entity with a life and meanings of its own, if you know what I mean.

Thanks to penicillin, Roger was well enough to go to the Retiro with his grandma, so I had no responsibility for him this morning. I performed thirty push-ups and stood on my head; then I shaved and dressed and strolled out. I left the grand boulevards and found my way into the back streets of the old city. My object was to buy a beautiful cloak for Renata but I remembered Julius's request for a marine painting and since I had lots of time I went into antique shops and art galleries to have a look. But in all the blue and green, foam and sun, calm and storm, there was always a rock, a sail, a funnel and Julius wasn't having any of that. Nobody cared to paint the pure element, the inhuman water, the middle of the ocean, the formless deep, the world-enfolding sea. I kept thinking of Shelley among the Euganean Hills:

> Many a green isle needs must be
> In the deep wide sea of Misery . . .

But Julius didn't see why there needs must be anything in any sea whatever. Like a reverse Noah he sent out his dove brother, beautifully dressed, greatly troubled, anguishing over Renata, to find him water only. Shop assistants, girls, all of them, in black smocks, were bringing up old seascapes from the cellars because I was an American on the loose with traveler's checks in his pocket. I didn't feel foreign among Spaniards. They resembled my parents and my immigrant aunts and cousins. We were parted when the Jews were expelled in 1492. Unless you were very stingy with time, that wasn't really so long ago.

And I wondered how American my brother Ulick was after all. From the first he had taken the view that America was that materially successful happy land that didn't need to trouble its mind, and he had dismissed the culture of the genteel and their ideals and aspirations. Now the famous Santayana agreed, in a way, with Ulick. The genteel couldn't attain their ideals and were very unhappy. Genteel America was handicapped by meagerness of soul, thinness of temper, paucity of talent. The new America of Ulick's youth only asked for comfort and speed and good cheer, health and spirits, football games, political campaigns, outings, and cheerful funerals. But this new America now revealed a different bent, new kinks. The period of pleasant hard-working exuberance and of practical arts and technics strictly in the service of material life was also ending. Why did Julius want to celebrate the new veins grafted to his heart by miraculous medical technology by buying a water painting? Because even he was no longer all business. He now felt metaphysical impulses too. Maybe he had had it with the ever-alert practical American soul. In six decades he had spotted all the rackets, smelled all the rats, and he was tired of being the absolute and sick master and boss of the inner self. What did a seascape devoid of landmarks signify? Didn't it signify elemental liberty, release from the daily way and the horror of tension? O God, liberty!

I knew that if I went to the Prado and asked around, I could find a painter to paint me a seascape. If he charged me two thousand dollars, I could get five from Julius. But I rejected the idea of making a buck on a brother with whom I had bonds of such unearthly satin. I looked over all the marine paintings in one corner of Madrid and then went on to the cape shop.

There I did business with the president of the international society Los Amigos de la Capa. He was swarthy and small, stood somewhat lopsided, like a jammed accordion, had tooth problems and bad breath. On his dark face were white sycamore patches. As Americans do not tolerate such imperfections in themselves, I felt that I was in the Old World. The shop itself had a broken wooden floor. Cloaks hung from the ceiling everywhere. Women with long poles brought down these beautiful garments, velvet-lined, brocaded, and modeled them for me. Thaxter's carabiniere costume looked sick by comparison. I bought a black cloak lined with red (black and red—Renata's best colors) and forked over two hundred dollars in American Express checks. Many thanks and courtesies were exchanged. I shook hands with everyone and couldn't wait to get back to the Ritz with my parcel to show the Señora.

But the Señora wasn't there. In my room I found Roger on the settee, his feet resting on his packed bag. A chambermaid was keeping an eye on him. "Where's Grandma?" I said. The maid told me that about two hours before the Señora had been called away urgently. I phoned the cashier, who told me that my guest, the lady in Room 482, had checked out and that her charges would appear on my bill. Then I dialed the concierge. Oh yes, he said, a limousine had taken Madam to the airport. No, Madam's destination was not known. They had not been asked to arrange tickets for her.

"Charlie, have you got chocolate?" said Roger.

"Yes, kid, I brought you some." He needed all the sweet he could get, and I handed him the entire bar. *There* was someone whose desire I understood. He desired his Mama. We desired the same person. Poor little guy, I thought, as he peeled the foil from the chocolate and filled his mouth. I had a true feeling for this kid. He was in that feverish beautiful state of pale child-hood when we are beating all over with pulses—nothing but a craving defenseless greedy heart. I remembered the condition very well. The chambermaid, when she found that I knew a lit-tle Spanish, asked whether Rogelio were my grandson. "No!" I said. It was bad enough that he had been dumped on me, must I be a grandfather, too? Renata was on her honeymoon with Flonzaley. Never having been married herself, the Señora was mad to achieve respectability for her daughter. And Renata, for all of her erotic development, was an obedient child. Perhaps the Señora, when she schemed on her daughter's behalf, felt herself more youthful. To do me in the eye must have made her decades younger. As for me, I now saw the connection between eternal youth and stupidity. If I was not too old to chase Renata, I was young enough to suffer adolescent heartache.

So I told the maid that Rogelio and I were not related although I was certainly old enough to be his *abuelo,* and I gave her a hundred pesetas to mind him for another hour. Even though I was going broke I still had money enough for certain refined needs. I could afford to suffer like a gentleman. Just now I couldn't cope with the kid. I had an urge to go to the Retiro, where I could abandon myself and beat my breast or stamp my feet or curse or weep. As I was leaving my room the phone rang and I snatched it up, hoping to hear Renata's voice. It was, however, New York calling.

"Mr. Citrine? This is Stewart in New York. We've never met. I know of you, of course."

"Yes, I wanted to ask you. You are publishing a book by Pierre Thaxter on dictators?"

"We have great hopes for it," he said.

"Where is Thaxter now, in Paris?"

"At the last moment he changed his plans and flew to South America. So far as I know he's in Buenos Aires interviewing Perón's widow. Very exciting. The country's being torn apart."

"You know, I suppose," I said, "that I'm in Madrid to explore the possibility of doing a cultural guide to Europe."

"Is that so?" he said.

"Didn't Thaxter tell you that? I thought we had your blessing."

"I don't know the first thing about it."

"You're sure now? You have no recollection?"

"What's this all about, Mr. Citrine?"

"To be brief," I said. "Only this question: Am I in Madrid as your guest?"

"Not that I know of."

"¡Ay, que lío!"

"Sir?"

In the curtained alcove, suddenly cold, I crawled into bed with the telephone. I said, "It's a Spanish expression like malentendu or snafu or screwed again. Excuse the emphasis. I am under stress."

"Perhaps you would be so kind as to explain this in a letter," said Mr. Stewart. "Are you at work on a book? We'd be interested, you know."

"Nothing," I said.

"But if you should get started . . ."

"I'll write you a letter," I said.

I was paying for this call.

Now very stormy, I asked the operator to try Renata again. I'll tell that bitch a thing or two, I thought. But when I got through, Milan said that she had gone and left no address. By the time I got to the Retiro, intending to express myself, there was nothing to express. I took a meditative walk. I reached the same conclusions I had reached in Judge Urbanovich's chambers. What good would it do me to tell Renata off? Fierce and exquisite speeches, perfect in logic, mature in judgment, deep in wise rage, heavenly in poetry, were all right for Shakespeare but they wouldn't do a damn bit of good for me. The desire for emission still existed but reception was lacking for my passionate speech. Renata didn't want to hear it, she had other things on her mind. Well, at least she trusted me with Rogelio and in her own good time she'd send for him. By brushing me off like this she had probably done me a service. At least she would see it in that way. I should have married her long ago. I was a man of little faith, my hesitancy was insulting, and it was quite right that I should be left to mind her kid. Furthermore, I suppose the ladies figured that Rogelio would tie me down and prevent pursuit. Not that I had any intention of pursuing. By now I couldn't even afford it. For one thing, the bill at the Ritz was enormous. The Señora had made many telephone calls to Chicago to keep in touch with a certain young man whose business was to repair television sets, her present *affaire de cœur*. Moreover, Christmas in Madrid, counting Roger's illness and his presents, gourmet dining, and Renata's cloak, had reduced my assets by nearly a third. For many years, since the success of *Von Trenck*, or about the time of Demmie Vonghel's death, I had spent freely, lived it up, but now I must go back to the old rooming-house standard. To stay at the Ritz I would have to hire a governess. It was impossible anyway. I was going broke. My best alternative was to move into a *pensión*.

I had to account somehow for this child. If I described myself as his uncle it would raise suspicions. If I called myself his grandfather, I would have to behave like a grandfather. To be a widower was best. Rogelio called me Charlie, but in American children this was normal. Besides, the boy *was* in a sense an orphan, and I was without exaggeration bereaved. I went out and bought myself mourner's handkerchiefs and some very fine black silk neckties and a little black suit for Rogelio. I gave the American Embassy an extremely plausible account of a lost passport. It luckily happened that the young man who took care of such matters knew my books on Woodrow Wilson and on Harry Hopkins. A history major from Cornell, he had heard me once when I gave a paper at a meeting of the American Historical Association. I told him my wife had died of leukemia and that my wallet had been stolen on a bus here in Madrid. The young fellow told me that this town had always been notorious for its pickpockets. "Priests' pockets are picked under the soutane. They really are slick here. Many Spaniards boast that Madrid is a world center for this picking of pockets. To change the subject—maybe you'd lecture for the USIA."

"I'm too depressed," I said. "Besides, I'm here to do research. I'm preparing a book on the Spanish–American War."

"We've had leukemia cases in my family," he said. "These lingering deaths leave you wrung out."

At the Pensión La Roca I told the landlady that Roger's mother had been killed by a truck when she stepped off a curb in Barcelona.

"Oh, what a horrible thing."

"Yes," I said. I had prepared myself fully, consulting the Spanish dictionary. I added with great fluency, "My poor wife—her chest was crushed, her face was destroyed, her lungs were punctured. She died in agony."

Leukemia, I felt, was much too good for Renata.

* • *

In the *pensión* were any number of sociable people. Some spoke English, some French, and communication was possible. An Army captain and his wife lived there, and also some ladies from the Danish Embassy. One of these, the most outstanding, was a gimpy blond of about fifty. Occasionally, a sharp face and protruding teeth can be pleasant, and she was a rather agreeable-looking person, although the skin of her temples had gone a little silky (the veins), and she was even slightly hunchbacked. But hers was one of those commanding personalities that takes over a dining room or a drawing room not because they say much but because they know the secret of proclaiming their pre-eminence. As for the staff, the chambermaids who doubled as waitresses, they were extremely kind. Black means much less in the Protestant north. In Spain mourning still carries a lot of weight. Rogelio's little black suit was even more effective than my bordered handkerchief and my armband. When I fed him his lunch we brought the house down. It was not unusual for me to cut up the kid's meat. I did this normally in Chicago. But somehow, in the small, windowless dining room of the *pensión*, it was an eye opener—this unexpected disclosure of the mothering habits of American men got to people. My fussing over Roger must have been unbearably sad. Women began to help me. I put the *empleadas del hogar* on my payroll. In a few days' time he was speaking Spanish. Mornings, he attended a nursery school. Late every afternoon, one of the maids took him to the park. I was free to walk about Madrid or to lie on my bed and meditate. My life was quieter. Full quietude was something I couldn't expect, under the circumstances.

This was not the life I had pictured in the little plush seat of the 747, rushing over the deep Atlantic stream. Then, as I had put it to myself, the little bubble in the carpenter's level might be coaxed back into the center. Now I wasn't sure that I had a bubble at all. Then there was Europe, too. For knowledgeable Americans, Europe was not much good these days. It led the world in nothing. You had to be a backward sort of person (a vulgar broad, a Renata—not to beat about the bush) to come here with serious cultural expectations. The sort of thing propagated by ladies' fashion magazines. I am obligated to confess, however, that I too had come this time with pious ideals, or the remnants of such ideals. People had once done great things here, inspired by the spirit. There were still relics of holiness and of art here. You wouldn't find Saint Ignatius, Saint Teresa, John of the Cross, El Greco, the Escorial on Twenty-sixth and California or at the Playboy Club in Chicago. But then there was no little Citrine family group in Segovia with the Daddy trying to achieve the separation of consciousness from its biological foundation, while the sexual, rousing Mommy busied herself with the antiques trade. No, Renata had given me my lumps and she had done it in such a way that my personal dignity was badly damaged. The mourning I wore helped me to recover, somewhat. Black garments put me on polite and

courteous terms with the Spanish. A suffering widower and a
pale foreign orphan touched the shop assistants, especially the
women. At the *pensión,* the secretary from the Danish Embassy
took a particular interest in us. She was very pale, and her pallor had origins very different from Roger's. She had a dry, hectic look and she was so white that the lipstick raged on her
mouth. She applied it after dinner with a violent effect. Yet her
intentions weren't bad. She took me for a walk one Sunday
afternoon, when I was not at my best. She put on a cloche or
bucket hat and we walked slowly, for she had a hip ailment. As
we followed the paths with the holiday crowds, she gave me a
talking-to about sorrow.

"Was your wife beautiful?"

"Oh, she was very beautiful."

"You Americans are so self-indulgent about grief. How long
has she been dead?"

"Six weeks."

"Last week you said three."

"You can see for yourself, I've lost all sense of time."

"Well now, you've got to get back on your feet. There are
times when you have to cut—cut your losses. What's the
expression? Spin the thing off. I've got some good brandy in
my room. Come have a drink when the boy is asleep. You have
to share a double bed with him, don't you?"

"They're trying to find us two singles."

"Isn't he restless? Children kick a lot."

"He's a quiet sleeper. I can't sleep anyway. I lie there reading."

"We can find you something better than that to do at night,"
she said. "What's the use of brooding. She's gone."

She was certainly gone. That was fully confirmed now. She
had written me from Sicily. On Saturday, only yesterday, when
I stopped at the Ritz to ask for mail, I was given her letter. This
was why I was not at my best on Sunday; I'd been up all night
studying Renata's words. If I couldn't attend very closely to
Miss Rebecca Volsted, this furiously white limping woman, it
was because I was suffering. I might almost have wished that
Roger weren't such a good child. He did not even kick in his
sleep. He gave me no headaches. He was a dear little boy.

Renata and Flonzaley had gotten married in Milan and they were honeymooning in Sicily. I suppose they went to Taormina. She didn't specify. She wrote, "You are the best person to leave Roger with. You've proved often that you love him for his own sake and never used him to get at me. Mother is too busy to look after him. You don't think so now, but you'll get over this and remain a good friend. You'll be sore and bitter and call me a scheming dirty cunt—that's how you talk when you're burned up. But you've got justice in your heart, Charles. You owe me something and you know it. You had your chance to do right by me. You missed it! Oh, you missed it! I couldn't get you started doing right!" Renata burst into mourning. I had spoiled it. "The role you got me into was the palooka role. I was your marvelous sex-clown. You had me cooking dinner in a top hat, and my behind bare." Not so, not so, that was her own idea. "I was a good sport and let you have your fun. I enjoyed myself, too. I didn't deny you anything. You denied me plenty, though. You wouldn't remember that I was the mother of a boy. You showed me off in London as your spectacular lay from Chicago, that Toddling town. The Chancellor of the Exchequer gave me a private feel. He did, the bastard. I let it pass because of the former greatness of Britain. But he wouldn't have done it if I had been your wife. You put me in the whore position. I don't think you have to be a professor of anatomy to connect the ass with the heart. If you had acted as though I had a heart in my breast just like your distinguished highness the Chevalier Citrine, we might have made it. Ah Charlie, I'll never forget how you smuggled Cuban cigars for me from Montreal. You put *Cyrus the Great* bands on them. You were kind and funny. I believed you when you said that a peculiar foot needed a peculiar shoe and that we were shoe and foot, foot and shoe together. Why, if you had only thought the obvious thing, 'This is a kid who grew up in hotel lobbies, and her mother never was married,' you would have married me in every city hall and church in America and given me some protection, finally. This Rudolf Steiner you've been driving me crazy with says, I think, that if you're a man this time, you'll be reincarnated as a woman, and that the ether body (not that I'm sure what an ether body is; it's the vital part that makes the body live, isn't it?) is always of the other sex. But if you're going to be a woman in your next life, you've got a lot to learn in between. I'll tell you something anyway. Many a woman would admit, if she was honest, that what she'd really adore is a man made up of many men, a composite lover or husband. She loves this in X and that in Y and something else again in Z. Now you are charming, delightful, touching, usually a pleasure to be with. You could have been my X and partly my Y, but you were a complete dud in the Z department.

"I miss you this minute, and what's more Flonzaley knows it. But one advantage of his business is that it's made him very basic. You once said to me that Flonzaley's point of view must be Plutonian—whatever that meant. I put it that his trade is gloomy but his character is roomy. He doesn't insist that I shouldn't love you. Don't forget that I didn't run away with a stranger. I went back to him. When we parted at Idlewild, I didn't know I was going to do it. But I got out of patience with you. There are too many zigzags in your temperament. Both of us need more serious arrangements."

Wait a minute. She said this and she said that, but was she giving me up because I was about to go broke? That would never be a problem with Flonzaley. Probably Renata knew that I was beginning to think about a more austere sort of life. I hadn't renounced my money out of principle. Urbanovich was taking it from me, and that was just as well. But I was beginning to see the American dollar-drive for what it was. It had assumed the proportions of a cosmic force. It stood between us and the real forces. But no sooner had I thought this than I understood one of Renata's reasons for giving me up—she gave me up because I thought such thoughts as this. In her own way, she was telling me so.

"Now you can write your big essay on boredom, and maybe the human race will be grateful. It's suffering, and you want to help. It's a wonderful thing to knock yourself out over these deep problems, but personally I don't care to be around when you're doing it. I admit you're smart. That's all right with me. *You* should be as tolerant toward undertakers as *I* am toward intellectuals. When it comes to men, my judgments are completely female-human, regardless of race, creed, or previous condition of servitude, as Lincoln said. Congratulations, your intelligence is terrific. Still I agree with your old sweetie Naomi Lutz. I don't want to get involved in all this spiritual, intellectual, universal stuff. As a beautiful woman and still young, I prefer to take things as billions of people have done throughout history. You work, you get bread, you lose a leg, kiss some fellows, have a baby, you live to be eighty and bug hell out of everybody, or you get hung or drowned. But you don't spend years trying to dope your way out of the human condition. To me that's boring." Yes, when she said this, I saw thinkers of genius throwing skeins of belief and purpose over the heads of the multitude. I saw them molesting the race with their fancies, programs, and world-perspectives. Not that the race itself was guiltless. But it had incredible abilities to work, to feel, to believe, which it was asked to bestow here, bestow there by those who were convinced that they knew best and abused mankind with projects. "And you never asked me," she went on, "but I have my own beliefs. I believe I live in nature. I think that when you're dead you're dead, and that's that. And this is what Flonzaley stands for. Dead is dead, and the man's trade is with stiffs, and I'm his wife now. Flonzaley performs a practical service for society. Like the plumber, the sewage department, or the garbage collector, he says. But you do people good and then they turn around and have a prejudice against you. In a way it's like my own personal situation. Flonzaley accepts the occupational stigma but there's a slight charge for that, and he adds it to the bill. Some of your ideas are spookier than his business. He keeps things in their compartments. The color of one frame doesn't leak into the next."

Here she wasn't being straight. This glowing person Renata, wonderful to me because she was in the Biblical sense unclean, had made my life richer with the thrills of deviation and broken laws. If Flonzaley, because of pollution by the dead, was comparably wonderful to her, why didn't she just say so—I took it that in the Z department, and Renata never told me what this was, he was all that I was not. This hurt me very deeply, it made my heart ache. In the old expression, she hit me where I lived. But she might have spared me Flonzaley's rationalizations for soaking the bereaved. I knew Chicago's business thinkers, I had heard many a rich Chicagoan philosophizing. I knew all of that would-be Shavian wit you could hear at dinner tables on Lake Shore Drive: they wanted to make an untouchable and a chandala of Flonzaley, a scavenger, but he would take their gold into the gloom with him, and he would be a Prince there—that sort of stuff I could do without. Still, Renata was wonderful. Naturally she wanted to say grand things to me and show how well she had done. I had lost a wonderful woman. I was suffering over Renata. She marched off in boots and plumes, as it were, and left me figuring, in pain, what was what, and how, and what to do. And trying to guess what Z was.

"You always said that the way life happened to you was so different that you weren't in a position to judge the desires of other people. It's really true that you don't know people from inside or understand what they want—like you didn't understand that I wanted stability—and you never may know. You gave this away when you told me how you tried to feel your way into little Mary's emotions over the ten-speed bicycle but couldn't. Well, I'm lending you Roger. Look after him till I can send for him and study his desires. It's him you need now, not me. Flonzaley and I are going over to North Africa. Sicily hasn't been as warm as I like it. Let me suggest, as long as you're going back to fundamentals of feeling, that you give some thought to your friends Szathmar, Swiebel, and Thaxter. Your passion for Von Humboldt Fleisher speeded the deterioration of our relationship."

She didn't say just when she'd be sending for the boy.

"If you think you're on earth for such a very special purpose I don't know why you cling to the idea of happiness with a woman or a happy family life. This is either dumb innocence or else the last word in kinkiness. You're really far out and you take up with a person who's far out in her own way, and then you tell yourself that what you really want is a simple affectionate relationship. Well, you had the warmth and charm to make me think you wanted and needed me. Always your affectionate friend." She had filled up the paper, and the letter ended.

I couldn't help crying when I read this. On the night when Renata locked me out George Swiebel had told me how much he respected me for being able to suffer agonies of love at my age. He took off his hat to me for it. But this was the vitalist youth attitude which Ortega, one of the Madrid authors I had been reading, disparaged in *The Modern Theme*. I agreed with him. However, in the back bedroom of this third-rate *pensión* I was just the kind of old fool who carried on like an adolescent. I was balder and more wrinkled than ever and the white hairs had begun to grow long and wild from my eyebrows. Now I was a forsaken codger snuffling disgracefully from a beautiful floozy's abuse. I was forgetting that I might also be a World Historical Individual (of a sort), that perhaps I was supposed to scatter the intellectual nonsense of an age or must do something to help the human spirit burst from its mental coffin. She didn't think much of these aspirations, did she, if you took her running off with Flonzaley, who dealt in stiffs, as an expression of opinion. And even as I wept I glanced at the clock and realized that Roger would be back from his walk in fifteen minutes. We were supposed to play dominoes. Suddenly life goes into reverse. You're in first grade again. Approaching sixty you must start from the beginning and see whether you can understand another's desires. The woman you love is making mature progress in life, advancing independently in Marrakech, or somewhere. She doesn't need a primrose path. Wherever she treads the primroses start growing.

She was right, of course. In taking up with her I had asked for trouble. Why? Maybe the purpose of such trouble was to turn me deeper into realms of peculiar but necessary thought. One of these peculiar thoughts occurred now. It was that the beauty of a woman like Renata was not entirely appropriate. It was out of season. Her physical perfection was of the Classical Greek or High Renaissance type. And why was this sort of beauty historically inappropriate? Well, it went back to a time when the human spirit was just beginning to disengage itself from nature. Until that moment it hadn't occurred to man to think of himself separately. He hadn't distinguished his own being from natural being but was a part of it. But as soon as intellect awoke he became separated from nature. As an individual, he looked and saw the beauty of the external world, including human beauty. This was a moment sacred in history—the golden age. Many centuries later, the Renaissance tried to recover this first sense of beauty. But even then it was too late. Intellect and spirit had moved on. A different sort of beauty, more internal, had begun its development. This internal beauty, manifested in romantic art and poetry, was the result of a free union of the human spirit with the spirit of nature. So Renata really was a peculiar phantom. My passion for her was an antiquarian passion. She seemed to be aware of this herself. Look at the way she swaggered and clowned. Attic or Botticellian loveliness doesn't smoke cigars. It doesn't stand up and do vulgar things in the bathtub. It doesn't stop in a picture gallery and say, "There's a painter with balls." It doesn't talk like that. But what a pity! How I missed her! What a darling woman she was, that crook! But she was a holdover from another time. I couldn't say that *I* had the new sort of internal beauty. I was a dumb old silly. But I had heard of this beauty, I got advance notice of it. What did I propose to do about this new beauty? I didn't know yet. At the moment I was waiting for Roger. He was eager to play dominoes. I was eager to get a glimpse of his mother in his face as I sat opposite with the dotted bones.

• • • •

The haggard Danish lady, Rebecca Volsted, came and walked with me in the Retiro. I walked slowly and she limped alongside. Her cloche hat was pulled low on her face. Her face with its bitter flashes was lightning-pale. She questioned me very closely. She asked why I spent so much time in my room. She felt snubbed by me. Not socially. Socially I was very friendly. I only snubbed her—well, essentially. She seemed to be saying that if I wrestled passionately with her in bed she could, bad hip or no bad hip, cure me of what ailed me. On the contrary,

experience had finally taught me that if I followed her suggestion I would only acquire one more (and possibly demented)
dependent.

"What do you do all day long in your room?"

"I have to catch up on my correspondence."

"I suppose you have to notify people of your wife's death.
How did she die, anyway?"

"She died of tetanus."

"You know, Mr. Citrine, I've taken the trouble of looking
you up in *Who's Who in the United States*."

"Why ever did you do that?"

"Oh, I don't know," she said. "A hunch. For one thing,
though you have an American passport, you don't behave like
a real American. I felt there must be something to you."

"So you found out that I was born in Appleton, Wisconsin.
Just like Harry Houdini, the great Jewish escape artist—I wonder why he and I chose Appleton to be born in."

"Is there an element of choice?" said Rebecca. In her cloche
hat, fire-pale, and limping beside me in the Spanish park
she spoke up for rationality. I slowed my pace for her as we
talked.

I said, "Of course, science is on your side. Still, it's rather
strange, you know. People who have been on earth for only ten
years or so are suddenly beginning to compose fugues and prove
subtle theorems in mathematics. It may be that we may bring a
great many powers here with us, Miss Volsted. The chronicles
say that before Napoleon was born his mother enjoyed visiting battlefields. But isn't it possible that the little hoodlum,
years before his birth, was already looking for a carnage-loving
mother? So with the Bach family and the Mozart family and
the Bernoulli family. Such family groups may have attracted
musical or mathematical souls. As I explained in an article I
wrote about Houdini, Rabbi Weiss, the magician's father, was
a perfectly orthodox Jew from Hungary. But he had to leave
the old country because he fought a duel with sabers and he
certainly was an oddball. Besides, how is it that Houdini and
I, both from Appleton, Wisconsin, struggle so hard with the
problem of death."

"Did Houdini do that?"

"Yes, this Houdini defied all forms of restraint and confinement, including the grave. He broke out of everything. They buried him and he escaped. They sank him in boxes and he escaped. They put him in a strait jacket and manacles and hung him upside-down by one ankle from the flagpole of the Flatiron Building in New York. Sarah Bernhardt came to watch this and sat in her limousine on Fifth Avenue looking on while he freed himself and climbed to safety. A friend of mine, a poet, wrote a ballad about this called 'Harlequin Harry.' Bernhardt was already very old and her leg had been amputated. She sobbed and hung on Houdini's neck as they were driven away in the car and begged him to give back her leg. He could do anything! In czarist Russia the Okhrana stripped him naked and locked him in the steel van it used for Siberian deportations. He freed himself from that too. He escaped from the most secure prisons in the world. And whenever he came home from a triumphal tour he went straight to the cemetery. He lay down on his mother's grave and on his belly through the grass he told her in whispers about his trips, where he had been, and what he had done. Later he spent years debunking spiritualists. He exposed all the tricks of the medium-racket. In an article I once speculated whether he hadn't had an intimation of the holocaust and was working out ways to escape from the death camps. Ah! If only European Jewry had learned what he knew. But then Houdini was punched experimentally in the belly by a medical student and died of peritonitis. So you see, nobody can overcome the final fact of the material world. Dazzling rationality, blazing of consciousness, the most ingenious skill—nothing can be done about death. Houdini worked out one line of inquiry completely. Have you looked into an open grave lately, Miss Volsted?"

"At this point in your life, such a morbid obsession is understandable," she said. She looked up, her face burning white. "There's only one thing to do. It's obvious."

"Obvious?"

"Don't play dumb," she said. "You know the answer. You and I could do very well together. With me you'd stay free—no strings attached. Come and go as you like. We are not in America. But what *do* you do in your room? *Who's Who* says you've won prizes in biography and history."

"I'm preparing to write about the Spanish–American War," I said. "And I'm catching up on my correspondence. Actually, I have this letter to post. . . ."

I had written to Kathleen in Belgrade. I didn't mention money but I hoped she wasn't going to forget my share of the option payment on Humboldt's scenario. The sum she had mentioned was fifteen hundred dollars and I was going to need it soon. I was being dunned in Chicago—Szathmar was forwarding my mail. It turned out that the Señora had flown to Madrid First Class. The travel bureau was asking me to remit, promptly. I had written to George Swiebel to ask whether the money for my Kirman rugs had been paid yet, but George was not a prompt correspondent. I knew that Tomchek and Srole would send in a staggering bill for losing my case and that Judge Urbanovich would let Cannibal Pinsker help himself from the impounded funds.

"You seem to be muttering to yourself in your room," said Rebecca Volsted.

"I'm sure you haven't been listening at the door," I said.

She flushed—that is, she turned even paler—and answered, "Pilar tells me that you're talking to yourself in there."

"I read fairy tales to Roger."

"You don't when he's at school. Or maybe you rehearse the big bad wolf. . . ."

◆ ◆ ◆ ◆

What was this muttering? I couldn't tell Miss Rebecca Volsted of the Danish Embassy in Madrid that I was making esoteric experiments, that I was reading to the dead. I already seemed odd enough. Supposedly a widower from the Midwest and father of a small boy, I turned out, according to *Who's Who*, to be a prize-winning biographer and playwright and a *chevalier* of the Legion of Honor. The *chevalier* widower rented the worst room in the *pensión* (across the air shaft from the kitchen).

His brown eyes were red from weeping, he dressed with high elegance although the kitchen smells made his clothing noticeably rancid, he tried with persistent vanity to comb his thin and graying hair over the bald middle of his head and was always disheartened when he realized that in the lamplight his scalp was glistening. He had a straight nose like John Barrymore, but the resemblance went no further. He was a man whose bodily case was fraying. He was beginning to wrinkle under the chin, beside the ears, and below the sad, warm-hearted eyes that gazed intelligently in the wrong direction. I had always counted hygienically on regular intercourse with Renata. I apparently agreed with George Swiebel that you were headed for trouble if you neglected to have normal sexual relations. In all civilized countries this is the basic creed. There was, of course, a text to the contrary—I always had a text to the contrary. This text was from Nietzsche and took the interesting view that the mind was greatly strengthened by abstinence because the spermatazoa were reabsorbed into the system. Nothing was better for the intellect. Be that as it might, I became aware that I was developing tics. I missed my paddle ball games at the Downtown Club—the conversation of my fellow members I must say that I didn't miss at all. To them I could never say what I was really thinking. They didn't speak their thoughts to me either but those thoughts were at least speakable. Mine were incomprehensible and becoming more so all the time.

I was going to move out of here when Kathleen sent that check, but meantime I had to live on a tight budget. The IRS, Szathmar informed me, had reopened my 1970 return. I wrote to say that this was now Urbanovich's problem.

Every morning powerful coffee odors woke me. Afterward came ammoniac smells of frying fish and also of cabbage garlic saffron, and of pea soup boiled with a ham bone. Pensión La Roca used a heavy grade of olive oil which took some getting used to. At first it went through me quickly. The water closet in the hall was lofty and very cold with a long chain pull of green brass. When I went there I carried the cape I had bought for Renata over my arm and put it over my shoulders when I was seated. To sit down on the freezing board was a sort of Saint

Sebastian experience. Returning to my room I did fifty push-ups and stood on my head. When Roger was at nursery school I walked in the back streets or went to the Prado or sat in cafés. I devoted long hours to Steiner meditation and did my best to draw close to the dead. I had very strong feelings about this and could no longer neglect the possibility of communication with them. Ordinary spiritualism I dismissed. My postulate was that there was a core of the eternal in every human being. Had this been a mental or logical problem I would have dealt logically with it. However, it was no such thing. What I had to deal with was a lifelong intimation. This intimation must be either a tenacious illusion or else the truth deeply buried. The mental respectability of good members of educated society was something I had come to despise with all my heart. I admit that I was sustained by contempt whenever the esoteric texts made me uneasy. For there were passages in Steiner that set my teeth on edge. I said to myself, this is lunacy. Then I said, this is poetry, a great vision. But I went on with it, laying out all that he told us of the life of the soul after death. Besides, did it matter what I did with myself? Elderly, heart-injured, meditating in kitchen odors, wearing Renata's cloak in the biffy—should it concern anyone what such a person did with himself? The strangeness of life, the more you resisted it, the harder it bore down on you. The more the mind opposed the sense of strangeness, the more distortions it produced. What if, for once, one were to yield to it? Moreover I was convinced that there was nothing in the material world to account for the more delicate desires and perceptions of human beings. I concurred with the dying Bergotte in Proust's novel. There was no basis in common experience for the Good, the True, and the Beautiful. And I was too queerly haughty to take stock in the respectable empiricism in which I had been educated. Too many fools subscribed to it. Besides, people were not really surprised when you spoke to them about the soul and the spirit. How odd! No one was surprised. Sophisticated people were the only ones who expressed surprise. Perhaps the fact that I had learned to stand apart from my own frailties and the absurdities of my character might mean that I was a little dead myself. This detachment was a sobering kind of experience. I thought sometimes how much it must sober the dead to pass through the bitter gates. No more eating, bleeding, breathing. Without the pride of physical existence the shocked soul would surely become more sensible.

It was my understanding that the untutored dead blundered and suffered in their ignorance. In the first stages especially, the soul, passionately attached to its body, stained with earth, suddenly severed, felt cravings much as amputees feel their missing legs. The newly dead saw from end to end all that had happened to them, the whole of lamentable life. They burned with pain. The children, the dead children especially, could not leave their living but stayed invisibly close to those they loved and wept. For these children we needed rituals—something for the kids, for God's sake! The elder dead were better prepared and came and went more wisely. The departed worked in the unconscious part of each living soul and some of our highest designs were very possibly instilled by them. The Old Testament commanded us to have no business with the dead at all and this was, the teachings said, because in its first phase, the soul entered a sphere of passionate feeling after death, of something resembling a state of blood and nerves. Base impulses might be mobilized by contact with the dead in this first sphere. As soon as I began to think of Demmie Vonghel, for instance, I received violent impressions. I always saw her handsome and naked as she had been and looking as she had looked during her climaxes. They had always been convulsive, a series of them, and she used to go violently red in the face. There always was a trace of crime in the way that Demmie did the thing and there had always been a trace of the accessory in me, wickedly collaborating. Now I was flooded with sexual associations. Take Renata, there was never any violence with Renata, she always smiled and behaved like a courtesan. Take Miss Doris Scheldt, she was a small girl, almost a blond child, although her profile hinted that there was a Savonarola embedded in her and that she would turn into a masterful little woman. The most charming thing about Miss Scheldt was her lighthearted bursting into laughter during the conclusion of the sexual act. The least charming was her dark fear of pregnancy. She worried when you hugged her naked in the night lest a stray spermatozoon ruin her life. It seems, after all, that there are no nonpeculiar people. This was why I looked forward to acquaintance with the souls of the dead. They *should* be a little more stable.

As I was only in a state of preparation, not an initiate, I couldn't expect to reach my dead. Still, I thought I would try, as their painful experience of life sometimes does qualify some people to advance more rapidly in spiritual development. So I tried to put myself in a proper state for such contact, concentrating especially on my parents and on Demmie Vonghel and Von Humboldt Fleisher. The texts said that actual communication with an individual who had died was possible though difficult but demanded discipline and vigilance and a keen awareness that the lowest impulses might break out and raise hell with you. A pure intention must police these passions. So far as I knew my intention was pure. The souls of the dead hungered for a completion of their purgatory and for the truth. I, in the Pensión La Roca, sent my intensest thoughts toward them with all the warmth I had. And I said to myself that unless you conceive Death to be a violent guerrilla and kidnaper who snatches those you love, and if you are not cowardly and cannot submit to such terrorism as civilized people now do in every department of life, you must pursue and inquire and explore every possibility and seek everywhere and try everything. Real questions to the dead have to be imbued with true feeling. By themselves abstractions will not travel. They must pass through the heart to be transmitted. The time to ask the dead something is in the last instant of consciousness before sleeping. As for the dead they reach us most easily just as we awaken. These are successive instants in the time-keeping of the soul, the eight intervening clock hours in bed being only biological. The one occult peculiarity that I couldn't get used to was that the questions we asked originated not with us but with the dead to whom they were addressed. When the dead answered it was really your own soul speaking. Such a mirror-image reversal was difficult to grasp. I spent a long time pondering that.

And this was the way I spent January and February in

Madrid, reading helpful texts, *sotto voce,* to the departed, and trying to draw near to them. You might have thought that this hope of getting next to the dead would weaken my mind, if it didn't actually originate in mental debility. No. Although I have only my own authority for saying so, my mind appeared to become more stable. For one thing I seemed to be recovering an independent and individual connection with the creation, the whole hierarchy of being. The soul of a civilized and rational person is said to be free but is actually very closely confined. Although he formally believes that he ranges with perfect freedom everywhere and is thus quite a thing, he feels in fact utterly negligible. But to assume, however queerly, the immortality of the soul, to be free from the weight of death that everybody carries upon the heart presents, like the relief from any obsession (the money obsession or the sexual obsession), a terrific opportunity. Suppose that one doesn't think of death as all sensible people in their higher realism have agreed to think of it. The first result is a surplus, an overflow to be good with. Terror of death ties this energy up but when it is released one can attempt the good without feeling the embarrassment of being unhistorical, illogical, masochistically passive, feeble-minded. Good then is nothing like the martyrdom of certain Americans (you will recognize whom I mean), illuminated by poetry in high school, and then testifying to the glory of their (unprovable, unreal) good by committing suicide—in high style, the only style for poets.

Going broke in a foreign country I felt little or no anxiety. The problem of money was almost nonexistent. It did bother me that I was a phony widower, indebted to the ladies of the pensión for their help with Rogelio. Rebecca Volsted, with her face of scalding white, was breathing down my neck. She wanted to sleep with me. But I simply went on with my exercises. Sometimes I thought, Oh, that stupid Renata, didn't she know the difference between a corpse-man and a would-be seer? I wrapped myself in her cloak, a warmer garment than the vicuña Julius had given me, and I stepped out. As soon as I hit the open air, Madrid was all jewelry and art to me, the smells inspiring, the perspectives lovely, the faces attractive, the winter

colors of the park frosty green and filled with vertical strokes of
the lightly hibernating trees and the mouth and muzzle vapors
of people and animals visible up and down the streets. Renata's
little boy and I walked, holding hands. He was a remarkably
composed and handsome little boy. When we wandered in the
Retiro together and all the lawns were a dark and chill Atlantic
green, this little Roger could very nearly convince me that up
to a point the soul was the artist of its own body and I thought
I could feel him at work within himself. Now and then you
almost sense that you are with a person who was conceived
by some wonderful means before he was physically conceived.
In early childhood this invisible work of the conceiving spirit
may still be going on. Pretty soon little Roger's master-building
would stop and this extraordinary creature would begin to
behave in the most ordinary or dull manner or perniciously,
like his mother and grandma. Humboldt was forever talking
about something he called "the home-world," Wordsworthian,
Platonic, before the shades of the prison house fell. This is very
possibly when boredom sets in, the point of advent. Humboldt
had become boring in the vesture of a superior person, in the
style of high culture, with all of his conforming abstractions.
Many hundreds of thousands of people were now wearing
this costume of the higher misery. A terrible breed, the educated nits, mental bores of the heaviest caliber. The world had
never seen the likes of them. Poor Humboldt! What a mistake!
Well, perhaps he could have another go at it. When? Oh, in a
few hundred years his spirit might return. Meantime, I could
remember him as a lovely man and generous, a heart of gold.
Now and then I shuffled through the papers he had left me. He
had believed so greatly in their value. I gave a skeptical sigh
and was sad and put them back in his briefcase.

● ● ●

The world checked in with me occasionally, reports arrived
from various parts of the globe. Renata's was the letter I most
wanted. I longed to hear that she was sorry, that she was bored
with Flonzaley and horrified at what she had done, that he had

vile mortician's habits, and I rehearsed in my head the magnanimous moment when I took her back. When I was less nice
I gave the bitch a month with her millionaire embalmer. When
I was angrily depressed I thought that after all frigidity and
money, as everyone has known since antiquity, made a stable
combination. Add death, the strongest fixative in the world,
and you had something remarkably durable. I figured by now
that they had left Marrakech and were honeymooning in the
Indian Ocean. Renata always did say that she wanted to winter in the Seychelles Islands. My secret belief had always been
that I could cure Renata of what ailed her. Then I remembered,
turning the point of recollection against myself, that Humboldt
had always wanted to do the girls good but that they wouldn't
hold still for it, and how he had said about Demmie's friend,
Ginnie, in the village, "Honey from the icebox . . . Cold sweets
won't spread." No, Renata didn't write. She was concentrating
on the new relationship and she didn't have to worry about
Roger while I was looking after him. At the Ritz I picked up
picture postcards addressed to the kid. I had guessed right.
Morocco didn't detain the couple long. Her cards now bore
Ethiopian and Tanzanian postmarks. He received some also
from his father, who was skiing in Aspen and Vail. Koffritz
knew where his child was.

Kathleen wrote from Belgrade to say how glad it made her to
hear from me. Everything was going extremely well. Seeing me
in New York had been unforgettably marvelous. She longed to
talk to me again and she expected soon to pass through Madrid
on her way to Almería to work on a film. She hoped to have
very pleasant things to tell me. There was no check enclosed
with her letter. Evidently she didn't suspect that I badly needed
money. I had been prosperous for so many years that no such
thought occurred to anyone. Toward the middle of February a
letter arrived from George Swiebel, and George, who knew a
good deal about my financial condition, made no mention of
money either. This was understandable because his letter came
from Nairobi, so he couldn't have received my appeals for help
and my questions about the sale of the Oriental rugs. He had
been in Kenya for a month hunting for a beryllium mine in

the bush. Or was it a lode? I preferred to think of a mine. Had George found such a mine, I as a full partner would be free forever from money anxieties. Unless, of course, the court found a way to take that too away from me. Judge Urbanovich had for some reason chosen to become my mortal enemy. He was out to strip me naked. I don't know why this was, but it was so.

George wrote as follows: "Our buddy from the Field Museum was unable to make this trip with me. Ben simply couldn't swing it. The suburbs wouldn't give him a release. He invited me for Sunday dinner so I could see for myself what a hell his life was. It didn't look too terrible to me. His wife is fat but she looks good-natured and there's a nice kid and a sort of standard mother-in-law and an English bulldog and a parrot. He says his mother-in-law lives on nothing but almond rings and cocoa. She must eat in the night because he's never yet seen her taking a bite, not in fifteen years. Well, I thought, a lot he's got to holler. His twelve-year-old boy is a Civil War buff and he and Daddy and the parrot and the bulldog have a kind of club. Besides, he has a nice profession looking after his fossils, and every summer he and the kid take a trip in the camper and fetch home more rocks. So what is he beefing? For old times' sake I let him into our deal, but he was not the one I took to East Africa with me.

"To tell the truth I didn't want to make that long trip alone. Then Naomi Lutz invited me to dinner to meet her son, the one who wrote those articles for the Southtown paper about how he kicked the drug habit. I read them and developed a real interest in this young fellow. Naomi said why not let him come with you? And I actually began to think he would be good company."

I interrupt to observe that George Swiebel conceived himself to be especially gifted with young people. They never saw *him* as a funny old fellow. He took pride in his readiness to understand. He had many special and privileged relationships. He was accepted by youth, by the blacks, by gypsies and bricklayers, by Arabs in the desert, and by tribesmen in every remote place he had ever visited. With exotics he was a hit, making instantaneous human contact, invited to their tents and their cellars and their most intimate private circles. As Walt Whitman did with the draymen, clam diggers, and roughs, as Hemingway did with the Italian infantry and Spanish bullfighters, so George always did in Southeast Asia or in the Sahara or in Latin America, or wherever he went. He made his trips of this sort as often as he could manage, and the natives were always his brothers and were mad about him.

His letter went on: "Naomi really wanted the boy to be with you. Remember we were going to meet in Rome? But when I was ready to leave, Szathmar still hadn't heard from you. My contact in Nairobi was waiting and when Naomi begged me to take her son, Louie—he needed adult masculine influences and her own boyfriend, with whom she drinks beer and goes to the hockey game, was not the type to help and, in fact, was part of the kid's problem—I was sympathetic. I thought I would like to learn about the dope scene anyway, and the boy must have some character, you know, if he got the monkey off his back (as they used to say in our time) without outside help. Naomi sets a good table, there was lots to eat and drink, I got pretty mellow, and I said to this Louie with the beard, 'Okay, kid, meet me at O'Hare, TWA flight so and so, Thursday, half past five.' I told Naomi I'd drop him off with you on the return trip. She's a good old broad. I think you should have married her thirty years ago. She's our kind of people. She gave me a thank-you hug and cried quite a bit. So Thursday at flight time this skinny young character with the beard is hanging around near the gate in his sneakers and shirt sleeves. I say to him, 'Where's your coat?' and he says, 'What do I need a coat for in Africa?' And, 'Where's your luggage?' I said. He told me he liked to travel light. Naomi provided his ticket but nothing else. I outfitted him from my own duffel bag. He needed a windbreaker in London. I took him to a sauna to warm him up and gave him a Jewish dinner in the East End. So far the boy was good company and told me a whole lot about the drug scene. Damn interesting. We went on to Rome and from Rome to Khartoum and from Khartoum to Nairobi where my friend Ezekiel was supposed to meet me. But Ezekiel didn't show. He was in the bush, collecting beryllium. Instead, we were met by his cousin

Theo, this marvelous tall black man, built like a whippet, and black, black, shining deep black. Louie said, 'I dig this Theo. I'm gonna learn Swahili and rap with him.' Okay, fine. The next day we rented a Volks Minibus from the German Tourist Agency lady Ezekiel had worked for. She organized the trip I took with him four years ago. Then I bought clothing for the bush and even a pair of suède desert boots for Louie and railroad caps and smoked glasses and lots of other stuff, and we took off into the bush. Where we were bound for I didn't know, but I developed a relationship with Theo very quickly. To tell the truth, I was happy. You know I always had the feeling that Africa was the place where the human species got its start. That was the feeling that came to me when I visited the Olduvai Gorge and met Professor Leakey on my last trip. He absolutely convinced me that this was where man came from. I knew from my own intuition, like a sense of homecoming, that Africa was my place. And even if it wasn't, it was better than South Chicago anytime and I'd rather meet up with lions than use public transportation. For the weekend before I left Chicago, twenty-five murders were reported. I hate to think what the real figure must be. Last time I took a ride on the Jackson Park El, two cats were slicing off a guy's pants pocket with razor blades while he pretended to be asleep. I was one of twenty people watching. Couldn't do a thing.

"Before leaving Nairobi we visited the game park and saw a lioness jumping on wild pigs. The whole thing was really glorious. Then we drove off and before long we were wallowing in the deep red dust of the back roads and driving under the shade of marvelous big trees, like with roots in the air, and all the black people looked to be sleepwalking because of their nightgown- and pajama-type of costume. We'd enter some village where a whole lot of natives would be working on old foot-pedal Singer sewing machines under the open sky, and out again among the giant anthills like nipples all over the landscape. You know how I love sociable, affectionate situations and I was having the time of my life with this marvelous black man Theo. It wasn't long before we really became very close. The trouble was with Louie. In the city he was bearable but as soon as we got into the bush, he was something else again. I don't know what's with these kids. Are they feeble, sick, or what? The generation of the Sixties, now about twenty-eight years old, already are invalids and basket cases. He'd lie there all day long, acting dazed. Dog-tired we'd arrive in some village in the Minibus and the young fellow who had been pissing and moaning for two hours would begin to cry for his milk. Yes, that's right. Bottled, homogenized American milk. He'd never been without it and it made him frantic. It was easier to kick the heroin habit than the milk. It sounded innocent enough, and even amusing, why shouldn't a kid from Cook County, Illinois, have his lousy milk? But I tell you, Charlie, the thing got desperate two days out of Nairobi. He learned the Swahili word for milk from Theo, and when we drove into any little cluster of huts, he leaned out of the window and began to shout for it. 'Mizuah! Mizuah! Mizuah! Mizuah!' as we bumped over the ruts. You would have thought he was in agony for his fix. What did the natives know about this damn mizuah of his? They kept a few little cans for the Britishers' tea and couldn't understand what he meant, had never even seen a glass of milk. They did their best with a trickle of evaporated stuff, while I felt—to tell the truth, I was humiliated. This was no way to travel in the wilds. After a few days this skinny character with his hair and beard and sharp nose and completely unreasonable eyes—there was just no rapport. My health went into reverse. I began to have a bad stitch in the side of my belly so that I couldn't sit comfortably or even lie down. The whole middle of me became inflamed, sensitive—horrible! I was trying to relate to the natural surroundings and the primitive life, the animals, etc. This should have been bliss for me. I could almost see the bliss ahead of me like heat waves in the road and couldn't catch up with it. I had fucked myself out of it by being such a do-gooder. And it only got worse. Ezekiel had left messages along the way and Theo said we should be catching up with him in a few days. I hadn't seen any beryllium yet. Ezekiel was supposedly making a tour of all the beryllium locations. We couldn't reach these in our Minibus. You had to have a Land Rover or a Jeep. Ezekiel had a Jeep. So we went along like this and every once in a while we hit a tourist hotel where Louie demanded *mizuah* and grabbed off the best food. If there were sandwiches, he seized the meat and left me nothing but cheese and Spam. If there was a little hot water, he bathed first and left nothing but dirt for me. The sight of his skinny ass as he toweled himself filled me with one complete hot passion, either to hit him on the butt with a two-by-four or give him a terrific boot.

"The payoff was when he got after Theo to teach him Swahili words and the first thing he asked for, naturally, was 'motherfucker.' Charlie, there is absolutely no such thing in Swahili. But Louie couldn't accept the fact that in the very heart of Africa this expression should not exist. He said to me, 'Man, after all, this is Africa. This Theo has got to be kidding. Is it a secret they won't tell the white man?' He swore he wasn't coming back to America without being able to say it. The truth was that Theo couldn't even grasp the concept. He had no difficulty with part one, the sex act. And of course he understood part two, the mother. But bringing them together was beyond him. Several long days Louie worked to get it out of him. Then one evening Theo at last understood. He put these two things together. When the idea became clear, he jumped up, he grabbed the jack handle out of the Minibus and swung at Louie's head. He landed a pretty bad hit on the shoulder and lamed him. This gave me a certain amount of satisfaction but I had to break it up. I had to pull Theo to the ground and get my knees on his arm and hold his head while I reasoned with him. I said it was a misunderstanding. However, Theo was all shook up and never talked to Louie again after this mother-blasphemy had struck home. As for Louie, he griped and bitched about his shoulder so long that I couldn't continue to follow Ezekiel. I decided that we would go back to town and wait for him. Actually we had been making an enormous circle and were now only fifty or sixty miles from Nairobi. It didn't look to me like any beryllium mine. I concluded that Ezekiel had been collecting or perhaps even stealing beryllium here and there. In Nairobi we X-rayed the young fellow. Nothing was broken but the Dr. did tie his arm in a sling. Before I took him to the airport we sat at an outdoor café while he drank several bottles of milk. He had had it with Africa. The place had become phony under civilized influence and denied its heritage. He said, 'I'm all shook up. I'm going straight home.' I took from him the outfit I had bought for his use in the bush and gave it to Theo. Then Louie said he had to bring African souvenirs home for Naomi. We went to tourist shops where he bought his mother a deadly ugly Masai spear. He was due to reach Chicago at 3 a.m. I knew he had no money in his pocket. 'How are you getting home from O'Hare?' I said. 'Why of course I'll phone Mother.' 'Don't wake Mother. Take a taxi. You can't hitchhike on Mannheim Road with that fucking spear.' I gave him a twenty-dollar bill and drove him to the airport. Happy for the first time in a month, I watched him in shirt sleeves and sling climbing up the stairs and carrying the Assegai for Mother into the plane. Then at about a thousand miles an hour ground speed, he took off for Chicago.

"As for the beryllium, Ezekiel showed up with a barrel of it. We went to an English lawyer whose name I had from Alec Szathmar and tried to set up a deal. Ezekiel needed about five thousand dollars' worth of equipment, a Land Rover, a truck, etc. 'Good,' I said. 'We've got ourselves a partnership and I'm leaving this check in escrow and he'll pay it over as soon as you give him a title to the mine.' There was no title forthcoming, nor any way to prove these semiprecious stones were legally come by. I'm going down to the coast now to visit the old slave towns and try to recover something from this double-disaster of Naomi's kid and our sour beryllium deal. I'm sorry to say that some kind of African con was going on. I don't think Ezekiel and Theo were on the level. Szathmar sent me your address, in care of his colleague in Nairobi. Nairobi is fancier than ever. Downtown it looks more like Scandinavia than East Africa. I'm getting on the night train to Mombasa. Coming home via Addis Ababa and maybe even Madrid. Yours with love."

While I was absorbed in boning a slice of *merluza* for Roger, Pilar came into the dining room and whispered as she leaned over me with her high-aproned bosom, that an American gentleman was asking for me. I was delighted. Stirred, anyway. No one had called on me before, not in ten weeks. Could this be Georgie? Or Koffritz, come to fetch Roger? Also Pilar, with cool apron, warm white face, large brown eyes leaning toward me with her powder fragrance, was being extremely discreet. Had she never swallowed the widower story? Did she nevertheless know that I had a deep legitimate sorrow and good reason to dress in black? "Shall I ask the señor to come to the *comedor* to take coffee?" said Pilar, and moved her eyes from me to the kid and back to me. I said that I would talk with my visitor in the salon if she would sit with the orphan for me and make him eat his fish.

Then I went to the salon, a room seldom used and crowded with old plushy dusty objects. It was kept dark, like a chapel, and I had never seen the sun in it before. Light now poured in, revealing many religious pictures and treasures of bric-a-brac on the wainscoting. Underfoot were rubbishy ensnaring scatter rugs. It all gave the effect of a period vanishing together with the emotions one had had for this period and the individuals who had felt such emotions. My caller stood by the window, aware that I was catching the dust-filled sunlight straight in the eyes and couldn't see his face. The dust swirled everywhere. I was as dense in these motes as an aquarium fish in bubbles. My caller was still pulling at the drapes to let in more sun and he sent down the dust of a whole century.

"You?" I said.

"Yes," said Rinaldo Cantabile, "That's who. You thought I was in jail."

"Thought, and wished. And hoped. How did you track me here, and what do you want?"

"You're sore at me. Okay, I admit that was a bad scene. But I'm here to make up for it."

"Was that your purpose in coming here? What you can do for me is go away. I'd like that best."

"Honestly I came to do you good. You know," he said, "when I was a little kid my grandmother on Taylor Street was laid out in a parlor like this with a ton of flowers. Wow, I never thought

I'd see another roomful of such old-time crap. But leave it to Charlie Citrine. Look at these branches from Palm Sunday fifty years back. It stinks on the staircase and you're a fastidious guy. But it must agree with you here. You look okay—better, in fact. You haven't got those brown circles you had under your eyes in Chicago. You know what my guess is? That paddle ball game put too much strain on you. You here alone?"

"No, I've got Renata's little boy."

"The boy? And where is she?" I didn't answer. "She blew you off. I see. You're broke, and she's not the type for a tacky boarding-house like this. She took up with somebody else and left you to be the sitter. You're what limeys call the nanny. That's a riot. And what's the black armband for?"

"Here I'm a widower."

"You're an impostor," said Cantabile. "Now that I like."

"I couldn't think what else to do."

"I won't give you away. I think it's terrific. I can't figure how you get yourself into these situations. You're a superintelligent high-grade person, the friend of poets, a kind of poet yourself. But being a widower in a dump like this is a two-day gag at most and you've been here two months, that's what I don't understand. You're a lively type of guy. When you and me were tiptoeing on the catwalk of that skyscraper in a high wind sixty stories up, hey, wasn't that something? Honestly, I wasn't sure you had the guts."

"I was intimidated."

"You entered into the spirit of the thing. But I want to tell you something a little more serious—you and that poet Fleisher, you really were a quality team."

"When did you get out of jail?"

"Are you kidding? When was I in jail? You don't know your own town at all. Any little Polish girl on confirmation day knows more than you, with all your books and prizes."

"You had a smart lawyer."

"Punishment is on the way out. The courts don't believe in it. Judges understand that no realistic sane person goes around Chicago without protection."

Well here he was. He arrived in a sort of torrent as if the

tail wind that drove his jet had gotten into him somehow. He was high, exuberant, showing off, and he transmitted the usual sense of boundlessness, of cranky dangers—chanciness I called it. "I just now blew in from Paris," he said, pale, dark-haired, happy. His chancy eyes glittered under the dagger-hilt brows, his nose was full at the bottom and white. "You know neckties. What's your opinion of this one I bought on the rue de Rivoli?" He was dressed with brilliant elegance in a double-knit sort of whipcord pattern and black lizard shoes. He was laughing, nerves were beating in his cheeks and temples. He had only two moods, this and the threatening one.

"Did you trace me through Szathmar?"

"If Szathmar could get you into a pushcart he'd sell you by the slice on Maxwell Street."

"Szathmar is a good fellow in his own way. From time to time I speak harshly of Szathmar, but I really love him, you know. You invented all that stuff about the kleptomaniac girl."

"Yes, but what of it? It could have been true. No, I didn't get your address from him. Lucy got it from Humboldt's widow. She phoned her in Belgrade to check out some facts. She's almost done with the thesis."

"She's very tenacious."

"You should read her dissertation."

"Never," I said.

"Why not?" He was offended. "She's smart. You might even learn something."

"I might."

"But you don't want to hear any more about your pal, is that it?"

"Something like that."

"Why, because he blew it—he goofed? This big jolly character with so many talents caved in, just a fucking failure, crazy and a deadbeat, so enough of him?"

I wouldn't reply. I saw no point in discussing such a thing with Cantabile.

"What would you say if I told you that your friend Humboldt scored a success from the grave. I talked to that woman Kathleen myself. There were some points I had to discuss with her and I thought she might have some answers. Incidentally, she's real keen on you. You've got a friend there."

"What is this about a success from the grave? What did you talk to her about?"

"A certain movie scenario. The one you described to Polly and me just before Christmas in your apartment."

"The North Pole? Amundsen, Nobile, and Caldofreddo?"

"Caldofreddo is what I mean. Caldofreddo. You wrote that? Or Humboldt? Or both?"

"We did it together. It was horseplay. A vein of humor we used to have. Kid stuff."

"Charlie, listen, you and I need to reach a preliminary agreement, have an understanding between us. I've already taken a certain amount of responsibility, put out money and effort, made arrangements. I'm entitled to ten percent, minimum."

"In a minute I'll ask what the devil you're talking about. But tell me first about Stronson. What happened to him?"

"Never mind Stronson now. Forget Stronson." Cantabile then shouted, "Fuck Stronson!" This must have been heard all over the pensión. After that his head shook a few times as if with vibration or recoil. But he collected himself, fetched his shirt-cuffs from under the coat sleeves, and said in quite a different tone, "Oh, Stronson. Well, there was a riot in his office by people who got screwed. But he wasn't even there. His big worry should be obvious to you. He lost a lot of Mafia money. They owned him. He had to do anything they said. So about a month ago they called the obligation in. Did you read about the Fraxo burglary in Chicago? No? Well, it was a sensational heist. And who should be flying afterward to Costa Rica with a bag, a big valise full of dollars to stash away?"

"Stronson was caught?"

"The Costa Rican officials put him in jail. He's in jail now. Charlie, can you actually prove that you and Von Humboldt Fleisher actually wrote this thing about Caldofreddo? That's what I asked Kathleen. Have you got any proof?"

"I think so."

"But you want to know why. The why is kind of strange, Charlie, and you'll hardly believe it. However, you and I have

to have an understanding before I explain things. It's complicated. I've taken a hand in this. I've laid out a plan. I've got
people standing by. And I've really done it mostly out of friendship. Now take a look at this. I've prepared a paper that I want
you to sign." He laid a document before me. "Take your time,"
he said.

"This is a regular contract. I can't bear to read these things.
What do you want, Cantabile? I've never read a contract
through in all my life."

"But you've signed them, haven't you? By the hundreds, I
bet. So sign this one too."

"Oh God! Cantabile, you're back again to hassle me. I was
beginning to feel so well here in Madrid. And calmer. And
stronger. Suddenly you're here."

"When you get into a tizzy, Charlie, you're hopeless. Try to
check yourself. I'm here to do you a major favor, for Christ's
sake. Don't you trust me?"

"Von Humboldt Fleisher once asked me that and I said, 'Do
I trust the Gulf Stream or the South Magnetic Pole or the orbit
of the moon?'"

"Charles" (to calm me he addressed me formally) "what's to
get so excited? To begin with this is a one-shot deal. For me it
provides like a regular agent's fee—ten percent of your gross up
to fifty thousand dollars, fifteen percent of the next twenty-five,
and twenty percent on the balance, with a ceiling of one hundred and fifty thousand. So I can't get more than twenty grand
out of this any way you look at it. Is that a colossal fortune?
And I'm doing it more for you, and for a few kicks, you poor
dimwit. A lot you got to lose. You're a fucking baby-sitter in a
Spanish boardinghouse."

These last weeks I had been far from the world, beholding it
from a considerable altitude and rather strangely. This white-
nosed, ultranervous, overreaching, gale-force Cantabile had
brought me back, one hundred percent. I said, "For just an
instant I was almost glad to see you, Rinaldo. I always like
people who seem to know what they want and behave boldly.
But I am very happy to tell you now that I will not sign any
paper."

"You won't even read it?"

"Definitely not."

"If I were really a bad guy I'd go away and let you miss out on a fortune of money, you creep. Well, let's have a verbal agreement. I put you on to one hundred thousand dollars. I manage the whole deal and you promise me ten percent."

"But of what?"

"You never read *Time* or *Newsweek,* I suppose, unless you're waiting to have a tooth drilled. But there is a sensational movie out, the biggest hit of the year. On Third Avenue the ticket line is about three blocks long and in London and Paris the same. Do you know the name of this hit? It's called *Caldofreddo,* and it's based on the scenario you and Humboldt wrote. It's got to be grossing millions."

"And is it the same? Are you certain?"

"Polly and I went to see it in New York and we both remembered what you described to us in Chicago. You don't have to take my word for it. You can see it yourself."

"Is it showing in Madrid?"

"No, you'll have to fly back to Paris with me."

"Well, Caldofreddo is the name we gave our protagonist all right. He's one of the survivors of the crash of Umberto Nobile's dirigible in the Arctic."

"Eats human flesh! Exposed by the Russians as a cannibal! Goes back to his Sicilian village! An ice-cream vendor! All the kids in town love him."

"You mean someone made something of such a farrago?"

Cantabile cried, "They're crooks, crooks, crooks! Those fuckers have stolen you blind! They've made a film out of your idea. How did they ever get it?"

"Well," I said, "all I know is that Humboldt gave the outline to a man named Otto Klinsky in the RCA building. He had an idea that he could reach Sir Laurence Olivier's hairdresser through a relative of some scrubwoman who was the mother of a friend of Mrs. Klinsky. Did they actually reach Olivier? Does he play the role?"

"No, it's some other Englishman, like the Charles Laughton or Ustinov type. Charlie, this is a hell of a good picture. Now,

Charlie, if we can prove your authorship, we've really got those guys. I told them, you know, I'm ready to slaughter them. I'm in a position to throw their balls into the Osterizer."

"You can't have many equals when it comes to threatening," I said.

"Well, I had to put heat on them if I didn't want a long business in court. We're looking for a fast settle. What kind of proof have you got?"

"What Humboldt did," I explained, "was to send himself a copy of the scenario by registered mail. This has never been opened."

"You've got it?"

"Yes, I found it among the papers he left me with a note that tells all."

"Why didn't he copyright the idea?"

"There is no other way in these cases. But the method is perfectly legal. Humboldt would have known. He always had more lawyers than the White House."

"Those movie bastards didn't have the time of day for me. Now we'll see. Our next move is this," he said. "We fly to Paris. . . ."

"We?"

"I am advancing expense money."

"But I don't want to go. I shouldn't even be here now. After lunch I generally sit in my room."

"What for? You just sit?"

"I sit and withdraw into myself."

"A hell of an egotistical thing to do," he said.

"On the contrary, I try to see and hear the outer world with no static whatever from within, an empty vessel, and completely silent."

"What is that supposed to do for you?"

"Well, according to my manual, if you sit quiet enough, everything in the outer world, every flower, every animal, every action, will eventually unveil secrets undreamed of—I'm quoting."

He stared at me with venturesome eyes and dagger brows. He said, "Damn it, you're not going to turn into one of those transcendental-type weirdos. You don't enjoy that, do you, just sitting quiet?"

"I enjoy it deeply."

"Come to Paris with me."

"Rinaldo, I don't want to come to Paris."

"You put your back up in the wrong place and you're passive in the wrong place. You've got everything arsy-versy. You come along to Paris and look at that picture. It'll only take a day or two. You can stay at the George V or the Meurice. It'll add strength to our case. I hired two good lawyers, one French and one American. We'll have to open that sealed envelope before witnesses under oath. Maybe we should get it done in the US Embassy and have the commercial attaché and the military attaché. So come on, pack your bag, Charlie. There's a plane in two hours."

"No I don't think I will. It's true I've got no money left, but I've been doing better without money than I ever did with it. And I don't want to leave the kid."

"Don't act like a granny about that kid."

"Anyway, I don't like Paris."

"You don't like Paris? What have you got against Paris?"

"A prejudice. For me Paris is a ghost town."

"You're out of your head. You should see the lines on the Champs-Elysées waiting to get into *Caldofreddo*. And it's your achievement. That should give you a feeling of secret power—a kick. I know you're sore because the French made a phony knight of you and you took it like an insult. Or maybe you hate them because of Israel. Or their record in the last war."

"Don't talk nonsense."

"When I try to guess what you're thinking I have to try nonsense. Otherwise it would take me a million years to figure out why to you Paris is a ghost town. Would old Chicago aldermen retire to a ghost town to spend their graft-money? Come on Charlie, we'll eat pressed duck tonight at the Tour d'Argent."

"No, that kind of food makes me ill."

"Well then give me the stuff to take back with me—the envelope Humboldt mailed to himself."

"No, Cantabile, I won't do that either."

"Why the hell not?"

"Because you're not trustworthy. I've got another copy of it, though. You can have that. And I'm willing to write a letter. A notarized letter."

"That won't do it."

"If your friends want to see the original they can come to me in Madrid."

"You irritate the shit out of me," said Cantabile. "I'm about to hit the ceiling." Incensed, he glared at me. Then he made a further effort to be reasonable. "Humboldt has some family yet, doesn't he? I asked Kathleen. There's an old uncle in Coney Island."

I had forgotten Waldemar Wald. Poor old man, he lived in kitchen odors, too, in a back room. He needed rescuing, certainly, from the nursing home. "You're right, there is an uncle," I said.

"What about his interest? What, just because you have a mental thing against Paris? You can pay a maid to look after the kid. This is a big deal, Charlie."

"Well, perhaps I should go," I said.

"Now you're talking."

"I'll pack a bag."

* * *

So we flew. That same evening Cantabile and I were on the Champs-Elysées waiting with our tickets to get into the vast movie house near the rue Marbeuf. Even for Paris the weather was bad. It was sleeting. I felt thinly dressed and became aware that my shoe soles had worn through and that my feet were getting wet. The queue was dense, the young people in the crowd were cheerful enough but Cantabile and I were both displeased. Humboldt's sealed envelope had been locked in the hotel vault and I had the claim check. Rinaldo had quarreled with me about possession of this brass disc. He wanted it in his pocket as a sign that he was my bona-fide representative.

"Give it to me," he said.

"No. Why should I?"

"Because I'm the natural one to take care of it. That's my kind of thing."

"I'll take care of it."

"You'll pull out your hankie and lose that check," he said. "*You* don't know what you're doing. You're absent-minded."

"I'll keep it."

"You were ornery about the contract, too. You wouldn't even read it," he said.

The ice beat on my hat and shoulders. I disliked intensely the smoke of French cigarettes. Above us in the lights were colossal posters of Otway as Caldofreddo and of the Italian actress, Silvia Sottotutti, or something of the sort, who played the role of his daughter. Cantabile was right, in a way, it was a curious experience to be the unrecognized source of this public attraction and to be standing in the sleet—it made one feel like a phantom presence. After two months of what was virtually a retreat in Madrid it felt like backsliding to be here, in the fog and glitter of the Champs-Elysées, under this icy pelting. At the Madrid airport I had picked up a copy of Baudelaire's *Intimate Journals* to read on the plane and to insulate me from Cantabile's frantic conversation. In Baudelaire I had found the following piece of curious advice: Whenever you receive a letter from a creditor write fifty lines upon some extraterrestrial subject and you will be saved. What this implied was that the *vie quotidienne* drove you from the globe, but the deeper implication was that real life flowed between *here* and *there*. Real life was a relationship between *here* and *there*. Cantabile, one thousand percent *here,* bore this out. He was acting up. He was feverish with me about the claim check. He fought with the *ouvreuse* who took us to our seats. She was enraged by the small tip he gave her. She took his hand and slapped the coin into his palm.

"You bitch!" he yelled at her, and wanted to chase her up the aisle.

I caught him by the arm and said, "Cool it."

Again I was part of a French audience. Last April Renata and I had come to this very theater. In fact I had lived in Paris in 1955. I quickly learned that this was no place for me. I need a little more fondness from people than a foreigner is likely to get here, and I was then still suffering from Demmie's death. However, there was no time now to think of such things. The picture was beginning. Cantabile said, "Feel in your pocket, make sure you've still got that check. We're screwed if you've lost it."

"It's here. Easy, boy," I said.

"Hand it over. Let me enjoy the picture," he said. I ignored him.

Then with great crashes of music the film began to roll. It opened with shots from the Twenties in the old newsreel manner—the first conquest of the North Pole by Amundsen and Umberto Nobile who flew in a dirigible from Scandinavia to Alaska. This was played by excellent comedians, highly stylized. I was enormously pleased. They were delicious. We saw the Pope blessing the expedition and Mussolini haranguing from his balcony. The competition between Amundsen and Nobile increased in hostility. When a little girl presented Amundsen with a bouquet, Nobile snatched it away; Amundsen gave orders, Nobile countermanded them. The Norwegians bickered with the Italians on the airship. Gradually we recognized, behind the *Time Marches On* style of these events, the presence of old Mr. Caldofreddo now in his ancient Sicilian village. These flashes of recollection were superimposed upon the daily existence of this amiable old gent, the ice-cream vendor who is loved by the kiddies, the affectionate father of Silvia Sottotutti. In his youth Caldofreddo had served with Nobile on two transpolar flights. The third, under Nobile's sole command, ended in a disaster. The dirigible went down in the Arctic seas. The crew was scattered over the ice floes. Receiving radio signals from the survivors, the Russian icebreaker *Krassin* came to the rescue. Amundsen was handed a cable telling of the disaster while he was drinking deeply at a banquet—according to Humboldt, who had private information about everything, the man had been drinking like a fish. Immediately he announced that he was organizing an expedition to save Nobile. It was all as we had laid it out in Princeton years and years ago. Amundsen chartered a plane. He quarreled violently with his French pilot, who warned him that the aircraft was dangerously overloaded.

He commanded him to take off, anyhow. They crashed into the sea. I was shocked to see how effective the comic interpretation of this disaster was. I remembered now that Humboldt and I had disagreed on this. He had insisted that it would be extremely funny. And so it was. The plane sank. Thousands of people were laughing. I wondered how he would have liked that.

The next portion of the film was all mine. It was I who did the research and wrote the scenes in which the rescued Caldofreddo ran wild aboard the *Krassin*. The sin of eating human flesh was too much for him to bear. To the astonishment of the Russian crew, he ran amuck, shouting gibberish. He hacked at a table with a large knife, he tried to drink scalding water, he hurled his body against the bulkheads. The sailors wrestled him to the ground. The suspicious ship's doctor emptied his stomach with a pump and found human tissue under the microscope. I was responsible also for the big scene in which Stalin directs the contents of Caldofreddo's stomach to be exhibited in a jar on Red Square under great banners denouncing cannibalistic capitalism. I added also the rage of Mussolini at this news, the calm of Calvin Coolidge in the White House as he prepared to get into bed for his daily siesta. All this I watched in a state of elation. Mine! All this had originated in my head in Princeton, New Jersey, twenty years ago. It was not a big achievement. It didn't ring bells in the far universe. It did nothing about brutality, inhumanity, it didn't clarify much or prevent anything. Nevertheless there was something in it. It was pleasing hundreds of thousands, millions of spectators. Of course, it was ingeniously directed and George Otway as Caldofreddo gave a wonderful performance. This Otway, an Englishman in his thirties, strongly resembled Humboldt. At the moment when he threw himself at the cabin walls, as I have seen maddened apes do in the monkey house, battering the partitions with heart-rending recklessness, I was stabbed with the thought of how Humboldt had fought the police when they took him away to Bellevue. Ah, poor character, poor fighting furious weeping hollering Humboldt. His flowers were aborted in the bulb. The colors never came into the light, they rotted in his chest. And the resemblance between Otway in the cabin and Humboldt was so uncanny that I began to cry. As the whole theater rocked with delight, shouting with laughter, I sobbed aloud. Cantabile said in my ear, "What a picture, hey? What did I tell you? Even you're laughing your head off."

Yes, and now Humboldt was spread out somewhere, his soul in some other part of the creation, there where souls waited for sustenance that only we, the living, could send from the earth, like grain to Bangla Desh. Alas for us, born by the millions, the billions, like the bubbles of effervescent drink. I had a world-wide dizzy glimpse of the living and the dead, of humanity either laughing its head off as pictures of man-eating comedy unrolled on the screen or vanishing in great waves of death, in flames and battle agonies, in starving continents. And then I had a partial vision of flying blind through darkness and then coming through a break above a metropolis. It glittered on the ground in icy drops, far below. I tried to divine whether we were landing or flying on. We flew on.

"Are they following your outline? Are they using it?" said Cantabile.

"Yes. They're doing it very well. They've added lots of their own ideas," I said.

"Try not to be so big about it. I want you in a fighting mood tomorrow."

I told Cantabile, "The Russians proved their case, according to the Doctor's statement, not only by pumping the stomach but also by examination of the man's excrement. The stools of the starving are hard and dry. This man claimed he had eaten nothing. But it was clear that he hadn't missed many meals, on the ice floe."

"They could have put that in. Stalin wouldn't have hesitated to put a crock of shit on Red Square. And you can do that nowadays in a picture."

The scene had changed to Caldofreddo's little town in Sicily where no one knew his sin, where he was just a jolly old man who peddled ice cream and played in the village band. As I listened to him tootle, I felt that there was something important about the contrast between his little arpeggios and the terrible modern complexity of his position. Lucky the man who has nothing more to say or play than these easy melodies. Are there still such people around? It was disconcerting also to see, as Otway was puffing at the trumpet, a face so much like Humboldt's. And since Humboldt had gotten into the film, I looked for myself as well. I thought that something in my nature might be seen in Caldofreddo's daughter, played by Silvia Sottotutti. Her personality expressed a sort of painful willingness or joyful anxiety which I thought that I had, too. I didn't care for the man in the role of her fiancé, with his short legs and his wide-angled jaw and flat face and lowish brow. It was possible that I identified him with Flonzaley. A man had once followed us at the Furniture Show who must have been Flonzaley. Signals had passed between Renata and him. . . . I had figured out, incidentally, that as Mrs. Flonzaley Renata was going to have a very limited social life in Chicago. Undertakers couldn't be very popular dinner guests, except with other undertakers. To be free from this occupational curse she'd have to travel a lot with him, and even on a Caribbean cruise, at the Captain's Table, they'd have to hope and pray that no one would turn up from the home town to ask, "You don't happen to be Flonzaley of Flonzaley Mortuaries, do you?" Thus Renata's happiness would be impaired, as the splendor of the Sicilian sky was stained for Caldofreddo by his dark act in the Arctic. Even in his trumpet-playing I detected this. I thought that there was one key of his trumpet which, when pushed down, drove right against the man's heart.

Now the Scandinavian journalist came to town, doing research for a book on Amundsen and Nobile. He tracked down poor Caldofreddo and began to molest him. The old fellow said, "You've got the wrong party. That was never me." "No, you're the man all right," said the journalist. He was one of those emancipated people from northern Europe who have expelled shame and darkness from the human breast, an excellent piece of casting. The two men had a conversation on a mountainside. Caldofreddo begged him to go away and leave him in peace. When the journalist refused, he fell into a fit similar to the one he had had on the *Krassin*. But this one, forty years later, was an old man's frenzy. It contained more strength and wickedness of soul than of body. In this seizure of pleading and rage, weakness and demonic despair, Otway was simply extraordinary.

"Was this the way you had it in your scenario?" said Cantabile.

"More or less."

"Give me that claim check," he said. He thrust his hand into my pocket. I realized that he was inspired by Caldofreddo's fit. He was so stirred that he had lost his head. More to defend myself than to keep the disc, I clutched his arm. "Get your hand out of my pocket, Cantabile."

"I have to take care of it. You're not responsible. A man who's been pussy-whipped. Not in your right mind."

We were openly fighting. I couldn't see what the maniac on the screen was doing because this other maniac was all over me. As one of my authorities said, the difference between the words "command" and "convince" is the difference between democracy and dictatorship. Here was a man who was crazy because he never had to persuade himself of anything! Suddenly it gave me as much despair to have thought this as to fight Cantabile off. This thinking would make a nitwit of me. As when Cantabile threatened me with baseball bats and I thought of Lorenz's wolves or of sticklebacks, or when he forced me into a toilet stall, I thought . . . All occasions were translated into thoughts and then the thoughts informed against me. I would die of these intellectual quirks. People began to cry out behind us, *"Dispute! Bagarre! Emmerdeurs!"* They roared, *"Dehors . . . !"* or *"Flanquez les à la porte!"*

"They're calling for the bouncer, you fool!" I said. Cantabile took his hand out of my pocket and we turned our attention to the screen again in time to see a boulder pried loose by Caldofreddo hurtling down the mountainside toward the journalist in his Volvo while the old man, appalled at himself, cried warnings and then fell on his knees and thanked the Virgin when the Scandinavian was spared. After this attempted murder Caldofreddo made a public confession in the village square. Finally he was given a hearing by a jury of townspeople in the ruins of the Greek theater on a Sicilian hillside. This ended with a choric scene of forgiveness and reconciliation—just as Humboldt, with *Oedipus at Colonus* in mind, would have wanted it.

When the lights came on and Cantabile turned toward the near aisle I made my exit by the far one. He caught up with me on the Champs-Elysées, saying, "Don't be sore, Charlie. That's just the breed of dog I am, to protect things like that claim check. What if you're mugged and rolled? Then who even knows what box the envelope is in? And five people are coming tomorrow morning to inspect the evidence. All right, I'm a high-strung fellow. I just want everything to go right. And you've been so hurt by that broad you're a hundred times more out of it than you ever were in Chicago. That's what I meant by pussy-whipped. Now why don't we pick up a couple of French hookers. I'll treat. Rebuild your ego a little."

"I'm going to sleep."

"I'm just trying to make up. I know it's hard for somebody like you having to share the earth with nuts like me. Well, let's go and have a drink. You're all ruffled and upset."

But I wasn't upset at all, really. A hard full day, even full of nonsense, acquits me of nonfeasance, satisfies my conscience. After four glasses of Calvados in the hotel bar I went to bed and slept soundly.

In the morning we met with Maître Furet and the American lawyer, a terribly aggressive man named Barbash, just the sort of representative that Cantabile would choose. Cantabile was deeply pleased. He had promised to deliver me and the evidence—I could see now why he had had such a fit about the check—and here we were, as prearranged, all beautifully coordinated. The producers of *Caldofreddo* knew that one Charles Citrine, author of a Broadway play, *Von Trenck,* later made into a successful film, claimed to be the source of the original story on which their worldwide hit was based. They sent a couple of Harvard Business School types to meet with us. Poor Stronson now in jail in Miami hadn't come within miles of the image. These two clean, well-spoken, knowledgeable, moderate, completely bald, extremely firm young men were waiting in Barbash's office.

"Are you two gentlemen fully authorized to deal?" Barbash said to them.

"The last word will have to come from our principals."

"Then bring the principals, the guys with the clout. Why are you wasting our time!" said Cantabile.

"Easy, easy does it," Barbash said.

"Citrine is more important than your fucking principals, any day," Cantabile shouted at them. "He's a leader in his field, a Pulitzer winner, a *chevalier* of the Legion of Honor, a friend of the late President Kennedy and the late Senator Kennedy, and the late Von Humboldt Fleisher the poet was his buddy and collaborator. Don't give us any shit here! He's busy with important research in Madrid. If he can spare the time to come up here so can your crummy principals. He won't throw his weight around. I'm here to throw it for him. Do this right or you'll see us in court."

To utter his threat relieved him wonderfully of something. His lips (not often silent) were lengthened by a silent smile when one of the young men said, "We've all heard of Mr. Citrine before."

Mr. Barbash now got control of the conversation. His problem, of course, was to subdue Cantabile. "Here are the facts. Mr. Citrine and his friend Mr. Fleisher wrote the outline for this film back in 1952. We are prepared to prove this. Mr. Fleisher mailed a copy of the scenario to himself in January 1960. We have this piece of evidence right here in a sealed envelope, postmarked and receipted."

"Let's go to the US Embassy and open it before witnesses," said Cantabile. "And let the principals get their asses down to the Place de la Concorde, too."

"Have you seen the film *Caldofreddo*?" said Barbash to me.

"I saw it last night. Beautiful performance by Mr. Otway."

"And does it resemble the original story by you and Mr. Fleisher?"

I now saw that a stenotypist sat in the corner at her tripod making a record of this conversation. Shades of Urbanovich's court! I became Citrine the witness. "It couldn't have had any other source," I said.

"Then how did these guys get it? They stole it," said Cantabile. "They might have to face a plagiarism rap."

As the envelope was handed around to be examined, a pang passed through my lower bowel. What if distracted, mad Humboldt had stuffed an envelope with letters, with old bills, with fifty lines on an extraterrestrial subject?

"You are satisfied," said Maître Furet, "that this is the unopened, original object? It will be so deposed."

The Harvard business types agreed that it was on the up and up. Then the envelope was slit open—it contained a manuscript headed, "An original movie treatment. —Co-authors, Charles Citrine and Von Humboldt Fleisher." As the pages passed from hand to hand I breathed again. The case was proven. There was no doubt about the authenticity of this manuscript. Scene by scene, shot by shot, the picture followed our outline. Barbash made an elaborate and detailed statement for the record. He had obtained a copy of the shooting script. There were almost no departures from our plot.

Humboldt, bless him, had done things right this time.

"This is thoroughly legitimate," said Barbash. "Authentic beyond dispute. I take it you people are insured against such claims?"

"What do we care about that!" said Cantabile.

There was, of course, an insurance policy.

"I don't think our writers ever said anything, one way or another, about an original story," one of the young men remarked.

Only Cantabile carried on. His idea was that everybody should be in a fever. But to business people it was just one of those things. I hadn't expected such coolness and decorum. Messrs. Furet, Barbash, and the Harvard Business graduates agreed that long costly lawsuits ought to be avoided.

"And what of Mr. Citrine's co-author?"

So that was all that the name Von Humboldt Fleisher meant to these MBAs from one of our great universities!

"Dead!" I said. This word reverberated with feeling only for me.

"Any heirs?"

"One, that I know of."

"We'll take this matter to our principals. What sort of figure have you gentlemen in mind?"

"A big one," said Cantabile. "A percentage of your gross."

"I think we're in a position to ask for a statement of earnings," Barbash argued.

"Let's be more realistic. This will be viewed mainly as a minor nuisance claim."

"What do you mean minor nuisance? It's the whole picture," Cantabile shouted. "We can kill your group!"

"A little calmer, Mr. Cantabile, please. We have a serious claim here," said Barbash. "We'd like to hear what you say after serious consideration."

"Would there be any interest," I said, "in another idea for a screenplay from the same source?"

"Is there one?" said one of the Harvard businessmen. He answered me smoothly, unsurprised. I couldn't help admiring his admirable schooling. You couldn't catch a man like this out.

"*Is* there? You just heard it. We're telling you so," said Cantabile.

"I have here a second sealed envelope," I said. "It contains another original proposal for a picture. Mr. Cantabile, by the way, has nothing to do with this. He's never even heard of the existence of this. His participation is limited to *Caldofreddo* only."

"Let's hope you know what you're doing," said Ronald, angry.

This time I knew perfectly well. "I'm going to ask Mr. Barbash and Maître Furet to represent me also in this matter."

"Us!" Cantabile said.

"Me," I repeated.

"You, of course," Barbash quickly said.

I hadn't lost tons of money for nothing. I had mastered the commercial lingo at least. And as Julius had observed I was a Citrine by birth. "This sealed envelope contains a plot from the same brain that conceived *Caldofreddo*. Why don't you gentlemen ask the people you represent whether they'd like to have a look at it. My price for looking—for looking only, mind you—is five thousand dollars."

"That is what we want," said Cantabile.

But he was ignored. And I felt very much in command. So this was business. Julius, as I've mentioned before, was forever urging me to recognize what he liked to call the Romance of Business. And was this the famous Romance of Business? Why it was nothing but pushiness, rapidity, effrontery. The sense it gave of getting your way was shallow. Compared with the satisfaction of contemplating flowers or of something really serious—trying to get in touch with the dead, for instance—it was nothing, nothing at all.

Paris was not at its most attractive as Cantabile and I walked by the Seine. The bankside was now a superhighway. The water looked like old medicine.

"Well, I got 'em for you, didn't I? I promised I'd make you money. What's your Mercedes now? Peanuts. I want twenty percent."

"We agreed on ten."

"Ten if you cut me into that other script. Thought you'd hold out on me, didn't you?"

"I'm going to write to Barbash to say that I want you to be paid ten percent. For *Caldofreddo*."

He said, "You're ungrateful. You never read the paper, you schmuck, and the whole thing would have passed you by without me. Just like the Thaxter business."

"What Thaxter business?"

"You see? You don't know anything. I didn't want to rattle you by telling you about Thaxter till the negotiations got started. You don't know what happened to Thaxter? He was kidnaped in Argentina."

"He wasn't! By whom, terrorists? But why? Why Thaxter? Have they hurt him?"

"America should thank God for its gangsters. The Mafia at least makes sense. These political guys don't know what the hell they're doing. They're snatching and murdering all over South America without rhyme and reason. How should I know why they picked on him. He must have acted like a big shot.

They let him send out one letter and he mentioned your name in it. And you didn't even know you were all over the world press."

"What did he say?"

"He appealed to the internationally famous historian and playwright Charles Citrine for help. He said you'd vouch for him."

"Those fellows don't know what they're doing. I hope they won't harm Thaxter."

"They'll be sore as hell when they find out he's a phony."

"I don't understand. What was he pretending? Whom did they take him to be?"

"They're very confused in all those countries," said Cantabile.

"Ah, my old friend Professor Durnwald is probably right when he says how nice it would be to hack off the Western Hemisphere at the isthmus and let the southern part drift away. Only there are so many parts of the earth of which that holds true now."

"Charles, the more commission you pay me, the less you'll have left for those terrorists."

"Me? Why me?"

"Oh, it'll be you all right," said Cantabile.

• • • •

Thaxter's captivity by terrorists oppressed me. It made me grieve at heart to imagine him locked in a black cellar with rats and terrified of torture. He was, after all, an innocent sort of person. True, he was not perfectly upright but much of his wrongdoing was simply delirium. Restless, seeking a piece of the action, he had now been cast among even more violently hallucinated parties who cut off ears and planted bombs in mailboxes or hijacked jet planes and slaughtered passengers. The last time I troubled to read a newspaper I noted that an oil company, after paying a ransom of ten million dollars, was still unable to obtain the release of one of its executives from his Argentine kidnapers.

That afternoon from the hotel I wrote to Carl Stewart, Thaxter's publisher. I said, "I understand Pierre has been abducted and that in his appeal for help he has named me. Well, of course, I will give everything I've got to save his life. In a way all his own, he is a wonderful man and I do love him; I have been his faithful friend for more than twenty years. I assume you have been in touch with the State Department and also with the US Embassy in Buenos Aires. Despite the fact that I have written on political matters I am not a political person. Let me put it this way, that for forty years during the worst crises of civilization I read the papers faithfully and this faithful reading did no one any good. Nothing was prevented thereby. I gradually stopped reading the news. It now appears to me, however, and I say this as a dispassionate observer, that between gunboat diplomacy at one extreme and submission to acts of piracy at the other, there ought to be some middle ground for a great power. In this regard, the flabbiness of the United States is disheartening. Are we only now catching up with the lessons of World War I? We learned from Sarajevo not to let acts of terrorism precipitate wars and from Woodrow Wilson that small nations have rights that great ones must respect. But that's it and we have gotten stuck some six decades back and set the world a miserable example by allowing ourselves to be bullied.

"To come back to Thaxter, however, I am wildly anxious about him. As recently as three months ago I would have been able to offer a ransom of $250,000. But that has been swept away by an unfortunate litigation. There is now more money on the horizon. I may soon be able to come up with ten or even twenty thousand and I am prepared to put up that much. I don't see how I can go beyond twenty-five. You would have to advance it. I would give you my note. Perhaps some way could be found to repay me out of Pierre's royalties. If these South American bandits let him go he'll write a whopping account of his experiences. That's the twist things have taken. Formerly life's bitterest misfortunes enriched only the hearts of wretches or were of spiritual value exclusively. But now any frightful event may be a gold mine. I'm sure that if and when poor Thaxter makes it, if they release him, he will strike it rich by writing a book. Hundreds of thousands of people who at this moment don't give a single damn about him will suffer with him intensely. Their souls will be wrung and they will gasp and cry. This is actually very important. I mean that the powers of compassion are now being weakened by an impossible volume of demands. We don't need to go into that, however. I'd be very grateful to you for information, and you may regard this letter as binding on me to come up with dollars for Thaxter. He must have swaggered and put on the dog in his Stetson and Western boots till he impressed those Latin Maoists or Trotsky- ists. Well, I suppose it's one of those World Historical things, peculiar to our times."

I got this letter off to New York and then flew back to Spain. Cantabile took me to Orly in a cab, now arguing for fifteen percent and beginning to make threats.

As soon as I reached Pensión La Roca I was handed a note on Ritz stationery. It was from the Señora. She wrote, "Kindly deliver Roger to me at 10:30 a.m. tomorrow in the lobby. We are going back to Chicago." I understood why she stipulated the lobby. I wouldn't lay violent hands on her in a public place. In her room I might go for her throat or try to drown her in the toi- let bowl. So, in the morning, with the kid, I met the old woman, that extraordinary condensation of wild prejudices. In the great circle of the Ritz lobby under the dome, I handed the kid to her. I said, "Good-by, Roger darling, you're going home."

The kid began to cry. The Señora couldn't calm him and accused me of corrupting him, attaching him to myself with chocolates. "You've bribed the boy with sweets."

"I hope Renata is happy in her new state," I said.

"She certainly is. Flonzaley is a high type of man. His IQ is out of this world. Writing books is no proof that you're smart."

"Oh how true that is," I said. "And after all burial was a great step forward. Vico said there was a time when corpses were allowed to rot on the ground and dogs and rats and vul- tures ate your near and dear. You can't have the dead all over the place. Although Stanton, a member of Lincoln's cabinet, kept his dead wife for nearly a year."

"You look worn out. You have too much on your mind," she said.

Intensity does that to me. I know it's true, but I hate to hear it said. Despair rises up. "*Adiós,* Roger. You're a fine boy and I love you. I'll see you in Chicago soon. Have a good flight with Grandma. Don't cry, kid," I said. I was threatened by tears myself. I left the lobby and walked toward the park. The danger of being struck by speeding cars, masses of them battering from all directions, prevented me from shedding more tears.

At the *pensión* I said that I had sent Roger home to his grandparents until I could readjust myself. The Danish lady from the embassy, Miss Volsted, was still standing by to do the humane thing for my sake. Depressed by Roger's leaving I was almost demoralized enough to take her up on it.

Cantabile telephoned every day from Paris. It was of the greatest importance for him to figure in these deals. I should have thought that Paris, with the many opportunities it offered a man like Cantabile, would distract him from business. Not a bit. He was all business. He kept after Maître Furet and Barbash. He irritated Barbash greatly by going over his head and trying to negotiate independently. Barbash complained to me from Paris. The producers, Cantabile told me, were now offering twenty thousand dollars in settlement. "They should be ashamed of themselves. And what kind of impression did Barbash make on them to get such a puny, insulting offer! He's no good. Our figure is two hundred thousand." Next day he reported, "They're up to thirty now. I've changed my mind again. This Barbash is real tough. I think he's sore at me and taking it out on them. What's two hundred to them, with such a box office? A pimple on the ass. One thing—we have to think about the taxes, and whether we should take payment in foreign currency. I know we can get more in lire. *Caldofreddo* is doing a tremendous business in Milan and Rome. The suckers are standing ten deep. I wonder why the cannibalism gets the Italians, raised on *pasta.* Anyhow, if you'll take lire you can get a lot more money. Of course, Italy is falling apart."

"I'll take dollars. I have a brother in Texas who can invest them in a good thing for me."

"You're lucky to have a kind brother. Are you feeling antsy down there in spic-land?"

"Not a bit. I'm very much at home. I read anthroposophy and I meditate. I'm doing the Prado inch by inch. What about the second scenario?"

"I'm not in on that, so why ask me?"

I said, "No, you're not."

"Then I don't see why I should tell you a damn thing. But I'll tell you anyway, out of courtesy. They are interested. They're damn interested. They've offered Barbash three thousand dollars for a three-week option. They say they need time to show it to Otway."

"Otway and Humboldt look very much alike. Maybe the resemblance means something. Some invisible link. I'm convinced that Otway will be attracted by Humboldt's story."

Next afternoon Kathleen Tigler arrived in Madrid. She was on her way to Almería to begin work on a new film. "I'm sorry to tell you," she said, "that the people to whom I sold the option on Humboldt's scenario have decided not to take it up."

"What's that?"

"You remember the outline that Humboldt bequeathed to both of us?"

"Of course."

"I should have sent you your share of the three thousand. Part of my purpose in coming to Madrid was to talk to you about it and draw a contract, settle with you. You've probably forgotten all about it."

"No, I hadn't forgotten," I said. "But it just occurred to me that I've been trying on my own to sell the same property to another group."

"I see," she said. "Selling the same thing to two parties. It would have been very awkward."

All this while, you see, business was going on. Business, with the peculiar autonomy of business, went its own way. Like it or not, we thought its thoughts, spoke its language. What did it matter to business that I suffered a defeat in love, or that I resisted Rebecca Volsted with her urgently blazing face, that I investigated the doctrines of anthroposophy? Business, sure of its own transcendent powers, got us all to interpret life through its practices. Even now, when Kathleen and I had so many private matters to consider, matters of the greatest human importance, we were discussing contracts options producers and sums of money.

"Of course," she said, "you couldn't be bound legally by an agreement I entered into."

"When we met in New York we spoke about a film outline Humboldt and I concocted in Princeton—"

"The one Lucy Cantabile asked me about? Her husband also phoned me in Belgrade and pestered me with mysterious questions."

"—to divert ourselves while Humboldt was scheming to get the chair in poetry."

"You told me it was all nonsense, and I thought no more about it."

"It was lost for twenty years or so, and then someone got around to stealing our original story and turned it into the picture called *Caldofreddo*."

"No! Is that where *Caldofreddo* comes from! You and Humboldt?"

"Have you seen it?"

"Of course I have. Otway's big, big hit was created by the two of you? It's not to be believed."

"Yes, indeed. I've just come from a meeting in Paris at which I proved our authorship to the producers."

"Will they settle with you? They should. You've got a real case against them, haven't you?"

"I die when I think of a lawsuit. Ten more years in the courts? That would be worth fees of four or five hundred thousand to my lawyers. But for me, a man approaching sixty and heading for seventy, there wouldn't be a penny left. I'll take my forty or fifty thousand now."

"Like a mere nuisance claim?" said Kathleen, indignant.

"No, like a man lucky enough to have his higher activities subsidized for a few years. I'll divide the money with Uncle Waldemar, of course. Kathleen, when I heard of Humboldt's will I thought it was just his posthumous way of carrying on more of the same touching tomfoolery. But the legal steps he took were all sound and he was right, damn it, about the value of his papers. He always had a wild hope of hitting the big time. And what do you know? He did! And it wasn't his serious work that the world found a use for. Just these capers."

"Also your capers," said Kathleen. When she smiled quietly she showed a great many small lines in her skin. I was sorry to see these signs of age in a woman whose beauty I remembered so well. But you could live with such things if you took the right view of them. After all, these wrinkles were the result of many many many years of amiability. They were the mortal toll taken by a good thing. I was beginning to understand how one might be reconciled to such alterations. "But to be taken seriously, what do you suppose Humboldt should have done?"

"How can I say that, Kathleen? He did what he could, and lived and died more honorably than most. Being crazy was the conclusion of the joke Humboldt tried to make out of his great disappointment. He was so intensely disappointed. All a man of that sort really asks for is a chance to work his heart out at some high work. People like Humboldt—they express a sense of life, they declare the feelings of their times or they discover meanings or find out the truths of nature, using the opportunities their time offers. When those opportunities are great, then there's love and friendship between all who are in the same enterprise. As you can see in Haydn's praise for Mozart. When the opportunities are smaller, there's spite and rage, insanity. I've been attached to Humboldt for nearly forty years. It's been an ecstatic connection. The hope of having poetry—the joy of knowing the kind of man that created poetry. You know? There's the most extraordinary, unheard-of poetry buried in America, but none of the conventional means known to culture can even begin to extract it. But now this is true of the world as a whole. The agony is too deep, the disorder too big for art enterprises undertaken in the old way. Now I begin to understand what Tolstoi was getting at when he called on mankind to cease the false and unnecessary comedy of history and begin simply to live. It's become clearer and clearer to me in Humboldt's heartbreak and madness. He performed all the stormy steps of that routine. That performance was conclusive. That—it's perfectly plain, now—can't be continued. Now we must listen in secret to the sound of the truth that God puts into us."

"And that's what you call the higher activity—and this is what the money you get from *Caldofreddo* will subsidize. . . . I see," said Kathleen.

"On the assumption commonly made the commonest events of life can only be absurd. Faith *was* called absurd. But now faith will perhaps move these mountains of commonsense absurdity."

"I was going to suggest that you leave Madrid and come down to Almería."

"I see. You're worried about me. I look bad."

"Not exactly. But I can tell you've been under a huge strain. It'll be pleasant weather on the Mediterranean now."

"The Mediterranean, yes. How I'd love a month of blessed peace. But I haven't got much money to maneuver with."

"You're broke? I thought you were loaded."

"I've been unloaded."

"It was bad of me then not to send the fifteen hundred dollars. I assumed it would be a trifle."

"Well, until a few months ago it was a trifle. Can you find something for me to do in Almería?"

"You wouldn't want that."

"I don't know what 'that' is."

"To take a job in this picture—*Memoirs of a Cavalier*. Based on Defoe. There are sieges and such."

"I'd wear a costume?"

"It's not for you, Charlie."

"Why not? Listen, Kathleen. If I may speak good English for a moment. . . ."

"Be my guest."

"To efface the faults or remedy the defects of five decades I'm prepared to try anything. I am not too good to work in the movies. You little know how much it would please me to be an extra in this historical picture. Could I wear boots and bloomers? A casque, or a hat with plumes? It would do me a world of good."

"Wouldn't it be too distracting, mentally? You have . . . things to do."

"If these things I have to do can't find their way around those mountains of absurdity there's no hope for them. It's not as though my mind were free, you know. I worry about my daughters, and I worry terribly about my friend Thaxter. He was kidnaped by Argentine terrorists."

"I wondered about him," said Kathleen. "I read it in the *Herald-Tribune*. Is that the same Mr. Thaxter I met in the Plaza? He wore a ten-gallon hat and asked me to come back later. Your name was mentioned in the article. He appealed to you for help."

"I'm upset by this. Poor Thaxter. If the scenarios do earn money I may have to pay it out to ransom him. I don't care too much. My own romance with wealth is over. What I intend to do now isn't very expensive. . . ."

"You know, Charles, Humboldt used to say wonderful things. You remind me of that. Tigler was lots of fun. He was an active, engaging person. We were always out hunting and fishing—doing something. But he wasn't much for conversation and nobody has talked to me like this in a long, long, long time, and I'm out of listening practice. I love it when you sound off. But it isn't very clear to me."

"I'm not surprised, Kathleen. It's my fault. I talk too much to myself. But human beings are far too deep in that false unnecessary comedy of history—in events, in developments, in politics. The common crisis is real enough. Read the papers—all that criminality and filth, murder, perversity, and horror. We can't get enough of it—we call it the human thing, the human scale."

"But what else is there?"

"A different scale. I know Walt Whitman compared us unfavorably to the animals. They don't whine about their condition. I see his point. I used to spend lots of time watching sparrows. I always adored sparrows. I do to this day. I spend hours in the park watching them bob and hop around and take dust baths. But I know they have less mental life than apes do. Orangutans are very charming. An orangutan friend sharing my apartment would make me very happy. But I know that he would understand less than Humboldt did. The question is this: why should we assume that the series ends with us? The fact is, I suspect, that we occupy a point within a great hierarchy that goes far far beyond ourselves. The ruling premises deny this. We feel suffocated and don't know why. The existence of a soul is beyond proof under the ruling premises, but people go on behaving as though they had souls, nevertheless. They behave as if they came from another place, another life, and they have impulses and desires that nothing in this world, none of our present premises, can account for. On the ruling premises the fate of humankind is a sporting event, most ingenious. Fascinating. When it doesn't become boring. The specter of boredom is haunting this sporting conception of history."

Kathleen again said that she had missed conversations of this kind in her married life with Tigler, the horse-wrangler. She certainly hoped I would come to Almería and work as a halberdier. "It's such an agreeable town."

"I'm about ready to get out of the *pensión*, too. People are breathing down my neck. But I'd better stay in Madrid so that I can keep track of everything—Thaxter, Paris. I may even have to go back to France for a while. I now have two attorneys there and that's double trouble."

"You haven't much confidence in lawyers."

"Well, Abraham Lincoln was a lawyer and I always venerated him. But he's nothing now but a name they put on license plates in the state of Illinois."

There was, however, no need to go to Paris. A letter came from Stewart, the publisher.

He wrote: "I see you haven't followed the papers for some time. It's true that Pierre Thaxter was abducted in Argentina. How or why or whether he's still in their hands I'm in no position to say. But I tell you in confidence, since you're his old pal, that it all puzzles me and sometimes I wonder if it's really on the level. Mind you, I don't care to suggest that it's a phony kidnap, out-and-out. I'm ready to believe that the people who grabbed Thaxter off the sidewalk were convinced of his importance. Nor is there any indication of a prearranged snatching as may possibly have been the case with Miss Hearst and the Symbionese. But I enclose an article from the Op Ed page of *The New York Times* by our friend Thaxter. It's supposed to have been sent from the secret place or dungeon where they keep him. How come, I ask you, was he able to write and send to the *Times* this little essay on being kidnaped? Perhaps you will note, as I did, that he even makes a pitch for ransom funds. I am told that sympathetic readers have already sent checks to the US Embassy in Argentina to reunite him with his nine children. Far from being harmed, he is even crashing the big time and, if I'm not mistaken, the experience has also sharpened his literary style. This is publicity beyond price. Your guess that he may have fallen into a gold mine is probably correct. If his neck isn't broken, he'll be rich and famous."

Thaxter wrote, in part, "Three men held pistols to my head as I was leaving a restaurant in a busy street in Buenos Aires. In these three muzzles I saw the vanity of all the mental strategies for outwitting violence that I had ever entertained. Until that moment I had never realized how very often a modern man anticipates this critical moment. My head, now perhaps about to be blown open, had been full of schemes for saving myself. As I got into the waiting car I thought, I'm done for. I was not subjected to physical abuse. It soon became apparent that I was in the hands of sophisticated individuals advanced in their political thinking and utterly devoted to the principles of liberty and justice as they understood them. My captors believe that they have a case to present to civilized opinion and have chosen me to state it for them, having ascertained that I was sufficiently well known as an essayist and journalist to command attention." (Even now he gave himself a plug.) "As guerrillas and terrorists they would like it known that they are not heartless and irresponsible fanatics but that they have a high tradition of their own. They invoke Lenin and Trotsky as founders and builders who discovered that force was their indispensable instrument. They know the classics of this tradition, from nineteenth-century Russia to twentieth-century France. I have been brought up from the cellar to attend seminars on Sorel and Jean-Paul Sartre. These people are, in their own fashion, most high principled and serious. They have, furthermore, the quality to which García Lorca applied the term *Duende*, an inner power which burns the blood like powdered glass, a spiritual intensity that does not suggest, but commands."

I met Kathleen at a café and showed her the clippings. There was more in the same vein. I said, "Thaxter has a terrible weakness for making major statements. I think I might just ask for the three guns to be applied to the back of my head and the triggers pulled rather than sit through those seminars."

"Don't be too hard on him. The man is saving his life," she said. "Also it's a fascinating thing, really. Where does he make the ransom pitch?"

"Here. '. . . a price of fifty thousand dollars which I am allowed to take this occasion to request my friends and members of my family to contribute. In the hope of seeing my young children again,' and so forth. The *Times* treats its readers to plenty of thrills. That's a really pampered public that gets the Op Ed page."

"I don't suppose that the terrorists would get him to write an apology to world opinion and then bump him off," she said.

"Well, it wouldn't be a hundred percent consistent. Who knows what those fellows will do. But I am a bit relieved. I think he's going to be all right."

Kathleen had questioned me closely, asking what I would like to do if Thaxter were out of the woods, if life became calmer and more settled. I answered her that I would probably spend a month at Dornach, near Basel, at the Swiss Steiner Center, the Goetheanum. Perhaps I could rent a house there where Mary and Lish could spend the summer with me.

"You should get quite a lot of money from the *Caldofreddo* people," she said. "And it seems that Thaxter is wiggling out of it, if he ever was really in it. For all you know he's free now."

"That's right. I still intend to split with Uncle Waldemar and give him Humboldt's full share."

"And how much would you estimate the settlement to be?"

"Oh, thirty thousand dollars," I said, "forty at the most."

But this guess was far too conservative. Barbash ended by bidding the producers up to eighty thousand dollars. They paid five thousand also to read Humboldt's scenario and eventually took an option on that as well. "They couldn't afford to pass it by," said Barbash, on the telephone. Cantabile was at that moment in the lawyer's office, talking loudly and urgently. "Yes, he's with me," said Barbash. "He's the most difficult bastard I ever had to deal with. He went over my head, he's been noisy, and lately he's begun to make threats. He's a real pain in the ass and if he weren't your authorized representative, Mr. Citrine, I'd have thrown him out long ago. Let me pay his ten percent and get him off my back."

"Mr. Barbash, you have my permission to disburse his eight thousand dollars immediately," I said. "What sort of terms are being offered for the second scenario?"

"They started at fifty thousand. But I argued that it was obvious the late Mr. Fleisher really had something. Contemporary, you know what I mean? Just the stuff the public was hungry for right now. You may have it yourself, Mr. Citrine. If you don't mind my saying so, I believe you shouldn't quit now. If you want to write the screenplay for the new vehicle I can make you one hell of a deal. Would you do it for two thousand a week?"

"I'm afraid I'm not interested, Mr. Barbash. I have other plans."

"What a pity. "Won't you reconsider? They've asked many times."

"No thanks. No, I'm engaged in a very different kind of activity," I said.

"What about consultation?" said Mr. Barbash. "These people have got nothing but money and they'd be glad to pay twenty thousand bucks just because you understood the mind of Von Humboldt Fleisher. *Caldofreddo* is sweeping the world."

"Don't say no to everything." This was Cantabile who had taken the phone. "And listen, Charlie, I should get a cut on the other thing because if it wasn't for me none of this would have started. Besides, you owe me for planes, taxis, hotels, and meals."

"Mr. Barbash will settle your bill," I said. "Now go away, Cantabile, our relationship has drawn to a close. Let's become strangers again."

"Oh, you ungrateful, intellectual, asshole bastard," he said.

Barbash recovered the phone. "Where shall we be in touch? Are you staying in Madrid for a while?"

"I may fly down to Almería for a week or so, and then return to the USA," I said. "I've got a houseful of things in Chicago to dispose of. Children to see, and I've got to talk to Mr. Fleisher's uncle. When I've taken care of these necessary items and tied up a few loose ends I'm coming back to Europe. To take up a different kind of life," I added.

Inquire a little and I'll tell you all. I was still explaining myself in full to people who couldn't have cared less.

• • •

So this was how, in warm April, it happened that Waldemar Wald and I, together with Menasha Klinger, reburied Humboldt and his mother side by side in new graves at the Valhalla Cemetery. I took a very sad pleasure in doing this handsomely, in real style. Humboldt had been buried not in potter's field but far out in Deathsville, New Jersey, one of those vast, necropolitan developments described by Koffritz, Renata's first husband, to old Myron Swiebel in the steam room of the Division Street Bath. "They cheat," he had said about those places, "they skimp, they don't give the statutory number of feet. You lie there with your legs up, short-sheeted. Aren't you entitled to a full stretch for eternity?"

Investigating, I found that Humboldt's funeral had been arranged by someone at the Belisha Foundation. Some sensitive person there, subordinate to Longstaff, recalling that Humboldt had once been an employee, had gotten him out of the morgue and had given him a send-off from the Riverside Chapel.

So Humboldt was exhumed and brought in a new casket over the George Washington Bridge. I had stopped for the old boys at their recently rented flat on the Upper West Side. A woman came to cook and clean for them and they were properly fixed up. Turning over a large sum to Uncle Waldemar made me uneasy and I told him so. He answered, "Charlie, my boy, listen—all the horses I ever knew became spooks years ago. And I wouldn't even know how to contact a bookie. It's all Puerto Rican up there in the old neighborhood now. Anyway, Menasha is keeping an eye on me. I want to tell you, kid, not many younger fellows would have given me the full split the way you did. If anything is left over at the end, you'll get it back."

We waited in the hired limousine at the New York end of the cabled bridge, the Hudson before us, till the hearse crossed over and we followed it to the cemetery. A blustery day might have been easier to tolerate than this heavy watered-silk blue close day. In the cemetery we wound about among dark trees. These should have been giving shade already but they stood brittle and schematic among the graves. For Humboldt's mother a new coffin also was provided, and this was already in position, ready to be lowered. Two attendants were opening the hearse as we came around to the back, moving slowly. Waldemar was wearing all the mourning he could find in his gambler's wardrobe. Hat, trousers, and shoes were black, but his sport coat had large red houndstooth checks and in the sunshine of a delayed overwarm spring the fuzz was shining. Menasha, sad, smiling in thick glasses, felt his way over grass and gravel, his feet all the more cautious because he was looking up into the trees. He couldn't have been seeing much, a few sycamores and elms and birds and the squirrels coming and going in their fits-and-starts fashion. It was a low moment. There was a massive check threatened, as if a general strike against nature might occur. What if blood should not circulate, if food should not digest, breath fail to breathe, if the sap should not overcome the heaviness of the trees? And death, death, death, death, like so many stabs, like murder—the belly, the back, the breast and heart. This was a moment I could scarcely bear. Humboldt's coffin was ready to move. "Pallbearers?" said one of the funeral directors. He looked the three of us over. Not much manpower here. Two old fuddy-duddies and a distracted creature not far behind them in age. We took honorific positions along the casket. I held a handle—my first contact with Humboldt. There was very little weight within.

Of course I no longer believed that any human fate could be associated with such remains and superfluities. The bones were very possibly the signature of spiritual powers, the projection of the cosmos in certain calcium formations. But perhaps even such elegant white shapes, thigh bones, ribs, knuckles, skull, were gone. Exhuming, the grave diggers might have shoveled together certain tatters and sooty lumps of human origin, not much of the charm, the verve and feverish invention, the calamity-making craziness of Humboldt. Humboldt, our pal, our nephew and brother, who loved the Good and the Beautiful, and one of whose slighter inventions was entertaining the public on Third Avenue and the Champs-Elysées and earning, at this moment, piles of dollars for everyone.

The laborers took over from us, setting Humboldt's coffin on the canvas bands of the electrical lowering device. The dead were now side by side in their bulky boxes.

"Did you know Bess?" said Waldemar.

"Once I saw her, on West End Avenue," I said.

He may have been thinking of money taken from her purse and lost in horse races long ago, of quarrels and scandalous scenes and curses.

In the long years since I had last attended a burial, many mechanical improvements had been made. There stood a low yellow compact machine which apparently did the digging and bull-dozed back the earth. It was also equipped as a crane. Seeing this, I started off on the sort of reflection Humboldt himself had trained me in. The machine in every square inch of metal was a result of collaboration of engineers and other artificers. A system built upon the discoveries of many great minds was always of more strength than what is produced by the mere workings of any one mind, which of itself can do little. So spoke old Dr. Samuel Johnson, and added in the same speech, that the French writers were superficial because they were not scholars and had proceeded upon the mere power of their own minds. Well, Humboldt had admired these same French writers and he too had proceeded for some time upon the mere power of his own mind. Then he began to look, himself, toward the collective phenomena. As his own self, he had opened his mouth and uttered some delightful verses. But then his heart failed him. Ah, Humboldt, how sorry I am. Humboldt, Humboldt—and this is what becomes of us.

The funeral director said, "Does anybody have a prayer to say?"

Nobody seemed to have or to know a prayer. But Menasha said he would like to sing something. He then did so. His style had not changed.

He announced, "I'm going to sing a selection from *Aida*, 'In questa tomba oscura.' " Aged Menasha now prepared himself. He turned up his face. The Adam's apple thus revealed was not what it had been when he was a young man operating a punch press in a Chicago factory, but it was there still. So was the old excitement. He clasped his hands, rising on his toes, and as emotionally as in our kitchen on Rice Street, weaker in voice, missing the tune still, and crowing but moved, terribly moved, he sang his aria. But this was only the warm-up. When he was done, he declared that he was going to perform "Goin' Home," an old American spiritual—used by Dvořák in the *New World* Symphony, he added as a program note. Then, oh Lord! I remembered that he had been homesick for Ypsilanti, and that he had pined for his sweetheart, back in the Twenties, longing for his girl, singing "Goin' home, goin' home, I'm a'goin' home," until my mother said, "For heaven's sake, go then." And when he came back with his obese, gentle, weeping bride, this girl who sat in the tub, her arms too fat and defeating her efforts to bring the water as high as her head, Mama came into the bathroom and washed her hair for her, and toweled it.

They were all gone but ourselves.

And looking into open graves was no pleasanter than it had ever been. Brown clay and lumps and pebbles—why must it all be so heavy? It was too much weight, oh, far too much to bear. I observed, however, another innovation in burials. Within the grave was an open concrete case. The coffins went down and then the yellow machine moved forward and the little crane, making a throaty whir, picked up a concrete slab and laid it atop the concrete case. So the coffin was enclosed and the soil did not come directly upon it. But then, how did one get out?

One didn't, didn't, didn't! You stayed, you stayed! There was a dry light grating as of crockery when contact was made, a sort of sugar-bowl sound. Thus, the condensation of collective intelligences and combined ingenuities, its cables silently spinning, dealt with the individual poet. The same was done to the poet's mother. A gray lid was set upon her too and then Waldemar took the spade and weakly dug out clods and threw one into each grave. The old gambler wept and we turned aside to spare him. He stood beside the graves while the bulldozer began its work.

Menasha and I went toward the limousine. The side of his foot brushed away some of last autumn's leaves and he said, looking through his goggles, "What's this, Charlie, a spring flower?"

"It is. I guess it's going to happen after all. On a warm day like this everything looks ten times deader."

"So it's a little flower," Menasha said. "They used to tell one about a kid asking his grumpy old man when they were walking in the park, 'What's the name of this flower, Papa?' and the old guy is peevish and he yells, 'How should I know? Am I in the millinery business?' Here's another, but what do you suppose they're called, Charlie?"

"Search me," I said. "I'm a city boy myself. They must be crocuses."